Indivisible

This is a work of historical fiction. While much of the details within this work are fictitious, some names, places, characters, and events are based on recorded historical incidences. Any trademarks, service marks, product names, or named features are assumed to be the property of their respective owners and are used only for reference. There is no implied endorsement if any of these terms are used. This book or any portion thereof may not be reproduced or used in any manner whatsoever without the express written permission of the publisher, except for the use of brief quotations in book reviews.

INDIVISIBLE

ISBN-13: 9781702822183

Copyright © 2020 Madison Flores

Cover Art by Madison Flores with imagery from Unsplash.

www.madisonflores.com

Indivisible

Book II of the Indivisible Series

By Madison Flores

This work is dedicated to my parents, Amy and Jeremy, my brothers, Brayden and Reece, and the love of my life, Moris. Without them, this duology never would have been possible, for they were my proofreaders, my editors, my muses, my first readers, and my biggest fans. Without their unwavering help and support, I never would have been able to achieve this crazy dream of mine.

Works by Madison Flores

Inalienable: Book I of the Indivisible Series

Indivisible: Book II of the Indivisible Series

Table of Contents

Chapter 1: Judas Kiss *9*
Chapter 2: Head Above Water *24*
Chapter 3: Home *38*
Chapter 4: To the Wolves *58*
Chapter 5: A Woman's Game *78*
Chapter 6: Forsaken *99*
Chapter 7: The Lion's Den *121*
Chapter 8: Monster *148*
Chapter 9: Long Live the King *175*
Chapter 10: Requiem *204*
Chapter 11: Only Us *229*
Chapter 12: Demons *257*
Chapter 13:Homeland *281*
Chapter 14: Tekariho:ken *305*
Chapter 15: A Bitter Truth *333*
Chapter 16: A Love Without End *361*
Chapter 17: Indivisible *380*
Chapter 18: A Breath of Heaven *410*

Chapter 19: Liberty *437*
Chapter 20: Do Not Weep and Wonder *457*
Chapter 21: He Lives in Us *490*
Chapter 22: World on Fire *513*
Chapter 23: Blood, Fire, and Fearlessness *542*
Chapter 24: A Generation Unafraid *570*
Chapter 25: The Heart of a Hero *594*

Chapter 1

Judas Kiss

November 1778

Theo Cunningham had never despised his father more, and over a month passed in which he refused to speak to, nor even look at the man after their falling out. He had always suspected that Alistair harbored a deep-seated shame and resentment towards him as a result of the circumstance of his birth, and in Theo's mind, the old man had essentially confirmed it. It was a regular occurrence for the two to butt heads, but this time was different, and no one but Theo could truly understand the depth of the scars that ran across his heart. And he could feel the scars grow ever larger now that Alistair had unwittingly spoken his truth. An uncomfortably tense silence thus fell between them, palpable to all who knew them, and there appeared to be no end in sight to their hostility as the winds of winter crept into New England.

While a storm seemed to be raging between the two men of the Cunningham household, Evie found herself consumed by thoughts of the future—more specifically, her and Theo's future. There was no doubt in her mind that she loved him more than she had ever loved another human being, and she looked at her reflection in the mirror every day to see Theo's reminder of his love for her hanging around her neck. Theo had already stated that he didn't think himself to be the marrying type, but that did not stop Evie from daydreaming of a proposal—a promise of a new life with a man she knew would never hurt her the way Silas Porter had.

But Silas was precisely the problem. So long as she was legally bound in marriage to Silas Porter, Evie would never be able to properly pursue a relationship with another man for the rest of her days. The world was already against her and Theo's relationship on the basis of the color of his skin, and that she was another man's wife only served to exponentially complicate the matter. Theo claimed it did not bother him in the slightest that she was married to another, but Evie knew he was only saying as much for her benefit. They both longed for her to be free of her binds to her previous life, but they were both at a loss as to how to go about freeing her.

On a cold and windy afternoon while Theo was out of the house, Evie shuffled into the sitting room to find Alistair and Johanna enjoying a cup of warm tea together. Alistair looked up upon hearing her incoming footsteps and bid her a warm greeting.

"Ah, Evie. We were just wondering where you were," Alistair said.

"I was upstairs putting Theo's laundry in his room."

"Come sit with us," Johanna said with a kind smile. "Have some tea. It is dreadfully cold outside, and the Earl Grey will do wonders to warm your weary bones."

Evie took a seat in the armchair next to Johanna while Alistair poured her a cup of tea. Gunner the hound, who seemed to have doubled in size and grown into his long floppy ears, followed close behind and plopped down under the armchair, tail wagging. Evie took the cup in both of her hands and thanked Alistair with a nod, but her eyes were settled on the floor and her lips were pressed into a thin hard line. She was distracted, the older couple could easily see, with something troubling plaguing her mind.

"What troubles you, dear?" Johanna asked with a thin brow quirked in concern.

Evie shrugged and began to fiddle with her fingers while staring at her lap. She nervously smoothed out the wrinkles in her skirt and swallowed.

"You can tell us, lass," Alistair coaxed gently after coughing into his fist. "We are here to listen."

Evie sighed heavily. "It's…about my husband."

Johanna frowned. "What about him?"

"I want to be free of him. I came here to start a new life, but I cannot do that if I am still bound to him in marriage."

"You want a divorce?" Johanna asked as she sipped her tea.

A determined look settled in Evie's bright blue eyes. "I want anything that will set me free from him. What can I do?"

Alistair looked up to the ceiling in thought and set his teacup on the table at his side. "I'm afraid there is not much you can do, lass. Colonial law is based in English Common Law. And the Common Law states that in order for a divorce to be recognized by God, and by the Crown, both the husband and the wife must consent to the separation. The wife may not initiate the proceedings without the husband's permission."

Evie's face fell with his words, and her voice broke in desperation. "He would never consent to a divorce. He is still out there looking for me, I know it."

Alistair continued after clearing his throat. "The only way to nullify a marriage outside of a divorce is for you to become a widow."

Evie's eyes widened nervously. As much as she hated Silas, she did not want to wish *death* upon him. He was still her late son's father, after all. She shook her head in sadness and opened her mouth to speak but was interrupted by a gruff voice emanating from the doorway to the sitting room.

"If that bastard shows his face anywhere near here, a widow is exactly what you are going to be."

Evie turned in her chair to see Theo standing in the doorway, his arms crossed over his chest and a sour look upon his face. His cheeks were flushed from the cold, and snowflakes were sprinkled in his hair and on his coat.

"How long were you standing there?" Evie asked quietly.

"Long enough."

Alistair cleared his throat again. "Why don't you join us for tea, Theo? I am sure you are cold after trudging through the snow."

Theo's sour expression deepened as he gave his father a sideways glance from the doorway. "I'll pass."

He then looked to Evie and motioned for her to follow him with a nod of his head and a crook of his finger. Evie bid Johanna and Alistair goodbye and thanked them for the tea before scurrying out of the room and following Theo up the stairs. Not surprisingly, Gunner scampered right behind them to the second floor, and Theo had to shoo him away before they entered his bedroom.

"That was rather rude," Evie commented as they entered his room. "You are going to have to speak to your father eventually. You cannot give him the cold shoulder forever."

Theo's back was to her as he gazed out the window, but he suddenly turned to face her with a stern expression upon his face. "Why were you asking my parents about the laws of divorce?"

Evie was slightly taken aback by the sternness of his tone. "I was just asking so that I may know the requirements for…leaving my husband."

Theo furrowed his brow in confusion. "You want to leave him permanently?"

"I do."

"...For me?"

Evie's lips twitched upward as she took a step toward him and placed a hand on his chest. "For you. And for me."

"You would do that for me?"

"In an instant."

Theo wrapped his arms around her and pressed a kiss to the top of her head as a warm feeling spread throughout his chest. He didn't think it possible to care so deeply for another person as he did her, and he never wanted to let her go from his arms.

"You heard my father," he mumbled in frustration. "If he will not grant you a divorce, the only way to be free of him is through his death."

Evie frowned and twisted her hands into the fabric of his shirt. "I wouldn't wish death upon anyone, not even him."

"Perhaps you don't have to. Perhaps he has passed since you left."

Evie scoffed and shook her head. "Not likely..."

"How do you know?"

Evie looked sadly into his eyes, longing to be able to tell him everything she was hiding. "I just know. He's still out there, looking for me. The only way for me to know for certain would be to go back to Boston and seek out my family...or his."

"You said your family disowned you when you ran away."

"They did. That is why I had nowhere else to go..."

Theo shook his head. "It is not safe for you to go to Boston to seek out anyone from your past. If your husband catches wind that you are in town, he can find you. I can't let that happen."

"So, I am just to leave everything about my past behind me?"

"You have for four years now."

Evie let out a deep sigh of sadness and buried her head in his strong chest. "What are we to do? The world will never accept us this way..."

Theo tightened his hold on her and rested his chin atop her head while staring longingly out the window at the falling snow. "The world will never accept us regardless, Evie. People hate what they do not understand, and as far as the rest of the world is concerned, we are an enigma. We will always have targets upon our backs. It is just the way it is."

"It isn't fair."

"Nothing about this world is fair."

***

Evie's heart pounded in her chest as she trudged through drifts of snow, ducking under low hanging tree branches and tossing a nervous look over her shoulder with every shaky step. Her breath billowed from her lips in a white, frosty cloud as she clutched at her skirts and continued on. Her cloak fluttered and twisted behind her as she ran through the woods on the edge of the homestead, and she jumped with a squeal every time the sound of footsteps or the snap of a twig touched her ears. When she wasn't looking over her shoulder, she was scouring the trees above her head for any sign of her pursuer, but every time she thought she caught a glimpse of him prowling from tree branch to tree branch, he disappeared into a blur of shadows, always remaining on the periphery of her vision, but never truly in her line of sight. She was haunted by the feeling of a pair of dark, predatory eyes on her as she weaved through the trees, and no matter how far she ran, she could not escape his gaze.

Evie yelped when her foot caught on a tree root buried in the snow, and she fell to her knees in exhaustion, her cheeks flushed and her chest heaving for a breath. Before she could throw up her arms to defend herself, a dark blur zipped from one tree branch to another overhead and bombarded her with a large cannonball made of tightly packed snow. The snowball hit its target with ease and exploded against the top of Evie's head, sending powdery shrapnel all throughout her hair and across her cloak and coat. The earth seemed to shake when the shadowy figure looming in the trees leapt down from the branch on which it was perched, landing in a crouched position in the snow just a few steps before her.

"I win again," Theo remarked triumphantly as he crossed his arms over his chest and smirked down at his prey. Despite having clambered through several trees to chase Evie halfway through the woods, he did not seem the least bit spent. Evie, however, was gasping for breath as she glared up at him, a pout upon her lips.

"It isn't far," she snapped as she brushed snow from her shoulders. "You can cover more ground by leaping through the trees."

Theo chuckled and extended a hand to help her stand, which she reluctantly accepted. "My legs are also twice as long as yours."

Evie crossed her arms with a huff. "This is a wretched game! Whose idea was it to chase each other around with balls of snow anyway?"

"Emma's, obviously."

As if on cue, a loud and shrill shriek shook the forest around them just as Emma came sprinting into the clearing, her curly blond hair flying behind her as Jacob came just on her heels with a clump of snow in hand.

"Mercy!" she cried as she ducked to hide behind Theo's large frame.

"Not a chance!" Jacob seized his wife be wrapping a large arm around her waist and holding her against him as he tried to shove the snowball down the back of her coat. Emma squealed in protest and immediately began to hop around to stamp the snow out of her clothes as soon as Jacob released her.

Upon noticing that Theo was distracted, Evie scooped up a large handful of snow and reared her arm back to throw it at the back of his head, but her movements were loud and clumsy, and he heard her coming for him long before she knew it. Just as she tried to sneak up behind him, he whipped around to face her and seized her wrist in his hand before pulling her into his chest by her waist. The snowball crumbled to bits in her hands as he smirked down at her with a mischievous glint in his golden eyes.

"You do not learn very quickly," Theo remarked slyly. "You have never been very sneaky."

Evie flashed him a smirk of her own as she stretched on the tips of her toes to press a kiss to his lips, but she was interrupted by the sound of someone clearing her throat just behind them. They both turned to look over her shoulder as Emma and Jacob froze in their attempts to shove snow in each other's faces to see Constance Baker's familiar figure gliding down the hill and into the forest clearing, her cloak billowing behind her in the cold breeze.

She wore a devilish sneer upon her painted lips, and her brows were slanted downward as if she was trying to send someone to their grave with just her eyes. It had been well over a month since she first snatched Evie's journal, well over a month that she had spent plotting exactly how she wanted to spill every last one of Evie's secrets so that she could plant the final nail in the Loyalist snake's coffin. Miraculously, Evie had been so preoccupied with her life that she hadn't even thought to write in her journal in as many weeks, and until this fateful day, she hadn't any clue it was no longer tucked under the corner of Theo's mattress.

Now that a courier had been sent with a message for Captain Silas Porter detailing exactly where he could find his runaway wife, the first and second components of her plan were in place. All that was left to be done was to administer the poison that would finally kill any and all affection that Theo held in his heart for Evie. And that poison was the little black book in her clutches.

"Constance," Theo greeted her less than enthusiastically. "Did you come to throw snowballs with us?"

Constance shook her head and tossed her snow-sprinkled hair over her shoulder as she entered the clearing. Her razor-sharp eyes never left Evie as she made a circle around the perimeter and then came to stand at Theo's side. "I do not indulge in such childish games. You should know that by now."

"Then why are you here?" Evie asked bitterly as she took a step back from Theo.

Constance shrugged and stuffed her hands in the deep pockets of her skirt. "Oh, I just happened to be strolling through the area when I heard you four frolicking about. I thought I would pay you a visit."

Theo rolled his eyes. "If you are here to start trouble—"

"Oh, I'm not the one who started the trouble," Constance snapped as she narrowed her eyes in Evie's direction. "Isn't that right, Mrs. Porter?"

Evie felt her heart leap into her throat and the color drain from her face as she glared at Constance in return. Theo furrowed his brow in confusion and looked between the two women before him.

"What did you just call her?"

"Mrs. Porter. That is her name, after all. At least that is what it says in here." Constance dug around in her pockets and produced a small black leather-bound book, holding it out for everyone to see. Her smirk was so wide that one feared it would have split her face in half.

Evie let out a sharp gasp as her eyes fell upon her journal in the hands of this snake of a woman. "Where did you get that?" she shrieked as she lunged forward to snatch it away.

Constance quickly ducked out of her reach and opened the book. "Oh, it doesn't matter where. What we should all be concerned about is what this little book of secrets contains."

"Give that to me!" Evie growled as she lunged for it again. "You had no right to go through my things!"

Constance let out a cackle and ducked away from her again, twirling to stand on Theo's other side. Theo stared at her in complete befuddlement.

"What are you talking about? What is that?"

"Just a compilation of every lie your precious little Evie has ever told us."

Theo turned to look at Evie, who had gone paler than the snow under their feet as she glared at Constance. "Evie?"

Evie looked nervously between him and the book in Constance's grasp as she began to wring her fingers. "It's…it's my journal," she whispered. "My *private* journal."

Constance began to flip through the pages of the book as she murmured, "Shall I tell him what is written here? Or would you like to do the honors, Evie? If that *is* your real name…"

Theo took an uncertain step in Evie's direction. His voice was low and strained, and he could already feel his heart creeping up into his throat. "What is she talking about? What have you done?"

Evie shook her head in defeat, her gaze falling to the frozen ground. "I'm so sorry, Theo…"

Theo's eyes narrowed in anger. "*What have you done?*"

"Evie?" Emma asked with wide, saddened eyes. "Have you been hiding something from us?"

Evie felt her heart begin to constrict in her chest as she was enveloped with a crushing wave of shame and regret. Never in a million years did she think this moment would come, and she was lost and confused as how to explain herself and her years of deception.

"Oh, she's been hiding many things," Constance snapped. "It is just a shame it took so long for her web of lies to come crumbling down. The list goes on and on, really. Where shall we begin? Should we start with the fact that her name is not Evie Greene as she says, but rather Evie Scarborough-Porter? Or that her father was an admiral in the British Navy and is currently an avid Loyalist? Oh, and let us not forget that he has offered thousands of pounds in financial support to the Crown during the war and continues to do so to this day." Constance flipped a few more pages as Evie felt her legs begin to give out underneath her. "And perhaps the most damning lie of all. Her husband."

Theo snatched the book from Constance's hands and scanned the page. Evie watched helplessly as he read, and she could feel her world come crashing down around her as his jaw began to clench and his eyes grew cold. After several agonizing moments, he looked up from the book and locked his eyes with hers.

"Silas Porter," he whispered in a broken voice. "Your husband...is Silas Porter?"

Evie squeezed her eyes shut as they began to burn with fearful tears. She swallowed thickly before weakly nodding her head. "He is..."

"Silas Porter," Theo repeated through clenched teeth as he took another step toward her and held the book high in the air. "The same Silas Porter that burned Kensington to the ground? The same Silas Porter that held me prisoner and permanently disfigured me?"

Evie gulped again as a tear escaped her eye. "I wanted to tell you...but I couldn't..."

"You couldn't? Or you *wouldn't?*" Jacob retorted angrily.

"Is all of this true, Evie?" Emma asked in a broken voice.

"You don't understand," Evie pleaded tearfully as she looked desperately between the angered crowd before her. Her voice grew weaker and weaker with every word she choked out under Theo's enraged gaze. "I...I didn't know how to tell you. I was afraid. I knew that if I told you my husband and father were Loyalists, you...you would not let me stay. I couldn't risk Silas finding me..."

"You used us," Constance corrected sharply. "You manipulated us."

"No! I...I was just so afraid of my husband finding me...that I would have done anything to protect myself and my baby. I didn't know what else to do..."

"You could have told me the truth long ago!" Theo growled. The familiar tingling of his blood boiling under the surface of his skin sent tremors up his spine as he stared down the woman that he once thought he knew so well. "Four years! Four years, Evie, you had four years to tell me the truth. But you chose to look me in the eye every day, year after year, and lie through your teeth! How could you do this?"

Another tear rolled down Evie's cheek as she stared at Theo with pleading eyes. "I didn't want you to be angry. I didn't want you to hate me…"

"And how well is that going for you now?" Theo hissed, his eyes cold and yet ablaze with anger and betrayal. Never before had he looked at her with so much resentment and so much rage, and it was truly terrifying to see.

"I'm so sorry," Evie repeated through her tears as she clutched at her chest. She could feel her heart pounding against her ribcage and the world began to spin wildly around her.

"You're sorry? You lied to my face for four years, you harbored knowledge of the monster that massacred our neighbors and nearly killed me, and you're *sorry*? Who are you? Was anything you've told me true?"

Evie reached forward and clutched onto the lapels of Theo's coat. "I'm still me. I'm still Evie. Everything I told you about my feelings for you was true, I swear it…"

Theo shook his head in disgust and pulled away from her. "No. No, you are a different person to me now…"

"Don't say that…" Evie begged. "You don't mean that…"

"I told you she was hiding something," Constance huffed triumphantly. "She's a liar and she's a whore. She seduced you so she would have a roof over her head while she spied on us for the Loyalists."

"I am no spy!" Evie sobbed. "Please, Theo, you have to believe me. I meant you and this community no harm. I only wanted to start over. I…I hoped that if I left the truth of my past behind me, I would never have to face it again…"

"Spy or no, you have still broken my trust beyond repair," Theo stated with words so cold they could have frozen the sun. "I can never trust you again…not after this…"

Evie sucked in a sharp breath, feeling as if she had just been punched in the gut. Her knees went weak as she stared at him with blurry eyes. "You can trust me. You know you can. Please don't do this…"

Theo shook his head solemnly and looked away, biting down on his lower lip as his hands clenched into fists at his side. "We're done," he whispered.

Evie's eyes widened in agony. "What?"

"We're done!" he repeated louder and with more force. "Whatever we had, whatever we were, we're done…"

"No. No, you don't mean that…"

"Unlike you, I mean every word I say. We're done. I never want to see nor speak to you again."

"Theo, please, I can explain…"

"Spare me."

"I am so sorry…" Evie desperately reached out to take ahold of Theo's coat again, but he was stiff under her touch. As soon as her fingers grazed his chest, Theo let out an enraged growl and roughly shoved her away much harder than he intended to.

"Get away from me!"

Evie let out a pained gasp when she stumbled backwards and fell to her knees in the snow at his feet, melting into a broken and crumpled pile as uncontrollable sobs began to wrack her thin body. She looked up to stare fearfully at him through her tears, expecting him to lash out at her in anger just as Silas would have, and she could feel herself shrinking under his despondent gaze. His eyes were cold as he stared her down, a frigidness she knew he only reserved for those who hurt him the most.

"Please, forgive me…" she choked out.

"I am out of forgiveness," Theo hissed, tossing the journal into the snow before her.

"Theo, please…"

Before Evie could eek out any more broken words between her sobs, Theo waved his hand dismissively and turned on his heel. Without another word, he stormed out of the clearing and up the road toward the homestead, his entire body rigid with an anger he couldn't comprehend. He had never felt so betrayed, so hurt, so wronged. And Evie was the last person he ever expected to be responsible for the raging storm of pain in his heart. With every step he took away from the clearing, he could feel the fracture in his heart grow wider and wider, until there was nothing left to keep him whole.

Evie watched helplessly as he stomped through the trees and disappeared over the hill before Jacob followed suit, but not before shooting her the most hateful glare he had ever given her. Emma glanced back and forth between him and Evie in confusion before shaking her head in sadness. She paused in the middle of the clearing as her husband began to follow after Theo, begging Evie with her eyes to tell her that none of this was really true. Jacob paused at the edge of the clearing when he realized Emma was not behind him.

"Emma," he snapped over his shoulder. "Come along. Now."

Emma tossed a sorrowful glance in Evie's direction before reluctantly turning to follow her husband back home. Constance stared down Evie's broken and crumpled form still collapsed in the cold snow with a malicious sneer upon her face. Tears streamed down Evie's pale face as she stared back, hopeless and confused. She was not angry with Constance—she was too shocked to be angry. She was *hurt*.

Constance crossed the clearing and stooped down to pluck the journal from the snow and stuff it back in her pocket. "You should not have underestimated me," she stated coldly. "I always get what I want."

"And what is it that you wanted?" Evie sobbed. "To hurt me? To poison Theo against me?"

"You're just sore because you do not want to admit that I *won*."

"You won? And what was the prize? Theo? If so, then congratulations, Constance, you have won a game that I never had any interest in playing!"

Constance flashed her a cheeky smirk and turned on her heel. "A victory is a victory," she sang as she began to skip out of the clearing. "Do not bother coming back to the homestead. Once word gets out about what you have done, you'll wish you had never come here in the first place."

Constance's figure soon disappeared behind the trees and the falling snow, leaving Evie alone on the forest floor, cold, alone, and heart broken. She was left breathless and nauseated, and she wanted nothing more than to walk off the edge of the cliff so that the sharp agony in her heart would be cured forever. She wished she could say that she was shocked by Constance's betrayal, but in truth, she was shocked it had taken so long for her to finally get her way. Evie knew from the beginning that Constance wanted to drive them apart, and with her final Judas Kiss, she had claimed her victory.

Violent sobs soon overtook Evie's body as she curled into a ball in the snow. She could feel the earth falling away underneath her as she quickly fell into an abyss of agony and despair, and she could not recall a time before this terrible day when she felt so betrayed and so broken. She watched her entire world slip away as she watched Theo storm off and leave her behind without a second glance, and her anguish was made all the more real by the realization that she deserved every bit of pain she felt.

She had brought it upon herself, all of it. She never should have hidden the truth from the man for whom she cared so deeply, and she never should have expected such happiness to last for so long. If she had learned anything in the twenty-one years she had spent on this earth, it was that any source of joy she found was ultimately destined to slip through her fingers.

Chapter 2

Head Above Water

December 1779

The coming winter was cold, but the heart beating in Theo's chest was even colder as the year drew to a close. Days passed, and then weeks, in which he refused to speak nor even look in Evie's direction as he added her name to the list of people with which he was not on good terms. As of now, Evie was joined only by Silas Porter, Alistair, and Commander Washington on that list, and it was not a place in which she expected she would ever find herself. The cold shoulder that he turned to her was sudden and unexpected, and every time she caught a glimpse of him only to see him angrily turn his back to her, she felt a thousand knives stab though her chest.

In the aftermath of her skeletons being dragged from her closet, word about her true identity and that of her family and husband spread through the homestead like wildfire, and within a matter of days, nearly every person that she had once considered a friend soon began to regard her with suspicious looks that cut through her heart like shards of broken glass.

After becoming so used to Theo's company, it was a shock to Evie's system to no longer be welcome in his room, in his bed, or in his life. She returned to sleep in her own room for the first time in months, and the bed felt cold and foreign to her. Her nights were restless as she tossed and turned, contemplating every mistake she had ever made to bring her to this point and desperately missing the warmth his body brought her when they slept side by side. She wanted desperately to be able to speak to him, to explain herself and why she had kept so many things from him and everyone else, but he would not give her the time of day.

After a fortnight of separation, Evie began to accept the fact that Theo would probably never forgive her for what she had done, and she knew she deserved it. She had hurt him deeply, perhaps worse than anyone else had ever hurt him before, and she deserved every hateful glare and wounded scowl he sent her way in the following weeks. She may not have physically scarred him, but as far as Theo was concerned, her crime was much worse than that.

She *lied* to him, day in and day out, for years on end, even after everything he had told her all that he had been through. Even after he had told her how much it pained him to be lied to and deceived. Theo had lived the first half of his life in the web of lies that his father had weaved to conceal the truth of his conception, and now, the one person that he trusted the most in this world, the woman with whom he had shared everything—mind, body, and soul—had dragged him through yet another entanglement of deceptions. And for what? To keep a roof over her head? To escape her past and a husband she didn't love? It didn't really matter, Theo decided, because no matter the motive, she lied to him. She betrayed him. She *used* him. She was the only person in the world that he trusted with his life, and she betrayed him in the worst way possible.

While the vast majority of Division Point became enveloped in suspicion and distrust of Evie, Johanna and Alistair remained steadfast in their love and support for her, even after the truth of her past reached their ears. They had both suspected for some time that she was keeping important details of her past hidden, but they rightfully assumed that she did so only out of self-preservation, rather than out of ill-will towards the community that had taken her in. Though had Theo turned his back on her in hurt and rage, Johanna and Alistair continued to accept her as the daughter they never had, urging her to give Theo time to cool off.

He will come around, Johanna promised. *He's just hurt. He'll see in time that you meant no harm.* But after weeks of cold and awkward silence, that time still had not come, and Evie began to lose hope that she and Theo would ever be able to look each other in the eye again. She wanted desperately for things to return to the way they were before, when he looked upon her with gentle adoration rather than hate and suspicion.

Constance Baker had never been so pleased with herself in her life, and it brought her great pleasure to watch the homestead turn on Evie overnight. She had never seen Theo so despondent, so angry, so hurt, and while it bothered her to see him so upset, it made her even happier to see the spell Evie had cast upon him broken like brittle glass. Almost as soon as Theo severed the ties that bound him to Evie, Constance attempted to swoop in and claim him for herself. She tried to speak to him, to woo him with sickeningly sweet words and coquettish smiles, but he was hardly in the mood to be flirted with. He rebuffed every one of her advances, just as he had before Evie's past had come to light, and this only served to confuse and infuriate Constance more.

She had been so certain that as soon as she revealed Evie to be the Loyalist snake she was, Theo would have come to his senses and come crawling to her, looking for a shoulder to cry on. But that was not the case. Instead, Theo became resentful and withdrawn, locking himself in his room for days at a time and refusing to speak to anyone. Before the storm of betrayal had blown through, Theo's heart filled with unspeakable joy and contentment every time he looked upon Evie's angelic face. But now, when he looked at her, or even thought of her, he felt nothing but hurt and hate. With every day that passed, he could feel his heart grow colder within his chest until it became frozen and brittle and shattered into a thousand icy shards that he could never hope to piece back together.

After over a month of awkward silence and resentful glares, Evie finally found the courage to try and speak to Theo again. She knew she owed him a full explanation, and she knew he craved it, but she also knew he was nothing if not stubborn, and it would be a miracle if he ever gave her the time of day again after what she had done. It was a cold day in late January when she dared to approach him, and she would be lying if she said that she wasn't at least a little afraid of him and the rage of which she knew he was capable. She had seen and heard firsthand what he was willing to do to those who he felt had wronged him, and of anyone in this world, she had wronged him the most.

She found Theo right where she expected to find him on that cold and snowy afternoon, wandering along the icy beach and staring wistfully out at the frozen expanse of water before them, like he always did when he was plagued by confusion or distress. He heard her coming from the start, as her footsteps against the slick and icy rocks as she descended the cliffside to reach the beach were loud and clumsy. His back was turned to her as he stared out over the water, and she could see his body stiffen as she approached.

She stood a few steps behind him in nervous silence for several moments as the wind whipped their hair mercilessly about their faces and her cloak billowed around her ankles. The cold wind cut through her clothes and penetrated her to the bone, sending shivers up her spine, and she wanted nothing more than for his arms to wrap around her and warm her tired body.

"Theo?" she eventually mumbled as she wrapped her cloak tightly around her body.

"What do you want?" His words were colder than the wind that sliced through their bodies, and they were the first words he had spoken to her in a month.

"I just wanted...I wanted to speak to you."

"I have nothing to say to you."

"You don't need to say anything. I just want you to listen..."

Theo abruptly turned to face her, and the action caused her to take a nervous step backward. His mouth was pulled into a tight scowl and his eyes had narrowed into slits.

"And why should I listen to anything you have to say to me? How can I trust anything you say?"

Evie shook her head and swallowed thickly. "I never meant to hurt you. That was the last thing I wanted..."

"No, all you *wanted* was to serve yourself. You did not care what you had to do, or who you had to hurt, to get there."

"No. You don't understand..."

"What exactly do I not understand? What did you really want when you came here? What did you want from me?"

"Exactly what I told you when we first a met. I meant everything I said when I told you that all I wanted was a chance to start my life over, as far away from my husband as possible..."

"And you just conveniently forgot to mention that your husband is the same man that murdered our neighbors and nearly took my life," Theo spat in return, eyes ablaze.

Evie gulped again as she became overwhelmed with the familiar sensation of tears burning in her eyes. "I hid the truth from the beginning because I knew you would never accept me if you thought I was a Loyalist.

And I had already waited so long to tell you… that I was afraid you would be angry with me. I was afraid he would find me and hurt me again. I didn't know what else to do…"

"Do you really think so lowly of me that I would not have understood if you told me the truth yourself? But no, instead of hearing the truth from you, I had to hear it from *Constance*?"

"No one was ever supposed to see that book. I was trying to leave everything about my past behind me…"

Theo took an angry step in her direction and pointed an accusatory finger in her face. "I can forgive your past and your family's connection to the Crown, I can even forgive that you bore a child by another man, but what I *cannot* forgive is that even after all you know I have endured, after all that Silas Porter has done to this community, and to me, you still could not be bothered to tell me the truth!"

"I was afraid…" Evie whispered, her words punctuated by quiet sobs.

Theo was unfazed by her tears. "You were afraid? How do you think the people of Kensington felt as they watched their world burn down around them and their families bleed out from Redcoat bullets on your husband's command? How do you think I felt as his prisoner, held captive and tortured for days on end under the threat of being sold into slavery like a dog? How do you think I felt when he whipped and beat me within an inch of my life and scarred me forever? He almost killed me, Evie, and you knew exactly who he was!"

Theo's words became harsher as the rage and pain he felt boiled closer to the surface, threatening to spill over in a fiery explosion. He took several more steps in Evie's direction until he was nearly chest to chest with her, leaning his face close to hers as he stared her down. Evie stared desperately into his eyes and watched with bated breath as they swam with agony and confusion. She felt her heart constrict painfully in her chest when those golden pools froze over into icy caverns, red and swollen with tears he wouldn't permit himself to shed in her presence.

"I'm so sorry," she gasped. "I'm so sorry. You have to believe me, Theo. Everything I told you about me, about how I feel about you, about my love for you is true. You have to believe me! What can I do to prove it to you?"

Theo shook his head and backed away when she shakily tried to reach out and place her hand against his cheek. He coldly shrugged out from underneath her touch as his scowl deepened.

"Nothing. I can never trust you again…"

Evie squeezed her eyes shut as her tears poured and froze to her cheeks. The world began to spin all over again and her knees buckled underneath her as she cowered under his cold gaze.

"You don't mean that."

"I mean every word. You mean nothing to me now…"

"How can you be so cold after everything we've been through together? After all we have shared, and all we have done? You know me, Theo! You know I would never do anything to harm you, your family, or anyone else here. You know me well enough to know that I only did what I did because I thought it was the only way I could protect myself…"

Theo shook his head stiffly, and his words broke as they escaped his lips with ragged breath. "No. I don't know you at all."

Evie clutched at the beaded necklace that hung at the base of her throat, the object that had once served as an enduring promise of love and devotion between them. "What happens now?"

"If you want to do something, do us all a favor and go back to wherever you came from. Go back to your mansion in Boston, go back to your aristocratic parents. Just go. Leave and don't come back."

"Would it make you happy if I left?"

"I will never be happy again, and I have you to thank for it."

"Theo, please—"

"Good day, *Mrs. Porter*. I wish you luck in all of your future endeavors."

Theo's final words were harsh and sharp, driving a wedge into the cracks of both of their hearts as he roughly brushed past her and stormed away, disappearing over the top of the cliff and leaving the woman he once loved alone on the beach. Evie's eyes went wide as she felt all of the wind knocked from her lungs with his words, and she stared out at the water in shock, gasping for breath. Violent sobs wracked her body as she slowly crumbled and collapsed to her knees in the icy sand, dropping her head in her hands in shame.

Nothing seemed real, and nothing seemed right. *This could not be happening*, a voice screamed in her head. Theo could not truly despise her this much, not after all of the love and all of the passion they had shared over the last year. But nonetheless, his heart had grown cold and he abandoned every feeling he ever had for her, leaving her alone to float aimlessly in a vast ocean of despair that only he could pull her out of if he ever had it in his frozen heart to forgive her.

Her body went numb as the feeling of emptiness overcame her, and she craved his touch and his affection like her lungs craved air. Watching him walk away put a dagger through her heart and sent her sinking into the bottomless ocean in which he had left her, and she tried desperately to claw her way back to the surface, but with every step he took away, she sunk further and further until there was no hope that she would ever see the light again. For the last five years, it was all she could do to keep her head above water, but now, the only thing that had been keeping her afloat had abandoned her for good.

Evie dropped her hands from her face and dug her fingers into the cold sand underneath her, feeling it slip though her grasp along with the only happiness she had ever known. She had woken up one morning on the top of the world, with everything she could have wanted in her grasp. She had a home and a community in which she felt safe and wanted, and she had a man whom she loved and who would do anything to protect her. But now, after a matter of a few devastating moments, once again she had *nothing*.

***

January 1779

    The freshly fallen snow cracked noisily underfoot as Evie shuffled through the Cunningham's' front yard and across the road to the church. The sun was low in the sky, looming lazily over the horizon as if it did not have the energy to rise for another day. Streaks of pink and orange shot across a deep indigo sky above her head, and she would have stopped to enjoy the view if her heart was not weighed down so terribly with an agonizing concoction of guilt, regret, and sorrow. Evie took a turn at the church and dragged her feet as she crossed into the Division Point cemetery. Her faithful companion, the only one that had remained by her side other than Johanna and Alistair during these past disastrous weeks, Gunner, followed close behind her, frolicking excitedly through the snow. He was now almost full grown and had turned into an enormous beast of a hound with massive paws and forever floppy ears.

    She did not need to look up from her feet to know the path to her son's grave, as it was a trek that she had taken many times over the last four years. Many times, she had come to see her boy since he passed through Heaven's gates, but it was still not enough. It was never enough.

    In the chaos that ensued after Constance had revealed her secrets to the world, Evie could not bring herself to leave the house long enough to come to the graveyard and visit Noah on the day that would have marked his fourth birthday. The guilt ate her alive, and so she snuck out of the house at the crack of dawn to pay him a much belated visit on the last day of January.

    Evie dropped to her knees in the snow before Noah's ice-covered headstone and flinched when she felt the frozen precipitation seep through her skirts and assault the skin on her legs. She wrapped her cloak tightly round her body and shivered against the cold wind as her red and swollen eyes roamed over the inscription on the headstone. Gunner came to sit protectively at her side, facing the entrance to the graveyard so that he could keep watch.

"Happy birthday, my son," she whispered weakly. "I know it has been far too long since I have come to see you. And for that I will never forgive myself."

She sniffled in order to swallow the mournful tears brimming in her eyes, but they began to fall regardless. She had never been good at holding back her sadness, and that was likely to never change.

"I suppose that is just one of many mistakes that I have made in my life, isn't it?" she asked aloud. "I thought I was doing what was best, for me, for you, for Theo, for everyone…but it seems that I only destroy everything good that I get my hands on.

"You deserve so much better, Noah. So much better than what I could give you. So much better than *me*. You deserved the entire world, but in the end, the only things I could give you were a shallow grave and a handful of excuses."

Evie's shoulders began to shake as sobs broke and punctuated her words. Her heart and lungs seemed to constrict tighter and tighter in her chest the longer she stared at the grave, and she gasped when she noticed something leaning against the headstone, buried in the ice and snow. She reached forward to brush the snow away, and a sad smile came upon her flushed face when she realized that it was the corn husk doll Theo had left for Noah nearly a year before. It was encrusted in ice and its colors had faded from being subjected to the elements, but miraculously, it remained undisturbed, just where it had been left, for all of these months.

Evie wistfully placed the doll back against the headstone where it belonged and reminisced on the day when it had first been left, back when Theo still wanted to hold her—during the calm before the storm. The storm that left her floundering in an abyss of guilt and regret with the weight of the world preventing her from keeping her head above the water.

"This was all a mistake," Evie whispered aloud to the gravestone as she shook her head and gave Gunner's head a gentle pet. "I never should have tried to run away. I never should have tried to make it on my own. What was I thinking? I've never done a damn thing for myself in all of my days, and here I was, thinking I could leave everything behind me and make a new life for myself. And now the only things I had—you and Theo—are gone. Nearly everyone has abandoned me...you, Theo, Emma, my parents. Perhaps Theo was right. Perhaps I have overstayed my welcome here. Maybe I...maybe I should just go back where I came from...back to Silas. Perhaps my past is where I belonged all along..."

Gunner's tail began to wag uncontrollably as gentle footsteps approached from behind. "How can you say such a thing?" a familiarly soft voice asked.

Evie gasped and glanced over her shoulder to see Johanna's short and curvaceous figure looming over her just a few steps behind. She was wrapped tightly in a cloak of her own, her dark hair tossed in a messy bun on the top of her head and her cheeks flushed from the cold. Johanna's eyes were as kind and soft as they always had been as she looked down upon the broken girl at her feet.

"What are you doing here?" Evie asked through her tears as she wiped the back of her hand over her eyes.

"Oh, you know I am always up with the sun. I was fixing breakfast in the kitchen when I happened to look out the window and see you across the yard. I didn't even hear you leave the house."

"You weren't meant to."

Johanna let out a heavy sigh and slowly lowered herself onto her knees next to Evie before the grave. "What is this nonsense I heard you speaking about going back to your husband?"

Evie shrugged apathetically. "There is nothing left for me here now. My friends hate me. Theo hates me. My son is dead. What reason do I have to stay?"

"Evie, this is your home. It has been for four years. This is your family. You can't go back to Silas. You know what he will do to you if he gets his hands on you again."

Evie's eyes were dark and empty as she gave Johanna a sideways glance. "I deserve whatever he has to give me. After everything I have done, I deserve every bit of his wrath."

"Don't you say that. There is nothing you could ever say or do to deserve that man's torture."

"How can you be so kind to me after what I have done, Johanna? How can you not despise me like everyone else? I lied to your face for years. My husband murdered your neighbors and nearly murdered your stepson…"

Johanna shook her head sadly and placed a hand on Evie's shoulders. Sadness danced behind her deep hazel eyes as she murmured, "Because I understand the motivations of a scared and desperate woman, love. I know you did what you thought you had to do to survive. No can fault you for that."

Evie's tears continued to pour as she dropped her head on Johanna's shoulder and wrapped her arms around her body. "Theo does not see it that way. He will never forgive me…"

Johanna rubbed her back and rocked from side to side. "You know how Theo is. He's stubborn and prideful. He has a short fuse on that temper of his and he refuses to admit when he's been hurt. It will just take him time to settle down. He'll see in time. He cares about you too much to let you go that easily."

"And what if he doesn't? What if he never speaks to me again?"

"Then you'll find another…"

"I don't want another! I want him! I…I love him…"

Johanna squeezed her tighter as she felt her own tears begin to burn her eyes, and thoughts and memories of her youth came back to flash across her vision. She could recall a time several decades ago, when she was just as desperate as this girl to escape her old world with the man she loved, motivated only by a desire to be happy and free from the binds of her past.

"And he loves you. I can see it in the way he looks at you. He is just hurt and confused. You know how angry he gets when he thinks he has been deceived. He has his father and myself to thank for that. We lied to him for the first thirteen years of his life about who he was, so I suppose it is only natural he would be furious when you lied to him about who you were."

Evie sniffled and wiped away the last of her tears, looking up to meet Johanna's gaze. "…Johanna?"

"Yes, love?"

"Do you think I am a terrible person? A terrible mother?"

"No, that could not be farther from the truth! I cannot think of many mothers who would go to the lengths you did to protect your child."

"And it was all for nothing, anyhow. The only two reasons I had for happiness are gone now."

Johanna placed a hand on Evie's cheek and smiled sadly. "I've told you about the struggles Alistair and I went through when we were your age. About running away together, about my inability to bear him a child, about…the affair…"

"I do not know how you endured it, Johanna…"

"There were times when I thought I wouldn't. Miscarriage after miscarriage after miscarriage…I thought I had given all I had to give when Alistair returned home from the war with another woman's child in his arms. I was so angry, so hurt, so betrayed. I told him I would never forgive him for his betrayal."

"But you did…"

"In time, yes. I knew Theo was my only chance to ever know the joys of motherhood, and I loved that fool Alistair too much to throw away everything we had built together. So, I swallowed my hurt and my pride and I grew to love his son as my own."

"Why…why are you telling me this?"

"If I have taught Theo anything, it is to have a forgiving heart. If I can forgive Alistair for his infidelity, Theo can forgive you for your deception. It will just take time. He'll see in time that his love for you far exceeds any anger he can harbor against you."

Chapter 3

Home

March 1779

Jacob's boots pounded heavily against the dewy earth as he sprinted across the homestead, cutting across the paved road and through several yards to save precious time. Sweat gathered upon his brow as he looked over his shoulder and then scanned the horizon before him, searching desperately for his friend as panic filled his heart. It had been a rather average springtime evening, and he had just been down at his father's forge when he happened to look toward the tree line at the end of the road and catch sight of something that stopped him in his tracks.

A cluster of red-coated men on horseback surrounding a horse drawn carriage poked through the trees just as the sun began to set. They were far off in the distance and barely recognizable as people, but their blood-red uniforms contrasted sharply with their dull green surroundings to give them away immediately. Feeling his heart leap into his throat, Jacob dropped his tools and made a mad dash toward the Cunningham house in search of Theo and Alistair, as anyone always did when strange visitors appeared in Division Point.

"Theo!" Jacob called frantically as he reached the front yard of the Cunningham home. Theo was slouched on the stairs of the front porch, whittling at a chunk of driftwood with his hunting knife.

Theo looked up with a frown. "What is it? You look like you've seen a ghost."

Jacob skidded to a stop in front of the steps and gasped for breath, pointing over his shoulder. "Down at the tree line...I saw...Redcoats...seven or eight of them..."

"*What?*" Theo leapt to his feet and furrowed his brow. "Redcoats? Are you certain?"

"Certain! They were carrying muskets and their uniforms were the color of blood. They are coming up the road as we speak!"

Theo tossed his whittling to the side and brushed past his friend to sprint toward the lighthouse. Jacob followed close behind as Theo took the spiraling stairs three at a time until they reached the catwalk at the very top, the only vantage point from which one could see the entirety of the homestead all at once. Theo scanned the tree line on the western horizon as he leaned over the railing, letting out an alarmed growl when he spotted a cluster of red marching up the road. He could not make out any faces at first, but he could see a large and ornate carriage drawn by two massive horses and flanked by two Redcoat soldiers on each of its four sides.

"What could Redcoats be doing back here again?" Jacob asked nervously as he peered over Theo's shoulder at the road below. "I thought the war had moved south..."

"It has," Theo snapped as he gripped the railing so tightly that his knuckles began to turn white.

"Are they here for quarter again, do you think?"

Theo hesitated before answering, taking another moment to watch as the carriage and its escort approached. Once the convoy was within less than a few hundred yards of the homestead, he squinted through the waning sunlight to see if he could gather any more information on their new visitors. That was when Theo saw *his* face, and he felt his blood run cold in his veins and his legs go weak underneath him.

There he was, sitting tall, proud, and arrogant inside the carriage, peering out the window at his surroundings with his face pinched in disgust. The large scar across his left cheekbone was unmistakable, even from the distance at which Theo had spotted him, as were his steely grey eyes and the repugnant smirk in which his lips seemed to be permanently twisted. *Captain Silas Porter, commanding officer of Fort Dumpling Rock.* Theo could recognize his eyes from a thousand miles away, and the sight of him, here on *his* land, approaching *his* home with an armed escort, sent his stomach churning and his heart pounding.

"No…" Theo murmured as he swallowed thickly. "It can't be. How…How could he have found us?"

"What? Who?" Jacob snapped.

Theo's hands tightened further around the railing as he ground his teeth, feeling every muscle in his body tighten as he stared at the ground below. "…Silas Porter. It's him. He's here."

"What? Are you certain? How can that be?" Jacob leaned over the railing to catch another glimpse of the approaching convoy, but he did not recognize a single face.

"I'm positive. I'd know his face anywhere…"

"Why would he come here? For you? How could he know you were here? Unless…" Jacob lowered his voice in anger. "Do you think Evie led him here?"

Theo's scowl deepened as he shook his head. "No. But I do not intend to watch from up here and wait to find out." He released his death grip on the railing and abruptly turned to sprint back down the stairs, leaving Jacob scrambling to keep up with him.

"Where are you going? What are you doing? Do you intend to confront him?"

Theo paused upon reaching the front porch of the house. Pointing a finger at Jacob, who had skidded to a stop in the middle of the yard, he sternly said, "Wait out here and keep watch for them. They will be here any moment. I will return shortly."

"Hurry!" Jacob whined as he looked toward the road. "Don't leave me out here alone!"

The carriage and its escort were now only about a hundred yards from the Cunningham house, and during the convoy's procession through the homestead, it had gathered the attention of many inhabitants, most of whom were now crowding at their windows or in their yards to watch what may unfold next. Fear and nervousness filled their hearts as the crowds began to gather, with vivid memories of the fiery remains of Kensington fresh in their minds. Would the same fate that befell Kensington befall them today, they wondered? Had the war truly reached their doorstep?

Theo stomped into the front room where Alistair and Johanna were sitting together to enjoy a cup of tea. Evie was also there, dusting the shelves and tidying up. Everyone in the room froze upon Theo's entry, taking in his stiffened posture and perturbed expression.

"What is it, son?" Alistair asked between coughs.

"Redcoats. They are coming up the road. Silas Porter leads them."

The porcelain vase Evie had been dusting slipped from her numbing fingers and crashed to the floor at her feet in a thousand shards as she felt the blood drain from her face and her body break out into a cold sweat. She suddenly became lightheaded and weak-kneed as she stared across the room at Theo in shock. His eyes were dark and cold as he stared back at her.

Swallowing, she stuttered, "It can't be."

"Are you certain it is him?" Alistair asked as he rose to his feet.

"I am certain. I do not know how, but he has found Division Point."

"What could he want?" Johanna asked fearfully as she brought her hands up to her face. "Could he be looking for you?"

Theo locked eyes with Evie again. Evie shook her head with a defeated sigh and brought a shaking hand up to her mouth.

"No," she whispered. "My husband would not waste his time looking for an escaped prisoner of war. He's here for *me*. He found *me*."

"How?" Johanna gasped. "How could he know you are here?"

Theo turned his back to them and made for the corner of the front room, taking up the pistol that he had stashed away behind one of the bookshelves. After checking to ensure it was loaded, he tucked it into the back of his trousers underneath his shirt.

"What are you doing?" Evie asked anxiously.

"I am going to see what he wants." Theo motioned for Alistair to follow him and then pointed to both Johanna and Evie, who were huddled fearfully in the corner of the room. "Both of you, stay inside where it is safe. Do not show yourselves for any reason."

Just as he turned to storm outside, Evie seized him by the shoulder. "You cannot face him alone. It is me he wants. I'm coming with you."

Theo glanced over his shoulder to shoot her a hot glare as he shrugged out from under her touch. "You are to stay inside with Johanna where it is safe."

"But—"

"That was an order, not a request," Theo spat hotly before turning away and stalking outside. Alistair followed close behind his son and reiterated the order for the women to stay inside. As soon as the men had left the house, Johanna and Evie both huddled together at the front window with their hearts in their throats.

Nearly every inhabitant of the homestead had now gathered outside or at the windows of their homes and shops as the large and ornate carriage rolled to a stop at the end of the road just before the Cunningham home. Jacob, Alistair, and Theo stood tall in the front yard, shoulders hunched defensively as the carriage door slowly opened and each of the eight Redcoat escorts stood at attention on horseback on either side of the carriage. The setting sun glinted ominously off of the musket in each soldier's hand, as well as the gilded carvings that covered the carriage's exterior.

Theo's body went rigid as he watched a tall and regal individual step out of the carriage, shiny black riding boots crushing against the gravel of the road as he slammed the door shut behind him and sauntered around to the front of his escort. Silas Porter stared sanctimoniously down the bridge of his nose at the crowd that had gathered to watch him, and his lips were pressed together in a thin hard line that bespoke agitation and boredom. His long, ashy blonde hair was slicked back and tied with a ribbon at the base of his neck, and everything about his red officer's uniform was polished and put together, with not a wrinkle nor a smudge to be seen.

It took several moments before Silas' eyes fell upon the three common folk that stood in the yard before him, as he was too busy taking in the sights and smells of a *lowly* fishing village, and when his eyes fell upon Theo, he looked quite taken aback, stunned into silence for several seconds before clearing his throat and blinking away his surprise. Narrowing his eyes and taking a step in Theo's direction, he said, "You. I have seen your face before…"

"And I have seen yours," Theo retorted. "I am sure we are both sights for sore eyes."

Silas cleared his throat again as a smirk slowly spread across his face. "Yes, that is right. You are the rebel prisoner that escaped my fort over a year ago."

"And you are the tyrant that tortured me and then tried to sell me into slavery."

"Yes, well…I like to think of myself as an opportunist. Tell me, boy, how is your *back*?"

Theo's fingers itched to reach for the pistol on his back as he ground his teeth and let out a low growl. He took an angry step forward as if to lunge in Silas' direction, but Alistair put up an outstretched arm in front of him to hold him back.

"What do you want from us?" Alistair asked. "I am sure a man as smart as yourself can figure out that you aren't welcome here."

Silas let out a breathy chuckle and dusted off the shoulders of his red coat. "I am here to collect my wife. I was told I could find her here in this…abysmal excuse for a settlement. Perhaps you have seen her? The last I saw her, she was a short, red-headed little thing with a smart mouth and my child in her womb. What a small world we live in, hm? What are the chances that my wife has found sanctuary with the very same rebel that I once had in my custody?"

"I don't know anyone by that description," Theo said through clenched teeth.

Evie peered through the front window while obscuring most herself behind the curtain, but even from a distance of nearly thirty yards, she could make out every feature of her husband's face. Time and the drink had not been kind to him, as he looked to have aged ten years in the span of five. His eyes were wild and beady, his face wrinkled by anger and stress. While the change in his face was striking, even more jarring was the very jagged and noticeable scar that extended across his left cheekbone, just under his eye.

In an instant, memories of the night of her perilous escape flashed across Evie's vision, and she was overcome by the vivid recollection of her shakily pointing a pistol in her husband's direction and watching in horror as it went off and the bullet grazed the left side of his face. Evie gasped and pressed her hand to the windowpane, chewing nervously on her lower lip as she watched Theo and Silas banter back and forth.

Silas rolled his eyes. "I know that she has been hiding out here for the last several years. I demand to know the whereabouts of my wife and my child, or else."

"Or else, what?" Theo snapped. "You'll flog me again?"

Silas bared his teeth arrogantly and placed his hands on his hips. "Produce my wife and child to me this instant, *or else*, history shall repeat itself and your miserable shanty town will meet the same fate as your neighbors in Kensington."

Theo would have been lying if he said he did not feel at least a little fear as he stared into the eyes of the man that had nearly taken his life, but he stood his ground, nonetheless.

"Bugger off, Porter. We have nothing for you here."

"Where is she?" Silas demanded again, this time with anger breaking through his once cool exterior.

"She isn't here," Theo repeated.

Evie looked back and forth between Silas and Theo in confusion as to why Theo would even consider trying to cover for her. As far as she understood, he hated her now and had even gone so far as to tell her to leave Division Point. At the threat of violence, why would he not hand her over to Silas the first chance he got and be rid of her?

Silas let out an enraged huff and looked back to nod to two of his escorts. Without hesitation, two Redcoats dismounted from their horses and marched across the grass in Theo's direction. Before Theo could even raise his hands to defend himself, the soldiers flanked him on either side and seized him by his shoulders, pinning both of his arms behind his back.

Alistair jumped and tried to reach out for his son, but Jacob wisely held him back so that he would avoid the business end of a musket that a third soldier on horseback was now pointing in his direction.

"Theo!" the older man called worriedly as Jacob held him back by his shoulders.

"No sudden movements," Jacob reminded him gently. "Don't give them a reason to hurt him."

Theo struggled against the soldiers' hold as they dragged him forward and held him while Silas closed the distance between them in two large steps. Leaning his face downward until Theo could smell the whiskey on his breath, Silas' lips curled back to reveal a set of perfectly white teeth that he clenched together into a menacing scowl. In one fluid motion, he pulled a pistol from his belt and held the barrel under Theo's chin.

"I'll ask again, *mongrel*. Where. Is. My. Wife?"

Johanna gasped tearfully behind the window and looked worriedly to Evie. "What is he going to do to him?"

Theo and Silas stared each other down in defiant silence until Silas abruptly curled his hand into a fist and forced it so hard into Theo's stomach that he doubled over in agony and let out a startled gasp. Alistair once again tried to come to his son's aid, but the moment he took a step in that direction, another Redcoat pointed a musket at his chest and warned him to step back. Theo dropped to his knees when Silas struck him in the stomach a second time, and before he could take another breath, one of the soldiers holding his arms behind his back bent down to snatch the pistol from underneath the back of his shirt.

Silas chuckled and tossed Theo's pistol to the side. "Tell me where you are hiding her, or I will tear this place apart and burn it to the ground to find her!"

Theo lifted his head to glare up at him through the hair that had fallen in his face. "Go to Hell."

Evie backed away from the window with a gasp as she watched Theo drop to his knees at Silas' feet. With a flourish she turned from the window and made for the front door, but Johanna reached out and took her by her arm.

"What are you doing? You cannot go out there!"

"I have to. He'll kill Theo and destroy the homestead if I don't!"

Evie tried to reach for the door again, but Johanna held fast to her upper arms, her eyes wide with tears and panic. "Please, Evie. You know what he will do when he gets his hands on you. He'll take you away with him! If you go out there, we can't protect you!"

Evie locked her eyes with Johanna's and touched a hand to the older woman's cheek. "We both know what happened to the last village that refused to give my husband what he wanted. I *won't* let that happen to Division Point."

Evie broke away from Johanna's hold and made for the door, leaving her surrogate mother to collapse back against the wall in tears. After taking a moment to collect herself, she followed Evie out the door, nearly tripping over Gunner as he came sprinting around the corner to remain by his owner's side.

Silas cocked his own pistol and held the barrel against the center of Theo's forehead, right between his eyes. His finger rested heavily on the trigger as he spat, "Last chance, boy."

Theo stared down the barrel of the gun with a smirk and opened his mouth to speak, but Evie burst through the front door a few yards behind him before he could utter another defiant word.

Coming to stand on the edge of the porch, she declared, "Silas! Let him go. It is me you want, not him."

Silas froze with his finger upon the trigger and looked up as a maniacal smile came upon his face. "Darling," he breathed, "it has been too long."

Evie straightened her shoulders and descended the steps as Silas pulled his pistol from Theo's face and ordered his men to release him. The soldiers flanking Theo on either side roughly pushed him to the ground and stepped away. Silas stared at her with a furrowed brow, taking notice of the fact that after almost five years, her womb was no longer swollen, yet she had no child upon her hip.

"I've come to bring you home, my dear," Silas continued. "I have been looking for you for five long years."

"I *am* home," Evie countered coldly at the bottom of the steps.

Silas frowned deeply and then smiled to conceal the anger bubbling in his chest. It was unlike her to talk back in such an assertive matter, and he did not like this change. Rather than staring at him with wide, fear-filled doe eyes and slumped shoulders, she stared him down with an air of confidence about her that betrayed every ounce of fear she felt in her heart. Though she may have appeared brave in the moment, on the inside she was cowering as she looked the source of her misery in the face.

Evie took a deep breath before crossing the yard and stooping down at Theo's side as he slowly pulled himself up onto his hands and knees and recovered from the blows to his gut. He met Evie's gaze with confusion and anger as she took him by the arm and helped him rise to his feet.

"I told you to stay inside," he hissed at her.

Evie shook her head sadly. "I can't let him hurt you in my name."

"Then come with me without a fight and I will spare this miserable wasteland," Silas snapped.

Evie looked at him sharply, but Theo interceded on her behalf. "No one leaves Division Point unless it is of their own volition."

Silas' steely eyes settled on his wife as he raised his voice. "Correct me if I am wrong, dearest, but I do believe that you were with child when you left me."

Evie swallowed nervously. "I was…"

"Then where is that child?"

Theo and Evie exchanged saddened looks before she lowered her head. Her voice dropped to a near whisper as she murmured, "He…he's dead."

Silas froze where he stood as his expression morphed from one of aggravation to one of shock and rage. "...*He?*"

She swallowed again and locked her eyes with his, painfully aware of the short distance of a just few yards that separated them. "I bore a son, Silas. His name is Noah. He...was stillborn. He is buried here in the cemetery by the church."

"You killed my son?" Silas bellowed in an abrupt explosion of anger, his voice echoing off of the surrounding buildings with enough force to make Evie cringe away.

Tears burned her eyes as she shook her head. "No. It was a tragic accident. He was dead before he was born..."

Silas let out a huff through his nostrils as he pinched the bridge of his nose to steady himself. Evie knew him well enough to recognize the signs of when he was about to erupt in a fit of rage, and she could see the vein in his forehead throbbing. After a moment of silence, he let out a breath and cleared his throat.

"Never mind that. What is done is done. I've come to collect you and bring you with me to the fort under my command. We will be leaving immediately. I'll allow you a few minutes to collect your things."

He expected her to immediately acquiesce to his command, as she had done so many times before in the past, but instead of cowering under the weight of his orders, she stood tall and defiantly crossed her arms over her chest.

"No," she said simply.

"No?"

"*No*. I left you for a reason. This is my home now. These people are my family. I want to stay here."

Silas was quiet for a moment before bursting out in laughter. "Oh, Evie. I never took you for the joking type."

"Do you see me laughing, Silas?"

Silas' amused smile faded back into a deep frown. "Perhaps I have not made my intentions clear. I will be leaving here today with you by my side, where you belong. Whether or not this homestead remains standing and its inhabitants alive when we leave is up to you alone."

Evie narrowed her eyes at him. "The people of Division Point have been nothing but kind and decent to me and everyone else that has come here for refuge. They have nothing to do with this. Your anger is towards me and me alone."

"Come willingly with me—as my wife—and no one will be harmed. Choose to resist me," Silas lifted his pistol and pointed it across the yard at Theo's chest, "and the savage and his home shall burn."

Evie turned to slowly pass her eyes over the faces of everyone that had gathered. She saw the faces of friends and family, the faces of people to whom she would forever be grateful and would never forget. Johanna and Alistair held each other as they silently pleaded for her not to go, and when her gaze fell upon Theo, her heart was broken to see the sadness swimming behind his eyes. After a moment of deliberation, she turned back to her husband.

"I will return to you on one condition."

"Name it."

"You leave Division Point and it's people as you have found them, and you give me your word that no harm will ever come to them. When we leave, you swear that you never return to hurt them."

A small smile slowly spread across Silas' face and he nodded curtly. "I am nothing if not an honorable man. You have my word."

"No!" Theo growled, taking several steps in Silas' and Evie's direction. As soon as he moved, all eight soldiers in Silas' escort raised their muskets and aimed them at his chest. "You can't go. Your home is here."

Evie passed a despondent look between Theo and her husband. "Tell them to lower their guns, and I will leave with you without a fight."

Silas motioned for his men to lower their weapons and back away towards the carriage. "Come along then, dearest. It is a long trek to Fort Dumpling Rock."

"Give me a moment to say goodbye at least," Evie begged.

Silas rolled his eyes up to the sky and waved his hand in annoyance. "Fine. Do it with haste."

Evie immediately turned and sprinted across the grass to throw her arms around both Johanna and Alistair, collapsing into them as tears streamed down her cheeks. They both held her tightly as their own tears came to their eyes, and they were forced to face the crushing reality that the daughter they had grown to love was being taken from them and they were powerless to stop it.

"Oh, my sweet girl," Johanna sobbed into Evie's hair as she held her tight. "I can't believe this is happening. We love you so much. Will we ever see you again?"

Evie gently pulled away and slowly shook her head. "I am afraid not. I'm so sorry. Thank you, thank you for everything…"

Alistair leaned down to kiss the top of her head, and as he spoke, his raspy voice began to crack. "If there was anything that I could do to stop this, you know I would, lass."

She shook her head again. "I couldn't let you put your community in danger for me. Silas has harmed enough people already. I won't allow anyone else to be hurt for me any longer…" '

After giving them each one last hug and kiss goodbye, Evie turned to see Theo staring her down from across the yard. His body was rigid and poised as if he was tensed and ready to pounce upon every Redcoat that surrounded him, but when his eyes fell upon her, they were tight and full of anguish. She gingerly shuffled across the grass and closed the distance between them, feeling Silas' eyes never leave her as she moved. Upon reaching her former lover, Evie threw her arms around Theo's neck and buried her face in his chest.

"I'm so sorry," she gasped into the fabric of his shirt. "I'm so sorry…for everything…"

Theo's eyes fluttered closed as he returned her embrace, and his body instantly relaxed underneath her touch—a feeling he had been missing for months now. "Why are you doing this?" he choked out. "Why are you doing this to me? You know what he will do once he has you again…"

Evie clutched onto his shirt and squeezed her eyes shut. "I would rather die a hundred times over than see you or anyone else here suffer. I've hurt so many already…"

"Don't go," he growled in her ear as he crushed her to his chest. "You can't go. I won't let you."

"This is what you wanted, remember? You told me to go…and now I am."

He shook his head in anger and through clenched teeth murmured, "No, I did not mean it. I did not mean any of it. This is the last thing I wanted!"

"I'm sorry… but it's too late for me now. He'll kill you and everyone else here if I do not go with him."

"How can you just leave like this, Evie? How can you go with him when you know what he is capable of?"

Evie pulled away from him enough to stare up into his red and swollen eyes. She swallowed her tears and with a gentle whisper, she said, "The things we do for the men we love…"

Theo's eyes widened momentarily as she pulled further away from him and reached for the back of her neck. She fumbled with the clasp on the bear-tooth necklace he had given her what seemed like ages ago, and after gently pulling it from her throat, she placed it in his hands. Theo did not think his heart could possibly break any more because it was not even whole to start with, but nonetheless, he felt an agonizing constriction in his chest as his hand became weighed down by the necklace she placed in his palm.

Evie closed his fingers around it and mumbled through another bout of tears, "Give this to a woman more deserving of your heart than I."

Theo let out a ragged breath as a single tear slipped down his cheek, and he closed his fist tightly around the necklace as his hands fell limply at his sides in defeat. Evie reached up on the tips of her toes to press a feather-light kiss upon his cheek before slowly back away. She took only three steps away from him before Silas suddenly appeared at her side and seized her tightly by her upper arm. Gunner immediately let out an aggravated bark at the hostile stranger, baring his teeth and lowering his head as if he was prepared to defend his master to the death.

"That is enough for goodbyes, I think," Silas snapped smugly as he locked eyes with Theo. "We should be off then. No need to pack any of your things, dear wife. You'll have everything you need at Dumpling Rock."

Evie sighed heavily at the mention of the fort. The last place to which she wanted to be dragged was a cold stone structure plagued by every vestige of a war and an empire she did not support, but she supposed it was better than to be dragged back to Silas' home, where there were fewer witnesses to her husband's fits of rage. She gasped in surprise when Silas suddenly pulled her into his chest and planted a hard, deep kiss upon her lips right before Theo's eyes.

Upon pulling away, a smug smirk graced the Captain's lips as he grazed his fingers across the pale and delicate flesh of her cheek. She winced away from his touch but had nowhere else to go to get away from him.

"God, I've missed you," Silas sighed.

"I cannot say the feeling is mutual," she retorted with her eyes averted to the ground.

Within an instant, she was taken by the arm and dragged away from Theo's grasp to be bundled into the waiting carriage. She looked frequently over her shoulder as she was led away, her eyes never leaving

Theo's deflated form. As soon as she was pushed into the carriage, she turned to stare out through the back window. Placing her hands upon the glass, she watched as Alistair, Johanna, and Jacob came to stand next to Theo to watch as she was driven off. Gunner tried to follow after her, but Silas swiftly kicked at him until he scampered away with a frightened whimper. The soldiers in the escort each returned to mount their horses, and after they did so, they kept their muskets trained on the Cunningham's. Silas tossed one last triumphant look over his shoulder in Theo's direction as he placed his foot upon the carriage's step.

"Thank you for showing my wife such hospitality," he called to him. "Consider our last encounter my thank you."

If Theo hadn't felt so defeated and destroyed, he would have had something snarky to say in return, but instead, he squeezed his eyes shut and looked away as Alistair placed a comforting hand upon his shoulder. Giving them one last salute, Silas stepped into the carriage and closed the door behind him, motioning for his driver to kick the horses into motion. The carriage lurched forward and began to roll bumpily down the road toward the tree line, and the escort immediately moved into formation to surround it on all sides. Theo and the others watched helplessly as their last glimpses of Evie rolled away and out of their lives forever, and tears that he had forced himself to swallow for an eternity began to stream down his tanned cheeks.

Once the carriage was a suitable distance down the road, the escort disengaged from pointing their weapons at the Cunningham's and faced forward, ready to guard the carriage from an attack from any side. Evie continued to stare wistfully through the back window, her hand pressed against the glass as the carriage rolled down the road, leaving Division Point and the new life she had created for herself further and further behind. She locked gazes with Theo until he disappeared in the distance, dried tears staining both of their faces, and she felt another devastating fissure crack across her heart when the homestead disappeared altogether behind the thick line of trees. Gunner refused to let her go without a fight, and he chased after the carriage and its escort for the entire length of the road, but he quickly fell behind and skidded to a stop at the tree line to let out a startled howl when Evie was lost to the dark wilderness ahead.

Once the carriage and its red-coated escort disappeared behind the horizon, Theo collapsed to his knees once again and dropped his head in his hands in shame, rage, and confusion. Never in a million years did he expect the love of his life to be taken right before his eyes when he was powerless to stop it, and though he still harbored anger in his heart towards her for the way she had deceived him, the love he had for her far outweighed anything else.

It was just a damn shame that he did not realize that he loved her until after she had departed permanently from his grasp. Her heart may have still been beating when she left, but everyone knew that now that Silas had her in his possession, she may as well have been sent to her death.

***

Evie remained turned towards the back window of the carriage for some time after Division Point vanished from her view, and the sun was now far below the horizon, leaving the carriage to bask in the thin silvery light of the moon high overhead. Silas sat in the seat across from her, slumped against the backrest as his eyes roamed over her body and his lips twitched upward. She could feel his eyes upon her, but she hadn't the desire nor the energy to acknowledge him.

"Turn around and look at me," Silas ordered after miles of silence. "The savage and his cesspool of a village are long behind us now."

Evie ignored his request. "His name is Theo."

"I know damn well what the half breed's name is. I am sure he told you just how familiar he and I became when he was my prisoner."

Evie's frown deepened as she slowly turned to sit correctly in her seat. She narrowed her eyes hatefully at she looked at him. "He mentioned it."

Silas's smirk morphed into a scowl when he realized that she was staring intently at the ghastly scar upon his cheekbone. Tilting his head, he asked, "What's the matter, love? Don't you recognize your handiwork? From the night you shot at me with my own gun."

"I never meant to hurt you, Silas. It was an accident…"

"You tried to *kill* me," he growled, leaning forward in his seat. "Just as you killed my son."

Evie squeezed her eyes shut in anguish and chewed nervously upon her bottom lip. "No," she whispered shakily. "Noah was stillborn. There was nothing I could do…"

"You could have never run away in the first place! Then I could have kept an eye on you to ensure the boy survived—"

Evie suddenly leaned forward and boldly pointed a finger in his face. "It would not have changed anything! We both know that I ran away to escape *you*! It was your drinking, your anger, your beatings, that killed our son, not I!"

Silas stared at her in mild shock at her brave outburst, his jaw slack. After a moment, he sighed and shook his head. "You've changed," he spat angrily.

"I cannot say the same for you."

Silas lunged forward and trapped her against the back of her seat, placing his arms on either side of her head as he leaned his face down until their lips were nearly touching. Evie gasped in surprise and coiled inward, turning her face away from his as he hissed in her ear, "Independence has turned you into a roguish, disrespectful little slut. I saw the way you and the savage boy were looking at one another—and I know that you have not been faithful to me during your absence. Any fool could see that you and he have become an item behind my back, and I have half a mind to bend you over my knee right here to remind you of your place in this world!"

"Do it!" she snarled back in his face, her eyes wide with hate and desperation. "Do whatever you want to hurt me, just as you have before, but it will not bring our son back, nor will it change the fact that I love Theo more than I could have ever loved you."

Chapter 4

To the Wolves

March 1779

March dragged on, and an uncomfortable silence fell upon Division Point, settling within every nook, cranny, and soul it could find like a heavy, suffocating blanket of sorrow. As angry as some of the homesteaders were that Evie had deceived them, her departure seemed to leave an emptiness in her wake that no amount of time could fill. In the name of love, and the name of war, even the most good and pure could be forced to do the unspeakable, and that notion was made all the more devastating by the fact that the entire community was powerless to stop the girl from being dragged back to Hell, lest they want the same fiery fate that befell their neighbors years prior.

Upon watching the love of his life disappear through the tree line, Theo was left in anguish in the middle of the road, clutching the necklace that Evie had tearfully returned to him. An enormous and jagged hole was torn through his chest when he lost the last glimpses of her in the darkness, and in the days afterward, he was inconsolable. Tangled in a swirling storm of anger, hatred, confusion, and sorrow, he lost all feeling in his mind and his body, and he began to float through the hours of the day with an emptiness in his eyes and a coldness in his heart.

He hated her for lying to him, he hated her for being the wife of his captor and his torturer, and he hated her most of all for leaving him behind. But he loved her for her kindness, he loved her for her gentleness, and he loved her most of all for the purpose she had instilled in him without even having to try. Until she had stolen his heart, he lacked all motivation to live a just and productive life, and now that she was gone with the wind, he could feel himself slipping back into a dark abyss of nothingness once again, with no hope and no end to his pain in sight.

The spring of that year was warm and pleasant, but it did little to lift Theo's spirits, and he spent the first few days following Evie's departure wandering the beaches, the docks, and the cliffs, staring out into the water and wishing that he had the power to save her from this terrible fate. But he was just one man, one lowly rebel mongrel, and he hadn't the strength to overpower the forces sent to tear them apart. He was weak, he was a failure, he was worthless. If he could not even protect the woman that he loved from the dangers that lurked outside their door, what purpose did he have on this earth?

As much as he hated her, and as much as he hated Silas, he hated himself even more for being so powerless to protect her. He would have fought her husband and his Redcoat goons to the death if it meant she would be safe, but he was outnumbered and outgunned, and he knew in his heart that he could not risk the lives of everyone in the homestead to save the life of one woman, no matter how angry and beguiled with her he was. He would have done anything to turn back time and pull his head out of his rear long enough to tell her how much he loved her before she left, but it was much too late for that, and she was miles and miles away by now, never to return and never to see the light of freedom again.

***

Theo let out an aggravated grunt as he tossed a stone into the ocean, his eyes narrowing as he stared into the sun to watch it skip several meters across the surface of the water before sinking to the bottom. The fact that the stone had only traversed a few meters out from the edge of the dock rather than the hundred or so feet he was looking for only added to his frustration, and he let out an enraged snarl as he turned to angrily kick the hull of *The Liberty*, which was tied to the dock and floated in the shallows just to his right.

Theo startled when the annoying sound of a barking dog touched his ears, and he looked over his shoulder to see Gunner barreling across the beach and onto the dock. The bloodhound, now a year old or so, skidded to a stop at Theo's feet and sat, wagging his tail wildly and staring up at him with big brown eyes. Gunner was perhaps the most devastated of all by Evie's absence, and he wandered the homestead aimlessly for hours at a time, sniffing for any sign of his master. It took him several days to realize that she was truly gone, after which he became rather lost and confused and began to follow Theo around like a shadow.

"What are you looking at?" Theo snapped at the dog as it stared up at him and beat his tail against the wooden boards of the dock. Gunner's only response was a pant and a confused bark, as if he was asking where his girl was and why she hadn't taken him with her.

"Evie isn't here," Theo grumbled. "She's gone. She's not coming back. I have to get over it, and so do you. So, quit following me!"

Gunner barked loudly in response and hastened the wagging of his tail before attempting to jump Theo's leg and lick his face. Theo angrily shoved him away. "I said, she's gone! Don't you understand? Gone! She's not coming back, so quit staring at me and get out of here! Go!"

Gunner whimpered at the sudden explosion of rage in Theo's raised voice and fearfully backed away, his tail tucked between his legs as he slowly turned and scampered out from underneath the man's large shadow.

"Stupid dog!" Theo hissed at him before turning back to face the ocean.

His chest heaved with anger as he bristled under the weight of his heartache, and with a defeated sigh, he plopped down to sit on the edge of the dock while allowing his feet to dangle and his boots to scrape the surface of the water. Normally, the feel of the wind and the saltiness of the air would have brought him joy and contentment, but now all it did was remind him of what he had lost and what may have been if he hadn't been so foolish and stubborn.

Gentle footsteps approaching from behind alerted him, but he didn't have the energy to turn and see to whom they belonged.

"Don't take it out on the dog," a high-pitched voice chastised playfully.

Theo frowned at the familiar trill of Constance's voice, and his entire body stiffened as she slowly crossed the dock and came to stand just behind him. He could feel her dark eyes on his back, and it sent unpleasant tremors down his spine.

"What do you want?" he asked somewhat bitterly without looking at her. He was in no mood for her flirtations, nor her quips.

"May I sit with you?"

He shrugged apathetically. "Do what you will."

Constance sighed and kicked off her shoes before lifting her skirts to take a seat on his right and dangle her bare feet into the cool water of the Bay. They sat in silence for several painful minutes before she spoke.

"It's been three days since she left. I didn't think you would still be so depressed…"

Theo furrowed his brow and cast her a sideways glare. "She was my best friend."

"*Was*. Until you realized what a liar and a whore she really was."

"Do *not* talk about her that way," Theo hissed as his fists clenched at his sides. "You didn't know her."

"Neither did you, apparently."

"Did you just come here to rile me up, Constance? What do you want?"

Constance flashed him a sideways smile before scooting closer and moving to kneel on her knees just behind him while he sat on the edge of the dock. He froze when he suddenly felt her hands upon both of his shoulders. She sighed heavily as she leaned forward and began to knead her fingers into his shoulder blades.

"I just came to see how you were faring," she said into his ear. "It pains me to see you so upset."

He did not enjoy when she touched him, but he would be lying if he said the way she was massaging the tension out of his shoulders wasn't relaxing him. After a moment or two, his eyes slipped closed and he let his head tip back just a bit as the wind blew through his hair and threatened to lull him off to a much-needed sleep.

"If you must know, I am not faring well at all."

"Forget about her, Theo. She is a liar and a Loyalist. You can do so much better. You'll find another and you'll forget she even existed."

"Not likely."

Constance increased the pressure of her grip on his shoulders and sighed in annoyance. "I thought her being gone would make you realize that she was no good for you."

Theo's voice dropped into a whisper. "She was *perfect* for me."

Constance scoffed. "Not if the contents of her little black book of secrets has anything to say about it."

Theo's frown deepened and he cracked his eyes open. "You had no right to take her journal, Constance. It was wrong, and you know it."

"And she had no right to lie to us all and take advantage of our generosity. Which, might I add, no one would have ever discovered if I had not brought it to the light. So, tell me, who has committed the greater crime?"

As she spoke, Constance leaned forward to rest her chest against his back and prop her chin upon his shoulder while her hands slid down his arms and across his chest. Theo froze nervously under her touch and his eyes flew wide open when he felt her fingers fiddle with the buttons on the front of his shirt.

"What are you doing?" he asked with bated breath.

She pressed a kiss to his cheek before whispering, "I'm just trying to remind you who has always been here for you."

Theo bristled under the sensation of her long dark hair falling over her shoulder and tickling his face, and he tried to shrug her away. "Constance. Stop it. I do not want to play this game with you any longer."

"What game?" she breathed into his ear. "I am only trying to show you how much I care for you. What I have done for you…for us…so that we could be together…"

Theo abruptly brought his hand up to capture Constance's wrist before her hand could slip under the top of his shirt, which she had so sneakily managed to partially unbutton while he was preoccupied. She felt his entire body go rigid as he tightly gripped her wrist and turned to stare at her in confusion.

"What did you just say?" he asked though clenched teeth as he glared at her over his shoulder.

Constance was slightly taken aback by the sudden blaze of anger in his eyes, and she chuckled nervously. "Whatever do you mean, darling?"

"Don't play coy with me. What exactly have you *done*?"

Constance's smug smirk faded as she murmured, "What I had to do. To get rid of that witch. To show you with whom you belong. To show you how much I love you…"

Theo suddenly leapt to his feet and pulled her upward with an iron-like grip on her wrist. "What. Did. You. Do?" he hissed in her face. Constance reached up to graze his face with her fingertips, but he turned his head away and shook her by her arm. "Tell me!"

"I did what needed to be done to rid us of that traitorous whore! As soon as I discovered her husband's identity, I knew exactly where to find him. So, I sent a courier to tell him exactly where he could find his runaway bride…"

Theo's grip on her wrist loosened before he let her go entirely and took a step backward, his jaw slack and his eyes ablaze with rage. He swallowed nervously before whispering, "You…you did what?"

Constance crossed her arms over her chest with a huff. "A good riddance, if you ask me…"

"Are you mad? Do you have any idea what you have done?"

"I got rid of her…so we could be together…" Constance tried to reach for Theo again, but he roughly shoved her back with an enraged growl.

"No, you sent her to her death! Don't you understand? Silas Porter is the monster that beat and raped her, and the one who nearly killed me, and you led him right to all of us!"

"I don't understand…"

"Silas Porter and all whom he commands now know exactly where Division Point is thanks to you, Constance! Now that he has what he wants, there is nothing stopping him from coming back and slaughtering all of us!"

Constance's eyes went wide with shock and confusion at his words. She lowered her head and mumbled, "I…I didn't think about that…"

"Of course, you didn't…because you never think of anyone but yourself!"

She suddenly looked up and narrowed her eyes angrily. "That isn't true. I did this for *us*."

"Us? Constance, there is no *us*! There never has been! What in God's name do I have to do to get that through your head? You didn't do this for us, or for me, you did this for *you*!"

"Well, none of this would have ever happened if that stupid girl had never come here and ruined our lives! I did everyone a favor by getting rid of her!"

"No, you threw Evie and everyone else here to the wolves by leading Silas Porter to our home!"

Constance crossed her arms again and turned her nose up in a pout. Theo glared holes into her face, feeling his flesh tingle with a white-hot rage; he could not think of an instance in which he had ever been angrier at her, or anyone else, really, and blood began to boil hot under his skin. The fact that she still appeared rather unfazed by the consequences of her conniving actions made him all the more incensed. A selfish brat, she was. Always and forever.

"Where is it?" Theo suddenly asked as he took a step toward her.

"Where is what?"

"The book, Constance. The journal that you stole from Evie. I know you have it."

She shrugged apathetically, hurt and confused by his burst of anger. Whether she was in the wrong or not, she did not want to acknowledge that his outrage was justified. "I may have it."

"Give it to me. Right now."

"Why?"

"If you got to read it, it is only fair that I know what it contains as well."

Constance tipped her head to the side and smirked while furrowing her brow. "It may or may not be on my person at this very moment."

"Then give it here." Theo outstretched his hand with a scowl.

She shrugged again. "No."

"*No?*"

"If you want it so badly, then come find it." She planted her hands defiantly upon her hips and pushed her chest outward while batting her eyelashes.

Theo stared her down from the edge of the dock before aggressively stalking towards her and seizing her by both of her arms. She gasped in surprise when he suddenly pushed her back against the side of the ship tied to the dock and put his hands on her waist. His golden eyes, now ablaze with an anger she never knew he was capable of, never left hers as he rather aggressively loosened the ties on the front of her corset and dug around the inside of her blouse before plucking the small book from underneath her breast. After finding what he was looking for, he quickly tied her corset back together and took several steps back, his eyes still locked with hers.

She had secretly hoped that the action of touching her body to find the journal would somehow arouse him, but it was very clear from his rigid posture and the even more rigid scowl upon his face that the only thing he felt toward her at that moment was hate.

"I just…I just wanted you to love me…" Constance murmured as her eyes fell to the dock under her feet.

Theo scoffed dismissively. "You put everyone in grave danger, and you betrayed my trust. How can I, or anyone else, ever love you after what you have done?"

His words stung like a thousand knives in her flesh, and Constance physically cringed under the weight of his glare. She gasped in shock at the poison with which his words were laced, and she looked away to the water while chewing on her lip in order to swallow the tears she could feel coming to her eyes.

Theo pointed a finger in her face. "If anything happens to Evie, I will *never* forgive you."

With her back turned to him, Constance stood in stunned silence as a single tear slipped down her cheek. She could feel his eyes boring holes through her back for several agonizing moments before he turned on his heel and stormed off of the dock and down the beach, journal in hand. Constance wrapped her arms around her body and slowly dropped to her knees on the end of the dock, leaning over the edge to peer at her reflection in the water. And she hated what she saw; a conniving witch with tears streaming down her cheeks, who had clearly gone too far to get what she wanted—what she thought she deserved.

How can anyone else ever love you, after what you have done?

***

"How long?" Theo snarled as he stomped into the Caldwell forge, an accusatory finger pointed at the man he had always thought to be his best friend.

Jacob looked up from his work and furrowed his brow in confusion, setting down his hammer. Mr. Caldwell paused in his attempt to pour a batch of molten steel into a mold when he saw Theo's large form approaching from the corner of his eye.

"Theo. What are you talking about?" Jacob asked as he wiped the sweat from his brow.

"How long have you known what Constance has been up to?"

"I don't know what you are talking about, mate."

"Don't lie to me. You and Constance have both hated Evie since they day she arrived. You had to know that Constance was trying to sabotage our relationship."

Jacob's eyes widened in mild surprise at the accusation and he looked away with a frown. "Why would I have any knowledge of such a thing? Constance and I are *not* friends."

"Oh, please. You and Constance have both admitted to thinking Evie was some sort of spy. Am I to believe that Constance hadn't recruited you to help her uncover this?" Theo held up the journal he had confiscated from Constance just minutes before, his eyes ablaze with hurt and anger.

Jacob shook his head and sighed. "Alright. Constance approached me with the idea to try and discover whatever it was that Evie was hiding. She wanted to try and drive a wedge between the two of you so that you wouldn't trust her, either. But I had no idea that there was even a journal to discover until Constance revealed it to all of us…"

Theo's scowl deepened as he stared his friend down from across the forge. Taking several aggressive steps in Jacob's direction, he growled, "And am I supposed to believe that you also had no knowledge about Constance's correspondence to Silas Porter?"

Jacob's dark eyes widened further in complete shock. "Her *what*?"

"She sent a message to Silas Porter telling him where exactly he could find Evie…and the rest of us! That is the only reason he was able to track her down. Do you expect me to think you didn't know about this as well?"

Jacob took a nervous step back and held his hands up in front of himself in a gesture of surrender. "I had no idea, Theo. She never mentioned anything to me about contacting Evie's husband. I never would have condoned such a thing if I knew."

"Cut the horse-shit, Jacob! You distrusted Evie from the very start, and you wanted her gone just as much as Constance did!" Theo took a few more angered steps in Jacob's direction and gave him a quick shove in the chest.

Jacob's expression of confusion quickly melted into one of aggravation as he returned the favor and shoved him back. "Clearly, I had every reason not to trust her! She lied to all of us for five years!"

"She was doing what she thought she had to do to survive! She didn't mean to hurt anyone!"

"So you say, but the truth is that you don't know her half as well as you thought you did!"

An enraged growl escaped from Theo's throat as he lunged forward in attempt to shove Jacob again, but Mr. Caldwell quickly slid in between them.

"That's enough! You two are grown men, and I expect you to comport yourself as such in *my* forge."

Theo sent a burning hot glare at Jacob over Mr. Caldwell's shoulder, his brows pinched together in anguish. "I knew her. I know her. I know she is not the villain she has been made out to be…"

"Would you still stay that if she hadn't lured you into bed? She's a *whore*, and a liar." Jacob retorted bitterly.

"Don't talk about her like that!" Theo lunged for his friend once again, only to be restrained when Mr. Caldwell took ahold of him by both of his arms and held him back.

Jacob sighed again as his expression softened ever so slightly. Clearing his throat, he said, "Listen, Theo. Everything I have ever done was out of love. I only want what's best for you. That's what we all want. I was just trying to…look out for you…"

Theo struggled against Mr. Caldwell's hold on his arms and snarled, "I don't need you or anyone else to protect me, Jacob! I am not a child! I am so sick of everyone thinking they know what is best for me!"

Jacob shook his head and looked away. "I'm sorry, Theo. I…I thought I was doing the right thing by keeping Constance's intentions a secret from you…"

Theo pulled his arms free from Mr. Caldwell's grasp with an aggravated snarl. His chest heaved with anger as his face tightened with a hurt one could only associate with betrayal. "I thought I could trust you. I thought you were my friend."

"I am your friend. The last thing I want is to see you hurt."

"She was the best thing that ever happened to me, and she's gone…and I have you and Constance to thank for that!"

"Hold a moment," Jacob snapped. "I never had anything to do with Constance luring Silas Porter here."

"No, but if you hadn't been so concerned with proving that Evie was some sort of Loyalist spy, you could have warned me before Constance crossed that line. Then perhaps Evie never would have been taken into the custody of the monster that nearly killed me! You are just as complicit in this as she!"

Jacob swallowed nervously as he ran a hand through his shaggy dark hair, and his eyes roamed around the forge as he searched for any combination of words that might offer some comfort to his despondent friend. He had never seen Theo's eyes so full of hurt and anger, and it pained him to know that he was partially responsible.

"If I had known she would be so mad as to reveal our location to the man that massacred Kensington, I never would have gone along with it. You have to believe me, Theo. I'm so sorry…"

"Everyone seems to be sorry once they have been caught," Theo coldly snapped. "But I have no forgiveness left to give."

"Theo, wait—"

Theo abruptly turned his back on Jacob and brushed past Mr. Caldwell to storm out of the forge. Jacob moved to go after him, but his father caught him by the arm and shook his head.

"Let him go, son. His fuse has been lit. Give him some time to cool down."

Jacob let out a disgruntled sigh and collapsed backwards to sit on a nearby overturned bucket. Dropping his head in his heads, he mumbled, "God help me, Pa. I think I've made a terrible mistake…"

Mr. Caldwell patted him on the shoulder. "I concur."

***

After a long and dreadful three days trapped in the carriage with no one to look at other than Silas' disgustingly smug face, Evie sat up in her seat when she realized that the convoy was rolling along the Rhode Island coast, with the towers and parapets of a heavily fortified stone structure peaking above the horizon. The shores of Rhode Island were just as craggy and rugged as those in Massachusetts, and after an hour or so of traversing the coast, the carriage rolled to a stop at the beginnings of a narrow bridge that connected the mainland to the large island in which the fort had been built.

"Ah, Dumpling Rock," Silas sighed as the carriage came to a sudden stop and he peered out the window. "You'll love it here, darling."

Evie crossed her arms over her chest and followed his gaze to the fort. It appeared to be ancient, covered in rust, moss, and algae on all sides, with the entire island surrounded by tall and jagged rocks. Large towers jutted into the sky at each of the four corners, and the catwalks were lined with stern-faced Redcoats.

"A fort, hm?" Evie hummed. "King George must have truly been desperate to trust you with a command."

Silas frowned. "Brazenness doesn't suit you, Mrs. Porter."

Evie gave the fort another cursory glance. "It looks dreadfully dull," she stated flatly. "No place for a woman."

"Well, if a certain someone did not have a propensity to run away, that certain someone would be allowed to go home."

Evie rolled her eyes up to the sky. "And you think keeping me locked in a tower will solve all of your problems?"

Silas smirked as he came to sit next to her and wrap an arm around her shoulders to pull her into his chest. He pressed his lips to her ear and murmured, "I know it will, love. No way in or out except the front gate, under my watchful eye at all times. You *won't* get away from me this time."

"And what about after the war?" she asked bitterly. "Do you intend to keep me locked away then, too?"

He leaned down to try and kiss her on the mouth, but Evie turned her face away in disgust. Suddenly aggravated, he captured her chin between his thumb and forefinger and forced her to look him in the eye.

"Do not worry, my dear wife. I will have broken you by then." Evie narrowed her eyes in confusion at his words, and he chuckled in her face. "By the time I am done with you," he whispered as he pressed his rough lips to her ear, sending shivers down her spine, "you'll have no reason left to run."

The carriage door was suddenly pulled open from the outside, causing Evie to jump with fright. Silas wasted no time in climbing out and ordering one of his men to help Evie out after him. After so many hours in the dim carriage, Evie was blinded by the sunlight streaming into her eyes as she stumbled after Silas. Silas quickly slipped an arm around her waist and held her tight to his side before motioning for them to walk together across the bridge to the front gate of the fort. Fort Dumpling Rock was large and imposing, and it cast a great shadow over them as they crossed the bridge, flanked on all sides by the same guards that escorted the carriage.

Upon reaching the front gate, Silas was greeted with a crisp salute by the two Ensigns stationed there, and he returned the gesture half-heartedly. The gate was constructed entirely of rotting planks of wood, thirty feet high, and it creaked horribly as it was opened, a sound so ghastly that Evie had to clamp her hands over her ears as she was led through. Just before the gates closed shut behind them, she took one last glance over her shoulder at the outside world, fearful that it would be the last time she saw freedom. The last thing she saw before the doors of her new life closed behind her was the rocky shore that surrounded the island, a sight that sent wistful memories of home rippling through her heart.

As soon as word reached the fort that the Captain was returning with his long-absent wife, every inhabitant of the fort quickly gathered in the courtyard to greet them. Servants, slaves, soldiers, and officers crowded around the perimeter of the courtyard just as Silas entered with a pretty young redhead on his arm. And it was painfully obvious straightaway that she did not appear excited to be there; she looked downright terrified, even.

"Welcome back, Captain Porter," a strapping young man in a red uniform and a crisp powered wig was the first to greet them. He had a boyish face and a kind voice, and he smiled warmly when his eyes fell upon Evie.

"Thank you, Sergeant Howell. It is good to be back. Especially now that I have my better half with me again."

Evie averted her eyes to the ground when she felt Howell's gaze fall upon her.

"My lady," Howell murmured as he gently kissed the back of her hand and bowed. "Sergeant Daniel Howell, at your service. Captain Porter has told us much about you."

Evie shyly nodded in reply but could not manage to meet his gaze. Silas roughly nudged her forward and snapped, "Do not be rude, Evie."

Evie shot him a dirty look over her shoulder before slowly curtsying to the Sergeant. "A pleasure to meet you, Sergeant Howell."

Howell chuckled. "Your wife is lovely, sir. Only you could find a lady so darling and beautiful."

Silas chuckled darkly as he pulled Evie back to his side by her shoulder. "Ah, for all her beauty, she certainly is a stubborn and slippery one. But that's nothing a bit of time and energy can't fix, hm?"

Howell raised his brow curiously, taking note of the way that Evie's eyes slipped closed in nervousness and her body tensed in fear whenever the Captain touched her. "Sir?"

"Step aside, Sergeant. I intend to introduce my wife to everyone else here."

Howell slowly backed into the surrounding crowd as Silas took Evie by the upper arm and led her to the middle of the courtyard under several hundred pairs of watchful eyes.

"Thank you all for your warm greetings," Silas bellowed to the crowd as he held his wife with a vice-like grip on her arm. "It is my pleasure to introduce you to the newest resident of Fort Dumpling Rock—my wife, Evie Porter, who is joining us after a very long absence."

A stunned silence fell upon the crowd as they eyed the skittish red-headed girl being displayed before them. Evie stared at the ground in embarrassment and tried to pull her arm free, but his grip upon her was iron tight. The more she struggled, the more he tightened his hold upon her in aggravation.

"And why was she absent from me, may you ask?" Silas continued. "Well, my young wife was overtaken by a mad desire to…see the world and live independently. Can you believe it? A woman, living on her own? What a notion!"

The crowd mimicked Silas' amused chuckle. "As amusing as it sounds, the crimes she has committed are no laughing matter."

Evie glared at him over her shoulder, but his smirk only widened. Suddenly, he pulled her backwards until her back was against his front and his hands were on both of her shoulders.

"What are you doing?" she asked in a fearful whisper.

"While she was away, I suspect that my wife seemed to forget that she was just that—*my wife*. A brief list of her transgressions includes an attempt to take my life, *adultery*, and of course, the murder of my unborn son."

The crowd gasped in shock, and Evie angrily tried to twist out of his hold, but he held her tightly to his chest with one hand while the other quickly moved to fumble with the ties on her corset.

"Let go of me!" she cried desperately.

Silas only chuckled as his hands made quick work of her corset and he tore open the front of her dress, baring her chest to the entire fort. Evie squealed in embarrassment and tried to wriggle free, but before she could even blink, he had torn her entire dress off of her body. She begged him to stop as tears of shame and terror filled her eyes, but her cries only served to amuse and delight him as he then stripped her of her undergarments until she was completely naked for the entire fort to see. Once he had her stripped, Silas roughly pushed her to the hard ground, chuckling with pleasure when she hit the stones with a painful cry. Evie cringed under the weight of hundreds of eyes staring at her while she was so vulnerable and so trapped, and she stared up into her husband's stern face in abject shock as he came to tower over her.

"What's the matter?" he snarled down at her. "No need to be shy now, love. Show everyone here what a whore you are!"

Quiet sobs escaped her lips as she slowly tried to pull herself up on her hands and knees, trying desperately to cover herself with her arms.

"Do you hear that, gentlemen?" Silas cackled. "A whore! I've married a whore, an adulterer, and a murderer!" Silas turned his attention back to Evie and asked, "Well, what do you have to say for yourself, girl?"

Humiliated and unable to speak, Evie shook her head and sobbed. For a brief moment, she locked eyes with Sergeant Howell, who stood at the front of the crowd and watched the madness unfold with mouth agape in horror. When Evie refused to offer any response, Silas growled in aggravation and delivered a swift kick to her side with the front of his boot, hard enough to double her over in pain and send her rolling across the cobblestones with a shriek of pain. The wind was immediately knocked from her lungs as she felt her bare flesh scrape across the hard ground, but before she could even attempt to take a breath, he was standing over her once again to deliver another kick, this time to her back. She cried out again and tried to curl herself into a ball, but Silas immediately knelt at her side to pull her up by a fistful of her hair.

He stared into her eyes for a brief moment before rearing his hand back and slapping her across the face with enough force to split her lip. Evie collapsed onto the ground, splayed out on her stomach at Silas' feet, chest heaving as she searched desperately for a breath. Her body was stained with dirt and several newly forming bruises, and her face was marred with trickles of blood and fresh tears. She sobbed loudly as the crowd watched on, too humiliated and too afraid to even care that so many men had now seen her bare. Her body instantly became overcome with a familiar ache—

the ache of the aftermath of one of Silas' outbursts. Only this time it was different; he no longer felt the need to reserve his tortuous punishments for behind closed doors.

Satisfied with his work, Silas rose to his feet and ran a hand through his hair, turning to address the crowd. His eyes were narrowed into slits and his teeth were bared as he paced a predatory circle around his wife's broken body. As possessive and domineering as he was over his woman, he felt no qualms about stripping her naked and humiliating her before hundreds of other men if it meant that she would finally learn her place as *his property*.

"Do you see this?" he cried. "*This* is the proper way to put a woman…or any other inferior creature…in their place! This is how you punish a whore!"

Evie let out another fearful cry and wrapped her arms protectively around her head when she felt him step over her body. "Let this be a warning to anyone, man or woman, who dares to cross me!" Silas turned and pointed to Howell, who had turned his head away in discomfort at the show being played out before him.

"Howell, get her out of my sight."

"…Sir?"

"Take her to my quarters and have the servants clean her up. Immediately. She and I will have much to discuss later."

"…Right away, sir."

Without hesitation, Howell stepped out of the crowd and into the middle of the courtyard, coming to kneel at Evie's side. She yelped fearfully and cringed away when he attempted to turn her over, and she could still feel Silas' eyes upon her. Upon realizing that there was nothing left to watch, most of the crowd dispersed to go about whatever business they had before the Captain and his wife had arrived.

"Come now, Lady Porter," Howell whispered gently. "Let us get you cleaned up."

With the help of another soldier and a slave woman who had been brought in from Silas' estate, Howell managed to slowly get Evie off of the ground. She limply dragged her feet as Howell and the others led her out of the courtyard and towards the barracks, but the throbbing pain in her ribcage made any movement excruciating and intolerable, and she continued to sob uncontrollably as she was taken away. Silas remained in the courtyard and watched her go with a smirk upon his face and contentment in his cold heart at the message he had sent.

If she was to act like a disgraceful whore, then she would be treated as such.

Just before Howell and the others took her to the barracks, Evie tossed one last glance over her shoulder at Silas, who smirked in return. It was then that the gravity of her new reality hit her like a ton of bricks collapsing upon her all at once. She was truly back in the Hell she had worked so hard to escape, and this time, Silas seemed even more determined to break her than he was before. Her worst fears had been realized with full force, and the wrath of God and her husband had come to strike with unending ferocity, punishing her for every mistake she had ever made. For running away, for losing the baby, for becoming entangled in an ill-fated and outlawed love. She may have been an adulterer and a runaway, but as far as the world was concerned, the worst crime she could have committed was wanting to be free and happy.

And now, thrown to the wolves with nothing to which to escape, she could see that this was only the beginning of a hellish payment for her misguided fight for freedom.

Chapter 5

A Woman's Game

March 1779

Evie collapsed to her knees in pain and exhaustion immediately upon being escorted to her husband's chambers in the heart of the fort. The room was spacious and dimly lit, furnished like a king's suite and cluttered with empty liquor bottles. Sergeant Howell barked an order at the other soldier and the slave woman that had helped him drag Evie out of the courtyard, but she could not hear his words over the pounding of blood in her ears. Howell shrugged out of his jacket and knelt down at Evie's side in the middle of floor before placing it over her shoulders to return to her some semblance of dignity, but it was far too late for the action to offer her any comfort.

She continued to sob as she locked her eyes on the floor in shame. She should have known that Silas was capable of such a cruel act of humiliation—to strip her naked and beat her in front of every man under his command—but she was still shocked and disoriented all the same, and the familiar tingle of fresh bruises rising to the surface of her skin sent shivers down her spine.

"Don't cry now, my lady," Howell said gently as he looked into her eyes. "We'll have fresh clothes brought to you right away. We'll get you cleaned at once."

Evie shook her head and choked back her tears as she wrapped the man's jacket tightly around her freshly bruised body. "How could he...do this to me?" she murmured. "I'm...I'm his wife."

Howell clicked his tongue. "I am sure I do not need to tell you that the Captain has a rather savage temper. I've served under him for the last five years and, unfortunately, I've seen him unleash his wrath many times."

Evie opened her mouth to speak but was interrupted when the soldier and the slave woman bustled into the room, a bundle of clothes and a tray with rags and a bowl of water in hand. Howell wasted no time in sliding his arms under Evie's legs so that he could lift her off of the floor and into the nearest armchair. He then turned his back while the slave woman removed the uniform coat from Evie's shoulders and took a wet cloth to her body to remove the dirt and blood her skin had accumulated. Once Evie had been cleaned, she was dressed in a loose-fitting blouse and long skirt that smelled like they had been stored away for ages.

Howell turned back to face her with a weak smile upon his face. "There, that's much better. Let us take a look at those cuts on your face."

Evie hissed and flinched away when he took up a fresh cloth and tried to dab at the cut on her lip, but he gently turned her face towards him and continued. After wiping the dried blood from her chin, he gingerly scrubbed away the dirt and tears on her cheeks, and she stared up into his olive eyes while he did so, never once blinking. Howell's kind and handsome face softened as he pulled the cloth away and set it back on the tray.

"I can see why you ran," he whispered.

"I'm not the things he said I am," she returned sadly. "Those things he said…they aren't true…"

"I know, Miss. You don't need to convince me." They stared at each other for several silent moments before Howell cleared his throat and took a few steps back from her chair. "Well, now that you've been cleaned up, I am sure the Captain will want you to stay here and wait for him. I'll have someone bring you supper shortly. I am sure you are famished."

Evie nodded curtly and painfully curled herself up into a ball in her chair, wrapping her arms around her legs and resting her chin upon her knees. Howell motioned for the soldier and the slave woman to depart before shrugging back into his coat and giving Evie a polite bow. He turned toward the door and said, "I bid you good evening, Mrs. Porter."

"Evie," she corrected as he halted in the doorway. "My name is Evie."

The corners of Howell's mouth twitched upward as he glanced at her over his shoulder. "*Evie*, then. And you may call me Daniel. But we'll keep that just between the two of us, hm?"

Howell flashed her a smirk and playful wink before taking his leave and closing the heavy door to Silas' chambers behind him. Evie's heart instantly sank when she heard the door lock from the outside and Howell's footsteps fade away. As soon as she was alone in the room, she slowly rose from her chair and groaned when her ribcage ached in protest.

Her eyes were immediately drawn to the vanity across the room, on top of which several bottles drained of their liquor were littered. Another object lay across the top of the dresser with the bottles, and she crossed the room with several hesitant steps before she realized that said object was a large leather flogger—a cat o'nine tails that was clearly meant to be on display.

Her hand shook as she tentatively reached forward and grazed her fingers across the smooth surface of the leather, and she swallowed the nervous lump rising in her throat before taking the object in her hands to observe it. It was heavy in her hands, and the long, thin straps that hung from its handle were hard to the touch. Evie gasped when she took a closer look at the tails of the whip and realized that they were encrusted with dried blood. Within an instant, memories of the large, ghastly scars that marred Theo's back flashed across her eyes, and she quickly tossed the flogger back onto the vanity before taking several fearful steps backward.

Her heart began to race as she brought her hand up to cover her mouth, and she slowly lowered herself into the nearest chair, her eyes locked on the flogger from across the room. She swallowed thickly and tried to shake away the haunting sight of Theo's scars that were no doubt the handiwork of that very instrument, and she suddenly began to feel very light-headed and nauseas at the thought.

Terror filled her heart as the possibility that her husband would be so cruel as to use such an implement on her echoed in her head. She did not want to believe he would have the gall to do such a thing to his wife and the mother of his child, but after all she had endured at his hands, she had learned to never underestimate his propensity for wickedness.

***

Several hours later, when the moon was high in the sky and shone through the single window of the room with a pale ray of light, Evie jumped as she heard the door behind her rattle. She hadn't moved from her spot in the chair by the window in hours, and she was curled up with her knees hugged to her chest as she peered out into the night, looking out over the water and longing for a way to be anywhere but there. The aching in her body was beginning to subside, but she knew the bruises on her face and her abdomen would surely darken with time, and she did not look forward to whatever Silas had up his sleeve when she saw him next.

Her heart leapt into her throat when the door to the Captain's chambers slowly creaked open and then slammed shut a moment later. She did not need to look away from the window to know who had entered—she could tell by the familiar sound of his heavy boots on the stone floor as he approached her chair. She tensed when she felt a presence just behind her, and she could smell the rum on him from several feet away.

Silas cleared his throat as he came to stand behind his wife's chair. "How do you like the accommodations here? Nothing but the best for the Porters."

Evie shrugged but offered to response. The thought of conversing with him after he so callously humiliated her made her sick to her stomach.

Silas cleared his throat again, louder this time. "I did not want to do what I did back in the courtyard, but you left me little choice. I had to prove a point. I had to send a message that no one, especially not my wife, shall cross me without serious repercussions. I am sure you understand."

"I don't understand a God-damned thing about you," Evie grumbled under her breath as she stared emptily out the window. "But I've given up trying."

"You dishonored me, and my good name, when you ran away and fell into the arms of that rebel savage. Such crimes cannot go unpunished."

Evie briefly took her eyes away from the window and passed him a cold glare before uttering, "How unfortunate it is that *your* honor lays between *my* legs, Silas."

She gasped in shock when Silas suddenly planted his hands on the arms of her chair and spun it around so that she was facing him. He then leaned forward and caged her into the chair with his arms locked on either side of her.

"I am perplexed, Evie," he spat. "What more must I do to demonstrate to you that you are my *wife*, and therefore my *property*? You shall comport yourself appropriately as my wife and lose any notions of running away again unless you long to suffer serious consequences. Am I understood?"

Evie narrowed her eyes into slits as she stared up at his face, which had become contorted with aggravation. "You've already taken everything from me. What more could you possibly do to hurt me?"

"Listen to me, you stubborn little bitch. I *own* you. Both in practice and in law, and there is nothing you can do to change that. I am your *king*, and your master. You can either choose to accept it, or to fight it tooth and nail. But I assure you, if you choose the latter, you are in for a lifetime of suffering."

"I choose the latter."

A swift backhand slap to the side of her face ripped a pained scream from Evie's throat before Silas seized her by a handful of her hair and pulled her face within inches of his.

"You do not want to play this game, girl. You are flirting dangerously with starting a war with me, and I can tell you with certainty that it is not one you will win. *War is not a woman's game.*"

"Let go of me," she hissed in his face as her eyes burned with tears.

Silas released her and allowed her to collapse into the chair before taking a step back. He began to pace the length of the room, consumed with thought, as Evie recovered from the blow to her face that had nearly knocked her sideways. She brought her hand up to caress her reddening cheek while sinking fearfully into the backrest of the chair, watching nervously while Silas paced back and forth in front of her.

"Tell me something," he said after several minutes of silence, pausing in his stride and locking eyes with her. "Tell me about the savage boy with whom you were cohabitating."

Evie frowned deeply. "What about him?"

"You said in the carriage that you love him. Is that true?"

Evie swore that she saw a flash of hurt and betrayal in Silas' steely eyes as he stared her down, but she could not be bothered to care. "I love him with all of my heart. He was everything to me that you weren't."

Silas scoffed snidely. "Let me guess. He promised you the world and told you that he loves you too?"

"...Not in those exact words."

"Did it work?"

"Pardon?"

Silas took an angered step toward her again. "Did it work? His pretty words and enchanting promises? You know he only said those things to get you into his bed."

Evie furrowed her brow in anger. "That is *not* true. He loved me."

"Ha! You really are as stupid as you look. Mongrels like him are not capable of *love*. They are savages. They live for raiding, pillaging, scalping, and raping!"

"You don't know Theo like I do. He is a good man."

"He isn't a man at all. You've become a whore to a half breed gutter rat!"

Evie defiantly stood from her chair. "I would rather be his whore than your wife."

Seething with rage, Silas quickly closed the distance between them in two large strides before seizing Evie by her throat and dragging her toward the large bed on the other side of the room. With a ferocious growl, he threw her backwards onto the bed and immediately moved to straddle over her, pinning her arms down to the mattress on either side of her head.

"I knew the moment I saw you with him that you had betrayed me," he hissed in her ear. "I could see how smitten he was. So, tell me the truth—were you unfaithful to me while you were away? And do not bother trying to lie to me either—I am no fool, and you are no angel. Did you allow that native beast to defile you despite your betrothal to me?"

Evie's eyes hardened into steel as she stared up at him. Her words were sharp like knives and more venomous than poison. "One hundred times over."

Silas tilted his head to the side as his lips pulled back to bare his teeth in a wicked snarl. "Then tell me, dear wife, which one of us was the better lover? I am dying to know."

"I think you and I both know the answer to that question."

Silas suddenly released his hold on her wrists and took ahold of her by the waist to flip her over on her stomach underneath him. She tried desperately to rise onto her hands and knees and wriggle out from underneath him, but he shoved a knee into her lower back before pinning her down by her shoulders. He hovered lowly over her and pressed his lips to her ear, and she cringed when she felt his pelvis graze against her back.

"Then perhaps I shall remind you to whom you truly belong, my dear. I think you owe me that much, after five long years."

Evie tried to kick against him, but he trapped her face down against the mattress with his knees on either side of her thighs. Her blood ran cold in her veins at the clinking of buckles and ruffling of fabric as he swiftly began to undress himself.

"I owe you nothing," she snapped viciously.

"You owe me a *son*," he growled lowly, pushing up her skirt to her thighs. "And now that I have you again, we will have plenty of time to produce another."

***

25 September 1774. I was given a second chance when a boy named Theo found me in the woods and offered me the one thing that I crave the most—my freedom. I have never met someone like him; he is brazen, impulsive, and hotheaded, but also passionate, kind, and generous. I have only known him for a few short months, since he brought me to Division Point to start my life over free from my past, but I already know he is everything Silas never was. He is handsome beyond comprehension, with a wildness about him that somehow draws me in. Everything I have ever been taught by my family tells me that I should fear and despise him for his heritage, that he is a savage and a heathen, and I should stay far, far away from him. But he is unlike anyone I have ever met before—gentle when he wants to be and ferocious when he has to be—and I want nothing more than to know more about him. I cannot understand why my father and many others despise the natives so, and it breaks my heart to see an entire race of people live as the targets of such hatred for the simple matter of the color of their skin.

20 February 1777. Theo has been away at war for nearly six months, and my heart breaks a little more with each day that he is gone. Words cannot describe how much I miss him and how sick I am with worry that he will not return. I pray for a swift end to this war, and a Patriot victory, so that I may never again have to worry about the Redcoats stealing him away from us. We have exchanged correspondence several times, and his letters are the one thing I have to look forward to as this war drags on and I continuously look over my shoulder. I am ever fearful that my worst fears will come true and the new life I have built for myself will come crumbling down around me—that Silas will somehow find me and drag me back to the Hell he created for me. I shudder to think what he will do to me should he ever get his hands on me again. His cruelty knows no bounds, and I have never been more fearful of another than I am of him.

3 August 1778. I never thought I would love again after what Silas had done to me. But then I met Theo. He has a heart of the purest gold—the rarest I am sure to ever find, and I am eternally grateful that he has given it to me. I have never loved another person as I love him, and I long for the day that I am free of my bonds to Silas so that I may be with my outlawed love wholeheartedly and with no hindrances. It pains me so that he has trusted me with every secret he possesses and I am unable to return the favor. But I fear that once he knows the truth about me—about my family, my husband, my Loyalist ties—he will hate me forever. He will surely never trust me again, and I will lose the best thing that has ever happened to me. He rescued me when no one else would, and he gave me a second chance at life when all hope seemed lost. For that, I will be forever grateful, and for that, I owe him everything. But I fear that my secrets must die with me.

Theo gently closed the little black book laid out in his lap and wiped at his eyes with the back of his hand. He had spent the last several hours combing through the journal and its contents, searching and scanning for answers in every page as to who this girl was that had stolen his heart. He thought that he knew her well, but after reading her writings, he realized that he had only scratched the surface of the tangle of troubles, toils, and triumphs that was Evie Scarborough-Porter. Saying her true surname out loud sent shivers down his spine, as did the thought that she was somewhere miles and miles away, trapped in Silas' clutches once again. He would have given anything to go back in time and kill the man where he stood before he could take her away, and he hated himself for waiting until she was gone to realize he could not live without her.

It had been three days. But it felt like fifty years since he had last seen her face and heard her voice. He missed her terribly, and he needed to feel her touch like he needed air to breath. With every day that passed that she was gone, his anger toward her subsided and was replaced with an agonizing worry for her well-being and a desire to have her back in his life. After having read her inner most thoughts, he felt like he understood her better than he ever did before—he could now fathom her motives for keeping the truth of her identity and her past hidden, and though he did not like it, he would have done the same if he was in her position.

She was desperate and afraid, willing to do anything to protect herself and her unborn child from the wrath of a wicked and vengeful husband. For a woman of the colonies, there was very little in the way of freedom and opportunity, and she merely did what anyone else would do—she survived.

Theo shoved the book into the breast pocket of his shirt and ran a hand through his long and messy hair in exasperation, a heavy sigh escaping his lips as he leaned back against the Liberty's center mast. With nothing to do but dwell on his mistakes and nurse the ache in his heart, he had wandered down to the docks and was now sitting cross-legged on the deck of the ship as she bobbed in the waves that lapped at the dock. He folded his arms behind his head and leaned back until he was lying flat on his back on the deck, staring up at the cloudless sky.

His mind raced with wild and reckless thoughts about what he could do to stop his pain. He had only a few options, as he saw it. He could take his own life, because a life without Evie was a life not worth living in his eyes; he could go back to the drink, the one constant in his life that always seemed to numb the agony that endlessly chipped away at his heart; or, he could stop wallowing in his sorrows and do whatever it took to bring Evie back home where she belonged. None of the aforementioned plans seemed reasonable or well-advised, but then again, he never claimed to be a reasonable man.

Theo was torn from his thoughts by the sound of footsteps shuffling down the dock, and he turned his head while still lying on the deck to see none other than Jacob Caldwell slowly approaching. Theo turned his eyes back to the sky with a huff, and Jacob paused at the end of the dock, placing his right foot upon the gang plank.

"I knew I would find you here," he commented dryly.

"Did you come to rub salt in my wounds?" Theo asked bitterly without meeting his friend's gaze.

Jacob shook his head with a sigh. "I just came to see how you were fairing. We haven't spoken since yesterday at the forge."

"There is probably a reason for that."

Jacob ascended the plank and stepped onto the deck of the ship. "I know. It doesn't take a genius to realize *I* am the reason."

Theo didn't respond, so Jacob took that as an implied invitation to take a seat next to his despondent friend on the floor under the shadow of the main mast.

"What do you want?" Theo asked quietly after a moment of silence.

"I wanted to apologize. I know I made a mistake."

"A mistake?" Theo repeated as he slowly sat up with a scowl upon his face. "You conspired behind my back to sabotage my relationship with the only girl I have ever loved."

"I'm sorry, Theo," Jacob murmured softly, placing a hand upon Theo's shoulder. "If I could take it all back, I would. I would make it so that Evie was never taken, so that she was still here with you."

Theo shook his head in disdain. "Well, you can't. She's gone. She's back in the clutches of that wicked monster, and she'll likely not survive the month."

"Do you really think he'd kill his own wife?"

Theo's eyes hardened as he met Jacob's gaze. "He'll do anything to get what he wants. And all he wants is wealth and power. Anyone that falls in his way, wife or not, is in danger…"

Jacob swallowed thickly, feeling his heart clench in his chest. "I'm so sorry. I had no idea. If there was anything that I could do to fix this, you know that I would."

Theo arched a brow and mumbled, "Well, I suppose there is something you could do."

"Name it."

"Come with me to get her back."

Jacob nearly choked on his tongue as he stared at Theo with wide eyes. "Come again?"

"Come with me to bring Evie out of her slavery and return her home with us where she belongs."

Jacob shook his head incredulously. "You mean, go to Dumpling Rock and conduct some kind of rescue operation?"

"That is exactly what I mean."

"You've lost your God-damned mind, Theo! You're mad! Going anywhere near Fort Dumpling Rock while it is swarmed with Redcoats is suicide."

"I have little choice, Jacob. It's the only way to save her. We have to save her before it's too late. We are all she has, and we cannot give up on her now."

"Theo, you can't be serious. It was a miracle that Silas chose to spare you when he came for Evie, but the moment he sets eyes upon you again, he will surely have you killed. He will never let you get near his wife now…"

The determination in Theo's eyes was unwavering as he looked up to the sky. "I don't care. I have to try."

"You know, people with any sense run in the opposite direction of danger, but you have a habit of charging straight into it."

Theo shrugged. "I never claimed to be a smart man."

"No, you are a foolish man who's fallen in love with a woman you were never meant to have."

"You can criticize me all you want in hindsight, Jacob, but that doesn't change the fact that I love her, nor does it convince me not to try and save her."

"You always have to be the hero, don't you? Theo, I am telling you this because you are my best friend and the last thing that I want is to see you hurt: you cannot save everyone. I know you have dreams of being everyone's hero and ridding the world of every shred of injustice, but I am telling you that if you pursue this course of action and go anywhere near Silas Porter or his wife, the only thing you are going to be is *dead*."

Theo looked to his friend with pleading eyes that swarmed with a tangling of emotions that Jacob could only assume to be desperation and fear. "I have to try," Theo whispered weakly. "I can't live without her."

"I have a wife. We are trying to start a family. I can't just…risk everything to save a runaway bride from her lecherous Redcoat husband."

"Then go back to your wife and your happy life and leave me alone. You have everything you could have ever wanted, but God forbid I have any shred of happiness. You will never understand what it is like to be in my shoes, watching the only woman I have ever loved dragged away while I am powerless to stop it…"

Jacob stared him down for several long moments before tearing his eyes away. With a heavy sigh, he shook his head and ran a hand down his face in exasperation. "And I suppose you have already concocted some sort of plan to rescue Evie and get us both killed in the process?"

Theo's lips twitched upwards with the beginnings of a smirk as he nodded. "I do."

"And that would be…?"

"We infiltrate the fort in disguise and sneak her out in the dead of night."

Jacob choked back his laughter. "Disguises? That is your master plan? Silas Porter is a lot of things, but blind and stupid he is not. No matter what disguise you concoct, you will be recognized immediately by your face and your complexion."

Theo's smirk widened ever so slightly. "I'm counting on it."

***

"I suspected you were mad before, but I am certain of it now," Jacob growled indignantly as he followed Theo up the stairs to the second floor of the Cunningham home. "You truly will be the death of me."

Theo rolled his eyes up to the ceiling and led his friend down the hall to the master bedroom, instructing him to be quiet by pressing a finger to his lips. "Johanna and my father are downstairs in the kitchen. Try not to alert them to what we are doing."

"You don't intend to tell them before we leave?"

"They'd only try to stop us."

"Emma is going to kill us both when she catches wind of what you have planned, Theo."

"She'll find it in her heart to forgive our recklessness when she has her friend back home safely."

"You seem pretty confident for a man who has willingly sentenced us both to die."

Theo waved him off as they quietly shuffled into Johanna and Alistair's bedroom. After tossing a nervous glance over his shoulder to ensure that no one had followed them upstairs, he knelt down next to the side of the bed and rummaged underneath for the war chest that Alistair had stashed away many years ago.

"Keep watch for my father," Theo instructed as he pulled the wooden chest out from underneath the bed.

"What are you looking for?" Jacob asked as he stood in the doorway and peered into the hallway.

Theo produced an old rusted key from his pocket that he had snuck from Alistair's possession the day before. He stuck it in the lock, and the lid to the old chest creaked loudly as he pulled it open. Jacob's curiosity was piqued as Theo opened the chest and he stepped into the room to observe the contents over Theo's shoulder.

"What is this thing?"

Indivisible

"My father's war chest. It contains everything he kept from his days as a soldier of the Crown during the Seven Years War."

Theo reached in and dug around for the object he was looking for, and the inside of the chest felt strangely empty without the sword and pistol that Alistair had gifted him several years ago. The weapons had been in storage under Theo's bed since he had returned from the battlefield, but they now resumed their places in the belt on his waist as he prepared to run into the inferno that was Silas Porter's domain. After a moment of rummaging, Theo produced a single article of old clothing—a red military coat that smelt of dust and gunpowder and hadn't seen the light of day in over twenty years.

"A Redcoat uniform?" Jacob asked in confusion. "This was your father's?"

Theo nodded curtly as he held the uniform up to the light. It was well worn and covered in a thin layer of dust, but it was perfectly preserved, a relic of a war and a time long lost to history. "It is old and out of style, but it will do for our purposes."

Jacob shook his head in confusion. "What exactly is your plan, then?"

"Think about it, Jacob. Who are the only people allowed into a fort in the midst of a war?"

"Soldiers?"

"And *prisoners of war*."

"I do not understand."

Theo sighed and closed the chest before folding the uniform over his arm. Rising to his feet, he held the coat up to Jacob's chest. "The plan is simple. You disguise yourself as a Redcoat soldier with this uniform and I will be your prisoner of war. We arrive at the fort and you deliver me straight to Silas as his captive."

"What? You want to crawl into the lion's den as a captive? You'll have no way to defend yourself!"

"This is the only way to get on the inside. He'll think I've come to foolishly try and take Evie back on my own, but he won't know that you aren't one of them."

"And what do you expect us to do once you are locked away in the hold of the fort?"

"Once Silas knows I am in his clutches again, his attention will be focused on me and me alone—he won't be thinking about Evie or anyone else. While he is distracted, find a way to get ahold of the Captain's keys, and in the dead of the night, you sneak Evie and myself out of the fort."

Jacob let out a snort of derision. "And how am I supposed to come into possession of these keys?"

Theo thought for a moment. "Get on Silas' good side. Secure a position as the one guarding my cell. If he trusts you, he will give you possession of the keys. Then, in the middle of the night when everyone is asleep, Evie will sneak away from Silas and meet us in the hold. Then we make our escape."

"That sounds like a brilliant plan," a gruff voice said behind them in the doorway, causing them both to nearly jump out of their skin. "But what happens if something goes wrong?"

Theo and Jacob whipped around with startled gasps to see Alistair standing in the doorway to the master bedroom, his hands planted on his hips and a curious frown upon his stern face. Jacob quickly tried to fold the uniform into a small bundle and hide it behind his back, but Alistair's old and keen eyes had already spotted it the moment he stepped into the room. He looked between the two young men with a brow raised in concern and curiosity and waited for an explanation.

Theo cleared his throat nervously. "Do not bother trying to stop me, Father. I have to do this. I have to save Evie before we lose her forever."

Alistair's expression softened as he took a few steps into the room. He was hunched over in exhaustion from coughing his lungs up the last several months, and he could feel his chest filling with anxiety as realization came upon him at what his son was planning. His eyes roamed over the looted chest next to the bed, to the old blood-red uniform behind Jacob's back, to the look of determination in Theo's golden eyes.

"I wouldn't dream of trying to stop you when I know your mind has already been made up," he croaked.

"You aren't going to call me a reckless fool and tell me not to risk my life for another man's wife?"

Alistair chuckled darkly. "I do not need to tell you that which you already know, son." Theo gave him a perplexed arch of his brow and Alistair slowly took a seat on the edge of the bed. "Listen to me, Theo. I have never seen you happier than you were when Evie was here. And it broke my heart to see you so devastated when she was taken away. She may have deceived us, but it is not our place to judge her struggles, nor her motives for doing so. Evie is just as much a member of this community, and this family, as anyone else."

"…What are you saying?"

Alistair reached forward and took his son by the hand, giving his fingers a gentle squeeze. "I would do anything in my power to protect that girl and bring her home, but I am in no condition to go charging into an enemy fort armed to the teeth with guns and Redcoats. But *you* are. You are stubborn and determined and you have never been one to run away from a fight, even when the odds are stacked against you. I know you love that girl, and I know she loves you. I could never live with myself I stood in the way of you doing what you must. Men will always do the bravest and most foolish things for the women we love."

"I love her," Theo repeated solemnly. "And I can't lose anyone else to this war…"

Alistair squeezed his son's hand again as his eyes slipped closed. "Take my uniform, take my old weapons, take whatever you need. Just bring Evie home where she belongs and give those Redcoats hell while you're at it."

***

Evie was awoken quite brutally the next morning by an intrusive ray of sunlight streaming into the room through the window and shining directly on her face. She cracked open one eye and then the other and took a moment to gather her bearings, only then realizing that she was sprawled out, naked and face down on Silas' bed in his quarters within the heart of Fort Dumpling Rock.

Part of her had hoped that when she woke it would be revealed to her that all of the agony from the night before was just a part of a ghastly nightmare, and she would wake up at home in Division Point, next to Theo as he slept soundly in her arms. However, the aching in her body and the sharp pain between her legs as she tried to roll over quickly reminded her that this was in fact her new reality. She was doomed to serve Silas' every sick and twisted whim, night after night, and endure his sadistic punishments so long as she insisted upon resisting him.

But at what point did it become fruitless to fight on? There was no way out of this hell now that she was locked away in the fort—no one would come to rescue her. Not her father, not her mother, and certainly not Theo now that he believed her to be a liar and a traitor. Yes, she could maintain her stubbornness and rebuff Silas at every turn, but nothing she could say or do would change him, nor would it stop him from unleashing his fury upon her whenever she disobeyed him. Men like Silas didn't change for the better—they only got drunker and angrier with time. If she was smart, Evie realized that morning, she would just give in an accept her fate as his wife and his prisoner and do everything in her power to ensure that he was happy. That was the only way she would live to see her next birthday, she was sure of it now.

She let out a pained groan as she turned over onto her back to see that the other side of the bed was empty. Silas had awoken long ago and went on his merry way to conduct his business as commanding officer of Fort Dumpling Rock, without a care in the world of the condition in which he had left his wife after he savaged her for hours on end the night before. The other men in the fort were not naive to his desires and predilections, and though they may have been able to hear the atrocities that took place in his private chambers that night, not a single one was able or willing to speak out on Evie's behalf.

Evie sucked in a deep breath and pushed herself onto her hands and knees in the middle of the mattress, wincing when every joint and bone in her body screamed in protest. Her long auburn hair was a tangled mess, and it fell in haphazard waves down her bare back as she slowly and painstakingly crawled to the edge of the bed. A jolt of pain ripped through the lower half of her body when her bare feet touched the floor and she tried to stand, but she ignored the pain and limped across the room to the standing mirror so that she could survey the most recent damage that had been done to her.

She gasped in horror and disgust when she peered through the looking glass at a pale and lifeless shell of the girl she had once been five years ago. Much like when she had first escaped her marriage, she was sickly white in the face, her eyes were swollen and red with tears, and her frail body was covered in bruises and welts in the shape of her husband's hands. Evie brought a trembling hand up to her mouth as a single tear escaped from the corner of her eye and rolled down her cheek. The girl staring back at her was not one she recognized after five years of freedom, and she was not one she had ever desired to see again.

But here she was, trapped and isolated once again, with nothing but solitude and misery to keep her company. As she stared into the empty blue caverns that were once her bright and captivating eyes, she replayed her husband's words over and over in her head.

You do not want to start a war with me. War is not a woman's game...

No, war was certainly not woman's game. War is bloody, war is dirty, war is painful. A good and proper woman must never resort to violence, nor vengeance, nor betrayal, nor should she ever expect to have her hopes and dreams fulfilled at the expense of a man's. She had never intended to start a war with Silas Porter when she ran away from him all those years ago, but yet, here she was, on the losing side of a game she never wanted to play in the first place. The stakes of the game were love, freedom, and a chance at a happiness she never thought possible, but now, the only prize she could see herself winning was a swift and painful end to a short and miserable life.

Chapter 6

Forsaken

March 1779

Evie let out a startled yelp when a loud knock sounded at the door to her husband's chambers. She abruptly turned and wrapped her arms around her body to cover herself as she asked in a raspy and deflated voice, "Who is it?"

"It's Sergeant Howell," a smooth voice replied from the other side of the door. "May I come in?"

"Hold a moment," Evie mumbled wearily as she searched the room for something with which to cover herself. The clothing she had been given the day before had been torn to shreds and strewn about the floor at the foot of the bed, so she settled upon one of Silas' shirts that he had discarded on a nearby chair. After slipping the large silk shirt over her torso, which hung loosely down to her knees, she cleared her throat and wiped at her eyes to destroy any evidence of her tears.

"You may enter."

Howell poked his head into the room to look around before entering fully with a gracious smile. His powdered wig was perfectly placed upon his head, but it looked out of place on a man whose face appeared so young and kind.

"Good morning, Lady Porter," he greeted as he stepped into the room. The same slave woman from the day before followed close behind and closed the door, keeping her eyes upon the floor.

"What is so good about it?" Evie retorted.

"Well, the sun is shining for the first time in a fortnight." Upon seeing the nascent bruises forming on the woman's cheek, as well as her busted lip, Howell's pleasant expression faltered. "I came to see how you were feeling."

"I've been better, Daniel. I would be much better if I was anywhere but here."

Howell sighed heavily. "I understand, my lady. I know I do not need to tell you that Captain Porter can be a cruel man."

"I am sure you did not come here simply to discuss my husband's violent predilections."

Howell cleared his throat and shook his head. "I was also instructed to notify you that Captain Porter requests your presence in the dining hall in in precisely one hour to share a meal, just the two of you."

Evie furrowed her brow suspiciously and crossed her arms over her chest. "If he wants to share a meal with me alone, why would we not eat here in his chambers?"

Howell shrugged. "That is the extent of my knowledge on the subject, my lady."

"Evie," she corrected again, with emphasis. "I told you to call me Evie."

Howell chuckled. "My apologies, Evie. You know Captain Porter would skin us both alive if he knew we referred to one other on a first name basis."

"He would skin you alive for simply looking in my direction without his permission."

"That is no doubt true as well."

Evie shook her head and began to pace across the room. "So, let me get this right. He humiliates me, he beats me, he rapes me, and then he has the gall to want to share a meal with me?"

Howell's voice softened in sympathy. "I am only following orders. I was told to inform you of what the Captain has ordered of you. He wants to see you in the dining hall in one hour."

Evie gestured to her haggard and battered appearance. "I am hardly in a presentable state."

Howell looked over his shoulder at the slave woman, who had come to stand in the corner with her eyes still fixed upon the floor. "We can be of assistance," he stated as he crossed the room and opened the doors to the large oak wardrobe. "When the Captain first learned that he would be bringing you here to the fort, he arranged for the finest dresses to be imported to the colonies."

Evie peered inside the wardrobe to see several of the most beautiful silken gowns she had ever seen hanging within. Each a different color, with intricate beading and embroidery that had to have taken months to construct by hand. "He bought these for me?" she asked in confusion.

"Imported from the best dressmakers in Paris. *Only the best for the Porters.*"

Howell motioned for the slave woman to come forward and help Evie dress before turning toward the door.

"Where are you going?" Evie asked nervously.

Howell smiled softly and reassuringly. "Worry not, Evie. I'll be just outside the door. Your husband has charged me as your personal guard and escort during your time at Dumpling Rock. I will not be leaving your side while you are here."

A wave of relief washed over Evie as she bashfully returned his handsome smile. She did not know Daniel Howell well, but she felt safe and comforted in his presence, which is more than she could say of her husband. Howell bid her adieu with a nod and a bow before backing out of the room and closing the door behind him. The slave woman joined her at the wardrobe as she scanned over the dresses within and tried to choose one.

"They are all so beautiful," Evie commented out loud as she ran her fingers across the smooth fabric. She hadn't seen such finery in her entire time at Division Point, and she had forgotten what it was like to live amongst the elite. "How could I possibly choose just one to wear?" She then glanced down at the petite dark-skinned woman at her side and asked, "Which is your favorite?"

The young woman looked up in surprise and swallowed nervously. "…My favorite?" she repeated in a mousy voice with a thick accent that Evie did not recognize. "You want…*my* opinion?"

Evie chuckled softly. "That *is* why I asked."

The small woman smiled shyly and scanned the row of gowns before them. There were at least eight from which to choose, and after a moment of thought, she said, "Well, I am partial to lavender. But I think the scarlet gown will suit your complexion the best."

Evie tapped her chin. "Scarlet it is then."

After choosing a gown, the woman helped Evie shrug out of the oversized shirt she was wearing and dressed her in the elegant silken garment, tying the corset tightly around her torso until she was nearly breathless. Evie then slowly took a seat in the chair at the vanity and stared emptily at her battered reflection in the mirror. She was dressed in the finest Parisian silks, but she had never felt so lowly and humble in all of her days as she took in the bruises forming upon her cheek and down her neck, and the despondency in her once bright blue eyes. She was silent for some time as the slave woman took up a brush and began to run it through her long red hair to rid it of its tangles.

Evie observed the woman as she worked through the mirror. She was young, probably no older than sixteen, with dark thick curls that fell down to her shoulders and dark chocolate colored skin.

After several minutes of silence, Evie softly asked, "What is your name?"

The woman hesitated before mumbling, "Tsipporah."

"Tsipporah? From the Bible?"

Tsipporah nodded with a slight smile. "Yes, Miss."

Evie smiled gently. "Moses' wife. She was always one of my favorites."

"Mine as well, Miss."

"…How did you come to serve at Fort Dumpling Rock?"

Tsipporah stiffened and set the brush down on the vanity. "I was purchased by Captain Porter from a plantation down south and then brought here three years ago."

"How far south?"

"Trinidad."

"Have you…always been a slave?"

Tsipporah nodded solemnly. "I was born in Trinidad, on the plantation. My mother was a slave, my father was her master."

Evie swallowed and closed her eyes. "Oh. I…I am so sorry. I should not have asked…"

Tsipporah shook her head and sighed before running her nimble fingers through Evie's long hair, separating it into sections so that she could braid the sides and then tie them back. "No need to apologize, Miss. You could not have known."

Evie's eyes fell to the floor. "…Do you long for your freedom?"

"I pray for it every day, Miss. But I fear it is not something I was ever meant to have, as both a woman and a slave."

"Why would you say that?"

Tsipporah shrugged and locked eyes with her through the mirror. "Women, Negros, Natives, peasants…God has forsaken us all."

"But the war…the tides of the war have turned in the Patriots' favor now. If they win, we will all be free from the Crown."

Tsipporah shook her head sadly. "No, Miss. Perhaps those that look like you will be free. But the same cannot be said for the rest of us."

"I read the Declaration that the Congress sent to King George back in '76. All men are created equal, are they not?"

"Perhaps in theory. But in practice, the colonies will be free, and those of us living our lives in bondage and servitude shall surely remain that way."

***

Sergeant Howell stood to attention when he heard the door to the Captain's chambers creek open, and he turned to see Evie take a tentative step out into the atrium of the officers' barracks. Tsipporah followed close behind and fussed with the long train of Evie's gown to ensure it did not snag on the rough cobblestone floors.

Howell's soft green eyes widened slightly as Evie came to stand in front of him, dressed in the finest of Parisian silks dyed a brilliant scarlet red and embroidered with golden threads. Her long auburn tresses were pulled away from her face in an intricate braided updo to reveal a weak smile masking a tempest of emotions.

"Simply stunning, Miss Evie," Howell stated as he lowly bowed before her. "You're a vision in red."

Evie shrugged and fiddled with the ties on her bodice while staring at the ground. She felt uncomfortable and out of place in such an extravagant gown, having spent the last five years of her life growing accustomed to the modest blouses and skirts available in Division Point. "I much prefer blue, I think," she mumbled wistfully.

Blue was Theo's favorite color. He had told her on multiple occasions it suited her complexion the best.

"Well," Howell sighed, "You look marvelous, nonetheless. Captain Porter has excellent taste, no?"

"In women, or in fashion?"

"Both, I suppose." Evie snorted in derision and resisted the urge to roll her eyes up to the ceiling. Howell offered his arm to her with a smirk and asked, "Shall I escort you to the dining hall? It's on the other side of the fort. It would not be proper for me to allow you to find your way on your own with so many wandering eyes about. The Captain would have my head."

Evie interlocked her arm with his and allowed him to lead her from the barracks. Tsipporah dutifully followed several steps behind them to ensure her dress did not get caught on any obstacles.

Evie kept her eyes trained on the ground as they went to avoid the lude, lecherous, and hostile looks she could feel boring into her on all sides from the many red-coated soldiers that surrounded them. Whether they were standing guard, doing chores, running drills, or simply sounding about, they all stopped to pass her a look as she went, and a vast majority were not of the friendly variety.

Evie could feel her fingers dig nervously into the rough fabric of Howell's uniform coat as they passed through the courtyard where she had been stripped and humiliated upon arrival the day before. It was crowded with soldiers and officers engaging in some sort of combat training, and they all paused to stare at her and her escort as they passed through.

"I do not think I am well liked here," Evie mumbled as she raised her eyes to meet Howell's.

Howell sighed and patted her hand. "It is not often that a woman comes to the fort, other than the occasional domestic servant. Most of these men have not seen a woman in months or years."

"They don't trust me. I can see it."

"Well, the Captain did not really give you much of a chance to give a first impression when you arrived. They think you are an adulteress and a traitor."

Evie locked her eyes with his for a brief moment. "Do you think that?"

Howell's lips pressed into a thin, hard line as his eyes softened. "No, Evie. I do not."

Evie smiled weakly at him, but it did little to calm the shivers running down her spine, and her tremors of nervousness only worsened as they reached the opposite side of the fort. "It is true that I betrayed my husband by falling into the bed of another man while I was away. But I will not apologize for it. Not after all that Silas has inflicted upon me…"

"You do not have to convince me to come to your side. I am already there."

Evie smiled weakly at him, but it did little to calm the shivers running down her spine, and her tremors of nervousness only worsened as they reached the opposite side of the fort. The last thing she wanted was to lay eyes on Silas or be forced into pleasantries with him, but it was painfully obvious that she had little choice in the matter as Howell led her through a large wooden door and into a dimly lit room filled with tables and chairs.

The room was dark and nearly devoid of life, illuminated only a few lanterns hanging on the wall. Silas was waiting in the middle of the room, impatiently tapping his foot with his arms crossed over his chest. Even in the dimness, his uniform coat and shiny black boots stuck out like bloody beacons in the night.

"Good morning, dear wife," Silas greeted as he approached them and pressed a kiss to Evie's cheek. "I see you have decided to wear my favorite color for today's meal."

"The dresses are beautiful, Silas," Evie returned dryly, not bothering to smile as she lowered into a deep curtsy and gathered her skirt in her hands. "Thank you."

"Only the best for the Porters, as I always say." Silas turned to Howell and gave him an approving nod. "Thank you for seeing my wife safely to the hall, Sergeant."

"Always a pleasure to serve you, Captain." Howell gave his Captain a crisp salute before turning to stand guard at the entrance to the dining hall. Evie looked nervously to him over her shoulder as Silas took her by the arm to lead her to the other side of the room.

"I am sure you are hungry after last night," Silas whispered in her ear. "I've had a lovely midday meal prepared for us."

Evie looked sharply at him. "Why would we not eat together in your chambers?"

"There is someone here that I want you to see."

Evie flashed him a confused raise of her brow as they came to the large oak table on the other side of the room. The table was set for three, rather than two, and a single individual sat at the head, partially obscured by the shadows. The man at the table cleared his throat and stood before stepping into the light to reveal himself. Evie felt her heart leap into her throat as he came into view, and she instantly recognized the rugged features of her father, Elliot Scarborough. He was just as tall and brooding as she had remembered, dressed in a velvet frock coat and silk trousers, his dark and greying hair slicked back to reveal a stern and battle-worn face. His eyes were steely and unkind as he stared his daughter down, and his posture was less than welcoming after five years of separation.

Tears came to her eyes as she shrugged out from under Silas' hold on her arm and sprinted the remaining distance to her father, throwing her arms around his shoulders in a tight embrace. She buried her face in his chest as tears of relief came to her eyes.

"Father…" she whispered. "I've…I've missed you so much. It's been so long…"

As a retired British admiral and colonial aristocrat, Elliot Scarborough had never been one for emotions nor sentiments. The only emotions he knew were greed and anger, and his body was as stiff as a board under Evie's touch as he made no effort to return her embrace. Sensing his tension, she slowly pulled away and looked up into his old eyes. Swallowing thickly, she murmured, "You are…angry with me, aren't you?"

Elliot scoffed and took an indignant step back. "Words cannot begin to describe my anger in this moment, Evie. Do you understand what you have done?"

Evie lowered her eyes to the floor and slumped her shoulders in shame. "I…I'm sorry, Father. I didn't mean to—"

"You're sorry?" the old man bellowed. "You ran away from your marriage and its commitments, soiled your reputation and that of your family, abandoned your responsibilities as a wife and daughter, and you are…sorry? Do you have any idea what your running away has done to my name, and to yours? Everyone in the Boston social circles thinks you are a sinful whore!"

"You don't understand. I had to run away. I was…miserable…" Evie could feel Silas' eyes boring holes in her back from a few steps behind, and she momentarily contemplated begging for her father to take her home with him.

Elliot shook his head and planted his hands on his hips. "You have a duty to your husband and your family. And you abandoned both, for what? To be with another man?"

"No. No…" Evie reached forward and clutched onto the lapels of her father's coat. "Father, you know Silas has never been good to me. He beats me… and he hurts me terribly!"

"As is his *right* as your husband. I thought I raised you better than to be so disloyal and selfish!"

Evie's eyes burned with tears as her father glared down upon her without a shred of empathy in his cold heart. "I did not mean to hurt anyone…" Evie whispered through her oncoming tears. "I just wanted to be free…and happy."

Elliot waved his hand dismissively and pried her hands off of his lapels. "It does not matter what you want, girl. You do not have the luxury of freedom or happiness. You are just a *woman*. It is your duty and your pleasure to serve the men in your life, as you have been raised to do."

Silas cleared his throat and stepped forward to place a heavy hand on Evie's shoulder. Gripping it tightly, he turned to Elliot and said, "As far as I am concerned, Mr. Scarborough, your daughter's greatest crime was not her adultery, nor her abandonment. Her greatest crime is what fate she allowed to befall the child she carried in her womb when she left."

Elliot narrowed his eyes in Evie's direction as Silas nudged her forward. "Tell your father what you have done," Silas grumbled. "Tell him what you did to our son."

A sob escaped Evie's throat as she squeezed her eyes shut and murmured, "The baby…he was stillborn. There was nothing I could do…"

Silas scoffed incredulously as Elliot turned away in anger. "You could have never run away," Silas snarled. "You could have stayed with me where you belonged, and then my boy would still be alive!"

"You killed my grandson with your treachery!" Elliot bellowed as he threw his hands in the air. "You have damaged and dishonored this family beyond repair…"

Evie sniffled and tried to swallow her tears, stiffening her lower lip and narrowing her eyes in hurt and anger as she asked, "Why are you even here, Father?"

Elliot cleared his throat and turned back to face her after recollecting himself. His once rageful expression had faded into one of apathy and coldness. "As soon as you were brought back into your husband's custody, he invited me to come see you. I simply came here to inform you of the damage your reckless and selfish behavior has done to your family, and to inform you of the consequences of your actions."

"...I do not understand."

"Then I'll put it in terms you do understand," Elliot snapped through clenched teeth. "You are dead to me. As far as I am concerned, I have no daughter any longer."

Evie swallowed thickly as she stared into her father's cold grey eyes. "Please don't do this..." she whispered. "I'm your daughter..."

"Perhaps once, but no longer. Not after you have forsaken your obligations to your family. Not after you have dragged the Scarborough name through the mud with your disloyalty."

"What...what does this mean?"

"Your husband shall still receive your inheritance and share of my estate and business, as per the pre-nuptial agreement. However, you shall no longer be associated with the Scarborough name in any way."

"What about...what about Mother?" Evie asked weakly. "Will I ever see her again?"

Elliot stiffened in anger as his voice lowered into a rasp. "Your mother is *dead*."

Feeling as if she had just been punched in the stomach and all of the air had been pulled from her lungs, Evie stared at him with wide eyes. Her knees went weak underneath her as she stumbled back a few steps into Silas' chest. Placing a hand over her heart, she whispered, "...She's *what*?"

"Dead," Elliot snarled. "She passed two years ago."

"...How?"

Elliot's eyes were ablaze with a deadly concoction of anger and pain. "She was never the same after we received word that you had run away. We searched for you for months and months, but never found any trace. Your mother worried herself sick over you day after day, never losing hope that we would find you. But when two years passed without a trace, she fell ill with worry and succumbed to her broken heart."

Evie collapsed to her knees at her father's feet and dropped her head in her hands as sobs began to wrack her body once again. The world began to spin uncontrollably around her as she became overwhelmed with a guilt and grief she had only ever experienced once before—when she had lost her son.

"No…" she wailed into her hands. "No, she can't be gone…"

"She is," Silas retorted coldly as he stood over her. "She died of a broken heart after you left. You killed her, just as you killed our son."

Evie looked up through her tears to see Elliot pass her one last look of disgust before turning away. "Goodbye, Evie," he stated icily. "I'll leave you and your husband to spend the rest of your days as he sees fit. I suggest you pray to God and beg that He does not forsake you as you have your family."

Evie watched helplessly as Elliot turned on his heel and stalked out of the dining hall, leaving her a crumpled mess on the floor at Silas' feet. She sobbed uncontrollably for several agonizing moments, wrapping her arms around herself and curling into a ball while Silas looked on. Upon hearing her agonized cries, Howell and Tsipporah sprinted into the hall and attempted to lift her from the floor, but she became a wild and inconsolable mess in their arms, kicking and fighting to get out of their hold. She let out a loud and mournful cry as rage and hatred filled the cracks in her crumbling heart; hatred for Silas, hatred for her father, and most of all, hatred for herself.

It was all her fault. Everything that had gone wrong in her life was her own doing, and she had no one but herself to blame for all of the anguish that bombarded her in that moment. If only she hadn't run away, if only she had tried to write to her mother from Division Point, if only she hadn't lost Noah, if only she hadn't lied to Theo and the others for so long…perhaps then none of this would have happened. Perhaps God would not have felt the need to punish her by taking away her mother and her son if she had accepted her fate long ago, instead of fighting it so ferociously. Perhaps then, God would have never forsaken her, as He had Tsipporah and so many others.

"Come now, Mrs. Porter," Howell murmured comfortingly in her ear as he lifted her off of the floor with his arms wrapped around her waist. "Come take a seat at the table. Eat with your husband, it will make you feel better."

After being forced into a chair at the table, Evie slumped lifelessly in her seat, staring emptily at the plate in front of her as silent tears streamed down her face. Silas waved Howell off and took a seat across from her, a triumphant air about him now that he had successfully severed the last of his wife's ties with her family. With no family to turn to, surely, she would have no desire left to run again.

Pleased with himself beyond belief, Silas began to eat the meal of boiled ham and vegetables that he had the servants prepare for them. Evie watched him eat without a trace of an appetite herself, now that the last person she had in the world was gone. Without Noah, and without Theo, Ophelia was her last hope. Now she was gone with the wind as well, and Evie truly had *nothing*. Nothing left to hope for, nothing left to lean on, nothing left to *live* for.

Silas looked up from his plate for a moment and caught a glimpse of her eyes before they fell to the floor in a final gesture of defeat. Her cheeks were stained with tears as she silently sobbed in her seat, and her eyes quickly became devoid of any life with every second that passed. Once bright pools of blue, they were now dark, cloudy, and glazed with a hopelessness and despondency that she never thought possible until now. Though her cries had quieted from a piercing wail to a pathetic mewling before fading altogether into silent sobs, Silas could see in her eyes that something had changed. Even after all he had inflicted upon her, he had never seen the light go out of her eyes the way it did in this moment.

He had done it, he told himself. The woman sitting across from him was not a girl nor a woman any longer; she was an empty shell—robbed of what remained of her hope and her spirit.

He had finally succeeded in his endeavor to make her his, and only his, with nothing left in the world to inspire her to try and escape again. She was distraught, she was hopeless, and she was lost.

Finally, she was *broken.*

***

Jacob gave his friend a sideways look as they rode side by side on horseback through the Rhode Island forest. It had been nearly three days since they left the homestead, Jacob dressed in a Redcoat uniform and Theo in his typical attire of a loose cotton shirt, trousers, and his trusty boots. If the plan were to work, Theo had to look himself, and Jacob had to appear as British as humanly possible.

Jacob pulled uncomfortably at the collar of his uniform coat, which still smelled of dust and gunpowder, and he wished he could be wearing anything else. He felt grimy and dirty wearing the attire of the enemy, but there was little he could do about it now that they were deep into Rhode Island and Division Point was long behind them.

"You never told me much about your friend Elijah," Jacob commented absently after a long bout of silence.

Theo looked up and momentarily froze, casting Jacob a side-eyed stare as he stiffened uncomfortably. His eyes then dropped to stare at Artemis' jet-black mane as his grip on the reins tightened.

"How did you know about him?" Theo asked quietly.

"Evie showed me some of your letters while you were away. You never mentioned him to me when you returned, though."

Theo shrugged wistfully. "There is not much to tell now. He is deceased."

"How? In battle?"

Theo shook his head and furrowed his brow. "No. He was murdered. Before my eyes."

Jacob's eyes widened as he looked up to the sky. "I'm so sorry, Theo. From the sound of your letters, you two must have grown quite close."

"He was my only true friend in the war. He saved my life on multiple occasions, and he died doing the very same."

"What happened?"

"A fellow soldier accused me of sympathizing with the Tories and pulled a pistol to shoot me. Elijah jumped in front of me and took the bullet himself. He bled out in my arms within minutes." Theo's voice grew quieter and quieter as he recalled the terrible day Elijah was taken, until it faded to a raspy whisper and his shoulders slumped in sadness. He hadn't thought about Elijah nor Washington in many months, and just as he suspected, recalling that time in his past brought back nothing but painful memories he longed to forget.

Jacob let out a long, drawn-out sigh. "He died a hero, then."

"He did."

"There are a lot of people in this world willing to risk their lives for you, Theo. I hope you realize that."

Theo looked up and briefly caught his friend's eye as a small smile tugged at the corners of his lips.

"I'm starting to."

***

It had been twelve hours since the rug had been pulled out from under Evie's feet and she had learned that the last person she had in the world was gone. Ophelia Scarborough had been her entire world growing up, and nothing pained her more than to be separated from her for the last five years. Evie had held onto the hope that she would someday be reunited with her mother when Silas was no longer a threat to her freedom, but now that she knew she was dead—dead from a worrisome and broken heart, no less—Evie could feel the last shreds of hope and light in her heart fading to an endless black.

She had nothing left in the world, as far as she was concerned, with no chance of ever escaping her misery again. Her father clearly had no intention of freeing her from her prison, and she was certain that Theo could never find it in his heart to come rescue her. Her last attempt at escape had clearly ended in disaster, with her ending up right where she had started, so she could no longer find any motivation to attempt it again. She couldn't bring herself to care that her father had disowned her—she didn't give a damn about his money, or his power, or her inheritance. She didn't want any of it.

All she wanted in that moment was her mother and her family in Division Point, the only people in the world that she had ever loved and trusted. And now, they were all torn from her grasp and blown away with the cold wind. With no one to turn to and nowhere to go, forsaken by God and all she had before the storm came through, she was doomed to spend the rest of her days floating aimlessly in a sea of hellish misery.

The sun had set just an hour before, casting a dim orange light through the window of Silas' chambers as Evie lay curled up on her side on the bed. She had discarded her fine scarlet gown long ago in favor of a rather humble skirt and blouse, and she spent the last several hours choking on silent sobs in bed while the world continued to turn around her. She refused to eat in the dining hall after hearing the news of her mother's passing, so Silas had Howell escort her back to his chambers and stand guard at her door for the remainder of the day. She had no desire to eat, nor socialize, nor even care for herself, so she spent the day wallowing in her husband's bed while he went about his merry way plotting the destruction of the Patriot's war effort.

Evie stiffened when she heard the door to her chambers creek open, and she remained curled up on her side on the bed as she slid her eyes over to see Silas entering the room. He hummed rather triumphantly to himself as he entered and closed the door behind him, not bothering to give her a greeting or even an acknowledgement before he began to shrug out of his uniform coat and toss it on a nearby chair. Evie rolled onto her other side to turn her back to him as she listened to the sound of rustling fabric; perhaps in the past she would have been fearful to be in his presence, but now, she felt nothing.

After dressing down to his shirt and trousers, Silas ran a hand through his long sandy hair to free it from the ribbon that tied it back at the nape of his neck. He then let out a heavy sigh and moved across the room to the table next to the bed that held a tray of his liquor bottles and a gilded decanter. He passed his wife a skeptical look as he poured himself a glass of rum.

"You seem more despondent than usual," he commented dryly.

Evie did not respond at first, but upon watching him pull up a chair to her side of the bed and take a seat while he swirled his drink in its glass, she quickly realized she was no longer going to be able to avoid him.

"I miss my mother," she murmured as she wiped at her red and swollen eyes with the back of her hand. "I wish I could have said goodbye…"

"Well, perhaps if you hadn't run away, you could have," Silas retorted as he sunk into the back of his chair.

Evie passed him a sharp look as his words cut deep into her already battered heart, but her hardened gaze quickly faded into one of defeat. Silas watched as her defiance seemed to melt before his eyes, and he tilted his head before setting the untouched rum back on the tray and leaning forward in his chair to lock his eyes with hers. Suddenly and without warning, his steely grey eyes took on a warmer quality that Evie could not recognize.

"I suppose I know what it is like to lose a mother," he mumbled forlornly as he folded his hands in his lap and stared into her eyes.

Evie quirked a brow in confusion and slowly sat up in the bed. "…What are you talking about?"

Silas withdrew another sigh and closed his eyes. "I never had the chance to tell you…but my mother died when I was just a boy. *Consumption*, I was told. She was fine one day, and then she began to cough. Within a month, she was gone. I was only eight."

Evie stared at him with wide eyes as she brought her hand up to her mouth. She felt her heart clench in her chest as she shook her head in sadness. "I…had no idea…"

Silas shrugged and held her gaze with eyes darkened by years of captive sadness. She had never before seen such vulnerability nor humanity within him before, and it was disconcerting to say the least. For the first time, she saw something dancing behind his eyes other than rage and drunkenness. She saw *pain*.

"My father moved on quickly," he continued with a voice made frail by a sudden wave of memories, "and he expected me to do the same. But I couldn't. I was never the same after she was gone."

Evie subconsciously leaned towards him, feeling the pain emanating from his tense form in a way that he had never once revealed to anyone before. Never before had he allowed her, nor anyone else, to witness him at his lowest. Emotions were a man's greatest weakness, he was convinced. To show them to anyone, even one's wife, was to reveal the vulnerabilities that anyone could use to destroy you, should they feel the need. But seeing his wife consumed by such a deep and overwhelming grief brought something out in him that he had never even known existed—was it compassion? Was it empathy? He didn't know. The feeling was so foreign to them both that they stared at each other for several moments in mutual silent confusion.

"…Are you drunk?" Evie asked after a moment of contemplation.

Silas scoffed with a dark chuckle. "No, actually. I haven't had a drink yet today. And I have a raging ache in my head to show for it."

Evie's gaze softened ever so slightly, and she swallowed nervously. "Do you drink to numb the pain?" she asked weakly, leaning forward in curiosity until their faces were only a foot apart.

Silas frowned. "I drink because I like the taste."

"No one drinks for the taste, Silas. They drink because they are searching for a reprieve from their suffering. To forget the things that haunt them..."

Silas' eyes narrowed into aggravated slits for a brief moment before softening once again. "So, what if I do?" he grouched as he suddenly stood from his chair. "It makes me no different than any other man! Don't we all have things we wish we could forget?"

Silas turned his back to her and began to pace across the room, his eyes roaming occasionally to the glass of untouched rum next to the bed. It was not until that moment that the realization hit Evie like a punch to the gut that Silas was still a human man with a beating heart...and a soul. Just like any other man, he was capable of feeling pain and betrayal, and that was exactly what she had inflicted upon him when she left him just as his mother had—he just refused to show it. A man as strong and reputable as Silas Porter could not let the world think he had lowered himself to feel something for a woman, nor could he tolerate anyone thinking he was so weak as to be *hurt* by her. So, the next logical choice was to drown every sorrow in a sea of liquor and harden his heart to anyone and anything that fell in his path. It was the only way for a man to survive in this world with his reputation intact, after all.

"I'm sorry that I hurt you, Silas," Evie murmured as she slowly stood from the bed and approached him. "If I had known...if I had understood you, as I do now, perhaps...things would have been different."

Silas spun around to face her with hardened eyes and his jaw tight. "Perhaps you would not have left me like my mother did, hm?"

Evie swallowed and hesitantly placed the palm of her hand on his chest, spreading her fingers across the bare flesh that poked out from the loose collar of his shirt. Underneath his warm skin, she could feel his heart beating—something she wasn't convinced he even possessed until now. A pang of guilt and regret shot through her heart as she looked up into his eyes, and for a brief moment, she questioned whether or not she ever had any business trying to flee from him. Silas locked his eyes with hers and reached forward to place his large hands on her hips, pulling her tightly, but gingerly, into his chest.

"I do not want to fight with you anymore, Silas," she whispered as a tear rolled down her cheek. "I just…want to be happy. That is all I have ever wanted."

"I could have made you happy," he returned lowly, his lips barely grazing hers. "If you had only given me a chance."

For the first time she could remember, Evie was not overwhelmed with the stench of whiskey nor rum rolling off of his breath. She could feel her heart begin to pound in her chest as he leaned down to press his lips to hers, and for the first time in their marriage, she did not try to pull away from him.

Despite his flaws, his anger, and his drinking, in that moment, she did not fear him. In that moment, he was not the monster that she knew, but a man. He was a human being, with a heart beating in his chest and blood coursing through his veins. As rough, ruthless, and hard-hearted as he was, she could see now that there existed within him the tiniest shred of humanity, buried deep under layers of grit and liquor that needed perhaps only a bit of tender coaxing to come to the surface.

Perhaps, she thought hesitantly to herself as Silas pulled away from the kiss and gingerly grazed her bruised cheek with his thumb, he and Theo were not all that different after all. They were both victims of forces in their pasts beyond their control, forced to navigate a world that told them exactly who they should be as men, and if they dared to deviate from those expectations, they ran the risk of losing everything.

The crucial difference between the two, however, was that the latter man had learned to cope with his sorrows much earlier than the other, for the consequences of his mistakes would always be higher as a privilege of the mixed blood that coursed through his veins. And as a result, *he* would always be the man that had her heart.

Chapter 7

The Lion's Den

March 1779

Jacob peered nervously around the large tree behind which he and Theo were crouched. The trees had thinned out along the Rhode Island coast that fell into the large, dark shadow of Fort Dumpling Rock, which seemed to jut up into the sky from the rocky island on which it sat like a stone-encrusted giant. Jacob took a moment to scan the coast and its nearby island fortress, feeling a dead weight settle in his stomach when he realized that the only way into the fort was across the narrow bridge that connected the island to the mainland, and it was guarded by four less than friendly Redcoats at the main gate.

Jacob slunk back behind the tree with a shake of his head. "I cannot believe you dragged me into this," he growled to Theo, who was crouched just behind him.

"Really now? I can believe it. It sounds exactly like something we would do."

Jacob passed him an unamused glare and pulled uncomfortably at his red uniform coat. It was hot and itchy and smelled of the enemy, and he wanted to be out of it as quickly as possible. "What do we do now?"

Theo stood to his full height behind the tree and looked up to the darkening evening sky in thought. "Your name is Thomas Black. You were instructed to transfer from Fort Halifax to Fort Dumpling Rock by your commanding officer. Upon arrival, you noticed me skulking about and trying to infiltrate the fort, and you captured me. I'm your prisoner."

"Would anyone really believe that you would try to infiltrate the fort single handedly?"

Theo smirked. "Silas would. He knows exactly why I would try to come back here. But there's just one more thing."

"What now?"

"They must believe that you captured me and that I put up a fight. I must look as if you roughed me up."

"How do we do that?"

Theo grabbed a handful of his own shirt and tugged on his sleeve until it partially tore away from his shoulder before collecting a handful of dirt from under his feet and smearing it all over his clothes and his face. "Now hit me."

Jacob widened his eyes in shock and confusion. "What?"

"Hit me. Come on, just once in the face. So it looks as if we scuffled."

Jacob shook his head, appalled by the suggestion. "Are you mad? I can't hit you! You're my friend…"

"You must, Jacob! They'll never believe that I just willingly gave myself up as a prisoner. Come now, just once. I won't hold it against you."

Indivisible

Jacob took a step back. "No, no. I can't. This is ridiculous, Theo. This will never work. This was a mistake. We are going to get ourselves killed! And for what, for that girl?"

"I *love* that girl," Theo snapped. "I will do anything to get her back. And you know I would do the same for you if the roles were reversed. So be a good chap and hit me in the face! We're losing time…"

"No. No. I can't do it, Theo. We have to turn back…"

Theo gave him a shove in the chest to aggravate him. "Come on, hit me. Hit me! Hit me!"

"No! Now stop it!"

Theo shoved Jacob again as he turned his back. "Hit me!"

"Stop it, I said!"

Theo paused, his shoulders slumping in defeat as Jacob shook his head with a dismissive sigh. After a moment of silence, Theo peered over his friend's shoulder with a mischievous smirk and mumbled, "James would have done it."

Jacob's hands immediately balled into fists at his side as he whipped back around to face Theo. "What did you just say?" he asked lowly through clenched teeth.

"You heard me. I said James, your brother, would have done anything to help me. *He* was my best friend, and he—" Theo was cut off when Jacob suddenly charged forward with an enraged growl, throwing a hard punch at Theo's face and smirking in satisfaction when he felt his fist connect with his jaw.

Theo let out a startled gasp as he felt his brain rattle inside his skull and his legs buckle underneath him. He hit the ground at Jacob's feet with a dull thud, and for a split second, the world was dark. A wave of pain scorched through the lower half of his face as he felt his bottom lip split open and his head hit the hard ground.

"Oh, God…" he moaned, feeling dazed and disoriented as stars danced across his eyes. Jacob came to stand over him, chest heaving in anger, and he watched as Theo slowly pushed himself up onto his hands and knees. He had seen the business end of a fist many times in his life, but he hadn't felt one coming his way that ferociously in a long while.

Theo hissed in pain and brought a hand up to nurse his throbbing jaw as he looked up to meet his friend's gaze, eyes wide in shock that he had actually done it. Jacob's eyes were ablaze with rage, but they immediately softened when he took notice of the trail of blood tricking down Theo's chin.

"Oh, Lord, Theo…I'm so sorry. I don't know what came over me. Did I…did I hurt you?"

Theo waved his hand dismissively and shook his head before spitting a mouthful of blood on the ground at Jacob's feet. "No, no…" he moaned. "That was perfect…exactly what I wanted…"

Jacob reached down to help him to his feet, brows pinched in concern. "Are you certain? You look…snockered."

Theo slowly tried to move his jaw and winced in pain as he did so. Jacob had hit him much harder than he was anticipating, but it did the job in roughing him up. Surely, a few bruises would soon come of the tussle to support their story. "I'm fine. Just a little surprised that you can actually throw a punch, I suppose."

Jacob's face fell as he gave Theo a shove. "Don't push your luck, mate."

Theo chuckled lowly as he turned away and held his hands behind his back. Jacob then produced a length of rope from the inner pocket of his coat and tied it tightly around Theo's wrists.

"Tight enough?" he asked.

"I've had tighter," Theo returned sarcastically.

Jacob tightened the bindings with an annoyed roll of his eyes before tying a black handkerchief around the lower half of his own face. He then lowered his tricorn hat to conceal much of his eyes and forehead and shouldered Alistair's old musket. "Are you ready?"

Theo shrugged. "As ready as I'll ever be to charge straight into the lion's den."

Ready to play the part, Jacob took a hold of his arm and roughly pushed him forward. "Then march."

***

Evie glanced between the plate of unfinished food in front of her and Silas' face, struggling to find an appetite. She had been trapped in Dumpling Rock for a week, but it felt like it had been ten years since she had known freedom. It was early evening, and Silas had retired early for the day to share a meal with his wife in his chambers, ordering explicitly that no one come knocking on the door unless someone was dead or the fort was in flames.

Ever since learning of the story of Silas' mother, Evie had found herself uncomfortably conflicted. She wanted to hate him after all he had done to her, to Theo, and to everyone else in the name of war, but after looking into his eyes that night and seeing a softness and vulnerability of which she didn't know he was capable, she found it more and more difficult to think of him as a monster. She knew she could never love him, not after how he had battered her and tortured Theo, but she found herself less afraid of him now than she had ever been before.

Silas set down his fork and reached across the table to pour himself a glass of brandy. Before he served himself, he offered her a glass.

Evie shook her head. "No, thank you."

"Come now, one glass won't hurt anyone. Imported from France, just like your gowns."

After a moment of hesitation, she accepted the glass from him and took a sip. It was bright and sweet on her tongue, as opposed to bitterness of the whiskey and rum that Silas usually consumed.

"Did your lover enjoy the drink, too?" Silas suddenly asked, peering at her over his glass.

Evie froze and stared at him in confusion. "Excuse me?"

"Your lover. The half breed. What did he call himself…Theo? Did he imbibe as well?"

Evie stiffened in her chair and cleared her throat. "No, actually. Not anymore. He quit the stuff a long time ago."

"Why would anyone want to do that?"

Evie's eyes narrowed ever so slightly as she crossed her arms on the table and leaned forward. "Because he could see it was destroying him. You would do well to do the same."

Silas scoffed and slammed his now empty glass on the table. "Do not presume to tell me what I should and should not do, woman. We both know who issues the commands here, and it certainly will never be you."

A frenzied knock on the outside of the door caused Evie to jump in her chair and clamp her mouth shut. Silas abruptly turned his head toward the door, and through clenched teeth, he growled, "Someone better be dying! I said I did not want to be interrupted!"

"It's Howell, sir," the voice on the other side said nervously. "I have urgent news."

Silas rolled his eyes and slicked back his hair in annoyance. *Enter.*

Howell immediately opened the door and strode in, pausing before the table to offer his Captain a salute and the Captain's wife a polite bow. A concerned look twisted his face. "Captain Porter. Mrs. Porter. I'm so sorry to interrupt."

Evie offered him a shy smile and tried to return the greeting, but Silas held up his hand to silence her.

"Make it quick, Daniel. We are obviously busy. What news do you have that could not wait until morning?"

"Just a moment ago, a fellow soldier of the Crown arrived bearing a prisoner of war. The soldier calls himself Thomas Black and says he was transferred here under orders from the commanding officer at Fort Halifax."

"Prisoner? Why is this any of my concern?"

"The prisoner is a native man. Black says he found him skulking about the outskirts of the fort, looking for a way in."

Silas shoved his chair back from the table and jumped to his feet as Evie froze in her seat. "How did this native man look, Howell?"

"Familiar, sir. I took the prisoner down to the hold and instructed Black to keep a close eye on him there."

"How familiar?"

"I questioned him briefly. I know his face from the last time he was held here, and he was very forthcoming in telling me his name is Theo Cunningham and that he had come to settle unfinished business with you, sir."

Evie gasped and slapped her hand over her mouth, feeling her stomach churn and the color drain from her face. She shook her head in shock and confusion, refusing to believe that it could actually be true. Theo couldn't possibly be foolish enough to come back here after all he had endured at her husband's hands, especially not after she had betrayed him.

Silas' expression immediately hardened, and he slowly turned to face her. "You wouldn't happen to know anything about this, would you, love?" he asked coolly as his eyes began to darken in skepticism.

Evie shook her head adamantly, just as confused as he. "No…I had no knowledge. I explicitly told him not to come anywhere near here…"

Silas looked unconvinced, and his scowl grew larger as he quirked his brow at her. "You expect me to believe you did not conspire with him to win your freedom again?"

"No, I've done no such thing. You must believe me, Silas," she begged fearfully, standing from her chair. "I had no knowledge he would try to come here at all, let alone…on his own."

Silas cackled skeptically and turned back to Howell. "Return to the hold and see to it that our slippery little friend does not slip away again. I will be there in a moment."

"Yes, sir." Howell bowed to them both before promptly exiting the room and closing the door behind him.

Silas sighed heavily and moved across the room to take up the red uniform jacket that he had discarded on the armchair. He shrugged into it and adjusted the lapels, but before he could make for the door, Evie took ahold of him by his sleeve.

"Silas, what are you going to do?" she asked frantically, her eyes wide with fear. "What will you do to him?"

Silas sneered at her over his shoulder, all remains of gentleness vanishing behind dark and nefarious eyes that stared her down without mercy. "Wouldn't you like to know? What's the matter, dear wife? Are you afraid I'll do something vile to your lover now that I have you both in my clutches again?"

"Please...do not hurt him. He doesn't deserve it. I'm the one who betrayed you, not him."

"Ha!" Silas angrily pulled away from her and bellowed, "He fucked my wife! And he took up arms against the Crown—he is a traitor, and a bastard, and an adulterer, just like the rest of his ilk."

He tried to turn away again, but she tugged on his sleeve with teary eyes. "Silas, you don't know him. Not like I do. You don't know his people. You cannot judge an entire group of people that you have never met and wave them off as uncivilized beasts. Theo is not a savage; he is a red-blooded man, just as you are!"

Silas roughly gripped her by both of her upper arms and snarled, "Might I remind you that both of our fathers fought these natives that you call your friends during the Seven Years War? Might I remind you that they have both told me stories of how they witnessed the savages raping, pillaging, raiding, and burning entire villages of colonists in the name of war?"

Evie jerked out of his arms and pointed an accusatory finger in his face. "And *you* burned an entire village of colonists in the name of war!"

"*Excuse me?*"

Evie clenched her teeth together as she glared up into his eyes. They were black empty pools staring back at her, sending shivers down her spine and forcing her to question how she could have ever seen any humanity within them. His tenderness the other night was nothing but a fluke, she could see it now. A ploy to get her to trust him, to convince her to forget about Theo, to trick her into loving *him*.

"Kensington. I wouldn't expect you to remember. You've probably razed a thousand villages by now. But you didn't burn them in the name of war…you burned them because you wanted to. Because it gave you pleasure to hear the screams of the wounded and smell the stench of burning bodies!"

Silas abruptly let out an enraged snarl and seized her by her shoulders, pushing her backwards into the nearest wall and caging her against it by slamming his hands against the stone on either side of her head.

"Yes!" he hissed in her face as she cowered against the wall. "Yes, it gave me immense pleasure to watch those traitors perish. Every last one of them, man, woman, and child! Nothing gives me more pleasure than to watch my enemies burn, to hear them scream, to hear them beg for their mothers and their God…to watch them beg me for mercy before I snuff out the minuscule remains of their pathetic lives!"

Evie's heart began to pound erratically in her chest as she stared back at him. His eyes were wide and wild in a way she had never seen before, not even when he had forced himself upon her or beaten her within an inch of her life. She could see the vein throbbing in his neck, the one that always throbbed when he became embroiled in a sea of blinding rage. In that moment, she was not looking into the eyes of an enraged man, but rather, a blood-thirsty animal.

"Then why didn't you burn down Division Point when you had the chance?" she asked in a whisper.

Silas smirked. "It would have been too easy. There would have been no satisfaction to it. No, I'll wait until the war is over and the Crown has emerged victorious, and then when I am no longer distracted by my obligations to His Majesty, I will take you back to that cesspool you called a home for the last five years and I will burn it, and all its people, to the ground. I will destroy everything you ever loved, destroy any reason you may have to run away from me again, starting with that half breed in my dungeon…"

Silas's smirk deepened as he watched Evie's eyes widen in horror and her body begin to tremble. After deciding his message had been effectively received, he stepped away and turned towards the door.

Evie swallowed thickly, and just as he opened the door, she murmured, "And to think…until now, I was beginning to believe that you might have had a heart beating in that chest of yours."

Silas laughed with no humor. "Silly girl. What a *fatal* mistake…"

***

"On your feet," Howell ordered coolly from the other side of the bars through which he was staring down the fort's newest resident. Just behind him stood the cadet that had somehow managed to capture the elusive rebel, and in front of him, slumped on his side with his hands bound behind his back, was a young man with long raven hair, golden brown eyes, and the complexion of a man of mixed blood.

Howell had seen him before; he had just arrived as Captain Porter's second in command in the fort when the man was captured and brought here the first time. He watched as the man and the other prisoners were flogged in front of everyone until their bare backs were torn open a thousand times over, left raw and dripping until each kiss of the cat o' nine tails eventually healed over into a hellish and garish welt. He was one of the ones that chased after the man and his accomplices, and one of the ones who shot at him as he disappeared into the wilderness. He was certain that Theo had succumbed to his bullet wounds over a year ago, and if he did somehow survive, that he would not be foolish enough to fall back into Silas' hands once again. But here he was, bound in the exact cell he was before; but this time, it seemed as if he had come *seeking* trouble.

Theo rolled over onto his back and slowly sat up before climbing to his knees and then onto his feet. It was a painful endeavor, as he had been welcomed into the fort in a less than friendly manner and roughed up a bit before being unceremoniously tossed back into the hold that he had come to know so well. Jacob could do little to protect him from the initial beating without putting his false identity in jeopardy, so he was forced to watch a group of three disgruntled cadets punch and kick at his friend's defenseless body before he himself was ordered to bring him to the hold.

Theo limped to the bars that separated him from Howell and Cadet 'Thomas Black,' shooting the former a confused furrow of his bruised brow. "I've seen you before," he commented dryly.

"Aye," Howell returned. "And I've seen you. I was there when you were flogged, and when you escaped the *first* time. I was told you had most likely succumbed to your wounds."

Theo pulled at the bindings on his wrists. "And yet here I am."

The door to the hold suddenly slammed open, and Silas' boots pounded mercilessly on the stone floor as he stormed in and approached the bars. A malicious smirk marred his face as he and Theo stood chest to chest, separated only by a few inches and a set of thick iron bars. Theo was rather ragged in his appearance, with his shirt torn in several places and his skin smeared with dirt and mud. His lip had been busted open and a fresh gash on his forehead sent a crisp trail of blood dripping down the side of his face. Despite this, he appeared just as cocky as the first time he stood before the Captain of Fort Dumpling Rock.

"Yes, here you are," Silas spat through clenched teeth. "And I would like to know exactly why that is. Certainly, you couldn't be foolish enough to willingly surrender to me a *second* time after I spared you at Division Point."

"Of course not. Does it look like I came to your hold on my own accord?"

"No. But I was told that you were found skulking about outside, looking for a way in. Why is that?"

Theo shrugged. "I came to kill you."

Silas looked mildly surprised, but barely fazed. He snorted in amusement and turned to Howell and Black, who shared an uncertain look. "*This* is why you interrupted my dinner with my wife?" He then turned back to his prisoner. "Let me guess. You came here, all on your own, with a grandiose idea to assassinate me in my own fort and reclaim my wife as yours, is that right?"

Theo scoffed. "I couldn't care less about your wife. She's a lying whore. You can have her. I came here for *you*."

Silas slammed his fists upon the bars hard enough to rattle the entire door. "And tell me how well that has worked out for you, welp! You're alone, in my dungeon, at my mercy, once again! And do not think I have not learned from my mistakes the first time. The only way you will be leaving this fort a second time is in a pine box!"

Theo did not flinch, but only smirked. "If I were a betting man, I would bet on myself, Captain. I've proven to be pretty difficult to kill."

Silas growled something unintelligible under his breath before running his hand down his face and turning his back to the cell. His eyes then fell upon the stranger in an outdated red coat on Howell's left.

"You," he grumbled as he pointed in the man's face. "You're the one that found this mongrel?"

Thomas Black cleared his throat and stuttered behind the handkerchief covering the lower half of his face. "Yes, sir. I was sent here from Fort Halifax. I found the rebel trying to infiltrate the fort from the back, and he was armed with a pistol, which I confiscated upon his surrender."

"And you captured the slippery bastard single-handedly?"

Black and Theo shared a fleeting look before he nodded. "Yes, sir. He realized he was out-gunned and surrendered after a minor scuffle."

Silas tossed a look over his shoulder at Theo. "You're losing your touch, boy. Bested by a single Cadet? How pathetic." He then turned back to Howell and Black once more.

"Tell me your name, Cadet."

"...Thomas Black, sir."

Silas scrutinized the young soldier for a moment, looking somewhat skeptical. "Who sent you from Halifax?"

Black froze in hesitation, and Theo dropped his head. He had forgotten to give him a commanding officer.

"Captain...Stone, sir." Thomas Black stuttered after looking around the hold, his eyes falling upon the stony floor under his feet.

"Captain Stone?" Silas repeated. "I am not familiar with a Captain Stone."

"He was just recently promoted, sir. He ordered me and several others to come south to Fort Dumpling Rock, but sadly I am the only one that made it here alive."

"What happened to the others?"

"...Indians, sir. We were set upon by Indians. I barely escaped with my life."

Theo resisted the urge to roll his eyes at his friend's clever on-the-spot fib. Of course, it had to be *Indians*.

Silas thought for a moment before shaking his head. "God-damned savages, every last one of them. Your brothers in arms will be remembered fondly for their sacrifice for the Crown."

"Yes, sir."

"Cadet Black, I am glad to have you under my command. We can use every man we can get in this war against the Rebels. I will be sure to thank Captain Stone for sending you at a later date. For the time being, go make yourself useful and stand guard outside my chambers. See to it that my wife, Evie, does not find a way to slip out." Silas dug around in his uniform coat before producing a ring of keys and inserting one into the door to Theo's cell. "Howell and I will continue our conversation with Mr. Cunningham in your absence before I have to leave for this evening's scouting mission."

Black gave Theo a nervous look before stating, "Yes, sir. At once."

He hesitated before slowly turning away and exiting the hold, but not before locking eyes with Theo one last time. Theo silently urged him to go with a pleading look in his eyes, assuring him that he would be fine. The door to the cell creaked open as Silas stepped inside and ordered Howell to follow suit. Theo took a nervous step backwards until his back hit the wall.

The last thing Thomas Black heard before he tore himself away and exited the prisoners' barracks was Theo's pained gasp as Silas shoved his fist into his gut and knocked him to the hard ground at his feet.

***

Evie curled herself tightly into a ball as she sunk into the armchair by her husband's bed. The very thought of Theo and herself being trapped together in this prison of a fort, so close, and yet still so far from one another, made her skin crawl and her stomach churn. She longed to see him, and she shuddered at the thought of what Silas could have been doing to him at that very moment. But she was also perplexed as to how and why he had found himself here again, especially after all he had endured the first time he was in Silas' clutches. He certainly would not have risked his life to come back here for her sake, would he? Not after she had hurt and betrayed him so terribly…

A sudden knock on her door startled her enough to pull her from her thoughts and tear a gasp from her throat. She glared at the door in aggravation, not caring who it could possibly be.

"I do not want any visitors," she snapped.

Another knock. "I want to be left alone," she repeated.

"Evie," a low voice whispered. "Come to the door. At once."

Evie furrowed her brow in confusion and stomped to the door. "Who is it?" she hissed. "I said I wanted to be left alone—"

"It's *Jacob*," the familiar voice whispered from the other side of the door. "It's me, Jacob Caldwell."

Evie gasped and pressed her ear to the door, not believing what she was hearing. It was Jacob's voice, she knew it instantly, but she could not fathom how or why he would be at her door. "Jacob?" she repeated shakily. "…Is it really you?"

"Yes, it's me. I swear it."

"H-How? Why? What are you doing here?"

"I do not have much time to explain. But I came here with Theo. We are bringing you home."

"*What?* How could you possibly think that would work? How did you even get in?"

"I'm in disguise as a Redcoat and Theo was my prisoner. I know, it's mad. Only he could come up with a plan so ridiculous."

Evie pressed both of her palms to the door and shook her head. "Jacob, you have to go. However you can, get Theo and go back home. It isn't safe for either of you here. If you are caught, you'll be executed."

"It's too late now," Jacob snapped, looking both ways down the long stone corridor to ensure no one was within earshot. "Theo is already in the hold, and only Silas has the keys. The only way we are leaving is with you."

"This was a mistake, Jacob. Silas will kill us all before he lets me go!"

"That is why we are sneaking you out of here. We just need time for me to get my hands on his keys to the hold."

"Silas always has those keys on his person. He never lets them out of his sight—"

Jacob cut her off by clearing his throat. From inside, Evie could hear a pair of footsteps approaching. "I overheard Silas telling his Sergeant that he will be away overnight on a scouting mission, taking the keys with him. Tonight, I will find a way to bring you to the hold when no one is looking so you can speak to Theo. For now, remain calm and do not give away my identity."

"But—"

Silas' voice echoing down the corridor startled her several steps back from the door, and she quickly moved to return back to her seat in the armchair. Her heart was pounding, and her mind was racing in confusion and worry. Whatever plan Theo had cooked up, it was doomed to fail. They would not be escaping the fort with their lives, that much she was certain.

"Black, thank you for guarding my chambers," she heard Silas say just outside the door, his words slightly muffled by the stone and wood that separated them.

"Of course, sir," Cadet Black replied with a salute.

"Sergeant Howell will be commanding the fort this evening during my brief absence, and he has retired for the evening. Our special prisoner is in no condition to attempt any type of escape, so I'm ordering you to stand guard here at my chambers until I return."

"As you command, sir."

A moment later, Silas came striding into the chambers with the smuggest of triumphant smirks upon his face. Squinting through the waning sunlight shining into the room, Evie could see that his hair was slightly amiss, and his knuckles were scuffed, as if he had spent the last half hour using his fists to beat someone or something into submission. Her stomach churned at the thought.

"You're leaving?" she asked, perplexed. "You did not mention a leaving to me before."

Silas straightened his jacket and smoothed his hair. "It was a last-minute decision, really. I received word from some of my scouts of rumors stating that there may be Indians in the area hostile to the Crown. I am leading a small squadron to scout out the surrounding wilderness. With luck, we will be able to *exterminate* any nearby threats."

Evie forced a smile to hide her disgust. "Then I wish you good health and safety on your mission, dear."

"As you should," he returned as he stepped forward to take ahold of her by her waist. He stared into her eyes briefly before pressing a kiss to the top of her head. She closed her eyes and tried desperately to pretend it was Theo that held her, but Silas' touch was cold and forceful, two words she never once equated with Theo.

After kissing her head, Silas bent down to whisper in her ear, "And you might as well rid yourself of any notions of trying to slip away while I am gone. I will be taking the only set of keys to the fort with me, and you will be under constant watch while I am away. And there will be no clandestine visits to your lover down in the hold."

Evie looked up into his eyes with a shy and broken smile, one that bespoke a newfound submission and a realization that she had nowhere to go but to him. There was little else for her in the world outside of the fort, outside of the suffocating walls her husband had succeeding building around her. Noah was dead, her mother was dead, and whatever plan Theo had concocted was doomed to fail. She was trapped, destined never to see the light of day outside of the oppressive shadow that Silas seemed to cast wherever he went. Whatever Theo and Jacob planned to do next, she would not be a part of it. She had lost too much already trying to forge a path to freedom that she was no longer convinced she was ever destined to have in the first place. Her place was here, with her husband, no matter how badly she craved to escape him.

"I wouldn't think of it, Silas. I know my place."

***

Evie paced the length of Silas' chambers, her heart in her throat and her stomach turning in knots. Silas had been gone for several hours already, and the moon was high in the sky. Jacob had yet to summon her with a knock on the door, and even if he did, she was not convinced she would risk punishment just to sneak away to see the man she knew she could never have again. She was not sure her heart could take it to see his face again and look into the eyes of a desperate and tortured man.

A faint knock on the door startled her from her thoughts, and she hesitated for several moments before eventually shuffling towards it. She returned the signal with a quiet knock of her own, pressing her ear to the door.

"I've been standing here for hours keeping watch," Jacob whispered through the wood that separated them. "Nearly every bloody Redcoat has retired for the evening or gotten piss-drunk and fallen asleep at their posts. Now is the time to sneak down to the hold."

Evie sighed and shook her head. "Jacob, I can't. I can't bear to look at Theo after what I have done…"

"If he can forgive you, I sure you can forgive yourself. Now quit your wallowing and come along. He wants to see you. I think you owe him that much after all that he has risked for you."

"I did not ask him to come and save me," Evie snapped. "I told him to stay far away. I've learned the hard way that my place is with Silas…and no one else."

"We are here now, and it is too late for us to turn back. Are you really going to abandon him like this after all he has done for you?"

Evie dropped her eyes to the floor in defeat. Her chest ached with fear and a longing to finally be free, but with every day that passed, the light of independence seemed to dim more and more, until it was nothing more than a pile of smothered embers. "And what if we're caught?"

"We won't be, so long as you do everything I say. Silas left the door to your chambers unlocked, should anyone need to get in to tend to you while he's away. Open the door and come with me. Quickly now, make haste."

After several painful minutes of deliberation in which she imagined every possible punishment that could befall her if Silas somehow got word of what she was about to do, Evie straightened her shoulders and wrapped a shaking hand around the cold metal doorknob. The door creaked meekly when she began to open it, causing her to cringe, but she continued on to open it just wide enough for her to slip between it and the doorframe. Jacob, also known as Cadet Thomas Black, was waiting for her just outside the door in the darkened corridor. Jacob's figure was tall and broad and coated in a crimson coat that Evie could tell he was itching to be free of. A musket was strapped to his back and a dark handkerchief covered the lower half of his face, but she could recognize him by his eyes in an instant.

She wanted to pause and ask him why he was there, why he would risk his own hide to save the girl that he never trusted nor even liked in the first place, but he wasted no time in taking ahold of her wrist and ducking around the corner.

"Stay close to my side and keep your head down," Jacob whispered, giving her a hard look of warning. "Make no sound and we will reach the hold without drawing any attention."

Evie's bare feet made little sound against the rough stone floors as they shuffled their way through the fort. Their surroundings became darker and more dank as they ventured deeper into the annals of the fortress, and Jacob's grip on her wrist was iron-tight as they bobbed and weaved through the long corridors, ducking behind several corners to avoid being seen by a straggling Redcoat who had not yet retired for the night. After narrowly avoiding several collisions with unobservant guards, Jacob led her around into the shadows of the cavernous prisoner's hold. The hold was vacant of any life, safe for one cell at the very end of the corridor.

Jacob paused at the entrance and released her wrist, gesturing to the end of the corridor with a jerk of his chin.

"Go to him. He's in the last cell. I'll stand guard here," he whispered before turning his back to her to face the entrance.

Evie's heart pounded in her chest as she made the long walk down the corridor of empty cells, dragging her fingers along the rusted bars as she went. She tried not to think about how many souls had come and gone through each set of iron doors, how much blood had been spilled and seeped into the stones, or how many cries for mercy fell on deaf ears.

Evie felt as if she had been punched in the stomach hard enough to knock the wind from her lungs when she finally came upon the final cell. Illuminated only by a single lantern hanging on the wall, Theo was curled up in the corner, his back against the wall as he sat on the cold floor with his knees hugged to his chest. His head was lowered, either in pain or exhaustion, his face concealed by a mess of long and tangled tresses. At the sound of bare footsteps heading his way, he slowly raised his head to reveal a battered face smeared with dirt and blood. His clothes were torn and stained, as if he had been beaten with a blunt object and then trampled on by a thousand wild horses.

Evie gasped when she took in his battered condition, and she felt her heart clench in her chest as his eyes fell upon her.

"Evie…" he rasped as he slowly and painfully unfurled himself and began to crawl towards her. Evie dropped to her knees outside of the cell with a saddened moan as he crawled to her. Separated by a wall of thick, rusted iron bars, they reached for each other through the gaps. "You came…"

"Theo," she gasped, clutching onto the remaining shreds of his shirt through the bars. "Oh, God, what did he do to you?"

"I've had worse," Theo mumbled weakly. Upon closer inspection, Evie could see an enormous bruise and laceration under his eye, as well as on his temple, and dried blood trailed down his face in several places, making him almost unrecognizable to her in the darkness.

Theo reached through the bars to place a calloused hand on her face, and she pressed her cheek into his palm while placing her hand over his.

She tried to savor every last moment of his touch, fearful that it would be the last time she would ever feel it.

"Why are you here?" she whispered tearfully. "I told you to stay far away, Theo. I told you not to come for me…"

"I couldn't let him take you away. You don't belong with him. You belong at Division Point. With me."

Evie shook her head. "No, not after what I've done. Not after I deceived you. How can you risk your life by coming here after I betrayed you?"

"I don't care about any of that, Evie. I don't. About your past, your family, your husband…I don't care! You did what you had to do to survive…"

"I thought you hated me. You said you could never forgive me…"

"I didn't mean it. I thought I could live without you, but after you were gone…I realized that my life was not worth living without you in it."

A single tear escaped Evie's eye as she murmured, "It's too late for that now…"

"I'm sorry, Evie. For everything that I said. You know I didn't mean it. Please, you have to come home with me. I already almost lost you once, I won't lose you again."

"This is my home now, Theo. I belong here, with my husband, and you belong at Division Point with your family."

"No!" Theo growled, reaching through the bars with his other hand to take ahold of her by her shoulders and pull her as close to him as he could manage. He leaned forward until their faces were only a few inches apart, separated only by the bars of his cell. "Your family is at Division Point. I can't let you go back to a life of misery with that monster. He'll kill you the moment he decides he no longer needs you."

"Perhaps we would all be better off."

"What? How can you say that?"

"Theo, listen to me..." Tears began to pour furiously down her pallid face as she stared into his warm golden eyes and placed a hand on his chest. "Noah is dead. My mother is dead. My father has disowned me. I have nothing left. I tried to escape once, and God punished me by taking my mother and my son from me. Losing everyone I have ever loved is not a price I am willing to pay for my freedom."

"You can't give up," Theo begged desperately, his voice breaking in a way she had never seen before. "I've lost too many people to war, Evie. James, Elijah, my mother...I can't lose you as well. Not you, too. Please, you can't give up on me. On us."

"There is no us," she cried as she tried to turn away. "There never was. I belong to another man, and I always will. Don't you see, Theo? Silas has won. He's got everything he ever wanted. You can't beat him. He's too strong, too powerful..."

Before she could pull out of his reach, Theo lunged forward and grabbed her hand, pulling her back into the bars and holding her there with both of his hands on her cheeks. Through the gaps in the bars, he rested his forehead against hers and looked into her eyes. He felt a twinge of agony shoot through his chest at the emptiness he saw in those once bright blue pools, and a wave of rage washed over him at the sight of the bruises on her face and neck.

"Evie, please..."

"You have to go, Theo. You have to leave, you and Jacob. If you stay, you will be caught, and you will be executed. And I could never live with myself if you died on my account. Please, just forget about me. You deserve so much better."

"If you won't do it for me, or for us, or for yourself, do it for your son. Everything you did, you did for your son. What would he think if he saw you give up like this, Evie? Wherever he is, he is looking down on you and watching you. Do you really want him to see you fall like this?"

"Noah is gone," Evie whispered tearfully.

"He isn't gone. He's with you, watching you, smiling down at you. Is this how you want your son to see you? Beaten, berated, humiliated, and miserable? That isn't the life you risked everything to create for yourself. If you give up now, Noah's death, and everything you've done for him, will be for *nothing...*"

Evie sniffled to try and swallow her tears as she raised her arms to place her hands atop his. "Do you just expect us to all slip out of the fort undetected? And even if we did, there is nowhere I could go where Silas won't find me."

"We have a plan. Jacob is going to find a way to get the keys to the hold. When he does, we will all sneak out under the cover of darkness."

Evie shook her head in disbelief. "Even if we got away alive, Silas would come looking for me again. He'll never let me go."

Theo's eyes hardened in determination. "Then I'll just have to make sure that he is no longer a threat."

"You mean...you mean to kill him?" she asked as she swallowed nervously.

"It's the only way for us both to be free."

"But he is too powerful—"

"Evie, this will only work if you trust me. Do you trust me?"

She paused as she felt another tear fall down her cheek, and he brushed it away with his thumb before pressing a kiss to her lips that seemed to breathe life back into her. After an eternity wandering in the hot desert, his kiss was like a fresh, cool oasis, offering her the sanctuary she so desperately craved.

"Do you trust me?" he asked again, softly this time.

"I trust you," she breathed, gasping for breath as the world seemed to spin around her.

The slightest of smirks tugged at Theo's busted lip as he brushed a stray lock of hair from her face, tucking it behind her ear. He pressed his lips to her forehead as his eyes slipped closed in contentment.

"I love you," he whispered weakly, just barely loud enough for her to hear.

She looked up to him in shock. Her heart skipped a beat in her chest, and her mind went blank as the words echoed inside her head. She had always longed to hear him say such a thing, but she struggled to believe she heard him correctly.

"How? How could you love me after all that I have done?"

"I of all men should know that people do whatever it takes to survive when their backs are against the wall. I understand that now, and I should have tried to understand that before. I'm sorry, Evie. For everything. I'm sorry I could not protect you."

"I'm sorry I put you all in danger. I never meant to hurt anyone—"

"It doesn't matter now. What matters is that we are getting out of here. All of us. Together."

"What can I do?" Evie asked as she wiped at her tears.

"Trust me. And give Silas no reason to believe that you are plotting an escape with me. Distract him, however you can. Bow to him, beg for his forgiveness, do whatever you can to gain his trust. Convince him you feel nothing for me. Promise him the world, just as I am doing to you now."

"I...I don't know if I can do that."

"You must, Evie. It's the only way for this to work. While he is distracted, we will find a way to get his keys."

Jacob turned from the door. "I think I hear footsteps. We have to get her back to the Captain's chambers before anyone realizes she has gone."

Theo locked his gaze with Evie's and released his hold on her. "Go now, quickly. Before you are seen."

"I can't leave you. What if Silas comes and does something horrible to you before we can escape? What if he kills you?"

"Do not worry about me. I am not an easy one to kill. Go now. I will be fine."

"But, Theo—"

"Go, Evie. Go with Jacob. He'll see you safely back to your chambers. Then we will both see you safely home."

"Do you promise?"

Theo placed a hand upon his chest. "Cross my heart."

After a few moments of hesitation, Evie pried her hands from his shirt and slowly rose to her feet. It pained her to separate herself from him, and fear and panic filled her heart at the thought that this may be the last time she could lay eyes on him if their ridiculous plan were to go awry. Theo have her a reassuring nod and sideways smile, one that crinkled his eyes and electrified her heart.

After lingering to stare into his eyes for a few more precious moments, Evie turned away and hurried down the corridor to meet Jacob at the entrance. Theo pressed his face against the bars to savor every last moment he had to watch her go before she and Jacob disappeared through the heavy door and into the darkness. The door closed softly but heavily behind them, leaving him to ruminate on every decision, triumph, and mistake that had led him to where he was now.

Jacob and Evie soundlessly exited the hold and rounded the nearest corner to sneak back the way they came under the cover of the early morning darkness. Within minutes, they successfully returned to the Captain's chambers without drawing any unwanted attention, as nearly all of the Redcoats who were supposed to be standing guard had dozed off or become otherwise intoxicated and preoccupied.

And while they may have avoided detection by the hapless foot soldiers that wandered the fort, they were totally unaware that a very keenly observant Sergeant happened to be strolling through the corridors in the wee hours of the morning when he caught sight of two dark figures slinking around a corner. Noiselessly, he followed them, remaining several paces behind until they slipped inside the prisoners' hold.

Sergeant Daniel Howell ducked behind a pillar as Cadet Black and the Captain's wife snuck into the hold, choosing to listen intently rather than apprehend them immediately. He held his breath and strained his ears to hear the muffled conversation between Mrs. Porter and the prisoner, making sure to keep himself concealed behind the pillar so as to not tip off their lookout. He felt his jaw go agape as he caught bits and pieces of their distant conversation, and he resisted the urge to leap out from his hiding place to catch them in the act of conspiring.

They were not just conspiring to escape. They were conspiring to commit treason. They were conspiring to assassinate a soldier of the Crown, which was grounds for an immediate execution for all parties involved, including the Captain's wife. Howell decided in that moment that it was purely providence that he felt restless that early morning and decided to take a stroll to clear his mind when he stumbled upon a conspiracy in progress.

Howell silently startled at the sound of quiet footsteps coming round the corner at the end of the corridor, as did Cadet Black, who turned to alert his partners in crime before slipping back into the shadows to lead Mrs. Porter to her chambers before anyone would notice her absence. Once they had gone, Howell emerged from behind the pillar and straightened out his uniform coat before turning back the way he came.

Two foot soldiers greeted him at the opposite end of the corridor from which Black and Evie had disappeared.

"Good morning, Sergeant," one of them greeted with a salute.

"Good morning, gentlemen," Howell returned, somewhat distracted by his thoughts. "And where are you heading?"

"We were just going to go check on the Captain's wife. To ensure she was still where he left her."

Howell held up a hand to halt them. Evie and her traitorous escort had just left the hold a few minutes before and surely would not have reached her chambers yet. "That won't be necessary. I was just there," he fibbed smoothly. "Cadet Black is seeing to her protection, as am I. I'd like you to go to the courtyard and see to guarding the powder stores."

"But what about the prisoner? That savage boy? Didn't he escape once already?" the second guard asked.

"He is in no condition to escape after the Captain's interrogation yesterday. Go now, at once."

"Yes, sir."

After the foot soldiers meandered down the corridor and disappeared out into the courtyard, Howell let out a breath he didn't realize he had been holding. He did not fancy himself a fantastic liar, but he could tell a fib when he deemed it necessary. And at that moment, it seemed *very* necessary.

He did not know Mrs. Porter very well, nor the Native prisoner who was very clearly the object of her affections, but he did know his Captain. And he also knew that the moment word reached Captain Porter that there was a traitor amongst his staff and a conspiracy brewing against his life between his own wife and a rebel prisoner, there would surely be hell to pay.

Blood would soon be spilled inside the Lion's Den, of that much Howell was sure. It was now merely a matter of whose blood, and unbeknownst to any of the traitors in his midst, he alone had the power to destroy their plan with a few simple words in his Captain's ear.

Chapter 8

Monster

March 1779

The next evening, Evie jumped from her chair under the window in Silas' chambers when she heard raucous footsteps approaching from down the corridor, followed by the door to her prison being forced open. Nearly leaping out of her skin at the sudden bombardment of noise, she put her hand over her heart, frowning deeply when she recognized Silas' familiar footfall and the smell of liquor that always followed him like an intoxicating shadow. Silas stood in the doorway to his chambers, a triumphant sneer upon his face, with one hand on his hip and the other clutching a tattered canvas sack that appeared to be stained red with blood.

"Silas," Evie cleared her throat nervously. "You've returned safely. I...I was waiting all day for you."

"Were you?" he asked with a scoff as he sauntered into the room and slammed the door shut behind him. "I was under the impression you'd be glad to see me leave."

Evie shook her head with a small smile and slowly approached him, placing hand upon his chest. Underneath her palm, she could feel his cold heart beating erratically, just under the rough woolen fabric of his uniform coat and the various straps of leather that held his weapons. He was a walking armory, guarded by a battalion of gunpowder barrels and a fiery temper just waiting to be ignited.

"Of course not. It would bring me no pleasure to see you harmed."

Silas eyed her skeptically before smirking. He then took ahold of her chin and pulled her face up to his so he could press a rough kiss to her lips. She accepted his actions without hesitation, but on the inside, she could hear herself screaming and begging to be free from his touch.

"It does my heart well to hear you say such things, Mrs. Porter," Silas said as he turned toward the table in the corner of the room and set down the canvas sack he had been clutching. He then began to whistle a meaningless tune as he unbuckled his weapon belts and set them on the armchair.

"...How did your scouting mission fair?" Evie asked after a few moments of silence, attempting to make conversation despite how much she disliked nearly everything he had ever said. "You said you were scouting...Natives?"

Silas looked up and flashed her another devilish smirk. "Aye. My scouts told me that they had seen evidence of some Oneida dogs that had traveled south to sabotage British encampments."

Evie furrowed her brow. "I am confused. I thought the Iroquois had allied themselves with the British."

Silas shook his head with a haughty chuckle. "Silly girl. The Iroquois are a *confederacy* of six tribes. From what I understand, they have been divided in their allegiance to the Crown. Half of the confederacy, the intelligent half, have allied themselves with the Crown. The Oneida and others have decided to side with the rebels. And they will pay the price for that in the end."

"…How do you mean?"

Silas plucked the canvas sack off of the table and held it up for her to see, his eyes alight with a lust for blood that sent shivers down her spine. He took a sudden step toward her, and she backed up until her calves hit the front of the bed. Upon closer inspection, she could see that the sack was indeed stained with blood, fresh blood, by the looks of it, and it dripped from the bottom of the sack and onto the stone floor in front of her.

"*This* is what I mean," Silas snarled as he turned the sack over.

The overturned sack spilled its bloodied contents onto the floor—a large, round, mutilated, object that was covered in blood, hair and skin. It hit the floor with a thud and rolled across the stones, coming to a stop at her feet to reveal what remained of a man's head and face, severed from its body at the neck as some sort of trophy of war. Evie gasped and let out a piercing scream, feeling her stomach churn at the grizzly sight. It was the severed head of a Native man, nameless to her and to his killer, whose face was pinched up in a gruesomely permanent and silent scream, mouth open, as blood trailed from the lacerations on its flesh and scalp. Long black hair tangled and matted with the fluids of death was splayed out upon the stones from what remained of the nameless man's head, but even in the dimness of the evening, she could see that the entire crown of the man's scalp was *missing.* Not only had he been slain, and then beheaded, he had also been *scalped.*

Evie turned away as fearful and revolted tears began to burn her eyes. The room began to spin with dizziness at the sight and smell of the blood, the look of agony permanently etched into the man's face, the pride in Silas' eyes as he looked upon his work with his chest puffed in triumph. Evie let out a disgusted sob as she ran to the window and unceremoniously vomited into the night air.

Silas scooped his bloodied war trophy off of the floor by what remained of its hair and grabbed her by the arm, forcing her to look into its dark and empty eyes. "What's the matter, darling?" he growled. "Can't stand to see the gruesome reality of war? You think you know what war is? *This* is war!"

Evie screamed again and tried to squirm out of his grasp, but his hold on her was vice-like as he grabbed her by her chin and forced her to look. She stared into the man's eyes as tears of horror streamed down her cheeks, and deep within those black and lifeless caverns, she saw her terrified reflection, which only seemed to frighten and horrify her more.

"Stop it," she begged between sobs. "Why are you doing this?"

Silas released her with an amused chortle and held the object up to admire it. Evie scurried to the other side of the room and cowered in the corner as he continued to cackle to himself, eyes wide like the mad man she was now realizing he truly was.

"Are you afraid?" Silas asked in a low whisper from across the room. "Does this terrify you?"

Evie swallowed thickly and pressed her back against the wall. "How could you?" she asked weakly. "You…you butchered him…"

"Yes, and I would do it again if I got the chance. He and his Oneida brothers were encamped just a few miles north of here. We found them and we destroyed them with ease. Every last one of their hunting party, *eradicated*. Then we took their heads as trophies of war, to celebrate our victory and send a message."

"How…how could you have even known they were your enemy?" Evie gasped. "They could have been innocent!"

"They were savages. There's no such thing as an innocent savage! And I'll display this mongrel's head on the pikes of the fort's front gate—a reminder to all of the fate that will befall those who cross me!"

"Whether they side with the Patriots or the Crown, they did not deserve *this*."

Silas shoved his trophy back in its bloodied sack and tossed it onto the table. His hands were now caked with blood and dirt as he took a predatory step in her direction and pointed a finger at her. "I was only doing to them what they have been doing to us civilized folk for decades. Why the tears? Can you not face the fact that your lover comes from a savage race? You've heard the stories, all they do is rape, pillage, and scalp, like the barbarians they are!"

"The only savage here is *you*!" Evie cried. "You are an unimaginable monster…"

Before she could blink, Silas strode across the room and caged her cowering form against the wall, leaning down to press his lips to her ear to whisper, "Monster or not, I am still your husband, and your master. I am your *king*. You haven't seen a monster *yet*. But if you want to see a monster, I'll show you one with haste."

"I hate you," Evie hissed in his face between clenched teeth. Any thoughts of trying to endear herself to him to throw him off of Theo and Jacob's plan went out the window as the visceral image of the man's severed head became burned into the backs of her eyelids. "You'll burn in Hell for what you have done…"

Silas smirked and took a step back, allowing her to collapse to her knees at his feet. "I'd advise you to pray for every Indian that falls in my path, girl, else you'll find that your precious mongrel down in the hold will soon meet a similar fate to the poor bloke in that bag."

***

Consumed with thoughts of the headless man rotting somewhere in the wilderness beyond the fort's walls, Evie could not find any rest that evening. Every time she closed her eyes, she saw his dead, black eyes, his bared scalp, his bloodied face frozen forever in an expression of terror. She wondered if he was truly an enemy of the Crown as Silas claimed, or if he was just an innocent man that happened to be in the wrong place at the wrong time. She wondered if he had a family, a wife and children waiting for him back in his village and none the wiser to his gruesome demise.

And whenever she could find sleep, she was haunted by nightmares of being chased down by ravenous and blood-thirsty monsters that jumped out at her from every corner, monsters with sandy brown hair, steely grey eyes, and crimson red coats.

Then her thoughts wandered to Theo, who remained imprisoned deep within the caverns of the fort, so close and yet so far from her touch. She thought of how much she missed him and how much she longed for both of their freedoms. As far as she knew, he and Jacob were still concocting a scheme to get their hands on the Captain's keys, but she hadn't the faintest idea how long they expected that endeavor to take. And with every day that passed, she could see Silas growing more and more restless to do something horrendous to his prisoner, something ghastly and permanent in order to send a message that she belonged to *him*, and only him. Her faith in the idea that Theo and Jacob would find a way to free her quickly began to wane as several more days came and went with no word from either of them, and she began to fear that by the time they found a way to escape, it would be too late for everyone.

It had been three days since she had last seen or spoken to Theo down in the hold, and her heart began to constrict in her chest at the thought that she may never see him alive again. If Silas did intend to finally execute Theo, Evie had no idea why he continued to wait to do so. Knowing him, she would have thought he'd end Theo's life the first chance he got in order to destroy any of her remaining desire to escape. And yet, the

Captain chose to hold off, dragging out the inevitable as long as he could in order to break their spirits once and for all.

Evie closed her eyes and shook away those terrible thoughts with a heavy sigh. It was early morning, and Silas had already left the chambers for the day to conduct his business as commander of the fort, leaving her alone once again to wallow in her sorrows and regrets. She turned sharply in her chair by the window when she heard a knock on the door, her spirits lifting ever so slightly at the thought that it might be Jacob, or even Howell, who had come to keep her company.

"Who is it?" she asked.

"Thomas Black," a familiarly gruff voice said from the other side.

Evie jumped to her feet and sprinted to the door. "Any news?" she asked in a whisper.

Jacob cleared his throat. "I was instructed to deliver you your breakfast, Mrs. Porter."

Evie slowly opened the door and poked her head out into the corridor. Seeing that it was empty, she beckoned him to come into the room. Jacob entered just behind her bearing a silver tray with a bowl of porridge. He set the try on the table in the corner of the room and gestured for her to sit, but she was too anxious to do so.

"The slave woman Tsipporah made you breakfast," Jacob said as his eyes wandered around the dim room and he played with the buttons on his red uniform coat. "She says you haven't been eating."

"I haven't had an appetite since I arrived," Evie admitted sadly.

"You need to eat. You'll need your strength for when we escape."

Evie gave him a confused sideways glance, puzzled by his out of character concern for her well-being.

Jacob began to pace the length of his room, removing his tricorn hat and running his hand through his shaggy brown hair. "Captain Porter showed us the…head."

"What?"

"His war trophy. When he slaughtered the native hunting party. He gathered every soldier into the courtyard and showed us the head he had severed from the leader's body." Jacob's words were tight and sorrowful as he spoke, and Evie could see a wrathful fire burning in his eyes. He slowly looked up from the floor and met her gaze. "I thought I knew what evil was after those Redcoats killed my brother, but your husband puts them to shame. *He* is evil personified."

Evie gulped and slowly sat on the edge of the bed as Jacob continued to pace. "I never knew evil until I met him."

Jacob hesitated. "I'm sorry, Evie."

Evie looked up with a furrowed brow to see that he had stopped just in front of her, his shoulders slumped in defeat. "For what?"

Jacob shook his head. "For everything. For distrusting you, for making you feel unwelcome in Division Point, for believing terrible things about you that I know now were never true."

"You don't have to apologize—"

"No, I do. I…After seeing the monster from whom you escaped, I feel terrible for how I have treated you."

"Why are you being so kind to me?" Evie asked in a broken voice. "Why are you risking your life to help Theo save me, after everything I have done, after all of the lies I have told?"

Jacob took another step toward her, his usually stern expression softening into one of empathy. "Because I understand you now. I understand why you ran; I understand why you did what you did. You were trying to protect yourself and your son from the man that hurt you. After seeing everything that he has done, all the damage he has caused you and others, I understand now. And I cannot fault you for it."

Evie's eyes fell to the floor as she began to twist her fingers. "I just wanted to be free."

"I know. We all do. And...I can see how happy you made Theo. You were the best thing that ever happened to him, and I could not stand to see him so heartbroken after you had been taken."

A sad smile touched Evie's lips. "I love him, Jacob. I love him more than anything. The last thing I want is for him to be hurt on my account..."

"We won't let that happen. We'll find a way out of here."

Evie stood from the bed. "But how? You've been here for days with nothing to show for it. I can see Silas growing more restless by the day. If we do not act soon, he will grow impatient and kill Theo before we ever have a chance to escape."

"I know. I am still trying to find a way to get his keys."

"He never lets his keys out of his sight. They are always with him, and he gives them to no one. Jacob, this will never work..."

"Peace, Evie," Jacob put both of his hands on her shoulders to steady her as her heart began to pound in her chest. "I just need more time to come up with something, a way to get to him when no one is around."

"We are running out of time. He will kill Theo the moment he grows bored with torturing both of us. Now that he has me, there is nothing keeping Theo alive in that hold other than Silas' will."

"We will kill Silas before he has a chance to do anything of the sort. And then we will escape together. But you have to remain calm and you have to trust us, just as Theo said."

Evie sighed heavily. "...How is he? I have not seen him in days."

"He is...holding on. He's growing restless, trapped in that dark and dank cage. Silas gave us instructions not to feed him more than once a day, but I have been sneaking him scraps of bread when I can. Silas comes to interrogate him every now and again, asking him what he knows about Washington and his army's current state of affairs. But he doesn't know anything now, and he won't talk."

"Just like the first time he was here..." Evie mumbled sadly.

"He is not easily broken. You and I both know that. He is strong enough to endure whatever Silas can deal out until we find a way to escape. And he'll have to."

Evie straightened her shoulders in resolution and tried to put on a brave face, though she could not shake the fear that continued to cloud her head. "Promise me you will keep him safe until we are free again."

"I promise. You know I'll protect him with my life."

Without a second thought, Evie lunged forward and threw her arms around Jacob's neck, holding him in a tight embrace as she buried her face in his coat. He was initially startled by her actions, and he stood there frozen in her arms for a moment before he slowly relaxed and returned her embrace. As he held her and she began to sob quiet tears of hope into his chest, Jacob could feel all of the anger, the distrust, and the hate he had once felt for her melting away. He kicked himself for letting himself become so entrenched in his hatred for the Crown that he had become blind to who Evie really was. She was no spy, no Loyalist, no liar. She was just a frightened girl searching desperately for a place in this world to call her own, a place where she could be free and loved, never again to live in fear.

"Thank you, Jacob," she murmured weakly into his coat. "Theo and I will both owe you our lives."

Jacob chuckled softly before pulling away. "Theo already owes me his life a hundred times over. As for you, we can call it even for the hard time I gave you these past five years."

Evie chuckled in return and wiped at her eyes with the back of her hand. After a few moments of tense silence, Jacob cleared his throat. "I should go back to my post at your door, before someone sees me gone and suspects something."

Evie nodded in agreement and watched him go, feeling her spirits begin to lift ever so slightly for the first time in days. She was still uncertain of what the near future would hold, but at least she could be sure that she could trust Jacob to fight until his dying breath to bring her and Theo home where they belonged.

***

Howell stood in the center of the cell and impatiently tapped his foot. The prisoner sat just before him, body slouched in exhaustion and bound to a wooden chair with his hands behind his back. Theo lowered his eyes to the stones under his feet as he weakly flexed his arms and tried to struggle against his restraints, but the ropes were iron-tight, and they dug into the flesh of his wrists every time he moved. His eyelids fluttered as the promise of unconsciousness danced through his head, and he swallowed thickly, his mouth and throat dry and begging for the relief of water. He could feel his body breaking out into a cold sweat underneath the shredded remains of his shirt, while a trail of blood trickled down the side of his face from a fresh laceration on his temple. He could feel Sergeant Howell's eyes burning holes in him, but he barely had the strength to lift his head in order to meet his gaze.

Howell sighed and crossed his arms over his chest. "You know this would all be so much less painful if you only told us what you know."

"I know nothing," Theo mumbled. "I deserted the army over two years ago."

"Why?"

Theo shrugged and then winced as the action sent a tremor of pain through his shoulders, which had been stretched uncomfortably by the ropes that bound his arms behind the back of the chair. "I lost the will to fight."

Howell scratched his chin and leaned down to catch Theo's gaze. Theo peered at him through the hair that had fallen in his face, and in his eyes, Howell saw nothing but stubbornness and rebellion.

"You seem pretty keen to fight to me. We could not break you the first time you were here, and you've proven to be just as determined to fight us every step this time."

The slightest of smirks touched Theo's chapped lips. "You'll kill me long before I turn against the Patriots. You're wasting your time yet again."

"Alright, fair enough." Howell reached up and took a hold of a fistful of Theo's hair, jerking his head back until he was staring at the ceiling. "Then tell me why you are really here."

"You captured me," Theo snapped through clenched teeth as he grimaced against the sensation of Howell gripping his hair at the root. "Or, rather, that cadet Thomas Black did."

"Ah, yes. Thomas Black. From Fort Halifax. Convenient that he found you lurking about the perimeters of the fort just a few days after the Captain returned with his runaway wife." Howell released his hold on Theo's hair and lowered his voice to an ominous whisper. "You are playing a dangerous game, Mr. Cunningham. I suggest you tell me your true motives for coming here, as this may be the last chance you have to confess."

Theo scoffed. "You want me to confess?"

"It would make everyone's lives much easier if you did."

"Fine." Theo adjusted himself in the chair to sit tall and straight, tossing his head back to remove the hair that had fallen in his face. "I came here to assassinate your Captain. But I've already told you that much."

"Yes, you did mention that. But why?"

"I wanted revenge."

"For his taking repossession of his wife, who we have recently discovered was also your former lover?"

A small scowl played at the corners of Theo's mouth as he swallowed his growing anger. "No. It has nothing to do with *her*. I wanted to kill him for what he did to me two years ago. For capturing me, for torturing me, for scarring me. That's it."

Howell began to pace the length of the cell as he tapped his chin. "You did not come to try and steal Mrs. Porter back? To take her back to your home so you two could continue to live in sin?"

Theo's furrowed his brow deeply and shook his head, his fingers itching to grab Howell by the throat and slam his head against the stone floor. "What I had with Mrs. Porter is in the past. Whatever we were, it was over before she left. I feel nothing for her now."

Howell stared him down over his shoulder, but something in his stern expression told Theo he was not convinced. "And you came alone?"

"Yes. I came alone, until Cadet Black found me and took me into his custody."

"You're quite a bit taller and larger than Cadet Black. How exactly was he able to overpower you and disarm you?"

"He attacked me from behind. My guard was down."

Howell chuckled in amusement. "Ah, well, I suppose the most frightening monster is the one that lurks in the shadow and attacks when you least expect it, hm?"

Theo nodded in reluctant agreement just as they were interrupted by the sound of heavy footsteps pounding down the corridor outside of the hold, intermingled with a muffled crying and a deep-voiced scolding. A moment later, the door to the hold was shoved open, and Silas stormed in, dragging Evie behind him by the wrist as she clawed and scratched in a desperate attempt to get away from him. Her hair was a mess and her dress was in disarray, suggesting that she had put up quite a struggle against Silas the entire time he had been dragging her to the hold. Thomas Black entered just behind them, a stern but nervous expression upon his young face as he stood watch just inside the door, his musket in hand.

Howell immediately stood to attention and Theo sat up straighter in his chair when the Captain and his wife entered.

"Captain Porter," Howell greeted with a salute. "You came just in time. I was just able to elicit a full confession from the prisoner."

"Oh?" Silas asked, intrigued. "And to what did he finally confess?"

"Your attempted murder, sir."

Silas chortled lowly in his throat as he approached the cell, his dark eyes meeting Theo's through the bars in a steely stare down. "I expected as much."

"What do you want from me?" Theo spat. "You have your confession now."

Silas cleared his throat with a smug smirk before tightening his grip on Evie's wrist and dragging her behind him as he entered the cell. She tried to pull against him, but he roughly pushed her into the cell before stepping in behind her and closing the door. Her eyes were wide with confusion and fright as she looked between Theo and her husband.

"Oh, I am far from done with you," Silas snapped. "You haven't outlived your usefulness to me just yet. I know you have information on Washington and his men."

Theo rolled his eyes up to the ceiling. "It's been two years since I served. Anything I knew before would surely be useless to you now."

"I'll be the judge of that." Silas paused just in front of Theo's chair and crossed his arms over his chest. "I'll give you one last chance. Now talk."

Theo spat a mixture of blood and whatever moisture remained in his mouth at Silas's feet before tipping his head back in stubbornness. "I'll talk when Hell freezes over."

Silas pinched his face up in disgust and took a step back, his brow furrowing in frustration. "Very well," he sighed. "I did not want to have to do this. But you have left me no other option."

Evie let out a fearful gasp when Silas suddenly turned around and seized her by her arm, pulling her until she was standing just before Theo's chair with her back against Silas' chest and his arm across her torso, holding her to his body. Before she could blink, Silas pulled the pistol from his belt and held the barrel to her temple, his thumb resting upon the trigger as a smirk came to his lips. Theo, Black, and Howell stared at him with mouths agape, but they were powerless to stop him, and Evie gripped Silas' arm for dear life, a quiet whimper escaping her throat.

"Silas," she whispered fearfully, "what are you doing?"

Silas cocked back the hammer on his pistol and held it harder against his wife's skull as he stared Theo down. "You are willing to gamble with your own life, but will you gamble with hers?"

Theo tensed in his chair and pulled against his restraints, his expression hardening as his eyes fell upon Evie's terrified face. "What are you going to do?" Theo asked in disbelief. "You expect me to believe you'll shoot your own wife?"

"That's exactly what I'll do!" Silas growled over Evie's shoulder. "You know I'll do it. I'll do just about anything to get what I want!"

Evie gulped and clawed at his arm as terrified tears came to her eyes. "Let me go," she begged. "Please, don't do this…"

Silas hissed in her ear, "Shut up, girl, or I'll give you something to cry about!" He then turned his attention back to Theo. "This is your final chance. Tell me what you know about Washington's army, or I will kill you and the girl right here and now! Give me what I want, and I will consider sparing you both!"

"Captain Porter, please consider what you are doing—" Howell tried to say from behind, but Silas glowered at him from over his shoulder.

"Silence!"

Howell cowered under the sound of Silas' deranged bellow and slunk back into the corner of the cell. A look of confusion, betrayal, and disgust twisted his face as he watched his Captain's every move.

"He's bluffing," Theo mumbled as he looked to Evie. "He won't do it."

"Oh, you think I won't do just about anything to win this war?" Silas snarled, shoving Evie down onto her knees in front of Theo's chair. He cocked the pistol once more and crouched down behind her, pressing the barrel to the side of her head again while his other hand went to clutch the front of her bodice.

Tears began to roll down Evie's face as he ripped open the front of her dress to reveal her corset, and she tried to fight against him, but every time she moved, he pressed the pistol harder against her skull. Theo and Howell both watched with wide eyes as Silas savagely pulled her dress from her shoulders and down her arms.

Silas locked his eyes with Theo as he continued to tear at Evie's dress and hissed, "You think I won't defile her right here and now, and then put a bullet in her head before your eyes? You think I wouldn't do it? I have no use for her anymore! I already have her father's money, her inheritance, her family's business! I'll find another whore to give me an heir, one that is obedient and loyal and doesn't commit adultery with half breed rebels…"

"Don't do it, Theo," Evie murmured through her tears as she stared him down. "Don't tell him a thing."

Theo looked desperately between her and Silas, swallowing nervously. He could feel the blood in his veins beginning to boil just under the surface of his skin, and he pulled with what strength remained in him against the ropes that bound him to the chair, trying in vain to free himself.

"Stop it," Theo growled. "Leave her alone. She has nothing to do with this…"

"Oh, she has everything to do with this." After tearing Evie's bodice off of her body, Silas pushed her onto her hands and knees, to which she protested with an anguished cry. "Last chance," he hissed as he reached for his belt, "or I have my way with her and blow her brains across these stones!"

"Tell him nothing!" Evie repeated through her sobs.

Theo squeezed his eyes shut and squirmed in his chair against his bindings as he felt his heart contract in his chest. Blood began to pound in his ears as he clenched his teeth together, and a wave of fury overcame him as he watched Silas slowly unbuckle his belt and push Evie's skirts up her thighs. He would have moved mountains to protect her, but in that moment, he settled with sacrificing himself.

"Stop it, I'll tell you everything!" Theo blurted out, dropping his head and slouching against the chair in defeat. "I'll tell you everything I know, just let her go. Please, don't hurt her…"

Evie whimpered when Silas pushed her onto her stomach and snapped his head up to stare Theo down. A look of triumph crossed his face as he slowly pulled his pistol from Evie's temple and stood, stepping over her trembling body to stand before Theo's chair. He pressed the barrel of the gun to Theo's forehead, right between his eyes, as Evie found the courage to push herself back up onto her hands and knees. While Silas was distracted, Howell came to her side and helped her to her feet before slipping out of his coat and wrapping it around her shoulders. She continued to sob uncontrollably as Howell held her comfortably in his arms, watching in horror as Silas stood over Theo's defeated form and pressed the pistol to his head.

"Talk," Silas spat.

Theo's chest heaved as he squeezed his eyes shut and swallowed thickly. His head told him he was making a terrible mistake, but his heart told him he had no other choice.

He stared at the floor in shame as he mumbled, "The last I knew, Washington had five Major Generals under his command, and a force of perhaps thirty thousand. But I am sure it has grown since then. After our encampment in Philadelphia back in '77, Washington intended to march south. That is all I know…"

Silas was silent for a moment before he pulled the pistol from Theo's head and placed it back in his belt with a click of his tongue. He then let out a maniacal chuckle, one that caused Theo to slowly look up from the floor.

"Your words are true. My scouts had already told me as much, and you have just confirmed it."

"I've told you all I know. You have what you wanted. Now let Evie go…"

Silas chuckled again. "Oh, I don't think so." He then reached inside his uniform coat and dug around in his pocket before producing a rolled-up piece of parchment and turning to beckon Evie to come stand by his side. She hesitated before returning Howell's coat to him and slowly approaching, wrapping her arms around her torso to maintain some sense of decency. Silas handed her the parchment. "Read this. Out loud."

Evie took the parchment from him with shaking hands and slowly unrolled it, and she felt her heart leap into her throat when she read at the top of the scroll the words "Death Warrant" in large dark letters. She looked to Silas in confusion, but he only nodded in confirmation. "Read it," he snapped again. "Out loud, so *he* can hear it."

"Please don't make me…"

"Do it!"

Evie cringed under his draconian snarl and cleared her throat before looking down at the page. Another tear slipped down her cheek as she began to read, and with every passing second, her words became more and more broken by the anguish and hopelessness that began to fill her heart.

"'By official decree of His Majesty and the Crown, this warrant hereby sentences Theo Cunningham to death for the crimes of treason, insurgency, attempted murder, adultery, and the possession of unlawful carnal knowledge of a woman who is not his wife. He shall therefore be hanged by the neck until dead at dawn on the twenty-fifth of March, 1779…'"

Theo felt the color drain from his face as he listened to Evie read his own death sentence out loud to him, and his eyes fell to the floor once more in defeat. His body slouched in his chair as any remaining strength or will to fight on drained into the cracks between the cobblestones under his feet. The twenty-fifth of March was *tomorrow*.

Evie gulped and looked up from the letter, a look of rage crossing her face as realization hit her like a slap to the face. "This...this warrant is dated March 18th. The day after Theo arrived here. You...you were never going to spare him! You were going to execute him all along, no matter what he said or did!"

Silas chuckled smugly and plucked the parchment from her hands, stuffing it back inside his coat. "My father did not raise a fool, dear wife."

"You bastard!" Evie cried, lunging forward to strike him with her fists. Silas easily dodged her attack just as Howell stepped in to take ahold of her from behind, holding her back by her arms as she struggled against him. "Let go of me!" she screamed. "You monster! How could you?"

Silas waved her off dismissively. "I told you, you did not want to start a war with me, Evie. It was not a war you could ever hope to win."

Evie kicked and screamed against Howell as he held her back. "You can't do this!"

"Oh, I can, and I will. The savage shall be hanged at the gallows at first light tomorrow, and that is final."

"No..." Evie wailed as she collapsed in Howell's arms. "God, no, please...."

"Howell, take my wife back to my chambers. I think she has received the message."

Howell tossed a conflicted look between Theo's hunched over form and the broken woman in his arms. After a moment of hesitation, he mumbled, "Yes, sir. At once."

Evie fought against him once again as he took her gently by the arm and led her out of the cell. When she refused to go willingly, he was forced to drag her along more forcefully. She kicked and pulled against his hold on her wrists, trying desperately to not let Theo out of her sight.

"No! Let me go!" she screamed, reaching out for Theo, who could not even bring himself to raise his head and look her in the eye.

Her sobs eventually faded from earshot as Howell took her away, and Theo squeezed his eyes shut when he heard the door to the hold slam shut behind them. He swallowed the anguished lump rising in his throat as his head begin to spin. He had never felt so defeated or betrayed in his life, and in that moment, he wanted nothing more than for the floor to open up and swallow him whole. He could feel his eyes begin to burn with tears of hatred and sorrow as Silas began to pace predatory circles around his chair, an air of triumph and smugness emanating from him as he went.

It was all for nothing. He had risked himself and Jacob to save Evie from her husband's clutches, only to have their plan fizzle out miserably when the days dragged on and they still had not found a way to escape. And now, he had less than twelve hours of his life left before he'd be marched to the gallows while his best friend and lover would be forced to watch on. He had hoped that by giving Silas what little information on the Patriots he had, he would somehow find it in his cold heart to spare them both, but he realized now that that was just a fantasy. Any thoughts of he, Jacob, and Evie escaping the fort alive and together were fantasy. And now, he had betrayed the Patriots for nothing. As much as Theo had begun to hate Washington and the cause he stood for, it still destroyed him to know that he had sold them out in a hopeless attempt to save his own skin.

"You know," Silas suddenly spoke, tearing Theo from his agonized thoughts. "Many people have underestimated me in my life." He then came around to stand before Theo's chair, leaning down to catch his weary gaze. "Most of them are in the ground now. You weren't the first, and you won't be last."

Theo's body began to tremble with anger as he slowly looked up to lock his eyes with Silas'. Though he tried to contain it, as much as his pride hated to let him do it, a single tear of defeat escaped from his eye and rolled down his cheek, mixing with the grime and dried blood that caked his face.

"Do not weep, dear fellow," Silas chuckled, "You put up quite a fight. It was a valiant effort, it really was. But you were never going to win against me. Our little game of cat and mouse ends tomorrow at dawn."

***

As soon as Silas had gone, Jacob sprinted back to Theo's cell and clutched onto the bars that separated them. Theo turned his head down and away, unable to look his friend in the eye. Jacob squinted into the darkness of the cell, feeling his heart ache when he heard Theo quietly sniffle.

"I betrayed Washington and the others for nothing," Theo murmured without looking up from the ground. "He was going to sentence me to death no matter what I did. He was just dragging out the inevitable."

Jacob shook his head. "It is not your fault. You did what you thought you had to do to protect Evie."

"It matters little now," Theo growled, sinking back against the chair to which he was still bound. "He won. Silas won."

"No, do not say that. This is not over yet, Theo. Do not give up."

"I am to be executed in the morning, Jacob! We've run out of time…"

"We can still escape tonight. We'll find a way."

"No. There is no way anymore. Silas is smarter than all of us." Theo squeezed his eyes tightly shut as he felt them continue to burn with sorrowful tears. "He is too powerful. We cannot all escape here alive, just as I…feared would happen."

Jacob furrowed his brow in confusion and tightened his grip on the bars. "What did you just say? Hold a moment. You…you knew all along that it would be impossible for all of us to escape together?" When Theo hung his head in shame once again, Jacob scowled deeply. "You never intended to escape this fort alive, did you?"

Again, silence. Theo locked his eyes on the stones, feeling his heart constrict in his chest as Jacob gasped in realization.

"Answer me," Jacob snapped. "Did you intend to sacrifice yourself for her this whole time?"

Slowly, Theo lifted his head and met Jacob's enraged gaze. "I'm sorry, Jacob."

"Theo, what have you done?"

"I just thought that…if Silas was focused on killing me, it would give you a chance to assassinate him and escape with Evie. That way she could finally be free."

"And you were willing to sacrifice yourself to give her a chance at freedom? How could you lie to me this entire time?"

"I knew you would never agree to help me if you knew I planned to sacrifice myself."

Jacob took a step back from the bars, a furious growl escaping his throat as he began to pace in front of the cell. "And what about me, Theo? I can't believe you would do this! I can't believe you would lie to me like this. I have a wife at home, remember? I have a family, and you have a family, and you just threw that all to the wayside to save this girl, never once considering the consequences for anyone but yourself!"

"It is too late for me, Jacob. But there is still hope for you and Evie. You two can escape under the cover of night."

Jacob paused in his pacing and shot his friend a hot glare. "Without you? Not a chance!"

"Jacob, you have to. Go home. Take Evie and go. You both have so much to live for, so just go and forget about me."

Jacob slammed his fist against the iron bars and bellowed, "I am not going to leave you here to die. We either leave this place together, or not at all!"

"Look at me, Jacob," Theo hissed in return. "I am in no condition to escape. I would only slow you down. Please, just promise me you will make sure that Evie makes it out of here alive…"

"Who the hell are you? The Theo Cunningham I know would never give up like this, even when his back is against the wall. He would fight for his life and the lives of those he loves until the very end—"

"That Theo is gone," Theo snapped viciously, "You can say goodbye to him at the gallows tomorrow morning."

"There has to be a way, Theo. Don't give up on me now. Come now, perhaps I could…sneak into Silas' chambers tonight and find a way to dispatch him in his sleep. Then Evie and I can take his keys, sneak back to the hold, and free you. This place is poorly guarded at night. We'll be able to sneak out under the cover of darkness and no one will know."

"That is a good plan," A smooth, deep voice suddenly said from the shadows near the entrance to the hold. Theo snapped his head up as Jacob whipped around to face the source of the interruption, their hearts leaping into their throats in shock and alarm. A moment later, a dark figure emerged from behind the cracked door and stepped into the light. "It's an optimistic plan," the man said as he revealed himself, his hands folded behind his back and his chin held high. "But it will never work."

Jacob and Theo gulped in unison as Sergeant Howell emerged from the shadows and approached the cell. His face was tight and stern, his eyes narrowed as he stared them both down. He was still dressed in his uniform, but he had removed his white powdered wig to reveal a head of long slicked back blonde hair. Without the wig, he appeared much younger and kinder, looking slightly out of place in his uniform.

Jacob swallowed nervously again and turned his back to the bars. "Sergeant Howell…how long have you been standing there?"

"Oh, just long enough to hear your plan. For the second time."

"…The second time?" Jacob repeated meekly.

Howell came to stand just outside of Theo's cell, a slightly smug look upon his face. "I was making rounds the other night when I overheard you and Mrs. Porter conspiring to kill the Captain and escape."

Theo sighed and shook his head, looking up to the ceiling in exasperation as he said to his friend, "You are an abysmal lookout."

Jacob rubbed the back of his neck in embarrassment and nervousness, hanging his head.

"What is your real name, Cadet Thomas Black?" Howell asked as he stared down his nose at Jacob.

Jacob squirmed uncomfortably under his stare. They had been caught, and there was no point in playing this game any longer now that Howell had revealed himself. "…Jacob Caldwell."

"And am I to assume that you two knew each other previously, or just met and decided to conspire together?"

"We came here together," Jacob confessed, his words flat with defeat. "All we wanted to do was bring Evie home where she belongs."

"What will you do now, Sergeant Howell?" Theo grouched from his chair. "Now that you know the truth, now that you know who Jacob really is, now that you know that Evie is trying to escape with us, will you turn us in to Silas? Will you sentence all three of us to death?"

Howell was quiet for a moment, running his hand through his hair as his eyes searched the stones under his feet. "No, no. I could have done that days ago."

"Then why didn't you?" Jacob asked.

"Did you just come to rub salt in my wounds?" Theo added bitterly.

Howell reached up to clutch the bars as he stared into the cell and met Theo's heavy gaze. "I do not want to harm any of you. I want to *help* you."

Theo furrowed his brow in confusion and skepticism, leaning forward in his chair as far as his bindings would allow him. "*What?*"

Howell sighed and passed a look between Theo and Jacob. "I have served the Crown in this war since the beginning. I have seen things, terrible things, nightmarish things, that I wish I could forget but know I never well. I have seen innocents slain in the name of the King and the name of our country. I…I have served under Captain Porter for nearly five years, and I have seen him slowly go mad with power and a lust for blood. He is not fighting this war for the British Empire anymore. He is fighting to quench his thirst for blood and torture. And that is not a cause I can support any longer."

Theo scoffed and shook his head. "Do you really expect me to believe anything you have to say? You helped him interrogate me for days!"

Howell's voice softened humbly. "Listen to me, Theo. Hear me out. I never joined this war to hurt innocent people. I joined the army because I thought it was the right thing to do. I thought I was preserving an empire run by a just and noble king, but now, I can see none of that is true. I was there when he burned that village of colonists in Massachusetts. I was there when he beat and humiliated his wife to punish her for her so-called crimes. I was there the last time you were here. I watched Captain Porter interrogate and torture you. I was there the day he flogged you and those other prisoners. I watched the way he cackled with pleasure as he beat you within an inch of your life. And it all made me sick to my stomach..."

"If you were so appalled, why did you do nothing to stop it?" Jacob asked angrily.

"I did not think I could at the time. I was afraid I would lose everything. I was afraid *I* would be tortured and executed for treason. I was a coward. And for that, I am greatly ashamed. Over these past five years, I have watched my commander become consumed with greed and bloodlust. I've watched him become a monster, and I cannot stand idly by any longer."

"Why now?" Theo asked weakly. "Why do you want to make things right now?"

"I have nothing left to lose but my pride and my honor. I would rather die an honorable man than live to be an evil one. And now, I can see that there is nothing honorable about this war any longer."

"You want to defect from the British army, then?"

A small smile graced the Sergeant's lips as he said, "I've spoken to Evie many times since she arrived. She spoke fondly of the home she had made for herself since she had run away, a homestead on the Massachusetts Bay. Where she met you. She said it was a place welcoming to all people looking for somewhere to start over. And I've seen the way

Silas has mistreated you, his wife, and everyone else in his life, and I know that you both deserve so much better. I want to help, and in exchange, I want to come with you to wherever it is you are going."

Jacob and Theo shared a skeptical look with one another, unsure if they could afford to trust him. At that point, Theo also had very little left to lose, other than his life. After a moment of quiet deliberation, Theo asked, "And I suppose you have some sort of plan to sneak us all out of here before the execution?"

Howell shook his head. "No. That is too dangerous. We would never be able to get Evie out of his chambers without him noticing, and he has the only set of keys to free you from your cell. No, we must wait until tomorrow morning."

"What?" Theo snapped in annoyance. "If you recall, I'll be hanging from a noose tomorrow morning, Howell."

"Listen closely," Howell murmured, lowering his voice to a near whisper. "Silas will have everyone in the fort gather in the courtyard to watch your execution. There will be a large crowd—an excellent opportunity to draw Silas' and his guards' attentions away from you. We will wait until just before your execution is to commence, I will create a distraction, and in the chaos and confusion, we take Miss Evie and we flee on horseback through the unmanned front gates."

Theo and Jacob shared another unsure look before Theo asked, "And what of Silas? He will surely chase after us when he realizes we have escaped. And he knows exactly where Division Point is."

Howell hesitated before smoothing out his uniform coat and steeling his gaze. "Then I suppose we will have to ensure that the distraction is a fatal one."

"You do realize that you are committing treason," Jacob said dryly. "If this plan fails, and we are caught, all four of us will be hanging from a noose tomorrow morning."

Howell cleared his throat and placed a hand on Jacob's shoulder while sharing a look of agreement with Theo through the gaps in the iron bars. "Then I suppose we shouldn't be caught."

Jacob looked up to the ceiling and slid a hand down his face. "This plan is just as dangerous and ridiculous as the first one…"

Theo chuckled dryly from inside the cell, and Jacob could tell from the tone of his voice that a renewed sense of hope and stubbornness had filled him as he and Howell shared a look of mutual agreement.

"Come now, Jacob," Theo said somewhat smugly, "it wouldn't be a plan of ours if it wasn't foolish, irresponsible, and potentially catastrophic."

Chapter 9

Long Live the King

March 1779

The early morning sun was blinding and merciless as it shone down upon Dumpling Rock, warming the surrounding earth and waters while beckoning a new day for some, and a last day for others. Theo cringed at the obtrusive light and squeezed his eyes shut, turning his head away from the sky as he stumbled out of the hold. He was flanked in either side by two stern-faced Redcoats, the ones that had torn him from a restless sleep at the crack of dawn, bound his hands behind his back, and were now not so gently nudging him through the corridors of the fort and out into the courtyard.

He lost track of how many days he had been in the hold—ten, perhaps—and during that time, his only glimpse of the outside world was through the tiny iron-barred window on the back wall of his cell. What little light that did stream in through those bars was nothing compared to that which assaulted him now as he got his first taste of fresh air in who knows how long.

The first thing he heard when he stepped unsteadily outside, other than his heart pounding in his chest, was the indistinct roar of a gathering crowd in the center of the courtyard. Every soldier, every servant, and every officer in Dumpling Rock had already gathered around a large wooden structure that had seemingly been erected overnight, hooting and hollering to demand the revelation of the prisoner whose life they were calling to come to a slow and painful end. The roar of the crowd became louder as Theo weakly stumbled forward, guided by the shoves of his escort and the barrel of a pistol being shoved into the middle of his back. His shirt had been torn to shreds long ago and hung from his body in pieces, and his skin and trousers were smeared with mud, blood, and grime. He could not remember the last time he had eaten anything of substance, and his body craved water so intensely that his mouth and throat felt like a desert. He had lost count of how many times he had been beaten, how many hours he had been interrogated, and he struggled to walk on his own without his body screaming in protest and begging for respite.

This is not the end, he tried to tell himself as the Redcoats shoved him along. *It isn't your time.* Howell was a good man, and he promised he would see that the execution was sabotaged with a diversion. But he never went into detail as to what exactly that diversion would be, and Theo could feel his stomach begin to churn as he reached the outer edge of the crowd. The sea of humanity that had come to see his demise slowly parted, and their taunting jeers became a thunderous tidal wave that engulfed him without mercy. Theo ducked with a startled grunt when a small stone was hurled at his head from somewhere in the crowd, followed by a torrent of curses and insults that he had certainly heard before.

"Kill the rebel!"

"Hang him dead! Put his head on a spike like the other savage!"

"Death to all Patriots!"

The trek through the crowd was long and arduous, and his body ached with every unstable step he took. He craved rest, water, and a hot meal, but at that moment, the only thing within his reach was doom. As soon as the gallows came within reach, another wave of panic washed over him. It was an enormous wooden platform inlaid with collapsing trap doors underneath a long beam; three nooses hung limply from the beam, swaying gently in the wind as if they were performing a mocking dance of death. On one end of the beam, a wooden spike protruded straight into the sky, and upon its point, the rotting remains of a decapitated head that had once belonged to an Oneida warrior was on display for everyone to see and *smell*.

Theo gulped and turned his head away from the grizzly sight just as he and his escort broke through the crowd. He squinted into the sunlight to peer up at the tall, crimson-clad figure that stood upon the platform and glared down at him with steely eyes devoid of anything other than madness.

Silas' lips pulled back to reveal his teeth set in a wide grin as he locked eyes with Theo.

"Bring him forward," he curtly ordered the escort. "The sun has already risen, and I've grown bored with dragging out the inevitable any longer."

Theo hesitated at the base of the steps that led up to the platform, swallowing thickly. His pause earned him a rough shove in his back by the guard just behind him.

"Move!" the man growled.

Theo shot him an icy glare over his shoulder before slowly and painfully climbing the stairs, each of which creaked ominously under his boots. The crowd continued to shout and curse at his back, but their cries had faded to a dull murmur in his ears once he reached the platform and looked out at the sea of men that had gathered to watch him perish. It was only then that he realized that he and Silas were not alone on the platform. Jacob was dressed in his uniform and stood just behind Silas while Evie stood by her husband's side, clutching onto his arm with her tear-flooded eyes locked on the planks under her feet.

She lifted her eyes to meet Theo's heavy gaze as soon as he reached the platform, and in that moment, it broke his heart to see the hopelessness and distress on her pretty face. As far as he knew, neither Jacob nor Howell had the chance to inform her of their plan to sabotage the execution before it commenced, and that she believed she was about to watch her lover's neck snap before her eyes was evident in her solemn expression. Her face was pale and hollow, as if sleep had eluded her for the last week or more and she had spent all hours of the day sobbing. Most jarringly, however, was the brokenness and despondency that clouded her dull eyes.

Theo tore her eyes from hers, as he could no longer bear to see her so miserable. He wanted desperately to reach out and take her in his arms, to comfort her and promise her that all would be well again soon enough, but instead, he began to scan the crowd for any sign of Howell. He had not seen nor heard from him since they had parted the evening prior, and the churning in his gut became all that much more intense when the morning came with no word from him.

Theo was surprised to see that Howell was not on the platform, and he supposed he should have found it somewhat comforting, but as he squinted into the sunlight to search the crowd for the man, he could find no trace. Time was quickly running out—he was mere minutes from his supposed demise now—and Howell was nowhere to be seen. Theo could feel his heartbeat quickening in his chest as Silas nudged Evie to stand next to Cadet Black before stepping forward to the edge of the platform to address his roaring audience.

Silas opened his arms to gesture to the crowd, his sneer widening as his chest swelled with pride. The murmurs and curses slowly died down to an ominous silence as he began to bellow. "My fellow soldiers of the Crown, I am sure you all know why I have gathered you here today. We have come to witness the long overdue demise of a traitorous enemy to the Empire."

Silas' words began to fade into white noise as Theo continued to search the courtyard for any sign of Howell, his eyes occasionally drifting over to see Evie burying her head in Jacob's chest as he looked on with a stiff upper lip masking a heart full of apprehension. Jacob nervously scanned the crowd for Howell as well, and he shared a fearful look with Theo when they both realized he was still nowhere to be found.

Silas continued, gesturing to his prisoner as the Redcoat escort not so gently guided Theo to stand upon the trap door in the center of the platform. "This man, and I use that term loosely, has been charged with many heinous crimes, not the least of which include treason, adultery, and conspiracy to murder one of His Majesty's soldiers."

The crowd gasped in disgust before another wave of disapproving murmurs washed through the courtyard. Silas looked over his shoulder to briefly lock his gaze with Theo's, a triumphant air about him as he continued.

"He is no stranger to me, nor the war, nor this fort. He escaped from our clutches once before, but I assure you, that is not a mistake I will allow to happen again." Silas took a few steps back to stand by Theo's side, clamping a hand upon his shoulder. His voice grew louder and louder with every word he spoke, his chest puffing with pride as if he had won some great victory now that his greatest enemy was minutes away from death.

"I have given him many chances to confess, as well as many chances to save himself by bending the knee. I gave him many chances to swear his allegiance to me, and to the Crown, and yet, at every turn, he has refused to cooperate, like the stubborn brute that he is.

"Before he came to us for the first time over a year ago, not a single prisoner had escaped from Fort Dumpling Rock under my command. But I made the mistake of offering him mercy, and he exploited that weakness, using it against me to escape when my back was turned so that he could return to his sinful life…with *my* wife in his bed!

"It is one thing to take up arms against the Crown. It is one thing to betray His Majesty's kindness and generosity to his subjects by entertaining the ridiculous notion of independence. Men have been executed for much less. But it is a whole other matter to commit the abominable crime of fornication with a man who is not his wife…and a white woman, no less! My wife is equally as guilty for betraying her wedding vows and willfully allowing herself to be defiled by a savage rebel, but she has already paid for her crimes. And now, the time has come for Theo Cunningham to pay for his."

Theo gave him a sharp sideways look, biting down on his bottom lip to swallow the string of insults he was tempted to hurl at him. No matter how badly he wanted to retort, he knew it was not in his best interest to anger the Captain further. He was running on borrowed time as it was, and he needed Silas to draw his rambling out as long as possible until that bloody Howell showed himself as he promised he would.

"As is my prerogative as commanding officer of this fort, I have hereby sentenced this man to hang until dead for his crimes, and this is exactly what he shall do." Silas turned to face his prisoner, a sickeningly smug grin twisting his lips. "Your years of heathenry, debauchery, and treachery have come to an end, Sergeant Cunningham, and nothing gives me more joy than to know I am the one that is bringing an end to your miserable life. I asked you long ago if you believed in God. Do you remember what you said to me that day?"

Theo's voice was low and unsteady, his eyes looking to the sky. "'It depends on the day.'"

Silas chuckled. "And what of today? I highly recommend you make amends with the Lord if you haven't done so already, else you will find yourself spending the rest of eternity in the fiery pits of Hell."

Theo flashed him another sharp look as he pulled fruitlessly against the bindings on his wrists. He would have given anything in that moment to be able to reach out and wrap his hands around the man's throat. "I know where I am going when my time is done, Captain," Theo stated boldly. "And I know where you are going as well. But I cannot say we will ever agree on that matter."

Silas' brow briefly furrowed in annoyance as he took a step toward Theo, who had now resolved to stare forward unflinchingly, even as Silas began to snarl in his ear. It was very clear that the Captain was less than appreciative of being disrespected before an audience, and it was also clear that Theo had struck a nerve in him.

"Let me make one thing very clear to you before I send you to the depths of Hell, boy. This fort is my castle, and I am the *King*. I will *always* be the King. And the girl you thought you were clever enough to bed behind my back is *my* property. *My* woman. *My* queen. I am the King, goddammit! I am the King, and this fort is my castle! And you will not be leaving it alive a second time!"

Silas' eyes grew wide with rage as he howled in Theo's ear, momentarily forgetting in his anger that he was standing before an audience. Despite the fact that Silas was spitting on his face with every word he hissed, Theo stared forward without flinching, his eyes scanning the courtyard as his heart continued to pound nervously in his chest. When it became clear that Howell was nowhere to be seen in the crowd or the rest of the courtyard, his eyes moved upward to scan the parapets and the battlements high above his head.

That was when he caught a momentary glimpse of a bright crimson coat against a dull backdrop of grey and brown stones. If he had blinked, Theo would have missed it as Daniel Howell stealthily slunk along the catwalks on the top of the fort's great walls, ducking behind watch towers and gunpowder barrels as he quickly went about setting his plan into motion.

Theo felt the churning in his stomach slowly dissipate when he noticed a large stack of crates and barrels, behind which he could now see Howell crouching. He could not be sure exactly what Howell was doing or planning, but he did catch a glimpse of a rack of loaded muskets. Silas was so consumed in his madness that he, and everyone else in the crowd, failed to take notice of the scheming taking place over their heads, and that, Howell prayed, would be their downfall.

"I am the goddamn King," Silas repeated again in Theo's ear, "and the King has spoken. You are hereby sentenced to death for your crimes against the Crown, and against humanity. For your sake, may God have mercy on your soul. Have you any last words before you make your final exit from this world? If so, now is the time."

Theo hesitated, swallowing the bile rising in his throat as he felt a Redcoat soldier appear behind him, reaching up to take ahold of the noose dangling above his head. The noose was heavy as it was placed around his neck, resting onerously upon his shoulders and collarbone before being tightened ever so slightly. Theo sent one last desperate look up to the parapet where he had last seen Howell disappear behind a stack of crates, feeling the last few minutes of his life quickly slipping away as the time for his demise drew ever near, and Howell still had not made his move to stop it. As Theo felt the noose settle around his neck and the trapdoor creak under his feet, he began to feel his luck, and his hope, slipping away once again.

But then, Howell appeared again, poking his head just above the crates behind which he was hiding. Theo caught a glimpse of something glinting in the sunlight in Howell's hands, and only then did he realize that he was holding a musket, perched upon a crate as he stealthily aimed it down toward the ground.

"I said, do you have any last words?" Silas repeated angrily, leaning close enough that Theo could smell the whiskey on his breath.

Theo glanced momentarily from Howell and then to Jacob and Evie before returning his gaze to Silas. Locking eyes with the Captain, he straightened his shoulders and narrowed his eyes into a dangerously smug glare.

"Long live the King."

Silas was quiet for a moment, slightly confused and taken aback by his choice of a last testament. Having decided that it was yet another attempt on the part of the savage to be cheeky, even moments before his death, Silas felt his blood begin to boil under his skin.

"A poor choice," Silas snapped as he took a step toward the side of the platform, crossing his arms over his chest. "Insolent until the end."

Before Theo knew it, his vision became obscured as a brown canvas sack was placed over his head. He felt panic briefly overtake him again, as he could no longer clearly see Jacob, Evie, Howell, nor anyone else, and the crowd became raucous again as Silas turned toward his wife and Cadet Thomas Black.

Black had the misfortune of being selected to do the deed of pulling the lever that released the trapdoor under Theo's feet, which would send his body falling a yard or so until the noose pulled tight enough to crush his windpipe and snuff out his life for good. Black's heart pounded in his chest as he looked nervously between Evie, Silas, and his friend. He had caught a brief glimpse of Howell slinking around the parapets a moment before, but it did nothing to calm his nerves. He was just as clueless as Theo was as to what Howell had up his sleeve, if he truly had anything up his sleeve.

"You are the one who captured the rebel and returned him to me," Silas told Black. "I'll allow you to do the honors."

Black nodded, shallowing thickly as he passed Evie one last glance before turning toward the lever. Tears streamed silently down Evie's cheeks as she looked desperately between her lover and her husband, pleading to Silas with her eyes to reconsider, to find it somewhere in his cold, empty heart to spare him. But she was no fool. Mercy was not in Silas' vocabulary, nor was honor, respect or compassion.

Howell looked down upon the courtyard from the catwalk with a skillfully trained eye, crouched behind a bulwark of stacked crates to give him a hiding place as he quietly gathered a cache of loaded muskets from the armory in the depths of the fort. He made sure not to let Theo, Jacob, or Evie slip from his gaze as he made his preparations for his reckless and ridiculous plan, and he felt his heart leap into his throat as he watched one of his former comrades place the noose around Theo's neck, followed by the canvas sack that he was accustomed to seeing upon the heads of those condemned to hang.

He had seen many men hang during his time in the army—hanging, if done right, could be a quick and rather painless affair. But there was always the occasional bloke who was too stubborn to die quickly, and instead of his neck snapping instantly as soon as the noose dropped, he would dangle there for minutes, or even hours, as his body convulsed, his feet kicked, and a ghastly gurgling erupted from his throat. In order to make the process less painful for those watching, it became customary to place a bag over the head of the condemned to conceal the horrific and gruesome expressions of agony that become permanently etched on their faces.

Howell rested his first musket upon a crate to steady his aim, and while keeping both eyes open, he pointed it downward, aiming the muzzle straight for the center of the Captain's chest. He hovered there for a brief moment as Silas made the motion for Cadet Black to finally pull the lever.

Evie gave Thomas Black one last pleading look, silently begging him not to go through with it, to which the Cadet replied with a sorrowful shake of his head. It hurt his heart to see her so forlorn, but in order for things to go smoothly, it was best that she believed she was going to see Theo's end as long as possible. Evie turned her back to the Cadet and let out an agonized shriek, gripping onto Silas' arm in grief when she heard the sound of the lever being pulled and a wooden door dropping underneath someone's feet.

Theo tightened every muscle in his body as he heard the lever creak, and he felt the floor give way underneath him. For less than half a second, he was weightless as he felt himself falling. He clenched his teeth and hands and let out a horrendous gurgle when he felt the noose tighten fleetingly around his throat, pressing harshly against his windpipe as the rope began to reach its full length. He closed his eyes and prepared for darkness to overcome him, sending a brief and desperate prayer up into the sky that God would somehow find it in His heart to spare him.

But the darkness never came, and the pressure on his throat was gone as quickly as it had come when the thunderous sound of a single gunshot touched his ears from somewhere off in the distance. Instead of feeling himself dangle after the noose had fallen and tightened, Theo felt his entire body hit the ground underneath the platform, hard enough to knock the air from his lungs and bash the back of his head against the cobblestones. For a moment, he was sure he was dead, and as he turned over onto his stomach and searched desperately for a breath, his head spinning and his chest heaving, chaos erupted all around and above him.

A satisfied smirk touched Howell's lips as he watched the bullet fire from his musket and down towards the gallows, slicing effortlessly through the length of the rope hanging above Theo's head just as the platform fell away from under his feet. Reloading the first musket would have wasted precious time, so Howell tossed it away and plucked up a new one from the cache behind him, sending a second shot into the ground in the center of the courtyard. The crowd looked up to the sky in fear, searching for the source of the shot, but they were quickly assaulted by three more quick rounds, all of which were aimed at the gunpowder barrels that were strewn about the courtyard. Once the barrels were struck, they immediately ignited into small, but fiery explosions that produced a thunderous clap and a thick cloud of smoke.

Silas stood upon the platform in shock and searched desperately around for an explanation as to why his affairs had been so rudely interrupted.

"Where did that shot come from?" he growled into the crowd before turning to one of his soldiers and barking, "Find whoever is responsible for this!"

Before the soldiers or the crowd could begin to disperse, Howell let off several more shots at the remaining powder barrels until over a dozen small fires had been ignited throughout the courtyard. Terrified and panicked screams erupted from the crowd as it become enveloped in the thick smoke from the fires before every soldier, officer, and slave quickly began to scatter like ants. Within seconds, the entire courtyard was covered in a blanket of grey smoke and clouds of gunpowder, and the people blindly fleeing in all directions down below only brought more confusion and chaos to the madness as Silas became overwhelmed with the sight before him.

"Now!" Jacob cried as he reached forward and took Evie's hand, pulling her back just as Silas leapt off the platform in search of the culprit responsible for the chaos.

"We're under attack!" Silas barked as he left his wife behind in the smoke. "At arms, men! Find the bastards and make them pay!"

Evie screamed when she felt a hand on her wrist, and through the clouds of smoke surrounding her she struggled to see Jacob just a foot or so in front of her. "What's happening?" she asked fearfully. "Are we being attacked?"

"We're escaping!" Jacob corrected as he led her quickly down the steps of the platform and underneath it. "Howell came through, and now is our chance!"

"What?" she screamed in confusion. "Daniel did this?"

"There is no time to explain. Come, we have to find Theo and run."

After trudging through the suffocating smoke, Evie and Jacob dropped to their knees on the ground next to Theo underneath the platform. They found him lying on his side, his arms still bound behind his back as he coughed, sputtered, and gasped for breath amidst the smog in the air and the pain in his throat. His disoriented moans were barely audible through the screams surrounding them and the canvas sack still covering his face, and Evie felt a breath of hope fill her chest when she realized that she was looking at a living, breathing man as opposed to a fresh corpse.

"Theo…" she gasped tearfully as she crouched by his side and pulled the sack away from his face.

Theo's eyes flew open with the action as he gasped for another breath and he stared up at her with clouded eyes.

"Evie…" he rasped lowly, barely able to speak. "…Am I…dead?"

Evie chuckled through her tears and placed a hand upon his cheek. "No, no, far from it."

"Did Howell…?" He was unable to finish the question before he began to choke on the smoke that surrounded them in a thick cloud.

"He came through," Jacob said anxiously as he pulled the noose from around his neck and tossed it to the side. "I don't know how, but he shot the noose before you could drop."

"And the smoke?"

"Gunpowder barrels, perhaps. I don't know. I haven't the faintest clue where he is now, but this is our chance to escape. Silas and the others have disbanded to find the culprit for the attack."

"You both knew he would do this?" Evie asked in abject confusion.

Jacob pulled Theo up into a sitting position by his shoulders before producing a knife from his belt and slicing the bindings on his wrists. As soon as his bruised and bloodied wrists were free, Theo brought a hand up to his neck and rubbed the font of his throat while he continued to cough and catch his breath. He was still seeing stars when Jacob and Evie each grabbed one of his arms and hauled him up to his feet, and the world seemed to be spinning around him as if he was floating on open water rather than standing on solid ground. His legs buckled underneath him, but before he could collapse again, Jacob and Evie each slid an arm around his shoulders and allowed him to lean against them.

"We'll take Artemis and my horse from the stables and slip out through the front gates," Jacob instructed as they began to blindly shuffle across the courtyard, dodging the occasional fleeing soldier who was too preoccupied to notice any kind of escape attempt.

"What of Daniel?" Evie asked nervously, looking over her shoulder for any sign of him or her husband.

"He'll catch up to us," Jacob returned.

Satisfied with his work of creating utter chaos, Howell peered down at the clouds of smoke filling the courtyard with a smugness he had not felt in a long while. He momentarily lost sight of Evie, Theo, and Jacob in the crowd, but they reappeared a moment later by the stables. Howell then destroyed any evidence of his hiding place by kicking over the musket racks and stacks of crates before taking the nearest staircase three steps at a time to descend into the madness.

"We do not have much time," Howell said to his conspirators as he reached the stables. "Silas will realize there is no real attack soon enough. We must escape now."

Silas pulled his sword from his sheath as he stormed throughout the courtyard searching in vain for any sign of an intruder, and his blood continued to boil as he become overwhelmed by the smoke filling every nook and cranny of the place. For a moment, he had completely forgotten that he left his wife and his prisoner at the gallows, and he abruptly turned on his heel to return back to the platform. He let out an enraged growl when the smoke had cleared just enough for him to see that the noose had been severed and there was not a soul to be seen at the gallows.

In that moment, Silas turned to look over his shoulder and caught a glimpse of his wife's skirts billowing behind her as she fled through the front gates, escorted by a haggard looking half breed and two Redcoats on horseback. As realization dawned on him that this mayhem was not the work of a foreign intruder, Silas clenched his teeth and took off after them.

"Son of a bitch," he snarled under his breath before snagging his own horse from the stables and riding through the front gates, sword drawn and thirsty for rebel blood.

Theo and the others paused in the wilderness just past the bridge that connected the island to the mainland. He was still struggling to catch his breath and the world still felt like it was spinning, but he was finally able to move on his own without collapsing.

Theo turned to Jacob and handed him Artemis' reins. "Jacob, you and Evie each take a horse and head toward home. Howell and I will go the opposite way on foot. Silas has surely noticed we are gone by now and will come looking. Go home and do not look back. We will catch up with you later."

"No," Evie protested, taking ahold of his arm. "I won't leave you."

"You must. Silas will come for me before anyone else. We will draw him away and finish him before he can come after you."

Evie shook her head as anxious tears continued to pour down her cheeks. "But—"

"Go!" Theo snapped, nudging her toward the second horse. "This is the only way we can be free of him. Please, Evie, you have to trust me."

Evie's eyes drifted to Howell, who stood by Theo's side with his hand upon the sword on his hip. "Promise me you will see that he is safe," she murmured.

"I'll let no harm come to him, Miss Evie," Howell said as he placed a hand over his heart. "Soon enough, we will all be free of this tyrant."

Evie hesitated, but after a moment of painful deliberation she threw her arms around Theo's neck. "Make him pay," she whispered in his ear before pulling away and pressing a short, sweet kiss to his lips. She then turned away with a flourish, and with Jacob's help, mounted the second horse.

"Take this," Jacob said to Theo as he handed him the sword he had been keeping on his belt. Alistair's sword. The very sword Theo had taken with him to war not too long ago. It had protected him many times before, and it would surely do it again now. "You will need it."

Theo clamped a hand on Jacob's shoulder and pulled him close. "Protect her with your life, Jacob," he murmured.

Jacob locked his eyes with his friend and nodded. "Come find us at the mouth of the river. We will wait for you there."

Howell glanced over his shoulder at the sound of horse hooves pounding against the earth in the distance. Silas' red coat stood out against the lush greenery of his surroundings as he crossed the bridge and hit the mainland, sword pointed to the sky.

"We must go," Howell shouted, taking Theo by the arm. "Silas will be upon us soon."

Theo and Evie shared one last longing gaze before he tore his eyes from hers and followed after Howell through the trees, as deep into the wilderness as they could manage in order to draw Silas far from Evie and Jacob's trail. After they had gone, Jacob and Evie kicked their horses into a gallop and took off in the opposite direction just as Silas reached the tree line.

Silas angrily looked between the path his wife had taken and the path his prisoner and former second in command had forged in the opposite direction. He clenched his teeth together and seethed as he contemplated which way to go, and after a moment of deliberation, a determined growl escaped his throat as he kicked his own horse into a gallop and followed Theo's trail deep into the wilderness, never once looking back.

***

"Get back here!" Silas snarled as he emerged through the trees right on Theo and Howell's heels. "Goddamned traitors! You'll wish you were never born once I get my hands on you!"

Theo and Howell resisted the urge to look over their shoulders, for fear that they would see Silas right behind them. The only advantage they had over him was that they were fleeing on foot while he was on horseback, allowing them to slip in between trees and over logs with ease. After a long while, Silas began to lose ground as his horse became confused and slowed by the many obstacles that Theo and Howell were able to avoid on foot. Within a few minutes after giving chase, Silas lost sight of them in the trees, which only served to further fuel his anger and desire to finally spill the savage's blood.

After their lungs and legs began to burn and they could run no more, Theo and Howell skidded to a stop in a large clearing in the depths of the forest, crouching behind a large tree trunk while they attempted to catch their breath and calm their racing hearts.

"I haven't had the chance to properly thank you," Theo mumbled as he leaned his back against the tree and gave Howell a sideways glance. "I did not think you would be true to your word. But…you saved my life. "

Howell chuckled lowly and raked a hand through his messy blonde hair. "There is no need to thank me, Theo. I am only doing what I think is right."

"If we survive this, I do not know how I will ever repay you…"

"If we survive this, perhaps I will let you buy me a drink."

Theo outstretched his hand in Howell's direction, which the Sergeant gladly accepted with a firm handshake. "I am not really the drinking type anymore, but you have a deal."

The thunderous explosion of a gunshot erupted in the distance, followed promptly by a bullet hurdling through the air in their direction and lodging itself in the tree just above their heads. Theo quickly grabbed Howell by the collar of his coat and threw him forward onto the ground before they began to crawl across the clearing to find cover once again, their bellies scraping the ground so that they could make themselves as small as possible. Silas' horse whinnied in the distance and pounded its hooves upon the ground, and Theo quickly looked around the surrounding trees for any sign of him. Another bullet ripped through the air from somewhere in the trees and Theo and Howell dropped even lower to the ground, throwing their arms over their heads. The hoofbeats became louder and louder with every second that passed until they sounded as if they were right on top of them, and they ducked behind the nearest tree just as Silas rode into the clearing.

Silas re-holstered his pistol and dismounted with his sword in hand. "I know you are both here," he snarled out loud as he began to circle the perimeter of the clearing. "Show yourselves at once, you cowards!"

Howell and Theo pressed their backs against the tree and shared a look, silently agreeing to emerge simultaneously with their weapons drawn. Within an instant, they both leapt out from behind the tree, swords held defensively in front of their bodies.

Silas immediately turned around upon hearing the snap of a twig under Theo's boot, and a sadistically cocky grin spread upon his face as their eyes met. "You've slipped away from me once, mongrel. You are a fool if you think I will let you do it again."

"You are outnumbered, Silas," Theo returned with a smug cock of his head. "You cannot defeat us both."

Silas scoffed indignantly, resisting the urge to chuckle. "Look at you. You've been beaten and starved for days. You can barely stand on your own, let alone best a seasoned commander in battle. You are in no condition to fight!"

"But I am," Howell returned as he stepped forward.

"*You.*" Silas's eyes narrowed dangerously as he turned his attention to Howell. "I must admit, Sergeant Howell, this is the kind of treachery I would expect of a brute like Mr. Cunningham. But from you? I trusted you. You have been my second in command for four and a half years!"

"Four years too many," Howell snapped. "I am sorry, Silas, but I can serve a tyrant no longer."

Silas' scowl deepened as he growled, "That's *Captain Porter* to you."

"You were never my Captain. You do not deserve such a title after all of the innocent blood you have shed in the name of this war!"

Silas' stern expression quickly morphed into one of madness as he charged forward without warning and swung his sword at Howell's head. Howell easily blocked his blade with his own and spun off to the side to avoid being run through. Silas' momentum sent him flying past both of his enemies and stumbling into the nearest tree before he quickly recovered and attempted another swing, this time at Theo.

"You are both traitors!" Silas growled as he and Theo crossed swords with devastating ferocity. "And you will both die a traitor's death!"

Theo may have had Silas beat in height and brute strength, but he had been weakened by days of beatings and near-starvation, and he struggled to wield his weapon properly and effectively block Silas' erratic and unpredictable attacks. Upon noticing that Theo was being beaten back toward the edge of the clearing, Howell recovered himself and set about joining the fray. While all three men were well trained in the use of a sword, Silas clearly had the most experience, and at the moment, the greatest strength. Mad with a lust for blood and revenge, every swing of his sword came quickly and powerfully, offering little time to his enemies to duck, parry, or stumble out of its path.

Silas' attention then became focused solely on Theo as he relentlessly pushed forward with his blade raised and locked against his, and Theo struggled to match his strength and skill, constantly stumbling backwards across the length of the clearing until his heel caught on a wayward tree root that knocked him off of his feet. Gracelessly, he fell onto his back while his sword skittered across the ground and came to rest several feet away.

Silas wasted no time in coming to stand over him, raising his sword over his head as if to come down upon him with one powerful cleave. Theo threw his arms up over his head and squeezed his eyes shut, waiting for the sting of the blade to come, but instead, Howell threw himself in between them and parried Silas' swing with his own blade, sending the Captain staggering back before he recovered again and charged toward Howell once more.

Theo scrambled up onto his hands and knees and attempted to recover while he watched Howell and Silas engage in a brief melee with one another, the clink of steel against steel echoing throughout the trees and intermingled with the grunts of exertion emanating from the combatants' throats. After several minutes of well-matched combat, Silas grew bored, and he decided to dispatch Howell once and for all so that he could devote his attention back to his true nemesis. When both of Howell's arms were raised while he held his sword to block his face, Silas took that split second to exploit his momentary vulnerability, and instead of trying to run him through, he effortlessly swiped his blade across Howell's exposed chest, cutting through his thick, wool coat and the top layer of his skin.

Howell cried out in pain and stumbled backwards until his back hit the nearest tree, his chest heaving as blood began to seep through his shirt and coat. Silas immediately charged at him once more, pinning him against the tree with their blades locked against one another once again. Silas pushed against him with all his might until their blades were mere millimeters from Howell's face, and as the laceration on his chest continued to bleed, Howell's strength quickly diminished until his grip on his sword faltered. Before Howell could blink, his sword slipped from his hands and clattered to the ground at his feet, leaving him open and vulnerable to the blade that Silas wasted no time in shoving into the center of his abdomen.

Howell let out an agonized, gurgling roar as he felt Silas' sword impale him straight through his stomach. Silas stared his former friend and right-hand man down with a dangerous glare, his eyes cold, dark, and wide with blind rage as he withdrew his blade from his abdomen. Howell stared back in complete and total shock, dropping to his knees as he wrapped his arms around his torso and warm blood began to pool through his clothing. Silas tore his eyes from Howell's crumpled body to admire the sight of the blood staining the length of his blade, his lips twitching into a sadistic grin that could only be brought about by the demise of another man by his hands.

"Howell!" Theo cried as he clumsily rose to his feet and staggered forward, searching for his sword. Howell let out another agonized moan and slumped back against the tree behind him, which was now also stained with his blood. Theo watched in horror as Howell stared blankly at him across the clearing, his eyes wide, as blood began to trickle from the corner of his mouth and he pressed his hands against the gaping wound in his abdomen.

Silas quickly turned away from his victim upon hearing Theo's distraught cry, charging toward him with his bloodied sword raised and ready to kill. Theo ducked under his first swing and swooped down to take up his sword, blocking a second swing meant to sever his head from his shoulders. Trapped in another duel to the death, he looked constantly over his shoulder to check on Howell, only to see each time that the man was still slumped against the tree on the verge of unconsciousness. The sight was ghastly and heartbreaking after all that Howell had done to save his life, and in that moment, Theo felt a wave of fury surge through him, strong enough to overpower his exhaustion and injury with a fiery onslaught of adrenalin that sent him charging Silas and, for the first time, sending *him* stumbling backwards.

Caught off guard by Theo's sudden burst of strength, Silas staggered back but maintained his grip on his broadsword, locking it against Theo's blade as they both leaned forward and rooted their heels into the ground. They pushed against each other with all of their might, teeth clenched and eyes narrowed into dangerous slits as they stared each other down through their crossed swords, trying in vain to overpower the other and leaning ever farther forward until their faces were nearly touching.

"Just give up!" Silas snarled through his teeth. "I've already taken down your conspirator, and I'll do the same to you! Surrender, and I will consider sparing you."

Theo scoffed at the audacity of his words. "Not a chance."

Theo and Silas both attempted to withdraw their swords at the same time, but their hilts had locked together such that when they attempted to pull away, both swords went flying from their grasp and clattered across the clearing, far out of their reach. Before Theo could even register that he had lost his weapon, Silas kicked a cloud of dirt into his eyes in an attempt to blind and disorient him and then took off toward their lost blades. Theo pawed at his eyes with a hiss and lunged after him, grabbing him by a fistful of his coat and jumping onto his back until they both hit the ground and tumbled across the dirt together.

Silas emerged on top when they came to a stop, straddling Theo's waist and throwing an unexpected punch that hit Theo's jaw and knocked his head against the ground hard enough to make him see stars. Silas took that split second that Theo was disoriented to lean forward and wrap his hands firmly around his throat, pinning him to the ground as he squeezed his neck with all of his remaining strength. A pained and gurgling yelp was ripped from Theo's throat as Silas constricted his large hands around his neck, and he could feel his windpipe being crushed under his enormous strength until the perimeters of his vision became dark and blurry and the world began to spin once again.

"You should have surrendered when I gave you the chance long ago, boy," Silas seethed from above, mercilessly tightening his grip on his throat as he stared him down through the strands of wayward hair that had fallen in his face in the scuffle.

"You and all your native ilk, you are all the same! Stubborn, repulsive, and simple-minded. You should have stayed in the forest where you belong instead of trying to pretend that you belong in the civilized world! All you savages do is rut around in the dirt, as you have done for centuries, resistant to change and improvement, headless of the progress being made in the world around you! You were foolish to ever think you could best me… for I am your better in every single way! You and every other Indian should do the world a favor and just *die*!"

Theo desperately stretched one arm out at his side, raking through the grass in search of his sword or any other item he could use as a weapon while he used his other hand to attempt in vain to pry Silas' hands from his throat. The pressure on his windpipe was crushing and agonizing, and he could feel the world starting to go dark as he kicked, clawed, and flailed underneath Silas' weight. When he realized that there was nothing on the ground within his reach that he could use to defend himself, he raised his arms to Silas' sides, and with the last remnants of his strength, he groped at the man's belt in the hopes of finding something, anything, which he could use to save himself.

A sliver of hope shot through his chest when his fingertips grazed what felt to be the hilt of a small blade, and with what remained of his consciousness, he plucked it from Silas' belt and plunged it into whatever flesh he could reach. Silas howled as he felt the knife plunge into the lower left side of his abdomen, all the way to the hilt. In an instant, Theo felt the pressure on his throat dissipate as Silas' hands fell away and he fell off to the side, collapsing to the ground at Theo's side and gripping the handle of the knife as he stared up at the sky in shock.

Theo gasped for breath and immediately turned over on his side, chest heaving and throat throbbing as the air slowly returned to his lungs. He pushed himself up onto his hands and knees and attempted to catch a much-needed breath. His head was still foggy, and the ground still seemed to rock underneath him as he tried to gather himself. He looked up when he heard Silas gasp and sputter, only to see that he was now crawling backwards across the clearing, knife still imbedded in his side, in a desperate attempt to find safety.

Theo narrowed his eyes as he watched the coward's pathetic attempt to slither away. Swiping the back of his hand across his mouth to wipe away the blood and dirt that had collected on his face, he slowly rose to his feet before taking an unstable step toward Silas' fallen form.

***

Evie looked nervously over her shoulder every few moments as she and Jacob trekked through the Rhode Island wilderness towards the mouth of the nearest river, where they planned to meet up with Howell and Theo. She knew she should have had faith in Theo and Howell's abilities to defend themselves, but she could not help but fear for them, knowing first-hand the brutality and cruelty Silas was capable of inflicting upon his victims. Jacob took notice of her anxiety from his horse on her right, seeing from the corner of his eye the way she incessantly peered over her shoulder in the direction from which they had come and gripped Artemis' reins so tightly that her knuckles had turned white.

"Theo will be fine, Evie," Jacob reassured, though from the tone of his voice she could not tell if he was trying to convince her or himself. "He knows how to use a sword. He and Howell will be able to take him easily."

Evie shook her head. "No. Something is wrong. I can feel it." Suddenly, she pulled her reins back until Artemis halted in the middle of the path. Jacob looked back at her in shock and brought his own horse to a stop.

"What are you doing? We have to keep moving! If we stop, the Redcoats could catch up to us."

Evie slowly looked up and met his gaze, her blue eyes swimming with resolve. "We have to go back."

"*What?* Go back? You're just as mad as Theo!"

Evie pulled on her reins again until her horse began to turn back toward the direction they had come. "I'm going back. I have to help them. I can't leave them to fight my battles for me any longer!"

"Evie, you can't possibly think you can fight your husband! If he gets his hands on you again, he will kill you!"

"I don't care. I'm going back."

Before Jacob could have even hoped to stop her, Evie kicked Artemis into a gallop and took off the way they had come without him, never once looking back.

Jacob let out a perturbed growl and rolled his eyes up to the sky before turning around and giving chase after her. "If Theo doesn't get us killed, it will surely be you who does me in!"

Evie rode her steed hard, pushing her to sprint as fast as she could while dodging trees, fallen branches, and other debris. Within a few minutes, Evie reached the clearing where they had parted, and after deliberating for a moment, she settled on a path to take, hoping it was the direction that Theo and Howell had taken. She could hear the pounding of Jacob's horse's hooves just a few paces behind her, and soon enough, he caught up to her. They rode aimlessly for a few minutes until the distant sound of clinking metal and pained groans touched their ears, leading them forward until they came upon a large clearing in which three men had been engaged in battle.

Artemis skidded to a stop at the edge of the clearing as Evie took in the sight of Daniel Howell slumped against a tree on one side of the clearing while Silas was splayed across the ground and Theo was crouched over his body on the other side.

"Daniel!" Evie dismounted her horse without a second thought and immediately ran to Howell, crouching at his side as he leaned against the bloodied tree behind his back and wrapped his arms around his torso. He was drifting in and out of consciousness with his head resting against his shoulder, but upon hearing Evie's voice, his eyes fluttered open just as she came to his side. Jacob dismounted his own horse and followed close behind her, stooping down on his other side.

"Miss Evie..." Howell murmured weakly as blood continued to trickle from the corner of his mouth. "What are you doing here? You are supposed to wait at the river..."

Evie looked down at the wound in the center of his abdomen, just under his ribcage, gasping at the ghastly sight of blood pouring over his hands in a river of red just below a deep slash across his chest that cut all the way through his flesh. "Oh, Daniel, you...you're hurt..." she mumbled tearfully, placing a shaky hand upon his cheek.

Howell's chest heaved as he searched for a haggard breath amongst the blood that he could feel slowly filling his lungs. "You must go...before Silas gets his hands on you..."

"No, I won't leave you and Theo."

"Miss Evie, please, do not worry about me..."

"Why did you do this, Daniel? Why did you save us? Why did you betray Silas?"

Howell sucked in a raspy breath as Evie reached forward and placed her hands upon his. She let out a weak sob as she felt the blood seeping from his wound pour over her own hands and stain her skin. "I could not watch him...hurt anyone else any longer. I had to do something...before it was too late...for you, for Theo, for everyone else in these colonies..."

Evie shook her head in confusion. "I do not understand. You will lose everything now that you have betrayed the Crown..."

"It will be well worth it, Miss Evie. I have come to realize that the colonies are destined...to be free...but with men like Silas Porter in power…there will be no such thing as freedom anywhere on these divided grounds. If my death is the price that I must pay to remove one more tyrant from this world, then so be it."

"No," Evie sobbed, "You will not die today. You will come back to Division Point with us. You can start over and—"

Howell let out a raspy groan and slowly shook his head as he stared up into her eyes. "I'm sorry, Miss Evie. I think my time has come…"

Though his words came slow and with a great degree of pain while blood continued to pour from his wound, he was still lucid, still breathing. Jacob and Evie shared a brief and knowing look, communicating with their eyes what they did not want to admit, but would surely come to pass.

Howell slid his eyes over to fall upon Silas' fallen form across the clearing. "Go to him," he told Evie in a whisper. "Do not waste anymore of your time on my behalf."

Reluctantly, Evie and Jacob slowly rose to their feet after giving Howell a grateful pat on the shoulder and crossed the clearing in several long strides. They silently came to stand over Silas as Theo remained crouched at his side.

Silas stared up into the sky with wide eyes glossed over with madness as he gripped the handle of the knife imbedded in his side. He choked and sputtered, gasping for a breath as blood began to trickle from his nose and mouth. Theo dropped to his knees in exhaustion at his side and leaned over him, close enough that their faces were only a few inches apart. They stared each other down in silence for a few long moments, the air tense and still between them.

After a long silence, Silas attempted to speak, but his words were punctuated by ragged breaths and wheezes. "Are you going to congratulate yourself now, mongrel? It looks like you've won…"

Theo shook his head in disgust. "Nothing worth celebrating has transpired today, Silas. You are mistaken if you think your death will bring me any pleasure."

Silas chuckled weakly as blood began to pour from around the blade in his side and stain his hands. "Of course, it will. Killing and conquering is what men thrive on. Perhaps...perhaps you and I are not so different in that regard, after all..."

Theo leaned further forward and took a handful of Silas' coat in his fist. "I am *nothing* like you. You derive pleasure from abusing and murdering innocent people under the guise of war."

Silas rasped out another dark chuckle. "Oh, do not look down at me from your high horse. You are no more righteous, no more just, no righter, than anyone else in this bloody war. You Patriots are all the same. You parade about, calling yourselves the champions of freedom, thinking that your cause is the one true, just cause, never stopping to think that...perhaps, your enemy thinks the same of their own convictions..."

"Nothing you say will change the fact that you are a monster. You call yourself a King, but you are no such thing. You are no leader. You are a tyrant, just like your King George, and you always will be..."

Silas' eyes drifted from Theo over to Evie, who had silently dropped to her knees on his other side. Their eyes met for a brief moment, but instead of finding grief or sadness on his wife's face, he was greeted only with coldness.

"And what of you?" he asked her weakly. "Will you celebrate my demise too?"

Evie curtly shook her head. "I would never want to give you the satisfaction."

Silas let out another raspy chortle, his eyes fluttering open and closed as darkness began to overcome his vision. "Perhaps you two were meant to be together, then. Dogs travel in packs, after all. I should have killed you both when I had the chance..."

"That was your fatal mistake," Evie countered as she leaned over his body, her face close enough to his that he could feel her breath on his skin.

She stared down into his eyes for a brief moment as her hand came to rest upon his own, gripping the handle of the knife in his side.

Silas sneered up at her and swallowed the blood that he could feel collecting in his throat. "May the Hell in which you both find yourselves be of your own creation, my dear…"

Evie's expression darkened as her grip on the knife handle tightened. As she looked into his eyes, she saw five years' worth of anger, pain, and nightmares coming to an end in such a surreal fashion that it took her breath away. Her eyes searched his face for any signs of emotion, but she saw none. She was staring into the eyes of a selfish, wicked man who, even in death, could not and would not admit his own defeat, nor atone for his wrongs. She had never known evil until she met him, and she hoped she would never again meet another as callous and as black-hearted as he. Evie swallowed thickly as she looked into his eyes for the last time—the cold, steely grey eyes of her husband, the father of her child, the villain she had been fleeing for what felt like an eternity.

"Have you anything left to say to me before we part?" Silas asked her in a whisper.

With a heavy and aching heart, she wrapped her hand tightly around the knife handle and twisted the blade sideways into his abdomen, ripping a ghastly groan from his throat before his head fell back against the ground and his body went still.

"Long live the King," she whispered in return as a single tear slipped down her cheek.

Chapter 10

Requiem

March 1779

Evie pulled her hands from the handle of the knife imbedded in her husband's side, her body trembling as she looked down upon the blood that stained her fingers, and she could feel Theo and Jacob staring at her with mouths agape. Slowly, she tore her eyes from her bloodied hands and met Theo's gaze as he swallowed thickly and reached forward to place a comforting hand on her shoulder. They both looked upon Silas' stilled body, his eyes having fluttered closed just a few moments before.

"You did the right thing," Theo mumbled as he attempted to catch his breath. "He had to be stopped."

Evie was silent as she reached forward and took Silas' left hand, still warm to the touch in her own, and slid the gilded wedding band from his finger. Wordlessly, she held the ring smeared with blood in her palm before tucking it into her bodice for safe keeping. The single tear that had slipped down her cheek as she twisted the knife in Silas' body had long since dried, and she rose to her feet as she passed another solemn look to Theo, who remained crouched at her side.

"That depends upon how you choose to define *right*," she said coldly before turning away and sprinting across the clearing to return to Howell.

Evie dropped to her knees at Howell's side once more as his chest laboriously rose and fell. Blood now trickled down his face from his nose and both sides of his mouth, and each breath he took was shallow and ragged. His hands had fallen away from his wound and come to rest on the ground at his sides, allowing the blood to flow more freely from his abdomen down into his lap, seeping into the grass around him. He slowly turned his head towards her and gave her a weak smile.

Evie placed a hand upon his cheek and returned his smile. "You saved us," she whispered.

"I could not…watch another tyrant…reign free," Howell choked out. "He's no better than King George. I did my part…to end this war. Now I may go in peace."

Evie shook her head. "No, you can't die today, Daniel. You'll come back to the homestead with us. You can start over with us."

"I'm sorry, Miss Evie. I don't think I have much time left."

Evie's eyes burned with tears of anger as she took him by the hand and attempted to drape one of his arms around her shoulder. "No, I won't allow it! We can get you home, and the doctor can treat you like he did Theo and—"

"Miss Evie, it is too late for me. I…I would only slow you down. I will be dead within the next few minutes, I fear. Go with Jacob and Theo. Go back to your homestead and resume your happy life there. Do not worry about me, please."

Another tear rolled down her cheek as she stared desperately into his eyes and squeezed his hand. "I won't leave you here. Not after what you have done for us."

"Do not waste your tears on me. I won't have it. All will be well soon enough, I swear it."

"Daniel…please, don't go…" Evie sobbed as she dropped her head to rest her cheek against his shoulder. "Please don't do this."

Howell turned his head to stare emptily up into the sky just as Theo and Jacob arrived on his other side. They watched in silent sorrow as the life slowly continued to drain from his eyes until they were nothing but dull pools of murkiness.

"I was supposed to buy you a drink," Theo mumbled mournfully as he clamped a hand on Howell's shoulder. "I can't do that if you keel over now."

Howell let out a weak, sputtering chuckle, one that sprayed blood out onto his chin and the front of his coat. "That's quite alright…I won't hold it against you when I reach Heaven's gates."

Theo squeezed his shoulder one last time. "Thank you, my friend. For everything. We owe you our lives. We owe you a debt we can never repay."

"Silas Porter's demise is payment enough. No matter who wins this war…the world is a better place without him…" Howell's eyes slid over to give Evie one last contented gaze before they finally slipped closed and his chest rose and fell for the last time.

A quiet, agonized sob escaped Evie's throat as she watched Howell's body still and felt his hand go limp within her own. Leaning forward, she placed a gentle kiss upon his cheek. A heavy silence fell upon the clearing as they lowered their heads in remembrance of the man whom they barely knew, but had sacrificed himself on their behalves, nonetheless.

Jacob eventually broke the silence when he quietly mumbled, "We should probably move on. If we stay here much longer, Redcoats will certainly stumble upon us. No doubt they've started looking for us…" He then began to unbutton his red uniform coat, and after shrugging out of it, he tossed it over his shoulder without a second thought.

Theo stood and offered his hand to Evie to help her to her feet. She did not acknowledge it, nor did she look away from Howell's face.

"We must go, Evie," Theo coaxed gently. "We can't risk being captured again."

"And what of Daniel?" she asked lowly without looking up.

Theo and Jacob shared an unsure glance before Theo mumbled, "He told us to go on without him. So that is what we will do…"

Evie's eyes snapped up angrily to meet his own. "I won't leave him like this. He was nothing but good to me from the moment I came to the fort, and he saved our lives. We cannot just leave him here to rot!"

"You expect us to carry his body with us all the way back to Division Point?" Jacob asked in confusion.

"We would have done the same for you," Evie countered coldly.

After a moment of thought, Theo let out a saddened sigh and looked to Jacob. "Help me lift him and strap him to the horse, Jacob. We will bury him next to the church as soon as we return home."

***

It was nearly dusk before the fires at Fort Dumpling Rock were contained, and only then did realization dawn upon the soldiers there that the prisoner was missing, and the Captain, his wife, and his second in command where nowhere to be found. A search party was immediately launched to hunt them all down, but Theo, Jacob, and Evie were long gone with Howell's body by the time the party set about looking for them.

The sun had just finished setting when the Redcoat search party stumbled upon the clearing, and they immediately dismounted their horses and drew their weapons upon noticing a dark figure that resembled a body strewn across the ground in a pool of blood.

The leader of the party, a young Cadet, was the first to approach the body, and he gasped in alarm when he got close enough to recognize it as the body of his Captain with a small hunting knife imbedded in his side.

"It's Captain Porter!" he called over his shoulder to the others lingering behind him and scouring the rest of the clearing.

The Cadet dropped to his knees at Silas' side and placed a hand on his neck to check for any signs of life. Silas was still for several moments before his fingers twitched and he let out a very faint moan as his eyes cracked open and then closed again. His pulse was faint, but it persisted.

"He's alive, lads!" The Cadet called to the others. "He's weak, and lost much blood, but he's still alive!"

A second Cadet came to stand over them, a look of relief upon his face as he scratched under his powdered wig. "Thank the Lord. We need to take him back to the fort immediately. The Royal Army doctor will have a look at him at once, and if God is with us, he will pull through."

A third soldier joined them. "Look at that wound," he said incredulously. "There is no way he can survive this!"

The first Cadet shook his head. "We still have to try! Come on, lads, help me carry him back to the fort. With haste!"

A fourth Cadet continued to scour the rest of the clearing for any signs of the other missing persons. "No sign of Mrs. Porter, Sergeant Howell, or the prisoner," he called. "But there's blood on this tree…and a uniform coat over yonder. Perhaps that savage kidnapped them both!"

Silas let out another quiet moan as he was lifted off of the ground. His clothes were soaked with blood and his body was dead weight as the soldiers struggled to carry him across the clearing and onto a horse. He opened his mouth to speak as his eyes fluttered open, but the world became dark again before he could formulate a coherent thought.

"What's that, sir?" one of the Cadets asked him as he leaned his head down to hear him better. "Who did this to you, Captain Porter? Was it the savage?"

Silas weakly shook his head before his body went limp again in their arms and his eyes fluttered closed once more. Despite the amount of blood that had poured from his body and the hours that had passed before he was found, he was still somehow clinging to his life by a thread, each breath coming long, slow, and painfully from his lungs. Dazed and disoriented, he could not recall where he was, how he had gotten there, or how much time had passed since he had last lost consciousness. But a red-headed siren specter remained burned into his memory as the rest of the world began to fade to black.

"Talk to us, sir," another soldier coaxed. "Who did this to you?"

Silas swallowed thickly and heaved out another ragged breath, and without opening his eyes, whispered so quietly that none but he could hear.

"...*Evie*..."

***

April 1779

The trek to Division Point was long and tensely quiet, with few words spoken by anyone other than the occasional quip. Evie was the quietest of them all, and she kept her eyes locked on the ground as her hands, still stained by the blood of both Howell and her husband, gripped the reigns of her steed with a vice-like hold. The only time she tore her eyes from the path below her was when she occasionally looked back to see Howell's lifeless body laid over Artemis' back.

She knew she should have been ecstatic that Silas was gone that and she was only a few days' ride from returning home, but the only thing she felt in her heart was sorrow. She had been dreaming of the day that she would be free from her husband's tyranny, and she had always imagined the occasion to be filled with happiness and relief, but even after all she had endured by his cruel hands, his demise brought her no joy whatsoever.

After over three days of silent trekking through the New England wilderness, Theo cleared his throat and spoke up. "Division Point is just on the other side of this hill," he said to Evie, hoping for some sort of reaction.

Evie nodded once without looking up.

Theo and Jacob shared a look of concern before Theo tried again. "Gunner will be excited to see you. You have no idea how much he missed you."

The slightest of smiles touched her lips, but Theo could tell that it was only for his benefit.

The sun was high in the sky when the horses broke through the tree line on the western edge of the homestead and cantered up the paved path. Both rider and steed were hunched over in exhaustion, but they felt an immediate sense of calm as soon as they stepped foot on the land.

They were home.

For what felt like weeks, Johanna and Alistair waited by the front window, squinting into the tree line for any sign of Theo's return with Jacob and Evie in tow. On the first day of April, their prayers were answered when Johanna happened to be sitting in front of the window, working on her sewing. She looked up to see three indistinct figures on horseback trudging up the path, battle-worn and in desperate need of a hot meal.

Johanna jumped to her feet and pressed her hands to the windowpane as she peered into the distance, startling Gunner awake in the process, who had been sleeping under her chair. It was not until they were one hundred or so feet from the front of the house that Johanna recognized the weary travelers as her boy, his lover, and his best friend, and she felt her heart fill to the brim with relief.

"They've returned!" she called excitedly over her shoulder to Alistair, who was busying himself in the parlor. "Theo and the others have returned safely to us!"

Alistair immediately poked his head into the front room, but Johanna and Gunner had already sprinted out the front door and down the path to meet them before they even reached the house. He followed after them, and upon his reaching the bottom of the front steps, Theo, Evie, and Jacob had already dismounted their horses and were locked in a tight embrace within Johanna's arms as Gunner pranced excitedly around them.

"Oh, God," Johanna cried out as she hugged the three youngsters tightly to her chest. "My prayers have been answered! I was so afraid that I would never see any of you again…"

"I promised you we would return, didn't I?" Theo said with a light chuckle.

Johanna ruffled his hair playfully before placing her hands on both of Evie's cheeks and kissing her forehead. It was only then that she noticed the faint bruises smattered across her and Theo's faces, as well as the dried blood that had caked to their hands. "Oh, dear Lord," Johanna sighed, "did that brute Silas do this to you?"

Evie and Theo shared a brief glance before they weakly nodded and shifted their weight uncomfortably between their feet.

"What is it?" Alistair asked as he came to embrace them all and immediately noticed Evie's morose disposition. He had expected to see her jumping for joy when she returned home, but instead, she seemed to be even more downtrodden than she was when she was taken. "What of Silas Porter? Does he still live?"

Theo shared another look with Evie before wrapping his arm around her shoulders and clearing his throat. "Silas Porter is exactly where he belongs now," he said curtly.

"And that place would be?"

"Hell," Evie finished, looking up with blue eyes darkened with a storm of emotions that no one could really decipher.

"You both look like you have been through Hell and back yourselves," Alistair noted with a sigh as he reached up to graze his finger across the nasty bruise under Theo's left eye, and then the gash upon his temple, and then the rope burn upon his wrists and the front of his throat.

Theo nudged away from his touch with a scowl. "You didn't really think we'd return completely unscathed, did you?"

Alistair cleared his throat nervously and approached the tired horses behind them, and it was only then that he realized that a man's body dressed in a blood-stained British uniform was strapped to Artemis' back.

"Dear God," Alistair exclaimed in shock. "Who is this?"

"The man that saved our lives," Jacob answered sadly. "He defected from the Royal Army and helped us escape the fort. He wanted to come with us to Division Point, but Silas killed him before he got the chance."

"He has a name," Evie corrected as she came to stand next to Artemis and placed a hand on Howell's back. "And it's Daniel."

"If it weren't for Daniel," Theo added, pointing to his throat, "I would be dangling from a noose right now."

"You would be, *what*?" Johanna snapped, her eyes going wide with fear.

"It doesn't matter now," Theo mumbled as he gave her a reassuring pat on the arm. "All that matters is that we are all home, where we belong."

"The man is a hero, then," Alistair stated as he began to unstrap Howell's body from Artemis' back. "And he will be buried as such."

***

After being away for nearly a month, it took Evie several days to readjust to her life in Division Point once again. Almost immediately upon her return, the community embraced her as if she had never left, as if she had never lied to them for last five years. She knew she should have been elated that she was welcomed back so readily, but it was hard for her to enjoy her new found freedom knowing that Howell was in the ground and Silas' body was God-knows-where, left to rot in solitude like the monster he was.

Though she had waited for the day that she could call herself free from him, becoming a widow did not bring her nearly as much joy as she thought it might. She was relieved that she would never have to live in fear of him again, but it hurt her heart to leave Noah's father's body behind the way they had. And in the days after his demise, she knew she should have mourned him, as any good wife would, but she could not bring herself to shed another single tear for him. She couldn't, she *wouldn't*, give him that power. He deserved no requiem, no remembrance, as far as she was concerned. And if she had the chance, she knew she would have twisted the knife in his gut all over again.

As soon as she returned home, she removed his bloodied wedding band from where it had been tucked into her bodice and tossed it into the drawer in the writing desk in her room where she had discarded her own wedding band years before. When the time was right, and when she was ready, she would properly dispose of them both. Only then, she knew, would she truly be able to move on from the darkness of her past. Only then could she live her life for herself, and no one else.

Theo found Evie's behavior strange in the days after their return home. He had expected her to mourn her husband's death with tears and lamentation, but he did not see her shed a single tear after his demise. In fact, she shed more tears for Howell after his burial than she ever did for Silas. He knew Evie well; she was not a cold and unfeeling person, so he thought her sudden aloofness to him and everyone else discomforting and concerning. She became rather cold and distant to him in the days after they came home, barely speaking, barely eating, and barely leaving her room. He had even assumed that they would be able to resume their relationship to its previous state before the storm of truth came and she was taken, but she did not seem interested in anyone or anything.

It was a humid day in mid-April when Theo found her sitting under a tree in the yard behind the Cunningham house, her back against the trunk and her long, curly auburn tresses blowing about her face in the wind as she became consumed with the book she was reading, *The Vicar of Wakefield*. He approached her slowly and cautiously, coming to a stop a few feet away from the blanket upon which she was sitting. Evie didn't look up from her book, but she could sense his presence.

"I thought I might find you here," Theo commented as he crossed his arms over his broad chest.

"And so, you did," she returned.

"...May I join you?"

Evie shrugged and turned a page in her book. "If it pleases you."

Theo sighed heavily as he took a seat next to her, crossing his legs and leaning his back against the tree. They sat in silence for several moments as she continued to read before he found the courage to speak.

"I wanted to give you something."

Evie slowly looked up, her brow arched in curiosity.

Theo reached into the pocket of his trousers and produced the small black leather-bound book that had once created an enormous rift between them. Upon seeing the journal in his grasp, Evie's face went pale and she shifted uncomfortably next to him. She looked at the object like it were a wild animal bristling and ready to attack her, and then looked to him.

"Take it," he said, holding it out to her. "It's yours."

Reluctantly, she took it from him and quickly tucked it away under her shawl as she looked away in embarrassment.

"You read it," she stated quietly.

Theo nodded and cleared his throat. "I did. While you were...away."

"How much?"

"All of it."

Evie shook her head and looked up to the sky. "Now you know everything there is to know about me."

Theo scooted closer to her on the blanket, but she seemed to shy away from his proximity. "I am glad," he said softly. "Now I finally know who Evie Scarborough is."

"Evie Porter," she corrected.

"Not any longer. You are a widow now."

A heavy silence fell upon them again as Evie tensed next to him, and Theo internally chastised himself for putting his foot in his mouth.

Of course, she knows she's a widow, you fool, he told himself. *You put the knife into him together.*

Searching for anything to change the subject, he peeked over her shoulder at the novel in her hands and chuckled under his breath. "How many times over have you read this book, hm?"

She shrugged again. "Maybe six or seven."

He sighed again. "Evie, I think…I think we need to talk."

"I disagree. There is nothing to talk about."

Theo placed a hand over her book, effectively blocking the pages from her sight. "Please," he said gently. "Put the book down and look at me."

Reluctantly, Evie tore her gaze from the book and looked up as she set it aside, her eyes roaming his face. She felt a twinge of guilt in her heart as she looked upon the healing bruises and lacerations upon his face, and she couldn't help but feel responsible for the torture he endured at Silas' hands once again. She felt so guilty, in fact, that she found it difficult to meet Theo's gaze.

"I did not get the chance to properly apologize…for the way I treated you just before…you left," Theo murmured as he stared into her eyes. "I said terrible things. I hurt you, I know I did. I'm so sorry."

Evie was quiet for a moment before she mumbled, "It matters little now. It is in the past. And I deserved every bit of it."

"No, you did not deserve it. I was too preoccupied with my own feelings to consider your own motives for what you did, and it was not fair of me to abandon you the way that I had. I hope you can forgive me…"

"There is nothing to forgive, Theo. I just want to forget any of it happened at all."

Theo furrowed his brow in concern. "You seem to want to forget a lot lately."

"Excuse me?"

"Are you angry with me? You have been cold and distant for days now. It is not like you."

"I have no reason to be angry with you," Evie snapped as she tried to reach for her book again.

Theo leaned forward and laid his arm across her torso to prevent her from doing so, bringing his face close enough to hers that their lips were almost touching.

"I killed your husband," he whispered. "And now you are angry with me."

Evie scoffed and turned her face away from his. "Why would I be angry about that? He was a monster. He deserved everything he got."

"He was still your husband. And your son's father. Do you really expect me to believe you feel nothing now that he is gone?"

Evie swallowed thickly and narrowed her eyes at him, feeling a confusing mixture of anger and sorrow boil in her blood. "I feel nothing for him. I always have. I am *glad* he's dead."

Theo's heavy gaze was determined and unwavering as he reached up and tucked a stray lock of her hair behind her ear. "No, you're not," he countered in a whisper. "You do not need my, nor anyone else's permission to grieve him, Evie."

"*Grieve?*" she snapped, suddenly jumping to her feet to stand over him. "You want me to grieve him? After all that he has done to me, to you, to Kensington, and everyone else? You expect me to *mourn* that beast?"

Theo slowly stood and held up his hands in a gesture of surrender. "I did not come to upset you. I am just worried for you. You have not been yourself since we returned."

Evie scoffed and turned her back to him. "I do not need you to worry for me. I can take care of myself."

"I know you can." Theo took a careful step toward her and stopped just behind her, placing his hands gently on each of her arms. "That is what I admire about you. Your enduring strength."

"Strength," Evie repeated sarcastically.

"I have never met a woman stronger than you. But you are still human. And I can see that you are hurting. Talk to me, Evie." He tried to lean forward to rest his chin upon her shoulder, but she shrugged out from under his touch before he could, whirling around to face him with an expression of agony upon her pale face.

"He does not get to hurt me anymore," she hissed through clenched teeth. "Not anymore."

"Of course. He can't hurt anyone anymore."

Evie shook her head and began to pace in front of him, her mind spinning in a hundred different directions, all of them leading to the pain that was festering in her chest. "No, you do not understand," she moaned quietly as she raised her hands to grip her hair.

"Then help me understand."

Evie paused mid-step and slowly turned to meet his gaze once more before her eyes fluttered closed and she let out a shaky, ragged breath that she didn't even realize she was holding. "If I allow myself to mourn him, to miss him, to grieve him, then he wins. So long as I feel anything for him, whether it be anger, hate, or love, he will always control me. He will always own me!"

"That isn't true, Evie."

Evie took several steps toward him until she was just a foot or so in front of him. "I can't give him the satisfaction of knowing, wherever he is, that he can still hurt me, even in death. I can give him no requiem. Not now, not ever."

Theo felt his heart crack when he watched a tear slip down her cheek, and without warning, he reached forward to capture her in his arms, crushing her against his chest. She hadn't the strength to fight against him, and she immediately fell limp in his arms, burying her face in his shirt as her resolve to remain stoic crumbled like an ancient wall and she began to sob into his chest.

"I'm sorry," Theo whispered as he ran a hand through her hair and held her head to his beating heart. "I am so sorry that I couldn't protect you…"

"How can he still cause me so much pain, even in death?" she asked through her tears. "It isn't fair! He was a bloody monster. So why do I feel so guilty now that he is gone?"

"Because *you* are not a monster, Evie. Even after all he has done, you still cannot bring yourself to hate him because he is your son's father."

"I just do not understand," she mumbled through her sniffles, "how fear and hate can be so strong in this world? Why must we always be so cruel to one another? Is that the world God meant to create, Theo? A world filled with greed, and hate, and anger, and suffering?"

Theo swallowed and rested his cheek against the top of her head. "I do not know much about God, but I do know there are some things we are never meant to understand. There are things we just endure because we have no other choice but to accept them…"

"It isn't right," she sobbed. "It isn't fair."

"Nothing about our world is right or fair. We've both learned that the hard way…"

After another few moments of silence only punctuated by Evie's occasional sobs and sniffles, she pulled away from Theo's chest and peered up into his golden-brown eyes. They were two large pools of comfort and contentment that she had once thought she would never have the pleasure of seeing again, but in that moment, they swallowed her whole until she became lost beyond reason.

"He had to die," she eventually choked out.

"So long as he lived, we were all in danger," Theo agreed. "There is a special place in Hell for men like him."

"You know," Evie mumbled as her eyes fell to the ground under their feet and she wiped at her eyes with the back of her hand. "For a brief moment, back at the fort, I thought I saw a shred of humanity in him. He told me about how he had lost his mother, and that he was never the same after that. For the first time in my life, I had seen him sober. He was a different man without the liquor, I could see it."

Theo's face tightened in discomfort as realization dawned upon him. "It could have been me, Evie. I could have become just like him. I could have become consumed by my sadness and anger, just like *him*."

"No," Evie said sternly, reaching up to place her hands upon his cheeks and forcing him to look her in the eye. "You are nothing like him. You will always be a stronger man than he ever was because you found a way to overcome the darkness in your heart. That is something that Silas could never do."

Theo's eyes seemed to be swimming with confusion as they stared at each other and a comfortable silence fell upon them. Nothing else needed to be said, as they both came to a silent agreement that there were no words in the King's English that could adequately describe the turmoil in their heads, nor the love in their hearts that still somehow remained steadfast in the face of the war raging on around them.

Theo eventually broke the silence as a smirk spread across his lips. "I only overcame it because I was waiting for someone like you to storm into my life and give me a reason to change."

"Storm in like a hurricane?" Evie asked playfully as she began to fidget with the ties on the front of his shirt.

Theo leaned down to press a gentle kiss to her lips, which she eagerly accepted, letting her hands slide up from his face to tangle in his long, dark hair.

"Like a hurricane," he confirmed with another smirk as he leaned down to plant a kiss on her forehead.

Before he could, however, they both snapped their heads up in alarm at the unsettling sound of a woman screaming and crying for help in the distance.

"Help me! Someone, anyone, please, you must help me! Please!"

Theo and Evie immediately circled around to the front of the house to find the source of the noise, and upon reaching the front yard, they found Mrs. Baker, Constance's mother. A tall and slender woman with dark raven hair like her daughter, Mrs. Baker was running wildly up the road, clutching at her chest as her eyes went wide in panic. She first came to Jacob and Emma, who happened to be walking along the path on their way home from visiting Emma's parents at the tavern. Theo and Evie quickly sprinted down the road to meet them and ascertain the cause of Mrs. Baker's distress.

Mrs. Baker immediately turned to Theo upon seeing him approach.

"Oh, Theo," she cried as she grabbed him by the shoulders, "You must help me. I am so worried!"

"What happened, Mrs. Baker?" Theo asked in concern.

"It's Constance," Emma answered as a solemn look came upon her face. "She's missing."

"She's *what?*" Theo stuttered as he and Evie shared a worrisome look. He and Evie had not seen nor spoken to Constance since their return from the fort some weeks ago, and he assumed she was actively avoiding them both after the words he had exchanged with her before he set out on his rescue mission.

"She's gone!" Mrs. Baker lamented, throwing her hands into the air. "She left the house last night without warning and I have not seen her since! Her father and brother have been looking for her all day, but there is no sign of her. What if something has happened to my girl?"

Theo placed a comforting hand on the older woman's arm at the sight of tears coming to her eyes. "Have you looked at the lighthouse and the beach?"

"Yes, and in every nook and cranny of the homestead. It's like she has disappeared!"

"I am sure nothing terrible has befallen her, Mrs. Baker. Perhaps she has just gone for a walk in the woods and forgotten her way."

"In the middle of the night?" Jacob questioned with a scratch of his head.

Theo gave Mrs. Baker a reassuring pat on her arm before taking Evie's hand. "Not to worry. We will help you look for her. All of us. And we will find her."

***

By the early evening, most of Division Point had been enlisted to join the search party for Constance Baker. The beaches and docks were scoured a second time over with no sign of her, as were the shops, the tavern, and the church. When those locations proved fruitless and the sun began to set, Theo and the others set out for the wilderness that bordered the homestead to the west under the assumption that she had gone exploring and somehow lost her way.

She had been missing for over half a day by the time dusk fell, and the Bakers were becoming more restless and more frantic with every minute that passed with no sign of her. It was very unlike her to venture anywhere on her own, let alone at night, and as the search dragged on into sunset, everyone began to assume the worst. Theories ranged from her getting lost and being eaten by some wild beast to her capture by straggling Redcoats or bandits. None of the scenarios playing out in anyone's heads were pleasant, and hopes of her safe return were beginning to wane.

Alongside the Bakers, Evie, Theo, Emma, and Jacob led the search effort. As much as Evie and the others disliked Constance's arrogance and selfishness, and as much as Evie resented her for stealing her journal and showing it to Theo, it did not bring her any happiness to think that something terrible may have befallen her.

"Only Constance would get herself into something like this," Jacob grumbled under his breath as he and Theo picked through the northern outskirts of the wilderness around the homestead. "She craves attention like she craves air to breath."

Theo nervously rubbed the back of his neck. "You think she got herself lost on purpose?"

"Anything to draw your attention now that you have returned home with Evie."

The shook his head doubtfully. "Not even Constance is that foolish—"

Jacob and Theo both froze at the sound of an ear-pricing scream traveling through the woods, shaking the trees and sending the birds scattering into the wind. Jacob spun around in alarm, feeling his heart leap into his throat.

"That sounded like Emma," he murmured fearfully. "Something is wrong."

Jacob took off through the trees in the direction of his wife's scream, and Theo followed closely behind. They came to a stop at the northern most edge of the wilderness, their stomachs churning at the sight of what lay before them. Emma and Evie stood before a large oak tree, clutching onto each other's arms as they stared up into the branches in horror. Emma had begun to cry hysterically as Evie held her in her arms and attempted to calm her, but she could not be consoled.

Before them, dangling from one of the lowest branches on the tree, was Constance Baker's lifeless body. A noose comprised of several silken shawls was wrapped tightly around her neck and to the branch, and a small stool was overturned in the dirt just under her hanging feet. Her eyes were closed to the world, her dark eyelashes in stark contrast to the pale and bluish complexion that had overtaken her once pretty face. Her thin body swayed lightly as a cool breeze blew through the trees, ruffling her skirts and her long raven hair. Other than the unnatural angle at which her neck was bent as a result of her own weight pulling against the noose, there were no signs of external trauma or injury upon her body. Her demise was, very clearly, self-inflicted.

"Oh my God," Jacob gasped, crossing himself with the sign of the Holy Trinity before rushing forward to take his wife into his arms.

Theo took several careful steps toward the tree, unable to tear his eyes from the sight of Constance's swaying corpse. The weight of one thousand bricks settled into the pit of his stomach as he felt the color drain from his face, and painful memories of his own would-be execution flashed through his mind. Evie remained frozen where she stood just a few steps in front of the branch, her hand clamped over her mouth as her eyes slipped closed in shock and disbelief at what she was seeing.

"How could she do this?" Evie whispered mournfully as Theo came to stand next to her. "*Why* would she do this?"

Theo swallowed thickly and ran his hand through his hair. As soon as he caught a glimpse of her body dangling just a foot or two above the ground, a rush of thoughts and explanations came to him as to how and why this could have happened. And every single explanation centered on *him*.

"Get her down from there!" Emma cried hysterically as Jacob forced her to turn and look away from the ghastly sight. "We can't just let her hang there!"

Theo tilted his head to the side in confusion as he surveyed the girl's body and noticed a folded piece of parchment tucked into her left hand, which hung lifelessly by her side. Gingerly, he reached up and plucked the paper from between her fingers, which, like the rest of her body, had begun to stiffen with the inevitable process of death. It was clear from the rigidity of her limbs, the coldness of her skin, and the pale blue of her complexion that it had been several hours since she took her last breath. The very thought that this girl whom he had once called a friend had been hanging alone for so long before she was found made Theo sick to his stomach.

Constance's flesh was frigid to the touch when his fingers grazed her own, much like, some would say, the heart beating in her chest when she was alive.

"What is that?" Evie asked in a whisper as Theo gently took the folded scrap of paper into his hands.

Evie looked over Theo's shoulder as he unfolded the scrap to find four words scrawled messily with ink in Constance's handwriting.

Tell them I'm sorry.

Theo quickly stuffed the note in his breast pocket at the sound of frantic footsteps approaching from behind. They turned to see Mr. and Mrs. Baker hurrying through the trees in their direction, followed closely behind by Alistair, Johanna, and several other homesteaders that had joined the search several hours ago. Upon seeing her daughter's lifeless body hanging from a noose as she broke through the trees, Mrs. Baker let out a harrowing shriek, dropping immediately to her knees as her husband tried and failed to catch her in his arms.

"Constance, no!" she bellowed as she clutched at her chest in agony and tears of mourning streamed down her face.

Her worst fears had been realized. *Everyone's* worst fears had been realized.

***

Constance Baker's funeral was short, but widely attended by every member of Division Point. At her family's request, she was buried in a pine casket next to the church in her favorite lavender dress, such that she would enter into Heaven looking her finest, just as she would have wanted. Though Constance had a reputation for vanity and indifference, her death came as a complete shock and devastating loss to everyone in the community. As Alistair had explained in his eulogy, she had spent her entire life in Division Point, just like Theo, Emma, and Jacob, and it would always be her home. No one at the funeral, not even her parents, had a plausible explanation as to why Constance felt the need to end her own life, at least not anyone that was willing to speak up in that moment.

Theo knew exactly why she took an early exit from this world many years before her time, but he could not bring himself to look her family in the eye at the funeral and confess to them that he felt he was to blame for their daughter's suicide. They had lost enough already.

"I do not understand." Evie mumbled under her breath as she stood before Constance's freshly covered grave many hours after the funeral had ended. "I do not understand why she would do this to her family…"

Theo, who was standing by her side, knelt down before the grave and placed a hand upon the front of the headstone.

Constance Anne Baker, it read.
12 July 1757—19 April 1779.
A wonderful daughter and an even more wonderful friend.

"This wasn't about her family," he said solemnly.

"How do you mean?"

Theo hung his head as memories of the last conversation he had ever had with Constance played through his mind. An overwhelming sense of shame, guilt, and regret overtook him with enough force to make his stomach churn and his hands shake as he knelt before her grave.

"She did this for herself, no one else."

"Even after all she has done, I would never wish this upon her," Evie murmured as she crouched at his side and placed a hand on his back. "It just pains me to know that we will never know why she did this."

Theo swiped a hand down his face and stared at the ground. "I know exactly why," he grumbled bitterly. "It's *my* fault."

"What? How can you possibly think that?"

"Because it is!" he snapped as he rose his feet. "I caused this. I did this!"

Evie slowly stood and watched in concern as Theo began to pace in front of the gravestones before them. "You cannot blame yourself for her decision to take her own life, Theo."

"You don't understand. You weren't there when I said what I said."

"What are you talking about?"

Theo paused mid-step and turned to face her, his head hung in shame. She could see the tension in his chest building as his hands clenched into fists at his sides. "After you were taken, she approached me at the beach. She told me she was the one who had informed Silas of your location. And that she did it because she loved me. But I told her that I could never love her after what she had done. I told her that *no one* could love her after what she had done."

Evie took a stunned step back, feeling as if she had just been slapped across the face.

Gulping, she asked, "*Constance* did that? She…she is the reason Silas found me? She is the reason you had to risk your neck to rescue me?"

Theo nodded slowly, his voice lowering to a weak whisper. "I told her I could never forgive her if anything happened to you. That no one could ever love her after the evil things she had done. But I never thought my words would hurt her so deeply. I never thought she was capable of this…"

"Constance Baker may have done evil things," Evie murmured as she scanned her eyes over the gravestone, "but she was not an evil person. She was troubled, and she was fighting her own private battles that none of us could have ever known."

"I pushed her to it," Theo argued as he felt his eyes begin to burn with guilt. He had known the girl since they were young children, and she had always been a bit hard to like, but he would have never wished such misery on her. "She just wanted to be loved. And I rejected her time after time after time. Until she broke."

Evie stepped forward and placed her hands on his shoulders as she stared resolutely up into his eyes. "No one could have known until it was too late. You will drive yourself mad with guilt if you allow yourself to shoulder the blame of every injustice in this world."

"But I—"

"Theo, this was Constance's decision, and her decision alone. In her mind, she believed that if she couldn't have you, then she couldn't have *anyone*. But we both know she is in a better place now. A place where she will never be hurt nor rejected again."

Theo was still unconvinced, and his heart continued to ache painfully in his chest. In his head, he contemplated every interaction he had ever had with Constance, every word exchanged, every rejection of her flirtations and advances, and every look of disappointment upon her face when he rebuffed her. But never once until now had he considered the fact that with every time he flippantly waved her off, he had been chipping away at her heart, one little piece at a time until there was nothing left to keep her alive.

"I could have been kinder to her," he mumbled sorrowfully. "But now I will never have the chance."

"We *all* could have been kinder. And you cannot carry this blame alone. What of the note we found with her body, Theo? 'Tell them I'm sorry.' This was not about you and you alone."

Theo suddenly began to dig around in the pocket of his shirt until he produced the crumpled scrap of parchment carrying her last testament. He hadn't really ruminated upon its meaning, nor had he really considered who 'them' was supposed to be. That is, until now.

"She was talking about us," he realized aloud as he looked down upon the paper in his hand.

"The guilt of what she did overcame her," Evie agreed solemnly as she reached to intertwine his fingers with hers.

"I didn't think she was capable of feeling guilt, after all she had done to tear us apart…"

Evie rested her head against his arm and squeezed his fingers. Looking up to the sky, she took a deep breath and searched the clouds. Her heart had felt heavy in her chest ever since they had discovered Constance's body, but now that the restless girl had been laid to rest and was on her way to Heaven's gates to find what she could never have on earth, Evie felt peace. She was no longer angry, no longer spiteful, no longer hateful. She did not have enough energy in her body to hold onto any more hatred. Not towards her father, not towards Silas, not towards Constance.

As she took the parchment with Constance's last words from Theo's hands and held it to her heart, she looked to the Heavens and whispered, "All is forgiven."

Chapter 11

Only Us

May 1779

E vie felt her jaw go slack and her heart leap into her throat as she looked into Emma's excited eyes. "You…you're what?" she asked in a stunned whisper.

Emma leaned forward in her chair and reached across the table at which they were sitting in the Cunningham's parlor, taking Evie's hand in her own with a wide smile threatening to split her face in half.

"I am with child," Emma repeated, nearly squealing with glee.

Evie jumped to her feet and rushed around the tea table to throw her arms around her friend in excitement. "Oh, I am so happy for you," she murmured into Emma's curly blonde hair. "You've been wanting to start a family for so long."

Emma sighed in contentment and placed a hand upon her belly. "Jacob and I have been husband and wife for nearly three years now. I was beginning to wonder if God would ever bless us with a child."

"How far along are you in your pregnancy?"

"Dr. Thorn told me ten weeks."

Evie paused in confusion and raised her brow. She, Theo, and Jacob had only returned from the fort a little over a month ago. "You were pregnant before Theo and Jacob left for Dumpling Rock," she stated with a twinge of guilt in her heart.

Emma nodded, looking down at her lap. "I did not realize I was with child until after Jacob had left…but I told him as soon as he returned. We decided to wait a while before telling everyone else the good news."

Evie squeezed Emma's hand affectionately before pouring her another cup of tea, looking for a way to distract herself from the thoughts dancing in her head. If anything had happened to Jacob on her account at the fort, especially now that she knew he was to be a father, she would have never forgiven herself.

"How did Jacob take the news, hm?"

Emma nearly rolled her eyes with a giggle. "He was a little taken aback at first, I will admit. But he is just as elated as I."

"Jacob never struck me as the kind to want to marry and have children so young."

"Oh, you don't know him like I do. He likes to pretend that he has no weaknesses, but behind closed doors, my husband is one of the sweetest and most caring men I have ever met."

Evie smiled gently and crossed her arms over her chest as she thought back to her time of captivity in Dumpling Rock, and the brief moment of tenderness that she had shared with Jacob in which she had seen a gentle side of him he had never shown her before. It was in that moment all those weeks ago that she realized she and Jacob had never truly been enemies. They had been allies along, but they were both too stubborn to see it.

"If it were not for Jacob, and for Daniel Howell, Theo and I would still be trapped in that fort."

"I will be honest with you, Evie. When Jacob told me that he was leaving home with Theo to rescue you, I begged him not to go. And while he was gone, I was so afraid something would happen, and he wouldn't return. I was terrified I would be a widowed mother at only twenty-two. But now that you are back home as well, I could not be more grateful that he went."

Evie flashed her a warm grin as she took her seat across the table once again. Chatting over tea with Emma was one of her favorite activities, and they had grown closer than ever once she returned to Division Point from the fort. It was as if she had never left, and now that she was back, Emma seemed to have forgotten all of the secrets that Constance revealed that had separated them in the first place.

"I am glad he went too," Evie said with a morbid chuckle. "I do not know how much longer I could have endured being Silas' prisoner again."

A saddened look came upon Emma's face as she slowly rubbed her belly. She was far from showing her condition, but she had already developed the habit. "I'm sorry we couldn't have protected you, Evie. I could not imagine how terrible it must have been for you to go back to him."

Evie cleared her throat before looking away and nervously playing with her hair. "It matters little now. It is in the past. And he is gone. None of us need to fear him any longer."

Emma hesitated before asking lowly, "What is it like to be a widow?"

Evie snapped her eyes up from the ground in mild irritation. Emma was nothing if not slightly oblivious to common social cues. "It is a relief, I must admit. I do not need to live in fear of my life any longer."

"Most important of all, you can marry Theo now."

Evie nearly choked on her tea, spitting it back into her cup and sputtering wildly as she tried to recollect herself and shake off the blood that she could feel rushing to her face. "Emma!" she whined. "Silas has barely been deceased for two months!"

"I know, I know. I just thought that…well, you and Theo always look so happy together. And with Silas gone, you are free to remarry anyone you choose."

"Well, I suppose," Evie stuttered with a flustered shake of her head. She could feel her face growing hot with embarrassment. "But I am nowhere near ready to consider a second marriage."

"Not even to Theo?"

Evie gave her friend an exasperated look over the table. "Perhaps when the time is right."

Emma giggled and clapped her hands in delight. "Oh, you and Theo are perfect for each other, Evie. I've never seen Theo happier than when he is with you. You'd make each other so happy as husband and wife. And you would make the most beautiful babies!"

Evie's face grew even redder as she stared at Emma across the table. She would be lying to herself and everyone else if she claimed she hadn't pictured herself married to Theo at least once in the past. The thought of being his wife and the mother of his children made her heart flutter in her chest, but she also knew that she could not possibly take on that role at this point in time. She was only twenty-two, and freshly widowed. It wouldn't be proper to move on so quickly. It wouldn't be right. What would her father and everyone back in Boston say if they were to find out? She shook her head at that thought—she didn't give a damn what anyone from her past would think about it anymore. They were in the *past*.

But then there was the matter of Theo himself. He had never once expressed an interest in marriage or children in the entire time she had known him, and he had never struck her as the type to want to settle down long enough to have a family. With those thoughts now running through her head, Evie let out a heavy sigh and rested her chin in her palm.

"I want nothing more than to spend the rest of my life with Theo," she murmured. "But the thought of becoming someone's wife again terrifies me to my very soul."

Emma passed her an empathetic look and reached across the table again to squeeze her hand. "I understand. But you know Theo would never hurt you like Silas did."

Evie shook her head. "That is not what I am concerned about."

"Then what?"

"Theo isn't the marrying type. Nor the fathering type. I know he loves me, but I fear that he would never want to marry me."

"Evie, do not be ridiculous. Theo isn't the same wild, reckless, and impulsive chap he was years ago. He will come around to it. Just give him time. Neither of you are ready now, and that is perfectly fine."

"I suppose so."

Emma's face brightened as an idea came to her suddenly after looking down at her stomach. "Well, there is one way to ensure he will marry you sooner rather than later."

"And what might that be?"

"Become pregnant with his child. He won't have a choice but to marry you then!" Emma cackled wildly.

Evie, quite unamused, rolled her eyes up to the ceiling after flashing Emma a deadpanned look.

"Emma, I love you dearly, but I think it is time for you to go home."

***

July 1779

"Where are you taking me?" Evie asked with a giggle as she pulled against Theo's hand. It was well past midnight on a hot summer night, and the moon was high in the sky as it shone its silver light down upon the waves of the Massachusetts Bay. Theo had convinced her to sneak out of the house once Johanna, Alistair, and Gunner were fast asleep, but she was beginning to question his motives once they reached the beach and he continued to lead her past the docks.

"You ask too many questions," Theo said cheekily over his shoulder as he gripped her hand and pulled her along the beach.

"You do not answer many," she shot back.

Theo rolled his eyes up to the sky and squeezed her hand. "You will see soon enough."

Evie's eyes roamed over the sand under her feet as Theo led her wordlessly along the shore, past the dock at which *The Liberty* was anchored, until they had ventured far past the usual stretch of beach to which she was accustomed to roaming. Following the curve of the shoreline, they trekked under the overhanging cliff on which the Division Point lighthouse was perched, until they came upon a small mountain of jagged rocks. Theo chivalrously helped Evie up and over the rocks by climbing over them first and then offering his hand to her.

On the other side of the rocks, they were greeted with the sight of a small paradise hiding underneath the overhang of the cliff, bathed in a silvery wash of moonlight from high up above. They had come upon an inlet, an indentation in the shoreline hidden behind a large mass of rocks that jutted out into the sea to create a small inlet bay and an accompanying beach isolated from the rest of the ocean. A tiny expanse of smooth sand extended out into the waves before them, free from any jagged rocks, driftwood, or other sea-born refuse that the rest of the beach typically displayed. The beach was pristine, seemingly untouched for many years, save for the small driftwood hut that had been erected against the face of the cliff.

"What is this place?" Evie asked past the breath that caught in her throat.

"My private little paradise," Theo murmured as he took a few steps forward into the sand.

"I thought that was Mariner's Cove."

Theo shook his head. "No, no. That's everyone else's paradise. This is mine. I found this little alcove many years ago when I was exploring. I am the only one who comes because no one else cares to climb over the rocks to get here. Nobody knows of it, save for me…and now you."

"It's beautiful. It looks as if it hasn't been touched in years."

Theo scanned the small stretch of beach as a contented sigh escaped his lips and a gentle nighttime breeze began to blow through his hair. "I have not come here in some time. Not since you first arrived here."

Evie took a few steps forward to stand by his side, lacing her fingers with his once again. "And why have you shown it to me now?"

"The timing was not right," he answered smoothly. "But it is now. I've trusted you with all of my other secrets, haven't I?"

"You have."

The slightest of smirks came upon Theo's face as he leaned down until their lips nearly grazed each other. "Come with me," he whispered as he kissed the back of her hand and led her across the sand to the driftwood hut tucked against the cliff's face.

The hut was small and crudely built, thrown together with driftwood, nails, and scraps of rope salvaged from the rigging of a fishing vessel. The roof was comprised only of the remains of an old canvas sail, and the floor was nothing but sand, but it comfortably housed two once they both ducked underneath the canvas roof to sit. In the center of the sandy floor was a fire pit that had not been ignited in years.

After ensuring that Evie was seated comfortably, Theo wasted no time in scraping together the embers and twigs in the pit and igniting them with the flint he had stashed in his pocket. The inside of the hut quickly became enveloped in a warm, orange glow as the small fire came to life and they both made themselves comfortable sitting cross-legged next to one another.

"This place is beautiful," Evie repeated as she leaned over to rest her head upon his shoulder. "Thank you for showing me."

"My pleasure."

A comfortable silence fell upon them in that moment as they both enjoyed each other's company in the warm glow of the fire that roared at their feet. Over the tips of the flames, they stared out toward the end of the beach, taking in the sounds of the water lapping against the shore, the smell of the salt in the air, and the sight of the stars in the sky up above. If there was one word that Evie would use to describe how she felt in that moment, nestled up against Theo's side on their own little private beach, hidden far from the war that was raging in the world outside their door, it was *peaceful*. She had never felt so peaceful in her life as she did in that moment.

Another sigh of contentment escaped Theo's lips as he wrapped his arm around her shoulder and slowly ran his hand up and down her arm, leaning his head against her own and taking in the delightful smell of her hair. He gave her a gentle kiss on the top of her head, and she turned to look up at him, their eyes meeting for a brief moment before she reached up to press a kiss to his lips, which he hungrily returned with his hand sliding down her arm to grip her waist and the other coming to rest upon her neck. Their eyes slipped closed as the kiss deepened for several blissful moments, until Theo suddenly pulled away with a devilish glint in his eye and a mischievous sideways grin upon his face.

"What is it?" Evie asked skeptically, slightly out of breath and a little disappointed that he had pulled away so soon.

"I have an idea," he said smoothly, getting onto his knees without warning and crawling out of the hut. He crouched just outside the hut's entrance and motioned for her to follow. "Follow me."

Evie rolled her eyes and reluctantly got on all fours to crawl across the sandy floor and out onto the beach. Theo extended a hand to help her to her feet as she brushed the sand from her skirts. After flashing her another smirk and a cheeky wink, he led her out to where the sand kissed the water of the bay.

"What are you doing now?" Evie asked in confusion.

Without a word, Theo turned his back to her and went about quickly unbuttoning his shirt, shrugging out of it and tossing it to the side with a flourish to leave him in just his boots and trousers. In the pale light of the moon overhead, Evie could still make out each individual muscle in his broad back as they rippled under the long, jagged scars that ran across his spine. The scars had faded considerably over time, but they were still there, still noticeable, still a permanent reminder of a memory best left forgotten in the annals of Fort Dumpling Rock.

Evie raised a brow skeptically, feeling her cheeks begin to tinge pink when, with his back still turned, Theo kicked off his boots and then made quick work of his trousers, tossing all of his clothing to the side before slowly turning to face her. Evie swallowed thickly, her face flushed hot, as she took in the sight of the silvery light of the moon playing off of the curves and planes of his naked body.

"What are you doing?" she stuttered, looking over her shoulder nervously for any sign of watchful eyes. "Put your clothes back on! Are you mad?"

Theo chuckled breathily and raked a hand through his hair to toss it out of his face. "Peace, Evie. I told you no one knows of this place. No one will see us."

"*Us?*" she repeated incredulously with an anxious squeak. "You expect me…to…to *join* you in your nudity?"

Theo chuckled again. "That *is* the idea, yes."

Evie took a step back with a shake of her head when he took a step toward her. She tore her eyes from his body before they roamed any further south and crossed her arms over her chest in stubborn defiance. "No, no, no, no. I will not! You are simply mad if you think I will undress outside…in public!"

Theo outstretched his arms at his sides and looked around. With a smirk, he said, "I see no public here. All I see is…us."

Evie swallowed again as her face continued to burn in embarrassment. She knew she should not have been shocked or embarrassed to see him this way, as she had done so many times before, but tonight, it was different. They were not in the privacy of *The Liberty's* captain's quarters, or behind the closed doors of a bedroom. They were on a *beach*! A good and proper lady did not make herself indecent outside the confines of the bedroom. Especially not outdoors. It was ludicrous!

"And what exactly do you think we will be doing, if I do undress, hm?" she asked with a curious tilt of her head.

Theo shrugged innocently and pointed toward the inlet bay. "A little night swimming, perhaps?" The idea may have sounded innocent enough, but the mischievous glint in his eye was anything but.

"You know I cannot swim."

"Then we will wade out only as far as you can stand."

"And what if we are caught?" Evie squeaked. "What if someone sees us? What will your parents think if they catch us in such an indecent position?"

Theo chuckled again and waved his hand dismissively. "You care too much of what others think of you, Miss Scarborough."

Evie almost cringed at the sound of her maiden name before she realized that it was indeed her name once again. It felt strange to hear him call her as such, especially since he had formerly known her as Evie Green for so many years.

"Will you join me for a swim, or not?" Theo asked somewhat impatiently, planting his hands upon his hips.

Evie deliberated for a moment before slowly shaking her head, although his body did look more and more enticing in the moonlight the longer that she stared at it. "No," she mumbled with another shake of her head. "You go ahead."

Theo shrugged his shoulders and turned away. "Suit yourself," he mumbled flirtatiously over his shoulder before he padded through the sand and began to wade into the bay. The waters were unexpectedly warm on his bare skin, considering how late in the night it was, but it was a welcoming sensation as he slowly emerged himself in the water, first up to his knees, and then up to his waist, before he stopped and turned back to face the shore.

Evie was just where he'd left her, lingering on the edge of the sand with her arms crossed stubbornly over her chest as she stared at him across the water.

"It sure is lonely out here," he called out to her. "Such a large bay for only one man."

Evie rolled her eyes and returned, "I can go fetch Jacob to join you if you like!"

Theo's face fell in annoyance. "I'd rather have a woman to keep me company. Perhaps one with red hair and freckles."

"Oh, you must mean the seamstress, Mrs. Thatcher? It is a bit late, but I am sure she will accept your invitation if I go and fetch her. She is a lonely old widow, after all."

Theo groaned in exasperation and slapped his hands against the water at his sides. "Evie…"

Evie smirked in satisfaction and batted her eyelashes at him in an innocently coquettish fashion. "Yes?"

Theo narrowed his eyes at her and arched his brow, beckoning her to come to him with a crook of his finger. "Join me. Please," he said softly, his voice low and as smooth as silk. His command was firm and confident, yet gentle and coaxing, the silkiness of his tone slowly breaking down her resolve and the walls she had tried to build around herself.

Evie let out a slow, shaky breath before turning her back to the water and undoing the ties on her corset with trembling fingers. After tossing her corset to the side, she let her skirts fall around her ankles and her blouse hang open, revealing her flesh to the salty night air just as another cool breeze blew through and sent a wave of goosebumps across her body. She could feel Theo's hungry eyes upon her back from almost thirty feet away as he waited, rather impatiently, for her to turn back to face him. With her skirts, blouse, and corset gone, Evie slowly turned back to face the water and tiptoed to the very edge of the sand, her shift billowing in the wind around her legs just as the tide came in to lap at her toes.

Their eyes met across the water for a brief moment and he beckoned her forward again with an expectant raise of his eyebrows. She swallowed thickly as her fingertips searched for the hem of her underclothes, and with one fluid motion, she lifted the shift over her head and let it fall into the sand behind her. Out of instinct, she immediately crossed her arms to cover her chest as she began to shuffle forward, letting out a quiet squeak at the sensation of the water slowly enveloping her.

A pleased grin spread across Theo's face as Evie came to meet him in the water, and he opened his arms to her as she looked down in nervousness. The water stopped just below his waist, but he was over a head taller than she, so by the time she reached him, she was submerged to just below her breasts. Theo gently took her by both of her wrists and pulled her arms away from her chest so that he could see every inch of her, and he felt a flood of warmth travel over his body at the sight before him.

"Beautiful," he whispered as he pulled her into his body, hooking his arms around her waist to hold her against him. "I think you are beautiful."

Evie stared bashfully up at him from under her eyelashes and placed her hands upon his smooth, hard chest. "The feeling is mutual," she mumbled as she began to chew on her bottom lip.

Theo smirked as his hands slowly traveled up her sides to cup either side of her neck before he leaned down to gingerly kiss her. "I missed this," he whispered as he pulled away and rested his forehead against hers. "You have no idea how terrified I was that I would never be able to do this again."

"Do what?" she asked with a cock of her head.

"Touch you. Hold you. See you, like this, so completely vulnerable to me and *only* me."

Evie's hands slid up from his chest to tangle in his hair, her eyes slipping closed as a contented sigh escaped her lips. "Only you," she repeated breathily before resting her head upon his chest and opening her eyes to look at the multitude of stars shining above their heads.

She untangled her fingers from the dark tresses that fell just past his shoulders and ran her fingertips up and down his spine, reveling in the way that his body tensed against hers when she grazed the scars that swathed across his broad back.

They stared up at the midnight sky in comfortable silence for many moments before Evie spoke. She could feel herself becoming overwhelmed by the beauty of the stars shining down from above; she had never seen a night sky so clear, so pristine, so unblemished by the sights, sounds, and smells of her former life as a British-American aristocrat's daughter. Perhaps the sky had always been that beautiful, but she was only now able to see it, without the clouds of her past hanging over her head.

"The stars are beautiful tonight," she commented absently. "I cannot remember a time when the sky was so clear."

Theo's chest rumbled under her cheek as he chuckled. "They pale in comparison to you."

"I could never see them so well back in the city. Too many distractions, too many clouds of smoke from all of the chimneys."

"You mean your father's mansion in Boston? I would kill to catch a glimpse of the city from a place like that."

Evie snapped her head up to meet his eyes. "It may have been a mansion to some, but to me, it was a prison. It did not matter how many people came or went, or how big the estate grew, I was still alone it. I was still a prisoner."

Theo's expression softened as he watched the storm of emotions swirling in her eyes, and he pressed a kiss to her forehead. "You'll be no one's prisoner ever again. Not so long as I have a heart beating in my chest."

"Do you promise?"

Theo hugged her tightly against him, enveloping her in the warmth of his body and his heart. "I swear it."

Despite the fact that she was bare to the world, standing chest deep in the waters of the Massachusetts Bay, Evie had never felt safer. "It seems too good to be true," she whispered as she nestled her head against his chest. "I have forgotten what it is like to live my life without constantly looking over my shoulder."

"That is called *freedom*."

Evie chuckled lightly. "Then call me free."

"We will all be free soon enough. The tides of the war turned in our favor after Saratoga. The end of this bloody war is in sight. I can feel it."

"Do you really think that will change anything? With the British gone, will anything really be different? Or will the rich continue to grow richer off the backs of the downtrodden while the poor only grow more destitute?"

Evie looked up again to see Theo's eyes momentarily harden before he looked up to the stars. He searched the sky for an answer to her question, the very same question that had been burning in his own heart since the beginning of this bloody conflict. He knew how he truly felt, but now was not a time for pessimism.

"If there is a God out there, He will see to it that this would be nation is forged in the fires of justice."

Evie nodded in solemn agreement, trying desperately to swallow the trauma and the pain that followed her husband's name. "We are one step closer now that my husband is…gone."

Theo cleared his throat uncomfortably. "Silas Porter is exactly where he belongs."

Evie shook her head with another pensive sigh. "Most men would not be so willing to have a woman who has been dishonored as I have."

"You were not dishonored when Silas raped you," Theo corrected sternly. "In my eyes, your honor rests not with a woman's body, but in her heart and her mind. All of which I find to be rather spectacular in your case."

Evie almost smiled. "I wish the rest of the world saw women the way you do."

"Maybe someday it will."

Another silence fell upon them for several minutes as they both looked back to the stars, but it was Theo who decided to speak first this time, in an attempt to draw the subject away from Evie's tortured past. "When I was a young boy, my father would take me up to the lighthouse late at night and we would count the stars. He taught me the constellations, and how to use the stars to navigate the sea. We would spend hours making pictures in the sky…"

Evie smiled gently and pressed her cheek to his chest, longing to have even one fond memory of her own father—the very father that had abandoned her time and time again. "That sounds so lovely."

Theo's body became tense against hers as his face and voice fell in disappointment. "That was before I found out the truth. About who I was, about what my father had done. After that, everything changed. Things were never the same between us after I learned the truth."

Evie wrapped her arms around his waist and squeezed him tightly. "They do not have to be different. You can reconcile with your father. You can start things over with him. You probably do not have much time left until—"

Theo pulled away slightly. "Until what?"

"Well, until…until Alistair…"

"Until he *dies*?" Theo snapped.

"Theo, his health has been declining over the last year. You and I both know that. With his coughing and his fatigue, I just fear that he does not have much time left."

Theo released his hold on her and pulled away further, his face twisted in a sudden burst of conflicted anger. "My father is *not* dying."

"I did not say that. That is not what I meant. I just meant—"

The held up a hand to cut her off, shaking his head with a heavy sigh. "I know what you meant," he mumbled softly.

Evie reached out to intertwine her fingers with his, feeling rather flustered by how upset he had become. "I did not mean to upset you. I would just hate to see something happen to him before you two have settled your differences…"

Theo squeezed her fingers and pulled her back into his chest, his expression softening as he looked down upon her. "I do not want to talk about me anymore. Or my father. Or my past. This is about us right now. Only us."

Evie relaxed in his arms as he leaned down to kiss her again, only to let out a startled squeak when he suddenly planted his hands on her hips and effortlessly lifted her into the air, holding her against his chest as she locked her legs around his waist. She threw her arms around his neck and held on for dear life when, without warning, he began to wade through the water in the direction of the beach while he held her against his body.

"What are you doing?" she stuttered nervously as they returned to the sand.

Theo did not answer, but instead dropped to his knees just in front of the driftwood hut, placing her on her back in the sand before leaning over her and straddling her waist. She stared up at him in mild surprise, her eyes wide and her face flushed. Even in the dim light of the moon now obscured by the overhanging cliff, she could see the hunger and wanting in his eyes. They had not been together like this in months, not since the truth of her past had come to light and not since she had been reclaimed by Silas. He hovered above her and leaned down to plant a deep, hungry kiss upon her mouth, his hands tangling in her hair and roaming up and down her sides.

She was breathless when he pulled away after what felt like an eternity, and she gripped his strong arms with all her might as he settled himself between her legs. She could already feel sand in places sand was not meant to be, but she couldn't bring herself to care as his eyes and hands continued to roam across her body, taking in the feeling of every curve, dip, and freckle he could find.

"I love you," he murmured as he pressed a kiss to the skin just above her heart.

"How can you?" she breathed, raking her fingers down his back when she felt their bodies unite for the first time in many long months. "After everything I have done? After all of the lies and—"

"Hush," he growled in her hear, effectively silencing her fears and worries when he rocked his hips against hers and sent her mind reeling in ecstasy. His words were raspy and came between heavy breaths as he asked, "What did I just say?"

"You love me."

"And that is all that matters. Us. And only us."

"Only us," she repeated in a ragged whisper whilst she looked up to the stars and he planted feather-light kisses up and down her neck.

***

The early morning sun was warm upon Evie's skin, gently coaxing her awake to the sounds of gulls squawking and waves lapping lazily at the shore. She cracked an eye open as she gathered her bearings, only to discover that she was curled up on her side on the floor of the driftwood hut. She could feel Theo sound asleep behind her, his arm draped over her hip whilst he nuzzled his face into her neck. Slowly, she turned onto her back and sat up, gingerly placing Theo's arm at his side so as not to wake him.

The flames of last night's campfire had burned out long ago, leaving behind hot embers in the fire pit just a few feet to her left. Upon looking down to examine herself, she realized that at some point in the night after she had fallen asleep, Theo had draped his shirt over her otherwise naked body but did not feel the need to cover himself before he drifted off to sleep next to her. Her long auburn tresses were a tangled mess, matted with sea water and sand as they fell down her back in waves. Her body was sore, but not in an unpleasant way. The aches she felt were welcomed remnants of the night before—a consummation of an outlawed love she would follow to the ends of the earth.

Evie turned to gaze upon Theo's face as he slept undisturbed next to her. His lips were just barely parted, and his eyes were gently closed, displaying his long dark lashes against his tawny cheeks. She envied how peaceful he seemed to sleep; there was no pain, no fear, no worry evident on his face. If he was having a nightmare or reliving some terrible memory, she could not see it in the sleepy expression he carried. A smile came to her face as she reached down to brush a lock of hair from his eyes and press a kiss to his forehead.

After watching him sleep for several minutes, she slowly rose to her knees and crawled out of the hut in search of her own clothes, which she had abandoned somewhere in the sand the night before. After a few moments of searching, she found her skirt and blouse in a crumpled heap down by the water, but she was not really in the mood to dress. She was quite comfortable in Theo's shirt, which nearly hung down to her knees, and nothing else. Just as Theo had said, their little cove was isolated from the rest of Division Point, hidden behind a wall of rocks and tucked away underneath the overhang of the cliff. No one could see them, and no one could hear them. If they had decided that day to shut everything out and never leave the cove, the rest of the world would have been none the wiser.

Evie crouched down in the sand and searched through the pockets in her skirt until she produced the item she was looking for, thankful it hadn't been lost in the fray of her tearing her clothes off the night before in the heat of unbridled passion. Breathing out a sigh of relief, she gazed down at the golden chain sitting in her palm, on which both her and Silas' gilded wedding bands were strung. Silas' ring still bared the bloody smudges from his fateful encounter with Theo and Howell in the clearing outside of Fort Dumpling Rock, and perhaps a month or two ago, she would have felt a twinge of pain in her heart upon looking down at the last remains she had of her departed husband. But now, as she looked upon the gilded chains that had once bound her to her past, she felt nothing.

Evie closed her fist around the pair of rings and rose to her feet before shuffling across the beach until her toes met the water. She looked out to the sea, a calm and contented breath escaping her lips as she raised her fist into the air. A cool morning breeze rolled in from the east, blowing her hair about her face as she reared her arm back and opened her fist to toss the chain and its rings as far into the Bay as she could manage. The chain hit the water with a tiny splash, giving out one last glint in the sunshine before it sunk beneath the surface of the water some fifty feet from the shore and was quickly taken away with the rolling tide.

She felt the weight of a thousand bricks lift from her shoulders when she watched the rings disappear below the waves—the last remnants of her old life, the last reminder of a past she was ready to forget. She jumped when she suddenly felt a presence just behind her, and she turned to see Theo approaching from behind, having just awoken and spending the last few minutes watching her from the hut. He was now dressed in only his trousers as he pressed his chest to her back and wrapped his arms around her waist, resting his chin atop her shoulder and following her gaze back out to the horizon. He had awoken just in time to see her toss her marital shackles into the sea, and he could not help but feel a sense of pride swell in his chest at the sight.

"How did you sleep?" he asked lowly in her ear.

Evie tipped her head back to rest it against his chest, folding her hands over his own. "Not well," she admitted cheekily. "I did not sleep much at all, actually."

She felt him smirk into her neck. "My apologies, Miss Scarborough. I did not mean to keep you awake."

"I am sure you will find a way to make it up to me."

A smile tugged at the corner of her lips at the sound of her maiden name upon his tongue. There was nothing more freeing to her in that moment than to come to the realization that she no longer needed to carry with her the crushing weight of her husband's name, a name she never wished to carry in the first place. And just as the rings were carried away with the tides, so too were Silas and Evie Porter. They were both dead now, never to be seen again. She was no longer just someone's wife or someone's daughter. She was her own person now, free to carry with her whatever moniker she pleased. She was not Evie Porter, and she was not Evie Scarborough. From that day on, she was just *Evie*.

***

November 1779

The remainder of summer quickly came and went, ushering in a quiet and uneventful autumn. With little activity in the homestead other than the everyday comings and goings, the residents looked to the newspapers coming from Boston, Plymouth, and New York for the latest news on the war. Despite his frequent coughing fits and failing health, Alistair made it a habit of collecting the latest edition of *The Boston Gazette* and standing atop the church steps to recount the news to those in the homestead who congregated before him. With the coming of fall came the news of an American-led massacre of native villages in Newtown, New York in retaliation for native raids on colonial settlements, as well as a failed attempt by the Americans to recapture Savannah, Georgia.

Despite the apparent setback in Georgia, most of the Patriot-minded folks in the colonies were confident that the Crown's days were numbered.

It was not new information that the tides of the war had turned in the Patriot's favor in the aftermath of the Battle of Saratoga back in '77, and the residents of Division Point, along with everyone else in the colonies, were growing restless for an end to the bloodshed on their soil.

The end is near, the newspapers promised. King George's army will fall. It was only a matter of time.

With little news of the war coming in towards the end of autumn, Emma's pregnancy became the focus of the homestead's attention, with everyone making the necessary preparations to welcome the newest member of Division Point into the world, come December. Emma was overjoyed to be the center of attention for months on end, but as she progressed near the end of her pregnancy, she became quite physically uncomfortable and anxious, resulting in a very moody young woman that nearly everyone soon wanted to avoid. When she was not obsessing over what to name the child, or whether she was having a girl or a boy, she was fretting about how much weight she had gained and how terrible she would look after the child was born. And then Evie made the terrible mistake of describing to her in detail the horrific pain of childbirth, and this sent Emma into even greater distress.

Not even Jacob was able to calm her riled nerves as the last months of her pregnancy came and went, so on one cool November afternoon, Evie decided to invite Emma on a walk around the homestead in order to take her mind off of her pre-natal anxieties. Emma had begun to experience an uncomfortable contracting in her womb, a symptom Dr. Thorn had assured her was just a sign of her pregnancy coming into its final few weeks. The good doctor thus prescribed a daily walk to alleviate her discomfort, and Evie was happy to join her.

"I have never felt so ugly in my life," Emma whined as she rubbed her massive belly and shuffled down the path that wound through the homestead. "Why didn't you warn me about how ugly I would be?"

Evie chuckled and shook her head, lacing her arm around Emma's. "You could never be ugly, Emma. And you had to have known your belly would grow. You watched it happen to me, for Christ's sake."

"Yes, but…but *this* big?" Emma extended her arms out to exaggerate the size of her rounded womb. "I am as big as a house, Evie! Jacob will never look at me the same again after this…"

"Don't be ridiculous. You are his wife and the mother of his child. He will love you to the moon and back no matter what your pregnancy does to your body."

Emma scoffed and waved her hand dismissively. "All men say that, until the child comes, and the love-making ends forever."

"Just try to take your mind off of it. I know better than anyone what worrying can do to you as you await the birth of your child."

A humble silence fell upon Emma for several moments before she cleared her throat and lowered her voice to a whisper. "…Evie?"

"Hm?"

"I'm afraid."

"Afraid of what?"

Emma halted mid-step and turned to face her friend. "I saw what happened…with you and Noah. I saw what it did to you, when you lost him. And…I'm afraid…the same thing will happen to me."

Evie tensed by Emma's side, her eyes falling to the ground. She was quiet for a moment as she searched the path under her feet for the words that always seemed to escape her when she tried to articulate the agony she felt when she put her baby in the ground.

"You have nothing to fear, Emma," she said quietly without looking up. "God would not let that happen to you or your child."

Evie tried to turn and continue walking, but Emma caught her by her arm and forced to look her in the eye. "He let it happen to you. Why would He spare me?"

Evie swallowed thickly, plastering a smile on her face that she knew Emma could see right through. "Our pregnancies were very different, Emma. You have been healthy and happy all the way through. Your child is strong and healthy, too. Please do not waste your time worrying about something like that."

As Emma looked into Evie's eyes, she could see the storm of sadness her friend was holding back. "I'm sorry, Evie. I should not have brought it up. I know how hard it is for you to discuss…"

Evie shook her head and motioned for them to continue walking. They had reached the end of the path and were just a hundred yards or so from the tree line that bordered the homestead. "It is alright. It has gotten easier with time."

Emma rubbed her belly worriedly. "I am so sorry you had to endure that. No parent should ever have to bury their own child. It isn't right."

Evie placed a comforting hand on Emma's shoulder. "I wouldn't wish it on my worst enemy. But that will never happen to you. You will give birth to a happy, healthy child, and you and Jacob will raise that child together and live the rest of your long lives with your perfect little family."

Emma giggled lightly. "You think so?"

"I know so."

"And what about you?"

"What about me?"

Emma raised her eyebrows suggestively. "You'll have a perfect little family someday too, won't you?"

Evie felt her cheeks tinge pink as she nervously chuckled. "I want nothing more than to have a family someday, just like any other woman."

"With Theo?"

Evie rolled her eyes up to the afternoon sky and groaned. "Emma! We've had this conversation before…"

"*Months* ago! And you are telling me that nothing has changed?"

"I've said it before, and I'll say it again. I would love to have a family with Theo. But now is not the time. We are not ready. I do not even know if Theo would *want* to have a family…"

"He would with you."

"How could you possibly know that?"

"I see the way he looks at you. Everyone in Division Point sees the way he looks at you."

"And how does he look at me?"

Emma paused as a gentle smile came upon her face. "Like he worships the ground you walk upon. Like he would die for you."

Evie looked away in embarrassment as she felt her stomach flutter and her heart skip a beat. "Really?"

"I've known Theo since we were children. I've never seen him look at another woman the way he looks at you. *Of course,* he wants to have a family with you. But he's too prideful to admit it, I'm sure. Like any other man."

Evie giggled childishly and began to play with a lock of her hair as she kicked at the ground. Nothing made her heart pound more than to think of her future, which seemed so much brighter now that the only man she could see on the horizon was Theo. She hadn't let herself admit it until now, but as she watched Emma's pregnancy progress, and as she saw how happy she and Jacob were together, anxiously awaiting the arrival of their bundle of joy, Evie had become more and more anxious to find that happiness for herself.

"Do you think he'd ever propose to me?" Evie asked in a near whisper.

Emma chuckled. "Surely he will. He just hasn't found the courage yet."

Evie furrowed her brow skeptically. Theo was the most generous, caring, and compassionate man she knew, but she had a hard time picturing him as anyone's father or husband. She had always seen him as wild, untamable, and unshakable. He had told her many times how much he loved her, but never once had he hinted that he desired anything more than what they had right now.

A wave of sadness overcame Evie as that realization hit her. Was this all he ever wanted? A wordless agreement of commitment, sealed with physical intimacy and whispers of promises that would never actually be? Would he ever allow himself to commit to her with anything other than his word? Or did he intend to keep her as his mistress forever?

Evie's troubling thoughts were interrupted when Emma suddenly gasped and froze where she stood, grabbing ahold of her belly before doubling over in pain.

"Emma! What happened? Are you hurt?" Evie rushed to her side and took ahold of her arm, her face pinched in concern.

Emma winced as her womb painfully contracted, much like it had been doing all day, only this time, the pains were much more intense. "My stomach…"

"I'm sure it is just contractions. Here, come sit."

Evie tried to lead her across the path to take a seat on a fallen tree trunk nearby, but upon taking one step, Emma collapsed to her knees and wrapped her arms around her belly, moaning in pain. "Something's wrong," she whispered anxiously. "It hurts…"

Evie crouched down at her side and rubbed her hand across her friend's back. "It's alright. They are normal pains, I'm sure—" Evie paused when she looked down to see a large wet stain on the front of Emma's skirt. "…Oh, God."

"What? What's happening?" Emma asked in alarm through clenched teeth.

Evie looked up to meet Emma's panicked stare, hiding nervously behind a comforting smile. "Stay calm, Emma. Everything will be alright."

"What is happening? Why am I in so much pain? Is something wrong with the baby?"

Evie let out a deep breath and smiled. "Nothing is wrong with the baby, Emma. Your water has just broken. You are in labor."

"What? Labor? That can't be possible! The baby is not supposed to come until December!"

"Sometimes they come early. Come now, we must get you back home. Can you walk?"

Emma shook her head with a grimace as another contraction rolled through her.

Evie climbed to her feet and pointed toward the homestead. "Stay here. I will go fetch Jacob, Theo, and Dr. Thorn."

Evie turned to hurry down the path, but Emma reached out and caught a fistful of her skirt as tears of pain and fear began to run down her face. "No, don't go! You can't leave me here!"

"Emma, we have to get help—"

Both girls jumped out of their skin when a loud growl and the rustling of leaves and twigs reverberated from the tree line just a few yards away. Evie slowly lowered down to her knees at Emma's side and wrapped a protective arm around her shoulders.

"What was that—?" Emma started to ask.

"Shh!"

They both fell silent as the trees and bushes continued to rustle, followed by another growl that sounded much closer than the last. After a moment, a large, black, four-legged creature slunk out of the shadows between two trees and sauntered towards the path, teeth bared.

The girls froze in fear, their hearts leaping into their throats as the creature revealed itself to be an enormous wolf with a solid black coat of fur shining in the light of the waning sun. Emma let out a terrified squeak, causing the animal to growl at them once more and slowly approach. Evie positioned herself in front of Emma's body, holding her arms up at her sides in order to block her from the wolf's line of sight. Emma continued to moan quietly behind her, biting her lip to keep from screaming as the contractions continued to intensify.

"Don't make a sound," Evie whispered over her shoulder. "Don't move a muscle."

"I...I can't..."

Evie's heart pounded against her ribcage as the wolf locked its amber eyes upon them both and bared its fangs once again before taking several more creeping steps in their direction. After sniffing the air, it started to tread a large predatory circle around them, never once taking its eyes off of them. Every nerve was alight in Evie's body as she remained frozen on her knees in front of Emma, her eyes following every move of the wolf as it continued its hunt. The wolf paced several circles around them before edging even closer, until only three yards or so separated it from its would-be prey.

"Evie...the baby is coming..." Emma whispered painfully, fighting back tears. "It hurts so much..."

"Stay calm. If you make a move or a sound, it will attack us—"

Without warning, an ear-piercing shriek was ripped out of Emma's throat as another agonizing contraction coursed through her, loud enough to shake the surrounding trees and send the wolf into a frenzy of growling and snapping jaws.

The wolf's entire body stiffened defensively before it charged forward, fangs glinting in the late afternoon sun. Evie squeezed her eyes shut and tensed, preparing herself for the onslaught of pain as the wolf latched its jaws around her neck. But the pain never came. After a moment of silence, she cracked one eye open while remaining completely frozen to see that the wolf had skidded to a stop just a few inches in front of her. Its nose was so close to her as it sniffed her that she could feel its breath on her face, and she stared so deeply into its amber colored eyes that she felt she was looking into the soul of a beast. Emma whimpered fearfully behind her while biting down on her lip and cradling her womb, an action that once again set the wolf on edge and prompted it to growl with teeth bared.

The wolf shifted its weight between its feet before rearing back with a ferocious snarl and arching its back to lunge forward in attack. Evie threw her arm up in front of her face as Emma let out another fearful shriek, both preparing for a horrifically bloody end to come. But before they could feel the sting of the beast's jaws clamping into their flesh, a single gunshot exploded just over their heads and shook the earth under their feet.

Chapter 12

Demons

November 1779

As the gunshot exploded overhead, the wolf snapped its jaws once more and let out an angered howl. Its attention was momentarily drawn from the girls to the source of the thunderous noise, and it suddenly leapt forward, skirting around Evie and Emma to charge at the presence approaching from behind. Evie looked hurriedly over her shoulder to see Theo and Jacob sprinting down the road, muskets in hand after being alarmed by the sound of the girls' distant screams.

Jacob quickly reloaded his musket after firing off the first shot as a warning to the creature, but the wolf was not the least bit intimidated as it began to sprint toward the two men coming down the road. Evie and Emma each let out another fearful shriek as the wolf charged at their men, coming within ten feet or so of them before Theo and Jacob each rang out a shot. The wolf immediately collapsed to the ground at their feet with a pained yelp, twitching and writhing for several painful moments before it eventually bled out from the two bullet wounds in its belly. Theo and Jacob did not bother to check to confirm the creature was dead before they hurried the rest of the way down the road and dropped to their knees at Emma's and Evie's side.

"What happened?" Jacob asked frantically as he wrapped his arms around his wife. "What are you two doing down here?"

"We were just taking a walk," Evie murmured, still in shock from her brush with death. "That thing came out of the trees…and it tried to—"

"You should not have wandered this far on your own," Theo scolded. "Especially not with Emma's condition! You could have been killed!"

"Are you hurt?" Jacob asked Emma gently as he placed a hand on her belly.

Emma shook her head, panting, "The baby…the baby is coming…"

All of the color seemed to drain from Jacob's face as he and Theo shared an alarmed look. "That can't be so! It isn't time yet!"

Emma grabbed ahold of Jacob's collar and pulled him in close. Through gritted teeth and narrowed eyes, she growled, "Tell that to the baby trying to rip me apart, you lobcock!"

Jacob held up his hands in a gesture of surrender. "Alright, alright. We have to get you home, then. Can you move?"

"No!" Emma wailed as she fell forward onto her hands and knees and then collapsed onto her side. Jacob reached down in an attempt to lift her into her arms, but she protested with another howl of pain before pushing him away.

"She can't give birth here on the side of the road!" Evie cried.

Theo shared another concerned look with Jacob before he looked around and scrambled for a solution. With no cart or wagon in sight, and with her unable to be carried without agonizing pain, there was no way to move her from the side of the road before she gave birth.

"She's going to have to," Theo stated sternly, his voice strained with worry. "I'll go fetch Dr. Thorn."

***

Dr. Thorn came immediately to the end of the road upon Theo's summons, followed closely behind by the O'Hara's and the Caldwell's, as well as Johanna. Emma's labor was fast and hard, and within several minutes of Dr. Thorn's arrival, he deemed her ready to start pushing. Sprawled out on her back in the grass on the side of the road was the last place Emma wanted to be when she gave birth, but she was so consumed by the hot flashes of pain ripping through the lower half of her body that she no longer cared where she was or who was around to see her private parts, which were now bared to the world as she began to push. While Dr. Thorn and Johanna were crouched between her legs to catch the baby, Jacob remained up by her head to hold her hand and shower her with words of encouragement that she was too agonized to hear. Evie and Theo were crouched on her left, and the Caldwell's and O'Hara's comforted her from her right side.

Whereas Evie could recall the birth of her son taking a few hours but feeling like an eternity, Emma's child was so determined to come into the world three weeks early that she barely had to push before everyone's ears were greeted by the angelic sound of an infant's first cries. Emma collapsed back, her head falling into Jacob's lap with a relieved cry when she heard her baby's startled shrieks. Jacob looked down upon her with adoration and brushed a lock of blonde hair from her sweaty forehead.

"You did it," he whispered with an uncharacteristically gentle smile. "You did it, my love. Our child is here."

After severing the umbilical cord, Dr. Thorn held up the newest addition to the homestead, a screaming, wiggling little thing still covered in blood and fluid, for everyone to see. "It is a boy," the doctor announced with a proud smile. "And he has the lungs of a giant!"

"He is so…small…" Jacob commented in worry.

"He is small," Dr. Thorn agreed as Johanna took the child into her arms and then placed him on Emma's chest. "He came three weeks too soon. But he is strong and healthy."

Emma and Jacob shared a jubilant look before looking down at their son in awe. Upon being held against his mother's breast, the baby's shrieking cries immediately quieted into a contented cooing. He was perhaps the smallest baby that the homestead had ever laid eyes on, but he was perfect in every way, with milky pale skin and a surprisingly thick head of dark brown locks reminiscent of his father's.

"He's so beautiful," Emma murmured through a renewed onslaught of tears. "How could we have created something so perfect?"

"God has blessed you," Mrs. O'Hara said with a tearful smile.

"What shall you name him?" Evie asked.

Emma looked up in thought for a moment before sharing another look with her husband, who nodded to her in approval.

"Levi," she said after a moment of deliberation. "Levi Jacob Caldwell."

Evie held a hand over her heart and giggled giddily as Theo wrapped an arm around her shoulders and held her to his side. "It suits him," Theo said to Jacob. "I can already see he looks just like you, my friend."

"For his sake, I hope not," Jacob chuckled as Emma reached up to allow him to hold his son for the first time.

Evie looked upon the happy couple and their bundle of joy with a wide smile upon her face, feeling a warm sensation of happiness spread through her chest the sight. She had never seen Emma or Jacob look happier than they did now as they welcomed their little one into the world, and she couldn't have been happier for them. But as she watched them dote on little Levi while Theo also watched on and held her close to his side, she couldn't help but feel a twinge if jealousy in her heart. Until she saw Emma holding her own child, Evie had never realized how much she wanted that for herself, and how much she wanted to have that with Theo. She had told herself and others that she wasn't ready to be a wife or a mother again after all she had endured with Silas, but the truth was that she wanted nothing more than to start her life over and build the family she never had.

Soon, the joy she felt in her heart for her friend was overcome with an intense envy. Why did Emma have everything she had ever wanted, and how did she seem to obtain it so effortlessly? Was Noah's death an omen of things to come? Was she not meant to have children of her own? And who is to say Theo even wanted the same things as she? Would he even want to have children with her, if she could? Did he want to spend the rest of his life with her, as she did with him? All of these questions and many more began to swarm in her head like a hive of angry bees, but she was far too terrified to ask him, worried that her worst fears would be realized in a matter of moments.

Evie swallowed thickly and looked up to see Theo staring affectionately down at her, rubbing her arm as a sideways smile came to his handsome face.

"They look so happy, hm?" he asked as he gestured to the new parents.

"So happy," she agreed.

Theo chuckled and leaned down to kiss her temple. "They certainly are lucky, aren't they?"

"Yes," Evie said with a feigned smile. "So very lucky…"

***

February 1780

Baby Levi's birth ushered in a period of much needed joy in Division Point after many months of loss and heartbreak. Levi was a charming little thing, with big green eyes and a toothless grin that could melt even the steeliest of hearts. And while he left an impression on anyone and everyone who met him, he seemed to leave the greatest impression upon Theo, who stopped by at the Caldwell home almost every day for the first three months of Levi's life to see the baby and chat with the new parents. Evie found it a little strange how interested Theo became in the baby so quickly, as he had never before given off the impression that he was overly fond of children, but she quickly learned that the opposite was, in fact, true. This new discovery filled her with an inexplicable joy and renewed hope that he would want a family with her in the future, but she still could not bring herself to actually *ask* him about it herself.

In fact, she was starting to grow a little impatient that he himself had not broached the subjects of marriage or children with her, considering they had been together for nearly three years and had shared so much together in that time. In her mind, they had become *de facto* spouses long ago, as they did many of the things a husband and wife did already. They shared a bed, they shared their secrets and their desires, and they had expressed their love in a physically intimate way more times than she could count.

So, it greatly confused her as to why he had not proposed to her yet, or even hinted at the idea of marriage. Not only was it confusing, it was also worrisome. For as long as she could remember, Evie had dreamed of being a wife and a mother, of raising a happy family in a happy marriage in a home that actually felt like hers. And now that all of those things seemed to be within reach, Theo appeared to be dragging his feet on taking their relationship forward.

"He may be content with having a mistress for the rest of his life, but I am not," Evie commented to Emma one February afternoon when the latter decided to stop by the Cunningham house to show off baby Levi once again, who was now nearly three months old.

Emma sighed heavily and handed the baby over so that Evie could hold him in her arms. They were sitting alone in the parlor while Johanna busied herself in the kitchen and Alistair and Theo went to the yard out back to chop firewood.

"Have you tried *talking* to him about marriage?" she asked as she leaned back in her chair in the parlor.

Evie slowly shook her head and smiled down at the baby, who reached up with his chubby little hands to try and grab onto a lock of her hair. "How could I, Emma? I do not want to frighten him away."

"You will never know unless you ask. And besides, Theo does not frighten easily."

"It isn't that simple. Theo is the best thing that has ever happened to me. If I were to drive him away with talk of marriage and children before he is ready, I will lose everything. No, I must wait for him to bring it up…"

Emma nearly rolled her eyes at her friend. "And what if he never does? Suppose he comes to you tomorrow and tells you he wants nothing to do with marriage and children. What would you do?"

Evie looked between Emma and the baby and swallowed nervously. She had tried her hardest not to think of that very scenario for months now.

"I…I would be devastated, I suppose. But I would learn to live with it."

Emma furrowed her brow in confusion. "You would give up everything you ever wanted to be with him?"

Evie looked down at Levi's round, cherubic face. He had opened his eyes from a little nap a few minutes ago and now beamed up at her, cooing happily. She felt her heart swell in her chest at the sight of his purity and his innocence, and she secretly wished that it was her own child she was holding instead of Emma's.

She swallowed thickly again before quietly answering, "Yes. I would."

***

Unbeknownst to anyone else, Theo was not that oblivious to the wordless signals Evie had been giving him the last few months. He could see the longing in her eyes whenever she looked upon Emma and Jacob with their son, and he could sense the discontentment in her disposition whenever the subject of family and children was brought up in discussion in her presence. He knew she longed to be a mother and a wife, but he also knew how horrifically devastated she was when her first pregnancy ended in disaster. He could never live with himself if he fathered a child with her that also met the same fate as Noah; that pain and guilt was something he wouldn't wish on his worst enemy, let alone on the woman he loved.

He had given her and everyone else the impression that he had no desire to marry or have children, and perhaps five years ago, that would have truly been the case. But he was a different man now than he was when he and Evie had stumbled upon one another in the New England wilderness, and now that he had lived nearly twenty-four years on this earth, he was finally starting to realize what he wanted in life. And what he wanted was *her*. He wanted her completely and whole-heartedly. He wanted to father her children, and he wanted her to take his name. Nothing would have made him happier than to spend the rest of his life with her, and he kicked himself for not realizing it sooner.

But those dreams and desires were being held prisoner in his heart by a crippling fear that he was never meant to have such happiness. He was terrified of repeating his father's mistakes and somehow doing something to break Evie's heart or lose her trust, and he was terrified of relapsing into his old self and going back to the bottle when things got rough. But most of all, he was terrified of cursing his offspring with his temper, his complexion, and his mixed blood. And he had yet to find the courage to tell Evie, nor anyone else, of these crippling fears that had kept him up for countless nights, for fear that he would drive her away with the burden of his sorrows.

"You know, none of us are getting any younger," Alistair commented dryly as he sat on the back steps and watched Theo finish chopping the firewood that same afternoon. "I would like to see a grandchild before I die."

Theo resisted the urge to roll his eyes up to the sky. Tossing his axe to the side, he wiped the sweat that had been accumulating on his face despite the chilly temperatures. "You have many years left to live, old man."

Alistair let out a wet, raspy cough into his fist, one loud enough to cause Theo to furrow his brow in concern. "I would not be so sure. I can feel my health failing me. Why can't you be more like Jacob and settle down with a wife and children soon? That way I can die knowing you've found a woman who's tamed your wild ways."

Theo planted his hands on his hips in annoyance. "Surely you mean Evie to be that woman, hm?"

"Well, I don't see any other women beating down our door to have your children."

"Enough talk of children," Theo snapped. "I do not want to discuss these things with you."

"You won't discuss them with me, with Johanna, or with Evie. Who else, then?"

"There is nothing to discuss." Theo raised the axe to strike down on the last chunk of wood to be chopped, but his father cleared his throat to get his attention. Looking over his shoulder, he could see Alistair beckoning him to come with a crook of his finger.

"Sit," his father commanded sternly, pointing to the empty space on the stairs next to him.

Theo hesitated, but eventually tossed the axe onto the ground and took a seat next to the older man, wrapping his coat tightly around himself to ward off the cold. It had been the coldest winter he'd ever seen, and snow was still falling even as they approached March.

"You don't want to have a family of your own?" Alistair asked after a moment of tense silence.

Theo's eyes fell to the snow crunching under his boots and he nervously began to play with his hands. "That isn't it, Father. I'm just…I don't know…just…" His thought trailed off into silence when he could no longer find the words.

"You're afraid," Alistair concluded simply.

Theo scoffed. "I've survived a multitude of battles against the strongest army in the world and narrowly escaped death on more occasions than I can count. I am not afraid of anything anymore."

Alistair raised a skeptical brow and chuckled, slapping a hand on Theo's back. "Those things may have been harrowing, but they pale in comparison to facing your own demons."

Theo swallowed and let out a long sigh, looking at his father from the corner of his eye. He may have been stubborn, but Alistair was even more so, and he was not likely to let this matter go anytime soon. "I have more demons than the average man, I suppose," Theo eventually admitted with a lowered head.

"I am not proud to say that I created many them, my son. But I'm afraid that only you can conquer them now."

Theo sighed again and shook his head. "And how can I? How can I possibly make anything of myself when I am haunted by what came before me?"

"How do you mean?"

Theo turned to face his father and slowly looked up to meet his wizened gaze. Alistair could see pain in his son's eyes, and it broke his heart to know he was responsible.

"I know Evie wants a family. And I want that too. More than anything. But…how can I live with myself if I subject her to the life of misery she will face if she becomes my wife?"

Alistair furrowed his brow again. "I do not understand."

"You understand *exactly* what I mean, Father. When you met my mother, the first thing to cross your mind had to have been what the rest of the world would think of your relationship. You had to have known that you would be shunned by both your world and hers because your tryst with her was outlawed, shamed, and forbidden."

"Of course, I considered that. But at the time, I did not care what the world thought of me. And I did not think you cared, either."

Theo jumped to his feet and began to pace through the freshly fallen snow in front of the steps. "I already know what the world thinks of me, and it isn't likely to change. I'm a bastard, an abomination, and a half breed dog. Why would any woman lower herself to take my name?"

Alistair shook his head sadly. "You know that no one here would ever think of you that way. Especially not your family. Especially not Evie."

"The moment Evie committed herself to me, she committed to a lifetime of ridicule. A lifetime of shame."

"It's obvious that none of that matters to her. And it should not matter to you. She made her choice long ago, and that choice was you. She loves you, Theo. She does not care what the rest of the world has to say. The world outside is cold and cruel, and we do our best to cope with it. And do you know how we do that?"

"No."

Alistair pointed a finger at his son. "We find that person we know will love us for who we are and nothing else. Someone who looks past all of our flaws and all of our mistakes and sees us for the men we were meant to be. I found that with Johanna. And you found that with Evie. So why are you still so afraid to accept it?"

Theo looked off into the distance and shook his head. "You do not understand."

"Then help me understand, son."

"I can't!" he growled, turning on his heel to face his father. "You will never understand what it is like to walk around with a target on your back as a privilege of the color of your skin. You will never understand what it is like to know that you curse everyone with whom you are associated with your very presence! And do you know the worst part of it all? My own father did this to me by bringing me into this world. You cursed me! You did this!"

Alistair fell silent for several long moments, his eyes falling to the ground in shame and regret. Theo immediately regretted his choice of words, but it was too late to take them back. He was angry and afraid, and he just wanted someone to understand. To *listen*.

"I know what you want me to say," Alistair eventually mumbled after another long coughing fit, "But I do not regret bringing you into this world. I never did, and I never will."

Theo swiped his hand down his face and let out a long, deep breath to recollect himself. "The thing I fear the most is bringing children into this world that will only hate me for cursing them with my blood."

Alistair's eyes slipped closed for a moment as he folded his hands in his lap. After a few moments, he sighed and said, "I implore you not to make the same mistakes I did, then, my son. I made the mistake of raising you to know only one half of who you are, and in the process, you have become ashamed of it. That is not right. And for that, I am sorry. Just like you, any children that you father will also carry your heritage, and there is nothing you can do to change that. You are, and will always be, a son of the English, and a son of the Mohawk. And because you cannot change it, you must embrace it. Embrace who you are. Teach your children to love and embrace who they are. Teach them what I never taught you."

Theo swallowed thickly and looked away, taken slightly aback by the warmth in his father's normally stern voice. He had never heard the man speak such words before, and he would be lying if he said it did not lift his spirits.

Alistair made an attempt to stand from the steps, but was overcome with another coughing fit that nearly doubled him over. Theo rushed to his side and wrapped an arm around his slumped shoulders. The corners of Theo's mouth twitched upward ever so slightly as their gazes met.

"Let's get you inside, Father. You'll catch your death if you stay out here any longer."

***

April 1780

The decision he had made weighed heavily on Theo's mind as the snow melted and the world began to bloom into spring. He knew what his parents would say; he knew they would discourage him, argue with him, rebuke him. But he didn't care. He'd been living under the shadow of the unknown for far too long, and he needed answers.

Though he didn't want to admit it, he could see Alistair's health decline with each passing day. Alistair was into his fifty-second year on this earth, and as the weeks and months went by, his friends and family could see that he was beginning to move slower and with more difficulty. His coughing only became more frequent, and he found himself short of breath with even the most moderate of activity. And being the man that he was, Alistair refused to ask for help in the things that had once been so routine but were now the most laborious of tasks.

Theo had known for many years that his father had not told him all there was to know about his mother, Kateri, or the circumstances that led up to their forbidden affair. He also knew that the old man was withholding valuable information as to why she really abandoned him, and where she could be found. Theo had spent most of his life resenting the woman that gave him life, while also growing more and more curious as to who she really was. He craved to know where she came from, and by proxy, where *he* came from. He could not go on any longer straddling two different worlds while one of them remained just out of reach on the other side of the horizon. He had been sometimes both white and native, and sometimes neither, the waters of his identity muddled by the confusion of his shadowed conception.

It was not fair. Everyone else around him had the privilege of knowing both halves of what made them whole, but not Theo. He was forced to grow up with only jagged and scattered shards of his past, following the pithy clues that Alistair fed him about his mother throughout his life. But now, he had to find those missing pieces so that he could feel whole for the first time in his life. He had to know who he was. He had to find the answers to his never-ending questions, and he had to hear *her* side of the story. He had to shine light on the enigma that was his maternal heritage, if not for his own sanity, then for the children he hoped to bring into the world in the future.

His heart pounded in his chest and his stomach churned as he shuffled across the house and into the kitchen on a cool April morning, in search of the man and woman he knew to be his parents. He had risen before the sun, much earlier than normal, and had left Evie still asleep in his bed upstairs. He found Alistair and Johanna exactly where he expected to, in the kitchen, where the aroma of hot porridge cooking in the hearth originated and began to waft throughout the house.

Theo paused stiffly in the doorway, watching silently for several moments as Johanna stirred the porridge and Alistair read a newspaper at the table. They both looked up when they sensed his presence.

"Oh, Theo, you have risen quite early," Johanna commented.

"The end must surely be coming if Theo is up before the sun," Alistair croaked with a cheeky smirk.

When Theo failed to return with a quip of his own, but instead remained in the doorway in stoic silence, Alistair's smile faded.

"What is it, son?" he asked.

"We need to talk," Theo returned quietly.

"Do we, now?"

Theo nodded and Alistair gestured for him to join him at the table. After taking the pot of porridge off of the hearth, Johanna took a seat with them.

"What troubles you, dear?" she asked worriedly.

Theo took a long breath through his nose, his eyes roaming the surface of the table as he searched for his words, which seemed to have suddenly escaped him now that he was sitting under the heavy gaze of the people that had raised him.

Slowly, he looked up and locked eyes with his father. "I want to find my mother. And I know you can help me."

A tense silence fell upon the room as Alistair shared a confused look with Johanna and then leaned back in his chair, folding his arms over his chest. Evie, who had risen just a few moments ago, shuffled down the stairs in her nightgown and paused in the doorway when she saw them sitting at the table.

Alistair was quiet for a moment before he cleared his throat. "And what brought this on, may I ask?"

"I am tired of living in the shadow of your secrets. I want to know who she is. I want to know who *I* am."

Johanna dropped her head with a sigh as Alistair looked pointedly at his son. "You are Theo Cunningham. Nothing will change that."

"I have to know, Father. I have to know where I come from. You've kept me in the dark for too long. It isn't fair."

"We've kept you distant from your native heritage for a reason. To protect you."

"From what? The truth of your mistakes?"

"From disappointment and heartbreak. You would surely be shunned by her people on account of your mixed blood," Alistair snapped, his voice stern. "Your mother and I agreed that it would be in your best interest for you to stay as far away from her and her people as possible."

Theo scoffed, feeling the blood under his skin beginning to boil. "My best interest? Or yours?"

Alistair's eyes narrowed dangerously as he said, "Watch your tongue. Remember to whom you speak."

"I'm speaking to a selfish coward," Theo hissed, slamming his fist upon the table. "You didn't keep me from my mother to protect me. You did it so that you would not have to face your mistakes."

"Enough." Alistair returned. "This conversation is over."

Theo shoved his chair back and jumped to his feet before leaning over the table and pointing a finger in his father's face. "This conversation is not over. I've spent my entire life listening to your sanctimonious preaching, while you silence me and keep me in the dark. But I am not a child anymore. I deserve to know both halves of who I am. So, I am going to talk, and *you* are going to listen…"

Alistair's brow furrowed in anger as he stared at his son. "I'm listening," he eventually mumbled.

Theo let out a breath to collect himself before saying, "Did it ever occur to you that I would want to know her? That I would want answers? Did it ever occur to you that I would not want to live my life in a state of constant confusion?"

"I did not know what else to do," Alistair admitted sadly. "Your mother wanted me to stay with her in her village, but I knew I had to return to Johanna. You would be shunned and outcasted by her people if you stayed with her…"

"I have been shunned and outcasted everywhere I go," Theo snapped. "Try another excuse."

Alistair slowly rose from his own chair and stared Theo down from across the table with eyes alight with anger and regret. "I have never met a more ungrateful excuse for a man in my life," he growled. "Everything I have done, I have done for you!"

"Then prove it," Theo returned coolly, outstretching his arms at his sides in a challenging manner. "I want to find my mother. I know you know where she can be found."

"I will not entertain these grandiose ideas, Theo," Alistair grouched. "I cannot let you risk your life to seek out a woman who may or may not even be alive. I haven't the faintest clue where she could be now, and I won't allow you to waste your life chasing after her throughout the entire frontier."

"Was it not you who had told me not so long ago that I should be unashamed of who I am? That I should embrace it?"

"You may embrace it from the safety of Division Point. And this isn't about shame. This is about protecting you from disappointment in the event that you never find whatever it is you are looking for."

"I do not need you to protect me! I am a man now!"

"And suppose you do find her and her people? What will you do then, when they become hostile, or when they cast you aside as a white outsider? They will not accept you as their own—that is why we kept you away. You know nothing of their culture, nothing of their language, nothing of them."

"And I have you to thank for that," Theo hissed coldly.

"Why can you not be content with what you have here? Why must you continue to push, and push, and push, past the point of no return? You have a family and a community that loves you here in Division Point. Why is that not enough for you?"

"Because this family is built upon a bed of lies."

Alistair stormed around the table to stand chest to chest with his son, pointing a finger in his face. "I will hear no more disrespect from you. Am I understood?"

"What are you so afraid of?" Theo challenged. "Are you afraid I will learn of some terrible secret you hoped would never come to light? Or are you afraid that I'll realize you aren't the saint you claim to be?"

"Stand down, boy," Alistair growled under his breath, leaning forward until their noses were almost touching as the vein in his neck began to throb with rage. He could not remember the last time he had been so angry with his son, and he did not like feeling as if he was about to lose control. But for the first time in a long time, Theo was pushing him past that point. "Do not give me a reason to rectify your behavior."

"And what will you do? Beat me with your belt? I am not afraid of you, nor anyone else! I deserve to know my mother. Tell me where her village is and how I can find it! Tell me! You owe me that much!"

Johanna suddenly stood from her seat as well, her voice uncharacteristically mousy as she said, "There is no reason for you to go out seeking disappointment, Theo. You do not know anything about this woman, or if she even wants to be found. Listen to your father. He knows what is best for you."

Theo scowled in her direction. "I used to think so. But now I am not so sure he does."

"You do not need to invite that woman into your life after all of these years," Johanna said pleadingly, her eyes becoming red with tears. "God gave you to me to raise for a reason. I have loved you as a mother for all of your years when no one else did."

Theo swallowed thickly in anger before coldly telling her, "You may be my father's wife, but you are *not* my mother."

He regretted the words as soon as they left his lips, and he could feel his heart ache at the look of hurt that immediately flooded Johanna's eyes as she gasped and turned away from him. Her body began to tremble with quiet sobs, but before Theo could open his mouth to speak again, Alistair was upon him, seizing him by the collar and slapping him so hard across the right side of his face with the back of an open hand that he stumbled sideways into the nearest wall. Evie let out a gasp of surprise from the doorway and hurried into the kitchen, but before she could get to Theo, Alistair had trapped him against the wall.

Theo raised a hand to cradle his throbbing cheek and slowly looked up to meet his father's gaze, both sets of eyes alight with unbridled hurt and rage.

"You will not speak to my wife in that manner ever again, or so help me, God, I will throttle you! Do I make myself clear?" Alistair spat in Theo's face, seizing him by a fistful of the collar of his shirt. Theo stared silently into the older man's eyes for several tense moments before turning his head away and brushing roughly past him to storm out of the kitchen. Evie tried to reach out for his arm, but he shot her a fierce glare before waving her off and stomping out of the house without looking back.

Taken aback by his sudden coldness, Evie took a step toward the front door to follow him, but she was stopped when Alistair placed a heavy hand upon her shoulder.

"Let him go," he rasped before breaking out into a coughing fit. Evie glanced at him over her shoulder to see the older man's face twisted with sorrow, the lines in his face deep with worry and regret. Evie stared at him in shock, stunned by what she had just witnessed.

"But—"

"He is a powder-keg waiting to ignite right now. Give him time to simmer down before he explodes on you as well."

Alistair shook his head with a ragged sigh, looking down at the hand he had raised to his boy for the first time in his life. He was immediately overcome with shame, but, just as when Theo first discovered the truth about his parentage, it was a bell he could ever un-ring. He was shocked at himself. He did not believe in raising his hands in anger to anyone, let alone his family. But in the moment, he had been so overcome by his anger and shame that he had lost control of himself for the first time in decades. Or perhaps, he was quickly realizing, he was just afraid to admit to himself that Theo's words, harsh as they were, had some merit. He *was* afraid for Theo to know the whole truth of his sordid past. He was terrified that Theo would no longer see him as his hero, like he did when he was a boy.

It was in that moment that realization hit the old man like a ton of bricks falling upon his head. He had made a grave mistake. He had made many mistakes in his life, wrongs that he had spent the last quarter of a century trying to right. Before he had found God, Alistair Cunningham had committed many crimes as a violent, impulsive, and drunken fool. But the worst crime he had ever committed was denying Theo the truth for so many years.

Theo didn't need excuses anymore. He needed the truth. He needed his *mother*.

***

Hours passed after Theo stormed from the house. The sun rose and reached its zenith, and then made its descent back down to the horizon, and during that entire time, Theo was nowhere to be found. Evie had considered going out in the afternoon to search for him, as he had already been given several hours to cool off, but Alistair discouraged her each time she suggested it. Alistair knew he had crossed a line when he raised his hands to his son, and with every hour that passed without his return to the house, he began to fear that something was wrong. Certainly, he wouldn't *run away* out of anger, would he? He was not that impulsive anymore…was he?

When dinner time came and went and Theo still had not returned, Alistair ordered Johanna and Evie to stay in the house while he left to go search for him. He went to the tavern, to the Caldwell's, and to the beaches, but found no trace until he stood on the dock to which *The Liberty* was anchored and looked up. Standing in the shadow of the lighthouse, he peered up to see Theo sitting on the catwalk, staring out at the Bay with his elbows resting on the lower railing and his feet dangling over the edge. It took him several minutes longer than when he was younger, but Alistair made the arduous trek up the spiraling staircase within the lighthouse tower and paused in the doorway that led out to the catwalk.

Theo sensed his presence but did not speak or look his way. Realizing that he was not going to be given an invitation, Alistair slowly took a seat on Theo's right and dangled his own legs off the edge of the catwalk. He followed Theo's gaze forward to the horizon on the other side of the Massachusetts Bay, where the sky was painted brilliant shades of orange and purple, but from the corner of his eye he could see the side of his son's face, upon which a large red mark had begun to form under the surface of his tanned skin. They sat in a tense silence for many minutes before Alistair finally cleared his throat.

"This had always been one of your favorite places to come and sit, you know. Do you remember when I would take you up here when you were a boy? And we would—"

"Draw pictures with the stars in the sky," Theo finished flatly without looking at him.

"Yes," Alistair said wistfully, thinking back to simpler times. "We would look at the stars and constellations for hours."

"That was a long time ago."

"Yes, a long time indeed. Before things changed."

"Before I caught you in your web of lies," Theo corrected.

Alistair sighed and reached out to place a hand on Theo's shoulder, but he immediately shrugged out from under his touch. Silence fell upon them again until Alistair said, "You owe Johanna an apology."

Alistair expected a defiant rebuttal, but instead, Theo nodded solemnly in agreement, kicking his feet as the shame of hurting the only mother he had ever known continued to wash over him. He didn't mean what he had said. At all. He just wanted someone to *listen*.

"I owe her much more than that," Theo whispered.

"And I owe you an apology as well."

Theo looked up with a furrowed brow to see Alistair staring at him with gentle eyes. "For hitting me?" Theo scoffed. "I've been hit harder."

Alistair shook his head and resisted the urge to roll his eyes. "You were right, son. You've always been right. It was foolish of me to hide the truth from you for so long, to try and pretend that there wasn't something that made you different. To keep hidden half of who you have always been. At the time, I thought it would be best for everyone if I pretended that Kateri never existed. And perhaps it was best for Johanna and I to believe that, but it was not what was best for you. It wasn't fair. I see that now because you helped me see that."

Theo hesitated and nervously fiddled with his hands. "You did the best you could," he admitted quietly.

"I could have done better. I know I could have. I...I—" Alistair was interrupted by a string of coughs, after which he continued to stumble as he searched for the words that he knew Theo needed to hear. Much like his son, he had never been particularly good at articulating his feelings to himself or others. "...I am sorry, son. I am so sorry."

Theo said nothing in return but flashed his father a brief look that told him nothing more needed to be said. The salty sea air grew quiet all around them again, save for the sound of a distant gull and the waves lapping the shore down below.

Theo settled his gaze back onto the waves but looked up again when Alistair suddenly uttered the words, "Mohawk River."

"What?"

Alistair slowly turned to face him, his eyes swimming with uncertainty. "The Mohawk River. Your mother's village is a place called *Atsa'któntie*. It is on the bank where the Mohawk River meets the Hudson. I have not laid eyes upon it in twenty-four years, and I do not know if it even still stands, but if you wish to find your mother, you should start there."

Theo blinked at him in shock and confusion. "I...I do not understand. Why are you telling me—?"

"You are your own man now. It is up to you alone to decide how you live your life. I can only guide you, but I cannot lead you. You must lead yourself."

"Father, I—"

Alistair held up a hand to interrupt him and shook his head. "No more needs to be said. Take this."

Alistair reached into the pocket of his vest and produced a very worn piece of parchment that had grown yellow with age and been folded and unfolded many times. Theo took it from him and unfolded it to reveal a hand-drawn map covered with sketches and scribbles he instantly recognized as his father's handwriting.

"What is this?" he asked with a raised brow.

"That damned village was a pain in the ass to find the first time, and I grew tired of getting lost, so I drew myself a map of the Mohawk Valley while my regiment was stationed there during the Seven Years War. I used it to find the village every time I went to see your mother. Hopefully it can help you now."

Theo gingerly ran his fingers across the smooth surface of the parchment, his index finger stopping at the junction of where the dark line labeled "Mohawk" intersected with the line labeled "Hudson." At that intersection was a single dot, labeled *Atsa'któntie*. He hadn't the slightest idea that this map existed, or why Alistair would have kept it all of these years if he had intended to put Kateri and his past behind him, as he had claimed.

"Why did you keep this?" Theo asked quietly.

Alistair shrugged, and Theo could see a wash of sadness swim across his eyes. "I suppose I knew that I could not keep you from her forever. No matter how badly *I* wanted to forget about her, and my past, I knew you wouldn't. And I couldn't force you to, either."

Theo folded the map in half and tucked it into the breast pocket of his shirt before turning to face his father. The old man looked tired and worn down, more so than usual, and it hurt Theo's heart to see him look so defeated.

"...Thank you, Father," Theo eventually murmured.

Alistair waved his hand. "Do not thank me. It is something I should have done a long time ago. But I must warn you that you should be prepared to find disappointment, should you decide to make this journey.

It has been many years, and she was never one to stay in one place for long. She could be anywhere by now."

Theo nodded curtly. "I understand."

"And tell me one thing. What exactly is it you hope to accomplish by tracking her down?"

Theo shared pointedly into Alistair's eyes with the slightest of sideways smirks tugging at his lips.

"I am conquering my demons."

Chapter 13

Homeland

May 1780

Evie squinted at the battle-worn piece of parchment that Theo had spread out across the desk inside The Liberty's captain's cabin. Tilting her head and tracing her finger across the dark line labeled 'Mohawk River,' she asked, "So this is how you plan to find your mother?"

Theo nodded and pointed with his index finger to the place at which the Mohawk and Hudson lines intersected in northern New York.

"This is her village. *Atsa'któntie.* Father says we can find it where the Mohawk River meets the Hudson."

"And your father drew this map himself?"

"Aye, a long time ago."

"What made him change his mind? He seemed so adamant that you stay away from her village…"

Theo sighed and raked a hand back through his hair before folding the map into fourths and placing it carefully in the inner pocket of his vest. "He realized he couldn't keep me from her forever."

"And will you really go? Will you travel all the way to New York to seek her out?"

Theo nodded. "I intend to set out for the frontier by the end of the month."

Evie nearly choked on her tongue. "So soon?" she stuttered. "The war is still raging in the frontier…"

"I am not worried. The war is drawing to a close. I can feel it."

Evie shook her head in worry and leaned back against the desk while folding her arms over her chest. "I don't know, Theo. This seems dangerous. And what if your father was wrong?"

"How do you mean?"

"What if he was mistaken? Or what if she has relocated? Or what if the village no longer exists? Or…what if she…"

"What if she, what?" he repeated curtly.

"…What if she has passed?"

Theo looked away and swallowed thickly, his eyes roaming the floorboards of the cabin. "Those are the answers I am trying to find. I won't live in uncertainty any longer."

Evie's gaze softened in sympathy as she took in the look of worry and sadness on his face. "I understand, Theo. I want that for you as well. I just do not want to see you hurt."

Theo wandered around from the other side of the desk to come chest to chest with her, grazing his hand against her cheek and tipping her chin up to look him in the eye. "Come with me," he breathed.

"What?"

"Come with me to *Atsa'któntie*. We can explore the frontier together. Just the two of us. It will be grand."

Evie quirked her brow skeptically. "Oh, Theo...I couldn't. I am needed to here. Alistair's health is declining, and Johanna needs my help with the chores—"

"The chores can wait. This cannot. Please, Evie..."

"How long would we be gone?"

"Weeks, most likely. Perhaps a month or two."

"It could be dangerous..."

Theo squeezed her arms affectionately and pleaded to her with his eyes. "I have been waiting my entire life to do this, and I can think of no one else I would want to have by my side for this journey than you."

Evie blushed at his words and smiled bashfully. Even after all of these years, she could still feel the blood rushing to her face in excitement whenever she looked into his golden-brown eyes.

"Really?" she asked in a whisper.

"Truly. Say you will come with me," he returned with a hopeful raise of his eyebrows and a flirtatious smirk. His hands moved down to hold her to his chest by her waist, and she now found it extremely difficult to deny his request as she caught the hopeful glint in his eye.

"...When do we leave?" she asked with a sigh.

Theo's smirk widened and he leaned down to press his forehead to hers. "As soon as we can."

***

Evie grunted in exasperation as she reached the bottom of the front steps, dragging her very full, very heavy, and very burdensome trunk behind her and wincing every time it thudded against the steps. Once she felt her feet touch the ground, she dropped the trunk with a groan and wiped the sweat that had accumulated on her brow with the back of her hand. It was early morning on the last day of May, and it was already unbearably hot and humid. Terrible weather for traversing the thick foliage and rocky terrain of the New England frontier, in her opinion, but there was no way she could convince Theo to delay his journey to find his mother until the fall. He had his heart set on leaving now, and there was no changing his mind.

On the other side of the yard, Theo's back was turned to her as he looked thoroughly over a large covered wagon. After inspecting the wooden wheels for any signs of cracking or rotting, he sauntered up to the front to give Artemis an affectionate pat on her flank. It was a single horse wagon, suitable for carrying two people on a long journey.

Evie shuffled across the yard to join Theo by the wagon. Upon hearing her footsteps behind him, he turned to greet her. "Good morning," he said cheerfully.

"It is far too early to tell if it will be good," she said with a yawn, pointing to the wagon. "This is quite a beautiful carriage. How did you come into possession of it?"

"It belongs to Jacob's father. He uses it to haul his blacksmithing tools and supplies back and forth from Boston. He loaned it to us for our journey."

"Well, that was very kind of him."

Theo outstretched his arms and gestured proudly to the freshly polished wagon. "Here it is. This will be our home for the coming weeks. It's no mansion, but it will see us through each day and night on our travels."

Evie raised her brow skeptically and wrinkled her nose. "Hold a moment. Do you mean to tell me that we will be *sleeping* in this thing?"

"Well, not entirely. We will stop by plenty of taverns along the frontier on our way north."

Evie still seemed hesitant. She did not find the idea of sleeping outdoors in any capacity very appealing, especially out in the middle of the frontier. The western edge of the colonies was infested with wild animals, Redcoats, bandits, and ne'er-do-wells of all sorts, and though she knew Theo would never leave her side on the journey, she was still nervous to leave the homestead. Silas may have been gone, but the rest of the British still lingered.

Theo took notice of the nervousness evident on her face and draped an arm around her shoulder, pressing a kiss to her temple. "Do not be afraid, love. This is an adventure. You know I will not let any harm befall you. So long as you are by my side, you are safe."

Evie looked up to him lovingly as a smile tugged at her lips. "I know."

Theo pulled away and traipsed back toward the porch to retrieve Evie's abandoned luggage, lifting the trunk off of the ground and into his arms with ease.

"Jesus Christ," he said as he carried it across the yard and loaded it into the back of the wagon. "I told you to pack for a month. Not three years."

Evie planted her hands on her hips and rolled her eyes. "I would not expect you to understand. You are not a woman."

Theo scoffed and lowered the canvas cover back onto the top of the wagon after loading the last of the luggage and supplies. "So, what do you think?"

"I think that I am very excited for you to finally find the answers you have been seeking."

"As am I. And do you know what else I am looking forward to?"

"What's that?"

Theo placed his hands on her hips and gently led her backwards until her back hit the side of the wagon and he trapped her against it with his broad chest. He pressed a chaste kiss to her lips and pulled away, staring into her eyes as he murmured, "Having you all to myself for the weeks to come."

Evie felt chills run up her spine and her face flush hot, but she tried to play coy. "Oh, is that so?"

"It will be just us, alone in the open wilderness, with no one around for miles…"

"That sounds…enticing," she whispered with a bat of her eyelashes.

Theo smirked before leaning down to request another kiss, this one much longer and deeper than the last, but after several moments, they were interrupted by the sound of someone gruffly clearing his throat behind them. They instantly pulled away from one another and looked over Theo's shoulder to see Alistair and Johanna standing at the bottom of the porch steps, tapping their feet and flashing them the cheekiest of grins.

"Did we interrupt something?" Alistair asked as he slowly made his way down the stairs. He was now leaning upon a wooden cane to move about, which considerably slowed his progress. Johanna looped her arm around his and led him down the steps and across the yard to the wagon.

"You always do," Theo shot back with a roll of his eyes.

"We just came to say our goodbyes and wish you good luck on your travels," Johanna said with an uncharacteristic sternness. Johanna was still hurt by what Theo had said during their explosive argument weeks before, and she made it known by acting rather short and indifferent whenever Theo was in her presence. Theo had yet to formally apologize to her for the hurtful things he had said that day, but it was not for a lack of trying. Johanna had simply been avoiding him. Rather than force her to speak to him, Theo decided to give her time to cool off while he was away and try clearing the air with her again when he returned.

In Johanna's other hand, she held a large wicker picnic basket. She handed it to Theo but looked to Evie as she said, "I've packed you both some dried meat, bread, fruit preserves, and cakes. It isn't much, but hopefully it will be enough to see you through."

"It's perfect. Thank you, Johanna," Evie said with a smile as she reached forward to take both Johanna and Alistair in a tight embrace.

"I want you to be weary," Alistair explained tiredly to his son. "Do not let Evie out of your sight. And be prepared for anything."

"I know, Father. This is hardly my first journey into the wilderness."

"This is different. You are venturing into unknown territory. And I want you to be prepared for the worst. Even if you do find your mother or her people, there is no guarantee they will welcome you with open arms."

"I know. That is a risk I am willing to take."

"Have you your sword and pistol that I gave you?"

Theo patted his belt, upon which his father's military broadsword and flintlock were sheathed. "I have them right here."

"May they protect you on this journey as they have all others, my son."

Theo stepped forward to hug both of his parents tightly.

Johanna returned his embrace, and after he pulled away, she took ahold of his hand and looked directly in his eyes, saying, "Be safe. I hope you find what you are seeking."

Theo smiled half-heartedly, a pang of guilt piercing his heart at the look of sadness in her eyes. He hated himself for saying the things he had said, and breaking her heart after all that she had done to raise him as her own was the last thing he wanted to do.

"Thank you, Jo," he whispered, leaning down to kiss her cheek. "For everything."

***

June 1780

A week of journeying along the trails that wound through the wilderness of New York came and went rather quickly for Theo, but for Evie, it felt like months had passed. She had never really been fond of the outdoors—she much preferred to be inside where she could read or sketch in her books—and the summer air was unbearably hot. It also did not help that two days into the journey she began to feel ill, with near constant nausea, lightheadedness, and cramping in her stomach. She tried her best to hide her discomfort for Theo's benefit; she could see how desperately eager he was to find his mother's village, and if God was with them, his mother too, and she did not want to dampen his mood with her petty complaints. So, she bit her tongue and pushed through her illness, spending much of her time sprawled out in the back of the wagon with the luggage, her head hidden from the unforgiving sun so that she could sleep the nausea away.

Theo, on the other hand, was nearly giddy with the anticipation of reaching *Atsa'któntie,* and as they followed the trails that ran parallel to the Mohawk River, he was thrilled to find himself out in the open after being cooped up in the homestead for so long. The sights and smells of the mountains, the river, and the enormous pines that dotted the frontier were a refreshing change of scenery from the beaches and the salty Bay to which he was accustomed.

The farther north they went, and the farther from civilization they ventured, the more at home he felt. He had called Division Point his home for as long as he could remember, but a strange feeling of contentment and belonging settled over him amongst the trees and the mountains far inland. While he had always been fascinated by ships and the sea, he also had that inexplicable feeling that he was one with the earth whenever he found himself in the wilderness.

He felt at home in the Mohawk Valley. Though he had never been this far north before, he felt connected to the earth in a way that he had never felt in Division Point. The flora, the fauna, the mountains, the crisp wild air—it felt familiar somehow, as if he had discovered a long-lost homeland that he did not know he had been missing, and the only direction he could see now was homeward bound. And this was exactly what he was hoping for. He hoped that the closer he got to his mother's village, the more whole he would feel. This woman named Kateri was a complete stranger to him, but somehow, her homeland felt like his homeland, too.

A week and a half after leaving Division Point behind, Theo steered Artemis and the covered wagon off of the trail and down a narrow path that took them into a small, sparsely populated frontier town in northern New York called Yarrowdale. Artemis was in desperate need of a rest, and

Theo and Evie had run low on the provisions Johanna packed for them. Evie's ability to hide her feelings of illness had also faded, and it had become very obvious that she needed a break from the trails and the constant jostling of the wagon. Perhaps after a day or two of rest in the town's inn, he reasoned, and she would be well enough to travel again.

Yarrowdale was sparsely settled and consisted merely of a tavern and inn, a hunting lodge, a general store, and a few scattered cabins, but it would suffice for a short rest before they continued on the remaining twenty or so miles to the junction of the Mohawk River and the Hudson.

"We will rest here for a day," Theo instructed as he pulled the wagon to a stop in front of the quaint yet lively Golden Finch Inn in the center of the town.

The wooden structure was alight with the glow of candles and lanterns in all of its windows, and the cheery notes of fiddle music intermingled with indistinct shouting could be heard emanating from inside. It was late evening when Theo and Evie arrived at the tavern, and the candlelight from the windows cast a warm and inviting yellow light upon the surrounding wilderness.

Evie poked her head out of the opening on the front of the covered bed of the wagon. Her hair was a frizzy mess and her face was pale from hours of nausea. "What if they have no rooms left for us?" she asked worriedly as Theo dismounted from the driver's bench in front of her.

"Then I suppose we will sleep under the stars," Theo responded with a chuckle.

Evie let out a sigh of relief when they entered the tavern and met with the innkeeper, a portly gentleman with a bushy black beard, who told them warmly that he had one vacant room to rent out for the night upstairs. Evie wasted no time in rushing up the stairs and collapsing on the bed in exhaustion while Theo dropped a handful of coins in the innkeeper's hand, unsaddled Artemis from the wagon and hitched her to the steed post out front, and then lugged their trunks up the stairs to their room.

He found Evie sprawled out on her stomach on the bed in the corner of the small room when he arrived with the luggage, her head buried under a pillow.

"You do not seem well," he noted worriedly as he sat down on the edge of the bed next to her.

"Just too many days on the road, I suppose," Evie said from under the pillow.

"We have not eaten much today. Perhaps you need something in your stomach."

Evie blanched as the thought of food made her stomach turn. "I am not hungry."

"You must eat, love," Theo urged as he placed a hand on her back. "You will need your strength if we are to make it to *Atsa'któntie*."

"I just wish to sleep…"

"Not until you have a hot meal in your belly. Come with me to the barroom and we will eat. Then we shall sleep."

Evie slowly pulled her head out from under the pillow and flashed him a defiant look. She was in no mood to be surrounded by frontier folk in a loud, crowded barroom while he forced food down her throat, but she could see by the determined look in his eye that he would not leave her be until she complied.

"It was not a request," Theo said with a smirk after several moments of silence. "It was an order."

With a roll of her eyes, Evie sat up on the edge of the bed. Her complexion was still paler than usual, and her cheeks were a rosy red. Theo leaned forward and kissed her forehead to look for a fever, but he found none. Taking her hand in his, he gave her fingers an affectionate squeeze and led her down the creaky wooden stairs to the barroom, which was still very loud and crowded with travelers despite the late hour. After nudging their way through the throngs of people drunkenly dancing and stumbling across the floor, they ordered two hot meals of mutton and stewed vegetables and then took a seat at one of the few empty tables strewn about the room.

Evie took immediate notice to the sudden change of Theo's posture as soon as they entered the barroom. Rather than just holding her hand and leading her through, he hovered protectively over her from behind, his arm looped tightly around her waist as he looked wearily about the room. She could feel many pairs of eyes upon them as soon as they entered the tavern, many of them less than kind, and it did not take a genius to realize why.

She was a fragile-looking white woman traveling in the company of a native man much larger and much darker in complexion than she, and no matter what she claimed, few would believe that she was traveling with him willingly. Theo may have been used to receiving sneers, glares, and curses wherever he went for the simple reason of the color of his skin, but Evie was not, and it set her on edge. She hated to be stared at, especially when many of those eyes belonged to some rather seedy-looking frontiersmen that possessed no love for natives and clearly had too much to drink.

Even once they were seated with their meals at the empty table, Theo nudged his chair as close to hers as possible and draped his arm around her shoulders, ensuring that their backs were facing a wall rather than the rest of the barroom.

Theo looked up from his finished plate and frowned as he watched Evie pick at hers. She had barely touched her food, and she still looked rather pale in the face.

"Still not hungry?" he asked worriedly.

Evie shrugged and pushed her plate away before placing a hand upon her stomach, which continued to churn and cramp uncomfortably. "I think I just need rest."

"It worries me that you will not eat—" Theo's thought trailed off into silence upon looking over Evie's shoulder and seeing a gruff looking man approach their table from behind her. He was tall, thin, and unimposing, but he smelled like a brewery. It was obvious from his appearance that he was a lumberer, and he had a rather lecherous glint in his eye as he stumbled drunkenly up to the table with a tankard of ale in hand.

Theo instantly tensed as the man approached and stood much too close for his liking over Evie's place at the table. Seemingly unaware of Theo's presence, the man looked Evie up and down with a tilted brow and sideways smirk.

"Hello, love," he slurred, "what's a pretty girl like yourself doing in these parts, hm?"

Evie looked up and wrinkled her nose at the foul smell of whiskey and ale the man was putting off as he towered over her. "Just passing through," she mumbled before turning her head away.

"Just passin' through, eh? How's about you come dance with me? The fiddles are lively tonight."

Evie quickly shook her head. "No, thank you—"

Theo abruptly cut in, grumbling through clenched teeth, "She is spoken for."

The man seemed to notice Theo for the first time in that moment, and he glared down his nose at him with an arrogant sneer. "Oh, is that right? And who are you supposed to be?"

"The one speaking for her," Theo shot back, tensing the arm that he had draped over Evie's shoulders. "Perhaps you should be on your way."

The man waved him off and looked back to Evie, placing a heavy hand on her arm. "Come on, girl," he leered, leaning down to whisper in her ear. "Come spend the evening with a real man."

As soon as the man's hand brushed her arm, Evie immediately flinched away and Theo jumped to his feet from his chair, stalking around the table to insert himself between them.

"I said, she is spoken for," he repeated with his chest puffed and eyes narrowed into dangerous slits. "Piss off."

The man laughed in his face. "And who's gonna make me? You? You're nothing but a blimey mongrel! Even worse, you're one of them damn Injuns, aren't you?"

"And what if I am?"

"I'm just trying to figure out what a pretty little thing like that is doing whoring herself out to the likes of you!"

Evie slowly rose from her seat and placed a hand upon Theo's arm to calm him, but he brushed her off. She could see his muscles tensing under his clothes and his hands clenching into fists at his side.

"Theo," she coaxed gently, "Step away. He is not worth it…"

Theo ignored her and remained toe to toe with the man before him. His blood had already begun to boil at the man's lewd comments, but he could now feel a rage stirring within his chest at the thought of the man nearly putting his hands upon what was clearly *his*.

"I suggest you walk away before I do something that you regret," Theo told the man pointedly, his arms crossed over his chest.

The man smirked maliciously before taking a swig from his tankard. "So, you are one of them Injuns, then? But you ain't no regular redskin, are you? No, I can see it in your face. You're one of those half breeds!"

Theo ground his teeth and swallowed thickly in order to resist the urge to break a bottle over the man's head. The gradual raising of their voices was enough the draw the attention of most of the tavern's patrons, and they all began to gather loosely around the table in order to catch a glimpse of the inferno that was surely about to ignite.

"So, tell me, mutt," the man continued arrogantly after taking another gulp of ale, "was it your father or your whore mother that got a taste of the forest fruits?"

A fleeting look of unadulterated rage flashed through Theo's golden eyes as he outwardly flinched at the man's words, and before the man could blink, a furious growl escaped Theo's throat. Sensing the fire that was burning just under the surface of Theo's skin, Evie tried to reach out for his hand, but before she could get a chance to try and hold him back, Theo lunged forward and landed a clenched fist easily upon his adversary's jaw. The man let out a pained howl and stumbled backward into the wall, dropping his tankard and spilling its contents across the floor at his feet. Despite the man's drunkenness, he collected himself rather quickly from the blow and charged back in Theo's direction with his arms raised and ready for attack.

"Theo, stop!" Evie cried fearfully.

"Dirty, rotten, Indian dog!" the man barked as he lunged forward and trapped Theo in a tight bear hug that knocked them both off their feet and sent them rolling across the floor. The crowd around them immediately began to hoot and holler in response to the outbreak of violence, half rooting for the drunken lout to smash Theo's skull in, and the other half begging for Theo to feed the drunkard his teeth.

Several minutes of senseless pummeling from both sides ensued, in which Theo and the man alternated throwing each other against any nearby object before landing another punch, whether that be a table, a chair, the wall, or the floor. As soon as the words left the man's mouth, Theo could feel a veil of red wash over his eyes, trapping him into another deafening fit of rage that he knew would only be quieted once the man was dead or otherwise silenced. He could handle a hurl of insults on his own behalf any day, but the moment Evie's or Kateri's names were mentioned, he felt the last strands of his self-control snap and wither away into nothing.

The drunken man may have been tall and strong, but Theo was taller and stronger, and he easily outmatched him in speed, strength, and stamina. Within minutes, the man had taken several well-placed blows to the face and groin, easily sending him onto his back on the ground before Theo leapt on top of him and attempted to land another punch to his nose.

"Theo," Evie begged from the inner edge of the crowd. "Stop, Theo, before you kill him!"

"The world would be better off if I did!" Theo growled up at her, his eyes wide and wild with a rage that frightened her to her core.

Evie took several nervous steps backwards, and Theo struck the man several more times about his face before looking up again. It was then that he saw that she had fearfully backed away from him, and even amongst the deafening shouts of the crowd and the sound of the blood pounding in his ears, he could hear her sniffle.

Their gazes met for a brief moment as she stared at him in fear. The sight of Theo beating a drunken man within an inch of his life after a brief exchange of ugly words cast a fear of him in her heart that she had never once felt before. She had seen him resort to violence in order to defend her many times—against the bandit in the woods, against the Redcoat officer that demanded quarters at Division Point, and even against Silas. But this time, it felt different to her. He seemed to be enjoying the man's cries of pain and his pleadings for mercy.

That is, until Theo suddenly paused and looked up to meet her gaze. The sight of her bright blue eyes wide with panic and fear *of him* instantly ripped him from the cloud of anger that hung over his head, pulling him back down to earth with a violent thud that reminded him where he was and what he was doing.

Theo looked down to see the man was pinned to the floor underneath him, blood streaming from his now broken nose.

"Please," the man begged in a raspy whisper, "Mercy, please. Mercy…"

Theo let out a gasp upon realizing what he had done, jumping to his feet and stumbling away from the man's body as he looked down at his bruised and bloodied knuckles in horror. Just then, the innkeeper stormed into the barroom and ordered the shocked crowd to disperse.

"What the hell is the meaning of this nonsense?" he demanded in a stunned rage.

His chest heaving, Theo searched for a breath and wiped the back of his hand across his mouth. The man had managed to land a single punch to his jaw in the mayhem, effectively splitting his lip open enough for blood to trickle down his chin.

"He started something he couldn't finish," Theo explained with a strange calmness.

The innkeeper knelt over the downed man and slid a hand under his neck to check for a pulse. The man was far from dead, but he would be out of commission for a good while after having his hide handed to him by a so-called "Indian dog."

"You've destroyed my barroom!" the innkeeper cried in distress, gesturing to the mess of broken glass and splintered wood spread across the floor.

Theo turned away from him and strode across the room to where Evie had backed herself into the crowd. He offered her a remorseful smile before outstretching his hand to her. After looking between his face and hand as if it were a wild creature ready to strike her, she hesitantly placed her hand in his and allowed him to lead her away.

Theo paused before the innkeeper and the now unconscious drunkard and dug around in his pocket, producing a rather large pouch of coins that Evie did not even know he had in his possession. He then tossed the pouch onto the floor at the innkeeper's feet.

"I'll pay for the damages," Theo started curtly before leading Evie by the hand towards the stairs that led to the second floor.

"And what of him?" the innkeeper asked angrily, gesturing to the man on the floor.

Theo and Evie paused at the base of the stairs and Theo sent one last glance over his shoulder.

"Put the rest on *his* tab."

***

Evie shook her head in exasperation as they entered their room and slammed the door shut.

"What the hell has gotten into you?" she snapped while planting her hands on her hips.

Theo dropped slowly onto the foot of the bed and hung his ahead, raking his bruised and bloodied hands through his long messy hair.

"How could you do that, Theo? You knew nothing about that man before you attacked him. You could have gotten us both killed!"

"I know…" Theo shook his head with disappointment in himself for once again losing control of his temper.

Vivid memories of that terrible night in the alley in Philadelphia several years ago flashed through his head and caused him to outwardly flinch. Had he not gained control of himself when he did, he was sure that the drunken lumberer would have joined that continental soldier in the grave, and it made Theo sick to his stomach.

"You know?" Evie repeated cynically. "Theo, you cannot just throw your fists at every man that insults you!"

Theo suddenly looked up, his eyes narrowed, and his mouth set in a snarl. "I would not expect you to understand."

"Excuse me?"

Theo slowly rose from the bed and came to stand face to face with her. He towered over her, and the heat held within his gaze was enough to tempt her to take a step back from him.

"When was the last time you were cursed at for merely existing?" he asked lowly. "When was the last time you were told that you do not have a right to walk this earth?"

Evie swallowed thickly, her gaze softening as she looked away sadly. "…Never."

"Exactly. But this wasn't about me. I can handle whatever curses and whatever names the world has to throw at me. But I will not tolerate a prick like that dishonoring *you* before my very eyes!"

Evie furrowed her brow skeptically. "So, you were defending my honor, was that it? Theo, I never asked you to defend my honor. I am a grown woman. I can defend myself, and I can *speak* for myself."

Theo scoffed sarcastically. "Oh, please. When have you ever been able to defend yourself? I have lost count of the number of times I have had to defend you, and if it weren't for me, you would still be a slave to Silas Porter, trapped inside that fort!"

Evie flinched away at his words as if she had been slapped across the face, and she immediately turned her back to him to walk across the room toward the window. Theo let out a remorseful sigh and followed her to the window.

"I'm sorry," he said softly after a long silence. "I did not mean that."

"Yes, you did," she corrected without facing him.

"I know you can take care of yourself. You are the strongest woman I know. But you know that I would go to the ends of this earth to protect you. You mean the world to me."

Evie's eyes slipped closed as she turned to face him. Immediately, she threw her arms around his neck and he returned her embrace by wrapping his arms around her waist and holding her to his chest. After a moment, she pulled away and looked up into his eyes.

"Where did you get that money?" she suddenly asked with a perturbed and skeptical glint in her eye.

"What money?"

"The enormous bag of coins you gave to the innkeeper just now. Where did you get it?"

Theo suddenly looked bashful, and he looked away nervously. "You needn't worry about it."

"Theo. Where did you get that money? I was not aware that you were independently wealthy."

After a moment of hesitation, Theo let took a step backwards, holding his hands up in surrender. "I earned it."

"How exactly?"

He sighed again, his face falling in shame. "The last time I was in Boston, I…I visited some old friends by the docks."

Evie bit down on her lip and shook her head. "I thought you had given up the brawls a long time ago. When we…became an item."

Theo scoffed under his breath. "I needed money for this journey. I needed money for my family. I did not know what else to do."

Evie crosses her arms over her chest with a huff. "Anything but resorting to fighting in the streets!"

"You know no one outside of Division Point would even consider giving me work because they think me a savage. And besides, fighting tooth and nail is what I'm best at."

"What of your apprenticeship with Mr. Caldwell?"

Theo waved his hand dismissively. "That is a pittance compared to what I earn by the docks. I was not going to let you or my family starve. How else do you think you've come to have food in your belly and clothes on your back?"

Evie let out a long breath in order to calm herself and began to rub her temples. "You are not a child anymore, Theo. You must give that life up. If not for yourself, then for us. Something terrible could happen to you the next time you pick a fight with the wrong stranger…"

"I've survived much worse than a drunkard's fists."

"Be honest with me," she said, attempting to return the conversation to the topic at hand. "You did not attack that man because he dishonored me or you. You attacked him because he insulted your mother."

Theo wrinkled his nose and hesitantly nodded. "She may have abandoned me," he said sadly, "but she is still my mother."

"Could you ever forgive her for leaving you, if you found her?"

Theo swallowed nervously and looked about the room for an answer that he didn't have. "I do not know. I have been angry with her for as long as I can remember. My father claims she gave me up for my own good, but I refuse to believe that. What kind of mother could do that so easily?"

"I am sure it wasn't easy."

"I want to hear that from her."

Evie reached up and forced him to look her in the eye by capturing his chin in her hand. "I know you are angry. You are angry at her, at your father, at yourself, at the world…but you cannot solve every problem you face with your fists. And tonight, in that barroom, you frightened me. I have never seen you so angry, and it frightened me to my core. It pains me to see you like that…"

"You know I would never hurt you—"

"I know, Theo. I know that. I do. But to see you beat that man within an inch of his life right before my eyes…it was so terribly frightening to see you so enraged…"

"I'm sorry," he whispered softly. "I never meant to frighten you."

Evie brushed her thumb across his cheek and stopped at his chin, upon which blood had gathered and dried after his lip had been split open.

"You're hurt," she mumbled worriedly.

"Only a flesh wound. I have survived worse."

Evie chuckled darkly and reached up on the tips of her toes to press her forehead to his. "Promise me you will never hurt anyone like that again," she said sternly as she stared up into his eyes. "Promise me you will never frighten me like that again."

Theo returned her heavy gaze for a moment before his eyes slipped closed and he pressed a kiss to the top of her head. Wrapping his arms tighter around her body, he whispered into her hair, "Never again."

***

Several hours later, Evie awoke to the feeling of her stomach churning so violently that she shot up to a sitting position in the bed she was sharing with Theo, her arms wrapped tightly around her middle. Theo was sound asleep next to her, buried under layers of blankets and completely oblivious to the fact that she had awoken. Hot and covered in a thin sheen of sweat, Evie threw the blanket to the side and turned to let her legs dangle over the edge of the bed. As soon as her bare feet touched the floorboards, however, a wave of dizziness washed over her that was powerful enough to drop her to her knees.

That was when the nausea struck her like a great wave crashing against the shore, and she immediately rose to her feet to stumble across the small room to the window. The crisp frontier night air was cool upon her face as she threw open the window of their room at the inn, and no sooner than she poked her head out did she begin to violently vomit. As soon as she evacuated what little was in her stomach, the nausea dissipated, seemingly disappearing as soon as it came. Placing a hand upon her stomach, Evie groaned painfully and closed the window before placing her back against the wall and sliding down to the floor where she curled her knees up to her chest. Her head was still spinning, and the floor seemed to be rocking back and forth underneath her like the deck of a ship on open water.

It was the middle of the night, and she could not bring herself to awake Theo from his deep sleep just to tell him that she threw up all over the outside of the tavern's wall. She could not remember the last time she had felt this ill, and as she sat on the floor under the window, she tried to think of anything she could have done or eaten within the last few weeks to make her so sick.

Nothing came immediately to mind—that is, until she looked up and froze in fear once she realized that she had not had her cycle in over two *months*.

Evie let out a startled gasp and stared at the ceiling, counting in her head the number of days and weeks that had passed since her last monthly cycle. Fear and anxiety filled her heart when she once again confirmed it had been nearly three months. It was now early June, but she was sure she had not bled since at least March. It was now over six years ago that she had last felt these symptoms—the nausea, the lightheadedness, the terrible cramping in her stomach—all just some of the many clues that told her when she was barely seventeen years old that she was carrying a child. And now, a woman of twenty-three years, she had been experiencing the same discomfort in her belly for going on two weeks, all while having missed two of her cycles without even realizing it.

Evie dropped her head into her hands as she became enveloped with shock, nervousness, and *anger*. How could she have not realized her condition sooner? How could she not have noticed her lack of monthly cycles for so long? How could she be so foolish? She had been with child before—she knew what it felt like. How could she let herself become so distracted by that which was going on around her that she completely ignored what was very clearly happening within her own body?

Evie slapped her hand over her mouth to muffle a sudden onslaught of sniffles as tears began to stream down her cheeks. *This could not be happening,* she told herself. *It couldn't be possible...*

But then she remembered that it was, in fact, *very possible* that she was pregnant with Theo's child. They had not been doing anything to prevent such a thing from happening the entire time they had been together, and now, it seemed, God had determined that they would have to endure the consequences.

She did not know exactly why she was crying, as she could feel a whirlwind of emotions flowing through her all at once. She was angry at herself for not discovering her condition sooner, and angry at Theo for his own carelessness in getting her into this situation before dragging her on a dangerous journey across the northern frontier. And how could she possibly tell Theo the news, should her suspicions be correct? He would surely be stunned, perhaps even angry with her, because they were not even close to being ready for the enormous change this discovery would bring to their lives.

He had told her before that he was not ready to be a husband or a father, but would that still be the case once he knew the truth? Would he stand by her and help her raise their child despite the ill timing, or would he grow sick of her and his responsibilities and cast her aside for the life of freedom he had always claimed to prefer? As these many thoughts swam in her head, Evie began to feel nauseas once again, and she buried her face against her knees to drown out the sound of her sobs.

But hidden deep underneath those layers of anger, confusion, and fear of the unknown, an incomprehensible joy and excitement began to bloom within her fluttering heart. If she was truly carrying Theo's child, it would be the greatest blessing for which she could ever ask. She wanted nothing more than to have his children, and the thought of that dream coming true much sooner than she expected began to fill her with joy. She remembered feeling nothing but fear and dread when she discovered that she was carrying Silas' child, but now, the feelings flowing through her were nothing of the sort. Her first pregnancy had felt like an omen of the end of the world, but this felt like the beginning of the future she had been craving for as long as she could remember. The only thing that could taint that future was Theo—should he decide that he did not want to he held back by the responsibilities of a family and wanted nothing to do with her or the baby.

But she couldn't tell him yet. Not now, while they were traveling alone through the middle of nowhere and he was on the cusp of making a life changing discovery of his own. His attention had been devoted fully to finding his mother and her village for the past weeks, and Evie could not bear the thought of distracting him from his quest with such dramatic news. This journey was about Theo and finding the closure that he so desperately wanted and needed. Now was not the time to turn his world upside down all over again. She, and the baby, Evie decided in that moment, would have to wait until they returned home, and Theo had the answers he was looking for.

Madison Flores

Whenever that was…

Chapter 14

Tekariho:ken

June 1780

Evie leaned to her side to rest her head upon Theo's shoulder as she sat next to him in the front of the wagon. It had been two days since they left the inn in Yarrowdale to continue their journey north, and a strange silence had settled upon them both ever since. It was not too long ago that she had made the discovery that she could be carrying Theo's child within her, but she could not bring herself to tell him while the anticipation of finding his mother hung over their heads. She was consumed with worry as to how he would react when he learned the news, and as much as it killed her, she decided it was best that she keep it to herself until the journey was over.

"Are you feeling any better?" Theo asked as he turned his attention away from the path in front of them.

Evie looked up at him with a faint smile and curled her arm around her middle. "I am," she fibbed. "I just needed some rest."

"Very good. I was worried you had fallen ill."

Evie cleared her throat and let her eyes wander about their surroundings, from the river flowing mightily on their right, to the great mountains poking over the western horizon. She had to admit that the more time she spent out in the frontier, the more she enjoyed the taste of the open air and the sights of the untouched wilderness. The Mohawk Valley was beautifully pristine, and a perfect place to settle a village for those who wished to put as much distance between themselves and the colonies as possible without crossing the Appalachian Mountains.

After another long silence, Evie spoke up, lifting her head from his shoulder to look at his face. "Theo?"

"Hm?" he returned without removing his eyes from the trail.

"Suppose we do find your mother's village and her people. Do you think they will speak English?"

Theo chuckled under his breath. "My mother does, so my father has told me. That was the only way they could communicate, as he could not speak *Kanien'kehá*."

"But what if no one else does?"

"Then I suppose it will be a very short conversation."

Evie shifted uncomfortably in her seat next to him, suddenly aware of the fact that they were traveling into Mohawk territory. She did not want to assume that Kateri's people were hostile or dangerous, yet she couldn't help but look over her shoulder to scan the surrounding forest for signs of disgruntled and distrustful native warriors lying in wait to attack them from all sides. Theo, however, did not seem the least bit fearful or worried that they were venturing into unfamiliar lands inhabited by a people he had never met.

"Do you think they will be...receptive to us?"

"Is that just another way of asking if they will be hostile?"

Evie shrugged. "I...suppose."

Theo thought for a moment. "There is no way to know. They welcomed my father into their community many years ago. But much has happened since then, and I suspect that they will not be too thrilled to be in the presence of a white woman and a half breed."

Evie furrowed her brow in frustration as she looked at him. "Why do you always call yourself such a terrible name?"

Theo was slightly taken aback as he gave her a sideways look. "...Because I *am* a half breed."

Evie shook her head in disgust. "No, you aren't. Such a word implies that you are only half-human. Do you really think that lowly of your mother's people?"

He shook his head somberly, his face falling. "No, of course not..."

"Suppose you and I were to have children in the future. They would share my blood, and yours. Would you look them in their eyes and call them half breeds as well?"

Theo's eyes widened in surprise and he vehemently shook his head while turning to face her. "I would never do such a thing."

"Then I do not want to hear that word escape your lips ever again, whether in reference to yourself or anyone else. Am I understood?"

Theo swallowed thickly as his eyes fell to his boots. He had never considered that the way he referred to himself could bother her. He had heard it flung his way so many times over the years that he had lost count, and to him, it had lost all meaning.

"I'm sorry, Evie," he mumbled, feeling rather foolish and ashamed. "I did not mean to offend you."

Evie crossed her arms over her chest and looked up to the sky, shaking her head. The thought of anyone referring to him or her own child as a half-blooded cretin made her blood boil under her skin. "You know you are more than the blood in your veins or the color of your skin," she said sternly.

The corners of Theo's mouth twitched upward as he looked at her. "I know that now. Thank you, *Ákskere'*."

Evie raised a brow in confusion. "What does that mean?"

Theo smirked and leaned over to kiss her cheek. "It means 'lover.' It was the only word my mother ever taught my father to say in *Kanien'kehá*."

Evie felt her cheeks turn pink as she murmured, "It seems fitting."

***

As Theo and Evie ventured farther north into the wilderness of New York, the mighty Mohawk River began to widen, and the trees around it thinned out. On the twenty-third day of the journey, the pair found their trail coming to an end at the point where two great rivers met. Theo pulled the wagon to a stop at the fork and paused to survey the area. The trees on each side of the river had thinned, but the terrain was too difficult to take the wagon any further. After much deliberation, they decided to cross the river on a crumbling bridge at the fork and make the rest of the way on Artemis' back in order to continue the search for *Atsa'któntie*.

They were met by another two miles of trees and untouched wilderness after crossing the river, an endless sea of green that Evie felt she had seen a thousand times over during the course of their journey.

"Are you sure we have come to the right place?" she asked in exasperation as they came to a stop under the shadow of a large evergreen. She had been sitting behind Theo on Artemis' back for the last several hours, and her rear end was beginning to go numb. "All I see are trees and deer. There could not possibly be a village here."

Theo pulled the hand-drawn map from the inner pocket of his vest and unfolded it to take another look. They had followed the trail his father had drawn many years before, taking every curve and bend laid out for them. After crossing the river at the great fork, they wandered north for another two miles, coming to stop at the face of a mighty cliff, presumably the one Alistair had drawn on the map and, for unknown reasons, had labeled "Cunningham Cliff."

"We are on the right track," Theo assured her confidently over his shoulder. "The map says that *Atsa'któntie* is just around this cliff."

Evie pointed to the sky, which had taken on a purplish hue as the sun began to dip below the horizon behind the cliff. "The sun has already begun to set. We do not have much time to find the village before nightfall."

"Then I suppose we should get a move on. Let us hope that we will come upon hospitable folk on the other side of the bluff."

Evie swallowed nervously. "And if we don't?"

Theo hesitated before shrugging and mumbling, "We see which one of us is the faster runner."

Evie gave an unamused shove to his shoulder as he commanded Artemis back into a gallop and they began the trek up the jagged face of the cliff. The cliff was surrounded on both sides by mountains of large rocks interspersed with the occasional evergreen tree, making it a difficult path for Artemis to take. After what seemed like an eternity, they reached the crest of the hill on the backside of the cliff and paused to take in the breathtaking scenery down below.

The sun was well below the horizon now, giving the sky above a golden indigo cast. From the top of the hill, Evie and Theo could see the wild frontier for miles and miles in every direction below them, an enormous sea of trees and mountains that had yet to be touched by a settler. In the great expanse before them, Theo could imagine village after village having come and gone over the centuries, and at the very bottom of the hill, as if hiding behind the wall of the cliff they had just overcome, there was a clearing in the otherwise undisturbed sea of trees.

"Look there," he said in awe as he pointed at the clearing and motioned for Artemis to slowly descend the hill. "We've found it."

Evie peered anxiously over his shoulder and tightened her arms around his waist as they reached the base of the mound. Upon reaching flat ground once again, they caught a glimpse of the sharp tips of a pointed, time-worn wooden palisade poking through the few trees that surrounded it. They came to a stop once again, perhaps one hundred feet from the outer palisade of *Atsa'kióntie* village. The protective wall, constructed of large wooden beams pointing to the sky, had clearly begun to rot away, and some beams were missing entirely, giving a tiny glimpse into that which was contained inside.

They expected to hear the chatter of a town full of people going about their business, with the smoke of many cooking fires billowing into the sky from inside, but the settlement, as well as the surrounding wilderness, was eerily silent. Theo felt a nervous lump rise in his throat as the silence became deafening, and images of the massacred village he and his fellow soldiers had found in the Watchung mountains years ago flashed across his eyes. In that moment, he sent a prayer to every God that ever lived that they were not too late, that an envoy sent by George Washington or another had not swept through and left a path of destruction in their wake in the name of "liberty."

"Why is it so quiet?" Evie asked in a whisper, looking nervously all around them. "Shouldn't there be villagers about?"

Theo swallowed the morbid possibility that they were about to walk into the aftermath of another massacre and began to dismount from the horse. "Night has come. Perhaps they are all asleep."

Evie raised her brow skeptically. "All of them? Really?"

Theo rolled his eyes and helped her dismount as well, gently setting her on her feet on the ground. "Stay here with Artemis," he told her. "I shall go in alone and investigate."

He tried to turn toward the front gates of the palisade, but Evie caught him by his sleeve. "You cannot leave me out here alone!" she screeched. "I could be attacked! Or taken! Or—"

Theo gripped her by her arm and pulled her into his side with an aggravated sigh. "Alright. You will come with me. But do not leave my side and let me do the talking. Do you understand?"

Evie nodded and gripped his arm as they slowly moved toward the opening in the palisade—the main entrance to the settlement. Just as they came to the main gate, Evie looked up and pointed excitedly to the sky.

"Look!" she whispered. "Smoke!"

Theo followed her gaze and spotted a single wispy column of smoke emanating from the center of the village and billowing over the top of the palisade and into the evening sky. The trail of smoke had not been visible when they first reached the village, which could only mean that the fire had just been started. And where there was a freshly started fire, there were *people*.

Theo tightened his grip on Evie's arm and led her through the opening in the palisade. Once inside, they found rows upon rows of large longhouses, each about thirty meters long and constructed of the same wooden beams as the palisade that protected them from the outside world. The inside of the village was just as still and silent as the outside, with not a soul in sight. Taking carefully slow steps forward, they both dared to venture deeper into the settlement, but with every longhouse they passed, they were met with more emptiness and more silence. Theo curiously poked his head through the front entrance of one of the longhouses to look for any sign of life, but what he found within it, as well as in every other structure nearby, was total abandonment.

The houses still contained many personal belongings of those who once inhabited them, including cooking pots, fur pelts, blankets, and weapons. But there was no indication that anyone had disturbed the items or lived in the structures for some time. Much like the palisade, the structures within the village appeared unused for many months or even years and were beginning to show signs of decay. But other than the obvious rot, the settlement appeared to be untouched and undisturbed. Not even a wild animal or passing bandit appeared to have made its way through. It was as if every inhabitant of *Atsa'któntie* had abandoned their homes and belongings or simply disappeared without a trace, leaving behind their homes as relics of the past, frozen in time as a memorial to that which once thrived upon these lands.

Theo stopped in the doorway of another emptied longhouse and lowered his head in defeat. They were gone, whoever they were, and with them, most likely, his mother. But where could they have gone? Why would they have gone? And why would they leave so many of their belongings behind when they went?

"I do not see the source of that smoke," Evie stated in confusion as she came to his side in the doorway of the longhouse. "Perhaps we were mistaken. Maybe the smoke was coming from somewhere else…"

Theo shook his head in disappointment and pinched the bridge of his nose between his thumb and forefinger. "No. This is the place. This has to be the place, Evie. The map says that—"

"Forget the map," she snapped in frustration. "Whether this is your mother's village or not, it is *empty*."

Theo's face fell in even greater disappointment. "Are we too late?" he asked in a whisper. "Where could they have gone? They could not just have disappeared!"

Evie swallowed thickly as the terrible thoughts she knew they were both trying to dismiss began to swim in her head. Neither wanted to believe that *Atsa'któntie's* people were somehow all dead or missing, nor that they had been forcefully displaced. But something had to have happened to make an entire community of people abandon their centuries-old homes.

Evie and Theo both nearly jumped out of their skin when they heard a twig snapping underfoot just behind them, as well as the sound of approaching footsteps and a wooden arrow being notched against a bow. A man's deep and gruff voice bellowed from just a few feet behind their backs, hollering in a language they didn't understand with a tone that bespoke anger and suspicion.

Theo instantly took ahold of Evie's arm once again and pushed her behind him as he turned to face the source of the noise. As soon as he turned, however, he was met with the sight of an enormous Mohawk warrior towering over them both less than a foot away, his eyes narrowed with deadly accuracy upon them as he pointed his bow and arrow directly at the center of Theo's chest.

He seemed to be as tall and broad as a tree, with a sharp jawline, chiseled cheekbones, and long black hair wrapped into a single braid that fell down to the middle of his back. His skin was several shades darker than Theo's and had clearly been aged by many years of toil and battle. Blood red warpaint was smeared across his cheeks, all the way from his eyes to his jawline. He wore only buck-skin breeches and thigh-high leather moccasins, leaving his abdomen bare except for a single wolf pelt shawl that he had wrapped diagonally across his chest from his right shoulder down to his left hip. Arms as thick as tree trunks held the bow and notched arrow with a clear confidence, and his hands were as steady as the river as he pointed his arrow at the heart of the invader that stood before him.

The man barked something at them, presumably in *Kanien'kehá*, eyeing them both up and down with his bowstring still pulled taught. Theo swallowed thickly and slowly raised his eyes to meet the man's hostile gaze as Evie hid fearfully behind his back.

They both cowered under the booming cadence of his foreign tongue before Theo found the courage to stutter out, "We...we are not your enemies. We have not come to hurt you..."

The man raised his brow curiously and hesitated before clearing his throat. "Then why have you trespassed onto my land?" he asked gruffly, his words assaulting their ears like claps of thunder.

Theo and Evie shared a startled look. "You...you speak the King's English?" Theo asked in mild relief.

The man nodded curtly without lowering his arrow from Theo's chest. "Just as well as you. Who are you, and why have you come here?"

"My name is Theo Cunningham. And this is Evie. We have simply come for answers. I am looking for someone, and I have it on good authority that she may live here."

The man's eyes widened ever so slightly, and his jaw tightened. "...Cunningham?" he repeated sternly. He then proceeded to look Theo up and down, seemingly scrutinizing his appearance. "Are you one of us? Are you *Kanien'kehá:ka*?"

Theo nodded hesitantly. "On my mother's side. I was born here. I am a friend. I mean you nor your village any harm."

Slowly, the man lowered his bow and arrow, his large body relaxing though his eyes remained fixed on Theo's face, as if he was intensely studying the younger man's features for an answer to a question that he feared vocalizing. Theo and Evie both let out a breath that they didn't realize they had been holding when the man strapped his bow onto his back and replaced the arrow into the quiver hanging on his shoulder.

"Follow me," the man barked before turning on his heel and stalking toward the center of the village. When Theo and Evie both hesitated in the doorway of the longhouse, he paused mid-step and glanced over his shoulder. "*Follow*," he repeated harshly before turning away again.

Theo tried to coax Evie to follow him out of the doorway, but she remained fixed where she stood. "Are you mad?" she whispered with wide and fearful eyes. "He could be leading us to our deaths!"

"We have to follow him," Theo shot back. "He is the only one who can help us find Kateri."

Evie's arm draped protectively across her abdomen as Theo tightly took ahold of her hand and urged her to follow him. The Mohawk warrior led them across the empty village into what appeared to be a communal courtyard surrounded on all sides by even more abandoned longhouses. In the center of the yard, a small fire was burning, sending a paltry tower of smoke up into the evening sky. The man took a seat upon the ground on one side of the fire and crossed his legs before silently motioning for Theo and Evie to do the same across from him. The rigidness in his posture and the coldness in his dark eyes told them both that it was not an offer of hospitality they wanted to refuse.

Theo and Evie took a hesitant seat across from their reluctant host. The three then proceeded to sit in an awkward silence for several moments as the man poked at the fire with a walking stick.

Theo dared to break the silence by clearing his throat and saying, "I was told that *Atsa'któntie* was a large and prosperous village…but it is empty now. What happened to the people?"

The man's expression soured from one of mild suspicion to unbridled anger and contempt. Setting his walking stick down on the ground next to him, the man leaned forward and propped his elbows on his knees before curtly stating, "*Atsa'któntie* was once the pride of the *Kanien'kehá:ka* nation. Our numbers were large and our power great, until we were forced to leave our homeland."

Theo's jaw went rigid. "*What*?"

The man violently cleared his throat and stared into Theo's eyes from across the fire, which cast an eerie golden glow upon the older man's face that made him appear twenty years older than he actually was.

"Two years ago, the colonial government sold the land upon which the village sits in order to fund their war. They sent an envoy who instructed us to leave within the month—or be exterminated. The same fate befell nearly every other village along the river."

"Sold?" Theo repeated incredulously. "That is *theft*. The Patriots cannot simply sell land that is not theirs to purchase."

The man nodded in agreement, a wash of sadness replacing the fire burning in his eyes. "Their envoy did not want to hear any such argument.

They came with their guns and their horses and threatened to massacre our women and children if we did not comply. Everyone took what they could carry and moved west."

"Except for you," Theo noted quietly.

"I was one of the few who refused to be displaced. On the day the envoy arrived, he ordered his men to shoot dead any who resisted. But I escaped, and as soon as they had gone, I returned. I was resolved to stay and protect my land. And now in the eyes of the colonial government, I am a squatter in my own home."

"Why would you return?" Theo asked in confusion. "Surely they will kill you when they realize you have come back."

"Let them try!" the man shot back with a raised fist. "I was born upon the lands of *Atsa'któntie*. I was raised upon the lands of *Atsa'któntie*. And I will die in *Atsa'któntie*. This is my home."

"That is very brave," Evie spoke up in a mousy whisper.

The man scoffed. "You may call it what you wish. Brave, or foolish, I do not care. I have watched the white men slowly overtake this continent, growing ever more numerous and powerful as they build their colonies and their plantations and push my people farther and farther west in the name of empire. Many natives have cowered in the face of these colonizers, but I refuse. The only way I will leave this village is when the Sky Woman takes me to her home amongst the spirits."

Theo was quiet for a moment as his eyes dropped into his lap and his heart and mind began to race. He could feel a renewed sense of rage beginning to bubble in his chest at the thought of the government for which he once fought having pushed his mother's people out of their homes with guns to their backs. Evie could feel his body tensing next to her, and she placed a gentle hand upon his shoulder in an effort to comfort him.

"I... I do not believe we ever got your name, sir," Evie mumbled upon realizing that Theo was too distraught to speak.

The man stared at her across the fire for several moments before uttering, "Call me Tehwehron." He then jerked his chin in Theo's direction. "Tell me who it is you seek."

Theo slowly looked up, his eyes glazed with sadness. "I am looking for a woman. My mother. She birthed a child with a Redcoat soldier during the Seven Years War."

Tehwehron froze in his place across the fire, a look of both confusion and realization upon his face. Suddenly, he rose to his feet. "Who is your mother, boy?" he asked urgently, his body rigid once again.

"Her name is Kateri," Theo murmured as he, too, slowly rose to his full height. "Do you know her?"

Tehwehron swallowed thickly, coming around to the other side of the fire in order to stand chest to chest with Theo. His voice dropped to a near whisper, his words catching painfully in his throat.

"Know her?" he repeated sadly. "Kateri was my *sister*."

Theo took a startled step backwards, brow furrowed skeptically, as Evie let out a gasp. "What?" Theo whispered. "How can that be—"

Tehwehron took another step closer, placing his large hands on both of Theo's shoulders. "*Cunningham,*" he mumbled as he searched Theo's eyes and face for the familial resemblance that he had first noticed when he set eyes upon him. "I could see it the moment I looked upon your face. You have your mother's eyes, and her complexion. You are Alistair Cunningham's boy…"

Tehwehron suddenly pulled Theo tightly into his chest, all of the tension and hostility in his body instantly replaced with relief.

"You knew my father?" Theo asked in confusion and disbelief, feeling both relieved and nauseas.

Tehwehron pulled away and clamped his hands on either side of Theo's face, his old eyes flooded with a strange and sudden warmth. "My sister and I were inseparable. I was there when he and your mother met, my nephew. I was there when you were born into this world. I was there when that bastard Cunningham took you away from us and never returned!"

Theo shook his head angrily. "What are you talking about? Explain yourself! My father never mentioned my mother having a brother…"

Tehwehron's eyes fell to the ground as a wistful sigh escaped his lips. "I am not surprised. He and Kateri were determined to remove any traces of your *Kanien'kehá:ka* blood."

Feeling as if he had just been slapped in the face, Theo slowly lowered himself back down to a sitting position on the ground. His eyes searched the flames burning before him for any sense he could make out of the chaos raging in his head. "You…you are my uncle," he repeated softly as he stared blankly into the fire.

Tehwehron cleared his throat and crouched down at Theo's side, his face pinched into a look of sorrow and regret. His voice was tight as he mumbled, "In the *Kanien'kehá:ka* nation, a boy's most important bond is with his maternal uncle. When you were born, I knew I was entrusted with a great responsibility to see you through your years and teach you the ways of our people. But that was taken away from me when Alistair Cunningham took you back to his world among the colonists…"

Theo swallowed thickly and shared a perplexed look with Evie, who had placed a comforting hand upon his back as she became just as overwhelmed with these revelations as he. Theo looked up and locked eyes with his uncle, searching his face for any indication that he may have been deceiving him. But he found none. All he found in the older man's face was a look of adoration, and a vague resemblance to his own facial features that sent chills down his spine.

"I begged him not to take you," Tehwehron lamented on. "I begged them both to reconsider. Begged them to let you stay where you belonged, with your people, in *Atsa'któntie*. But they had already decided that it would be in your best interest to live among your father's people. They knew when you were brought into this world that you would carry with

Indivisible

you a terrible stigma as a child of both the forest and the colonies. They believed you would be spared years of heartache and confusion if you grew up to believe that you had no native blood at all."

Theo frowned deeply. "They were wrong."

"I have known that all along, my nephew," Tehwehron whispered as he reached out to place a hand on Theo's shoulder. "I knew there was no way to deny you the truth of your heritage. But they could not be swayed. Surely your mother knew this, deep down, but your father convinced her otherwise. And when he took you away, I feared I would never see your face again. But here you are, right before my eyes…"

Theo shook his head in anger and confusion. Tehwehron's words more or less corroborated what his father had told him over the years, but it still did not explain how easily Kateri was convinced to give up her firstborn child with the understanding that she would never see him again.

Before he could articulate one of the million questions summing in his head, Tehwehron squeezed his shoulder and softly murmured the word, "*Tekariho:ken.*"

"What?" Theo questioned. "What does that mean?"

A wistful smile came upon his uncle's face as he repeated, "*Tekariho:ken,* my boy. Tekariho:ken. This is the name your mother gave you when you first came into this world. She knew from the moment you were born that you were a magnificent creation—the offspring of two worlds that were never meant to meet but found each other nonetheless. That is why she named you Tekariho:ken. Because you were born between two worlds…"

Theo shrugged out from underneath the man's touch. "My name is Theo," he corrected curtly.

Tehwehron shook his head sadly. "No, nephew. Until you were taken from this village, you were Tekariho:ken. Your father gave you an English name because he knew you would be living among the English, but *here*, you are my nephew, Tekariho:ken. When they are born, each

Kanien'kehá:ka child is given a unique name meant for them, and only them. This name is meant to tell a story of who they are, who they are destined to be. And you were destined to be *between two worlds*."

Theo released a trembling breath and pinched the bridge of his nose, trying to make sense of the world that had just been ripped out from underneath his feet. In that moment, he did not know who he was or who he was supposed to be. Tekariho:ken or Theo, *Kanien'kehá:ka* or English, half breed or not, he was just as confused now as when he arrived. Tehwehron's revelations had left him with more questions than answers, as well as a newfound frustration building in his chest.

Suddenly, Theo stood again and pulled Evie to her feet to stand by his side as he wrapped an arm protectively around her waist. "If you truly are my uncle, then you can help me find Kateri."

Tehwehron rose to his full height with a deliberate slowness, and when his and Theo's eyes met again, his face was contorted with a renewed sorrow. "I...I wish I could, nephew. But I do not think that is possible."

"Why not?"

Tehwehron let a breath out through his nose, reaching forward once again to place a comforting hand on Theo's arm. "You have come too late, Tekariho:ken. Twenty years too late."

Theo stiffened and frowned skeptically. "Explain yourself."

"Kateri passed away twenty years ago. She died here, in this village, with her people surrounding her."

Theo felt as if he had simultaneously been punched in the stomach and stampeded by a herd of wild horses, and he stumbled backward, shrugging away when Evie attempted to reach out to take his hand. His eyes fell to the ground under his feet as the weight of one thousand tons settled upon his chest, suffocating him with a sadness that he could not comprehend. He could not believe it. He did not want to believe that she was dead, that she had *been* dead for so many years, while he carried the unbearable weight of his anger and resentment toward her, all the while none the wiser to the truth.

"...How?" he asked in a barely audible whisper without raising his eyes from the dirt.

Tehwehron sighed again. "I am so sorry..."

"*How?*" Theo repeated through clenched teeth as his hands balled into fists at his side.

"Twenty years ago, when you would have been four years old, the Seven Years War was still raging. Much like this war for independence, the *Kanien'kehá:ka* allied ourselves with the British. We had little love for King George's men even then, but we hated the French even more. In the summer of 1760, a convoy from the British army arrived at our village. The officer leading the convoy told us that they had been ordered to bring us supplies so that we may continue to provide them with our men to fight their battles. They brought us rations, guns, clothing, blankets...

"Except, we discovered quickly that those blankets were infested with smallpox. Sickness and suffering spread through the village like wildfire, taking more than half of our people with it. Most of the men were away on the warpath, fighting for the very men that had poisoned us, and when we returned, many of our wives and children had been taken by the pox."

Tehwehron paused, his words catching painfully in his throat as he recalled the terrible fate that had befallen his people two decades before. Theo's and Evie's eyes were wide with shock as they stared him down, waiting breathlessly for him to continue.

"Kateri, my sister, my closest friend in this world, she fell ill in the summer, and by autumn of that year, she had wasted away to nothing. She fought so hard, she refused to give in to that terrible plague, but in the end, after three months of suffering, she finally succumbed and joined the realm of the Sky Woman, along with many others. I returned home just before she passed, and I stayed by her side until the end. I held her frail body in my arms as she died, and I watched the light fade from her eyes until…until finally, she was gone…

"We were at a loss of what to do to help the sick. Our medicines and our prayers to the Sky Woman proved fruitless, so we burned the blankets and everything else from the convoy. And suddenly, the sickness stopped. That was when we knew we had been sabotaged by those who claimed to protect us. By the end of the autumn, nearly half of our people had been taken by the pox. We became weak and vulnerable, and our population never recovered. That is why we were unable to prevent the Continental Congress from selling our land and forcing us westward."

When Tehwehron looked up, a single tear slipped from his eye and rolled down his rugged cheek, smearing the warpaint upon his face, but he quickly wiped it away with the back of his hand. To see such a large and proud man reduced to such sadness before her eyes knocked the wind out of Evie and left her breathless. Theo felt her tighten her grip on his arm and bury her face in his chest, and though he wanted to comfort her, he found himself so overwhelmed by grief that his knees buckled underneath him, and he took an unsteady step backwards from her, bringing his hands up to clutch at his hair.

"I…I do not understand," he murmured after several moments of silence whilst he tried to swallow the rage bubbling in his blood. "Why would the British intentionally poison their allies?"

Tehwehron crossed his arms over his broad chest and bowed his head. "To remind us that we are dispensable as a people and living on this land at their mercy. The British may be our allies in wartime, but that does not make them our friends. No matter who sits on America's throne, whether it be a King or a Congress, the people who have inhabited these lands for thousands of years will always be seen as second class, and we will never be safe."

Feeling nauseas, Theo leaned forward and placed his hands upon his knees. He wanted nothing more than for the earth to open up and swallow him whole. He could feel what remained of his heart shattering even further into shards so small and so sharp that they could never hope to be put back together, and under the heavy gazes of both Evie and his uncle, he felt as if the weight of the entire world had been dropped upon his shoulders.

"…Who was the officer?" Theo suddenly asked, looking up through the strands of hair that had fallen in his face.

"Pardon?"

"The officer that led the convoy with the tainted blankets. Did he give a name?"

Tehwehron nodded once. "He called himself George Washington. He said he was given orders by his commanding officer to deliver rations and supplies to the Crown's native allies."

Theo shook his head in defeat as he ground his teeth together. He wanted to be shocked, but in truth, he was not. Every misfortune that befell his people seemed to come in the wake of destruction that Commander Washington left behind. No matter the war, no matter the side, the *Kanien'kehá:ka* suffered at the hands of a man that claimed to fight for the freedom of all.

Tehwehron stepped forward, taking a stick up from the ground and plunging it into the fire to light himself a torch before pointing his walking stick into the darkness over Theo's shoulder. "Come with me, nephew. There is something I want you to see."

Though he lacked the desire to hear or see any other heartbreaking revelations, Theo followed close behind Tehwehron and urged Evie to join him as the older man led them away from the fire and to the northern edge of the village. The moon was now high in the sky but hidden behind thick clouds that obscured most of its light. Theo was silent, his eyes fixed on his feet, as Tehwehron wordlessly led them along a winding path that snaked around several hollowed-out longhouses that stared emptily back at them like lifeless skeletons of the past. Tehwehron eventually stopped before the entrance of a longhouse along the northern edge of the village, just inside the palisade. Much like the others, it was in a state of decay and disrepair, a hollow shell of the home and sanctuary it once was.

"What is this?" Evie asked.

Tehwehron turned to face them and pointed his torch inside the doorway. "This was my sister's longhouse. This is where she spent her final days. I thought you should see it."

Without hesitation, Theo brushed past both Evie and Tehwehron to stalk inside the longhouse, and much as he expected, he found himself swallowed in darkness. Tehwehron and Evie entered just behind him, and the light from the torch managed to illuminate the inside of the house enough for Theo to catch a glimpse of the confines of his mother's world. Rather than being picked over and abandoned, this longhouse appeared as if it had been lived in just yesterday. Pelts, pots, clothing, and other trinkets, as well as a bed constructed of furs, littered the floor, covered in dust but otherwise undisturbed, as if its inhabitant had disappeared off of the face of the earth without warning and left behind all of her worldly possessions.

"This house has remained untouched since she passed," Tehwehron spoke up solemnly. "A person is only truly gone when they have been forgotten. And I refuse to forget."

"She really lived here?" Theo asked softly.

"She did. Until the end. She loved this village, and her people. She wanted nothing more than to raise you here. But she knew you would be safer with your father. She lived in constant fear that the village would be attacked by outsiders that want to see us all destroyed. The farther you were from the Kanien'kehá:ka, the better."

"I had always tried to picture her in my head. What she looked like, how she spoke. How she lived. I hoped finding this place would give me some clue as to what she was like, but I am left with just as much emptiness and confusion as when I began this journey. This place feels strange and foreign to me, but also, somehow…familiar…"

"You were born in this longhouse. I was there, holding your mother's hand. As was your father. This is where you spent the first few weeks of your life."

Theo looked around the empty shell of a home with a heavy heart. He was still disoriented by the fact that his mother had been gone for most of his life, and he hadn't had the slightest clue until now. Guilt ate ferociously at the inside of his chest as he thought back to all of the times he had cursed the woman's name, all of the times he claimed to have hated her for her selfishness, all of the times he had wished he had never been born.

His eyes searched the walls and the floor for anything that looked or felt remotely familiar, anything that spoke to him and told him he was home. The moment he crossed the threshold into Kateri's longhouse, Theo was assaulted by a strange feeling of both comfort and despair. For as long as he could remember, he had longed to know Kateri as more than a faceless stranger, and now that he was surrounded by the confines of her world, this foreign place seemed familiar, like a distant dream he could reach but not quite hold onto. He could sense her presence here though he had never met her—he could sense her like both a guardian and a friend that he had always known.

Eventually, his gaze settled on a dust-covered shelf upon which a small toy sat amongst several other trinkets. It was a small object, only as long as the palm of his hand, and it appeared to be a statue of the likeness of a wolf carved out of a chunk of wood and polished smooth.

Tehwehron smiled sadly when he noticed Theo pluck the toy off of the shelf and study it. He stepped forward to offer him the light from his torch and said softly, "That was a gift from me. I carved it myself. I was heartbroken when your father did not take it along when he took you away."

Theo ran his thumb across the surface of the statue's back. "She kept it," he mumbled.

"Of course, she did. She kept anything and everything that reminded her of you."

Theo looked up in mild confusion and quirked his brow. "Why would she do such a thing?"

"Because she loved you more than anything."

Theo shook his head in disbelief. "If that were true, she would not have given me up so easily."

Tehwehron sighed heavily. "You must understand, my boy, that it was not easy. It was the hardest decision she had ever made. She did not give you up because she did not want you, she let you go because she loved you and she thought she was giving you the best chance to have the happiness that she never had."

"How could I possibly be happy living a lie?" Theo snapped. "How could she possibly think I would be happier without her in my life?"

"She knew your life would be difficult, no matter who raised you, because the world does not yet accept those of mixed blood. She wanted to keep you with her, and raise you here in the village, and she wanted your father to stay here with her. But he refused. She did not think she could properly raise you on her own with our enemies so close outside our gates, so they came to the mutual agreement that you would be better off in his world, with Alistair and his wife. I disagreed completely, but their minds could not be changed."

"So that was it, then? How could she be content with sending me away and never seeing me again?"

Tehwehron shook his head. "She was far from content. But she was willing to sacrifice anything for you. She did not give you away with the intention of never seeing you again, Tekariho:ken. She wanted to find you, when the time was right, and you were older, old enough to understand why she had to make such a sacrifice. She never gave up hope that one day you two would be reunited, but…the sickness took her before she could even begin to look for you…"

Feeling his legs buckle underneath him once again, Theo slowly dropped to his knees on the floor of his mother's longhouse, clutching tightly at the wolf statue in his hands. His eyes began to burn with the tears he had been holding back for his entire life, and he wanted desperately to let them flow freely down his face. But in that moment, he was too shocked, too dismayed, too confused, to do so. All he could do was collapse to his knees as his chest constricted around his heart and he clutched onto the last remaining shred he had of the woman named Kateri.

He had dreamed for as long as he could remember of the day that he would find her, look her in her eyes, and hear her tell him she loved him. And with every year that passed, his faith that he would ever see her continued to wane, until now, as he came to the crushing realization his dream was just that—a dream. It would never be reality. It could never have been reality, as she had been gone from this world for most of his life, leaving him hopelessly wandering the earth in search of a person he would never be able to find.

It was not the fact that she was dead that destroyed him, he decided in that moment. It was the fact that she had been dead for all of this time and he had been none the wiser, left to assume that she had simply abandoned him with no intention to reunite. He had hated and resented her for all of these years because he did not know how else to feel. But now, he was beginning to consider the possibility that the decade of anger he held in in heart may have been misplaced. She would not have kept a memento of her son if she wanted to forget he ever existed—she would not have kept anything that remained of him to keep him in her heart until the day came that they could finally be reunited. Yet that is exactly what she did, holding onto it into her dying days.

Evie moved to crouch next to him, wrapping her arms around his torso as she watched his shoulders begin to shake. Theo dropped his head into his hands, feeling somehow both defeated and vindicated while also feeling his heart crumble into pieces as he watched the world that he thought he knew disappear from under his feet, leaving him stumbling for a soft place to land. That soft place was Evie, and he rested his head against her chest while squeezing his eyes shut to swallow the tears he wanted to shed, but still couldn't allow himself to reveal. He had the answers he had been waiting for all of his life, but the discovery was bittersweet and left a sour taste in his mouth.

After several moments of tense silence, Tehwehron crouched at his nephew's other side and placed a large hand upon his back. "Your mother loved you. She loved your father, and she loved her people, but she loved you so much more. I know there is nothing that can be done to bring her back, but I hope this brought you some peace."

Theo looked up and met his gaze, his eyes red and swollen. His mouth twitched upward as he weakly nodded. "It did. Thank you, Tehwehron."

"Call me Uncle," the man corrected with a sideways smile. "We are family, Tekariho:ken. We are *Kahwá:tsire*. And in *Kanien'kehá*, we thank others by saying *Niá:wen*."

"Uncle," Theo repeated, slowly rising to his feet and wiping at his eyes with the back of his hand. "*Niá:wen*."

He would be lying if he said it was not slightly overwhelming to be looking at the only family he had left on his mother's side—the only person in the world that carried her blood other than himself. Tehwehron was rough and unrefined, if not a bit boorish like his nephew, and Theo had just met him, but when he looked into the older man's eyes, he saw family. He saw a connection. He saw part of what he had been missing his entire life, part of what he had been craving for as long as he could remember. He saw his mother, without ever having laid eyes upon her, and he saw a people he never met but somehow felt he now knew. It pained him to think that when they parted, it may be for the last time.

"Now that you have your answers, what shall you do?" Tehwehron asked as he led Evie and Theo both out of the longhouse. "You are welcome to stay here as long as you wish, as I have been rather lonely here by myself. But I fear for you and the girl's safety, should any hostile parties come through."

Evie and Theo shared a brief look before he said, "We plan to return home to Massachusetts as soon as possible. That is our home."

"To Boston?"

Theo shook his head. "We are not city folk."

Tehwehron smirked and clapped him on the back. "Neither are the *Kanien'kehá:ka.*"

"Come with us," Theo blurted out suddenly. "Come back with us to our homestead on the Bay. You said yourself that you are lonely here. Come with us and start your life over."

Tehwehron shook his head with a wistful smile. "No, nephew. I thank you for the invitation, but I cannot do that. I told you I was born in *Atsa'któntie* and that I would die in *Atsa'któntie.* This is my home. I refuse to leave it."

"But, Uncle, if the Patriots return to this land and see that you have not left, they will surely have you killed."

"Let them try."

"Please, be reasonable—"

"Listen to me," Tehwehron interrupted him sternly. "If I let them push me out of my homeland, I let them win. They have already taken my sister, and my people. I will not let them take the home that our ancestors built thousands of years ago."

Theo sighed in defeat. "Will I ever see you again?"

"This is not the last you will see of me, I swear to you. We will meet when the time is right."

Theo nodded in agreement, but he hung his head sadly. He had finally been reunited with the only remains of his mother's bloodline, and he could not fathom leaving him so quickly. Upon seeing the disappointment in Theo's eyes, Tehwehron beckoned them to follow him again, this time towards the entrance of the village.

"Come, both of you. There is one last thing you should see before you go."

Tehwehron led them back to the main entrance of the village, stopping inside the opening in the palisade. He held up his torch to illuminate one of the larger posts in the walls of the palisade, and that was when Evie and Theo both noticed a large tomahawk embedded into the post at waist level, its handle intricately engraved and decorated with an array of beads and feathers swaying in the wind.

"What is this?" Theo asked with a raised brow.

"Of all things you should know of your people, this is the most crucial. When our people go to war, an axe is buried in a post to signify its beginning. The axe is removed only when the conflict ends, and the threat is exterminated. You need to understand that a war has been raging on these contested lands long before the first shots were fired at Lexington and Concord. The war began when the white colonizer first stepped on this land and claimed it as his own, not caring who he stepped on and who he destroyed on his journey to create his empire. This war will not end when a treaty is signed and the British return to their island across the great sea. This war will only be over when people who look like you and I no longer need live in fear that their way of life will be vilified simply because it is *different*."

Theo swallowed thickly, feeling his body tense as his uncle echoed the words that he had repeated to himself many times since the war for independence had begun. It was foolish of him to ever think that his or any other downtrodden person's life would improve just because the British were soon to be defeated and gone. Nothing would change, because the men who would inevitably be put in charge of this fledgling nation were raised in the same society, with the same doctrines and dogmas, as the oppressors they had pushed back across the sea. The only difference was, these new oppressors would lack a London accent and consider taxing white landed men a crime against God.

The Patriots were fighting for their independence, but what was independence? What did it mean to be free? Did it mean reprieve from burdensome taxes and the right to bear arms, or was it much more than that? Was it the chance to live unburdened by the fear of your own destruction at the hands of those in power? Was it freedom from persecution on the basis of creed or color? Theo did not yet know, and he hadn't the courage to dwell upon it in that moment.

"Why did you show me this?" Theo asked softly.

"Because I want you to understand that you symbolize an end to this war, Tekariho:ken. Your name signifies that you are trapped between two worlds, that much you understand. But it also means that you are living proof that those of farer skin need not be enemies to those who possess foreign tongues and foreign practices. We *can* live in peace. We can love one another as our fellow man, regardless of the color of our flesh. Your father, as foolish and misguided as he was when he was young, was not an evil man. I truly believe that he loved my sister at one time. And you are the eternal proof of that love, of that unity, of that momentary peace between two opposing worlds."

Theo grazed his fingertips across the handle of the axe and looked up to meet his uncle's heavy gaze. It was not until then that he realized he was still clutching the wooden wolf trinket, and he tried to offer it for the man to take. Tehwehron shook his head and refused. "No, nephew. You take it with you. It is yours, after all."

The slightest of smiles touched Theo's lips as he tucked the trinket into the inner pocket of his vest. Before Tehwehron could blink, Theo suddenly threw his arms around his neck in a tight embrace that nearly knocked the large man off of his feet. Caught off guard by the sudden display of affection, he hesitated for a moment before returning the embrace and holding his nephew to his chest.

"*Niá:wen*, Uncle," Theo mumbled quietly as a single tear slipped down his cheek.

Tehwehron pulled away slightly and gripped him by his shoulders. "There is no need to thank me. I wish you safe travels on your way home. And promise me you will give your father my warmest regards when you return. Tell him that all is forgiven."

Chapter 15

A Bitter Truth

June 1780

The journey home from the Mohawk Valley was long and mostly silent. The initial contentment Theo felt from meeting his uncle and finally discovering the fate that had befallen his mother began to wear off the moment he pulled the wagon away from the bank of the Mohawk River and onto the trail, and he was left with days to dwell upon the devastating truth that had had been thrust upon him.

Though he had just met Tehwehron, he felt an instant connection with him, and it saddened him greatly to have to say goodbye so quickly, especially now that he had been forced to come to terms with the fact that his mother was gone, not just from his life, but from this world, and had been for most of his life. It was a miserable feeling to know that he would forever be denied the chance to know her, to show her the man he had become despite the many trials, toils, and tribulations he had faced. In fact, his contentment quickly morphed into a wordless melancholy, which then spiraled into a deep depression as the third day of the journey back drew to a close. He had gotten some of the answers he had been seeking, but they did little to comfort him like he had hoped, and they stirred up a new onslaught of questions he was terrified to ask.

Evie took instant notice of the way his mood soured the farther they traveled from the village, and she attempted to make conversation to keep his mind occupied, but he did not seem interested in discussing the weather in the frontier or scouring the wilderness for wildlife with her like he had on their way up north. She had told herself that she would find the courage to tell him the secret she had been keeping in her womb as soon as their journey was over, but she could feel that courage leaving her every time she looked into his eyes and saw nothing but devastation. She could see that his life had been turned upside down and then ripped out from underneath him the moment he learned that Kateri was gone, and she could not bring herself to disturb his world any further. At least not yet. Not now. Not while he was still so distraught and freshly hurt by her loss. She would give him until they returned home, and then maybe a few days or weeks after that, until his wounded heart was no longer so raw and battered.

A week into the trek back to Division Point, Evie could handle the silence that had settled upon them no longer, and she turned in her seat next to him on the front bench of the wagon.

"Theo...?"

"Hm?" Theo did not look away from the path before them to meet her gaze, nor did the inflection in his tired voice indicate he was really interested in talking.

"Do you...feel better, now that you know what fate befell your mother? Now that you no longer have to wonder what happened to her?"

Theo was quiet for a moment, and she could see his throat move as if he was swallowing the words he actually wanted to say. "I feel betrayed," he eventually said in a quiet and defeated mumble.

"How do you mean?"

Theo's grip on the reins that guided Artemis down the path tightened as he slowly turned to meet her eyes. "I cannot even be angry at myself for waiting so long to try and find her. Whether I had set out yesterday or five years ago, it still would have been too late, because she died long before I even knew she existed. Long before I would have ever been able to find her."

Evie's eyes fluttered closed as she shook her head in sadness. If anyone understood the pain of discovering one's mother's death second hand long after it had already occurred, it was she.

"It is not your fault," she said quietly. "You never could have known."

"I know," he returned coolly. "I can only blame the people that kept her a secret from me for all these years. And the one that killed her."

Evie swallowed uneasily and wrapped her arms around her middle. "Do you think George Washington knew the blankets were diseased when he brought them to the village?"

Theo snorted in derision. "If you had asked me that question five years ago, I would have told you it was impossible. But now I realize that the Commander, just like any other man, is capable of both great heroism...and great evil."

Evie placed a hand gently on his back and leaned her head against his shoulder. "I am so sorry, Theo. I am sorry you were never able to meet her like you had hoped."

"As am I," he returned meekly.

"But I hope it brings some joy to your heart to know that she loved you. She never stopped thinking about you. She wanted nothing more than to find you when she thought the time was right. God…God just had different plans…"

"God had nothing to do with it," he grumbled through clenched teeth before abruptly pulling on the reins and bringing Artemis to a sudden stop that violently jolted the entire wagon. Evie sat upright and turned to Theo with eyes wide in shock.

"What the hell are you doing?"

After having pulled the wagon to a stop on the side of the road, Theo turned his back to her and released the reins before stepping down from the front bench. "Stay here," he ordered quietly.

"Where are you going?" Evie asked nervously as he began to walk toward the back of the wagon.

"Just give me a moment!" he snapped back before disappearing behind the wagon.

Assuming that he had gone to ensure that their luggage was still secured in the bed of the wagon, Evie turned back in her seat to face forward, crossing her arms over her chest in a huff. She did not like when he raised his voice at her—it was not a frequent occurrence, but when it did happen, it made her heart skip a beat in a very unpleasant way.

Several minutes of silence passed before Evie began to grow impatient that he had not yet returned. She ached to be home, and whatever he was doing in the back of the wagon was just delaying them further. Impatiently tapping her fingers on the bench, she decided to climb down from the wagon herself to investigate whatever it was that was taking him so long. It had grown quiet behind the wagon several minutes ago, and she was starting to wonder if he had disappeared all together.

It was not until she shuffled around toward the rear of the wagon that the sound of muffled sobs touched her ears, urging her to quicken her pace. When she reached the back of the wagon, she found Theo sitting in the dirt, his knees hugged to his chest and his back leaning against one of the wagon's wheels as he clutched onto the polished wooden wolf statue he had been keeping in his pocket since they left the village. Evie immediately dropped to her knees at his side when she saw the cascade of infuriated tears running down his cheeks, and she threw her arms around him.

"Oh, Theo," she whispered soothingly. "Please do not cry."

Theo found himself unable to speak past the violent sobs that escaped his throat—sobs that had suddenly overcome him after so many years of holding them deep within himself. He had always prided himself on his ability to bury his sadness until it was invisible to those around him, but now, he found himself overwhelmed by an inconsolable sorrow that shook him to his very core. He did not know who he was angry at the most—his father for keeping his mother a secret for so long, Washington for bringing about her demise, the Patriots for stealing the Mohawks' land and forcing them west to fund their fight for freedom, or himself for getting his hopes so high in the first place. He should have known from the beginning that he was never destined to have her in his life. It was too good to be true.

He hadn't the energy to try and swallow his tears before Evie came to his side, nor did he care to hide them from her after she wrapped her arms around him. Instead, he welcomed her tight, comforting embrace and dropped his weary head upon her breast, taking in her lovely scent and continuing to sob into her bodice the tears of years and years of disappointment that had culminated into the greatest defeat he had ever faced. Perhaps the most painful part of all was that the very people he had trusted, the very people for whom he had given his life in this bloody war, had been his people's greatest enemy all along. Washington, Putnam, the Continental Congress, and all who followed them, had betrayed him *once again*. They had been betraying him for the last twenty years, and he had just been too foolish and too stubborn to want to see it.

And how could those who claim to fight for the freedom fund their war by denying that very thing to so many others? How was that fair? How was that just? How was that *right*?

He was so angry that he could not fathom it nor articulate it into words. He had been angry for as long as he could remember—at his mother, at his father, at the Crown, at the world, at God, at everyone that gave him a dirty look in passing or made a snide comment about his past. Yet, he was so tired of holding such anger in his heart. So tired of hating. So tired of fighting. He just wanted to forgive, and to be happy. But he had been at war with himself and the entire world for so long that he hadn't the faintest clue how begin.

Evie held him tight and allowed him to sob in her arms until there were no more tears to cry, whispering whatever comforting words she could manage as she felt herself become overwhelmed in her own sadness on his behalf. She wanted to tell him that things would be alright, but in truth, now that she had seen some of the true horrors of their world, she knew she could not guarantee that. No matter who won the war, nor who held the power, and no matter what Washington and the others preached, life and liberty were not yet truly inalienable rights on these contested lands.

It was a sad and terribly bitter truth, but a truth, nonetheless.

***

July 1780

Wordlessly, Theo steered the wagon up the road that snaked through the middle of Division Point. He expected to feel some sort of relief upon returning home, but his heart still felt heavy in his chest, as if he was carrying the weight of ten thousand stones upon his shoulders with no one near to help lighten the load.

After pulling the wagon to a stop in front of the Cunningham house, he immediately climbed down from the front bench and made his way through the front door, leaving Evie outside, puzzled and slightly irritated that he had abandoned her to unload their luggage on her own. Rather than putting up a fuss, however, she followed him inside, where she found him standing silently in the doorway to the parlor as Gunner pawed excitedly at his legs and yipped with glee that they had finally returned home.

Alistair was seated in his armchair in the parlor and looked up from his newspaper at the sound of the front door slamming open and then two sets of hurried footsteps.

"Oh, Theo," he said in surprise, taking in the solemn look on his son's face with a concerned frown. "I am so glad you two have returned. I did not expect you back for another week or so…"

Theo waved off his pleasantries. After discovering the extent to which Alistair had hidden the past from him, he was in no mood for small talk. He had more important things to do.

"Where is Johanna?" Theo asked pointedly.

Between two violent coughs, Alistair said, "She's in the kitchen, preparing supper—"

Theo did not stick around to hear the end of his statement, and instead turned on his heel to rush into the kitchen. Evie and Gunner followed curiously behind him, stopping in the doorway as Theo entered and Johanna looked up from the hearth where she was making the preparations to bake a loaf of bread. Her face tightened when her eyes fell upon Theo and Evie, and she could tell in an instant by the tension in their bodies that something terrible had happened.

"Evie? Theo?" she asked worriedly. "I did not hear you return. If I had known you'd return today I would have prepared more food for supper."

Abruptly, Theo crossed the floor of the kitchen in two long strides, throwing his long arms around Johanna's small frame and crushing her against his chest while he buried his face in her shoulder. She was briefly startled by his sudden display of affection, and a little puzzled, but she immediately returned it, nonetheless.

"Theo? What has happened? Are you alright?"

Her heart ached when she heard the beginnings of a quiet sob muffled by the fabric of her blouse. Without looking up, Theo tightened his arms around her and murmured tearfully, "I'm so sorry, Johanna...I am so sorry. I did not mean it. I didn't mean it; I swear to you. I am so sorry. Please forgive me..."

Johanna held him to her chest and placed a hand on the back of his head to cradle him. "Oh, my boy, there is nothing to forgive. You know nothing you say or do could ever change my love for you."

"I am so sorry," he repeated through quiet sobs into her shoulder. "I have taken you for granted all of my life. It wasn't right. You've done so much for me. You have made me the man I am today. I do not know how I could ever thank you..."

Johanna chuckled lightly. "That is what mothers are for, is it not?"

She could not remember the last time she had seen him shed a tear, or even embrace her. After what had been said between them, and the time that had passed since he had left for the Mohawk Valley, the last thing she expected was for this towering man of twenty-four years to fall to pieces in her arms. In that moment, as she held him while he sobbed, he was not the man she had watched grow throughout the years. He was the boy she had nurtured, loved, and raised out of the kindness of her heart. The boy she had loved as her own, unconditionally and irrevocably, despite the terrible betrayal that had resulted in his birth.

She would have given anything to go back in time to when he was a little chubby-faced boy with bright eyes and an even brighter smile. She would have given anything to rewrite history and make it so that he had never been hurt, never been lied to, never been betrayed. If she could do it all over, she would have told him the truth herself, long before he ever had the chance to discover it on his own. Then, perhaps, they would have all been spared such heartache and despair.

Theo slowly raised his head from her shoulder, and a tear rolled down his cheek as their eyes met. Johanna reached up to wipe away the tear with the pad of her thumb, feeling her own eyes begin to burn with a mutual sorrow.

"Yes," he agreed in a whisper, "That is what mothers are for…"

Johanna cupped his cheek with the palm of her hand and smiled wistfully. "No more tears, darling. All has been forgiven. Tell me, what happened? Did you find Kateri or her village?"

In that moment, Alistair appeared in the doorway next to Evie, leaning heavily upon a cane as he waited anxiously for the news that they had all been waiting weeks to hear.

Theo pulled away from her and cleared his throat, hesitating for a moment before mumbling, "We found what was left of it."

"How do you mean?" Johanna asked.

Theo looked between her and Alistair as he stated, "The people of *Atsa'któntie* were forced out of their home and to the west when the Continental Congress seized their land and sold it to pay for the war. There was no one left, save for…*Tehwehron*." Theo's heavy gaze settled upon his father as he finished his statement, his eyes narrowing dangerously as he uttered his uncle's name. Alistair tensed next to Evie at the sound of the name, swallowing thickly as his eyes fell to the floor in shame.

"Who is that?" Johanna asked in confusion.

Theo did not look away from Alistair as a deep frown settled upon his face. "Ask my father. He knew him well," he muttered bitterly. "He is my mother's brother."

Johanna gasped in confusion and shook her head. "How can that be? I hadn't any clue that your mother had a brother."

"No one knew but my father," Theo retorted, crossing his arms over his broad chest. "Tehwehron told me everything that *he* didn't."

Alistair sighed heavily and shuffled into the kitchen with the aid of his cane. "I am so sorry, Theo…" he rasped.

"Is that even my name, Father? Or is it Tekariho:ken?"

Alistair narrowed his eyes at Theo and pointed at his chest. "Your name is Theo Cunningham. Nothing Kateri's brother told you will change that."

"Why didn't you tell me I had family other than my mother in *Atsa'któntie?*" Theo asked him angrily. "How could you hide that from me? But I suppose that is only a drop in the bucket of all of the secrets you chose to keep!"

Alistair was quiet for several moments as he slowly settled himself into a chair at the kitchen table and rested his hands on the top of his cane. His old, wizened eyes were swimming with sadness and regret as he stared at the floor and searched for his words. "I was afraid," he eventually whispered.

"Afraid of what?"

Alistair raised his eyes from the floor to meet his son's angered gaze. The look of sorrow evident in his father's eyes momentarily made Theo consider softening his tone, but he was too enraged in the moment to be rational or civil. The lies had to stop. Now, and forever.

"I was afraid that if you went to the village and found your mother, or her brother, you would realize that you belonged there. That you would not want to come back," Alistair morosely confessed, his voice breaking. "I was afraid. I did not want to give you another reason to leave me…"

Theo let out a deep sigh to collect himself. His father's confession managed to soften his anger ever so slightly, but he would be lying if he claimed he was not still frustrated. He was slightly taken aback by Alistair's explanation, as he had honestly believed that he would be doing his father a favor if he disappeared from his life. Perhaps then he would no longer be a source of shame, or the proof of how he had betrayed his wife all those years ago.

"How many more secrets do you intend to keep from me?" Theo asked curtly.

Alistair sadly shook his head. "None. There are no more secrets left to tell. You know everything now…"

"Well, I have a secret of my own now," Theo coolly returned. "But I have chosen not to repeat your mistakes. You should know that Kateri is dead, Father. She has been dead for twenty years."

Alistair snapped his eyes up again, his jaw clenched. A look of pain fleetingly crossed his face before he pressed his lips into a thin, hard line. "...She...she's gone?" he asked in a mournful whisper that was barely audible to everyone else.

Theo nodded. "And do you know what fate befell her?"

Alistair weakly shook his head and leaned heavily on his cane, his heart aching in his chest as he tried to comprehend that his one-time lover was truly deceased. He had tried to banish her from his memory long ago, but she had always maintained a place in his heart, no matter how hard he resisted. And now he struggled to fathom that she was *dead*, not just to him, but to the rest of the world. It wounded him to his very core to realize in that moment that the last glimpse he had of her twenty-four years ago was truly the last glimpse he would ever have.

"No, I do not know," he mumbled.

"Your good old friend, George Washington, led a convoy to *Atsa'któntie* twenty years ago. And within that convoy was a supply of blankets, blankets deliberately infested with smallpox. My mother, along with so many other women and children, was dead within three months of his visit."

Evie sadly hung her head in the kitchen doorway as Johanna gasped and placed a hand over her heart. "Oh, good God...how despicable..."

Alistair's eyes widened in both shock and disbelief as he leaned back in his chair. He shook his head incredulously as his hands began to tremble in his lap. "No...no, that can't be true. That is impossible. George would never do such a thing..."

Theo took a perturbed step in his father's direction, hands and jaw clenched. "Just as it is impossible for him to have ordered the deliberate destruction of the native village in the mountains three years ago?" he bellowed. "Just as it is impossible for him to have enslaved numerous human beings for his own profit in Mount Vernon? That man is no better than the tyrants he claims to oppose! What more must he do before you finally see him for what he is, Father? My mother is dead and her blood stains his hands!"

The entire house fell silent under the thunderous power of Theo's raised voice, and Alistair seemed to shrink within his shadow as he slumped morosely in his chair. He hadn't even made peace with the fact that the mother of his child was dead before he was bombarded with the fact that she was supposedly *murdered*, and he could feel his head swimming with a sorrow that he hadn't felt since he and Kateri parted ways for the last time.

He took several moments to collect himself before speaking, clearing his throat before dropping his eyes to the floor and quietly rasping, "I do not understand. Why would the British do something like that to those they claim to be their allies?"

Theo straightened his shoulders and scowled. "The Mohawk and the British may be 'allies,' but they were never *equals*."

Alistair shook his head in disgust as his eyes roamed the floor. "I...I am so sorry, Theo. I do not know what to say."

"Do not say anything. There is nothing you can say to make this right, to turn back time and give me back all of those years of deceit, or to bring my mother back from the dead. I do not want an apology from you. It will mean nothing now."

"Theo," Evie said gently, stepping into the room to place a hand on his shoulder, "your father had no way of knowing that she had passed. You cannot blame this all on him. You told me yourself that it would have been too late to find her no matter how long he waited to tell you about her."

Theo scoffed angrily and crossed his arms over his chest, narrowing his eyes at Alistair one last time. "He could have left me where I belonged. *With her*."

Alistair pointed an accusatory finger his way. "Don't you dare say that, boy. You belong here with us, with your family. If you had stayed in that village, you would have surely met the same fate as your mother!"

Theo leaned down until they were staring into each other's eyes, fiery golden oceans locked against grayish blue pools. "Perhaps we all would have been better off, then," he murmured softly before abruptly turning away and storming out of the kitchen toward the front door.

Immediately, Evie, Johanna, and Alistair followed after him, concerned by the cryptic implication in his words. They followed him out the front door and around to the back of the house, calling after him as he kept his back to them and their pleas to halt fell on deaf years. They all froze in fear when he easily plucked the heavy axe off of the wood-chopping block behind the house and took it into both of his hands, eyeing it carefully with his back still facing them.

"Theo, what in God's name are you doing?" Alistair asked through labored breaths as he leaned heavily on his cane. If he didn't know his son better, he might have feared that the boy had finally snapped and was now preparing to hack them all to pieces.

Wordlessly, Theo stalked toward them, axe heavy in his hands, but instead of raising it to them, which, of course, he would never do, he brushed in between Johanna and Evie and made his way back toward the front of the house, stomping up the steps of the front porch. Taking in a deep breath, he faced one of the supporting pillars of the veranda and raised the axe high over his head just as the others came around the corner of the house.

"Theo, what are you—?" Evie tried to ask, but before she could get the words out, Theo swung the axe as hard as could into the thick wooden post, lodging the head of the weapon deep into the pillar until it stuck. When he pulled his hands away, the axe head was still embedded in the wood, and its long handle jutted awkwardly into the air.

"For God's sake!" Alistair crowed. "Have you gone bloody mad? Are you trying to destroy the house I built?"

Slowly, Theo turned to face them from the top of the porch steps. He looked between his parents, his lover, and the damage he had done to the wooden post, his chest heaving with a swarm of emotions he wished he could toss away.

"When my mother's people go to war," he explained to them with a sudden and unsettling calmness, "they embed an axe into a wooden post, and it remains there until the war is over and the threat has passed. My war started long before Lexington and Concord, long before the Intolerable Acts, and long before I was born. It started when a man on a throne across the sea decided that it was his right and his destiny to conquer the rest of the world, and that his people would be the measuring stick against all others would be judged. It started when a line was drawn demarcating who was worthy of life and liberty and who wasn't, and that criteria ultimately became our native tongues, our creeds, and the colors of our flesh.

"I've learned the hard way that people like me will always be left to fall through the cracks, and that is not going to change when the British are gone. A new king and parliament, an American king and parliament, will ultimately continue the bloody cycle in which we have been living for the last two and a half centuries. I've spent my entire life blaming the British and their King for my misfortunes, but I see now that they are not the only ones to blame. The ones at fault are those on both sides who believe that they have something to gain from conquering, pillaging, and exploiting the most vulnerable.

"I was told by my uncle that I am living proof that two people from completely different worlds can coexist in peace. I pray that he is right, and his words will ring true one day, but I also fear that he may have confused the exception with the rule. The war does not end when the British surrender. The war ends when the people of this fledgling nation finally see that there is strength in unity, strength in equality, and strength in diversity. The axe will remain here until that day comes."

Another solemn silence fell upon the three onlookers as they exchanged glances with one another and then looked back to Theo. Evie was the first to climb the stairs to join him on the porch, and when she did, she stood by his side, raising her arm to gently graze her fingertips across the length of the axe's handle. She swallowed thickly, her knees feeling week under the weight of his intense gaze.

Slowly, she looked up at him from underneath her eyelashes and reached forward to intertwine the fingers of her free hand with his. With the action, she could immediately sense the tension in his body dispersing.

"If you are at war," she murmured as her thoughts trailed to the creature that she was sure was growing inside her body, "than so am I."

If Theo's existence was proof that peace and prosperity were possible between the native people of these lands and the neighboring colonists, she told herself in that moment, then so too was the life growing within her. The life she could feel blossoming in her womb carried both his blood and hers, a beautiful mixture of two souls that were destined to find one another despite the obstacles that society had placed before them.

She just hoped Theo would come to see things the same way.

***

August 1780

Much to Evie's dismay, a month passed since she and Theo arrived home from *Atsa'któntie* and she still had not found the courage to tell him or anyone else the secret that she was harboring. Her initial suspicions about her pregnancy were confirmed when she missed yet another one of her monthly cycles after returning to Division Point, in addition to the fact that she was continuously nauseas and fatigued, much like the beginning of her pregnancy with Noah.

There was no doubt in her mind now that she was with child, perhaps two months along, she had calculated, but she was so fearful of how Theo would react that summer came and went before she could manage to tell him. She had initially waited because she did not want to distract him from his mission of tracking down Kateri, and then she had put it off because she was afraid to upset him during the first few weeks of his mourning his mother's death. And now so many weeks had passed since she first discovered her condition that she feared telling him *because* she had waited so long.

She had told herself that she was waiting for the right time, but it was obvious now that there was no right time, especially not after the devastating news of Kateri's death had come to light. Theo was still not fully himself a month after returning home, and after embedding the axe into one of the front posts of the house, he refused to speak of her further with anybody. After all of the trials and tribulations he had suffered with his family, surely the last thing he would want now was to learn that he was about to be burdened with the responsibility of a family of his own.

However, Evie was about ready to burst after holding in her secret for so long, and though she was not ready to have that conversation with Theo, she thought it necessary to confide in her best friend. So, on a warm and muggy August afternoon, she shuffled down the road to Jacob and Emma's cabin, located just behind Mr. and Mrs. Caldwell's home.

Emma answered the door with little Levi perched on her hip after Evie gave it a few quick raps.

"Evie, how nice of you to stop by! I haven't laid eyes on you in over a week," Emma beamed, though the tired bags under her eyes betrayed her giddiness. She had taken to motherhood quite well over the last few months, but her sunken in face and messy blonde tresses clearly stated that she was running on very little sleep while caring for her home, her husband, and an infant of ten months.

"It is wonderful to see you too, Emma. Did I catch you at a bad time?" Evie asked, gesturing to the fussy infant on Emma's hip.

Emma shook her head as she bounced the baby in her arms. "Not at all! Please, come in, come in. I've been trapped in the house for days with the baby. I'm aching for some adult conversation."

Evie chuckled and followed her into the cozy cabin, closing the front door behind her and peering around for signs of any other guests in the house.

"Jacob and his father went to Boston for a spell," Emma explained as she led Evie into the sitting room and offered her a seat in one of the two armchairs by the fireplace. "Something about supplies for the forge. So, it has just been Levi and I for a few days."

Evie gazed adoringly down at baby Levi as he sat in his mother's lap and peered back at her with a pair of big hazel eyes that mirrored his father's. He had grown so much over the last few months that he now sported a fair bit of fatness in his cheeks, legs, and arms that made him all the more adorable. He also had a head of thick dark curls nearly to his ears, also like Jacob. Levi smiled widely at her, a slobbery toothless grin, and raised his arms as if he wanted her to take him from Emma's lap.

Emma took notice of the grin that had unconsciously snuck its way into Evie's face. "Do you want to hold him?"

"I would love to," Evie returned eagerly.

Emma gladly plopped the baby onto Evie's lap before letting out a sigh and collapsing against the backrest of her chair.

"God love him, but I gave birth to a wild animal."

Evie bounced the baby on her lap until he began to giggle. "How do you mean?"

"He never stays still! The moment I think I can have a moment to myself to sit, he decides to go crawling about and leaving a trail of chaos in his wake!"

Evie chuckled and shook her head. "Welcome to motherhood."

Evie looked down at the giggling infant in her lap and thought back to the reason she had come here in the first place. She had always adored baby Levi, but now as she peered at him while knowing that she was carrying a miracle of her own, there was a different sort of joy in her heart. A joy mixed with fear, worry, and anxious anticipation that quickly became visible on her face, even to the rather oblivious Emma.

"Something troubles you," Emma noted with a raised brow.

"What makes you say that?"

"Your smile disappeared rather quickly. What is on your mind?"

Evie hesitated and looked away, feeling her cheeks begin to tinge pink. "I...I have something I want to tell you. But you must swear to me that you will not tell a single soul."

Emma leaned forward with wide eyes and clasped her hands together excitedly. "Oh, I love a good secret. Go on, tell me, tell me."

Evie let out a long and heavy sigh as she stroked the top of Levi's head. She could feel her chest tightening at the thought of uttering her secret out loud for the first time. Deciding she could no longer keep it within, she squeezed her eyes shut and blurted out, "I am with child."

When Emma did not immediately react, Evie cracked her eyes open to see her friend staring at her with wide, doe-like eyes and a wide smirk. She didn't look all that surprised or concerned. If anything, she appeared rather smug. "With whose child?" she asked slyly.

Evie rolled her eyes and groaned. "Emma!"

Emma snickered and patted her on the shoulder. "Oh, you know how I love to jest. Lighten up! Isn't this exciting news? You and Theo are to be parents!"

"Yes, I suppose...but...I have not told him yet. Or anyone else, for that matter. You are the first to know."

"Well, how long have you known of your condition?"

Evie shrugged in embarrassment. "Nearly two months..."

Emma nearly choked on her tongue. "Dear God...why have you waited so long? Aren't you happy to be with child again?"

Evie began to nervously fidget with her fingers as she wrapped her arms around the baby in her lap. Looking down, she mumbled, "Of course I am happy. I'm elated. But...I am also terrified, Emma. I do not have a husband anymore like you did when you had your child. And you and Jacob were trying to have a child. Theo and I are not married, and this was the last thing I was expecting to happen right now."

"You don't think he will share in your excitement?"

Evie shrugged again. "I do not know. I know that he does not want to start a family at the moment. And I fear he will be upset with me, especially now that I have waited so long to tell him. I'm...I am afraid that he will be so angry that he will...leave me."

"You know Theo would never do that. You must tell him soon. You know how much he hates to be kept in the dark."

Evie groaned and tipped her head against the back of her chair, rubbing her temples to alleviate the headache brewing there. "Emma, I do not know what I am going to do. I am not ready to be a mother. I certainly wasn't ready when Noah was born, so how could I possibly be ready now? Oh, God, and what if...what if God takes this child as He took my first? I can't lose another child, Emma, I just can't—"

Emma immediately stood and placed her hands upon Evie's shoulders, leaning down to look her in the eye. "Evie, that is not going to happen. This pregnancy is going to be nothing like your last. You have a man who loves you, and who will undoubtedly love your child. Everything will be fine. But you must tell Theo now. You cannot hide the truth any longer."

"I suppose you are right..."

"Of course, I am! Listen, Evie. I did not think I was ready to be a mother either. But when Levi was born, all of those fears and worries melted away. It came naturally to me, and it will for you as well. You will be a wonderful mother."

Evie attempted a weak smile. "Do you really think so?"

"Of course! Oh, this will be so exciting! Our children will surely be the best of friends, I just know it. And if you have a girl, someday she and Levi will marry and have children of their own and we will be one big family, and—"

"Emma," Evie cut her off with a raised hand. "Don't you think you are putting the cart before the horse just a bit?"

"Well, perhaps," Emma sighed as she reached down to take Levi back into her arms. "I am just so excited for you and Theo. You will finally have the family you always wanted."

Evie's smile widened as a warm feeling spread across her chest and she placed her hands upon her stomach. After having confided in Emma, she could feel some of the weight of her secret lifting from her shoulders. "I just hope Theo will be as excited as I."

"Of course, he will. He loves you."

"But you must promise me that you will not tell anyone what I have told you today until after I have told Theo. He will be furious if he hears about this from anyone but me."

"I cannot even tell Jacob?"

"Especially not Jacob! He and Theo are close—surely he'd tell Theo immediately if he caught wind of the news."

"What if I swear him to secrecy—"

"No, Emma. Not a soul. Please. I'm trusting you. Promise me you will keep this between us for now."

Emma let out a sigh. "Fine. But you cannot hide the truth from Theo any longer. He deserves to know."

***

As the summer drew to a close, Evie could feel her world beginning to close in around her. Theo, so consumed by his own thoughts and grief, had been completely oblivious to the fact that she had been behaving differently since they returned home, or the fact that she was desperately searching for the courage to tell him something that had been on her mind for weeks.

As much as Evie loved Emma, she immediately regretted telling her before anyone else. Emma was known to be a bit dense at times, and very talkative, and Evie feared that it would only be a matter of time before her decision to confide in her friend came back to bite her. Unfortunately, the fear of her enormous secret catching up with her became realized only three days later, and the ensuing chaos seemed to rip the ground out from underneath her feet and send her reeling to find her balance.

It was a humid evening in late August when Jacob happened upon Theo, who was distracting himself from his melancholy by lounging on the dock to which *The Liberty* was anchored. He was sitting cross legged at the end of the dock, staring at the horizon as the sun dipped below and sent hues of purple and orange across the sky, when Jacob approached from behind.

"I see you have returned from Boston," Theo stated without having to look to see who was coming.

Jacob took a seat next to him on the edge of the dock. "I just returned yesterday with my father. We have not spoken much since you returned from New York a month ago, my friend."

Theo shrugged and maintained his gaze on the bay. "We have both been preoccupied, I suppose."

Jacob sighed and turned to face his friend, reaching out to clamp a hand on Theo's shoulder. "I heard the news about your mother. I am so sorry."

"What's done is done," Theo murmured quietly without looking up. "There is nothing I can do to bring her or anyone else back."

"How are you faring? Emma tells me you haven't been yourself since you returned."

"I am still trying to understand it all," Theo mumbled with a sigh. "It is just difficult to grasp the fact that I will truly never have a chance to know her now. She has always been, and will always be a stranger to me, but I also feel as if I am mourning the loss of someone that I have known for all of my years..."

Jacob squeezed his shoulder affectionately. "She would be proud of the man you've become, Theo. And she would be even prouder to know that you are creating a family of your own."

Theo abruptly looked up, an eyebrow raised in confusion. "What are you talking about?"

Jacob chuckled. "I'm talking about the happy news, of course. I hear a congratulations are in order for you and Evie!"

Theo narrowed his eyes and furrowed his brow even deeper. "Congratulations for what?"

"Well, for the baby..."

Theo nearly choked on his own tongue as he felt all of the air leave his lungs. "...Baby?" he stuttered. "*What* baby?"

Jacob's chuckle melted into a nervous cackle as he mumbled, "The baby in Evie's womb..."

"*What?*" Theo hissed, feeling as if he had just been punched in the stomach so hard that he was seeing stars. "What the hell are you talking about?"

At the sight of all of the blood draining from Theo's face, Jacob swallowed thickly. "She...she did not tell you?"

"Tell me, what?"

"That she is with child..."

"No! Evie has told me nothing!" Theo snapped harshly, his voice breaking in shock and surprise. He could feel himself quickly becoming lightheaded as a million anxious thoughts began to race through his mind.

Jacob slapped his hand over his face in embarrassment and shook his head. "Oh, God...I never should have said anything. I thought she would have told you by now—"

Theo turned to face him and reached forward to grab him by the shoulders. His golden-brown eyes were wide with worry and panic as he asked, "Are you telling me that Evie told *you* before she told me?"

"No, no. Not at all. I heard from Emma. She was bursting with a secret and told me the moment I returned from Boston. But I didn't know it was a secret from *you*. I assumed that if Emma knew, you surely would have known as well…"

Theo immediately jumped to his feet in rage. "No! I knew nothing of this! Who else knows?"

"No one that I am aware of. Theo, I am so sorry. If I knew Evie hadn't told you, I never would have said anything. I feel like such an ass."

"How could she not tell me this?" Theo bellowed, his eyes nervously scanning the horizon as his heart began to race in his chest. "Why would she hide this from me?"

"I... I haven't any clue. The extent of my knowledge is that she is pregnant and has been keeping it to herself for two months."

"Two *months*?" Theo repeated in a howl. Abruptly, he turned on his heel and began to stalk back toward the beginning of the dock. He could feel a white-hot anger beginning to boil under the surface of his skin, and the weight of one thousand tons settled in the pit of his stomach.

Jacob stood and hurried after him. "Where are you going?"

"To find the mother of my child," Theo hissed over his shoulder through clenched teeth.

Jacob tried to reach out for him, but Theo quickly shrugged away from his touch and waved him off before sprinting across the beach at full speed. Jacob helplessly watched him go, kicking himself for unknowingly putting his foot in his mouth.

Dammit, Emma, he thought to himself with a heavy sigh and a shake of his head. *What Hell have we created now?*

***

Evie nearly jumped out of her skin when the door to Theo's bedroom slammed open that evening. Letting out a startled squeak, she whirled around from the armoire, where she had been placing Theo's freshly laundered clothes, to see none other than Theo lurking in the doorway. She could tell immediately from his posture that something was wrong; his entire body was stiff, his hands were clenched at his sides, and his jaw was set, while his eyes appeared to be swimming with anger and confusion.

"Theo, you frightened me," she stuttered with a nervous chuckle. "I was just putting away the last of your laundry—"

Theo cut her off by taking several heavy steps into the room and crossing his arms over his broad chest before snapping, "How long?"

"...I'm sorry?"

"How long?" he repeated harshly. "How long were you planning to wait until you told me?"

Evie swallowed the lump rising in her throat. "I...I do not understand—"

"Do not play coy with me, woman. We both know that you are pregnant. How long did you plan to keep me in the dark while you told everyone else?"

Slowly, Evie placed the last stack of garments in the armoire and closed the door before leaning her back against it while her eyes fell to the floor. She could feel herself cowering under the weight of Theo's gaze from across the room, and the anger radiating from his body made her knees weak with worry.

"I...I can explain," she murmured quietly, slowly encircling her arms around her stomach. "I am so sorry, Theo..."

"Sorry for what?" he returned coldly as he crossed the room in three long strides and came face to face with her, trapping her against the armoire with the sheer size of his rigid body. "Are you sorry for keeping the news from me for so long, or for telling everyone else but me?"

Evie held up her hands in a gesture of surrender. "Please, Theo, you must understand. I told only Emma because I was afraid to tell you. I swore her to secrecy, but that was clearly a mistake…"

"No, the mistake was thinking that I did not deserve to know first!"

"Of course, you deserved to know first…but I knew how terribly distraught you were after we returned home from New York, and I did not want to further burden you with this news until you were starting to feel better. Please, you must believe me. I did not mean to keep this from you for so long. Time just got away from me, and I was only trying to protect you while you were grieving—"

"I do not need you to protect me!" Theo growled, taking another step in her direction. "If I am the father of your child, I deserved to know as soon as you discovered your condition. But instead, I had to hear the news that I am to be a father from *Jacob*! Do you have any idea how that makes me feel, Evie?"

Evie reached forward and attempted to place her hands upon his chest, but he immediately took a step back and shrugged away from her, his face pinched up in anger. "I'm so sorry, Theo. I wanted to tell you, I was going to tell you, I just wanted to wait until the right time…"

"What happened to not keeping secrets?" Theo barked. "No more secrets, remember? I thought you trusted me. I thought I could trust *you*."

"You can trust me. I was just afraid that you would be…upset."

"Upset? You feared I would be upset? I am not upset, Evie, I am furious! I am hurt that you would even consider keeping something so important from me, *again*!"

Evie swallowed thickly as she felt regretful and nervous tears beginning to burn her eyes. "Please do not be angry," she whispered.

Theo scoffed and shook his head. He was quiet for a moment as he looked about the room that they had shared for the last three years—the room in which the child she carried had surely been conceived. He *hoped*.

"Is this child even mine?" he suddenly asked as he turned to face her with a gaze colder than ice.

The words felt like knives in Evie's flesh as she outwardly flinched. "What did you just say?"

"Is this child even *mine*?"

Evie gasped and turned her head away, the burning in her eyes intensifying before a tear slipped down her cheek. She was shocked that he would even think such a thing, and her heart began to crumble in her chest as she turned back to face his steely glare.

"How could you even ask me such a thing?" she snapped with a shake of her head. "Do you really think that lowly of me?"

Theo cleared his throat, immediately regretting his choice of words. He knew he had no reason to suspect she had been unfaithful, but the thought began to nag at him as soon as he discovered how long she had been keeping the truth of her condition from him.

"I am sure you can understand my concern, given the way our relationship began. Why else would you hide this from me for so long?"

It was Evie's turn to scoff as she pointed an accusatory finger in his face. "And who else's child might this be? Silas'? In case you have forgotten, my husband has been dead for over a year! Or did you just want to hurt me by throwing everything he did to torture me back in my face?"

Theo stumbled over his thoughts and his words as he searched for a rebuttal, but he could find none. He immediately realized he had crossed a line, but he was so angry, disoriented, and confused that he could not manage to find any words of apology. He could see the hurt in her eyes, and it pained him to know he had caused it once again. He had an uncanny ability, he was discovering, to find the most hurtful words when he became upset with the people he cared most about. He never meant to hurt her, he just found himself so enraged by her secrecy that he lost all control of his thoughts. He just wanted all of the lies and the secrets to stop, whether they be from her, or his father. No more lies. No more shadows. No more secrets.

"I didn't mean that, Evie. I just—"

"Spare me," Evie hissed tearfully as she held up a hand to silence him before turning her back to him and quickly storming out of the bedroom. Theo followed her as she stomped across the hallway and into the room that had once been her own bedroom, slamming the door shut in his face before he could join her inside.

Theo rapidly knocked on the door after he heard the lock on the other side click to keep him out. "Evie, please come back out here so we can talk," he said as he tried to breathe deeply through his nose to calm himself.

"I have nothing to say to you," she snapped through the door. "Leave me be!"

"We have to talk about this. You are carrying my child…"

The door to the bedroom opened a crack, just wide enough for Evie to peek at him from the other side without opening it enough for him to get inside. "You clearly do not think so," she hissed. "You think I am some sort of cheap whore, don't you? Is that what Silas told you? Or did you develop that opinion on your own?"

"You know I could never think that of you. I did not mean what I said. I was just upset—"

Evie slammed the door shut again before he could finish and locked it. "Leave me alone!" she cried from the other side. "I never want to speak to you again!"

Theo let out a heavy sigh when he realized that the damage had already been done. She was too upset to give him the time of day at the moment, so he resolved to give her some time to recollect herself. Pressing his back against her door, he slowly slid down to the floor and dropped his head in his hands. It never ceased to amaze him how skilled he was in hurting those he loved, whether it be with his fists or his words. But now, he had gone and said the worst thing he could have possibly uttered to the woman carrying his child, and he would be lucky if she ever chose to speak to him again. If time was what she needed to forgive him so that they could discuss how their lives were about to change, that was what he would give her. She had to come out of the room sometime, and when she did, he would try to make things right. Until then, he planned to park himself on the floor at her door.

"Well done, Theo," he whispered to himself as he tipped his head back against the door and stared up at the ceiling. "You've really cocked it up this time…"

Chapter 16

A Love Without End

August 1780

Leaning heavily on his cane, Alistair gingerly made his way down the stairs in the wee hours of the morning. The sun would not rise for at least another few hours, but he had awoken himself with a rather terrible coughing fit that left his throat dry and tasting of blood. After tossing and turning for what felt like hours, he resolved to shuffle his haggard body downstairs in order to fetch something to drink.

His health had taken a dramatic turn for the worse within the last several months, though he did not want to acknowledge it, and the coughing fits were becoming more and more frequent, to the point that he was barely able to leave the house without assistance. The coughing and accompanying throbbing in his chest had been keeping him up at night for months, as had the news that his son had brought home with him when he returned from the Mohawk Valley.

The old man still could not bring himself to believe that Kateri was truly gone, and it sent an ache through his heart to know that she had been dead for so long and he had been none the wiser. Though it had been twenty-four years since he had last laid eyes on his one-time love, her name was still carved upon his heart, and it always would be. Their affair was brief, but fiery and passionate in a way he could not even fathom, and it resulted in the greatest thing that had ever happened to him—his son. But their love was never meant to last, and his love for Johanna had, and always would, run so much deeper than what he had ever felt for Kateri.

Alistair was torn from his thoughts when he reached the bottom of the stairs and saw the light of a single lantern burning within the kitchen. He knew for a fact that he did not leave a lantern alight before he and Johanna retired for the night, which could only mean that someone else was up. Slightly alarmed, he hobbled into the kitchen with a vice-like grip on his cane in case he needed to be prepared to use it as a weapon against an intruder. He let out a sigh of relief and relaxed, however, when he crossed into the room and spotted his son slumped forward at the table, alone, his head buried under his arms as the lantern burned brightly next to him.

"Good God, Theo," Alistair croaked. "You gave me a fright! I nearly bludgeoned you with my cane!"

Startled, Theo immediately raised his head and looked over his shoulder. In the light of the lantern, Alistair could see that his face was creased with worry and sleeplessness. "I'm sorry," Theo murmured quietly as he laid his head back upon his arms. "I did not mean to frighten you."

Alistair was slightly puzzled by his morose tone and hobbled across the room to take a seat across from him at the table.

"What are you doing down here, son?" he asked with a sigh. "You are never up before the sun."

"I could ask the same of you," Theo countered without looking up from the table.

"I could not sleep. I decided to come down here to clear my mind."

"As have I," Theo mumbled, raising his head again and sliding a hand down his face.

"I can see that something is bothering you. I have always been able to see it on your face. What troubles you?"

Theo shook his head dejectedly and let out a deep sigh, burying his face in his hands as he rested his elbows upon the table.

"It is your mother, isn't it?" Alistair rasped, clearing his throat sadly. "You have not been the same since you returned from her village."

A sound escaped Theo's throat from behind his hands that resembled a quiet sob, and Alistair reached across the table to pry his hands away from his face. The action revealed that Theo's eyes were squeezed shut and his mouth was pinched up into an agonized scowl.

"I'm so sorry," Theo mumbled as he shook his head again and clenched his teeth. "I'm so sorry. I've…I've ruined everything…"

"What? What are you talking about? Why would you say that?"

Slowly, Theo opened his eyes and looked up to meet Alistair's concerned gaze. "Was I a mistake?" he asked in a whisper.

Alistair furrowed his brow. "You were *never* a mistake."

Theo shook his head incredulously. "How could I not be? My existence nearly destroyed your marriage and your family."

Alistair abruptly stood and limped around to the other side of the table, where he pulled a chair out and took a seat on Theo's right. Taking his son's wrists in his hands, he cleared his throat and said lowly, "Listen to me. *I* nearly destroyed my marriage, not you. In my younger years, I was a terrible excuse for a man. I drank, I fought, I stole, and I cheated my way through life. I don't know how Johanna found the strength to stay with me after all I had done. But you, you changed everything. *You* were the reason I gave up my hellish ways. You were the reason I found God. You were the reason I became a better man. You *saved* my family, Theo."

Sniffling, Theo stared into the old man's eyes with a perplexed look. All of his life, his father had been a man of few words, and the words he did say were not often affectionate. "Do you really mean that?"

Alistair squeezed his wrists. "Of all of the mistakes I have made in my life, you were not one of them. And I have made more mistakes than I can count. I know I have not been the best father to you over the years, but I want you to understand that everything I have ever done was for you."

"I know," Theo returned as he dropped his head.

Alistair reached forward to take his chin in his hand and raise his head until their eyes met. "I should have told you this so many years ago, but my life changed for the better when I became your father. I would do anything to protect you from the consequences of my mistakes, because a father's love for his child is a love without end. I need you to know that I meant well in keeping you from your mother and her people, but I know now that it was not the best decision for you."

"It doesn't matter now," Theo murmured glumly. "She was gone long ago."

"It does matter. I had hoped that by isolating you from half of who you are, I would protect you from the persecution that your mother's people have faced since the first colonists arrived here. But instead, I only bred hate, hurt, confusion, and resentment within you, and for that, I will never forgive myself."

"I've resented you for as long as I can remember," Theo admitted. "But I could never hate you."

The slightest of smiles tugged at the corner of Alistair's mouth as he placed a hand upon Theo's cheek. "You know, I had hoped that you would grow up to resemble myself so that no one could question your heritage, but you look more and more like your mother with every day that passes, and I am grateful. I see her every time I look into your eyes, my son."

Theo quietly scoffed. "I always wished I resembled you."

"Do not say that. I do not want you to be ashamed of any part of who you are."

Theo began to chew on his bottom lip as he stared into his father's eyes. He could not find the words to express how much he had longed to hear these words leave Alistair's lips, and he could feel his eyes beginning to burn with long-buried tears. Before he could stop it, a single tear slipped down his cheek, and Alistair wiped it away with his thumb.

"I do not expect you to forgive me for the mistakes I have made," Alistair whispered, "but I hope someday that when you become a father yourself, you will understand why I made them."

Theo suddenly pulled away and squeezed his eyes shut while clenching his teeth together. He dropped his head into his hands again with a sigh, prompting Alistair to state, "Something else troubles you."

"I've made a terrible mistake," Theo whispered after several moments of tense silence. "I've ruined everything..."

"I do not understand."

Theo raised his head to stare up at the ceiling, suddenly feeling too ashamed of himself to look his father in the eye. Crossing his arms over his chest, he let out a long breath and murmured lowly, "Evie is pregnant."

Alistair did not speak at first, as he was stunned into a silence, but after a few moments, he cleared his throat uncomfortably and pinched the bridge of his nose between his thumb and forefinger. "I see," he mumbled quietly. "I take it you just discovered this."

Theo nodded curtly. "This evening."

"Does she know how far along she is?"

"Two months."

Alistair let out a sigh and rubbed his chin as his eyes fell to the floor. This had not been the first thing he expected to hear so early in the morning, but he had to admit that he was not entirely surprised. Despite his protests and heeding, Theo and Evie had been sharing a bed together for over two years, and he was not naive to the ways of passionate young lovers.

"And how does she feel about that?" Alistair asked.

"I would not know. She is not speaking to me."

Alistair scoffed. "That upset, hm?"

Theo rolled his eyes and mimicked his father's habit of pinching the bridge of his nose. "We had an argument last night. I said something terrible because I was angry that she had kept it a secret from me for weeks, and now she has locked herself in her room."

"And what did you say?"

"I...may have suggested that the child was not mine."

Alistair audibly groaned. "For God's sake, Theo, what would possess you to say that to a pregnant woman? Are you touched in the head?"

Theo angrily pushed his chair away from the table and jumped to his feet while emitting a perturbed growl from his throat. Alistair watched from his seat as Theo began to pace nervously across the kitchen floor, his hands gripping his hair. "I did not believe I was until now," he grumbled. "I do not know why I said such a terrible thing. But I suppose it is just like me to ruin everything I touch."

"Do you really believe she could be unfaithful to you?"

Theo paused with a sigh and shook his head. "No. Not at all. I was just...angry."

"Were you angry that she is with child, or angry that she hid it from you?"

Theo furrowed his brow and grumbled in confusion. "No. Yes. I don't know. I was just angry."

"And are you angry now that you have had time to dwell on it?"

Theo looked up to the ceiling in thought and relaxed his tensed shoulders with another sigh. "No. I am just afraid."

"And I am sure she is as well. What are you so afraid of?"

"I do not fear many things, Father, but repeating your mistakes ranks high on that list."

Alistair frowned and rested his hands on the top of his cane. "How is this repeating my mistakes?"

"Don't you see? I've ruined Evie's life! She and that child will forever be cursed by my tainted blood. How could I be so selfish to bring a child into a world that so hates people like me?"

Alistair made to stand as quickly as he could manage and crossed the kitchen floor to stand chest to chest with Theo. Pointing a finger in the boy's chest, he sternly stated, "Don't you ever say such a thing. Now, you listen to me, young man. You may not think you are ready, or even capable, of being a father, but that matters little now. No man is *ready* for that responsibility. But I know you have a good head on your shoulders and a heart of the purest gold in your chest. You've created this family, and now you'll do what you must to care for it."

Theo swallowed thickly and raked his hand nervously through his hair. "What if I can't?" he asked in a broken voice as his eyes fell to the floor under his feet. "What if I fail? What if my child hates me for bringing him into this world?"

Alistair reached forward to place a gentle hand on Theo's shoulder, his eyes softening with fond memories of his son's long forgotten childhood. "You will drive yourself mad asking yourself such questions. You and Evie will make wonderful parents."

Theo scoffed. "I do not know the first thing about being a father."

"Tell me something. Do you trust yourself?"

"Not one bit."

"Do you trust Evie?"

After a moment of thought, Theo murmured, "With my whole heart."

"Then you must trust that she chose to be with you—to have a child with you—because she saw something wonderful in you. You may not believe it now, but I can tell you from experience that becoming a father is the greatest thing you will ever do."

Theo looked up and felt a warm feeling spread through this chest as he stood under the enormous weight of Alistair's gaze. The old man's eyes were tired from a lack of sleep but filled to the brim with a tenderness that Theo had been longing to see for many years. Before Theo could speak, Alistair reached forward and pulled him into a tight embrace, wrapping his arms around the boy's waist and holding his head to his chest. Theo was initially caught off guard, but he quickly relaxed against his father's body and returned the embrace. He could feel his eyes beginning to burn again, so he buried his face in Alistair's shirt and silently sobbed into his chest.

"Your life will never be the same," Alistair said gently as he stroked Theo's hair. "But it is soon going to change in the most wonderful way. Do you remember what I just told you about a father's love, son?"

Theo pulled his head away enough to mumble, "It's…a love without end."

"A love without end," Alistair repeated softly. "You will know that love soon enough."

Theo squeezed Alistair one more time, feeling the slightest of smiles come to his face for the first time in weeks. He could not remember the last time he felt as safe as he did now in his father's arms, and he did not want the feeling to end. He could feel the lightest of weights being lifted from his shoulders now, but the fact that Evie was still not speaking to him made his heart ache.

"Not unless Evie forgives me for what I said," he stated as he pulled away. "I hurt her greatly."

"I am sure you did. You must understand that for as difficult as this will be for you, it will be infinitely more so for her. After what happened with her son, she is surely terrified to be with child again. She needs you to be by her side with words of comfort, not hurt. She needs to know that you will provide for her and your child, not because you are obligated, but because you *want* to."

Theo nodded in agreement and sighed. "I must speak with her. I must make it right."

"Go to her. Promise her everything that she wants and needs, and then deliver it. You two are a family now. Do you understand me?"

Theo placed a hand on Alistair's arm and gave him a sideways smirk. The thought of family, especially with Evie, brought a joy to his heart that he had never before experienced. "I will. You have my word."

Alistair opened his mouth to speak, but was interrupted by the sound of footsteps creeping down the wooden stairs around the corner. A moment later, Johanna appeared in the doorway, still in her nightclothes. "Oh, good morning, gentlemen," she said with a yawn. "I was not expecting you two down here so early. I just came down to get breakfast started." Sensing the strange tension that had begun to dissipate from the room, she then asked, "Did I interrupt something?"

Alistair and Theo shared a sheepish look before the former asked his son, "Do you want to tell her, or shall I?"

***

Evie sat up abruptly in her bed when she heard the sound of rustling outside the door. She had taken refuge within the room that had once been her bedroom for nearly a day now, curled up upon the otherwise empty mattress to stare blankly at the bare walls as tears of sorrow and regret stained her cheeks. At that moment, she hated Theo for the cruel things he had said and the way he had reacted to the news of her condition, but she hated herself even more for setting the chaos into motion.

Nearly half a day had passed since she slammed the door in Theo's face after he had accused her of being unfaithful to him, and she had yet to speak to him, nor even leave her room. If Emma had been foolish enough to tell Jacob the secret, and Jacob had told Theo, it was only a matter of time before the news spread like wildfire throughout the rest of the homestead, leaving her powerless to watch as everything seemed to burn to the ground around her.

Throwing her legs over the side of the bed, she peered across the room to see a small scrap of parchment being slid under her door amidst a fleeting shadow on the other side. Evie forced herself to her feet and shuffled to the door, bending down to take up the paper from the floor. It was late afternoon, and the sun was preparing to make its descent to the horizon, giving her room a dimness that made it difficult to see what the parchment contained. She moved to the window and held the scrap up to the minimal light shining through the glass to see a carefully crafted note, written in ink with Theo's characteristic chicken-scratch.

Please forgive me. I need you both.

Evie ran her eyes across the words several times and swallowed thickly. Normally, such a sentiment would have brought a weakness to her knees and a skip in her heartbeat, but she was still so vexed by Theo's cruelty and Emma's apparent betrayal that she could not allow herself to be swooned by pretty words on parchment. Before she realized what she was doing, she tore the note into several small pieces and made for the door, her skirt whirling around her legs as she strode into the hallway. She found Theo immediately down the hall, his back turned as if he was caught in the middle of making his exit after having slipped the note under her door. He turned upon hearing her door creak open and found her standing in the middle of the hall just a few paces behind.

She looked tired and rather ragged as she stared back at him, her eyes red and swollen from hours of silent sobbing. Her cheeks were rather gaunt, and her face was paler than usual; her long auburn tresses had gone unbrushed that day and her dress unchanged, as she had not found the desire to get out of bed until now. Theo's gaze softened apologetically as he looked upon her sad and bedraggled state, and his heart ached knowing that he was the one who had caused her sorrow.

"Evie..." he started to say as she approached him.

But instead of welcoming him with open arms, as he had greatly hoped, she held up the torn note before shoving it into his chest. He stared at her in shock for several moments before she said, "You cannot fix this by dressing it up with pretty words. Not this time."

"What do you want me to do?" he asked softly, letting the scraps of parchment flutter to the floor at his feet.

Evie leaned forward with narrowed eyes, her voice dropping to a whisper as she murmured, "Prove me wrong."

He furrowed a brow in confusion. "What does that mean?"

Evie scoffed and took a few steps back before placing her hands on her hips in derision. She began to nervously chew on her bottom lip for a moment, her eyes roaming about the hall as she found the courage to say, "Had my son lived, he would be six years old. Six years ago, I told my husband I was carrying his child, and do you know what he said to me?"

"I haven't any clue..." Theo admitted sheepishly.

Evie hesitated before muttering, "My husband looked me in my eyes and accused me of adultery when I told him I was with child. He was certain I had betrayed him. I tried to tell him otherwise, begged him to believe me. But he was drunk and paranoid, and he refused to believe that I was an honorable woman worthy to be his wife and the mother of his child. But the only time, *the only time*, I ever betrayed that man was with *you*, and only you! And that still isn't enough for you!"

"It is more than enough," Theo returned. "I had no idea that Silas had said that. If I had, I never would have—"

Evie held up a hand to silence him. "You promised me you would never hurt me like he did. *You promised.*"

When Theo was too stunned and ashamed to offer a rebuttal, Evie shook her head in disappointment and brushed past him to storm down the hall. At the last second, he spun around and caught her by her arm to pull her back.

"Wait," he pleaded. "Please, I'm sorry—"

"Do not touch me!" she barked in return, ripping her arm from his grasp and marching toward the end of the hall. She paused at the top of the stairs and tossed one last wounded glance over her shoulder at him before turning away and storming down the stairs, leaving him alone in the hallway, a heart weighed down by shame and regret. Angrily, Theo let out a deep growl and threw his fist at the nearest wall in aggravation.

Evie took the steps two at a time to reach the first floor, nearly running into Johanna in the front room on her way out of the house. Johanna tried to stop her with a kind greeting and excited smile, having just heard the news of her pregnancy the night before from Theo and Alistair, but Evie silently brushed past her and left the house, slamming the front door closed behind her. Johanna turned back toward the stairs in confusion just as Theo reached the bottom landing. She could see the anger and frustration on Theo's face as they met at the bottom of the stairs.

"The apology did not go so well, I take it?"

Theo collapsed into a seated position on the bottom stair and dropped his head in his hands. "How can I properly apologize if she won't even speak to me?"

Johanna sighed heavily and lowered herself onto the step next to him, smoothing out her skirts as she said, "I would tell you to give her time. But no amount of time will assuage the sting of what you said to her last night."

Theo pinched the bridge of his nose in frustration. Perhaps the worst part of this entire mess was that he now had to live with the fact that Evie had just compared him to Silas Porter, the saddest excuse for a husband, a father, and a man, that had ever walked this earth. The thought of himself resembling that bastard in any capacity in Evie's mind made Theo sick to his stomach as he sat upon the staircase.

"She told me that Silas had said something similar to her before. I feel like a God-damned fool. How do I fix this? How do I get her to see how much I love her?"

Johanna reached back to wrap an arm around his broad back and leaned her head upon his shoulder. "Give her what Silas couldn't," she said simply. "He may have been her husband by law, but in every other way, he was her slaver. Prove to her that you are different."

Theo slowly raised his head as Johanna's words began to sink in. Suddenly, he jumped to his feet and began to climb back up the stairs. "You're brilliant, Johanna," he said with a renewed excitement.

"Well, I do try my best. Now, where are you off to so quickly?"

Theo paused at the middle of the stairs and returned to the bottom to press a quick kiss to Johanna's cheek before ascending them once again. "I'm making things right. I'm going to give her what he never did."

***

Once outside, Evie made her way down the road toward the lighthouse. She wanted peace and she wanted quiet, and the only place she could think to get such things was high in the sky, overlooking the homestead and the Bay. Just as she reached the door to the winding staircase within the lighthouse's tower, however, she heard a voice calling her name just behind her. Glancing over her shoulder, she saw Emma scampering up the road to meet her at the lighthouse.

"Evie!" Emma called exhaustedly as she skidded to a stop. "Evie, I'm so sorry. Jacob told me that Theo was going to confront you about the baby, and I've been trying to find you all day…"

Evie curtly folded her arms over her chest. "I told you *not* to tell a soul."

Emma nervously wrung her hands together and chewed on her lip. "I'm so sorry! I was just so excited for you that I couldn't contain myself. I told only Jacob, but I did not think he would go to Theo so quickly!"

Evie rolled her eyes up to the evening sky. "How could you betray me like this? You promised! I thought you were my friend…"

"I am your friend, Evie. It was a mistake. I'm so sorry."

"No, the only mistake was trusting you to keep your promise! Theo and I are not speaking, and I have you to thank for that!"

Emma's eyes widened in shock. "You aren't speaking?"

"We fell into a terrible argument because he believed that I am pregnant by another man!"

Emma dropped her head in her hands in shame. "I never should have said anything. Please, forgive me. I never meant to make such a mess of things…"

"Emma, this is supposed to be the happiest time of my life, but now it has been ruined because you took away my chance to tell Theo he is going to be a father! How can I ever forgive you?"

Emma dropped her eyes to the ground and shifted her weight between her feet as a look of hurt flashed across her face. "I suppose you shouldn't. I've spoiled everything. Is there anything I can do to fix this?"

Evie roughly pulled open the door to the lighthouse tower and turned her back to her friend before coldly stating, "Yes. You can stay out of my life."

Before Emma could open her mouth to speak, Evie stepped into the tower, slamming the door shut behind her. Dejectedly, Emma stared at the door for several moments, feeling tears of regret burn her eyes as she slowly turned away and made her way back to her home with her head hung low.

Emma paused in the middle of the road when she heard the front door to the Cunningham house open and close. Looking up, she saw Theo hurrying down the road toward her.

"Have you seen Evie?" he asked her worriedly as he approached.

Emma sadly pointed to the lighthouse. "She went up there."

Theo glanced at the top of the lighthouse nervously, catching a glimpse of a small figure standing on top of the catwalk and looking out over the water as the wind blew her skirt about her legs. Immediately, he was haunted by memories of seeing Evie stand on that very catwalk several years ago, overcome with such grief and despair that she was ready to end her own life.

"Why would she be up there?" he asked as he swallowed the lump rising in his throat.

Emma shrugged. "She is furious with me for spilling the secret. Perhaps she just wanted to clear her mind…"

Theo placed a comforting hand on her shoulder. "You are not the only one."

"Go to her, Theo," Emma said with a sigh as she looked to the lighthouse. "She needs you right now more than ever."

After bidding Emma goodbye, Theo turned to the lighthouse and rushed up the spiraling stairs, pausing in the doorway that led out to the catwalk. Evie stood before him just a few paces away, her back turned to him as she stared out across the water of the Bay. A gentle wind blew through to ruffle her long auburn curls about her shoulders as she looked down and placed a hand upon her belly, completely unaware that a visitor had made his presence just behind her.

"I'm sorry, little one," she whispered to her womb as her eyes fluttered closed. "I promised myself this time would be different, but it seems that I've made a bloody mess of everything…once again."

Slowly, she began to turn away from the Bay in order to lean back against the railing, but she was met with the sight of Theo's imposing figure just a few paces away as she did so. Her soft expression immediately hardened when she laid eyes upon him, and she instantly turned her back to him again.

"We need to talk," Theo said gently.

"I have nothing to say to you."

"Then do not speak," he returned as he stepped forward to stand by her side at the railing, "Just listen."

"I have been listening to men flap their jaws my entire life. Why should I believe you have anything worth hearing?"

Theo let out a long sigh as she turned her head away from him, and he leaned back against the railing while folding his arms across his chest. Leaning his head down to get as close to her face as she would allow, he murmured, "What I said to you last night was inexcusable. It was not fair, and it was not right. You have given me no reason to believe you would ever betray me like that, and I have no excuse for my foolishness. But I suppose I was just...shocked by the news."

"Then I'm sure you can imagine how I felt when I discovered it myself," Evie returned coolly as she gently stroked her stomach.

"Tell me something," Theo whispered. "Tell me why you really kept the news from me for so long."

Evie swallowed thickly and looked away, chewing nervously on her lip. "...I was afraid," she eventually responded.

"Afraid of what? Afraid of me? Did you think that I would be angry with you for carrying my child? Did you think I would abandon you?"

Evie did not respond, but instead lowered her head sadly, closing her eyes as the wind continued to blow strands of her hair into her face. Gingerly, Theo reached forward to brush a wayward lock of her hair from her eyes and tuck it behind her ear. Much to his surprise, she did not pull away from him when he did so, but instead cracked her eyes open to look up at him.

"Come now," he said softly, "you know me better than that. You know there is nothing you could do to rid yourself of me now."

"I just...I just knew that you did not want a family right now," she admitted bashfully. "I was afraid to burden you..."

Theo looked slightly taken aback, if not hurt. "What would make you think such a thing? Evie, a family is the only thing I have wanted as long as I can remember. The family from which I come is as dysfunctional as it is complicated, and I swore to myself long ago that I would never let any children of mine live the way I have. And if you thought for a moment that I would not want this child, then you are wrong."

Evie sniffled as she stared up into his golden eyes, feeling her resolve to be angry with him begin to dissolve the longer their gazes locked.

"Do you mean that?" she asked in a breathless whisper.

She felt her knees begin to grow weak when he reached down to splay one of his large hands across her stomach, leaning his head down to rest his forehead against her temple.

His voice was soft and soothing as he told her, "A man much wiser than I told me that a father's love for his child is a love without end, but he failed to mention that a man's love for the mother of his child runs just as deep and unending."

Evie sniffled once again before letting out a quiet sob, feeling the walls she had tried to build around herself quickly crumbling as Theo pressed a kiss to her forehead and held her body against his.

"I am just so afraid," she admitted in a fearful whisper as she squeezed her eyes shut to hold back a new onslaught of tears. "I do not know what it is like to be a mother. That feeling was taken from me before I even had it. I do not know what to do…"

"This will not be like last time. You are not doing this alone. And you never will. Forgive me, please, for my thoughtlessness. I need you. I need our child. I need you by my side, and I want every part of you for the rest of my life."

Evie looked up at him in surprise as a single tear escaped the corner of her eye, and he immediately wiped it away with his thumb before stroking her cheek with the hand that was not placed upon her stomach. Suddenly, she pulled away from him and turned away to begin pacing across the catwalk, her mind reeling in one thousand directions as she tried to calm her racing heart.

"I can't lose this baby, too," he heard her mumble, though he was not certain he was meant to hear it.

"I won't let that happen," he promised her as she turned to face away from him again. "So long as I have a heart beating in my chest, no harm will come to you or this child. And I want you to know, that when you betrayed your husband to be with me, that was the best thing you could have ever done. Because if you hadn't, we would not have had the chance to create the family that we have both wanted our entire lives. Be with me. Spend the rest of your days with me."

"What are you saying?" she asked as she began to turn to face him. Just as she turned around, she found him kneeling before her on one knee, his arms spread out at his sides as he stared up at her.

"Marry me," he whispered pleadingly from his knees.

"*What?*"

"Marry me. I know that I cannot offer you some of the things that Silas did—I have no ring, no titles, no inheritance, no mansion in the city. I am a bastard, and a half breed, a traitor, a Patriot rebel, and a God-damned fool, but nothing would make me happier than to be your husband as well, if you will have me."

Evie stared down at him, her eyes wide with shock and her mouth slightly agape as she brought her hand up to her chest. She could feel her heart leap into her throat to choke away the few words that she had managed to string together in her head. Her knees felt week underneath her as their gazes locked and he stared pleadingly up at her. She could see the warmth and vulnerability as plain as day in his eyes, two things that he saved exclusively for her, and only her. Another bout of tears began to roll down her cheeks as a sob racked her body.

"You took care of me when I needed you the most," Theo continued when it became evident that she was unable to speak. "Three years ago, you were there for me when I needed you. When I was on my deathbed, you never left my side. You took care of me until I could stand on my own. And I would be honored if you would allow me to return the favor for the rest of our lives. And I know I said I did not have a ring for you, but I do have this. You had told me once to give it to a girl that deserves it, and that is what I wish to do now."

Theo's eyes did not leave her as he reached into the inner pocket of his vest and produced a shimmering piece of jewelry. Evie immediately recognized it as the necklace that he had given her several years ago, the necklace that belonged to his mother once upon a time, and that Evie returned to him just before Silas had reclaimed her and taken her away. The turquoise beads glinted beautifully in the light of the setting sun as he held it up for her to see, and once again, she was breathless.

Evie took several small steps in his direction and slowly lowered herself to her knees in front of him before reaching up to place both of her hands on either of his cheeks. Pressing her forehead to his, she let her eyes slip closed and cried several more silent tears before mumbling a quiet, "Yes."

"What?" he asked.

"I said yes," she gasped as the slightest of smiles tugged at her lips. "Yes, I will have you. For the rest of my days and a thousand years after…"

A sideways smirk made its way onto Theo's face as he reached behind her to secure the necklace around her neck, where it rightfully belonged. He had forgotten how beautiful it looked laying across the pale flesh of her collarbone, and it brought him great happiness to see it back in her possession after so long. After the necklace was fastened around her throat, Evie threw her arms around his neck and buried her face in his chest as tears of unspeakable joy began to stain her cheeks.

"The rest of our days and a thousand years after will still never be enough," he murmured into her ear as he held her body against his, "but it is a start."

Chapter 17

Indivisible

September 1780

Their lives finally seemed to be falling into place. The world seemed right again, and all past transgressions had been lost to the wind now that summer was cooling into a blessed autumn, and Evie and Theo had never been more content now that they had sealed their commitment to one another and were engaged to be married.

It was not until late September, when Evie was well over five months pregnant and her belly had grown substantially to the point that she had outgrown many of her dresses, that she realized she did not have a gown in her possession elegant enough for her upcoming nuptials, which were decided to take place on the seventeenth of October that year. Not wanting to try and squeeze herself into an old gown borrowed from Johanna, she decided to visit the homestead's resident seamstress, Mrs. Thatcher, to see if she could put together a special gown that was both large enough to accommodate her growing belly and beautiful enough to do justice to the momentous occasion to which it would be worn.

Johanna accompanied her on her walk down to the road to Mrs. Thatcher's tailor shop on a crisp autumn afternoon in order to offer her input on the design of the wedding gown. They were both happily chatting about the excitement of the upcoming ceremony, but they paused in the middle of the road when they nearly ran directly into Emma, who had little Levi perched on her hip as she traveled from her parents' tavern to her home.

Emma's face immediately fell when she and Evie locked eyes for a moment, and she bashfully lowered her head, as if afraid to even speak to her. She and Evie had not spoken in over a month, not since their falling out in the aftermath of Emma's inability to keep a secret, and though they both missed each other terribly, neither girl had found the courage to confront the other in order to make amends. Though Evie was still upset by Emma's blunder, she was growing tired of avoiding her closest friend, and she no longer had the energy to give her the cold shoulder. Emma may not have been the sharpest pitchfork in the shed, but she was still her best friend, and she wanted her back in her life, especially now that she had a wedding to plan.

Johanna greeted Emma warmly. "Good afternoon, dear. Where are you and your little one off to?"

Emma averted her eyes from Evie as she mumbled, "I was just visiting my parents with the baby. I was on my way home…"

"Well, we are off to see Mrs. Thatcher to inquire about a dress for Evie's big day."

Emma smiled sadly and kept her eyes to the ground. "That is wonderful. I hope she can make you something as beautiful as you, Evie."

Evie cleared her throat and took a step in Emma's direction. "Why don't you join us?"

Emma looked up and furrowed her brow in confusion. "Me? You want me to come with you?"

"Of course. We could use an extra opinion."

"I don't know…I do not want to intrude. Especially after we, well, you know…"

Evie shook her head and placed a hand upon Emma's arm, smiling warmly. "I want you to come. How could I plan my wedding without my best friend by my side?"

Emma's brows knitted together hopefully as she readjusted Levi on her hip. "I'm still your best friend? Even after the mess I made?"

Evie chuckled and ruffled Levi's thick dark hair, coaxing a giggle from him. "You always have been. Come with us. It wouldn't be the same without you."

"Are you still furious with me for letting the secret slip?"

Evie sighed and shook her head. "Everything turned out well in the end. And I cannot tolerate our separation any longer. I want my friend back."

A wide smile of relief spread across Emma's face as Evie looped her arm through the one that was not currently balancing a baby on her hip.

"Come along then, girls," Johanna cooed as she led them down the road toward the tailor shop. "Let's hurry now. The wedding is less than a month away, and we still don't have a dress!"

***

October 1780

Evie gently stroked her growing belly with a contented smile upon her face as she made her way down the road toward the Caldwell home and its adjacent blacksmithing forge. By the beginning of October, she had reached her sixth month of pregnancy according to Dr. Thorn's estimations, and her womb seemed to grow more and more with each day that passed. She could not deny that this pregnancy felt much different from the first in nearly every single way, and as it continued to progress, she could feel her fears of a stillbirth waning.

Within weeks of discovering that he was to be a father, Theo became even more protective of her than he had been before, carefully monitoring nearly every step she took and every move she made so as to ensure nothing was done to harm the child growing within her. He became more reluctant to let Evie leave the house on her own the bigger she got, should something happen and she would need assistance returning home, and it took quite a bit of convincing for her to be able to engage in the simple errand of visiting the Caldwell house without Theo's presence. While she appreciated his doting concern, his hovering was beginning to drive her mad, and she wanted desperately to get away for him for just a few minutes.

The sound of hammers pounding against anvils touched her ears as she reached the front of Mr. and Mrs. Caldwell's home, and she wandered around back to the forge, where she found Jacob working alone on one of his many blacksmithing projects. Jacob's back was turned to her as she approached, and he failed to hear her footsteps amidst the pounding of his hammer, so when she suddenly appeared just behind him and tapped his shoulder, he quickly spun around with a startled cry, hammer raised as if he was prepared to use it against whomever had disturbed him.

Evie let out a gasp and stumbled backwards, instinctively throwing her hands up in front of her stomach.

"Jesus Christ!" Jacob cried out in annoyance when he realized who had startled him, immediately lowering his hammer to his side. "You scared me out of my wits, Evie! Do not ever sneak up on a man with a hammer in his hand!"

"I'm sorry," Evie stuttered as she placed a hand over her now racing heart. "I did not mean to startle you…"

Jacob's expression softened and he let out a sigh, laying the hammer down on a table nearby. "It's alright. No harm done. How fares the baby these days?"

Evie looked down at her now protruding belly with a contented smile. "She is well. She has begun to kick within the last few weeks. Keeps me up at night while Theo snores up a storm."

Jacob chuckled. "That's wonderful to hear."

Evie attempted to stand on her toes in order to peer over his shoulder at what he was shaping on the anvil. "What are you making over there?"

Jacob immediately stepped squarely in front of the anvil in order to block her view. "Nothing," he mumbled much too quickly to be convincing. "Nothing you need worry about."

Evie arched her brow curiously. "You wouldn't happen to be secretly crafting weapons for the British, would you?" she asked jokingly.

Jacob scoffed and shook his head. "You'll see me aiding the British when my brother is brought back from the dead and Hell freezes over." Upon seeing a saddened look come to Evie's face at the mention of his fallen brother, he attempted to change the subject. "Did you come to see Emma? If so, you just missed her. She took Levi to see her parents over at the tavern."

Evie shook her head. "I wanted to speak to you, actually."

Jacob almost groaned. "Is this about letting the secret slip to Theo? Because that happened months ago…"

"No, no. Nothing like that. It is about the wedding, actually."

"What about the wedding?"

Evie sighed wistfully and looked for a place to take a seat—her ankles were swollen and feet sore from carrying the extra weight in her womb, and she was desperately tired. Sensing as much, Jacob overturned an empty apple crate and told her to sit while he leaned back against his anvil with his arms folded over his chest.

"It recently occurred to me that, as per colonial custom, the bride is supposed to have a man walk her down the aisle at the ceremony to deliver her to her groom. And that man is typically her father."

"Yes, that is how it has worked in my experience."

Evie nervously began to play with her fingers, her eyes falling to her lap as she said, "Well, seeing as I have been formally disowned by my father, I do not really…have anyone to play that part on my wedding day."

Jacob arched his brow. "And?"

She took a deep breath before mumbling, "I was wondering…I was hoping that…perhaps you would consider…taking on that responsibility?"

Jacob's eyes widened in shock and he felt his jaw go slack as he stared at her. When he did not respond at first, she slowly raised her eyes from her lap to meet his gaze.

"You want *me* to walk you down the aisle?"

Evie smiled bashfully and nodded. "I could think of no one else I would like to give me away."

"What about Alistair?"

"He is preforming the ceremony, so he would not be able to accompany me down the aisle. And besides, Alistair did not save my life the way you did back at the fort."

Jacob waved his hand dismissively. "Oh, please…"

"Jacob, if it weren't for you, Theo and I would both be dead. Theo and I would not be together now if it weren't for you."

The corners of Jacob's mouth began to twitch upward. "I was just trying to help my friend. As anyone else would have done."

"Not anyone else would have risked his life to save me after everything I have done. But you did. You are Theo's closest friend. I would love it if you could join me down the aisle."

After a moment of thought, Jacob's smirk widened, and with a single nod, he said, "I would be honored to give you away."

Evie rose to her feet as quickly as she could manage and threw her arms around Jacob's neck without warning, nearly knocking him off balance. "Thank you, thank you. You have no idea how much this means to me…"

Jacob chuckled lightly and returned her embrace as best as he could around her belly. "I am honored to be a part of your special day. Was this Theo's idea?"

Evie shook her head with a smirk of her own. "No. I thought of you on my own."

Jacob would have been lying if he said he didn't feel a warm feeling spread across his chest at that moment. Ever since their return from Fort Dumpling Rock, he and Evie had been on much better terms, but he did not think they were close enough that she would even consider him to play the part of her father on her wedding day. Even six years after the red-headed hellcat had found her way into Division Point, she still found ways to surprise him and everyone else around her. And he could think of no woman more perfect for his best friend than her.

"Speaking of Theo," Jacob said as he cleared his throat to whisk away the emotion beginning to show on his face. "Did he tell you what I have planned for him the night before the wedding?"

Evie frowned. "No. He did not mention anything of the sort. What is it you have up your sleeve?"

Jacob smirked again. "Some of the other fellows in the homestead and myself are going to take him out for a night of merriment so that he may savor his last few hours of freedom."

Suddenly appearing concerned, Evie furrowed her brow at him. "And what does this merriment entail, exactly?"

"Oh, nothing too wild. Just going down to the tavern for some ale and cards. No ladies allowed, I'm afraid."

"You know Theo doesn't drink."

"Of course, I know that. I won't let him get near any of that stuff, I assure you."

Evie looked unconvinced. "Is that a typical prenuptial activity for a groom? To drink and behave foolishly with his friends the night before his wedding?"

Jacob shrugged. "It is tradition around here. Didn't your first husband do such a thing? Or was fun beneath him?"

Evie frowned again, not ready or willing to dwell on such memories. She had a crystal-clear memory of what Silas did the night before their wedding, and she did not want to bring it back into her consciousness. "He preferred to drink alone," she answered tightly, her eyes falling to the ground. "And he did not really have very many friends."

"After meeting him at Dumpling Rock, I am not the least bit surprised."

Desperately trying to change the subject, Evie cleared her throat. "Please just promise me that whatever you have planned for that night, it does not get Theo into any trouble."

"Of course. Don't you trust your fiancé?"

"I trust Theo plenty. It is you I am not so certain of."

Jacob placed a hand over his heart as if he had just been mortally wounded. "I'm hurt."

Rolling her eyes up to the sky, Evie turned away in order to make her way out of the forge. "If anything happens to Theo that night, I suppose I will know who to blame, hm?"

Jacob also rolled his eyes and turned back to his anvil as she wandered away.

Taking up his hammer once she was nearly out of sight, he sarcastically shot back, "Theo certainly has his work cut out for him with you, doesn't he?"

***

Evie felt her heart leap into her throat when she heard a knock at the door, and she momentarily paused her anxious pacing across the parlor in order to answer it. Upon opening the front door, she found Jacob standing on the front porch, joined by several other young men from the homestead whom Theo considered good friends.

"We've come to collect the groom," Jacob stated. "So that we may celebrate his last night of freedom."

Evie rolled her eyes up to the ceiling with a smirk and motioned for all five men to come into the house. She then shuffled across the front rooms and paused at the base of the stairs, calling up to the second floor, "Theo, your entourage of hellions is here."

After several moments of hesitation, Theo appeared at the top of the stairs, looking not at all excited to have been summoned. Reluctantly, he shuffled down the stairs and paused at Evie's side, shoving his hands in the pockets of his trousers. Within the last few weeks, the reality of the impending wedding seemed to have hit him like a ton of bricks, and he could feel his heart begin to race in his chest at the thought of meeting the love of his life at the altar. He knew that he wanted to spend the rest of his life with her, but the thought of becoming legally and spiritually tied to one person for the rest of eternity suddenly snuck up on him like a monster in the night, and before he knew it, he could feel the walls beginning to close in on him. And when Jacob suggested that he and the other young men from the homestead gather together for his last night of bachelorhood, the walls became that much more suffocating. Naturally, he could not share that hesitancy with Evie while she was six months pregnant with his child, and he didn't have the courage to talk to his father about his mounting anxieties, so he decided to keep them to himself until after the wedding, after the birth of the baby, and perhaps for the rest of his days.

He was also not looking forward to the hours of teasing he was about endure. As the last of his friends in the homestead to settle down and marry, and the only one who did not drink, he was sure to be the butt of several hundred jokes over the course of the night.

"Don't look so bothered by our presence," Jacob teased as he slapped Theo on the back. "We will have fun tonight, you'll see."

"And where do you fine gentleman plan on taking our boy tonight?" Johanna asked as she and Alistair waltzed into the room from the kitchen. "Nowhere seedy, I should hope."

"Of course not, Mrs. Cunningham," Gabriel, Mrs. Thatcher's nephew, cut in, "We were just going to go to the tavern for a spell. Play some cards and have a drink or two."

Evie, Johanna, and Alistair all flashed Theo a mildly concerned look, to which he rolled his eyes and said blankly, "I know, I know. I'll stay away from the liquor."

"Promise?" Evie asked worriedly.

Theo flashed her a devilish smirk and placed a hand upon her protruding stomach. "I swear it."

"If anyone knows how to resist temptation, it's Theo," Jacob joked sarcastically, earning himself a smack on the back of the head from Theo, who was less than amused.

Evie reached forward to wrap her arms around Theo's waist. "Be careful. I want you to come home in one piece so that we may still have a wedding tomorrow."

Theo chuckled under his breath, somewhat nervously at the mention of the wedding, and pressed a kiss to the top of her head and then to her belly. "You know I will."

After giving her another kiss, Theo bid both of his parents *adieu* and reluctantly let his friends lead him out of the house.

"How much trouble can one really get themselves into in the homestead?" Jacob asked with a chuckle as the group of rowdy young men made their way towards the front door to leave. "There's nothing here but docks and cliffs."

"Neither of which pair well with liquor," Alistair noted.

Before Theo and the others could leave, Evie grabbed Jacob by the arm. "Keep an eye on him," she mumbled lowly to him once Theo and the other men were out the door. "I can see that he is anxious about tomorrow. Do not let him fall into his old ways."

Jacob patted her comfortingly on the shoulder. "I'll look out for him, you needn't worry."

"I'm trusting you, Jacob," Evie said whilst pointing a finger at his chest. "Don't make me regret it."

"You have my word, *Mrs. Cunningham*."

***

Shortly after the men left and made their way down the road to O'Hara's Tavern, another knock sounded at the front door, only this time, it was Emma, who was practically ready to burst with excitement over tomorrow's festivities. Because Theo and Jacob would be absent all night doing God knows what, Evie decided that the best way to spend the evening before her wedding was to have her closest friend spend the night so that they may chat and gossip like they used to before they were busied with the responsibilities of children and husbands.

"If I'm not mistaken, Emma," Evie said when she answered the door and noticed the wide grin upon Emma's face, "it seems as if you are more excited for the wedding tomorrow than even the bride and groom."

Emma chuckled giddily and stepped into the house, hanging her coat on the nearby coatrack. "Nonsense. I am just overjoyed to see you and Theo finally tying the knot. I can think of no two people more perfect for each other than you."

Evie looked away when she felt her cheeks tinge pink. "Where is little Levi this evening?"

"I let him spend the night with my mother in law. I needed a respite from motherhood for a moment. God love that boy, but he was beginning to drive me mad!"

Evie chuckled again as she led her friend up the stairs and to Theo's room, where they would be sleeping.

Emma immediately collapsed backwards onto the bed with a sigh. "Can you believe that by this time tomorrow, you will be Mrs. Theo Cunningham?" she asked as she crossed her arms behind her head and looked up to the ceiling.

Evie slowly lowered herself onto the other side of the bed and laid down on her back next to her, sighing in relief when she felt the weight of her body being lifted from her swollen and tired feet. "I still cannot believe it," she admitted as she gently stroked her belly. "It all seems to be happening so quickly now."

"But isn't that a blessing? You have been waiting so long for this. You will finally have the family you wanted."

"Of course. I want nothing more than to be a family with Theo. It's just that…my last experience with marriage…and pregnancy…was not exactly pleasant. I suppose I am just afraid of history repeating itself."

Emma propped herself up on her elbows and gave her friend a confused look. "Theo would never hurt you or the baby as Silas did."

"I know that. But I cannot help but be afraid of what the future holds for us. What if…what if I turn out to be a terrible wife, or a terrible mother?"

Emma scoffed at the suggestion. "Why would you even think such a thing?"

Evie shrugged and let out a long sigh. "Theo has been acting strangely for the last few weeks. He's trying to hide it, but I can see that he is just as nervous as I for the future. I am worried that…perhaps he is regretting his choice to marry me. I fear that once the baby comes, everything will change, and he will grow bored with me…"

"Theo loves you. And the baby. More than anything. He would not have proposed if he didn't."

"He does *now*. But what happens when my body changes after the baby? What happens when he no longer finds me attractive, and all of my time is devoted to caring for our child, rather than to him? Will he become resentful? Will he just leave us?"

Emma placed a comforting hand on Evie's hands, which were folded over her stomach. "Evie, I thought the very same things when I was with child. I feared the same things you do. But you were the one who talked me off of the ledge. And you have to trust that you have a good man by your side who will love you through thick and thin. These fears and anxieties you are having are just the pregnancy playing tricks on you."

"And what of Theo's fears? He doesn't have the excuse of carrying a child to explain his anxieties."

Emma chuckled and waved her hand dismissively. "Theo is just a *man*. All men have a moment of madness before they marry. And after the initial shock of never being with another woman again wears off, they transform from lovers to husbands."

Evie let out a deep breath as she stared up at the ceiling. As much as she did not want to admit it, Emma's words had merit. She was surely fussing over nothing, letting her premarital and prenatal jitters overwhelm her.

"Emma?" she asked quietly after a few minutes of silence had settled over them both.

"Hm?"

"What is motherhood like?"

A wide grin spread across Emma's face as she turned onto her side to face her friend, resting her head upon her hand as she said, "It is the best thing that has ever happened to me. I did not know I could love anything so much until I held Levi in my arms, until I saw him smile for the first time, until I heard him laugh for the first time…"

"Really? I…I never got the chance to know that feeling with Noah."

"But you will now. In just a few months' time, you will hold a miracle in your arms."

Evie swallowed thickly and looked down at her belly, feeling a strong kick on the right side of her womb. Though she and Theo had taken every precaution to ensure that this pregnancy went as smoothly as possible, she could not shake the fear in the back of her mind that something could still go wrong, just as with Noah's birth. It was no secret that babies died frequently. Women in labor died frequently. Children died frequently. And there was little that could be done to prevent it. No matter what she did, she could not abandon the fear that she, much like Johanna, was not meant to have a child of her own.

"I know. You are right. I am surely worrying for nothing…" Evie said aloud, though she was not sure which one of them she was trying to convince.

"I know the unknown is frightening now, but soon enough, all of those worries will melt away. And you and Theo will go on to have many more beautiful, happy, healthy babies." Emma said as she reached over to pat Evie's belly.

Evie giggled at the thought, feeling the weight of her worries on her heart momentarily drift away. "Thank you, Emma. I needed to hear that."

"Anytime, friend. Anytime."

"When did you become so wise?"

Emma shrugged smugly and smirked. "I've always been *wise*. People just rarely ask for my opinion."

Evie chuckled and rolled her eyes. "Of course, of course."

Emma then laid down on her back again and asked, "What do you think our men are up to down at the tavern?"

***

"I fold," Jacob mumbled in annoyance, slamming his hand of cards down on the surface of the table around which he and the other men sat.

It was well past midnight and several hours into their celebration of the end of Theo's bachelorhood, and they had played what felt to Theo like several hundred hands of poker whilst drinking and having a laugh at his expense. Just as he had promised both himself and his family, Theo didn't allow himself to even look at the tankards of ale that his friends were imbibing, and surprisingly, despite the anxiety that was still swirling in his chest, he didn't feel an urge at all to partake in their drinking. Jacob and the others were well past the point of intoxicated as they sat together in the otherwise empty tavern, and as expected, their logic and inhibitions began to wash away with the ale as the night went on.

"Full house," Theo stated simply, revealing his hand to coax frustrated moans from all of the others as they tossed their cards down in defeat.

"That's the sixth hand in a row you've taken!" a young man named Phillip Smith, the son of one of the many fishermen in the homestead, grouched as he pointed a finger in Theo's direction. "You must be cheating!"

Theo shrugged with a smug smirk. "Or you're just shit at cards."

Phillip jumped to his feet and leaned over the table, knocking over Gabriel's tankard of ale in the process. "Say that again, I dare you!"

"And what would you do if I did?"

Jacob immediately stood and clamped a hand on Phillip's shoulder, forcing him back down into his chair. "Easy now, lads. No need for hostility. We're just playing a friendly game of cards to send Theo off to the rest of his life. Sit down, Phillip, you've clearly had a bit too much to drink."

"And I'll have some more," Phillip snapped as he took another swig from his mug. "Too bad Theo can't partake without falling into an abyss."

Theo furrowed his brow in annoyance. "Consider yourself lucky I don't, Smith. Else I might be inclined to feed you your teeth."

"What did you just say to me?" Phillip growled as he tried to jump to his feet again, but he was immediately held back by Jacob once again.

"That's enough, Phil. Perhaps that's enough cards for tonight."

"Fine by me. I need more ale," Phillip growled as he pushed his chair away from the table and stumbled to the bar, tankard in hand, to help himself to another round.

Once he was gone, Theo sighed heavily and slouched against the back of his chair, tipping his head back to stare up at the ceiling. He was not sure of the time, but he knew only a few more hours remained until he was meant to meet Evie at the altar.

"So, tell us, Theo," Gabriel said as he attempted to wipe up the mess that Phillip had made when he spilled the ale, "how are your last few hours of freedom treating you?"

Theo shrugged. "Fine, I suppose. But you say that as if I am being shipped off to a prison for the rest of my life."

"Because you are," one of the other men, Henry Jenkins, butted in. "You can say goodbye to life as you know it once you say 'I do'."

Theo raised his brow in concern, feeling a nervous lump rise in his throat. "How do you mean?"

"Listen, friend," Henry sighed, "I married my lady three years ago. I love that woman, but, God, do I wish I had waited. Because now I have a wife, two little ones, and barely enough time to myself to take a piss! If the wife doesn't require my attention, the twins do, and every time I turn around, I'm pulled in a hundred different directions! If I had known how much my life would change, perhaps I never would have settled down."

Theo swallowed again, feeling his heart begin to race in his chest. "You regret having your family?"

Henry sighed once more, deeper this time as he leaned back in his chair and took a swig of what was left of his drink. "Depends on the day. I spend more hours than I can count slaving away at the docks, toiling under the baking sun, and when I return home, all I want is to be able to sit and have a moment to myself. But, no! What do I get in return for my hard work?

A nagging wench of a wife and two screeching banshees for children! God, I miss the days when I had no one to care for but myself…"

Theo watched in angst as Henry ran a hand down his face and stared tiredly at the ceiling, seemingly watching as his life passed before his eyes. Every word Henry spoke was slurred with liquor, so it was difficult to know if he truly meant anything he had just said. But what Theo knew the man meant, judging by the exhaustion evident on his young face, was how tired and run down he was. And as Theo looked around the table, he could see that same tiredness on all of his friends' faces. He was the only man at the table not yet married, and now that he knew what he was looking for, he could see how much they had all changed over the years. They were not young, irresponsible boys anymore. They were men, with families and homes of their own, who no longer had the luxury to worry about only themselves.

Theo lowered his head and pinched the bridge of his nose between his thumb and forefinger, squeezing his eyes shut as the room began to spin around him. Henry's description of marriage and fatherhood was anything but inviting, and within a few moments, Theo could feel his chest constricting nervously around his heart. Suddenly lightheaded and panicked, he could feel the walls collapsing in on him once again, to the point that it became a chore to even take a breath.

"Oh, God," he whispered to himself between heaving breaths. "Oh, God, what have I done?"

Taking notice of Theo's palpable nervousness, Jacob cleared his throat. "Come now, Henry, I'm sure you are exaggerating…"

Henry scoffed and slammed his fist on the table. "I wish! And as if it isn't hard enough being dog-tired at all times, once those children came, my wife barely ever let me touch her again!"

Theo slowly looked up, gesturing with his hands to allude to the words he couldn't find in that moment. "You mean…she doesn't let you…anymore?"

"Once a month, *if* she's feeling generous! We used to make love almost every day, but now, nothing! And when we do, it's over within a minute! How's a man supposed to get what he's after in a minute? She claims it's because she's tired as well, but what about me? After a long day on the docks, the least she could do is give me—"

Jacob groaned and rolled his eyes, holding up a hand to silence Henry before he could finish his thought. Theo's eyes widened in panic before he dropped his head in his hands.

"I think we all get the point, Henry," Jacob admonished.

Abruptly, Theo stood from his chair, mumbling the words "Excuse me" under his breath before scurrying across the barroom and out the back door, where he collapsed onto the steps of the building's back porch. The others watched him go in shock, and once Theo was out of the room, Jacob reached over the table to give Henry a hard smack on the back of the head.

"What the hell was that for?" Henry asked furiously, sitting up in his chair and rubbing the back of his head.

"Are you daft?" Jacob hissed lowly. "Are you trying to scare him out of his wits?"

Henry shrugged and crossed his arms over his chest. "Don't you think the boy should know what he's in for?"

Jacob rolled his eyes again and stood before also excusing himself out through the back door. There, he found Theo sitting with his back to the building on the porch steps, his head in his hands and his foot tapping nervously. Wordlessly, Jacob took a seat next to him and cleared his throat.

"Pay Henry no mind, Theo," he said gently. "He's drunk, and he's a fool."

"Is he right though?" Theo asked as he raised his head. "Is everything really going to change that much after tomorrow?"

"Of course, it is. But not for the worse, like Henry implied."

Theo shook his head in disbelief and rubbed his temples. "I...I don't think I can do this, Jacob."

"What?"

"This. Marriage. Fatherhood. I...I don't think I'm cut out for it. I'm going to fail, just as I have failed at everything else in my life. I just know it."

"You cannot sell yourself so short. Of course, you are nervous. It is natural to be nervous when life changes. But you cannot run away from the changes this time, Theo. You can't escape your reality with alcohol, and you can't abandon the family you've created."

Theo raked his hand through his long, wild tresses while continuously tapping his foot on the step, his eyes locked on the horizon before them. Jacob could see in his friend's eyes that his mind was racing even faster than his heart, and he could also see a battle raging within him. A battle between the desire to do what was right, and the fear of destroying everything he ever loved.

"I would never abandon them," Theo whispered. "But what am I supposed to do when that child comes into this world and I do not have the slightest clue of how to raise him?"

"You learn as you go. That is all you can do."

"It is just so much happening at once," Theo mumbled as he gripped his hair. "I am terrified that I will destroy the family I have created. I am terrified that I will fail as a husband and that my child will grow to resent me for bringing him into a world so cold and cruel. I am terrified I will not be able to protect my family from the evils that surround us. Everything is falling into place, Jacob, and I could not be happier. But I still find myself living in fear that something will happen to take it all away from me..."

Jacob placed a gentle hand on Theo's shoulder. "God has blessed you with a beautiful wife and a beautiful child. After everything you have endured, you deserve this happiness."

"If God could give it to me, He could take it away just as easily."

"You know, I remember your father telling us when we were boys that we are not meant to understand God's plans for us. What I do know is that you and Evie were meant for one another. And that is all you need to understand. Your father used to always tell us that we do the best that we know how with what we have been given. And you have been given an amazing gift—the opportunity to create the family you wish you had."

Slowly, Theo turned to look Jacob in the eye. "Were you this nervous…before your wedding?"

"I was a trembling mess before the wedding, and even more so before Levi was born. But when I saw Emma walking down the aisle to spend the rest of her life with me, and when I laid my eyes on my son for the first time, nothing else mattered. I thought I knew what love was, but it was not until I became a father that I realized how much I could love another person. And you will find that feeling too, soon enough."

Jacob watched as the confusion and fear in Theo's eyes slowly morphed into a newfound contentment—a realization that he was much more fortunate than he had ever realized. Millions of men would kill for what he had, he realized in that moment, and he would fight to the death to protect what was his. The traces of a smile began to touch Theo's face as he said, "I do not know what I would do if I did not have you to keep me together, friend."

Jacob chuckled softly. "And I do not know what I would do if I did not have you to drag me into trouble."

"Well, that ends now. I have more than just myself to think about. I can't afford to slip into my old ways of fighting and drinking and running amuck."

"That's a good man, Theo. That's the first step to becoming a man. Realizing that your world no longer revolves around yourself." Jacob then began to dig around in his pocket as he said, "I was going to wait until tomorrow to give these to you, but I figure now is as good of a time as ever."

Theo looked at Jacob curiously as he pulled his fist from his pocket and opened his hand, revealing two polished golden wedding bands sitting in his palm.

Theo's eyes widened momentarily in disbelief as he stared at his friend. "You made these?" he asked in awe.

"Aye. Been working on them at the forge since your engagement. I figured you and Evie would like a symbol of your commitment at the ceremony tomorrow."

Theo was nearly speechless as he gazed down at the rings glimmering in the moonlight. "Jacob...they are perfect. You shouldn't have. And I haven't any money to pay you for your hard work—"

"You know how things work in Division Point. We take care of our own. Take them. Surprise Evie tomorrow."

A wide smile quickly spread across Theo's face as he took the rings from Jacob's hand and held them up to examine them in the light of the full moon overhead. They were immaculately crafted, one significantly larger than the other, and it wasn't until he held them up to the light that he realized that a single word had been etched by hand into the inside of each ring.

"*Indivisible?*" he asked as he squinted into the ring and read the inscription out loud.

Jacob nodded in satisfaction. "I thought it was a nice touch. I could not think of a better word to describe you and Evie. *Indivisible.* The rest of the world may forever be divided, but not you two."

Theo stuffed the rings into his breast pocket and leaned over to capture Jacob into an enormous bear hug. "Thank you, my friend. I will find a way to repay you for this. I do not deserve your friendship."

"Of course, you don't," Jacob returned with a smirk and a wink, "but you will always have it regardless. Now go home. Rest up. You will need all of your strength for the important day to come."

Theo gave his friend one last embrace before leaping to his feet. After bidding Jacob goodnight and instructing him to thank the other men for a good time on his behalf, he headed for home with a renewed vigor in his step. He could feel the pair of wedding bands in his breast pocket resting over his heart as he walked, and it now brought a child-like smile to his face to think of what would be taking place in only a few hours' time. A residual nervousness still remained in his heart as he quietly entered the house and found both Evie and Emma fast asleep in his bed, but as he kissed his bride to be on her forehead and then settled into the armchair in the corner of his room to catch a few hours of sleep, that nervousness was quickly overshadowed by an indescribable excitement for what the future had in store.

***

Evie's stomach fluttered in beat with the pounding of her heart in her chest as she slowly made her way down the stairs of the house, the skirt of her wedding gown in hand so that she would not trip over the hem. Though her womb protruded quite noticeably from her tired body, she could not remember a time she felt more beautiful. The gown that Mrs. Thatcher had created was simply stunning, and she could not have asked for anything better to wear on her special day.

"Oh, Evie, you are a vision!" Johanna gushed as Evie reached the bottom of the stairs, dress on and hair fashioned for the approaching ceremony. "The most beautiful bride I have ever seen…"

Emma nodded in excited agreement, twirling the skirt of her own gown as she watched her friend cascade down the stairs like a dream. The dress Mrs. Thatcher crafted by hand over the last month was a lovely peach color, with a plunging neckline that left Evie's shoulders bare, but her arms cloaked in long wispy sleeves of silk. Kateri's necklace was on full display around her neck, the glimmering turquoise beads a stunning compliment to the soft hue of the gown. The skirt of her gown was long and flowing behind her in waves of silk and lace trimmings, and the waistline of the dress was specially crafted so as to sit just under her breasts and flow elegantly over her swollen belly. Her long auburn tresses were gently curled and left to fall freely down her back, and a crown of autumn flowers was placed upon her head in lieu of a long, heavy veil. She had worn a veil at her first wedding and hated it—she didn't want to be hidden from the world as she made her way down the aisle toward the rest of her life. She wanted all who were present to see the wide smile upon her face as she met her better half at the altar, freely and without reservations.

"Do you think Theo will like it?" Evie asked nervously as she paused at the bottom of the stairs and examined herself. She could not decide if the fluttering in her stomach was due to her anxious anticipation, or the baby giving her a good kick to say that it, too, was ready for this day to come.

"He will not be able to take his eyes off of you, my girl," Johanna said as she dabbed at the tears forming in her eyes. "No one will."

Evie furrowed her brow in concern upon noticing Johanna's eyes red with oncoming tears. "Jo, please do not cry. You will make me cry."

Johanna chuckled and waved her hand dismissively. "Oh, I'm not crying. The autumn wind has just carried a bit of dust into my eyes. And…and you just look so beautiful…and I could not have asked God for a better woman to take care of the boy that I have spent all these years raising…" As Johanna went on, her stiffened bottom lip began to quiver, and soon she could no longer contain her tears of happiness. Evie blinked rapidly to swallow her own whirling emotions and leaned forward to wrap her arms around Johanna's waist.

"And I could not have asked for a better mother in law," she said gently in the woman's ear. "You raised a fine man. A man with a heart of the purest gold. And we both owe that to you."

Johanna returned her embrace with a sob before pulling away and fanning her face to rid herself of the tears. "You do not know how much it means to me to hear you say that, love," she murmured, "But enough about me. This is *your* day."

Emma held out a small bouquet of peach, plum, and burgundy flowers that matched those in the crown on Evie's head. "Shall we be on our way to the church, then? We don't want to keep your groom waiting."

Evie gladly took the bouquet and gave Emma a hug of her own, blinking her eyes again to stave off another bout of tears. The last thing she wanted was to sob with joy right before she walked down the aisle and leave her face a red and swollen mess. Taking a deep breath, she said with a smile to her matrons of honor, "Lead the way."

Emma and Johanna looped an arm around each of Evie's and carefully led her out the front door and across the road to Division Point Church. The entire community had gathered inside and were waiting anxiously for the ceremony to commence, leaving it peacefully quite outside as the women made their way to the chapel. As promised, Jacob was waiting just outside the front doors of the church, dressed in his finest clothes for the occasion and prepared to walk Evie down the aisle. His eyes widened slightly as he watched Johanna, Evie, and his wife approach. He could not deny that Evie looked stunning in her gown, seemingly glowing underneath the October sun overhead.

"How does she look?" Emma asked her husband cheekily as they reached the front doors of the church.

"You're beautiful," Jacob said to Evie with the slightest tinge of red dusting his cheeks. "Stunning."

Emma loudly cleared her throat in mock jealousy and raised her brow at him, to which Jacob rolled his eyes and pressed a kiss to her cheek. "Of course, you are also stunning, my dear."

"Come," Johanna said to Emma as she took her by the hand, "Let us go find our places inside."

Jacob waited until Emma and Johanna had slipped inside the chapel and closed the doors behind them before turning back to face Evie with a smug smirk upon his face. Offering her his arm, he asked, "Are you ready?"

Evie anxiously shifted her weight between her feet and squeezed the stems of her bouquet. "Is Theo really in there?"

"No, he decided to go down to the docks for a spell. *Of course,* he's in there. He is waiting for you at the altar, just as he promised he would be."

Evie swallowed the lump rising in her throat and let out a deep breath as she looped her arm around Jacob's and the traces of a smile tugged at her lips. "Thank you, Jacob. For everything."

Jacob leaned down to kiss her cheek and patted her arm. "Say no more. Shall we take a walk?"

Evie eagerly nodded. "Promise me you will not let me fall."

Jacob pulled open the heavy wooden door to the church whilst whispering, "I wouldn't dream of it," and just as he did so, the air became filled with the gentle music of an organ that floated outside from within the church and filled Evie's heart with unspeakable joy.

As Evie and Jacob took their first steps into the building, everyone inside rose from their seats in the pews and turned to watch them make their grand entrance. After scanning the pews for the faces of the people that had become her closest friends and family, she looked forward to the alter to find Alistair, leaning heavily on his pulpit with a Bible in hand and a wide smile upon his face. Immediately to the right stood her husband to be, dressed in the finest clothes and boots she had ever seen him wear, looking so polished and refined with the sides of his wild dark hair pulled back that she wasn't sure she recognized him.

He had a stern look upon his face as he stood there waiting, but as soon as the chapel doors opened and he looked up to see his bride slowly floating down the aisle to meet him, his golden eyes lit up with the light of one thousand suns and his lips twitched upward into a bashful smile that brought a deep blush to his cheeks. Their eyes met almost immediately, and simultaneously they felt their hearts skip a beat. He had yet to see what her gown looked like, but now that he had, he decided that she had never looked more beautiful to him than in that moment. Not only was she wearing a fine gown that hugged her body perfectly, she was also carrying his child within her as they both prepared to formally give themselves to one another—mind, body, and soul.

Not only was Theo wowed by her beauty as she walked down the aisle toward him, he was also taken aback at how easily he felt all of his previous fears and worries melt away once he laid eyes upon her within the church. Seeing the purest expression of excitement in her eyes when she first entered the chapel, and watching the way her cheeks turned more and more pink the closer that she came to the alter, sent a warm feeling through his chest that he could only describe as adoration and awe. Seeing her not just as Evie, but his bride, his wife to be, assured him instantly in that moment that no matter what he had feared before this day came, they would endure it together.

Evie's heart seemed to leap into her throat when she and Jacob arrived at the alter in what felt like an instant after making their journey down the aisle. As soon as they arrived, Theo offered out his hand to his bride and she took it without hesitation, allowing him and Jacob both to help her up onto the first step of the altar as she handed her bouquet off to Emma. After exchanging a quick embrace with Theo, Jacob ducked off to stand behind him. Theo's gaze never left Evie's face as she made the symbolic journey to meet him at the front of the church, and now that they were standing chest to chest and hand in hand, the only distance separating their bodies being her swollen womb, he could feel an undeniable burning of tears in the back of his eyes. Never before he met her did he think that he would ever find himself in this position, but he could not have been more grateful that she had crashed into his life like the waves breaking on the shore to sweep him out of his hopelessness.

Before her, there was nothingness. But now that they were minutes away from being permanently united, all he saw was their future, and all he felt was hope.

"You look breathtaking," Theo whispered under his breath as they stood face to face and took each other's hands.

Evie beamed up at him through teary eyes and bashfully red cheeks, squeezing his hands as she returned smugly, "You also clean up rather well."

There was not a dry eye in the church as Alistair cleared his throat and bid everyone to sit before turning his attention to the Bible sitting open on his pulpit. The old man could not deny that he, himself, was already overcome with emotion as he watched Evie float enchantingly down the aisle toward his son, and he took a moment to collect himself before he was able to begin the ceremony. Naturally, Johanna was already a blubbering mess in one of the front pews, constantly dabbing at her eyes with a handkerchief as Alistair began the ceremony by reading a passage from the Bible.

"'They are no longer two, but one. Therefore, what God has joined together, let no one separate.' *Matthew 19:6*."

After reading, Alistair cleared his throat and closed the Bible before pushing the pulpit aside. Theo, Evie, and everyone else looked at him in minor confusion as he leaned heavily on his cane and addressed them candidly.

"I had a speech prepared for this occasion," the old man said with a voice rasped by months of coughing fits, trying desperately not to let his tiredness show on this special day. "I wrote it down and everything. I was going to read several more passages from the Holy Text about the beauty and sanctity of marriage as God sees it, but out of respect for my son, who has never really been a God-fearing man, I have decided in this moment not to bore you all with another Bible reading. Instead, I will speak from my heart."

Theo resisted the urge to roll his eyes at his father's innocent jab, and instead smirked and shook his head. His smirk faded, however, when Alistair turned and locked eyes with him. "It is both an honor and a privilege to watch you begin the rest of your life today, my son," Alistair murmured, clearly struggling to find his words amongst the storm of emotions in his heart as he then turned to look at Evie. "And I can think of no better woman to have captured his heart than you, my dear. I know you will make an honest man of him. Someday."

Theo almost rolled his eyes again as several chuckles emanated from the pews and Alistair's amused expression slowly faded into a more serious one. "We are gathered together here in the sight of God, and in the face of this congregation, to join together this man and this woman in Holy Matrimony, and we will begin with the vows."

Looking to Evie, he asked pointedly, "Evie Scarborough, do you take this man as thy wedded husband, to live together after God's Ordinance, in the holy Estate of Matrimony? Will you obey him, serve him, love, honor, and keep him in sickness and in health, and forsaking all other, keep thee only unto him, so long as you both shall live?"

Evie let out a short breath, rapidly blinking away the tears in her eyes before murmuring the words she had so longed to be able to say of her own volition.

"I do."

"Theo Cunningham, do you take this woman as thy wedded wife, to live together after God's Ordinance, in the holy Estate of Matrimony? Will you protect her, love her, honor her, and keep her in sickness and in health, and forsaking all others, keep thee only unto her, so long as you both shall live?"

"*I do.*"

His words were strong and powerful, without a trace of hesitation. They felt like silk rolling off of his tongue, and nothing felt more right in the world than to say them. As soon as the words left his lips, he watched a single tear escape the corner of Evie's eye and slip down her cheek, and as if out of reflex, he reached forward to wipe it away with his thumb. It hurt his heart to watch her cry, no matter if they were tears of joy or tears of sorrow, and he knew that if he hadn't perfected the art of swallowing his own tears years ago, he, too, would have been a sobbing puddle before her eyes.

"Let us have the rings, then," Alistair stated before coughing violently into his fist.

Evie looked between Theo and Alistair in confusion. "Rings?" she asked in a whisper. "We haven't any rings—"

Her words trailed off into silence when Theo dug around in the breast pocket of his vest and then opened his fist to reveal two golden wedding bands sitting in his palm. Evie was speechless as Theo took her hand and effortlessly slid the smaller of the two onto her left ring finger and then placed the larger one on his own hand. Upon glancing over Theo's shoulder, she caught Jacob giving her a smug smirk.

Shaking her head in amusement, Evie looked down to admire the ring upon her finger, finding herself in awe at how much she loved to admire it. She could recall her previous wedding band feeling as if it weighed a thousand tons when she wore it, dragging her down to the bottom of an abyss with the weight of its accompanying unwanted obligations. But as she gazed upon this ring, a golden band of long sought after promises that seemed to fit her finger so perfectly, she felt weightless.

A contented smile spread across Alistair's face as he watched the young couple exchange the rings that would make them no longer just lovers, but also spouses, and before he knew it, he was rubbing at his eyes with the back of his hand in order to keep his composure. He could not remember the last time he shed a tear of happiness—perhaps the day his son came into this world? At any rate, he knew that if he did not conclude the ceremony soon, he was going to lose control of the floodgates.

"Dearly beloved," Alistair stated proudly, his voice threatening to break under the weight of the joy he felt for his son, "I now pronounce these two husband and wife. May I present to you, Mr. and Mrs. Theo Cunningham. You may now kiss your bride."

"Gladly," Theo returned smoothly as he reached forward to place his hands upon Evie's waist and pull her as close to his body as he could manage. In an instant, she melted into his arms, her eyes fluttering closed as she stood on the tips of her toes to press a longing kiss to his lips.

The first kiss of their marriage, the first kiss of the rest of their lives.

They are no longer two, but one. Therefore, what God has joined together, let no one separate. Theo repeated the words in his head as he took his wife in his arms and kissed her passionately, not one care in the world as to how many were watching.

It was perhaps the first verse from the Bible that resonated with him. The first one that made sense to him. Whether it was God that had joined them together, or fate, or luck, he didn't care. So long as they remained indivisible in a world so terribly torn and divided, he would die a happy man.

Chapter 18

A Breath of Heaven

December 1780

Evie looked down at her hand as she sat in one of the armchairs in the parlor room, a contented smile tugging at her lips as she admired her golden wedding band and simultaneously stroked her swollen belly. It had been two months since the wedding, but she still found it surreal to think that she was someone's wife once again. Not just anyone's wife, however. Theo's wife. And he was her husband. And the father of her child, who was due to enter the world in less than eight weeks. So many changes seemed to be coming her way all at once that she found herself constantly out of breath and in need of a moment to recollect that this was not some wonderful dream she was having—this was her life, and it finally felt worth living.

"You seem to be captivated by that ring of yours," Johanna spoke with a smirk from her place in the armchair across the parlor, pulling Evie suddenly from her train of thought.

Evie looked up bashfully from her lap and immediately dropped her hand to her side. "It is just beautiful," she said quietly as she felt her cheeks tinge pink in embarrassment at being caught admiring something as trivial as a wedding band.

The ring did not have a single stone—it was a simple golden band—but to her, it was worth more than all of the diamonds and rubies in the world. It was more than just a ring; it symbolized her second chance at life, as well as her eternal union to the man who made that second chance possible.

Johanna smiled warmly and looked at Evie over her knitting. "I have never seen you smile so much in all the years I've known you as you have these last two months."

Evie shrugged with a light girlish giggle. "I just have so many reasons to smile now, I suppose."

"I felt the same way when Alistair and I first married. It was still so new and unfamiliar, and we were still learning how to navigate our lives together. Eventually, though, the novelty wears off, and you forget what your life was ever like before you were together. But the love that brought you together, that never wears away."

Evie smiled widely, a warm feeling spreading across her chest as she watched Johanna speak with a far-off dreamy look in her eyes. She loved discussing all things marriage and family with Johanna, as she was the only mother that she had known for the last six years, and would be the only mother she had for the rest of her life. But as much as she loved Johanna and her life in Division Point, there was still a part of her that longed to have her own mother back. But sadly, she would have to be content with knowing that Ophelia was watching over her above and sharing in her newfound happiness from Heaven.

"You still love Alistair the way you did when you first met?" Evie asked in an attempt to distract herself from the thoughts of her mother that had begun to creep into her head.

Johanna nodded softly. "Even after all these years, and all the trials and tribulations we have faced together, my heart still beats for him like it did thirty years ago."

Evie looked down once more at her wedding ring and watched as it glinted in the light of the candles on the walls above their heads. "*Indivisible.* A perfect word for this family, no?" she asked, recalling the inscription that Jacob had chosen to etch into the inside of her and Theo's rings.

Johanna chuckled in agreement, but before she could speak, they were alerted by the sound of the front door opening and closing with a thud.

"I'm sure Theo will find a way someday. Speaking of the devil, it looks like he has just returned home."

Evie and Johanna both looked toward the doorway to the front room as the stomping of feet to remove the snow that had accumulated on a pair of boots echoed through the house. Gunner immediately alerted to the sound of the front door opening by raising his ears and wildly wagging his tail whilst lounging on the floor underneath Evie's chair. A moment later, Theo appeared in the parlor doorway, donning a thick woolen coat, windswept and snow-speckled hair, and tanned cheeks tinged red by the cold. He looked frigid and exhausted, and the women could tell he was struggling not to shiver in front of them.

"And where have you been, traipsing through this blizzard?" Johanna asked in concern.

Theo stepped into the room and shrugged out of his coat before tossing it onto an empty chair. "I was discussing the building plans with Mr. Drake," he replied with a sigh as he came to stand next to Evie's chair.

"He has drawn up a design for the house. All we need now is to arrange for the lumber from Boston."

"And that could not have waited until the snow stopped?" Evie asked worriedly as she took in her husband's haggard appearance. Ever since the wedding, it seemed as if he was always on the move, always finding something to busy himself with little rest in between.

Theo bent down to press a kiss to the top of her head and placed a hand gently atop her belly. "The sooner the arrangements are made, the sooner we will have a home of our own."

It was not until Christmas time rolled around and snow began to fall to the earth in blankets that the thought occurred to Theo that he and his new family may soon outgrow their lodgings in the house his father had built. His bedroom was adequate when it was just Evie and himself sharing his bed at night, but now that they were soon to be caring for a newborn, it seemed appropriate that he should follow in his father's footsteps and see about building a home for his own family. Just before the snows and blistering winds of winter blew in, Theo took it upon himself to visit with various members of Division Point to arrange for their help in gathering the needed supplies and manpower to construct a house from the ground up. And naturally, he found many friends and neighbors who were more than willing to help with the project once the winter was over and the ground began to thaw with the coming of spring. Naturally, Mr. Drake, the homestead's resident master carpenter, offered both his tools and his expertise without hesitation.

Evie sighed heavily and rested her hand on top of his. "I just worry for you. I do not want you to overwork yourself with this grand vision you have for the house."

"It will all be worth it soon enough," Theo returned excitedly. "Can't you just see it? A house all to ourselves, just down the road, where we can spend the rest of our lives and raise all of our children? They will have a place where they can grow, and play, and explore to their hearts' content!"

"...*They?*" Evie repeated with an arched brow. "That is to say...more than the one child we have now?"

"Of course."

Evie shared a confused look with Johanna before asking, "And how many more children do you expect of me after this?"

Theo chuckled lowly and crouched down by her chair, placing a hand on her arm and smirking as he whispered, "As many as you can give me."

At the sight of Evie's eyes widening in mild fear, Theo's smirk widened, and he leaned down to playfully kiss her lips. As much as he loved to make her smile, he also liked to ruffle her feathers.

"Let us not put the cart before the horse, Theo," Johanna warned with a knowing grin, "Don't you think you are asking enough of that woman to spend the rest of her life with you and bear just *one* of your children? And why are you so eager to escape out from underneath our roof?"

Evie flashed her husband a smug smirk whilst he resisted the urge to roll his eyes at her and Johanna both.

"If I didn't know any better, Jo," Theo teased, "I would think that you do not want us to live apart."

Johanna frowned slightly and set aside her knitting work, folding her arms over her chest. "It will just be strange not to have you around," she admitted sadly. "You've lived in this house your entire life."

Theo smiled wistfully at her and stepped across the room to place a hand on her shoulder. "We will be building our home just down the road, not across the ocean. You will still see us every day."

"And the baby?" Johanna asked hopefully.

"Especially the baby," Evie agreed.

Without warning, Alistair appeared in the doorway that separated the parlor from the kitchen. He was leaning heavily on his cane with his shoulders hunched, taking very small, slow steps as he made his way into the parlor.

Between clearing his throat and taking shallow, ragged breaths that seemed to take everything out of him, he mumbled cheekily, "It surely will be strange without you living in the house, son. And it will certainly be less chaotic."

Theo crossed his arms over his chest, clearly unamused, but his grumpiness immediately disappeared when Alistair fell into a particularly violent coughing fit in the middle of the parlor that stopped him in his tracks and doubled him over in pain. Alistair let out a pained groan after coughing several times into his handkerchief and placed a hand over his chest whilst he felt his knees begin to buckle underneath him. When he pulled his handkerchief away from his mouth, he found several speckles of blood on the white cotton fabric and the taste of iron on his tongue.

"Father?" Theo asked worriedly, gasping in unison with Evie and Johanna when Alistair's eyes slipped closed and his cane slipped from his hand. Within an instant, the old man dropped onto his knees with another wheezing cough.

"Al!" Johanna cried as she, Evie, and Theo all rushed to her husband's side and worked together to hold him up on his knees. Alistair pitched forward with a pained groan and clutched at his chest whilst continuing to choke on the air he struggled to pull into his lungs. Theo immediately placed himself on his father's right and allowed him to lean against his side while placing his arm around his waist.

"Alistair, what happened? Are you alright?" Evie asked in a panic as she struggled to crouch down with them in the middle of the floor.

Alistair was yet unable to speak as he gasped for a breath and remain hunched against Theo's side. Slowly, they watched as his complexion began to pale, as if his body was struggling to keep his heart beating and his lungs breathing at the same time. After several agonizing moments of wheezing and gasping, his eyes began to flutter until closing completely as his head dropped onto Theo's shoulder.

"Oh, my God," Johanna cried in terror. "Theo, go fetch Dr. Thorn at once!"

Theo gingerly slid Alistair's unconscious body from out of his arms and placed him on his back on the floor before they all huddled over him. They could see the old man's chest continuing to rise and fall under his shirt, but the breaths were shallow and not without considerable struggle. His complexion continued to grow pale right before their eyes while the smallest amount of blood began to pool at the corner of his mouth, and Theo found himself frozen in a crouched position at Alistair's side. His head became cluttered with terrorized thoughts that he may be watching his father's last moments transpire before his eyes, and soon, he could feel his own breathing become labored with fear.

"Make haste!" Johanna screeched at him again with tears in her eyes, pointing toward the door. "He needs a doctor immediately!"

Theo flinched under the intensity of her cries, and after a bit of nudging from Evie, he reluctantly rose to his feet and sprinted across the room, but not before stopping once more in the doorway and looking worriedly over his shoulder at his father's body laying lifelessly on the floor.

He could feel the fearful lump rising in his throat as he stood there, and he struggled to swallow it, along with the other nagging fear that today would be the day that Alistair finally succumbed to his sickness. It was painful to watch the strongest man he had ever known slowly weakened by a war of attrition against the illness in his lungs, but it was even more painful yet to see him look so frail and broken as he lay across the floor.

After another moment of anxious hesitation, Theo squeezed his eyes shut and turned his back to the room, his hands clenching into fists of anger at his side as he stormed out of the house and out into the blistering cold in order to find Dr. Thorn.

***

A frustrated sigh escaped Theo's lips as he paced up and down the hallway outside of his parents' room. It had been nearly an hour since Dr. Thorn arrived, and Theo, Evie, and Johanna were made to wait outside the master bedroom while the doctor examined Alistair's condition. With every minute that passed while they waited for him to emerge with hopeful news, they could each feel their heart rates quickening with anxiety.

"Theo, you are making me nervous with all of that pacing," Evie mumbled as she slumped in her chair by the door to the master bedroom.

"What else do you suggest I do?" he returned rather sharply. "My father's life is hanging in the balance."

"He will be fine," Johanna interjected with a sniffle as she dabbed at her eyes with a handkerchief. "Alistair is strong. He will pull through this sickness."

"He has been ill for years," Evie said forlornly. "And he only seems to be deteriorating with time…"

Johanna abruptly stood from her own chair with a distressed huff. "I'll hear no more of this. It is not my husband's time to leave this world. God shall not take him yet."

Evie dropped her head sadly as Theo turned away in frustration, taking his hands through his hair while nervously tapping his foot. A heavy silence fell on them all for several moments before they were startled by the sound of the bedroom door creaking open. They looked to the door with expectant eyes as Dr. Thorn appeared with a bowed head, but their hearts immediately sank when they saw the morose look upon his wrinkled face.

"What news?" Theo asked gruffly.

"He is awake and lucid. Still very weak and groggy, however."

"What happened?" Evie asked. "He was fine one moment, and then the next, he just collapsed."

Dr. Thorn let out a sigh before saying, "He has been battling this sickness for several years, and it has begun to progress quite violently now.

From what I can tell, fluid has filled his lungs, and he is struggling to breathe as a result. He has grown weaker and weaker over time, and today, his body gave out."

"What can we do?" Johanna asked desperately. "How can we heal him?"

Dr. Thorn's expression soured further as he ran a hand down his face and hung his head. "There is no cure. He has shown slight improvement over the last hour, but I am afraid that there is nothing we can do to help him other than keep him comfortable."

Theo's brow furrowed angrily as he asked, "Are you saying that my father is *dying*?"

Dr. Thorn curtly nodded his head, earning a devastated whimper from Johanna, who immediately turned to Evie and collapsed into her arms in a puddle of tears.

"The fluid has already filled most of his lungs. There is nothing that can be done to reverse it. And this bitter winter only serves to make his condition worse."

"Alistair has always insisted that he was fine," Evie murmured in confusion. "He never let us see that he was so sick."

"He has been battling this sickness for a long time. But you know how Alistair Cunningham is. He puts all others before himself, even at his own expense."

"How long?" Theo asked through clenched teeth. "How long does he have?"

"Months, at the most, I am afraid. His body is exhausted from fighting this illness, but soon, I fear he will have nothing left with which to fight."

"Can we see him?" Johanna asked through her tears. "I must see him!"

Dr. Thorn stepped out of the doorway to give her access to the room. "He is well enough to converse. But I insist that he remain bedridden. He does not have the fortitude to be up and about without collapsing."

Johanna did not stick around to hear anything more, for as soon as Dr. Thorn stepped aside, she breezed by him to sprint into the bedroom and drop to her knees at Alistair's bedside. Evie followed close behind her, leaving Theo and Dr. Thorn in the cold and empty hallway.

The two men remained in a heavy silence for several moments as Theo looked away with eyes narrowed into angered slits. He could not articulate who or what he was angry at—Dr. Thorn for not giving him better news, Alistair for falling ill and keeping the true severity of his condition hidden for so long, or himself for only being able to watch as his father wasted away into nothing.

"There has to be a way," Theo whispered once Evie and Johanna were out of earshot. "There has to be something we can do to help him…"

"I'm sorry, Theo," Dr. Thorn sighed. "You know I would cure him in a heartbeat if I could. I wish I had been able to examine him sooner. Perhaps I would have had better news…"

"He is a stubborn man. A prideful man. He refused to admit he was sick."

Dr. Thorn reached forward and placed a sympathetic hand on Theo's shoulder. "The best we can hope for is that he remains comfortable until the end. See to it that he stays in bed and moves about as little as possible. I will return to check in on him every day."

Theo swallowed thickly and nodded his head in reluctant agreement. "Evie is to give birth at the end of February. Please tell me he will at least live long enough to meet his grandchild…"

Dr. Thorn's expression remained grim as he mumbled, "I cannot promise anything, but I believe he will be able to hang on until then."

Theo wished that the doctor's words gave him some sort of comfort, but they did not in the least. Nothing could have given him comfort in that moment, now that he was face to face with the terrible reality that Alistair Cunningham was not the indestructible hero whom he had looked up to for as long as he could remember.

A heavy silence fell upon them as Theo's eyes drifted emptily to the floor, and Dr. Thorn cleared his throat before saying, "He wanted to speak to you when he came to. I suggest you go and see him while he is lucid."

Theo nodded stiffly as Dr. Thorn bid him a heavy-hearted goodbye and showed himself out of the house. He waited a minute before entering the master bedroom and simply stood speechless in the middle of the hallway, glaring harshly at the wall as if doing so would somehow reverse the clock and bring them all back to a simpler time, before the war, before the sickness, and before the weight of the world seemed to have fallen upon his shoulders.

After lingering in the hall for several more minutes, Theo let out a long breath and shuffled into the room, gently closing the door behind him. Evie and Johanna were each seated at Alistair's bedside, gingerly grasping his hands as he laid propped against several pillows with a thick blanket pulled up to his chest. Theo immediately felt his chest constrict around his heart at the sight of Alistair lying in bed. He had never before seen him so feeble, so weak, so small. Alistair's complexion was still sickly pale, but his skin no longer held the bluish tint it did when he had first collapsed, and he stared forward with half-lidded eyes that bespoke tiredness and a desperate desire for relief from the pain in his lungs.

"Theo," Alistair rasped, his words barely audible and nearly dying before they left his throat. "Do not look so forlorn, my son. I do not like to see you frown."

Theo cleared his throat and slowly approached the bed, pausing next to Evie and trying fruitlessly to replace the frown on his face with a half-hearted grin. It was pointless. There was no reason to even fake a smile now.

He hadn't any clue if Alistair was even aware of the severity of his illness, or if Dr. Thorn had explained to him that he hadn't much time left, but hearing the old man choke out another wheezing cough made him physically flinch.

"How do you feel?" Theo asked softly.

"Better now," Alistair replied between wheezes. "I suppose I just needed some rest…"

"You pushed yourself too hard," Johanna corrected sternly. "You must put aside your pride and allow us to help you. You are sick, my love. Please, you must take care of yourself…"

Alistair stubbornly shook his head. "Is that what Dr. Thorn told you? That I am old and frail?"

"He told us that you are *dying*," Theo suddenly snapped, much harsher than he had intended. But he didn't care. He was furious. "You are dying because you refused to admit to us or yourself that you had fallen ill. And now it is too late!"

"Theo…" Evie chastised quietly, placing a hand on his arm.

Another silence fell upon them all for several moments as Alistair's eyes slipped closed, seemingly in realization that Theo was not exaggerating. Letting out a deep sigh, he meekly asked, "How long did the good doctor give me?"

"Months, at the most," Theo replied shortly. "And you are to remain in bed at all times."

Alistair shook his head sadly. "That is no way to live. It is no way to die, either."

"Well, you haven't left us much choice, now, Father. There is nothing we can do now but watch you waste away. Is that what you wanted?"

"That is the last thing I wanted…"

Johanna let out a devastated whimper and wiped at her eyes again, squeezing Alistair's hand as she lowly bowed her head. "Oh, dear God, please let Dr. Thorn be wrong. This is the worst news we could possibly receive so close to Christmas time…"

Alistair turned his head to look at Johanna with a tender look in his glossy eyes. The corners of his mouth twitched upward in a contented grin as he mumbled, "No more tears, my dear. I cannot bear to see you cry on my behalf."

"We cannot lose you," Johanna whispered as a stream of tears rolled down her cheek. "Not now. Not yet…"

"You must promise that you will hold on enough to see the baby," Evie tearfully begged as she squeezed her father-in-law's other hand. "Please, Alistair. You cannot leave this world without meeting your grandchild."

Alistair's grin widened ever so slightly as he turned his head on the pillow to meet her gaze. It was plain to see that he struggled to speak as he murmured, "You know I will do my best, dear girl. Nothing would bring me more joy than to hold my grandchild in my arms."

Feeling the surface of his skin become hot and his eyes begin to burn with tears of anger and hopelessness, Theo dropped to his knees next to his wife at Alistair's bedside, his head falling onto the bed as the weight of the world seemed to crush him into the floor. Squeezing his eyes shut and clenching his teeth, he tried to swallow the firestorm of pain swirling within his heart, but before he could find the strength to stifle his tears, he felt one escape the corner of his eye and slip down his cheek. Evie desperately wrapped her arms around his waist in an attempt to comfort him, and both Johanna and Alistair watched helplessly as his shoulders, and eventually his entire body, began to tremble with the devastated sobs he had been trying so desperately to suppress.

"How could you do this?" Theo asked through clenched teeth as he slowly looked up to meet Alistair's tired gaze. "How could you leave us like this?"

"I have not gone anywhere, my son. I am right here…"

"No!" he cried, slamming his fists upon the mattress. "The sickly thing in this bed is not the man I call my father. You have let this sickness waste you away into nothing because you were to stubborn to admit that you needed help! And now you have left us with no choice but to watch you die a slow and painful death. How could you do this to your family? How could you be so selfish?"

Alistair swallowed thickly before raising his arm in order to place a shaking hand upon Theo's cheek, gently wiping away the tears that stained his face with the pad of his thumb.

"I am so sorry, Theo," he whispered weakly. "I never meant to hurt you, any of you. I thought that if I pushed through the illness, God would reward me. I thought he would cure me…"

"How could you be so naive, after all of these years?" Theo barked. "God was *never* going to cure you! God was never going to protect you! The only person who could ever do that was yourself…"

Alistair shook his head again. "I refuse to believe that."

"Then you are a fool. A *dying* fool."

"Theo!" Johanna cried. "Now is not the time for such spite. We must cherish the time we have left with your father, not waste it away with bitterness and anger."

Abruptly, Theo rose to his feet, allowing Alistair's hand to fall limply away from his face and back into the bed. "If you are asking me to stand idly by and watch as my father's life slips away, the answer is no."

Just as he turned away in an attempt to storm out of the room, Alistair summoned the last of his strength to reach forward and grab ahold of his hand before collapsing into his pillows and pulling Theo back toward the side of the bed.

"Listen to me," Alistair croaked as sternly as he could manage whilst clutching his son's hand so tightly his knuckles began to turn white. "I know I have made many mistakes. And I know that those mistakes have all come back to hurt you. But I am begging you, do not see *this* as a mistake. Please do not be frightened or saddened by my passing. I have spent many years upon this earth, and I have done what I can to atone for my wrongdoings in the last decades of my life. My only hope is that I have left the world better than how I had found it, for you, and the generations to come…"

"Do not see this as a great and terrible loss. God has simply decided that my time on earth has come to an end, and that I have done all I can do. I am not afraid, and neither should you be. I am relieved that that I will soon be with God, and I will be free forever to walk with him through Heaven's gates."

Theo swallowed thickly and wiped at his eyes with the back of his hand, squeezing Alistair's fingers as he whispered, "It isn't fair…"

"I know, my son. But we must do the best that we know how with what we have been given, and I have been given over fifty wonderful years on this earth. And I would not trade any of them for all of the riches in the world. But I have a feeling that it is my time, and I will soon be called home."

"Your home is here," Theo returned. "With us."

"Division Point is our temporary home. Just a stop on the way to where we are all meant to be in the end. That is why I am not afraid."

"What do you think it is like," Evie asked softly as she leaned forward in her chair and rubbed Alistair's arm, "leaving this world behind?"

Alistair closed his eyes with a peaceful smile before opening them again and looking up to the ceiling whilst still clutching onto Theo's hand. "I would imagine it is just one more step forward, and when I blink my eyes, I will be home on the other side with the songs of a million angels in my ears. And when that breath of Heaven fills my chest, and I see His face, I will finally find the peaceful rest I have always sought…"

Johanna attempted a weak smile and leaned her head down upon her husband's shoulder as mournful tears continued to gather in her eyes. Nothing could soothe her devastation, but for the remainder of Alistair's days, she would face the inevitable with a brave heart, for his sake, and for everyone else's. "If what you say is true, my love, then none of us have anything to fear…"

Theo gently released his hand from Alistair's grip and stepped away from the bed, his head hung low while he ran his hands through his hair and attempted to make sense of everything that had been thrown at him. He had never been a God-fearing man, and for a moment, after his close brushes with death, he had begun to wonder if he was wrong—if there was something, or *someone*, up above to guide them in this world and the next.

But he still struggled to understand how a just God could create a world filled with so much pain and suffering, and now that he was watching his own father waste away into nothing after only spending fifty years on this earth, he was more confused than ever. Was this illness God's punishment for the mistakes Alistair had made when he was young? Would He punish Theo the same way in the years to come for the many mistakes he had made in his own past? Was there any way to know? And if there was such a thing as Heaven, would Theo be granted access when his time came, too?

Would he ever feel the breath of Heaven fill his own chest, just as Alistair had promised?

***

February 1781

"I'm coming with you," Evie stated sternly as she placed her hands on her hips and stood at the end of the dock with a small trunk packed for travel by her side. The early February winds were still bitterly cold as they whipped her hair about her face, and a light flurry of snow filled the frosty air.

Theo frowned at her from where he stood on the deck of *The Liberty*, which he was currently in the process of preparing for a short trip to Boston. "It is not a safe journey for you to make in the last month of your pregnancy. And I will only be gone three days or so. Please, stay here and help Johanna look after my father."

Evie shook her head stubbornly. "I am your wife now. If you are going to Boston to collect the lumber for our home together, I should be joining you."

Theo rolled his eyes up to the dreary grey sky above their heads and smirked. "And as my wife, you should do as I request. You did agree to love, honor, and *obey* me, remember?"

Evie crossed her arms over her chest and rested them atop her swollen belly, shifting her weight impatiently between her feet. "That was merely a suggestion, not a hard and fast rule."

"The only reason I am taking the schooner to Boston through the harbor is because the ground is still too frozen to safely travel by wagon. But that does not mean it is safe for you to be traveling in this frigid weather."

Evie flashed him a pleading look and puffed out her bottom lip. "I will stay plenty warm in the cabin. Please, Theo, let me come along. I need to get away from the homestead for a spell…"

"And what of my father?"

"Johanna told me that she could manage his care on her own while we are away."

Theo let out a sigh, watching his breath cloud before him in the cold air as he deliberated. After a moment, he shrugged his shoulders in defeat. "Alright. You may come. But you must stay in the cabin during the entire journey. And you are to stay by my side at all times while we are in Boston. Understood?"

"Understood, Captain Cunningham," she returned slyly before stepping onto the gangplank.

"There could be pirates, you know," Theo teased as he offered her his hand in order to help her waddle up the rest of the gangplank and step onto the deck of the ship.

"Pirates between Division Point and Boston? Perhaps five or six years ago, I may have been foolish enough to believe you," Evie returned with a smirk as she made her way to the captain's cabin with her trunk in hand.

***

After bidding Johanna and Alistair goodbye, Theo and Evie set sail from the dock at Division Point and cruised north through the icy waters of the Bay along the Massachusetts coast. The winds were strong and carried them without incident to the Boston Harbor in a little over a day's time. A wiser plan would have been to wait until closer to the spring time to make the journey, but Theo was not a patient man, and he was itching to gather supplies needed to build his new family's home as soon as possible so that he would have them on hand when construction began in April.

And while he was anxious to get to Boston to meet with the lumber tradesmen that were supplying him with the wood, he was reluctant to leave the homestead. Evie was due to give birth at the end of the month or in early March, but there was always the chance that she could enter into labor at any time. That was the only reason he agreed to let her join him in Boston. If she were to give birth early, even away from home, he wanted to be there.

And much like they had expected, Alistair's condition had continued to deteriorate since December, to the point that he was completely unable to move himself from his bed under his own power. It caused him great discomfort to speak or even take a breath, but miraculously, he retained his lucidity with every day that passed. His body may have been failing him, but his mind was still as sharp as ever, and that gave his family some comfort as they tended to his every need day after day.

After arriving in Boston, Theo and Evie anchored *The Liberty* at one of the many docks in the harbor. The lumbermen that Theo had secured to provide the timber for the house were expecting to meet with him that same day at a tavern near the wharf, and after disembarking, the meeting commenced.

Theo expected he would need to haggle with the men a bit to lower the lumber's price down to what he could afford, but he was not expecting was for the lumbermen to be two very large and less than accommodating Frenchmen with very broken English. After nearly twenty minutes of back and forth at a table in the barroom with many words exchanged and not a single message being delivered, Evie, who had been sitting silently by Theo's side at the table, dared to clear her throat and interject.

It was clear that Theo's skills as a diplomat, as well as his knowledge of the French language, were quite limited, and his patience with the pair of grubby frontiersmen before them was wearing thin. Evie had been instructed to sit quietly and let him do the talking, but that had clearly gotten them nowhere, and she was growing tired with having to sit in an uncomfortable wooden chair whilst cradling her swollen belly.

"*Excusez-moi, messieurs,*" Evie said gently from her seat by Theo's side, causing all three men to turn and look at her with rather wide eyes. "It appears we have reached an impasse in our negotiations, and I would like to return home before I go into labor."

The lumbermen shared a confused look before whispering to each other under their breath. They were gruff and boorish looking men, with unkind expressions upon their unshaved faces that bespoke an unwillingness to haggle.

"Your husband…is cheap," one of them grumbled to her with a clenched fist. "No pay, no lumber."

Theo rolled his eyes and ran a hand down his face in exasperation. "They are trying to take us for a ride," he mumbled to Evie from the corner of his mouth. "And I told you to let me do the talking."

"And look how far we have gotten with your negotiations," Evie shot back before clearing her throat again. "Let me have a go."

"Evie, I do not think you should—"

Evie cut off Theo's warning by turning her attention from him to the men sitting across from them. "*D'où êtes-vous?*" she asked the men kindly.

One of the men hesitated before stating, "Québec."

"Ah, Québec. I have never been, *mais j'entends dire que c'est charmant.* And you are right. *Mon mari est un avare.* But with good reason. *Comme vous pouvez le constater, je suis avec mon enfant. Tout notre argent ira au soin du bébé et nous voulons désespérément construire notre propre maison pour notre famille.*"

The lumbermen shared another look, but their expressions had softened slightly as they bantered back and forth indistinctly. Meanwhile, Theo remained frozen in his seat, staring at Evie in complete shock as she effortlessly transitioned between English and French without skipping a beat, a skill he was completely unaware that she possessed.

"We can go no lower on price," one of the men said firmly. "750 pounds for lumber. *Je suis désolé.*"

Evie smiled sweetly and folded her hands before placing them upon the top of the table. "*Avez-vous des familles? Des épouses et des enfants?*"

The men both hesitantly nodded. "*Oui.*"

Evie's smile widened ever so slightly, and she placed a hand upon her belly. "*Ensuite, vous pouvez comprendre notre lutte. Pouvez-vous trouver dans vos cœurs d'aider une jeune famille à se remettre sur pied?*"

The men shared another uncertain look before leaning close and mumbling together for several moments. Evie flashed Theo a rather smug look over her shoulder as the men conversed, and he continued to look at her in both awe and confusion. He spoke not a lick of French, so their conversation was quickly lost on him, and after a minute or so, the men separated and looked at the young couple with softened gazes.

With a single nod of his head, one of the men stated, "500 pounds for lumber. *C'est le plus bas nous pouvons aller.*"

Evie did not bother to clue Theo in on the conversation or even look his way before she stood from her chair and said with a pleased smirk,

"*Oui, vous avez un accord. Merci pour votre gentillesse, messieurs. Au revoir.*" She then leaned forward over the table to shake each of the men's hands before turning away and sauntering across the barroom toward the exit. "Come along, Theo," she sang triumphantly as she brushed past his chair. "Our work here is done."

Theo blinked in befuddlement and looked back and forth between Evie's retreating form and the men across the table, and after taking a moment to collect his thoughts, he nodded to the lumbermen in thanks before following after his wife.

It was late evening when they left the tavern and stepped out into the bitterly cold wharf, and the air was crisp with a light wind.

"What the hell was that?" Theo asked, perplexed, as he helped her shrug into her coat before they both braved the cold together. "What did I just watch transpire?"

Evie chuckled lightly, smugly, and bid him to follow her back to *The Liberty*. "That was a business transaction, my love. I watched my father complete hundreds of them throughout my youth. Perhaps some of his skill impressed upon me."

Theo shook his head in confusion. "But…how long have you been conversant in French?"

Evie chuckled again. "Father insisted I learn from the best tutors that money could buy when I was a young girl. In addition to mathematics and religion, I had French and Latin beaten into my head by the time I was twelve years old."

Theo looked at her in amazement. "And how did you convince them to lower the price of their lumber?"

"I merely appealed to their sensibilities as family men. Now, for 500 pounds, they will have ten tons of lumber shipped to Division Point, come springtime."

It was Theo's turn to smirk as he hooked an arm around Evie's shoulders and pulled her into his side. "You never cease to amaze and surprise me, Mrs. Cunningham."

Evie returned his embrace by wrapping her arm around his waist as they wandered through the wharf under the silver light of the full February moon overhead.

"Perhaps it was a good thing I tagged along, hm? Without me, you may have never secured the lumber."

Theo resisted the urge to roll his eyes, but instead leaned down to kiss the top of her head and place a hand gently upon her belly. They stopped when they came to the end of the dock to which *The Liberty* was anchored and shared a brief and tender kiss as the busy sounds of the wharf played on all around them. Wood creaking, sailors shouting, gulls cawing, and waves breaking against the shore all danced in the air to create a beautifully chaotic backdrop to their moment of solace on the docks—a much-needed moment of peace after all that they had both endured over the past several months.

Back in December, Alistair had mentioned something about the breath of Heaven filling his chest when he passed from this world into the next. And everyone had always spoken of this place called Heaven as if they could not wait to die and make their ascendance into that castle in the sky. But standing there on the docks, surrounded by the sights and smells of the city with his wife in his arms and his child in her belly, Theo could not imagine any other place he would rather be in that moment, Heaven or otherwise. And as far as he was concerned, he felt a breath of Heaven fill his chest every time he looked into her eyes.

"Now what?" Evie asked in an almost breathless whisper after Theo pulled away.

The corners of his mouth twitched upward as he looped his arm around hers in order to lead her down the dock and to the gangplank.

"Now, we go *home*."

***

The air over Massachusetts Bay was cold, but not unpleasant, and a light flurry of snow hung over the water as *The Liberty* cut through the icy waves on her journey to Division Point. Just like the trip to Boston, the trip back had been rather uneventful, with Evie spending the day resting in the cabin while Theo braved the cold at the helm to ensure the ship stayed its course along the coastline.

Six hours into the journey, Evie grew bored with lounging inside the captain's cabin and wrapped a shawl around her body before poking her head out through the door and scanning the deck.

Upon hearing the door to the cabin creak open, Theo glanced over his shoulder to see Evie shuffling across the deck to meet him at the helm. In that moment, the wind picked up to ruffle their clothes and blow their hair wildly about their faces.

"It is much too cold for you out here," Theo commented while passing her a chastising look. "You are already shivering."

Evie wrapped her shawl tightly around her body and shook her head. "I cannot lay about in the cabin any longer. The baby will not stop kicking."

"You may join me for a few minutes. Then you must go back inside to rest. I do not want you to push yourself."

Evie nodded in silent agreement and turned to lean backwards against the nearest railing while cradling her belly. They stood in comfortable silence for a few moments, the only sounds in the air being the wind filling the sails and the squawking of gulls on the shore. It was midafternoon, and the sun was high in the sky behind a thin veil of clouds, bringing a little warmth to an otherwise bitterly cold day.

Evie was the first to break the silence when she cleared her throat and asked, "May I ask you something?"

"Anything."

"…How much time do you think Alistair has left with us?"

Theo hesitated, his body tensing as he clutched tightly onto the spokes of the helm wheel. He swallowed thickly before quietly stating, "Your guess is as good as mine."

"He has only gotten worse since Christmas. He cannot even stand on his own any longer."

"My father is nothing if not a strong man. He will pull through."

Evie shook her head sadly. "You heard what Dr. Thorn said. He is not going to get *better*."

"You do not know him like I do. He has a lot of living left to do before he goes. It will just take time for him to recuperate."

"Why do you insist on denying the inevitable?"

Theo turned his head to shoot her a sharp glare with eyes narrowed in annoyance. "My father wanted to live long enough to see the birth of his grandchild, and that is what he is going to do. Then he will live for a long time after that."

"Theo, please be realistic—"

"Realistic? You want me to be realistic? If you are waiting for me to say that I am going to blindly accept that my father is dying, then you are more foolish than Dr. Thorn. I will not sit and dwell on such terrible things, and I do not want to discuss his sickness anymore. You may be content to give up on him, but *I* am not."

Evie turned her head away as a look of hurt crossed her face, and another silence fell upon them for several minutes. Crossing her arms over her chest with a frustrated huff, her eyes fell to the wooden boards of the deck crusted with patches of ice under her feet.

"I'm sorry," Theo eventually mumbled after sighing heavily. "I did not mean to lose my temper…"

Evie shrugged her shoulders. "I am just worried for you. You and Alistair have always had your squabbles, but I know his sickness has hurt you most of all. And when he does pass, I fear you…you will never be the same."

"No one will be the same when he is gone," he admitted softly, his eyes fluttering closed in sadness. "Alistair Cunningham touches the lives of everyone he meets."

Evie opened her mouth to speak but was interrupted when she suddenly let out a squeak of discomfort and looked down at her womb. Theo gave her a sideways look of concern when she placed both of her hands on her belly, her face pinched up in a sudden rush of pain.

"Are you alright?"

She nodded her head curtly as she continued to stroke her stomach. "I am fine. Just…uncomfortable."

"Perhaps you should go back to the cabin and lay down—"

Evie groaned again and sunk back against the railing while cradling and rubbing her stomach, which had begun to churn and contract intensely over the last several hours. Thus far, she had been able to ignore the discomfort, but now, the pain was so intense that her legs were beginning to buckle.

That was when the realization hit her like a stampede of wild horses and knocked the wind out of her lungs—this was the exact same painful contracting she had felt just before she had gone into labor with Noah all those years ago.

"Oh, God," she gasped fearfully as she used one hand to cradle her stomach and the other to grip the railing. "Oh, no…not now. Please, God, not now…"

"What is the matter?" Theo asked in alarm as he stepped away from the helm and came to her side. "Are you in pain?"

Evie clenched her teeth and weakly nodded, gasping out, "The baby…the baby is coming. I can feel it…"

"*What? Now?* We are still a day's sail away from home!"

Evie moaned painfully once more as her legs gave out underneath her, but Theo was at her side in an instant and immediately let her lean against his side as he wrapped an arm around her waist.

"Theo," she whispered as fearful tears began to burn her eyes, "I am afraid. I do not know what to do..."

Theo effortlessly swept her up into his arms and sauntered across the deck toward the captain's cabin whilst attempting to swallow the panic he could feel rising in his own chest.

"It will be alright," he promised her as he kicked open the door to the cabin. "Everything will be fine."

"No!" she cried out and clutched at her belly. "It will not be alright! We are miles and miles from home! I cannot give birth here!"

Theo set her down gently upon the bed in the corner of the cabin and quickly set about lighting several candles around the room. "Stay here. I will anchor the ship where we are and return shortly."

Before Evie could object, Theo sprinted out of the room to let the ship's anchor unravel and fall to the bottom of the Bay. He hadn't any clue how long they would need to remain anchored before they could set sail again, but he did not care. With luck, they would be able to continue their journey shortly, before any Redcoat ships came through. After ensuring that the anchor had been properly deployed at the bow of the ship, Theo rushed back into the cabin to find Evie writhing in pain in the bed, collapsed back against the mattress with her eyes squeezed shut as she continuously whimpered in agony.

Much like her first experience with birth, her stomach seemed to be trying to turn itself inside out within her body, creating an enormous pressure in her pelvis that seemed to come and go every few minutes. While Theo was gone, she felt the mattress underneath her suddenly become soaked in a large puddle that also stained most of her skirt. That was when she knew.

"Theo!" she whined as he came to the side of the bed and gripped her hands. "The baby is coming. Something is wrong. We cannot have the baby on the ship...we just can't!"

"You are going to have to, love," Theo said resolutely. "We have little choice now. There is no way to reach home before you give birth."

Tears began to stream down Evie's face as she shook her head and groaned. "But the baby…"

"The baby will be fine. But you are going to have to push. And I…I will have to deliver it."

"You don't know the first thing about delivering a baby!"

Theo raked his hands nervously through his hair before moving onto the end of the bed and reaching for both of her ankles so that he could gently push her skirt over her knees and pull her legs open.

"Then I suppose I am going to learn today," he mumbled, his confident smirk betraying the whirlwind of panic he could feel flooding his chest.

Chapter 19

Liberty

February 1781

E vie dropped her head back against the mattress with an agonized cry, feeling sweat gather upon her brow and a sharp pain undulate in her abdomen. It had been three hours since her water had broken, three hours of painful contractions, and three hours of The Liberty bobbing in the Bay like a sitting duck; and there was still no sign of her labor progressing any further.

Theo remained at the side of the bed, stroking her hair and rubbing her arm as she clutched as tightly onto his hand as she could manage.

"I can't do this…" Evie moaned, "I can't give birth on this boat! We must go home!"

"We aren't going anywhere until this is over. I am not leaving your side. Now, come, you must try to push again."

Evie shook her head and tried to close her legs when Theo slid down to the end of the bed to push her skirt up over her knees again. He hadn't any clue what he was supposed to be looking for, or the proper way to deliver a baby, but he was present for both Noah's and Levi's births, so he reckoned that he could feel his way through this one. They had few other options at this point, after all.

"I do not want you to see me like this," she whined.

Theo placed his hands on her thighs and gently pulled open her legs, looking up at her from over her swollen belly. "Evie, I am your husband, and I have watched you give birth once before. This is hardly the time for bashfulness."

"What if something goes wrong? What if something is wrong with the baby? What if—"

"The only way we can know is for you to push. That is the hardest part, but you must do it."

Evie clenched her teeth together in order to gather the strength to push, but the attempt was weak, and she could feel no movement in her womb as a result.

"Harder, Evie. You have to push harder."

"I can't! It hurts so much…"

She tried to push again, but she could feel herself becoming overwhelmed by the agony coursing through the lower half of her body. Every time she squeezed her eyes shut to push, she was assaulted with painful memories of the last time she had been in this position over six years ago, and the memory still stung as if it had been yesterday. Noah would have been six years old in January, but instead, he remained six feet under in a small coffin next to Division Point Church.

As Evie tossed and turned on the bed in the captain's cabin that cold afternoon, her thoughts were quickly pulled away from the terrible pain in her body to the horrible fear in her heart that this birth could end in the same tragic way Noah's had. The fear of losing another child in the womb had plagued her since the beginning of her pregnancy, but only now that she was in labor did said fear seem all the more real.

"Nothing is happening," Theo grumbled from between her legs.

"Theo, I am afraid…"

"I know you are. But it will all be over soon. You just have to push. Do it for the baby, do it for me, do it for us. It's only us, remember? Only us. Nothing else matters…"

"What if I'm not strong enough?"

Theo's voice softened as he flashed her a smile. "You are the strongest woman I know. Do you remember what I said to you all those years ago, before Noah was born?"

Evie nodded weakly as tears of fear and exhaustion began to well in her eyes. "A few moments of pain…for a lifetime of joy…"

Theo's sideways smile widened as he said, "That's right. Just a few moments. And then we will have our family. You can do this, love. Please, for us. Be brave for us."

Evie nodded again, this time as the slightest of smiles spread across her face, before tipping her head back and closing her eyes in order to gather the strength to push again. She could recall Noah's birth coming and going with extreme haste, but this time around, God had decided that it would be humorous to torture her with hours of labor. If He was trying to test her faith over the last six years, it was certainly working.

With an ear-piercing shriek, Evie pushed once more with all of her might, feeling the pressure in her abdomen begin to move even lower in her body until she was assaulted by a searing pain between her legs.

"I see it," she heard Theo say hesitantly, though his voice seemed distant over the sound of the blood pounding in her ears. "I can see it, Evie. I can see the head. Keep going."

She pushed again, overwhelmed by an agony even greater than that she remembered feeling the first time she was in labor, and if her shrieking howls were any indication of her pain, Theo concluded that she must have felt as if her body was being simultaneously turned inside-out and ripped in half.

He tore his eyes away from the gory sight between her legs to look at her over the curve of her belly, catching a glimpse of her normally angelic face twisted in agony and covered in a sheen of sweat, and he made a mental note to never underestimate a woman's physical strength or power ever again. He could not even imagine the fortitude required to grow another living thing in one's body before bringing it into the world, and as he watched his wife give the last few pushes she could manage, he had found an all new respect for her and every other woman in the world. She never ceased to amaze him, Theo said to himself with a smirk.

After looking away for only a moment or two, Theo looked back down to see an infant's head and shoulders, covered in a sticky, reddish substance, protruding from between Evie's legs. He sucked in a sharp breath before shouting, "You're almost there, love, you're so close. Come on now, just one more push…"

Evie did not have to be coaxed again, for with one last push, she could feel the immense pressure in her pelvis melt away and disappear as if it had never been there in the first place. Falling back against the mattress in exhaustion, she let out a gasp of relief when she realized the pain was gone, and she squeezed her eyes shut to wait in anxious anticipation for a sign of life.

Theo caught the slippery little creature in his outstretched hands without hesitation and reached for the knife on his belt to sever the umbilical cord, the last physical connection between mother and child after birth. The air was deathly quiet inside the cabin as Theo and Evie both held their breath, and after several agonizing moments, their ears were touched by the beautiful and miraculous sound of a baby's first cry, a tiny little squeak at first that gradually turned into a strong, piercing screech as air filled the child's lungs for the first time.

Evie let out another gasp, this time one of unspeakable joy and relief, when she heard her baby's cry fill the cabin, and she brought her hand up to cover her mouth as tears began to stream down her flushed face once more. After severing the umbilical cord with his knife, Theo held the tiny little creature, still covered in afterbirth, up in the air for Evie to see.

"It's a girl," she heard him utter excitedly over the baby's cries, his voice threatening to break in what she could only assume to be paternal pride and joy.

"A girl," Evie repeated between heaving breaths and sobs, "We have a girl…"

Theo's hands shook with an overwhelming mixture of happiness and shock at what he had just witnessed as he clutched the crying baby to his chest and searched for something with which to wrap her in order to keep her warm. His eyes eventually settled on his cloak, which had been tossed onto a nearby chest, and he slid off the edge of the bed to collect it before using it to wipe the blood off of the baby's tiny body and swaddling her tightly within its warmth.

Evie was still gasping for breath and sobbing uncontrollably when he took a seat on the edge of the bed next to her and placed the baby on her chest, whose cries had quieted into a soft whimper once she was clean and warm.

"Oh, God, she is so small," Evie said with a light giggle as she felt the baby's weight settle onto her breast, and she immediately wrapped her arms around her to hold her close. "And so beautiful."

"She's perfect," Theo agreed in a whisper, squeezing his eyes shut in order to swallow the tears he could feel brimming within. If someone had told him only a few years ago that he would be brought to tears by the birth of his own child, he would have called them mad, but now, he found himself overwhelmed with a happiness he could not possibly articulate as he looked down at the tiny creature in Evie's arms. A tiny creature that they had both created, together, and would love, together, for the rest of their days.

Now that the baby was clean, and the redness from the shock of birth was beginning to fade from her skin, it was easy to see that her complexion was a rich tan color, much like her father's. The top of her little head was awash with thin wisps of dark hair, and they both knew in that moment that she would favor Theo in her appearance from this day forward. Within moments of being swaddled in the cloak and nuzzled against Evie's chest, the baby's whimpers began to fade until she fell asleep completely, leaving the cabin in a beautiful and peaceful silence.

As he sat on the edge of the bed, Theo leaned down to rest his head against Evie's and gently raised his bloodied hand in order to stroke the baby's cheek with his finger. The child stirred slightly when his skin made contact with hers, but after he began to stroke her face with a touch as gentle and light as a feather, she nestled comfortably back against her mother's breast. Theo looked down at the girl with wide and teary eyes, unable to recall a time in his life he had ever been so in awe. As soon as he heard his daughter's cries pierce the air for the first time, he could feel his chest begin to swell with an intoxicating wave of pride and contentment that only seemed to grow the longer he gazed at her sleeping face.

All those months ago, Alistair had told him that his life would never be the same once his child was born, and that a father's love for his child was a love without any end; at that time, he could have never hoped to understand what the old man really meant. But now, as he sat by Evie's side and wrapped his arms around her as she nuzzled their sleeping child to her chest, he knew in his heart *exactly* what Alistair meant. He had only known the little girl for a few minutes, and thus far only held her in his arms for a few moments, but he already knew that never would love anything more deeply than he loved her. She was so small and so fragile,

Indivisible

but she had already captured his heart and taken his breath away, and she would forever have him wrapped around her finger.

Suddenly, Theo turned his head away and wiped at his eyes with the back of his hand, sniffling under his breath. Evie tore her eyes away from the baby to look up at him with a quirked brow.

"Are you...crying?" she asked with a breathless giggle.

Theo considered denying it, but there was no point. Instead, he vehemently nodded his head and pulled his arm away before looking down at her again to reveal two streams of hot tears staining his cheeks.

"She is just as beautiful as you," Theo whispered as he leaned down to press a kiss on Evie's temple. "What good could I have possibly done in my life to deserve what I have now?"

Evie leaned her head tiredly against his shoulder and gently rocked the baby in her arms. Her face was still flushed red and slick with sweat, and several strands of her hair were matted to her cheeks and neck, which Theo brushed away with his finger and tucked behind her ear.

"I could offer an explanation," she said with a yawn, "but you would just tell me that God had nothing to do with it."

Theo chuckled gently and stroked her hair with one hand while placing the other under the baby's back. "Some things in this world just can't be explained by mortals," he murmured. "That's when we turn to God, hm?"

"Only God could have created something so beautiful and perfect," Evie concluded as she gazed down at their sleeping daughter.

"I'd like to think that *I* had a little something to do with it..."

Evie opened her mouth to give him a sassy retort, but she was interrupted when Theo turned his head to look out the porthole near the bed and suddenly jumped to his feet with enough vigor to startle both her and the baby. Theo wordlessly peered out of the porthole, his body visibly beginning to tense.

"What's wrong?" Evie asked worriedly. "What's happened?"

Theo held a hand up to silence her as he slowly stepped away from the porthole. When he turned back around to face her, his face was pale, as if he had seen a specter or some other entity that had suddenly frightened him out of his wits.

Theo swallowed thickly and pointed to the window. "Redcoats," he whispered, his eyes wide with shock. "A British warship, just off the starboard side."

"*What?*" Evie gasped, clutching the baby tightly to her body as a wave of fear washed over her. She tried to peak through the porthole herself, but only caught a glimpse of the top of a tall mast. Attached to the top of that mast was the flag of the British Empire. And from what she could see, the warship was only a few hundred yards away and continuing to approach them. "What would a British warship be doing in the Massachusetts Bay?"

Theo's voice was tight with concern as he continued to peer out of the porthole and mumbled, "To deliver troops and supplies, I am sure." He was sure now, the warship, a great wooden vessel with three masts and more guns in her hull than he could count, had spotted them and was now slowing down as she headed their way. That could mean only one thing. "They want to board us."

"What could they possibly want with us?" Evie asked tensely.

"To ensure that we are not rebels." Theo stepped away from the porthole and made his way across the cabin to the door.

"Where are you going?" Evie's voice was small and her words hesitant as she watched him go, and she could feel herself sinking back into the bed in fear once she realized that he intended to leave her and their newborn child alone in the cabin.

"I am going to see what they want. Stay here with the baby. And keep her quiet. I will return shortly."

Evie helplessly watched him open the door to the cabin and protested, "Theo, please don't leave us here alone…"

"Do as I say," Theo ordered sharply as he stepped onto the deck and began to close the door behind him. "Make no sound. I will take care of this."

His words evoked both confidence and fearlessness, but they both knew that he was now just as afraid as she. British warships did not board small fishing boats just to engage in friendly chats. But it mattered little how fearful he was for his own safety in the face of the enemy—he had a family to protect.

Unable to get out of the bed on her own and without the strength to even move, Evie was helpless as she sat in the dim light of the cabin and listened intently to what was unfolding outside on the deck. Just as Theo stepped outside, the warship whose hull was emblazoned with the words *HMS Leopard*, had sailed within a hundred yards of *The Liberty* and had now come to a stop on her starboard side. The flag of the British empire flew tall and proud at the top of the main mast, as if it was staring down tauntingly at the tiny schooner underfoot.

A large man in a powdered wig and red admiral's uniform stood at the railing on the main deck of the warship and glared down at Theo with an unkind frown. Theo returned his gaze with a nod of greeting, his hand hovering over the handle of the pistol that he had placed on his belt just before exiting the cabin.

"State your business in these waters, sir," the Admiral called out sternly as the warship weighed anchor on *The Liberty*'s starboard side.

"Just stopping to fish on my way home from Boston, Admiral," Theo replied as he approached the railing of his own ship.

"These are hostile waters. The war continues to rage on. How do I know that you are not a rebel in disguise?"

Theo crossed his arms over his chest. "I mean no one any harm, sir. Just trying to make a living."

"Then I'm sure you will have no objections to my men and myself coming aboard to take a look at your catch?"

Theo swallowed thickly and nodded, stepping back from the railing and glancing nervously over his shoulder at the cabin as several Redcoats began lowering a gangplank between the decks of the two ships. The Admiral wasted no time crossing the gangplank onto the deck of *The Liberty*, accompanied by a soldier on each side.

The Admiral stared down his nose at the small schooner, his eyes raking across the deck as a look of mild disgust twisted his face. Before he had boarded the ship, he seemed only mildly inconvenienced, but once he was on board and got a clearer glimpse of Theo's appearance, his expression soured.

"I haven't caught anything yet," Theo explained with a shaky voice, shifting his weight uncomfortably between his feet.

The Admiral ordered one of his men to descend into the hull and search its contents before turning back to Theo. A sickeningly sweet smirk tugged at his lips as he said, "We are just ensuring that you are not carrying any weapons or supplies that the Patriot rebels may get their hands on. I'm sure you understand, given the circumstances of the times."

"You'll find no weapons down below. Only fishing gear."

The Admiral nodded and gazed around the deck again, his eyes landing on the cabin. "Are you alone on board today, boy?"

Theo slowly looked from the Admiral to the man on his right, his second-in-command. The man was much younger than his commander, a Commodore with a much kinder face that did not exude nearly as much disdain as the Admiral's.

"I am alone," Theo stated, folding his hands still bloodied from his daughter's birth behind his back.

The Admiral turned to his Commodore. "Search the cabin. Inform me of what you find."

The Commodore nodded and stepped toward the cabin, ordering Theo to follow him. Theo sheepishly followed him to the door as the Admiral turned away to walk the deck, and when they reached the captain's cabin, the Commodore paused and stared Theo down with an unexpected softness and compassion in his eyes.

"Tell me what I will find in the cabin," the Commodore whispered lowly. "I can see from your nervous disposition that you are not alone here."

Theo's eyes fell to the deck below his feet as a defeated sigh escaped his lips. "My wife and newborn child," he returned softly. "Please, take whatever you want from the ship, but don't hurt them…"

The Commodore nodded once in understanding before clearing his throat and reaching for the handle on the door. Wordlessly, he pulled open the door and stepped into the threshold, his entire body blocking the view of the cabin from the outside. He peered inside the dimly lit quarters, his watchful eyes immediately falling upon a young woman sitting on the blood-soaked bed in the corner, clutching a bundle tightly in her arms as she stared back at him with wide terror-filled eyes. She let out a meek whimper when their eyes met, and the Commodore immediately put his finger to his lips to order her to be silent. The bundle in her arms was beginning to stir at the sound of footsteps on the deck outside, and she tried desperately to cradle and rock the child in order to keep her quiet. The look in Evie's eyes was pleading and desperate as she silently begged him to spare her and her family.

"Commodore," the Admiral called from the other side of the ship. "What did you find in the cabin?"

The Commodore hesitated as his eyes remained locked with Evie's, and after a moment of deliberation, he called back, "Nothing of interest here, sir," before stepping backwards out of the cabin and quickly pulling the door shut behind him.

Theo waited anxiously just outside the door, and as soon as the Commodore exited the cabin, he let out a breath of relief he didn't realize he had been holding in. He and the Commodore shared a fleeting look, one of gratitude on his part and mutual understanding on the part of the

Redcoat. Instead of saying anything, the Commodore simply nodded once before crossing the deck to meet with the Admiral.

"The cabin is empty, save for some rods and bait, sir," Theo heard the Commodore tell the Admiral.

"Nothing but rubbish in the hold," another Redcoat said as he emerged from the hull.

"This man is just a civilian—clearly no threat to the war effort," the Commodore concluded in a whisper that was still within Theo's earshot. "I think it best that we move on so that we may reach the Chesapeake in a timely manner."

Theo raised his brow at the mention of the Chesapeake, a bay down south that he had never seen himself, but had overheard Commander Washington tell his generals was a strategic location for the navies on both sides of the war—a priceless port for importing and exporting weapons, troops, and supplies.

The Admiral passed Theo another disdainful and distrusting look, the same kind of look that he had received countless times over the years and would surely receive many times more in the future.

"Very well. We shall be on our way. And you," the Admiral pointed to Theo with a sour frown, "I suggest you pack up and get to wherever it is your going before trouble finds you again."

Theo nodded vehemently. "Yes, sir. I will raise my anchor immediately and return to shore."

The Admiral waved him off in disinterest and turned away to make his way back across the gangplank and onto his warship. The Commodore and the other Redcoat followed close behind, giving the ship one last glance over before boarding and raising the gangplank. Just before crossing the gangplank, the Commodore tossed one last glance over his shoulder in Theo's direction, a gentle smile gracing his young face. Theo gave the man another nod in silent thanks before he disappeared onto the deck of the warship, feeling his stomach flip in relief when the *Leopard's* sails opened up to catch the wind.

Theo remained frozen in place on the deck and watched until the warship was in motion and began to sail away, not allowing himself to relax until he could no longer see the main mast over the edge of the southern horizon. When His Majesty's ship was a safe distance away, Theo felt his legs buckle underneath him in both relief and shock; he was certain that his family was doomed when the Commodore made his way towards the cabin, but instead of revealing the location of the young mother and her mixed blood newborn to the Admiral, he displayed a moment of unexpected compassion that made Theo's heart skip a beat.

Theo did not know who the Commodore was or why he had decided to spare his family from the wrath of his commander, but he made a mental note to thank him earnestly should their paths ever cross again in the future. He could not remember the last time he had experienced such compassion from a stranger, and a Redcoat, no less, other than Daniel Howell, but it lessened the weight on his shoulders to know that not every bloke in a blood red uniform coat was a dastardly fiend. Perhaps there was hope for the world after the war, after all...

Wiping the sweat from his brow that had accumulated despite the cold that hung in the air, Theo turned on his heel and sprinted back into the cabin, immediately taking Evie and the baby into his arms as he collapsed onto the edge of the bed in relief.

"Have they gone?" Evie asked through her tears as she clutched the now fussing baby to her chest and buried her face in his neck.

Theo wrapped her arms tightly around her body and kissed the top of her head. "They're gone, love. They won't hurt us."

"I was so afraid...I was so afraid that they...would take us away..."

"I know. I know. But everything is fine now. We're safe. All of us."

"I want to go home," Evie sniffled as she looked down at her daughter, who had awoken enough to crack open her eyes just the slightest and peer back up at them.

Theo stared back down at the girl in amazement at her beauty, once again lifting a finger to gingerly stroke her cheek. "I'll get us home soon," he whispered to them both. "You have my word."

***

"I've never seen anything like it," Dr. Thorn mumbled whilst scratching his chin and taking another look over the small infant in Evie's arms. "I'm tempted to call it a miracle."

Evie sank back deeply into the pillows against which she was propped on her and Theo's bed, her newborn daughter clutched tightly against her breast as Theo, Johanna, and Dr. Thorn surrounded her bedside. It had been only a few hours since they had returned home from their trip to Boston, and Johanna nearly fainted when Theo stormed into the house with his hands stained with blood and Evie and a screeching newborn baby in his arms. Dr. Thorn rushed to the house with haste as soon as he received word that Evie had delivered her child on board *The Liberty*, and given the cold temperatures and the fact that she had no one but Theo to assist her in her labor, he was expecting the worst for both her and the infant when he arrived.

But he was pleasantly shocked to find both Evie and the infant in perfect health when he entered the house. The little girl had been born two weeks early, and she was smaller than the average newborn, but after a thorough examination, the doctor could find nothing to indicate any complications as a result of her premature birth in the middle of the icy Massachusetts Bay. Evie, surprisingly, suffered no serious injuries or infections from the birth either, leaving Dr. Thorn stunned and puzzled as to how Theo had managed to deliver the child safely without having had any medical training whatsoever.

When asked how he had done it, Theo simply shrugged and stated, "I did what I knew I had to do. Instinct took over, and I thought of nothing but getting my family home safely."

The baby was fast asleep in Evie's arms when Dr. Thorn finished his examinations, and everyone in the room looked down at her in awe as she dozed.

"God was looking out for you, all of you," Johanna said with a grateful smile as she stood by Evie's bedside and reached down to stroke the baby's head. Looking up, she caught Theo's eye from the other side of the bed where he stood.

"Perhaps He was," Theo agreed softly as he gazed down at his wife and daughter.

"I'd like to think Kateri was watching over us too," Evie added with a giggle as she looked up at Theo. "She made sure we all made it home safely."

"You think so?" Theo asked with a sideways smile as he took a seat on the edge of the bed and wrapped his arm around her shoulders.

"I know so."

Johanna's smile widened as she dabbed at her teary eyes with the back of her hand. "She looks just like you, Theo," she murmured. "I can already see it."

Theo chuckled lowly. "Then we shall pray that she has Evie's temperament."

"Have you seen your father since you arrived home?" Johanna asked. "I know how happy he will be when he sees the baby."

Theo shook his head. "Not yet. I wanted to ensure Evie and the baby settled in properly. But I will bring her to see him shortly."

In truth, Theo was putting off visiting Alistair since he had returned because he could not bear to see how terribly the old man had deteriorated in his short absence. This was supposed to be the happiest time in his life, and he could not bring himself to taint it with thoughts of Alistair's imminent demise.

"Does the little one have a name yet?" Dr. Thorn asked as he began packing up his medical case.

Evie and Theo shared a brief knowing look with one another, their smiles widening before Theo glanced in the direction of the nearest window, through which his trusty schooner could be seen bobbing in the water by the docks down below the cliff.

"Libby," Evie stated proudly as she pressed a kiss to the baby's forehead.

"Libby," Johanna repeated in satisfaction. "Short for Elizabeth?"

Theo shook his head with a smirk. "*Liberty.*"

Johanna's own grin widened until it threatened to split her face in half as she held her hand over her heart. "It suits her," she whispered.

"Would you like to hold her, Jo?" Evie asked. "She is your granddaughter, after all."

Johanna giggled with a gleeful nod and held out her arms to receive the baby, who settled comfortably against her chest without even stirring in her sleep. Johanna then began to softly hum a tune under her breath as she paced across the room and bounced Liberty in her arms. She had witnessed the birth of many babies throughout her life, held many babies over the years, but none brought her so much joy to hold as little Liberty Cunningham. For as long as she could remember, she had dreamed of having a family and children of her own, to hear the words "I love you, Ma," and to bring a dream to life that carries her blood in its veins, but in that moment, as she gazed down at the most perfect little cherubic creature she had ever seen, none of that compared to what she had now. Libby may not have carried Johanna's blood, but she had captured the woman's heart nonetheless, much like her father had twenty-five years before.

Theo looked on as his stepmother rocked his daughter back and forth and sang to her for several moments, feeling his heart swell in his chest.

Until then, he did not know he could feel such happiness, such fulfillment, such contentment as he did now. And every time he gazed upon that sweet angel's face, all of the fears, the worries, and the anxieties he had felt over the last several months became meaningless and seemed to drift away with the winter winds.

After several minutes, Johanna placed Liberty's tiny body in Theo's awaiting arms and patted his shoulder, telling him with a voice weakened by tears of both happiness and gloom, "Take her to your father so that he may meet her. Before his mind leaves him as his health has."

Theo looked down and closed his eyes as he nodded in solemn agreement. Standing from the bed, he gave Evie a kiss on her temple and said to her, "Get some rest. Libby and I will return shortly."

***

Theo gave the master bedroom door three short raps with his knuckles before opening it and poking his head into the room. Alistair was just where he had left him several days ago, propped up against a stack of pillows in his bed clothes with a blanket pulled up to his chest. He had been drifting in and out of sleep for the last several hours, frequently interrupted by violent coughing fits that left a metallic taste in his mouth and a searing pain in his throat and lungs. Upon hearing his bedroom door creak open, Alistair slowly opened his eyes, the slightest of smiles spreading across his pallid and sunken in face when he recognized his son standing in the doorway.

"Theo," he croaked, his words nothing more than a hoarse whisper. "How was Boston?"

The old man attempted to sit up in bed but was stopped when he doubled over with another hacking cough and collapsed back into his pillows. Theo opened the door fully and stepped into the room, and it was only then that Alistair was able to see the small, blanket-wrapped bundle in his arms.

"I think it was a success," Theo replied with a sideways smirk as he gently rocked the bundle and approached Alistair's bedside.

Alistair's eyes widened in shock when he finally wrapped his sickness-plagued mind around what exactly it was Theo was holding in his arms. When the bundle let out a mewling whimper, and a tiny arm shot out from within the confines of the blanket, he let out a startled gasp.

"The baby?" he asked tiredly, but with a smile that brightened his wizened eyes. "The baby is here?"

Theo nodded proudly and took a seat in the empty chair next to the bed, adjusting his arms so that Alistair could clearly see Liberty's face from his reclined position. The baby's eyes were wide open now, and she stared blankly at her grandfather for several moments as he stared back in amazement. It was clear to him from first glance that she had her father's complexion, but her mother's ocean-blue eyes. Though Alistair's head was clouded and groggy, he could see plain as day how beautiful she was, and he could feel the pride radiating from his son as he held her in his arms.

"This is her."

Alistair tore his eyes away from the baby to look up at Theo. "She's the most beautiful little thing I have ever seen, my son. I could not be prouder of you."

"Here name is Liberty. Liberty Kateri Cunningham."

Alistair stared at his son in silence for a moment, his eyes becoming glossy before another smile broke out across his face and his heart swelled with mirth. "A beautiful name for a beautiful miracle, no?"

"You were right, you know," Theo said softly. "She is the best thing I have ever done. I already know it."

Alistair tipped his head back against his pillow and loudly cleared his throat before chuckling. "I had a feeling you would feel that way. No matter the man, fatherhood will always change him…"

"Would you like to hold her?"

"I would be honored."

Theo stood from his chair and gently placed Liberty in Alistair's awaiting arms, helping to support her weight by keeping his hands under her back. Alistair's smile widened further when he cooed down at the baby, and she stared back at him once again with big, round eyes full of curiosity.

"How is Evie fairing?" Alistair asked after several moments of silence.

"She is tired, but in good spirits."

"She has every reason to be. You two have everything you could have wanted now."

Theo chuckled quietly in agreement. "And I am grateful that you were able to share in this happiness with us, Father."

"I can die in peace now. I know my granddaughter is in good hands."

Theo shook his head sadly. "Do not speak such things. I can't bear to hear it."

Alistair turned his face away from Liberty and let out another string of violent coughs, prompting Theo to take the baby from his arms and back into his own.

"Come now," Alistair rasped after roughly clearing his throat again. "We have both known for some time that my time is coming to an end. It would bring me nothing but happiness to live another fifty years to watch you and your family grow old, but I am content to go whenever the Lord calls me home. And I need you to be content as well."

Theo's expression soured considerably as he began to chew on his bottom lip. "How could I ever be content without you in my life, Father?" he asked as his voice began to break and he gazed down at the infant in his arms. "Johanna needs you. Liberty needs you. I need you. Please, don't do this to us now."

Upon watching Theo's eyes become red and glassy, Alistair summoned what little strength he had to slowly raise his arm and place a hand on his son's cheek. "I know you need me, my son. But I think that Heaven may need me more. I need you to let me go, so that I may leave this earth with peace in my heart. Please...promise me you will forgive me when my time comes."

Theo's eyes fluttered closed as he dropped his head in defeat, holding the baby tightly to his chest as a single sob escaped this throat. He could hear the shallowness of Alistair's labored breathing just beside him, and he could feel the old man's tired eyes lingering on him as he tried to collect himself. He could only imagine how sick and tired his father was of being sick and tired, and it broke his heart to think of the pain he endured with every shallow breath he took. He did not want to see the man in agony any longer. He did not deserve such torment, after all the good he had done in the last half of his life. No matter how badly it would hurt his own heart, Theo told himself in that moment, he would give his father the peace he deserved. He owed him that much.

The man was a hero to everyone he met, and there wasn't one life in Division Point that he hadn't touched in one way or another. It was not fair that such a kind and pure soul was being taken from the world long before his time, and Theo had been trying to make sense of it in his mind for months. But the only conclusion he could come to was that after all of the bloodshed and sorrow to stain the earth during this God-forsaken war, Heaven needed a hero. And that hero was Alistair Cunningham.

Theo placed one of his hands upon his father's cheek as a tear escaped the corner of his eye. Alistair gazed at him sorrowfully from the bed, pleading with his eyes for his permission to move on from this world to the next. He had lived long enough to meet his grandchild, and now the only thing left he longed to do was ensure that he had his son's forgiveness. It was all he wanted in the world.

Theo let out a short breath and squeezed Alistair's cold hand, the slightest of smiles tugging at his lips. "There is nothing left to forgive, Father," he breathed shakily, his words punctuated with muffled sobs. "You do not have to suffer for our sake any longer. Just promise...that you and Mother will save a place for me up there after you've gone."

Chapter 20

Do Not Weep and Wonder

April 1781

The snow that coated the earth finally began to melt with the coming of March, and once the ground was no longer frozen and the lumber was delivered, construction finally began on Theo and Evie's home on an empty patch of land between the lighthouse and Division Point Church. With Alistair still bedridden, Theo relied heavily on the kindness of Jacob and several other men from around the homestead to help him in the raising of the house's structure, and he insisted on somehow trying to find a way to repay the friends that had come together to help him in his time of need. But naturally, they all refused any sort of monetary reimbursement, insisting that it was the least they could do after Theo had risked his life for their freedom years ago by serving with the Continentals. By the middle of April, construction on the house was half-way completed, with estimations that Theo would be able to move his family into their new home by the end of May.

Though the spirits of the homestead had been dampened by the dreary winter weather and the news that Alistair's health was in a continuous decline, a ray of light found a way to shine down on Division Point through the thick clouds of melancholy—and that ray of light was the arrival of Liberty Kateri Cunningham. She was a miracle, not just to her parents, but to everyone in the homestead, and she was living proof that purity and goodness still existed in world that had been fraught with bloodshed for so many years. She was proof that a man and woman of two different worlds could come together to create an indivisible union, and she was proof that color and creed need not be points of irrevocable division.

Liberty grew quickly in the coming weeks, and with every day that passed, it became undeniable to everyone that laid eyes upon her that she was Theo's spitting image. She carried his richly tanned skin and thick, dark curls, as well as his infectious charm. Her eyes, however, remained a clear blue that only became brighter with time.

When he was not busying himself with the construction, Theo spent the days of his daughter's first few months of life doting on her more than he ever thought himself capable. She had instantly become his world, his entire reason for being, and the motivation that encouraged him to wake every morning with a smile on his face and contentment in his heart. With Libby and Evie in his life, Theo could not think of another place in the world he would rather be than with them, and for the first time in his twenty-five years, he had found his purpose. It was to be a husband and a father, a caretaker and a protector, and he would not have traded his new roles for all of the riches or adventure in the world.

While fatherhood seemed to come more easily to Theo than he had initially predicted, Evie also took to motherhood like a natural, and all of her previous fears and worries quickly became meaningless as Liberty grew bigger, stronger, and more beautiful with every day that came and went. Every day of Evie's pregnancy had been haunted by an aching fear that Liberty would befall the same fate as her older brother, and the world would never know her light. But by the grace of God, instead of asking who their child might have been, her parents were gratefully spending their days wondering who she was going to be in the future to come.

***

It was a warm afternoon at the end of April when Evie took a moment for herself in her in-laws' home. Johanna was out running errands, and Alistair was where he had been for the past several months, in bed, drifting in and out of a restless sleep. Theo had just returned home from spending most of the day working with Jacob and the other men to finish the interior of the house, and Liberty was napping in her bassinet upstairs, while Evie took time to herself to read the most recent edition of *The Boston Gazette*. The house was both quiet and serene, so much so that one could hear a pin drop, until Evie's eyes landed on the front page of the paper, where she read a headline that nearly knocked her out of her chair at the kitchen table.

ARTICLES OF CONFEDERATION ADOPTED AFTER FINAL RATIFICATION IN MARYLAND

Confused, Evie scanned the article for several moments before leaping to her feet and sprinting up the stairs to the bedroom she shared with Theo and Liberty. She expected to find her husband resting in bed after a long day of work in the hot sun, with Liberty still asleep in her bassinet nearby, but instead, what she found when she tip-toed into the room was Theo laying on his back in the middle of the mattress, his dirty shirt having been discarded so that he was in just his boots and trousers, while Liberty laid curled up on his bare chest, her little head tucked under his chin. Theo had one arm folded under his head while his other large hand rested tenderly upon Liberty's back, dwarfing her tiny body while also holding her snugly to his chest. Evie paused in the doorway to the bedroom as soon as she caught sight of the sleeping pair, and she could not help the warm feeling spreading through her chest as she watched father and daughter nap together in solace.

Not wanting to disturb them, she carefully shuffled into the room and lowered herself onto the edge of the bed, leaning down to press a gentle kiss to the top of Liberty's head, and then to Theo's cheek. Theo's eyes immediately began to flutter at the sensation of her lips on his skin, and with a quiet yawn, he cracked one eye open.

"I'm sorry, love, I did not mean to wake you," Evie whispered as she brushed a wayward lock of hair from his face and smiled down at him.

The corner of his mouth twitched upward into a smirk, and his words were raspy from grogginess. "You are forgiven."

"I did not expect to find you two like this."

Theo chuckled under his breath and gently rubbed Liberty's back as she continued to doze on his strong chest, the steady rhythm of his heartbeat under her head lulling her comfortably as she slept. "I intended to let her sleep in her bassinet. But then she began to fuss. And I could not bear to hear her cry. She fell back asleep immediately when I placed her on my chest."

Evie giggled in amusement. She would never not enjoy the sight of this big bear of a man exuding the gentleness that he only reserved for his wife and daughter. If she had been asked six years ago if she thought she would be sharing a child and the rest of her life with the wild boy that had rescued her from her past and given her a new future, she would have called the idea daft. But now, as she watched that wild boy—now, an equally wild young man with a family and a purpose—caress and comfort their infant daughter with a tenderness that she didn't even know was possible, she realized that this was exactly where she was meant to be all along.

"She already has you wrapped around her finger," Evie noted with a smirk as she placed a hand upon the baby's back.

"Did you really expect anything different?" Theo retorted playfully.

Evie began to respond, but was interrupted when Liberty began to fuss again on her father's chest. Immediately, she leaned forward and motioned for Theo to place the baby in her arms, but Liberty continued to whimper despite her mother's attempts to comfort her.

"She is probably hungry," Evie noted with a sigh. "She needs to nurse."

"What is that you have?" Theo asked as Evie stood and he sat up in bed, pointing to the folded newspaper tucked under her arm.

Evie unfolded the newspaper and handed it to him before rocking the baby in her arms and wandering across the room to settle in the wooden rocking chair in the corner. After sitting down and removing her breast from the top of her blouse, she gently coaxed Liberty's head to her chest and encouraged her to nurse.

"I thought you should see the paper," she said once Liberty successfully latched into her breast and began to hungrily suckle.

Theo rubbed at his eyes and let out another yawn before scanning the front of the paper himself, and Evie watched him in anticipation of his reaction from her chair across the room. He was quiet for a moment after he finished reading, but eventually broke the silence by stating, "This must mean that the war is truly drawing to a close."

"But what are these Articles?" Evie asked with a quirked brow. "Some sort of…constitution?"

Theo scanned the paper once more. "It says here that they were written back in '77, but it was not until March of this year that they were finally ratified when Maryland voted in the affirmative. The Articles are to provide for a federation of thirteen *states,* united under a single government."

"That seems a bit ambitious, doesn't it?" Evie asked skeptically. "Is it wise to assume that thirteen colonies, all so different in their interests and histories, will be able to so easily unite under a single flag so quickly after the British are expelled?"

Theo scoffed without taking his eyes off of the newspaper. "If we can unite to overthrow a tyrant, we can unite to forge a nation."

"You still appear to have a lot of confidence in the men who started this war, and then betrayed you in the name of it…"

Theo looked up and raised his brow at her from over the top of the paper. "I do not have any confidence in Washington and the others. But I do have confidence in the men and women who will elect the leaders of this would-be nation."

"Elect?"

"Of course. There will be no monarchy here once the British are gone. The paper says that Articles became the law of the land on March 2nd of this year, and under this law, there shall be a single house of Congress, with each state having one vote, and a president shall be elected to chair the assembly."

"Is a president and congress not just another way of saying king and parliament?"

Theo shook his head with a sigh. "No, this is different. Much different. *The Gazette* says that Congress does not have the right to levy taxes upon its people, but shall have authority over foreign affairs and the ability to raise an army and declare war. Amendments to the Articles shall require approval from all thirteen states."

Evie listened intently as he read, but she was still skeptical. "It is a wonderful plan on paper. I just fear that men of nefarious ambition will quickly come to power and tear it to shreds."

"That is why we must elect men of benevolent ambition to lead us."

Indivisible

"That is why *you* must elect such men," Evie corrected almost bitterly. "Of all of the revolutionary writings I have read over the years, I have not seen one mention of *women*."

Theo blinked as he closed the newspaper and tossed to the side, his eyes roaming the room for a response. Her concern was valid, he just now realized—he had never heard nor seen any mention of the rights of the fairer sex at any point during the war. What did that mean for women in this new nation, they both wondered silently? Would they still be prisoners within their own families for the years to come? Or would this concept of *freedom* that everyone had been fighting for extend to those who needed it most?

"...May I ask you something?" Theo asked after several moments of silence as he moved to sit on the edge of the bed.

Evie looked up from watching the baby nurse, fixing her eyes upon the wispy scar that trailed across the center of Theo's bare chest. "Of course."

"Are you happy here?"

Evie almost laughed. "Of course, I am happy here. I have never been happier than I am now. Why would you ask such a question?"

Theo shrugged his shoulders and peered down at the golden wedding band upon his left hand. "When you speak like that, I just worry…that you are not content with your life as a wife and mother."

"Theo, I love my life as a wife and mother. This is what I was meant to do. I just wish…that it was not the only thing expected of me. I wish for a world in which a woman is valued for more than her ability to serve the men in her life. I wish for a world in which a woman…has a choice. Where she no longer spends every day of her life as someone's property."

"You know how much I value you, don't you?" Theo asked worriedly as he rubbed the back of his neck. "I do not see you as…my property, or anything of the sort. I see you as my…equal. My partner."

463

Evie chuckled lightly and flashed him a smirk. "That is because you are not like most men."

Theo let out another sigh and wandered across the room to the window, where he gazed out over the crystal blue waters of the Bay that stretched out before him.

"I pray that we can build the world that you seek in the coming years," he mumbled, deep in thought. "Or, at least, protect our daughter from the world that already exists."

***

May 1781

Evie let out a squeak when she felt herself stumble over a stray stone that had fallen underfoot, clutching her daughter to her chest so as to ensure that she did not drop her.

"Careful, now," she heard Theo chastise playfully from just behind her, his lips at her ear as he held his hands over her eyes and slowly led her across the uneven ground behind the lighthouse.

"Why must you be so dramatic?" Evie asked in mild annoyance at not being able to see where she was walking. "I could just amble on my own…"

Theo chuckled in amusement as he guided her across the grass. "To savor in the suspense."

After several more steps, he stopped and positioned her to face the wooden structure before them, perched upon the cliff in the shadow of the lighthouse with a view of the Atlantic stretching out for an infinite number of miles past the horizon.

Construction on their home was finally complete, and he could not bear to wait any longer to unveil the fruits of his labor to his wife and daughter. Liberty was now three months old, just barely able to hold her head up on her own, and her big blue eyes were wide with wonder as she gazed upon her surroundings and relished in her first adventure outdoors.

"I cannot wait any longer," Evie whined as she stamped her foot. "Show me the house already!"

Theo chuckled again and pressed a kiss to her temple. "Are you ready?"

"More than ready."

Theo let several more moments pass before he finally pulled his hands away from Evie's face, allowing her eyes to flutter open and gaze upon the sight before them. Upon laying eyes on their new home for the first time, she felt her jaw go slack and her knees wobble underneath her, for she could not believe what she was seeing. It was a beautiful four room, single story cabin, constructed of both cedar logs and stone bricks which caught the light of the setting sun just so to give them a warm and cozy glow. She could have never imagined such a charming cabin to be built from the ground up in such a short amount of time, and though it was certainly no mansion in the city, it was already home. She could think of no other place where she would rather raise her family than the home her husband built with his own two hands.

Theo glanced nervously between Evie's stunned face and the newly completed cabin, shifting his weight between his feet as he waited for her to say something—anything. "Well?" he coaxed after several moments of silence. "What do you think?"

"What do I think?" Evie shook her head in awe and took several steps across their new front yard until she was standing just before the steps leading up to the quaint front porch. Liberty began to wiggle in her arms as if she, too, was anxious to explore their new home. "Theo…it's beautiful. I cannot believe you built this with your own two hands!"

"Well, he did have a little help," a familiar voice stated from seemingly out of nowhere, causing her to spin around and find Jacob emerging from around the corner of the house.

Evie flashed him a smug grin as he sauntered around to the front of the house and slung an arm around Theo's shoulders. "Of course, he did.

Thank you, Jacob. This would not have been possible without you and the other men that gave us your aid."

Jacob shrugged. "Anything to help my friend's family get on their feet."

Theo shrugged out from under his friend's arm and gestured toward the front door of the house, which glistened with a fresh coat of ivory paint. "Shall I show you the inside of our estate, Mrs. Cunningham?"

Evie resisted the urge to roll her eyes as she placed Liberty in his awaiting arms. "Lead the way, good sir," she returned coquettishly.

The interior of the home was just as warm and inviting as the exterior, with each and every wall stained a dark mahogany brown and illuminated by a mounted candle. Evie's attention was immediately drawn to the kitchen at the back of the house, and she was elated to find a large hearth for cooking, just like the one she had grown used to in Johanna and Alistair's home. In addition to the spacious kitchen, she also found a master bedroom, a smaller second bedroom, and a parlor for lounging, all of which exuded a rustic charm that she did not know she loved until that moment.

Theo puffed out his chest with pride as he held a squirming Libby in his arms and followed Evie throughout the house to survey his work with a fresh pair of eyes. There were times over the last few months when he thought the house would never be finished, and he had even considered abandoning his dream of building his own home several times, but he was elated to see how beautifully it had all come together in the end. And now, as he watched Evie skip giddily from room to room to explore her new sanctuary, he knew that there was no better place to spend the rest of his days than with her and their child, safe within the walls of their little piece of Heaven on the cliff.

***

July 1781

"So, they are calling it the Articles of Confederation, hm?" Johanna asked with a sigh as she took her seat at the dinner table. It had been nearly two months since Theo, Evie, and Liberty had settled into their new home across the road, and it was on this humid night that they had returned to Johanna and Alistair's home for a family dinner to celebrate the occasion of Liberty's fifth month of life.

Theo nodded as he took a bite of stew from the bowl in front of him. "The new law of the land."

"Well, I hope it works as well in practice as it does on paper," Johanna retorted with a shake of her head, sharing a look with Evie from across the table.

Evie hummed in agreement as she bounced Liberty in her lap with one hand and attempted to feed herself with the other. Libby had just learned how to babble and reach for anything that caught her interest, which always made any meal an adventure for anyone involved.

"We would all do well to keep in mind that the war is not over yet," Evie noted. "As of yet, there has been no surrender nor treaty. We may write as many constitutions and articles as we wish, but they hold little weight until we are able to call ourselves a nation."

"We already are a nation," Theo corrected pointedly. "What is a nation, if not a union of states under one flag and a mutual desire for independence?"

Evie rested her cheek against her palm and gave her husband a sideways glance. "I will never grow tired of your unflinching optimism, my love, but I beg you not to count your chickens before they hatch."

"The war has already been won," Theo insisted. "The British are outmatched—they may have more troops and guns, but we have knowledge of the land and a burning desire to protect it. We have already worn them down to the point of no return. It is only a matter of time until Cornwallis and his lap dogs cut their losses and surrender."

Evie sighed in defeat and decided to drop the subject. "I am sure you are right. You have seen more of the war than any one of us."

"It is not something I should ever want to see again. War is hell, and I have no intention to return to it."

Johanna shook her head morosely. "I no longer wish to discuss such things. We should be focusing not on the gloomy facts of life, but rather the things for which we are grateful. Like that little angel over there," she stated whilst pointing across the table at Liberty and flashing her a wide grin in order to coax a giggle from the infant. "She is a miracle child—a refreshing ray of light after the storms you two have battled together."

"Johanna is right," Evie said as she smiled down at her daughter, her face glowing with pride. "We have much for which to be grateful, and it does not do us well to dwell on the things we cannot change."

"Speaking of which," Johanna sighed, "we all should be grateful that God has granted Alistair the strength to stay with us despite his sickness. Dr. Thorn did not think he would live past winter, but here we are on the cusp of summer, and he fights on."

Theo nodded in melancholy agreement, his spirits suddenly dampened at the mention of the man wasting away in the bedroom just above their heads. He could sense the end was coming—everyone could sense it, but no one dared speak it into existence.

"Alistair has not eaten much today," Johanna noted after a long period of silence. "Perhaps I should bring him a bowl of stew and see if he is well enough to eat."

"You sit and relax, Jo," Evie said as she stood from her chair with Liberty on her hip. "I shall go check on him. Hold the baby."

Evie then placed Liberty in Johanna's awaiting arms before flitting into the kitchen to fetch an empty bowl into which she ladled several hot spoonfuls of the stew that remained in the pot hanging in the hearth.

"Thank you, dear," Johanna sighed tiredly and wiped her brow as she placed her granddaughter in her lap and allowed her to attempt to reach for the various objects on the dining table. "Caring for him constantly has begun to take its toll on me, I'm afraid."

Evie gave Johanna's shoulder a sympathetic pat before sauntering out of the dining room, bowl of stew and a rag in hand.

"Libby looks more like you every day," Johanna commented as she stroked the girl's head of thick, dark curls, which had begun to grow at an astounding rate over the past several weeks.

Theo flashed Liberty a smirk from across the table when their eyes met, and she immediately threw her chubby arms into the air to reach for him with an amused giggle. With every day that passed, her lightly tanned skin seemed to take on a deeper and richer tone that only emphasized the wash of freckles that had begun to appear across her cheeks. Looking at her now, there would not be a single doubt in anyone's mind that she carried Mohawk blood in her veins, and for that, Theo could not have been any prouder.

"I'd like to think she resembles Kateri," Theo replied as he crossed his arms on the top of the table, "But sadly, I will never know."

"No matter who she resembles, she is breathtaking. And God could not have blessed you more when he placed her on this earth."

For once in his life, Theo did not feel the urge to correct her and tell her that God had nothing to do with bringing the light of his life into the world. Instead, the corners of his mouth twitched upward, and his expression softened as he murmured, "I could not agree more."

Johanna opened her mouth to speak, but she, Theo, and the baby were all startled out of their skin by a piercing scream that cut through the evening calm like a knife through flesh, sending them on edge immediately when they realized that the shriek had come from above their heads.

Theo jumped to his feet, the hairs on the back of his neck standing on end. "That sounded like Evie," he gasped as he made an immediate escape toward the staircase to investigate the source of the noise. Without hesitation, Johanna stood from her chair and followed after him up the stairs with a fussing Liberty on her hip.

The initial shriek was followed by several more, unmistakably belonging to Evie and becoming quieter and quieter until they were eventually replaced all together by a horrendous sobbing. Theo sprinted up the stairs, taking them two at a time as his heart began to race in his chest and he tried to wrap his mind around what she could have possibly found upstairs to make her scream so terribly. Upon reaching the second floor, he followed the sounds of his wife's muffled cries, sprinting down the hallway until he came face to face with the door to the master bedroom. The bedroom where Alistair had been sequestered as a condition of his bedrest for the last several months.

Suddenly, Theo's heart was no longer pounding in his chest—it was now well up into his throat, choking and suffocating him until his knees felt weak. The rest of his body was numb as he gripped the doorknob and threw the door open, stumbling in awkwardly with Johanna and Liberty not far behind. Inside the bedroom, they found Evie on her knees at the side of the bed in which Alistair laid, the bowl of stew she had brought spilled all over the floor from when she had dropped it at her feet in shock and dismay. And instead of sitting upright against the pillows as he usually did, Alistair was slumped limply to one side, his arms resting lifelessly at his sides whilst he gripped his Bible in one of his hands. Evie reached up to grip the old man's arm, shaking him desperately as tears streamed uncontrollably down her cheeks.

"Alistair…" she sobbed breathlessly, "Alistair, wake up, please, it is time for your dinner…" Upon hearing Theo and Johanna stumble into the room, Evie whipped her head around to stare up pleadingly at them, her eyes wide with shock and devastation as she shook her head. "He…he won't open his eyes…" she whispered.

Gunner the hound sat by her side and anxiously pawed at the blankets hanging off the edge of the bed, whimpering to alert that something was terribly wrong as he watched Evie's shoulders shake with grief.

"No…" Johanna gasped as realization trampled over her like a herd of stallions. She shuffled weakly toward the bed in which her husband lifelessly lay. "No, that can't be…"

Theo charged toward the bed as he felt his stomach churn within him, suddenly feeling the urge to vomit when he came to the side of the bed and found his father both completely still and cool to the touch. The old man's skin was a ghastly shade of pale blue, the veins under his flesh visible as crimson red rivers that no longer had the strength to carry the blood throughout his body. Alistair's eyes were closed, and his purplish lips gently parted as Theo rested his head against his chest in a desperate search for a heartbeat or any other sign of a fleeting life. But after several heartbreaking moments of stillness and silence, he found *none*.

Not wanting to believe it, Theo raised his head from Alistair's motionless chest and gripped him by the shoulders as he stood over him. Shaking the man's body, which now felt small and emaciated in his hands after so many months of sickness, he shouted, "Father! Father, wake up, come now, wake up! This is not funny…wake up! Wake up!"

When Alistair failed to respond, move, or even take a breath, Theo shook him harder, clenching his teeth together in rage as he tearfully snarled, "Get up, old man! Get up! It isn't time yet! Get up!"

Without even realizing it, Theo had begun to shake Alistair with so much force that his head snapped back and forth against the pillows. Evie rose to her feet with another sob and reached for Theo's arms in order to pull him away, telling him through her tears, "Theo, stop! Stop, it is too late. It's too late…"

"No!" Theo hissed at her, his eyes red and glassy as he glared at her over his shoulder and shrugged her away. "No, he can't do this! He can't be gone…"

Evie turned from him and stepped away just as Johanna rushed to the side of the bed with Liberty still in her arms, collapsing to her knees as she let out a terrible lamenting wail. Evie crouched down at her side and wrapped her arms around both Johanna and the baby, resting her head upon her mother-in-law's shoulder as they began to sob together.

Theo tightly gripped Alistair's shoulders for several more moments as his eyes roamed over his lifeless body. He begged him once more to open his eyes, to take a breath, but his pleas fell on dead and deaf ears, for the man had already taken his last breath an hour before, allowing for his spirit to finally ascend to the home he had been seeking in the sky, while leaving his body behind to grow cold and stiff.

Though he had been preparing himself for this moment for months, Theo still found himself frozen in shock at the side of his father's deathbed, his entire body enveloped in a red-hot wave of mournful anger and sadness. No matter what he had told Alistair, or himself, he was not ready for this day, and within an instant of prying his hands off of Alistair's shoulders, Theo collapsed to his knees beside Johanna and Evie, dropping his head in his hands as his entire world began to crumble all around him and disappear into the surrounding darkness.

They sobbed in unison for several minutes, holding each other wordlessly as their tears fell from their cheeks to stain the floorboards under their feet. But suddenly, Theo pulled away from them, rising to his feet as he wiped the back of his hand over his red and swollen eyes. Without a word, he approached the bed once more and reached for the Bible that Alistair still gripped in his right hand, prying it from deathly cold and stiff fingers before turning away.

"What are you doing?" Evie asked as she took Liberty from the arms of a distraught and devastated Johanna, who had become overwhelmed with grief and collapsed onto her side on the floor.

Theo held the Bible the in his hand, gripping it so tightly that his knuckles began to turn white as his face fell to the floor. Several moments passed before he spoke, and when he did, his voice was empty and hollow.

"I am going to find Dr. Thorn," he responded as he turned toward the door, the tears in his eyes suddenly gone as if he had banished them away before they could even fall. "And make the preparations for his funeral at once."

"Theo, please wait," Evie begged as she tried to grasp his hand, but he pulled it from her reach before they could touch, storming out of the bedroom to leave her, Johanna, and Liberty to mourn in solitude. He knew they had done nothing to deserve his sudden callousness, but in that moment, he did not care. A coldness had washed over him the moment he realized Alistair's heart had stopped—the moment he felt his motionless chest and cold, pale skin against his own. He wanted to be furious and sorrowful, but as he numbly made his way out of the bedroom, he felt everything all at once so intensely that it felt like *nothing*. A frigid, black cavern of nothingness had been ripped open inside his chest, and he could feel everything he had left in him slowly pouring out of the wound. He felt numb, cold, and empty, just like the body lying in the bed that had once been his father.

"Cover his body until Dr. Thorn can get here," Theo barked over his shoulder, pausing in the doorway before storming off again. "Give him some God-damned dignity."

***

Alistair Cunningham's funeral was short and simple, just as he would have wanted. Theo made the arrangements with haste, and his father was laid to rest in a large mahogany casket three days after he passed, surrounded by every member of the Division Point community as they came to pay their respects to the man that built their home with his own two hands. There was no point in a long, drawn out mourning ceremony—Alistair would not have wanted so many tears shed on his behalf, and no words could be found that would have adequately articulated the weight of devastation that had fallen upon the homestead and everyone in it.

With the reigning patriarch of the Cunningham family and Division Point's only preacher gone, Theo took it upon himself to conduct the funeral, little as he knew about religious ceremonies. He would not entertain the thought of bringing in a man of the cloth from the nearest town to conduct a formal ceremony, because there was no way a stranger could have done Alistair's final farewell justice.

In addition to the blanket of sorrow that had settled over the homestead, dark and malignant storm clouds hung heavily in the sky on the day of the funeral, as if to communicate to the rest of the world that Division Point had lost one of its brightest rays of light. The clouds opened up to send a spitting of rain onto the earth just as Alistair's casket was carried into the graveyard on the backs of Theo, Jacob, Mr. Caldwell, and Mr. O'Hara, and that spitting gradually became a light shower just as he was lowered into the ground.

Theo stood at the head of the grave, just behind the freshly carved headstone that bore his father's name, a name forever etched in stone as lost to the world, but not lost in the hearts of those who knew him. Evie stood by his side with Liberty asleep in her arms, while Johanna stood on his other side with her head bowed and her hands clutching her husband's most prized possession—his Bible. The cemetery soon became crowded as a processional of black swarmed in behind the casket and surrounded Alistair's burial plot—a great flood of family and friends with tear stained cheeks dressed in their mourning clothes.

Thunder rumbled menacingly overhead when Theo cleared his throat to speak after the casket had been lowered into the grave, an ominous and unneeded reminder of why they had gathered in graveyard.

"I am sure I do not need to say that this place will never be the same without my father," Theo began with his eyes set on the ground, his voice both tight and weak. His voice was ghostly, an empty echo amid the thunder and the rain that began to pour over them.

"Not only did he build this settlement from the ground up, but he also welcomed with open arms anyone and everyone who needed sanctuary or a chance to start over. Without him, none of us would be who we are today. Like many of us, he made his share of mistakes, but unlike many of us, he had the grace and courage to devote the rest of his life to rectifying them. After he came to Division Point, he became a man of God and spent the rest of his days bringing all who he met into a congregation. Not just a congregation of worshippers in a chapel, but a congregation of friends and family whose lives were made better because they could call Alistair Cunningham an ally. He was a father, a husband, a war veteran, and a minister, but he was also a leader and a teacher to us all."

Theo paused and cleared his throat in an attempt to swallow the overpowering urge to collapse, searching desperately for the words he didn't think he had to describe just how much Alistair meant to him.

"My father and I spent much of my life squabbling, but I hope to God he knows how grateful I am for every scolding, every disappointed sigh, and every tear shed over these years, for they are what made me the man I am today. *He* made me the man I am today. Without him, I would still be a reckless, drunken lout, sleeping in gutters and fighting in the streets for a few coins while believing that I was never meant to be anything greater.

"It is true that one of Alistair's greatest mistakes resulted in my birth, and I have spent far too much of my life resenting him for it. But I know now that if it were not for that mistake, I would have never been put on this earth, and I would have never had the pleasure to be raised by such a pure-hearted man and his saint of a wife. And I never would have met my beautiful wife, nor had my daughter, the two best things that have ever happened to me.

"I had always hated him for bringing me into this world. I believed for the longest time that I was a curse to all who knew me, and that my existence brought nothing but shame and suffering to those who I loved most. For the longest time, I was ashamed of who I was, and I blamed him for it. Every failure and misfortune, I placed upon his shoulders. But now, I only wish I had the chance to look him in the eyes and *thank* him for bringing me into this world. I wish I that I could thank him for teaching me what it means to be a father and a husband, and for teaching me what it means to be a man. I would thank him for my life and so much more, but sadly, I will go to my grave regretting how terribly I treated him in the past.

"If I were a man of God, I would beg the Lord for one more chance. Just one last chance, one more moment of time, to take him in my arms and tell him everything that I have said to you today. If I had known I would lose him so soon, I would not have wasted so much time giving him gray hairs, and instead I would have made sure that he went to bed every night knowing how much he meant to me."

Theo let out a shaky breath and roughly dragged the back of his hand across his face to banish the tears he could feel brimming in the back of his eyes, but a single one escaped and cascaded down his cheek to mingle with the rain that now soaked his face and everyone around him.

"If I were to pray for anything, it would be more time to tell him that I love him, that I always have and always will, and that I had just been too stubborn to see it until now. It is a mistake among many that I will live with for the rest of my days, but I hope he entered Heaven's gates knowing just how many people he touched, and how many broken-hearted loved ones he left behind. He may be gone from this world, but he shall never be forgotten."

A heavy silence punctuated only by the sound of rain beating against the soft earth fell over the graveyard once Theo finished. He had so much more he wanted to say, but he could not find the strength to utter the words publicly; those words, he would reserve for between himself and God, if He was out there.

Wordlessly, Theo turned to Johanna and outstretched his hand, allowing her to place Alistair's Bible in his palm. As the downpour continued, he tossed the worn book between his rain-slicked hands, running his thumbs along the frayed gilded edges of the vellum pages as he flipped through it one last time. Just before he reached the end of the text, however, he paused when he caught sight of something out of place.

Tucked between the last few pages of the book, Theo found a small piece of parchment, folded several times over as if it was meant to remain hidden inside the book until the right person found it. Confused, he plucked the folded parchment from between the pages and tucked it into his vest pocket before it could become anymore soaked by the rain, and with a final sigh of goodbye, he crouched down at the edge of the grave and placed the Bible on top of the closed lid of the casket.

Each mourner then took their turn tossing a single flower into the grave before silently filing out of the cemetery. After the cemetery was emptied, leaving only Theo, Evie, Liberty, Emma, Jacob, little Levi, and Johanna surrounding the burial plot, Theo wasted no time in taking up a shovel to begin replacing the dirt back into the grave while the others watched on. He would not have known if anyone was crying silently to themselves as he worked to fill his father's grave with the soil that had turned to mud, for any tears that they may have shed became quickly lost amongst the rain streaming down their faces.

After several minutes of shoveling, Theo ordered the women to return home so that they could shelter themselves and the children from the cold rain. They were reluctant to leave him, but they did as they were told and hurried through the mud to take shelter from the storm. Gunner stubbornly remained, however, and curled up in front of Alistair's gravestone with his ears sagging sorrowfully, as if he, too, was mourning a great loss. Theo expected Jacob to follow the women to shelter, but he remained also, standing next to the burial plot as the rain continued to drench them both. His eyes were fixed on the mud, and his shoulders slumped as if the weight of the world was dragging him deep into the earth. Alistair had been a second father to him for as long as he could remember, and it stung greatly to know the patriarch of their community would never be there to give him guidance again.

After the women had gone, Theo worked nonstop for nearly half an hour, groaning in exertion as the ground under his feet turned to a slippery vat of mud into which he could feel himself sinking.

Noticing that Theo's strength was waning and that he was beginning to struggle, Jacob spoke up and asked, "Do you need help?"

Theo briefly paused his work, slowly raising his eyes to his friend's heavy gaze. "No. Go back inside with the women," he answered more sharply than he intended.

Jacob stepped forward and offered his hand to take the shovel. "Let me help you. This is not a job for one man."

Theo stubbornly continued to dig, shaking his head and waving him off. "No!" he shouted over the rain. "This is something I must do alone. He was my father, and I will be the one to lay him to rest. Go home—be with your family while you still have them, and leave me be..."

Jacob reached out to clamp a hand on Theo's shoulder, forcing him to look him the eye. "He was a father to us all, Theo. You do not have to shoulder this burden alone. Please, let me help you. You helped me bury my brother; the least I can do is return the favor."

After a moment of silent deliberation and staring into his friend's eyes, Theo heaved out a sigh of submission. Wordlessly, he handed Jacob the shovel and took a few steps back to wade out of the mud before standing over the burial plot to watch as his friend finished the morbid task. As Jacob continued to fill the grave, Theo could feel what little strength remained in him quickly draining from his body. He wanted sleep. He wanted peace. He wanted to go to sleep and wake up to discover that this was all a terrible dream, but instead, he found himself in a perpetual nightmare from which there was no escape.

By the time they finished, the mud had reached their shins and their clothes were soaked all the way through to their skin. With an exhausted sigh, Jacob planted the head of the shovel into the ground and took a step back to look over what had been done. Theo remained silent by his side, his eyes fluttering closed as he gritted his teeth together. He reached forward to take ahold of the shovel before leaning heavily on the handle, using it to hold his weight as he fought the urge to collapse and let the earth swallow him up.

He had not allowed himself to shed any tears in front of his family or anyone else since they found Alistair's body—he told himself that he had to be strong for the others, because that was what a man did, and he was the man of the Cunningham house now. But now that everyone else but Jacob had gone, and he was alone with the swirling tempest that was his thoughts as he stood on top of his father's freshly filled grave, he could feel the strength he had been exuding pouring from his body and washing away with the rain that flooded the earth.

A tired gasp escaped his lips as he felt his legs give way underneath him and his knees sink into the mud. He was cold and exhausted, but he hadn't the strength to rise back to his feet against the weight of the world that had suddenly fell upon his shoulders.

Jacob knelt down next to him and draped an arm around his friend's shoulder as his body began to quiver despondently. "You do not have to do this alone," he gently reminded Theo, "and no one will think any less of you if you shed a tear. I know it is exhausting to be everyone's pillar of strength, but on occasion, you need someone else to hold *you* up."

"Now is not the time for weakness," Theo mumbled. "I have to be strong for my family. If I fall apart, so will they."

"Vulnerability does not make you weak. It makes you human. Surely you remember Alistair teaching us that when we were children."

Theo squeezed his eyes shut once more and clenched his hands into fists, feeling the urge to scream with the anger and agony that had accumulated in his chest. He had silently endured so much throughout his life, and now, he just longed to be heard. When he was sure any sound would be drowned out by the rain, Theo slammed his fists against the ground and let out an excruciating howl into the sky—a terrible, mournful lamentation that he could only bear to utter when no one else but his father and closest friend were listening.

Hopefully, wherever he was, Alistair could hear his son as he cried for him and see the tears of sorrow and regret stream down his mud-stained cheeks. Perhaps then he could find his eternal rest and know just how badly his boy ached to have him back. Perhaps then he would know how much he was missed, and how greatly his life had impacted those he left behind.

***

Thunder rumbled continuously within the confines of the dark clouds overhead, sending an unending downpour of rain onto the New England coast. By the time Theo found the strength to pull himself to his feet after he and Jacob filled in Alistair's burial plot, the cemetery's ground had become a wasteland of mud into which they sunk deeper and deeper with every move they made. Their clothes were soaked completely through and stuck uncomfortably to their skin as they slowly shuffled out of the cemetery and back toward the cabin behind the lighthouse, with Gunner following close behind them with his head hung low in shared grief.

Evie and Emma were waiting for them in the front room of the small home, watching out the window for what seemed like hours until they finally caught sight of their husbands exiting through the cemetery's gates and shambling home. Not a single part of them wasn't soaked with rain or smeared with mud when they walked through the front door, but Evie didn't care, for she immediately threw her arms around Theo's neck and pulled him as close to her body as possible. Theo gave no resistance, and sunk immediately into her embrace, locking his arms around her waist and clutching at the fabric of her dress as he buried his face in her neck. Evie could feel the moisture from his clothes, skin, and hair soiling her dress, but it mattered little to her as she bit down on her bottom lip to hold in her own sobs and held Theo in her arms.

"I miss him already," Theo breathed into her shoulder as he tightened his grip around her waist.

"I know," she whispered as she stroked his wet hair. "I miss him as well."

They held each other in silence for several more moments, the only sounds in the air being the thunder that shook the sky and the rain pounding against the roof of the house. Theo broke the silence when he lifted his head and locked gazes with her. Her eyes were red and swollen, much like his own, but they were gentle and full of compassion as she stared up at him.

"I'm cold," he whispered shakily.

"Go change into some dry clothes, love, and come join me by the fireplace to warm up. You will catch your death otherwise."

He nodded tiredly in agreement. "And what of Johanna?"

Evie sighed heavily and ran her hand through her hair. "She is in the parlor with Libby, sitting by the fire. I could not bear to let her stay alone in that house right now. She is despondent and beside herself with grief…"

Theo gave his wife an appreciative pat on her shoulder before turning away to lumber across the hall to the master bedroom in search of warm and dry clothes, shivering as he went. He was still ringing rainwater from his hair when he eventually wandered into the parlor after changing, and there he found a fire roaring in the fireplace and both Evie and Johanna sitting in front of it. After drying himself off, Jacob took a seat in the parlor to warm himself with a cup of tea while Emma sat by his side with their son, Levi, sleeping in her lap.

Johanna had barely spoken a word since they found her husband's body three days prior, and she was still speechless as she sat in an armchair by the fire with her head bowed and her hands folded in her lap. Evie attempted to offer her a cup of tea to warm herself, but she simply shook her head in refusal.

"Come sit down and have some tea," Evie said to Theo when he entered the room. She tried to put on a brave face and smile, but even a blind person could see that her heart was not in it.

Wordlessly, Theo traipsed across the floor of the parlor and took a seat in the empty chair by the fireplace, feeling an immediate relief when he was enveloped by the warmth of the flames. After handing him the cup of tea that Johanna had refused, Evie placed a fussing Liberty in his lap. Almost immediately the baby's whimpers quieted into a contented babbling as she nuzzled her head against his chest and reached up to place one of her small hands on his face.

"She was crying for you when you did not come back to the house with us," Evie explained.

Theo gazed down at his daughter and felt the slightest urge to smile as she stared back up at him with her big blue eyes. He envied her; her youth, her innocence, her purity, and most of all, that she had both of her parents. And it pained him greatly to realize that she would have no memory of her grandfather as she grew older. She would never know his face, nor his voice or his kindness, as he passed long before she would have had the ability to remember him. She would only know Alistair from the stories her parents and others would tell her, and never once would she be able to hear his many life lessons in his own voice.

A heavy silence had fallen over the parlor after Theo began to sip his tea and bounce the baby on his knee, but that silence was abruptly punctuated when Johanna suddenly looked up and locked eyes with Theo from her chair.

"What was that, that you took from Alistair's Bible before his burial?" she asked meekly, her voice strained and barely louder than a whisper.

Theo shared a confused look with Evie and arched his brow, initially shocked that Johanna had found the strength to speak. "What?"

Johanna cleared her throat and stared pleadingly at her stepson. "That parchment. Tucked in the pages of the book. I saw you take it out before you put the Bible in the grave. What was it?"

"Oh." Theo muttered as he thought back to the ceremony. He had taken a folded piece of parchment from the Bible and tucked into his pocket, but he had been so consumed with sadness after finishing the burial that he had not thought of it since. "It is still in my vest pocket. I have not looked at it."

"I wish to see it."

Theo sighed heavily. "Johanna, it was probably just a note that he scribbled to himself. It is probably nothing—"

"I wish to see it," Johanna repeated sharply. "If it contains my husband's hand, I want to have it."

Deciding it was best to humor her request rather than continue to upset her, Theo stood from his chair and placed Liberty back in her mother's arms before sauntering out of the parlor to retrieve the paper from the pocket of the clothes he had discarded on the floor of the master bedroom. Digging around in his clothes for several minutes, he eventually found the parchment, which was now quite damp and crumpled.

He quickly returned to the parlor and handed it to Johanna, who took it without hesitation and hastily unfolded it.

"What is it?" Evie asked as she stood behind the chair and peeked at the parchment over Johanna's shoulder.

The face of the paper was covered in lines and lines of script written with ink in Alistair's unmistakably elegant handwriting. The ink had begun to run and seep in blotches into the aged paper once it became dampened by the rain, but the words were still legible. It was obvious that the parchment had been hidden away in the Bible for some time, as evidenced by how faded the ink had become.

Johanna's eyes scanned the parchment for a moment before a shaky breath escaped her lips. "It is a letter," she murmured tearfully.

"A letter to whom?" Theo asked.

Johanna looked up from the paper as a tear slipped from the corner of her eye and down her cheek. Her lips and hands trembling, she held the letter out to him.

"To you."

***

To my son,

If you are reading this, it must mean that my time has come, and I have been called home. I am sure you must be angry with me, and you must think that I have abandoned you. But nothing could be further from the truth. I have known I was ill for several years, but I could not bring myself to admit to you, Johanna, or even myself. I had always feared that God would find a way to punish me for the wrongs I committed when I was young and foolish, and it appears now that He has chosen to punish me by taking me from my family long before I thought I would ever be ready.

I have privately battled this sickness for as long as I possibly could, but I can see that my time left in this world is waning, as is my strength to keep fighting. That is why I am writing to you now, in the hopes that I can put quill to paper to tell you all of the things I could never bring myself to say before. I can only die in peace knowing that I am leaving you strong enough to face the cruelties of this world without me there to guide you, and I believe with all of my heart that you have found that strength now.

I beg you, my son, do not lose yourself in grief when I am gone. Do not stand at my grave with a broken heart, and do not weep and wonder what might have been if I had been given more time on this earth. Instead, be at peace knowing that I have found my rest, and that I will spend the rest of eternity with your mother in a place of eternal light.

I have so many things I want to tell you, but I will try to be brief, so that you may not waste your time dwelling on things over which you have no control. This is a letter to you, my son, but it is also a letter to my younger self, and everyone else in the world who needs to hear what I am about to say. Consider this my final sermon, an open letter to the lost, the broken, and the outcasted.

We do the best that we know how with what we have been given, and the only difference between you and I is that I have been given time to reflect. In time, you will see that you and I were never quite so different, and we have made many of the same mistakes. And I know that you have never taken to the Word of God as I have, but you should know that there is nothing you could ever do or say to separate you from the love of our God, for he made you just exactly as he intended to. And you cannot imagine all the places you will find Him, if you only try to look. You will find Him everywhere you thought He was not meant to be.

For the rest of your days, I implore you to live your life with an endless supply of love in your heart and know that for all of your struggles, you have been blessed. Use your time on this earth to make the world a better place than how you found it. Lord knows there is a plethora of injustices that remain to be rectified.

Hold in your arms all of the mothers whose babies have been lost, and feel the hunger that rages on every street corner and in every alley. Shout for the prisoners, and use your voice to cry for justice, loud and long, until you are heard. March with the victims, hear their stories, remember their plights. And dance to the music of the world around you, even if you cannot sing its native tongue. Raise your children with a father's unending and unconditional love. Cry for the empty arms and empty hearts and hold high the warriors like you who fight on for our freedom.

And most importantly, love like everyone you meet is your own blood. Love as you have been loved. Hatred has no place in our hearts. And from now on, when you are faced with prejudice and ignorance, hatred and injustice, hold your head high and prove them wrong.

Carry this message with you until your dying days, share it with all who will listen. I can think of no one better than you to understand my struggles, my triumphs, and my message to the world.

Indivisible

I did not learn these things in a day, or two, or even three. It took me fifty years to learn what I know you have already discovered in your short time on this earth.

God loves us all, this much I know, and I love you, this much I am certain, and there are no exceptions. You are the greatest gift I have ever been given, that this world has ever been given, and I will forever be proud to call you my son.

I had always prayed that I would live to see the colonies finally freed from British rule, but I am content to know that you will live to see such liberty. Do not weep and wonder, for I am always with you, beaming with pride as I watch you usher this would-be nation into a new era.

With all of my love,

Your father and your friend,

Alistair Theodore Cunningham

P.S.—I am reminded of an old Irish drinking song that I learned from my mates during my enlistment in the Seven Year's War. It has always been one of my favorite tunes, and I hope that if my own words cannot give you some comfort, these will.

The Parting Glass

Madison Flores

Of all the money that e'er I had
I spent it in good company
And of all the harm that e'er I've done
Alas it was to none but me

And all I've done for want of wit
To memory now I can't recall
So fill to me the parting glass
Goodnight and joy be with you all

And of all the comrades that e'er I had
They are sorry for my going away
And all the sweethearts that e'er I had
They would wish me one more day to stay

But since it calls unto my lot
That I should rise and you should not
I'll gently rise and I'll softly call
Goodnight and joy be with you all

A man may drink and not be drunk
A man may fight and not be slain
A man may court a pretty girl
And perhaps be welcomed back again

But since it has so ordered been
By a time to rise and a time to fall
Come fill to me the parting glass

Indivisible

Good night and joy be with you all...

Chapter 21

He Lives in Us

August 1781

Alistair's open letter remained tucked away in Theo's breast pocket for the weeks to come, and though the words that stained the paper were everything Theo thought he needed to hear, they did little, if anything, to console him. A dark mirage of clouds had settled over him and the rest of Division Point, with no hope for a break in the storm any time soon. And though he felt as if his heart had been ripped from his chest and then stomped on repeatedly before his eyes, Theo could not bring himself to shed another tear after Alistair's funeral.

Perhaps he wanted to be strong for his wife, his daughter, and his father's despondent wife, or perhaps, he simply did not have the strength to even cry for the man. As the days after the funeral turned into weeks, and the hot summer gradually cooled into autumn, he could feel the grief in his heart morphing into something much more agonizing—it was morphing into an *unbridled rage.*

And the last thing he wanted was to lash out that anger on the ones he loved most, so he retreated, away from the world and into himself, spending most hours of the day ruminating in the house, while the rest of Division Point attempted to move on. He spoke few words, to Evie, to Jacob, to Johanna, and he saw little of Liberty as he found himself sinking deeper and deeper into an all too familiar abyss of darkness. It killed him inside to withdraw from his family, but in those moments, he could not find the strength to look them in the eye and tell them just how broken he had so quickly become.

If there was one person more devastated by Alistair's departure than his son, it was Johanna, and she had become so inconsolable that she could not bear to even reenter the home in which he had passed. Perhaps, in time, she would be able to live in that house again, where so many memories had been made between her, her husband, and their son, but that time was a long way off. She had spent the last twenty-five years of her life making that house, and this community, her home, but now, it was tainted. Tainted by the death of the only man she had ever loved, and tainted by all of the years that they would never have together now that he was gone. She would never love again, that much she was sure, and she could never be happy in that home now that she had no one with whom to share it. No, she could not go back to that house, not yet. So, for the time being, while she tried to put herself back together, she would stay with her son and daughter-in-law and distract herself from her pain by pouring herself into being the grandmother she had always wanted to be.

It was a crisp afternoon in late August when Evie left little Libby with Johanna in the parlor of their home to go to her bedroom in search of Theo, who she expected to find sequestered away as he had been for the past several weeks. He had not eaten all day, and she was attempting for the third time to coax him to have a meal before he began to waste away. But when she opened the door to the bedroom, she found no trace of him. The bed had been made, and the curtains pulled shut. There was no sign of Theo having been there, and she could not recall ever hearing him leave the house.

Wandering back to the parlor, Evie asked Johanna, "Have you seen Theo? He is not in our bedroom."

Johanna shook her head as she held her granddaughter of six months on her lap. "No, dear. I have not seen him all day."

Evie placed her hands on her hips in befuddlement. "I would swear he was there just an hour ago. And I did not hear him leave. Where could he have gone?"

Johanna sighed emptily and brushed a stray lock of her hair behind her ear, hair that had once been chocolate brown but seemed to have greyed exponentially over the last month. "Perhaps he went over to the house."

"Why would he do that?"

Johanna shrugged. "Your guess is as good as mine."

"Perhaps we should go look for him at the old house…"

Johanna shook her head firmly and held Liberty tightly to her chest. "You go. I will stay here with Libby. I shall not go back to that God-forsaken house now or anytime soon!"

Evie placed a hand on Johanna's shoulder in an attempt to calm her. "Peace, Johanna," she said softly. "You do not have to go back to the house until you are ready. I will go look for him. Then we will all have supper together."

Johanna nodded in discontented agreement, sighing again as her eyes fell to the floor. Evie gave her one more pat on the shoulder before kissing the top of Liberty's head of thick, dark curls and sauntering out of the house in search of her husband. Surely, he would not just up and disappear without telling her, and he would not leave the homestead without his family, so he could not have gone far.

The sun was beginning to set when Evie checked Jacob and Emma's home, the docks, and the lighthouse, but she found no trace of him there. That was when she decided that the next most likely place was in fact Alistair and Johanna's home, as Johanna had suggested, but she could not comprehend why he would willingly go there when the wounds from the old man's passing were still so fresh.

Nevertheless, she pushed open the front door and stepped into the house on the other side of the lighthouse, feeling a rush of cool air envelop her body as she entered. The place was dim, and everything appeared to be covered in a thin layer of dust from not having been touched in weeks. Evie also felt a strange, discomforting tenseness in the air as she cautiously made her way deeper into the house, as if the place had been enveloped by the stench of death and grief.

The house was silent, save for the creaking of the floorboards under her feet, and the muffled sound of footsteps and furniture shuffling across the floor above her head. She could recognize her husband's footsteps anywhere—they were strong and heavy, surefooted and confident. But the ones she heard lumbering across the second floor were nothing like that—they were slow, quiet, and weak, as if they were waning in both strength and the will to go on. Evie took a deep breath and picked up the hem of her skirt before traipsing up the rickety staircase to confront the source of the noise. Upon reaching the top of the stairs, the sounds of footsteps and heavy objects being dragged across the floor became clearer, and she followed them down the hall until she was in the doorway of the master bedroom—the room where Alistair had taken his last breath.

She let out a sigh of relief she didn't know she had been holding when she peered into the room and instantly recognized Theo's tall and muscular frame in the corner, illuminated only by a single lantern hanging on the wall above his head. He had not noticed her arrival, for his head was hung low as he wandered back and forth across the room, which was now littered with old chests and crates that had been torn open and rummaged through.

"What in God's name are you doing?" Evie asked, loud enough to startle him.

Theo whipped around to face her, his body tense as if he was preparing to defend himself from an attack. When he saw Evie lingering in the doorway, staring at him with wide and worried eyes, he relaxed and let out a sigh. "You startled me," he snapped. "Do not sneak up on me like that again."

Evie crossed her arms over her chest and stepped into the room. "I have been looking everywhere for you. We are about to sit down for supper."

"I am not hungry."

"Theo, you must eat. You have not eaten in days."

Theo shrugged and turned away from her before resuming his business of what appeared to be packing away a large assortment of items into the chests and crates, from books and manuscripts to clothing items and other knick-knacks.

"What does it matter, anyhow?" she heard him mumble under his breath, though she wasn't sure she was meant to hear it. "We are all going to die regardless."

Evie furrowed a brow in concern at his words, sadly shaking her head. "Come home with me, love. We'll eat together as a family."

"Not until I am finished here."

"What are you doing?" She watched him work for several minutes before she realized that the mess of objects scattered around the room were all belongings of Alistair's, and that Theo was packing them away, as if he was trying to rid the place of any trace of his father's existence. "Why are you packing away all of Alistair's things?"

Theo did not look up from the tattered old war chest into which he was placing several ancient books. "He is gone now. There is no need to keep his things around to remind us of what we have lost."

Evie sighed again and began to rub her temples, closing her eyes in frustration. She knew exactly what he was doing, and why, and she understood exactly the feelings that were running through him. She could see him silently breaking down right before her eyes, fighting a private battle within himself that he refused to share with anyone. She could see it in his eyes that he was masking the darkness brewing within him, and she recognized that darkness instantly. It was the same darkness she had become trapped in all those years ago when she lost Noah, and now, she was watching Theo fall into the same hopeless abyss. The withdrawal, the grief, the anger, the confusion, the denial—she had seen and felt it all before in herself, and now she could see it in her husband.

And she also remembered distinctly that Theo had always been the one by her side during that terrible time, and he had been the one to quite literally pull her out of the darkness that had nearly drowned her. But now, the roles were reversed, and as she watched him work tirelessly to hide away all traces of Alistair Cunningham's life, she could see him standing on the precipice of that same abyss. And if something was not done to pull him out of it, he could end up slipping from that icy edge and falling to his demise just as she had nearly done years before.

No thought terrified her as terribly as the thought of losing Theo to that darkness, so she stepped further into the room and attempted to reach out for him, her fingertips grazing the fabric of his sleeve before he abruptly pulled away from her.

"Just go home," Theo grumbled as he glared at her with golden brown eyes that had been dulled to a tarnished bronze by weeks of grief.

"Not without you."

"I do not want you here. I want to be left alone."

Evie placed her hands on her hips and narrowed her eyes at him, resisting the urge to become frustrated by his stubbornness. "I can see you are hurting, Theo," she said gently, her eyes softening. "You have barely spoken since the funeral. Perhaps talking about your pain will help you—"

"I am not hurt." Theo cut her off as he began to anxiously move about the room again. "I am *angry*."

"Angry at whom?"

"I do not know."

"Yes, you do."

Theo halted mid-step and whirled around to face her again, his face pinched up in a look of annoyance. Within an instant, that annoyance shifted into sorrow, and his face fell as his shoulders slumped in defeat. The books he held in his hand to pack away slowly slipped from his fingers and clattered to the floor at his feet as he lowered his gaze to his boots.

"I'm angry at everything," he eventually confessed in a whisper. "I am angry at my father for leaving me behind, just as my mother, James, and Elijah did, and I am angry at myself because I was powerless to stop it…"

"Oh, Theo…" Evie gingerly murmured, closing the distance between them to embrace him. She tried to wrap her arms around his waist, but he took an unstable step backwards and stumbled back into the nearest wall as he dropped his head into his hands.

"It's my fault," she heard him mumble into his palms. "It's all my fault…"

"What? How can you say that?"

Theo pulled his hands from his face to glare down at her, his eyes suddenly red with anger. "Don't you understand?" he bellowed. "He had always told me that my recklessness gave him grey hairs and took years off of his life. He had always told me that he worried himself sick over me whenever I fell into trouble! Don't you see it, Evie? It is my fault. If I hadn't been so reckless, so disobedient, so headstrong, he would not have worried himself into his grave! I killed him. *I killed him!*"

"You know that is not true," Evie countered tearfully. "Your father was sick, but you did not make him sick. There was nothing you could have done to—"

Theo interrupted her by letting out an enraged grunt from deep within his throat and brushing past her to storm across the room, where he stood before a full-length mirror leaning against the wall. Evie watched worriedly as he stared into the looking glass for several moments with a cold, empty look in his darkened eyes. He wanted to see a familiar reflection looking back at him from within the glass, but instead he saw a tired stranger, with bloodshot eyes and a haggard posture. And, God, was he *tired*. Tired of hurting, tired of losing, tired of grieving, and tired of portraying an aura of strength and resilience that he was no longer sure he had.

Evie let out a startled gasp when Theo suddenly clenched his teeth and raised a fist to smash it against the surface of the mirror with all of his might.

"Theo, stop!" she cried as the sound of shattering glass filled the air, but her words fell on deaf ears.

Another growl escaped his throat as he threw his fist against the glass several times over, only stopping when the mirror was shattered into a thousand tiny shards at his feet and his knuckles were covered in several lacerations from which his blood began to trickle and drip onto the floor. He felt no pain when he threw his fists against the sharp glass, but he did feel the slightest sensation of relief when the shards slashed through his knuckles and sent warm blood tricking across his skin. It was the only relief he had felt in weeks.

"Theo, what have you done?" Evie asked between sobs as she hurried across the room and pulled him away from the mirror. Instead of resisting her, Theo clutched his wounded hand to his chest and collapsed into her arms, his legs giving out underneath him as he fell to his knees. He was numb to the stinging pain in his bloodied hand, but the agony in his heart was unbearable, and it was all he could feel. Evie lowered herself to the floor while holding him in her arms, feeling her heart shatter even more than it already was when she heard a single sob escape his throat as he closed his eyes and clenched his teeth.

"It's all my fault..." he whispered again, pressing his face into her chest as his fist continued to bleed onto their clothes.

Evie took his bloodied and trembling hand in hers and searched the floor for anything to wrap around his wounds. She eventually found an old shirt of Alistair's hanging out of a chest, which she snatched up and immediately used to soak up the blood that continued to flow from the cuts that the glass had left in his flesh.

"It is not your fault," Evie whispered in his ear, tangling her fingers comfortingly in his hair. "You cannot shoulder every wrong in this world. God, and only God, is to blame for this, because He took Alistair away..."

Theo lowly looked up to meet her gaze, the self-inflicted wounds on his hand forgotten as he asked, "And are we just supposed to live with the consequences?"

"There are things in this world we are meant to understand..."

"That is not good enough for me anymore!" Theo tried to pull away from her embrace again, but she held him tight until his head eventually fell back upon her breast, and she began to rub circles across his broad back.

He was quiet for several moments, silently sobbing into the fabric of her dress until he eventually murmured, "I cannot bear the world taking one more person from me, Evie. I have lost too much to this war already..."

Evie tightened her arms around his large and muscular frame, burying her face in his neck as she could feel her own tears brimming in her eyes. Her heart ached in her chest like no other time before, not for her own pain, but for that of her husband. She would have given anything to take his pain away. It was not fair how much he had suffered in his short time on this earth. He had endured enough sorrow for a hundred lifetimes, yet it seemed God was still not satisfied.

"I am so sorry, Theo," she whispered painfully, unable to find any other words of comfort.

"Who is next?" Theo asked angrily. "Who will be the next to leave me? Johanna? You? Liberty? Will you leave me too, just as everyone else has?"

Heartbroken, Evie vehemently shook her head with a sob, unaware until then that in their sorrow, they had both begun to rock their bodies back and forth while holding each other in their arms.

"We are not going anywhere, Theo. God will have to tear you from my cold, dead hands before he takes me away. We are not going anywhere without you. I swear it…"

***

September 1781

Theo winced in pain and let out a hiss under his breath as he attempted to close his bandaged right hand into a fist. The blood had long stopped flowing from the cuts in his knuckles after he destroyed the mirror in a fit of anger, but a week later, he still found it difficult and painful to use his right hand for much of anything. The cloth bandage was wrapped tightly around his palm and the first set of knuckles, leaving his fingers free to move, but even the slightest movement sent a stinging pain through his entire hand and into his arm, leaving him once again in a state of regret for having lost control of his temper.

After packing away much of Alistair's belongings and storing them away in the attic of his childhood home, Theo found himself no less content or relieved of his bereavement from when he had started. He thought removing any trace of his father's existence from the house would bring him some sense of peace and make it easier to grieve, but it only left him hollow. Nothing he could do would ever remove Alistair's legacy from the house he built or the community he nurtured, and Theo found himself slipping further and further into the pit of sorrowful darkness that he had tried so hard to claw his way out of years before. Every beat of his heart sent a shockwave of pain, guilt, and regret through his body, and he wanted nothing more than to feel any sort of relief.

He could still remember the tingle he felt whenever he got a taste of the liquor he used to love so much, and shivers went down his spine at the thought of losing all feeling all together once the sweet nectar reached his bloodstream. He had not tasted alcohol in nearly ten years, not since he had quit the stuff for good and taken a new path away from vice, but with Alistair gone, he could feel the urge to imbibe creeping up on him like a monster in the shadows. Alistair was the one who had convinced him to turn his life around after spending most of his teenage years drunk and disorderly, but now that the old man was gone forever, what was the point?

Theo's self-destructive thoughts were interrupted when he heard footsteps approaching him from behind, and he snapped his head up to glance over his shoulder. He was sitting on the back porch of his home, watching the sun set behind the horizon in an attempt to calm the tempestuous thoughts that had been plaguing him since Alistair's funeral, while Evie and Johanna watched after Libby inside; but his solace was interrupted when he heard the back door creak open and hesitant footsteps click against the wooden boards of the porch.

Looking over his shoulder, he found Johanna standing just behind him as he sat on the porch steps. For the first time in weeks, she appeared to have some color to her cheeks and a little more pep in her step, and she was no longer dressed in black garments. The slightest traces of a hopeful smile touched her lips as she said, "I thought I might find you out here."

Theo shrugged and turned back to face the edge of the cliff. "Just came to clear my head, I suppose. You look as if you are starting to feel a little better."

Johanna sighed and nodded while smoothing out her skirt. "I will never be content with your father gone, but I think I have finally accepted that…he has found a better place. I believe I am starting to make peace with it."

"I wish I could say the same for myself."

Johanna sighed again. "May I join you for a moment?"

"Of course."

Johanna picked up her skirt and took a seat next to him on the back steps. They sat in silence for several moments, staring at the horizon as the setting sun sent a cascade of orange, purple, and indigo paint strokes across the sky.

"It is plain to see that you are struggling the most out of all of us," Johanna eventually said, breaking the silence.

"What would give you that idea?"

Johanna gave him a sideways glance and gestured to the bandaged hand resting on his knee. "Evie told me about the mirror. And that you packed away all of your father's things into our attic."

"I had to. For you, and for all of us. How can we possibly move on when we are constantly reminded of him everywhere we look?"

Johann's gaze softened sympathetically. "You know, I thought the same thing when he first passed. I told myself that I never wanted to be reminded of him again, because I feared it would hurt too terribly to even think of him. But then I realized that forgetting him would be far more agonizing than remembering."

Theo quirked his brow at her incredulously. "What changed?"

"I realized that forgetting my husband would mean forgetting all of the wonderful memories we made together. Of course, there were unpleasant memories as well, but they were always overshadowed by the moments I could never put into words."

Theo pinched the bridge of his nose between his thumb and forefinger and shook his head, his gaze falling to his feet. "It is easier said than done, Johanna. You may be able to move on with your cherished memories, but every time I think of my father, I feel nothing but shame and regret. I think only of the mistakes I made and the pain I caused him. That is why I want to forget him. I do not want to be reminded of my sordid past at every turn."

Johanna frowned and shook her head. "Theo, you will never be able to remove every trace of Alistair Cunningham from this place. He built Division Point from the ground up. He is in every building, every person, and every family on this land. He was our friend, our mentor, and our patriarch. He lives on in each and every one of the people in the homestead. *He lives in us.* He lives in *you.*"

Theo looked up to catch her gaze, which was glassy with tears that had not yet been shed. But they were not tears of sorrow or bereavement—they were tears of contentment.

"What are you saying?" he asked with a furrowed brow. He had always found it frustrating when Alistair spoke in riddles and anecdotes, and now Johanna seemed to have picked up the habit.

"I am saying that Alistair was a pillar of this community, and he was a leader. He led us through good times and bad, and even through a war. We both know that he died wanting to leave the fruits of his labor in good hands."

Theo could see where she was going, and he shook his head. "Johanna, please—"

Johanna turned in her seat to face him fully, reaching forward to place her hands on his broad shoulders. "I have read his final will and testament. He left everything, the entire homestead and all of its assets, to you. Because he could think of no one better than his son to ensure that Division

Point will always be a safe haven for the downtrodden and the outcasted. It is your destiny to pick up where he left off and lead this community into a new era of independence..."

Theo turned away and rose to his feet, pacing nervously in front of the steps. "I could not possibly hope to fill his shoes," he argued as he ran a hand through his hair, "Alistair Cunningham was a war hero, and a preacher, and the most generous man to have ever stepped foot on this land. And I am just...me. We are nothing alike."

Johanna reached forward as he paced by her and snagged his hand, pulling him down until he took a seat next to her again. "You and your father are alike in all of the best ways possible. You are both headstrong, and fearless, and passionate, and you wear your heart on your sleeve."

"I've repeated nearly all of his mistakes, Johanna. How can I possibly be fit to lead or mentor anyone?"

"But you have both learned from those mistakes. And you have become a better man because of it. Listen to me. You have spent so many years trying to avoid repeating your father's mistakes that you have become blind to his triumphs, as well as your own. And you have become so consumed by your fear of becoming who he used to be that you have forgotten who *you* are."

Theo sighed heavily and looked down once more at his bandaged hand and the healing cuts that littered his knuckles. As much as he didn't want to admit it, her words had merit, and as he looked back over his last twenty-five years, he could pinpoint a thousand instances in which her claims rang true. He had been consumed by a desire to avoid becoming the fool that Alistair once was, but he had failed to realize until now that it had been at a detriment to himself.

He had always been Alistair's son, Alistair's boy, Alistair's *bastard*. And now that Alistair was gone, Theo did not know who he was without him. He had always longed for the day he could stop being Alistair's boy and just be Theo, but he had never imagined that when that day came that it would be so bittersweet.

And what was he to do now? He had a family to care for—a wife, a daughter, and a stepmother, all dependent upon him and only him. How could he possibly care for an entire community while the war for their independence raged on? Alistair's death had brought the weight of a thousand tons into his shoulders, but now that it was expected of him to continue his legacy as the patriarch of Division Point, he could feel that weight transforming into the weight of the entire world.

A heavy, suffocating weight that only dragged him further into the dark abyss lurking on the other side of the precipice.

***

The walls were caving in. The ground was crumbling under his feet. The world was spinning, but not nearly as fast as he could feel himself spiraling out of control, quickly losing touch with everyone and everything around him. He had never known sorrow like this, not when he learned the truth of his parentage, not when James had passed, not when Kensington burned, not when Evie had been taken by her husband, and not even when he discovered that his mother had been dead for most of his life. None of it compared to the emptiness Theo felt in his soul in the weeks after Alistair's funeral, and what frightened him the most was that he could think of nothing capable of pulling him out of his darkness. Not his friends, not his family, not even his wife and daughter could bring him joy. And the mere thought of Division Point's care falling upon his shoulders and his shoulders alone while he grappled with supporting his mourning family made him want to fall asleep and never wake up.

It was too much. Too much weight to bear, too much sorrow to withstand. And as the days of autumn dragged on, Theo could feel his body beginning to crave that which he had not entertained in many years, simply because it was the only thing left that he thought could possibly numb his pain. Friends and family may have come and gone with the tides, but the liquor had always been there when he needed to drown his sorrows.

And it was here now, staring him right in the face like a minion of the dark, beckoning him to take just one sip. Theo sat slumped at the kitchen table in the middle of the night, the room illuminated by a single lantern sitting next to him on the table. It was well past midnight, and his wife and daughter were fast asleep. Johanna had finally found the courage to go back to her own home, now that nearly two months had passed since Alistair's death, which left Theo's house strangely quiet without her presence. Theo was thankful that she was no longer staying with them, for she certainly would have heard him awake and lumber out to the kitchen in the middle of the night. And he did not want any witnesses to what he was ready to do this evening.

Theo lowered his head and slumped further back against his chair, his eyes fixated upon what sat before him on the table—a single bottle of rum, unopened and untouched, which he had pilfered from behind the bar of the O'Hara's tavern earlier that day when no one was looking. He did not remember taking it, that moment was a blur between the memories of walking into the tavern on a sunny afternoon and then returning home to stash his stolen goods in the back of one of the cupboards in the kitchen. And now, here it was, sitting upon the table and glowing in the light of the lantern, it's parchment label beckoning him to break its seal.

Not once since he had quit liquor ten years ago had he contemplated going back to the stuff, but now in his bereaved and hopeless state, it was all he could think about. It was all he craved. The satisfyingly sweet, yet freshly tart taste on his tongue, the mild burning in the back of his throat, and of course, the unforgettable numbness that overtook his mind and body and sent him adrift upon an ocean of tranquility.

In these desperate moments of utter misery and despair, he was sure that nothing but the liquor could bring him that peace that he so desperately craved. But every time he lifted his hand from his lap and reached forward to take the bottle to his lips, he was stopped by a nagging voice rattling in the back of his head, a familiar, deep, and raspy voice that sounded suspiciously like Alistair and always seemed to materialize when Theo least expected it.

Do not be foolish, the voice said. *You are better than this. Do not throw the last decade away for me.*

"And of all the harm that e'er I've done, alas it was to none but me..."

But that was easier said than done. He had already been tempted enough to steal the cursed drink—what made him think he still had the strength to resist the urge to consume it now that it was staring him right in the face? And Theo knew himself well enough to know that he could not take just *one* sip and toss the rest away. No, once he got a taste, the bottle would be empty within the hour and he would be well on his way to the bottom of the abyss he had spent so long trying to escape.

Think of your wife. Think of your daughter. They need you. You have too much to lose to give it all back to the liquor.

"And all the sweethearts that e'er I had, they would wish me one more day to stay..."

But he could not go on like this, that much he was certain. Something had to change, and something had to give, for Theo knew that he could not live another day with this much anger and grief in his heart. It hurt too much.

Theo reached out for the bottle once more, this time allowing his fingertips to graze the cool glass until he clutched it tightly in his hand and pulled it toward him. He held the bottle to the light of the lantern and turned it, watching as the dark liquid swish around inside. He licked his lips as he watched; he could taste it on his tongue already. Ten years later, and he could still taste it as if his last drink had been yesterday. Time seemed to stand still as he popped the cork and tossed it over his shoulder, savoring the pungent aroma that arose from the freshly opened spout. Oh, how he had missed it.

"A man may drink and not be drunk, a man may fight and not be slain..."

His eyes slipped closed as he let out a long breath through his nose and raised the bottle to his lips. He froze then, before any of the rum could come near his mouth, feeling his heart clench painfully in his chest and the nagging voice in the back of his head screaming at him, begging him to pause and consider the consequences of the decision he was about to make.

With an enraged growl, he suddenly pulled the bottle easy from his lips and slammed it down before using his arm to swipe it off of the table. The bottle flew across the kitchen and collided with the nearest wall where it disintegrated into a million pieces, filling the air with the sickening crunch of shattering glass and sending the rum within all across the wall and floor. The resulting noise was much louder than Theo had anticipated and, he clamped his hands over his ears while dropping his head upon the surface of the table. He squeezed his eyes shut and clenched his teeth as his blood began to pound in his ears, searching desperately for relief from the deafening whirlwind raging inside him.

"But since it calls unto my lot, that I should rise, and you should not..."

He could feel his shoulders begin to shake as a set of startled footsteps hurried across the house and skidded to a stop in the kitchen doorway.

"What has happened?" Evie gasped as she reached the kitchen with her night gown swirling around her legs, disoriented and groggy from having been awoken by the sound of shattering glass.

That was when she saw Theo, slumped at the table before her, and the remains of a bottle of rum scattered upon the floor across the room, the liquor dripping down the wall and gathering between the cracks in the floorboards like crimson pools of blood.

"Theo, what happened? Are you alright?" she asked again, more alarmed than before when Theo did not answer nor look up from the table.

She placed her hands on his trembling shoulders and leaned over to place her lips at his ear. Her heart began to race in her chest when she could smell the rum in the air, and she tried to force him to sit up so that she could see his face, but he refused.

"Look at me," she begged in a panicked whisper. "Please, Theo, please tell me you didn't. Please tell me you did not take a drink…"

Theo's body continued to tremble under her touch, and after a moment of hesitation, he shook his head and slowly looked up to meet her gaze. When his face finally became visible in the dim light of the lantern, she could see his sunken cheeks were stained with tears and his eyes were red and glassy.

"Tell me you didn't," she whispered again, kneeling down next to his chair and taking his face in her hands.

"I couldn't do it," he confessed emptily. "I wanted it. I wanted it so badly…but I couldn't do it."

Evie glanced back over her shoulder at the mess of broken glass and rum on the floor behind her, and then looked back into his crestfallen face. "Where did you get it?"

"O'Hara's," Theo rasped shamefully, dropping his head again. "I stole it."

"Oh, Theo…why would you do that?"

He shrugged and let his head rest upon her shoulder. "I have nothing left to lose…"

"What? How can you say that? You have everything left to lose!"

Theo abruptly pulled away from her embrace, standing with enough force to knock his chair backwards against the floor. He then began to frantically pace before her, his hands clutching at his hair as he stared sorrowfully at the floor.

"My father is dead—he was the entire reason I gave up the drink, and now he is dead! What is the point, Evie? Why should I try to hold myself together anymore?"

Evie stated at him with eyes wide in shock, feeling as if she had just been slapped across the face. His words pierced her heart like a dagger, but she knew it was not him she was talking to anymore. The being in front of her was not her husband, nor the man she fell in love with. He was an empty shell that had become so fully entombed in darkness that he could no longer see the light. It was not Theo talking to her now—it was the grief. The Theo she knew would not give up so easily, nor throw away everything for which he had worked so hard just to have a taste of the vice he had given up long ago.

"What is the point?" Evie repeated dejectedly. She pointed to the golden band on her left ring finger. "*This* is the point. How can you say that you have nothing left to lose? You have *us* to lose! Your family. Remember us, the wife and daughter that have remained at your side through thick and thin?"

Theo let out a heavy sigh and paused in his pacing, slowly turning to face her. He regretted his words as soon as they left his lips, but it was too late to take them back.

"I just wanted it to stop," he told her quietly. "The pain, the guilt, the anger. I just wanted to be me again…"

Evie slowly closed the distance between them, stopping just a few feet before him. "I want that, too. But *this* is not the way to go about it. You just need time to grieve. We all do. But the moment you take another drink, you will throw the last ten years away."

"And so what if I do? The old man isn't around to scold me anyhow…"

"Theo! Alistair would not want you to give everything up for just one night of numbness."

Theo narrowed his eyes at her and crossed his arms over his chest. "You don't know what he wanted. You don't know him like I did."

Evie shook her head in frustration and took another step in Theo's direction, poking a finger in his chest. "Perhaps not. But I do know you. And I know that the man I married would not give up like this. Think of your family. Your wife, your daughter. What would we do without you?"

"Perhaps you'd all be better off without me..."

Evie suddenly took ahold of his wrist and pulled him close, causing him to stumble clumsily into her. Their gazes locked in an instant, blue eyes staring into golden brown.

"I'm not going to let you fall into the same abyss that I did all those years ago," she whispered as her eyes searched his face for any sign of the man she knew before Alistair's death. "You have too much to lose."

Theo stared her down harshly for several moments before his expression slowly began to soften and his eyes slipped closed as a shaky breath escaped his lips. Wordlessly, Evie gripped his wrist and began to lead him out of the kitchen and across the house until they reached the door to Liberty's nursery.

"What are you—" Theo tried to ask, but she silenced him with a finger pressed to his lips before pushing the door open and leading him into the room. Inside, Libby was fast asleep in her bassinet in the corner, completely unaware of the storm that had been raging in the kitchen.

Evie brought him to the corner of the room and made him to stand before the bassinet. They both watched their daughter sleep peacefully for several silent moments before Evie whispered, "This is what you have to lose, Theo. If you absolutely cannot go on for yourself, go on for her. For me. For us. For Alistair. Do you remember what you said to me when I was standing on the edge of the lighthouse all those years ago?"

Theo slowly shook his head, his eyes still fixated on Libby's sleeping form. She was so small, so innocent. So pure. She had yet to be scarred by the trials and tribulations of life, and he would go to the ends of the earth to keep it that way.

"You told me...that there are so many reasons not to give up. You just have to want to see them. And if the little girl in that crib isn't an adequate reason, I don't know what is."

Theo swallowed thickly, feeling the tension in his body begin to release when Evie intertwined her fingers with his own as they stood side by side over Libby's bassinet. His eyes dashed back and forth between his wife and his daughter for several moments before he dropped his head in his hands. He could feel nothing but shame for having even contemplated taking the bottle to his lips again, and he would have given anything to turn back time and stop himself from stealing it in the first place.

"I'm so sorry," he whispered into his palms. Whether it was to Liberty, Evie, or his father, he wasn't sure. But it needed to be said.

"Drinking yourself to death won't bring Alistair back, and it won't rewrite the past, but it surely will destroy our future," Evie murmured softly, her eyes burning with tears.

Theo's legs suddenly went weak underneath him, and he dropped to his knees before Liberty's bassinet, resting his head against the edge. "I'm so sorry," he repeated shakily to the sleeping infant. "I'm sorry..."

Evie knelt next to him before the crib and leaned her head on his shoulder while wrapping her arm around his waist.

"We will get through this," she promised him. "Together."

"Together," Theo repeated, reaching forward to place his hand gingerly upon Liberty's small body. He could feel her tiny heart beating against his palm, and she stirred quietly under his touch before reaching forward to clutch one of his fingers in her sleep.

The traces of a smile touched Theo's lips as he felt her little fingers wrap around his, a sensation he had surely taken for granted until he had slowed down enough to feel it for himself. In that moment, he was struck by another pang of guilt, not for stealing the rum, or nearly consuming it, but for the fact that he had allowed himself to be so consumed with his own problems over the last few months that he had barely been able to enjoy his time as a father. Liberty was well into her sixth month of life, and yet, Theo felt as if he barely knew her. One thing after another had diverted his attention from her since she was born, whether it was building the house, searching the papers for news on the war, or burying his father.

But that ended now. Nothing mattered more in this world than his family, and he would spend the rest of his life showing them as much. And as he looked down into the bassinet and watched his little girl sleep, he knew everything Evie and Johanna had been telling him was right. They had been telling him everything he needed to hear in the aftermath of Alistair's passing, he had just been too stubborn to listen until he came face to face with the bottom of the abyss.

His family was his reason for trudging on through this life, the reason he never gave up despite the numerous reasons he had been given to quit. And the reasons to keep fighting far outnumbered the reasons to roll over and die, he could see that now. Alistair may not have been with them any longer, but his spirit lived on in the hearts and minds of everyone he knew. He lived on in his wife, in his son, in his granddaughter, and in the community that he had forged with his own two hands so many years ago. Just as he would have wanted, Division Point and its people would live on into the new era of prosperity and independence, and his name would forever remain synonymous with peace, freedom, and hope. So long as his name was not forgotten, he was still alive.

"He lives in us," Theo mumbled to himself as he tore his eyes away from his daughter to look out the window and up to the night sky.

Staring down at them, a full moon hung high in the clear indigo sky, a much-needed beacon of light in a sea of darkness and heartache.

"I'll gently rise, and I'll softly call, goodnight and joy be with you all..."

Chapter 22

World on Fire

September 1781

"Come on now, Libby. You can do it. I know you can," Theo coaxed gently, resting his chin on his palm as he laid out on his stomach on the floor of the nursery.

Liberty stared at him with her big blue eyes from across the room, where she was also lying on her stomach upon a blanket that had been spread out on the floor. Her face split into a wide, toothless grin at the sound of his voice, and she pushed herself up onto her elbows while letting out an excited squeal.

"Come to me," Theo repeated as he clapped his hands. "Crawl to your papa."

After muttering something that sounded like the word "Pa-pa," Liberty squealed again and began to clap her hands against the wooden floorboards. Theo watched for several more minutes as she bounced up and down on her stomach, kicking her legs and waving her arms as if she was contemplating whether or not she was capable of completing such a task.

Theo let out a defeated sigh and pushed himself up onto his hands and knees before crawling across the room to her. As soon as he reached the blanket, she giggled giddily and reached up to him with both of her chubby little hands. Taking a seat on the floor in front of her, Theo took Liberty in his arms and placed her in his lap, where she happily began to reach up and tangle her fingers in his tousled, shoulder-length hair.

"Worry not, little one," he told her with a smirk. "Your time will come soon. We can't give up yet."

As if on cue, Evie appeared in the doorway to the nursery, her arms folded over her chest and a contented grin upon her face. "No luck with the crawling yet, hm?" she asked as she tilted her head in curiosity.

Theo shook his head. "Not yet. But when the time comes, I will be there to see it. I swear it."

Evie chuckled in agreement and opened her mouth to speak, but she was interrupted when Johanna suddenly sprinted into the room from the kitchen.

Johanna's face was pale, as if she had seen some sort of specter, and her eyes were wide with confusion and worry.

"What is it, Johanna?" Theo asked in alarm as he rose to his feet with Liberty in his arms.

"There is someone at the door," Johanna mumbled. "He looks like a Continental soldier. He asked to see you, Theo."

Theo and Evie shared a startled look. "Did he give you his name?" Theo asked suspiciously.

"He spoke with a French accent," Johanna said as she shook her head in befuddlement. "Young and polite, but insistent that he see you immediately."

"What would a French soldier be doing at our door?" Evie asked with a furrowed brow.

"I intend to find out. Both of you stay here," Theo muttered in mild annoyance, handing the baby off to his wife before sauntering out of the nursery and into the front room.

Theo's jaw went slack when he opened the front door to see a familiar young man standing on his porch, decorated to the hilt in French military regalia. His face was kind and his smile inviting, just as Theo had remembered him, but there was also a noticeable tension in the man's posture as he stood before the entrance to the house. As soon as Theo opened the door, the visitor's smile widened, and he held open his arms in a welcoming gesture.

"Sergeant Cunningham," he said smoothly, his Parisian accent still just as strong as the day Theo had met him. "Oh, how I am glad to see you, *mon ami*."

Theo's body relaxed as he quirked his brow in confusion and scratched his chin. "Lafayette?"

"The one and only!"

"What in God's name are you doing at my front door? Is the war still not raging as we speak?"

Lafayette let out a pensive sigh and adjusted the powdered wig that sat atop his head. "*Oui*, the war rages on. That is why I am here. I need to speak with you, urgently."

Theo crossed his arms over his chest and leaned against the doorway after recovering from the initial shock of seeing the young military hero he had met years prior. As much as he personally liked Lafayette, it had been over four years since they last spoken, and he really had no interest in discussing the war with him. The war was the last thing on his mind now that his life revolved around his wife and daughter.

"I no longer have any interest in the goings on of the Patriots, Lafayette. I am not a Sergeant anymore. I fear you have wasted your time by coming all this way."

Lafayette shook his head. "I did not just come for a friendly chat. The Commander sent me personally to come see you, and to deliver a message on his behalf."

Theo's expression immediately soured as he pushed himself away from the doorway. At the mention of Commander Washington's name, both Evie and Johanna pressed themselves against the wall that separated the nursery from the front room so that they could better hear what was being said between Theo and the visitor.

"If the Commander wanted to speak to me, he should have come himself," Theo grumbled.

"As you can imagine, he is…otherwise engaged at the moment. That is why he sent me. Please, I request only a few moments of your time. May I come in?"

Theo hesitated for a moment before silently nodding and stepping to the side to allow Lafayette entrance into the house. "I am sorry, Lafayette," he sighed. "But I am sure I will also have no interest in whatever message the Commander has to give me."

"I would not be so sure," Lafayette returned as he reached inside the inner pocket of his military coat and produced a folded piece of parchment—a correspondence written in Commander Washington's own hand and addressed to Sergeant Theo Cunningham.

Theo took the letter from his hand, rubbing his thumb across the wax seal that enclosed it. The seal was emblazoned with the letters GW, a monogram he recognized from when he had rifled through Washington's desk at their encampment near Philadelphia four years ago. It was most definitely the seal of the Commander. Theo opened the correspondence and scanned over it quickly, his heart contracting in his chest and his blood boiling under his skin by the time he finished.

Theo looked up from the letter with narrowed eyes. Surely, this was a *joke*. "The Commander is personally requesting my appearance in Virginia?" he asked, his words coated in venom.

Lafayette nodded and cleared his throat. "Near Yorktown, by the end of the month. We are currently preparing for a battle of epic proportions—perhaps the battle that will end this war for good. Commander Washington wants you there, fighting alongside your brothers in arms."

"The man is daft if he thinks I will entertain this ludicrous request after everything he has done to betray me!" Theo snapped, shoving the letter back into Lafayette's hands.

"Theo, please take a moment to consider what is being asked," Lafayette pleaded. "The Commander would not ask such a thing of you if he did not have faith in your capabilities as a soldier."

"Or if he was not desperate," Theo added with a roll of his eyes. "You will have to tell Washington that I politely refuse his request. I ceased being a soldier four years ago, and I told myself I would never take up arms again."

"You may think you have given up being a soldier, but you have not given up being a Patriot."

Theo shook his head stubbornly. "Even if I wanted to go to war again, I couldn't. I have a family now. I have too much to lose."

"We all have families. We all have too much to lose. And that is exactly why we fight."

Theo opened his mouth to argue once more, but he was interrupted by the sound of frantic whispering and shuffling on the other side of the nearest wall. Before he could speak, Evie and Johanna stumbled out of the doorway to the nursery in unison, as if they had been nudging to get closer to the door without revealing themselves and then tripped over each other's feet. Their faces immediately turned red in embarrassment at being caught eavesdropping, and Johanna handed Liberty off to Evie before straightening out her skirts and averting her eyes to the floor.

"Speaking of which," Theo snapped, sending a harsh glare across the room to Evie. "This is mine. Lafayette, allow me to introduce you to my brown-nosing wife, Evie, and my meddling step-mother, Johanna. Evie and Johanna, this is Major-General Lafayette."

Lafayette let out a charming chuckle before bowing his head to Johanna and taking Evie's free hand in his own. He kissed the back of her hand with a smile after murmuring the words, "A pleasure to meet you, *Madame* Cunningham."

Evie felt her cheeks turn an even darker shade of red under the young man's coquettish gaze, and she lowered into a curtsy before returning, "*C'est un plaisir de vous rencontrer.*"

Lafayette's eyes lit up and his grin widened. "Oh! *Vous parley français?*"

"*Juste un peu,*" Evie returned with a girlish giggle.

Lafayette's eyes landed on the baby in Evie's arms. "And who is this little one?"

"That is my daughter, Liberty," Theo answered somewhat tensely. He was not sure how keen he was to see Lafayette so brazenly flirt with his wife, especially after he had shown up unannounced with such an outlandish request.

Lafayette smirked again, his young eyes wide with wonderment as Liberty smiled back at him and reached out to try and take ahold of one of the medals pinned to his uniform coat. "Ah, *Liberté*...what a beautiful name for such a beautiful girl."

"I am sure you overheard our conversation," Theo said to Evie with a noticeable discomfort in his voice.

Evie nodded before turning to look pointedly at Lafayette. "I'm sorry you had to come all this way, *Monsieur* Lafayette, but my husband must decline your request. He is needed here, not on the battlefield."

"I beg you not to dismiss this so quickly," Lafayette said to Evie and Theo both, clasping his hands together. "The impending meeting between the British and the Patriots at Yorktown could end the war for good, and you have a gift for battle. I have seen it. The Commander has seen it. Please, Theo, take a moment to consider what is at stake."

Evie did not look the least bit convinced, but Johanna seemed to be ruminating on something.

"Perhaps he is right," Johanna mumbled quietly. "Perhaps it is something worth considering."

Evie and Theo both looked to her with mouths agape. "Johanna!" Evie gasped. "How can you even entertain such an idea? The last time Theo went to war, he returned on death's doorstep! No, I will not consent to this. You cannot go back to the war. I won't have it!"

Johanna placed a hand on Evie's shoulder with a wistful, gentle smile. Her voice was tight as she said, "If there is a chance to end this bloody war once and for all, I do not think we should be so hasty to reject it. If there is one thing Alistair would have wanted to see before he passed, it would be the colonies finally *free*…"

Evie shook her head with an exasperated huff, feeling her stomach churn when she looked across the room to see Theo looking up at the ceiling in deliberation. As soon as Johanna had mentioned Alistair's name, Theo's eyes went to the sky, and his expression morphed from one of defiance to one of confusion and contemplation.

"You cannot be serious," Evie snapped at him, Layette, and Johanna. "This is madness! You were captured and nearly killed the last time you went away! We cannot lose you, Theo—"

Theo silenced her with a raised hand, closing his eyes with a pensive sigh. Turning to Lafayette, he mumbled, "You are welcome to stay until I make a decision, but I cannot promise anything."

Clutching Libby to her chest, Evie turned away in anger, hurt that Theo would even consider returning to war after all the misfortune that had befallen them. Liberty was barely seven months old, and they, along with the rest of Division Point, were still reeling from Alistair's death. It was not the right time. It would never be the right time.

"You can't do this to us," she hissed at her husband. "You cannot abandon us now!"

"Evie, please..." Before Theo could stop her, she stormed out of the front room and into the master bedroom with the baby in her arms, slamming the door shut behind her with a wounded whimper.

Silence fell upon those that remained in the room as Theo hung his head in defeat, pinching the bridge of his nose with a heavy sigh. He had not planned to entertain the idea of accepting Washington's request to rejoin the Patriots in Yorktown, but the moment Johanna had mentioned his father's name, he could feel his heart skip a beat. Though Alistair had been reluctant to let him join the war five years ago, he had never made his support for independence and equality a secret. Suddenly, Theo's thoughts became consumed by whether or not the old man would have given him his blessing to take up arms against the British again, or if he would have fought him the whole way as Evie appeared to be doing now.

Lafayette broke the silence by clearing his throat. "Your wife is very lovely," he mumbled as he awkwardly rubbed the back of his neck and dropped his eyes to the floor.

Feeling lightheaded, Theo invited Lafayette to join him in the parlor so that they could take a seat and talk further. His heart and mind were racing as he numbly made his way to the next room, and he could feel sweat beginning to bead on his forehead at the mere thought of returning to the battlefield.

There was so much to consider before he made this decision, but his immediate thought was still to decline and send Lafayette on his way. The last thing he wanted was to abandon his family when they needed him the most, but he also loathed the thought of disappointing his father. Would the old man tell him to go, or beg him to stay? Or would he tell him that he was his own man now, the man of the house, and that he needed to make this decision for himself and no one else? And what was truly at stake now? His life? His family? His future?

***

"How did you even find me?" Theo asked as he leaned back in his armchair in the parlor, rubbing at his temples as he tried to shoo away the migraine he could feel coming on.

Lafayette crossed one leg over the other as he sat in his own chair. "The Patriots have eyes and ears everywhere, *mon ami*. It was not difficult to track you down."

Theo paused when he heard footsteps behind him, and he glanced over his shoulder to see Evie sauntering into the parlor with a tray in her hands. Upon the tray, a steaming teapot and two teacups, which Theo had requested she prepare for their guest. She was silent as she entered, her eyes averted to the floor and her lips pressed in a thin hard line. She set the tray down on the table between Theo and Lafayette's chairs and poured two cups of hot tea before wordlessly excusing herself from the room, but not without shooting a skeptical glance at Lafayette over her shoulder. He had seemed so charming and polite when he first arrived, but now that she knew his motive for coming—to whisk Theo away on another suicide mission—she had no love for the Frenchman, and even less for the Commander.

"The Commander has some nerve asking for my help after all he has done," Theo noted sharply after Evie had gone. "Why should I even consider sticking my neck out for the man that ordered the execution of my people behind my back on multiple occasions?"

Lafayette quirked his brow in confusion. "Pardon me?"

Theo leaned forward in his chair, his jaw set tightly. "He did not just order the demise of that village in the mountains four years ago. During the Seven Years War, he destroyed another native settlement by infesting it with smallpox. One of his victims…was my *mother*."

Lafayette swallowed thickly and uncomfortably shifted his weight in his chair. Pulling at the lapels of his coat, he mumbled, "The Commander never mentioned that to me."

"Of course, he didn't. He did not want you to see him for who he really is. But I know actually what he is. He is a hypocrite and a murderer."

Lafayette sighed heavily and also leaned forward in his chair, taking a sip of tea. His face was pinched together in befuddlement, but after a few moments of silence, he shook his head. "Commander Washington may have made terrible mistakes in the past, as have we all. I am terribly sorry for what fate befell your mother and her people, but that was a different time. A different war. Please, I beg you to put aside your personal hostilities and help us end this bloodshed."

Theo's jaw clenched tighter and his eyes narrowed into slits. "And why should I risk everything I have to help him after what he has done?"

"Because the world is on fire, Theo. And it is finally time to extinguish the flames of war once and for all. This can only be done at Yorktown, and only with your help."

"Why me?"

"You seem to have made quite the impression on Commander Washington. He says he has seen something in you from the beginning, and you are one of the most promising Sergeants he has ever had the pleasure to meet."

Theo raised his brow skeptically. "Did he tell you to say that?"

"He did not have to. It was plain to see."

Theo shook his head and raked a hand through his hair. "I do not understand why he would ask for me. I disrespected and disobeyed him, I accused him of treason and tyranny, and I deserted his army. Men have been *executed* for less."

"What can I say? The man admires your convictions and your passion for justice. The world would be much better off if there were more men like you around."

"Lafayette, I am flattered, but I cannot leave my family behind. Not now. My daughter is still young, my father just passed—" Theo cut himself off and allowed his statement to trail into silence, clearing his throat and turning his head away when he felt his body become tense with anxiety.

"I am sorry, Theo. I understand. I really do. But I fear that nobody's family is safe until the British are defeated. Not yours, not mine, not anyone's. If you truly want to protect your family and their future, you will come to Yorktown to fight one last time for our freedom."

Theo slowly rose from his chair and began to pace the length of the floor. He was suddenly very aware of the multitude of ragged scars that ran across his back, now fully healed after four years, but still very noticeable as a permanent reminder of the horrors of war.

"I fought for my freedom once before. I believed in Washington and everything he promised once before, and he stabbed me in the back. So now I do not know what I believe. And the last time I left for war, I almost did not return."

"You were captured," Lafayette speculated, taking note of the tenseness in Theo's posture as he stood before him.

"I was captured by the British on my way home from Philadelphia. I barely escaped the fort with my life. I won't take that risk again."

"You say you do not know what you believe in anymore, but you would not have named your daughter *Liberty* if you did not believe in it whole heartedly."

"Of course, I believe in liberty. But I fear that what Washington promises is just another monarchy in disguise, where men who look like him succeed and people who look like me fall through the cracks."

"I believe in Washington. I believe that he is a good man, with a good heart, and though he may have made some misguided mistakes in the past, I can see that he has learned from them."

"Mistakes? You call the slaughter of an entire village in the name of freedom a *mistake*?"

Lafayette shook his head. "I would never condone such a tragedy, even in the name of freedom. And I do not know what the future for this would-be nation holds, but the only way to truly know is to pave a way toward it. That starts and ends with Yorktown."

"How can I possibly look him in the eye and call him my commander after what has been said and done between us?"

"I am asking you to put aside your distaste for the man and look at the bigger picture. Please, Theo. We need you. I would not have come this way if I didn't think so…"

Theo let out a long and heavy sigh, lowering himself back into his chair and resting his head in his hands while he thought. There was so much at stake. No matter whether he stayed or went, there was so much to lose. But Lafayette was right.

They were surrounded by a world on fire, and it was only a matter of time until the flames swallowed his home. He could either sit idly by and watch as the land around him burned, eventually surrounding him and everyone he loved in a suffocating prison of smoke and tyranny, or he could take the call to action and extinguish the fire himself. After a great conflagration, there was always a rebirth, a renewal—a chance to begin anew, unchained and unafraid of the years to come.

"And what of my family?" Theo eventually asked in a husky whisper. "If I am to go to Virginia, who will protect my family while I am away?"

"I can arrange for some Minutemen to encamp nearby if you are concerned, but all of Cornwallis' men and supplies are concentrated in Virginia."

Theo folded his hands together and stared up the ceiling as he continued to argue with himself. His eyes briefly roamed from the ceiling to the nearest window, where he caught sight of the sun beginning to dip down toward the horizon. Every time he looked to the sky, he saw Alistair's face and heard his voice, and this time, the old man was telling him that which he was desperately looking to hear.

You do not always have to be everyone's hero. But you wouldn't be Theo Cunningham if you didn't try.

Theo's eyes fluttered closed in resolution as he let out a shaky breath before muttering, "Send word to Washington that he can expect to see me by the end of the month."

Lafayette jumped to his feet in excitement, barraging Theo with an unprovoked embrace that nearly knocked him out of his chair.

"*Dieu merci!*" he cried out. "*Merci beaucoup,* Sergeant Cunningham. The Commander and the Patriot army will forever be in your debt, sir."

Theo awkwardly patted him on the back before nudging him away. "I am not doing this for Washington, or the Patriots. I am doing this for my family."

"For your family, hm?" Evie spat, suddenly emerging from around the corner of the parlor doorway, her eyes wide with betrayal and her lips curled into a snarl. Unbeknownst to either Theo or Lafayette, she had been eavesdropping on their conversation once again from the other side of the wall, and the moment that Theo verbalized his decision, she stormed into the parlor with tears already burning in her eyes.

Theo and Lafayette both nearly leapt out of their skins at the commotion of her sudden entry, and Theo held up his hands in a gesture of peace and surrender as she approached him.

"Evie, please do not be upset—"

"Upset? You think I am upset that you went against my wishes and agreed to go back to war? I am not upset. I am hurt and devastated! How could you possibly agree to this? What about your daughter? And Johanna? And me? How could you be so reckless?"

Theo sighed heavily and took her hands in his own in an attempt to calm her. "Lafayette is right. The war needs to end here and now. We cannot move forward until the British are gone for good."

"I do not give a damn about the British, or the war, or anything else! I care about my family, and you are trying to tear it apart by leaving when we need you the most!"

Theo tried to pull her into his chest and hold her shaking form, but she roughly pulled her wrists free from his grasp and turned on her heel to storm out of the room once again. When she had gone, Theo dropped his head in his hands and let out an unsteady breath.

"Let me go speak with her," he mumbled to Lafayette before excusing himself from the room.

"Of course, *mon ami*. Take your time. This is never an easy decision to accept for the ones we leave behind."

***

Theo followed the sound of Evie's enraged footsteps out of the house and past the lighthouse, where he found her sitting upon a rock near the edge of the cliff, staring out across the water as the evening wind blew her long auburn tresses about her face. He slowly approached her from behind, but the moment he reached her, she harshly turned to face him, revealing the tears that had just begun to roll down her cheeks.

They were not tears of sadness, but rather anger, confusion, and fear. She finally had the life she wanted, and she finally had her family. But she could feel that safety and sanctuary slipping away now that she could see his mind was made up.

"You know I would never abandon you, or my daughter," Theo told her as he crossed his arms over his chest. "You know I always have and always will do everything in my power to keep you safe."

Evie shook her head and turned away from him again. "You are not trying to keep us safe. You are trying to relive your glory days. We finally have everything we could have wanted, and it is still not enough for you. You still feel the need to risk everything so that you can call yourself a hero."

Theo took a seat on the rock next to her and leaned forward, resting his elbows on his knees. "I am begging you to try and understand what is at stake, Evie. If the British are not defeated, they will rule over us with an iron fist for the rest of eternity."

"I am done trying to understand this war," Evie spat tearfully. "I am done trying to understand man's unrelenting desire to compete to see who can shed the most blood."

"This is not about a competition—it is about creating a better future for our family, and creating a world in which we no longer live in fear of a tyrant. This is about creating the world for our daughter to grow up in that we never had."

Evie released a sob from her throat before turning to face him once again. Deep in her clear blue eyes, Theo saw a terror that he had not seen in her in many years.

"I cannot bear to see you on your deathbed as I have before," she murmured. "You have no idea how unimaginably horrid it was to see you so weak and broken when you stumbled back home from the war. I cannot go through the pain and the worry again."

Theo reached forward to place both of his hands on her cheeks and pull her close, until their noses were nearly touching. "I am not the same man I was when I left the first time," he told her in a gentle whisper. "I will return to you and Liberty again, I swear to you."

"And what am I supposed to tell Liberty if you don't return? Will your sentiments about honor and independence be any comfort to a girl who must grow up without her father?"

Theo pulled her even closer, crushing her against his strong chest and stroking her hair with one hand while rubbing her back with the other. He held her in silence for several moments as she sobbed into his shirt and he fought back the tears of his own that he could feel creeping into the back of his eyes.

"Liberty is still so little," he heard her mumble against the fabric of his shirt. "If something were to take you from us, she would never remember you…"

Theo tightened his arms around her petite, quaking body and rested his head atop hers. "And when I *do* return, victorious and unscathed, she will be so proud to know what her father was willing to sacrifice to protect her and her mother."

Evie slowly looked up to meet his gaze, wiping away at the tears that continued to roll down her cheeks. "Why must you always have to be the hero?" she asked weakly.

"Because no one else will."

A long, drawn out sigh escaped Evie's lips as she dropped her head back onto his chest. "You could get yourself killed, thinking like that. But perhaps that is why I fell in love with you…"

The traces of a lopsided grin tugged at Theo's mouth as he pressed a long kiss to her lips and continued to hold her close. He never wanted to let her go. He never wanted their embraces to end.

She returned his embrace by tightly wrapping her arms around his waist, savoring in his touch and his scent as if she feared it was last chance that she would have to do so. She loathed the idea of him leaving on another suicide mission, but the longer she sat in his arms, the more she realized how crucial it was to end the war once and for all. If his leaving now meant he would never have to take up arms in their defense again, then it was worth it.

"I cannot leave for Virginia knowing you are upset," he told her gently. "I need you to trust that I will do everything in my power to return to you."

Evie sniffled before mumbling, "I trust you with my life. It is every other soldier on the battlefield whom I resent."

"This is hardly my first battle. You know I have always been a fighter."

Evie nodded with a humorless chuckle. "That, you have. You have always tried to do what is good and right. And…if you believe that you truly must go, then I will support you. Go and bring us our final victory, knowing Liberty and I will be waiting here for you when you return, counting the moments until we can hold you in our arms again."

Theo's sideways smirk widened ever so slightly as he took her face in his hands again, pulling her forward until her lips crashed into his in another passionate, feverish kiss that neither wanted to end.

"I love you," he breathed against her skin.

"I know," she returned with a smirk of her own as she tangled her fingers in his hair. "Just promise me one thing before you must depart."

"Anything."

Evie pressed another kiss to his lips before capturing his chin in her hand forcing him to look in her eyes. Her words rolled off of her tongue like silk as she narrowed her eyes and whispered, *"Give them Hell."*

***

The blue and white uniform coat was heavy with memories Theo would rather forget as he pulled it from the trunk under the bed and shrugged it over his shoulders. It smelled of dust and stale cotton, having sat untouched and undisturbed for nearly five years. After shrugging into the coat, Theo stood before the mirror in the master bedroom and took a moment to stare at the man in the reflection; he looked like a stranger wearing this uniform for the first time after so many years, but he did not look as frightened and guileless as the boy who wore it before him. This was not new territory by any means—he knew what to expect of the battlefield, of the enemy, of the Commander. But that did little to comfort the storm of anxiety raging within him. It had been so much easier to leave the last time, but now, he had so much more tying him to home that the thought of being away from his wife and daughter for even a day made his heart ache.

His eyes trailed from the pensive expression on his face, down to the uniform that cloaked him, taking in the sight of the multitude of bullet holes and slashes in the fabric of the coat that Evie had mended years before. He grazed his fingers across the stitches that held together the tear over his heart, and then the hole over his right side. They had been stitched closed with meticulous precision, and the dried blood had been scrubbed away, but he could still remember the ordeal that had nearly killed him like it was yesterday.

After straightening out the lapels of his coat and brushing off the remaining dust, Theo tied his hair back from his face with a black ribbon and picked up the small wooden bowl sitting on the vanity nearby. The bowl contained a mixture of clay and powdered red paint, into which he dug three fingers before swiping them down each of his cheeks, leaving behind three distinctive and menacing crimson lines that ran from under his eyes and down to his jaw.

His maternal uncle, Tehwehron, had warn such warpaint when they first met the previous year, and now it was Theo's turn to do the same. He *was* going to war, after all. Once the paint had dried to his skin, Theo took his father's sword and pistol from the trunk—which had also not seen the light of day for some time—and slid them both into his belt. The weight they added to his body was somehow both foreign and familiar, both daunting and comforting.

Theo emerged from the bedroom after ensuring he had everything he needed for battle, and he found Evie and Libby, Johanna, Emma and Jacob, and Lafayette waiting for him in the front room of the house as he closed the bedroom door behind him.

"How does it feel to wear the uniform again, soldier?" Jacob asked with a smirk that masked his worry.

Theo shrugged and looked down to inspect his uniform again. "Better than I am sure it felt for you to wear a Redcoat uniform."

"Are you nervous to return to the battlefield?" Johanna asked, slightly startled by the jarring contrast between the blood red warpaint and Theo's tanned skin.

Theo shook his head. "Only nervous to be away from home."

Lafayette clapped him on the back. "Have no fear, *mon ami*. I will do everything in my power to ensure we both return home to our families when this is over."

Theo looked across the front room to see Evie hovering near the front door, averting her eyes to the floor anxiously as she held Liberty in her arms. Theo quickly closed the distance between them with outstretched arms, his heavy uniform boots pounding across the floor as he went.

"Well?" he asked his wife, coaxing her to look up at him. "How do I look?"

"Like a warrior," Evie murmured with a tinge of a smirk, though fear and sadness were visible in her eyes. "Tehwehron would be proud."

"As would your father," Johanna added, dabbing at the corners of her eyes with a handkerchief, "And your mother."

Theo grinned wistfully at his stepmother over his shoulder before she quickly scuttled across the floor to throw her arms around his neck.

"You will always be my mother," he whispered as she buried her face in his chest.

"And I am so proud to call you my son," Johanna returned between muffled sobs. "Promise me you will return to us in one piece this time."

"You have my word."

Theo turned back to face Evie and the baby, feeling his chest tighten as he looked down into their eyes and they stared expectantly back at him, pleading wordlessly for him to stay. Theo cleared his throat while fighting back the urge to tear up himself—he had shed far too many years over the past months. Now was not the time for tears. Now was the time for strength and bravery, and he plastered a confident grin upon his face as he bent down to look Liberty in the eye. She immediately tried to reach out for him and wiggle out of her mother's grasp, and Theo took her in his arms before pressing a kiss to her forehead. He then took the last of the paint that remained on his fingers and drew three small lines down both of her tanned and chubby cheeks.

"Protect the homestead while I am away, little warrior," he whispered to her gently. "Take care of your mother and grandmother for me. I will be back before you know it."

A tearful whimper escaped Evie's throat as she squeezed her eyes shut and wrapped her arms around both Theo and the baby, holding them tightly against her small body. "Please be safe, my love," she told him before pressing a tender and passionate kiss to his lips. "And promise me you will return."

Theo leaned down to kiss her again before reluctantly placing Liberty back in her arms. Once his hands were freed, he placed them on each of Evie's cheeks and pressed his forehead to hers.

"To you, I will always return."

***

"We estimate to have over sixteen thousand allied troops between the Americans and the French in Yorktown," Lafayette stated with his chest puffed with pride. "Our spies tell us that the British have…maybe six thousand."

Theo let out a low whistle and adjusted his grip on the reigns of his horse as he followed Lafayette down the road that led them south from Massachusetts. It had been nearly a week and a half since they had set off from Division Point, and they were only just now reaching the northern borders of Virginia.

"And Cornwallis still intends to fight with those odds?"

Lafayette shrugged with a smirk. "Lord Cornwallis is a foolishly ambitious man, and it has served him well…until now. He does not know when to surrender. But we will surely give him good reason soon enough."

"You sound rather confident that this will be the final battle of the war, Lafayette."

"Because I am confident. We will have Cornwallis outmanned and outgunned, surrounded on all sides with nowhere to escape. He will realize he is outmatched and surrender, I am sure of it."

"If you and Washington are so sure of yourselves, why did he insist you travel all the way to Massachusetts to recruit me? Surely I will make little difference in the outcome if your numbers are true."

Lafayette shrugged again. "That is something you will have to ask of the Commander. He was adamant that you be present for the endgame."

"The *endgame*," Theo repeated with a sigh. "I hope your words are true. Enough blood has been shed, and enough mothers have lost their babies to enemy bullets."

"*Oui*. And when my work is done in America, I will be able to return to France and see her revolution come to fruition just as it has here."

"Lafayette…may I ask you something?"

"Ask away, *sergent*."

"Do you think things will really change for the better when the colonies are freed? Or will the rich remain rich and the poor remain poor? Will the downtrodden remain downtrodden? Will the prejudiced continue to hate? Will a flag and government of our own really unite us as one?"

"That is an intriguing question you pose, sir. But the only answer I can offer is this: Washington and the other founders of this revolution believe in something called *democracy*, something called a *republic*. A society by which supreme power is held by the people and their elected representatives, who work together to elect a leader that embodies the values they seek to perpetuate. I believe Washington could be that man, but he is yet undecided if he will take on such a role when the time comes to assemble an independent American government. If justice, equality, and liberty is what you seek, then a republic is where you can find such things. My hope is that once the American republic is established, a French republic, free from nobles, aristocrats, and monarchs, may soon join her in the ranks of the free."

"I read about this concept of a republic once, long ago, before I joined the Continentals. Thomas Paine, Voltaire, Montesquieu, and Rousseau. I have read their writings many times over the years, and I have always admired such a vision. But I did not think it possible, given how ambitious and selfish powerful men can be."

"That is why it is up to the people to choose their leaders wisely."

"When you say people, I have a feeling you mean, *landed white men*."

Lafayette cleared his throat uncomfortably and began to stumble over his words. "Well...ah...that has been the tradition. But we are living during a time of great change. Who knows what is possible?"

***

It was the nineteenth of September when Theo and Lafayette finally reached the outskirts of the allied French and American encampment between Yorktown and Williamsburg. Upon reaching the camp, they were greeted warmly by a small group of French cavalries who escorted them deeper into the camp, past the seemingly endless columns of infantrymen running drills, cleaning cannons, and loading muskets, until they reached a large collection of tents interspersed between groups of conversing officers.

Theo took a deep breath as they entered the camp and inhaled the scent of gunpowder and sweat, a distinctive smell of war he had never truly forgotten, and which brought him immediately back to his previous enlistment as if it had ended only the day before. He could not say that he was elated to be back in a Continental encampment, but it felt strangely comforting to hear the sounds and see the sights of a life he thought he had left behind long ago. He had never seen so many soldiers gathered together in one camp before, and the sheer number of men that had agreed to take part in this battle put the army's numbers from four years ago to shame.

Upon hearing the beating of horse hooves on the earth, the sea of soldiers quickly parted to allow Lafayette, Theo, and their escort access to the center grounds of the camp. Theo and Lafayette wasted no time penning up their horses and meandering through the crowded camp until they reached the crest of a hill where the Commander's quarters were located. Washington was standing just outside his tent, conversing with a large man in a French uniform coat emblazoned with the trappings of a General, but he paused when he caught sight of Lafayette and Theo trudging up the hill.

"Lafayette," Washington greeted with a smirk, "I see your journey was a resounding success."

"*Oui*, Commander, Sergeant Cunningham has graciously agreed to join us for the final battle."

Washington bowed his head ever so slightly in Theo's direction, his posture rigid and his voice tight, as if he was somewhat nervous now that Theo had arrived but didn't care to show it.

"Sergeant Cunningham. It is so wonderful to see you back in uniform after such a long hiatus."

"Commander," Theo returned curtly, also bowing his head.

The Commander looked as if he had aged ten years over the last five, the pressure of leading a country to independence having taken a great toll upon him. His hair was nearly completely gray, and his face pallid, but he retained the same air of regality and prestige that he had the last time they had spoken.

Washington gestured to the French General with whom he had previously been conversing. "Lafayette, you and General Rochambeau are well aquatinted, but I would like to introduce Sergeant Cunningham to General Jean-Baptiste Donatien de Vimeur, comte de Rochambeau. He will be commanding the French forces here in Yorktown."

Theo bowed his head again. "General, a pleasure to make your acquaintance."

Rochambeau was a tall and rotund man, perhaps in his fifties, with a powdered wig reminiscent of Lafayette's, but a much less friendly disposition. The General's expression soured almost immediately upon Theo's arrival at the top of the hill, and he greeted him with a curt nod of his head. He then looked to Washington and mumbled, "Is this that Indian boy you had mentioned? Can he really be trusted as a *Sergeant*?"

Theo's eyes narrowed into aggravated slits, but instead of barking back, he bit down on his tongue and passed both Lafayette and Washington an unamused glare. Washington cleared his throat uncomfortably and told the General, "Sergeant Cunningham is one of my most trusted officers. He is an excellent strategist and an even better leader. That is why I asked him to join us for the siege."

"Siege?" Theo repeated with a raised brow.

"Yes. A siege." Washington pointed at the horizon on the other side of the hill, where a small fortification had been erected against the bank of the York River. "Cornwallis has sequestered himself and his troops within that fortification, but he made the fatal mistake of pressing his back up against the river. We have already surrounded his fortification, and he has no means of escape by land or sea. We merely need to lay siege to the fort until he surrenders."

"And I suppose you have already detailed a course of action?" Theo asked as he folded his hands behind his back.

Washington nodded his head and motioned for Theo, Lafayette, and Rochambeau to follow him into his tent. Inside, Theo was introduced to Major Generals Benjamin Lincoln and Baron von Steuben. All of the men gathered around a table in the center of the tent, across which a large parchment map detailing the landscape of the area had been laid.

Theo was quite surprised that Washington so willingly invited him into a meeting among Generals, considering both his rank and that he had just arrived after having been absent for so long, but the Commander ordered him to join the gathering as if no time had passed from the last time they had spoken. It was as if nothing had changed, nothing had transpired, and no one had been betrayed.

"De Grasse has anchored his flagship in the York River near Gloucester Point, where he will halt any and all seaward advances by the British," Washington explained as he ran his finger across the map. "Rochambeau will command the French infantry and cavalry, while Lafayette, Lincoln, von Steuben, and myself will command the American regiments. The plan is to encircle Yorktown and bombard it with heavy siege guns from De Grasse's ships. We will dig trenches to approach Cornwallis' fortifications and mount new artillery batteries. The defenses of Yorktown extend in a circle with seven redoubts and six artillery batteries connected by trenches, and Gloucester is protected by another small line of trenches. We may have to storm the strong points of the defenses, but our hope is that the British will be drawn out of the fort in order to halt the digging of our trenches, which gives us the opportunity to take their fortification when they have become distracted. With his fortification destroyed and his army reduced to pittance, Cornwallis will have no choice but to surrender to us. And that is when negotiations for peace can finally begin."

Theo listened intently to Washington's plan, nodding along and following the map with his eyes. Based upon the sheer difference in numbers and guns between the two sides, he could see little chance for this plan to fail. Siege warfare ended almost exclusively in favor of the attackers, and Cornwallis had sealed his fate when he holed himself up against the riverbank with no other means of escape now that French ships had taken residence there. For the first time in a long while, Theo had faith in the Commander standing before him.

After explaining the battle plan in detail once more, Washington dismissed his Generals to get some rest, leaving himself and Theo alone in the tent. A heavy silence fell between them as Theo looked over the map on his own and Washington began to anxiously pace back and forth past the table.

"I want to thank you for returning to the army," Washington eventually said, his voice uncharacteristically quiet. "I am sure it was not an easy decision for you to make, given our…history."

"I did not do it for you, Commander," Theo stated without looking up from the map. "I am simply here to finish what the Crown started, and to ensure my family has a safe place to call home. When the siege is finished, I am returning home immediately."

Washington nodded tightly. "I understand. I would do the same if I could."

Theo suddenly looked up and crossed his arms over his chest. "Why me?"

"Pardon me?"

"Of all the men in the colonies, why did you take the time to track me down and drag me back to help you with your siege?"

Washington sighed again and motioned for Theo to follow him back out of the tent, where they stood at the very crest of the hill and looked down upon the expanse of empty field that sat separated their encampment from Cornwallis' fortifications. In the distance, Theo could make out a few lines of cannons and columns of tiny, red figures marching in formation within the fort, no doubt preparing for their inevitable defeat.

"I was not content with the terms under which we last parted ways, if I must be honest," the Commander said as he looked out over the Virginia countryside below. "I have been haunted by what was said and done between us, by the unfortunate death of that friend of yours—"

"Elijah," Theo cut in harshly. "His name was Elijah Cutler."

"Elijah. Yes, he was a good soldier. A good man. His death was an unnecessary tragedy."

"As was the demise of the Iroquois villages you ordered to be destroyed."

"...Villages?" Washington mumbled in confusion.

Theo straightened his shoulders as a deep frown settled upon his face. "I have not forgotten what happened in the Watchung Mountains, nor am I naive to what you did to *Atsa'któntie* twenty-one years ago."

Washington still appeared perplexed as he stared Theo down. "I am unfamiliar with a place called *Atsa'któntie*."

"I would not expect you to remember. You did not see them as people, but rather an inconvenience in need of disposal. Twenty-one years ago, you waltzed into *Atsa'któntie* and gave its people rations and supplies infested with smallpox. The village was nearly destroyed, and my mother was among the dead."

Washington stared at him with an expression that bespoke both total shock and unbridled shame. The name of the village meant nothing to him, but he remembered delivering supplies to an allied native village many years ago as the Seven Years War was drawing to a close. The Commander hung his head and rubbed his forehead, his face tight with regret.

"I...I hadn't any clue that the supplies were contaminated, Sergeant Cunningham. You must believe me. I was merely given orders from my commander to deliver a convoy to our allies. If I had known of the pox, I never would have gone—"

Theo cut him off with an enraged growl. "Do you really expect me to believe that you were unaware of the sickness that convoy contained, especially after you so casually ordered the execution of the natives in the mountains?"

Washington sighed heavily, his eyes glazing over in sorrow as a haunted look came upon his face. He remembered the day the convoy rolled past the *Atsa'któntie* palisade like it was yesterday, but he hadn't any clue until this moment what had transpired after he left the village for good.

"I am so sorry, Theo. Your father was one of my closest friends, and if I had realized what our commander had planned, or that your mother called that village home, I would have never let those convoys reach their destination. But I was young and foolish. I did what I was ordered to do…"

Theo nearly snorted in derision, but instead bit his tongue once again. He may have been able to put aside his distaste for the man long enough to fight under his command one last time, but he was not yet ready to forgive him. "I did not come here to hear your apologies, Commander. I came to end this bloody war."

Washington held up his hands in a gesture of peace. "Fair enough. I understand. It is too soon for a reconciliation. In that case, I suppose I should give you your orders…and your promotion."

Theo nearly choked on his tongue. "Promotion?"

"Yes. I hereby promote you from Sergeant Cunningham, to *Captain* Cunningham."

"But…why?"

"I need you to lead a battalion of infantry men behind the trenches. Your men will defend our engineers as they dig the trenches and run off any Redcoats that try to stand in our way."

"Commander, I surely do not deserve such a distinction—"

Washington chuckled under his breath and shook his head. "This is not about who deserves what rank. This is about doing everything in our power to protect what is ours." He then gestured to the open field beginning at the base if the hill with an open palm. "This battlefield is the last thing standing between us and our freedom."

Theo followed his line of vision down to the battlefield and the fortifications behind it. As a light breeze blew through to rustle his hair and uniform, a strange sense of peace settled over him. This was it. The end was finally coming.

"Then we will take it with blood, fire, fearlessness, and everything else we have."

Washington nodded in agreement, the slightest of smirks tugging at his lips. "The Crown chose the wrong people to rule, no?"

Theo cocked his head to the side, feeling his own smirk beginning to form as he looked down from the crest of the hill. "No," he murmured, "they merely chose the wrong voices to *silence*."

Chapter 23

Blood, Fire, and Fearlessness

October 1781

Theo released a shallow breath through his nose, tightening his grip on the reigns of his trusty steed, Artemis, as he guided her to trot back and forth across the length of the firing line. It was the middle of October, and a chilly breeze blew through to tousle the stray locks of hair that had fallen into his face. Days before, he had received word from Washington that Cornwallis ordered his men to abandon the outer works of their fortifications and to retreat further inward. Almost immediately, Washington gave the command to his infantrymen to scramble forward and occupy the deserted areas, and that is where they began their entrenchments, within one hundred yards of Cornwallis' main fortifications on the bank of the York River.

The large open field before the fortified village of Yorktown became a sea of liberators, with lines of infantry and cavalry interspersed around the winding trenches and artillery batteries in order to block all means of escape for the British. Frenchmen and Americans fought, dug, and defended side by side, with no regard for the differences in their flags, their faiths, nor their native tongues. It mattered little that they hailed from different lands; in Yorktown, they were fighting under one banner, as one army, with one purpose—to forge a path toward freedom.

As ordered, Theo led a small battalion of bayonet-wielding infantrymen, positioned in a line behind fresh trenches as the diggers worked tirelessly to extend the entrenchments forward. From the first day of October onward, American batteries mounted in the outer works pounded Yorktown, earning a half-hearted return fire from the British guns within. The siege quickly became a wild, fast-paced dance between the two armies, much more chaotic and disorienting than any open-field battle in which Theo had participated before. In addition to dodging the heavy exchanges of cannon fire flying just over his head, he was also made to orchestrate the defense of the trenches from various British detachments that occasionally slithered out of the fort, guns blazing in an attempt to halt the progress of the diggers.

Dozens of Tory men had already been killed by artillery fire or violent melee clashes outside of abandoned and captured redoubts, and the smell of blood and gunpowder hung heavy in the air amidst the smoke clouds and downpours of dirt that fell from the sky every time a cannonball hit its target. The sound of cannon fire and musket balls soaring through the sky was much louder than Theo had remembered, rattling his brain inside his head and sending his heart aflutter with a fear he didn't dare let show. A single stray bullet from either side could do him in, and his sitting astride his horse left him a much easier target than those digging or defending the trenches at his feet.

Blood, fire, and fearlessness. Those were the words that he repeated in his head over and over to calm his frazzled nerves when he was not calling out for another volley of musket shot to be released upon an approaching British detachment. Those were the things that would win this God-forsaken war. Without them, they were hopeless. The odds had been against them from the beginning; the revolution had begun as a coalition of disgruntled farmers wielding pitchforks and rioting in the streets, demanding justice and independence from the largest and most powerful empire in the world. And now, nearly seven years later, those farmers had become soldiers, and they were toe-to-toe with that empire's unconquerable army on the battlefield once again—and they were *winning*. His Majesty's elite fighting force had been reduced to shambles, and they hid within the confines of their Yorktown fortifications like cowardly dogs with their tails tucked between their legs while the Americans relentlessly barraged them from the outside with everything they had.

"On my mark!" Theo called out, trotting down the length of his firing line and raising his arm in the air. Looking over their heads and across the trench, he could clearly see the main fortifications in the center of Yorktown, much of which had been reduced to rubble and ash after two weeks of artillery fire. The protective barriers around the village were far from a brick and mortar fort, but rather scattered barricades of wood, stone, and whatever else Cornwallis' haggard army could scrape together. Hunkering down in the village was a last ditch effort to preserve what little fight the British had left in them, and with each successive capture of a segment of the fortifications, Cornwallis retreated even further inward, trapped with his back against the river and with no means of escape as cannon fire continued to rain down upon his head.

Theo waited until a detachment of twenty or so Redcoats scattered out of the nearest redoubt like ants and began to move toward their segment of the trenches, squinting his eyes to stare into the sun ahead. He held his arm in the air with bated breath, waiting patiently until the detachment scuttled within range of his men's guns. Once a majority of the battalion was within range and forming a firing line of their own, he lowered his arm and strongly bellowed *"Fire!"* over the cacophonous sounds of gunshots, cannon fire, and wounded howls filling the air.

Three-fourths of the detachment on the other side of the trench fell after the shots rang out, the remaining scattering to the wind in an attempt to escape the growing chaos. The longer the siege drug on, the easier it became to frighten the Redcoats away before even putting a shot into them. Of those Redcoats that had not yet been killed by allied American and French combat, fewer and fewer were willing to venture outside of the fortifications to meet their enemies in the open field. And those that did emerge were either killed or quickly chose to flee for their lives, abandoning both the battle and their commander in the process.

Theo could not help but feel a newfound confidence swell in his chest as he watched the remains of the British detachment flee, and while his men reloaded their muskets, he briefly thought back to the last things he had said to the men under his command, words he wished someone had told him long ago during his first battle.

"We cannot go home until the last shot has been fired. Do not relent until you see their white flag waving, and do not forget why you joined this fight. We are not just fighting for our freedom; we are fighting for our lives, for our families, for our futures. The rest of our lives depend upon the choices we make right now on this battlefield. We have fought too long and too hard not to be victorious today. We did not come this far to only come this far. They have doubted us from the beginning, called us peasants, servants, and subjects, but we are no one's subjects. We are our own people, an American people, and His Majesty and all else who follow him will see that today. If they want our freedom, they'll have to come and take it!"

The traces of a smirk touched Theo's lips as he recalled those words, but he was suddenly pulled from his thoughts by the sound of horse hooves pounding the earth just behind him. Looking over his shoulder, he was greeted with the sight of Commander Washington riding on horseback toward the trenches, emerging from behind clouds of smoke with his sword in hand. Washington maneuvered his horse between the lines of infantrymen and skidded to a stop on Theo's right, his chest heaving in exhaustion. The Commander's splendid uniform coat was smudged with gun powder and dirt, and much of his greying hair had fallen into his face under his hat. Beads of sweat gathered upon his brow as his and Theo's gazes met, and they attempted to converse over the sounds of battle raging around them.

"What news?" Theo hollered with a salute, though they were barely over a yard apart.

Washington took of his hat and ran a hand through his hair, sighing. "We have made excellent progress with the trenches and successfully fought off every attempt by the British to slow us down. But in order to extend the trenches to the river, we must take two more redoubts. I have ordered Hamilton and de Deux-Ponts to lay siege to them with a bayonet charge. If all goes well, we shall have those redoubts incorporated into our system of strongpoints by the morning. And then we will be that much closer to taking Yorktown for ourselves."

Theo nodded in satisfaction. "I will have my men continue to dig toward the river, then."

"Very well. You have led your men bravely thus far, and I trust you will do the same until the end."

"And when is the end, Commander? How long do you expect Cornwallis to hide within his fortifications like a coward while his men fight his battle for him?"

Washington scoffed indignantly. "He cannot hold out much longer. He has been hiding away for two weeks already, but he is running out of men and ammunition. I estimate that he will surrender within the month."

"Cornwallis does not strike me as the surrendering type."

"He will be, soon enough. We will give him little other choice once our trenches reach the river and we close the distance to the main fortifications. I can see the light at the end of this long and bloody tunnel, Captain Cunningham. We are so close to victory that I can *taste* it."

Theo smirked and raised his arm once again to order his infantrymen to fire a volley at another approaching British detachment. He and Washington shared a brief look of agreement and bid each other goodbye with a salute before the Commander rode off, disappearing into the clouds of smoke once again in order to spread the news to the other officers.

Cornwallis had already sealed his fate when he trapped himself in the confines of Yorktown, but that would not stop the Patriots from giving him one last show of their strength. They were no longer colonists; they were Americans now, and Yorktown would be the site of the final display of what it meant to fight like an American—with blood, fire, and fearlessness.

***

Just as the Commander had predicted, the allied forces under Hamilton and de Deux-Ponts were able to capture two more redoubts and incorporate them into the growing trench system by the next morning, giving the Patriots unhindered access across the field and up to the York River while further diminishing any chance for Cornwallis' men to escape. With the French and the Americans closing in on Yorktown from all sides, it was expected that Cornwallis would put an end to the madness by admitting defeat and waving his white flag—he was surrounded, outgunned, and outnumbered two to one—but two and a half weeks into the siege, he remained steadfast and refused to emerge from his hiding place in the annals of the fortified village. Instead of surrendering, he continued to send what little men he had left out onto the field in small detachments with the hopes of gradually cutting away at the thousands of Patriots awaiting outside the fort, only to have them quickly pushed back by both artillery fire and frenzied bayonet rushes.

Lord Charles Cornwallis was nothing if not a stubborn and prideful man, refusing to accept that he had been bested on the battlefield by a ragtag army of colonists, many of whom had never seen battle until now. He could not return to London empty handed—His Majesty would surely have his head. And he did not understand what had gone *wrong*. Just six and a half years ago, England's military was an unbeatable force, able to intimidate and conquer all who stood in their way, including those rowdy colonists who suddenly craved a foolish taste of independence.

In the early stages of the war, the Patriots were clearly in over their head in every way possible, and Washington had lost nearly every battle in which he had taken part. But now, his "army" of commoners had become just that, an *army*, and they were fighting with far more ferocity than any Loyalist could have anticipated. They fought as if they had everything to lose and were fighting for their very lives; and that unwavering fortitude had proven to be far more effective in guerrilla-style warfare than the British could ever hope to match.

Rather than fighting their oppressors on their terms, the Patriots created their own style of battle, one that was much more suited to the rugged American wilderness than traditional European battle tactics. Rather than relying solely on highly disciplined regiments organized meticulously in firing lines, the Americans did what they knew best. They took to the battlefield as both one unit and as individuals, taking on each Redcoat with a ferocious mettle that could only be forged in the heart of a colonist who longed to be a citizen. That mettle had gotten them this far, surrounding the last British stronghold and waiting patiently for the impending surrender, and it would take them through until the last shot was fired.

But Cornwallis was not done quite yet. On the sixteenth day of October, the cowardly Commander chose once again to remain hidden behind his fortifications while he sent a force of three hundred and fifty men out onto the battlefield in one last attempt to fight off the sea of Patriots surrounding him. This was the largest group of Redcoats that had emerged from Yorktown together, and upon seeing them charge toward the trenches, Theo felt his heart leap into his throat.

Immediately, he ordered the men under his command to emerge from behind the trenches and charge forward to meet the approaching Redcoats before they could reach the entrenchments. The forward-most American batteries were quickly overrun by the British detachment, forcing Theo to order his men and all those around him to make ready for hand to hand combat in order to drive them back toward Yorktown.

Chaos quickly erupted in a frenzied storm of gunfire and smoke, and the sound of metal clashing against metal filled the air amidst the hellish and blood-curdling battle cries emitted by both sides. Taking his sword from the sheath on his belt, Theo kicked Artemis into a trot and guided her to leap over the trench line just as the first Redcoats had begun to overrun it. He charged forward at full speed into the sea of red and ordered his men to do the same behind him, slashing his sword with all his might at any and all men in red uniforms that fell in his path.

The chaos of the new melee quickly filled his ears and sent his heart pounding in his chest as he slashed his father's sword across the chest of a Redcoat that had charged straight at him with a loaded musket in hand, dropping the man with a fatal gash in his abdomen just before he stuck his bayonet into Artemis' chest. The air became heavy once again with the smell of blood and gunpowder, and he could hear the batteries behind him making haste to reload their cannons in order to fire into the swarm before them.

But Theo froze where he stood, sword raised, as the world seemed to turn around him, and his eyes landed on the form of one British officer on horseback charging wildly amongst the other British infantrymen. He was perhaps fifty yards ahead, turned slightly away as he pulled a pistol from his belt and began shooting at every Patriot he saw, but Theo could see his face quite clearly through the smoky haze that had filled the air. He appeared to be in his mid-thirties, with long, sandy-blonde hair flowing wildly out from underneath his tricorn hat, and a large and unmistakable scar running down his left cheekbone. As the officer rode closer whilst reloading his pistol, their eyes briefly met—golden brown locked against steely grey. And then they both froze in unison, twenty yards apart as swords and guns continued to clash all around them.

The officer's face immediately tightened before souring into a devilish snarl when his and Theo's gazes met, and Theo felt every nerve in his body begin to fire, the hairs on the back of his neck rising as a cold chill swept across his flesh. He was not staring into the eyes of just any British officer, he was staring into the eyes of a Captain, *Captain Silas Porter*. There was no mistaking it; Theo would know that scar and those cold, piercing eyes anywhere. They were all he saw both times he had been in the man's clutches, bound and tortured for days on end, and they were the eyes of the man that had hurt Evie so terribly over the years that she had become afraid to let herself be loved.

But how could that be? Silas Porter was dead! He had been dead for nearly three years. Theo remembered distantly plunging the knife into Silas' abdomen, and watching Evie twist it with all of her might before the man began to bleed out. They had killed him together and left him to die in the wilderness before fleeing back to Division Point. So how was he here, in Yorktown, leading the last desperate charge of Cornwallis' men? It did not seem possible, and for a moment Theo thought he was mistaken, but the way the man's snarl deepened the moment their eyes met across the fray told him everything he needed to know. He was, in fact, staring into the eyes of Silas Porter. But he would be damned if he let him leave this battle alive once again.

After staring Theo down for several tense moments, Silas' lips curled back in a hateful snarl that bespoke an unwavering desire for bloodshed and vengeance, and the officer suddenly leapt into action and kicked his horse into a sprint. Turing around, Silas bolted toward the way from which he had come in a cowardly and desperate attempt to flee back to the safety of the main fortifications, while the rest of his men charged forward in the opposite direction. Theo immediately took off after him, ordering his men to continue fighting before kicking Artemis into a gallop to charge toward Yorktown.

Silas continuously looked over his shoulder as he fled toward the remaining British redoubts, shooting off his pistol in Theo's general direction without ever successfully finding his target. Theo ducked his head and hugged his body lowly against Artemis' back to narrowly dodge the bullet as he gave chase, wincing when he felt it rush just over his head. He quickly gained several yards on the fleeing Captain, getting within less than ten feet of his horse, and they were within fifty yards of the fortifications before he made the sudden decision to release his hold on Artemis' reins and stand in her stirrups before leaping forward off of her back.

Silas did not see it coming, and he let out a startled wail when he felt Theo's body slam into him from behind. Theo wrapped his arms tightly around Silas' waist and let the weight of his body and the momentum of his jump pull them both sideways off of the horse's back; they hit the hard ground together, tumbling in a tangle of arms and legs several yards across the battlefield before rolling to a painful stop. The rest of the chaos continued on around them, unaware and unbothered by their collision. Artemis and Silas' horse continued to gallop aimlessly around them, disoriented and confused now that they had both lost their riders in the smoky haze.

They both laid on their backs in the dirt for several moments, stunned by the harsh impact of the fall and the wind being knocked from their lungs. Theo blinked several times and hissed at the dull ache that began to throb in his side, and he rolled over onto his stomach before rising to his feet and dusting himself off. Silas slowly did the same until they were both standing just ten feet apart, staring each other down with icy gazes that could freeze over Hell.

"I must admit that I did not expect to see you here," Silas snarled between heaving breaths as he brushed the dirt from his uniform and held a hand to his side, the side where Theo recalled plunging a knife into him.

"I could say the same of you," Theo growled back, his body immediately tensing into a defensive stance as he placed a hand on the pommel of the sword he had placed back in his belt.

Silas' hand also lingered on the sword in his own belt. Simultaneously, they both began to pace in predatory circles around one another, their eyes never leaving each other as they tried to size each other up.

Silas shrugged his shoulders and tilted his head to the side with a cocky smirk. "I told you already, boy, you cannot defeat me."

"I killed you," Theo hissed, his mind racing in confusion as his heart began to pound once again. "I put the knife into your body, I watched your eyes close, I watched you die! How are you here?"

Silas chuckled darkly. "I was never dead, you imbecile! Just after you fled with my wife, my men found me and carried me back to Dumpling Rock. I nearly succumbed to my injuries, but I pulled through."

Theo's frown deepened into a scowl. "If you have been alive all this time, why did you not immediately come back for us? You knew exactly where to find us…"

Silas chuckled again and took another predatory step in Theo's direction. "Oh, that will come soon enough. So long as the war continued on, I would be distracted and unable to devote my full attention to keeping my wife where she belongs. No, I planned to wait until the war was won before returning to that cesspool you call a village to collect what is mine. Then, I would make you watch as I destroyed everything you ever loved!"

Theo's scowl slowly morphed into a smirk. "That is a wonderful plan, Silas, but you are too late. Evie does not belong to you anymore."

Silas' arrogant smirk faltered momentarily. "What?"

Theo raised his left hand into the air, the golden wedding band upon his ring finger glinting in the late afternoon sunlight. "She is my wife now. And the mother of my child."

Silas' steely eyes widened in shock and rage as his grip upon the handle of his sword tightened. "You think you can claim what his mine?" he hissed through clenched teeth. "How dare you! You are a half breed Patriot dog! And today I will kill you like a dog!"

"I have surrendered to you twice before, Silas. I will not do it again."

Silas pulled his sword from its sheath with a furious growl, immediately charging forward with his face pinched into a look of madness. "Bold words for a man about to bleed out at my feet!"

Theo unsheathed his own sword in an instant and threw it up in front of his face to block Silas' incoming strike, the clash of steel against steel echoing amongst the other deafening sounds of battle.

"Hold a moment!" Theo suddenly cried out with a grunt as he pushed Silas back. "It does not have to end like this…"

Silas cackled maniacally and swung at Theo's head once more. "Oh, I think it does. You nearly *killed* me!"

Theo parried Silas' next attack and once again forced him to stumble back, feeling a newfound rage boil just under his skin as he stared into the man's seething gaze. It was the gaze of a madman, someone who had lost all reason long ago and now craved only the blood of those who had crossed him.

"Consider us even, then," he hissed back, landing a quick strike of his own on Silas' thigh as he attempted to spin out of his reach.

Silas let out an agonized howl as the blade sliced through his trousers and the flesh of his thigh, and his knees buckled underneath him. He did not remember this so-called half breed being quite so skilled with a sword the last time they had dueled.

"We will not be even until I deliver your head on a platter to Lord Cornwallis myself!" Silas growled through clenched teeth as he stumbled forward with his sword raised, hacking downward with a mad and mighty roar.

"I have a family to return to," Theo quipped as he easily ducked out of the way, holding up his left hand once more so Silas could gaze upon his wedding band once again. It was clear that Silas was distracted and disoriented by his own growing anger, and the more enraged he became, the less polished and precise his swordsmanship became. "I suppose you would not know what that is like, would you, Silas? Your wife left you for dead and married another man, and your only son is...well, *dead*."

"Shut your gob, you useless shite!" Silas snarled ferociously, his face turning just as red as his uniform coat. He attempted yet another sloppy downward cleave with his blade, but Theo was once again able to parry his attack and slip out of his reach.

"When will you learn that you cannot so easily bend everyone to your will? Perhaps that stubbornness is why Evie came willingly to me and *ran* from you!"

Before Silas could gather himself enough to deliver another pitiful swing with his sword, Theo locked his sword against his and pushed him backwards with all of his might. Silas stumbled back several steps before tripping over the body of a fallen solider, landing flat on his back in the mud as his sword fell just out of his reach. Theo leapt upon him before he could even blink, straddling his waist and holding his sword to the Captain's throat. Silas stared up at him with mouth agape and eyes wide in shock, completely flabbergasted as to how he had so quickly been taken to the ground by the likes of *him*.

"It's over, Silas," Theo told him calmly, bending his head down such that their faces were mere inches apart. Silas struggled under his hold, but Theo held the blade closer to the flesh of his throat until his squirming ceased. "You've been beaten. Surrender now, and I will consider sparing you."

Silas let out an enraged growl before spitting upward into Theo's face. "It will be a cold day in Hell before I surrender to a rebel mongrel!"

Theo wiped the saliva from his face with the back of his hand before throwing his fist against Silas' jaw. He no longer desired to play any games. The man had to die. He was too prideful to surrender, and too dangerous to leave alive.

"Tell me something, Captain," he murmured snidely as Silas's head bashed against the hard ground. "Do you believe in God?"

Silas sneered up at him with a mouthful of blood dribbling from the corner of his lips, quickly recalling that he had asked Theo the very same question years ago when he was bound to a whipping post and completely at his mercy.

"I've never been a man of God. Perhaps that is the one thing we have in common…"

"Well, I suggest you pray to Him and beg His forgiveness," Theo hissed in his face as he clamped his hand around Silas' throat to hold him still and raised his sword above his head. "Because I have none left for you…"

With an infuriated grunt, Theo squeezed his eyes shut and turned his head away, swinging the blade of his sword down with all of his might. He could not find the fortitude to watch as he ended his torturer's life, so he looked away and waited for the sensation of his blade embedding itself into Silas' skull. But before he could complete the strike, he was startled by the sound of a cannonball flying just over his head and crashing into the nearest British redoubt, creating a thunderous and deafening explosion that tore him from Silas' body sent him skyward. He yelped when he felt the shockwave of the blast throw him off of Silas' body, and it felt as if he flew nearly fifty yards through the air before hitting the ground stomach first and tumbling painfully across the field for several more yards, stopping only when his back hit the body of a British soldier who had been killed by a musket ball to the heart.

The world around him went dark for what felt like an eternity as time slowed to a stop. Theo could hear nothing but the sound of his own blood pounding in his ears, and he could feel nothing but a searing pain pulsating in his head. He laid still on the ground for many moments, staring at the back of his eyelids as the battle continued to rage around him. He was still, which meant to everyone else still standing that he was dead, and just another obstacle to step over.

After several minutes in which he was sure he was dead, Theo let out a gasping breath as his eyes flew open. He slowly turned over onto his stomach with a pained groan, his entire body protesting with the action. His head was throbbing, and the world was blurry as he began to choke on the clouds of dust, gunpowder, and smoke that enveloped him in the aftermath of the explosion. It took a full minute of laying splayed across the ground on his stomach for him to realize that he was, in fact, still alive and on a battlefield, rather than deep within the pits of Hell, like he had initially suspected when he opened his eyes. If he were to give Hell a description, it would look like the battlefield stretching out before Yorktown.

Theo painfully raised himself up onto his elbows, clamping his hands over his ears as the pounding in his head continued. He still could not see clearly, nor could he really hear anything, but when he pulled his hand away from his right ear, he noticed that his palm was smeared with blood. He let out another gasp when he collected enough of his senses to realize that his sword had been lost in the chaos of the explosion and he had never gotten the chance to plunge it into Silas' head before he was blown into the air. A cold sweat broke out upon his brow as he squinted into the smoke in a panic, searching desperately for any sign of the deranged Captain. Surely, he had also survived the blast, but there was no doubt he would be just as dazed and disoriented—the perfect opportunity to land the killing blow, if Theo could manage to get back onto his feet.

Clenching his teeth together to choke back another pained groan, Theo began to pull himself across the ground with his elbows in attempt to return to the place where he had last seen the Captain. The smoke clouds resulting from the explosion gradually began to clear, revealing that the Patriot cannonball responsible had hit its intended target, reducing an entire redoubt and its surrounding barricades to rubble while also igniting an enormous fire in the western most battery that quickly began to engulf the village behind it. Theo was still seeing double when he spotted Silas just ten or so yards before him, his back turned as he tried desperately to crawl away toward the destroyed redoubt. Squinting into the distance, Theo could see that Silas was clutching at a gaping shrapnel wound in his side, and blood had quickly soaked through his uniform to leave a trail behind him as he attempted to flee to safety in what remained of the British fortifications.

Theo summoned what remained of his strength and forced himself onto his hands and knees, and then rose slowly onto his feet, still clutching at his pounding head as blood trickled from the inside of his ear and down his neck. He limped forward for several steps, searching desperately for his sword, but he quickly abandoned that endeavor. There was no time to waste on that—he had to make do with what he had left, and that was his father's trusty pistol, the remaining half of the dynamic duo that had gotten both Alistair and his son though their time in battle. Theo continued to limp toward the fortifications as he watched Silas stumble deliriously past the rubble of the destroyed redoubt and wander into the burning village. There were still several dozen yards between him and where Silas had disappeared into the shadows, and he began to slow his pace, the pain in his head and ears making it nearly impossible to continue on foot.

As if on cue, Theo just barely made out the sound of Artemis' hooves pounding against the earth as she charged forward from behind him, startled by the explosion and lost without her master. Just as she came rushing past, Theo reached out to take ahold of her reins, allowing her to drag him toward the main fortifications for several yards before he was able to pull himself up onto her back. As soon as he was balanced in her saddle, he kicked her into a full gallop and guided her toward the heart of Yorktown.

And that was when he saw it. The body of a fallen young man, dressed in the blues of the Patriot uniform, splayed out across the ground just in front of the recently destroyed redoubt. He was one of the flag bearers for Washington's army, and he had been instructed once the chaos broke out to traverse the battlefield and plant the flag of the thirteen united colonies into the earth within Yorktown in order to further compel a British surrender. The boy was barely in his teens by the look of his young, blood-splattered face, and he had been within a few yards of reaching the fortifications when his short life was snuffed out by a cannon blast from his own brothers in arms. He held tightly onto the flag of his country as his body went rigid on the muddy ground of the battlefield, the red, white, and blue of the Patriot banner waving tattered and bloodied, but still somehow intact, in the wind.

Theo urged Artemis to gallop harder and faster, steering her in the direction of the fallen boy, and just as she sprinted past the body, he leaned over to one side with an outstretched arm to snag the flag by its pole from the boy's cold, dead hand. He then charged forward toward the rubble behind which Silas had escaped, planting the base of the pole into the earth once he entered into Yorktown.

That boy had died serving the Patriot cause, and Theo would be damned if he didn't see to it that the colors of freedom flew tall and proud on these contested grounds by the time the last shot was fired.

***

Theo was met with little resistance as he stormed past the rubble of the outer works and deeper into the village that had become Cornwallis' sanctuary. He had half a mind to go look for the British commander and end him with his own hands for being such a coward, but Silas had to be dealt with first. His life, and that of his family, would forever be in danger so long as the man lived, no matter if these lands were colonies or free states.

Theo found that much of Yorktown had been abandoned by its inhabitants, most likely when Cornwallis had taken it for himself, and many of its structures were either damaged by cannon fire or engulfed in flames, creating a scene of smoke-filled chaos reminiscent of Kensington and so many other pillaged settlements across the land. After several minutes of searching and dodging the occasional straggling Redcoat, Theo caught a glimpse of Silas' bloodied uniform from the corner of his eye. He watched from around a corner as Silas deliriously stumbled through the entrance of an abandoned chapel whose thatch roof had just been set ablaze by a neighboring building.

Theo deliberated for a moment before dismounting from Artemis' saddle, leaving her in an empty alleyway as he limped toward the church. The air was hot and uncomfortably heavy as he entered the building, and the sight of the rafters above his head becoming engulfed in flames set his heart pounding in his chest. He could distinctly remember the last two times he had found himself surrounded by fire in the heart of burning villages, and the memories put a deep scowl upon his face as he made his way inside.

Inside the chapel, he found Silas slumped against the pulpit before rows and rows of empty pews, his arm draped over the gushing wound in his side. Slowly, he raised his head to reveal a tired, empty gaze as Theo limped down the center aisle and stopped just a few feet before him. The only sound in the air was that of the flames licking the wooden structure, and the occasional creak of a beam that was beginning to give way under the stress and heat of the fire.

"If you came to kill me, you are too late, I am afraid," Silas rasped as blood trickled from the corner of his mouth and onto his coat. Raising his arm, he revealed a massive hole that had been ripped in his side by a piece of shrapnel from the explosion. Instead of flesh under the torn fabric of his uniform, all Theo could see was bloody tissue. "I am on my way out as we speak, it seems..." His eyes fluttered closed before opening a moment later, and his head bobbed as he struggled to maintain consciousness.

"It's over, Silas," Theo whispered as he took a step closer to the pulpit against which Silas was leaning his head. "The colonies will be free. *Evie* is free."

Silas scoffed before choking on the blood collecting in his throat. Sweat had begun to gather on his skin from the intense heat of the flames around them, but he felt nothing. His body was numb, his cold heart even more so.

"You can have her," he hissed.

Theo knelt down before him with a hardened gaze. "She was never yours to *give*."

Silas tried to roll his eyes, but he hadn't the strength. He could feel his life slowly draining from his body, and the whole endeavor was made all the worse by the fact that his sworn enemy was standing over him and *watching*.

"Go then. Go back to your Commander and tell him of your great victory here today. Go home and tell your wife and child of your bravery. Just leave me be. Leave me here to die."

Theo looked around him at the growing flames traveling down the walls. "This is where you want to die? Alone and consumed by flames?"

"Just go!" Silas growled, spitting bloodied saliva at Theo's feet. "I will die a hero here. His Majesty will hold high the same Silas Porter, a faithful servant to the Crown who was slain in service to his country..."

Theo quirked his brow in mild amusement. The man was clearly delirious from blood loss. "I suppose it is a fitting end for you, after sending so many innocents to die the same way…"

Silas sneered remorselessly at him, baring a set of blood-stained teeth set within a battered and scarred face. The flames had now nearly caged him in against the pulpit, and both he and Theo could feel the intense heat beginning to singe their uniforms and cook their skin. Silas let out a weak breath before growling, "They were far from innocent. They were rebels, traitors…"

"They were civilians!"

Silas tipped his head back in resignation against the front of the pulpit. "Soldier or civilian, I don't care. I don't discriminate against my enemies…"

Theo wrinkled his nose in disgust and shook his head. After a moment of intense deliberation, he held out his hand. "You do not have to die this painful death. If peace is what you seek, you can find it outside, away from the flames. Let me help you."

Silas angrily slapped his hand away, snarling, "I'd rather die a thousand painful deaths than accept anything from the likes of you, mongrel! Now get out before the flames take you, too!"

Theo swallowed thickly and shook his head. As much as he hated Silas Porter with every fiber of his being, the sight of him so defeated, broken, and helpless made his stomach churn. Not necessarily for him, but for Evie. She would be devastated to know the father of her son had died in such agony.

Crouching before the Captain's body, Theo attempted to reach for Silas' arm to help him to his feet, but Silas once again pulled away and angrily reached for the pistol upon Theo's belt. Theo let out a yelp and squeezed his eyes shut when he felt Silas rip Alistair's pistol out of its holster, and he wrapped his arms around his head in an attempt to protect himself from what appeared to be Silas' last-ditch effort to snuff him out.

But instead of feeling the searing pain of a bullet ripping through his body, he was startled by the deafening sound of a single shot ringing out just before him, followed by the dull thud of a body hitting the floor.

Theo cracked one eye open to see Silas' body strewn across the floor at his feet, the pistol clutched in his right hand. But instead of finding a lifeless look upon the man's face, Theo found *no* face. The entirety of his face had been blown apart by a single gunshot after he placed the pistol in his mouth and pulled the trigger, leaving behind only a large, jagged, and bloody cavern in what remained of his skull. Theo stumbled backward, letting out a disgusted yelp at the sight of blood and brain matter splattered across the floor and his own uniform while clamping his hand over his mouth to stifle a scream. His heart continued to race in his chest as he stared at the headless body in horror, his stomach turning at the smell of death and burning wood filling the air within the church.

He had little time to dwell on Silas' last act, however, because his attention was diverted to the deafening sound of one of the main pillars of the structure beginning to give way now that the flames had begun to crawl across the floor. The floorboards under his feet began to shift as the rafters pulled loose and fell onto the pews in a downpour of splinters and ash. Without the time to turn back and retrieve his beloved pistol, Theo turned and bolted down the main aisle as the building began to collapse all around him, tossing one last glance over his shoulder at Silas' corpse as he reached the entrance to the chapel. The body, however, had already been crushed and buried by several fallen rafters, leaving only a pale hand clutching a pistol visible amongst the rubble.

Summoning the last of his strength, Theo kicked the front door open and stumbled out into the street, gasping for a breath of fresh air after his lungs had filled with smoke. Just as he hit the hard stones of the blood covered street, he looked back to see what remained of the chapel cave in on itself and fall into a large burning heap of wood and brick. The smell of burning flesh began to fill the air as the church's remains continued to burn, and Theo pressed his nose into the crook of his elbow to endure the wretched odor he had come to know so well.

Artemis scuttled around the corner from the alleyway and skidded to a stop at his side, nickering in alarm and nudging at his shoulder with her nose. Theo placed a hand upon her snout to calm her before taking a hold of her reins and pulling himself onto the saddle. His head was still throbbing, and his ear was pounding, but he was alive. The same could not be said for Silas Porter. He had made his choice to die by his own hand rather than accept the help of someone he considered his enemy, and he would pay the price for his crimes for the rest of eternity, wherever it was that he spent it.

"A coward until the end," Theo mumbled to himself as he ordered Artemis into a gallop to take him across enemy lines and back to his own men. "May the Hell you find be of your own creation, Captain Porter…"

***

The British overrun of the Patriot trenches was brief, as they were almost immediately beaten back with the help of a regiment of French grenadiers under the comte de Noailles. Within a matter of a few hours, the remains of Cornwallis's last-ditch sortie had either been killed, captured, or run off, and both sides retired from the battlefield by the late afternoon.

It was a crisp morning on October 17th, and the air was filled with the smell of a fresh rain as Commander Washington paced anxiously around the encampment behind the Patriot lines. Nearly all of Yorktown's fortifications had been destroyed or captured the day before, and much of Cornwallis' army had been taken prisoner in the chaos of the siege. Once the British had been forced back into their main works once again, Commander Washington ordered his men to retire back to their own encampment for a much-needed rest, with the hope that they would receive news of a surrender before any more sieging could take place.

It was midmorning when Washington visited the infirmary tent in his encampment, expecting to find the worst when he arrived. Rather than finding a crowd of injured, dead, or dying soldiers, however, he found only a few that had suffered injuries from the previous day's campaign, as most of the casualties had come from the British side. Inside the tent, he did, however, find Captain Cunningham sitting upon an overturned crate as an army doctor stood before him and examined his head. Washington could see a sizable gash on Theo's forehead, as well as blood caked in and around his right ear. His face was covered in small scrapes, and the red warpaint upon his cheeks had been smeared with blood, dirt, and sweat. Lafayette sat next to him on another crate, seemingly keeping him company as the doctor worked to clean the dried blood from his skin and then wrap his forehead and ear with a bandage.

Theo looked up from the ground as soon as he heard the Commander enter the tent, and Lafayette immediately stood to salute him.

"Commander," Lafayette said excitedly, "I am happy to report that yesterday's campaign was a resounding success. I also received word from my scouts that Cornwallis and his men attempted an escape across the river to Gloucester late last night, but they were halted by the storm and forced to return to Yorktown by early morning."

Washington nodded once in satisfaction, crossing his arms over his chest. "My scouts just told me the same thing. He has exhausted all of his options. The only thing he has left to do now is wave the white flag." Peering over Lafayette's shoulder, the Commander gave Theo another once over, taking note of his rather haggard appearance. "And how do you fair, Captain?" he asked in concern.

Theo shrugged his shoulders and prodded at the bandage wrapped at an angle across his forehead to cover his ear. He found it difficult to hear much of anything out of that ear, and the doctor had told him that it was possible the explosion had ruptured his eardrum.

"I will survive. The same cannot be said for Captain Silas Porter."

"Ah, Porter. I have heard his name before," Lafayette noted. "He is one of Cornwallis' most favored officers."

"*Was*," Theo corrected.

"You killed him?" Washington asked with a raised brow.

"I did not have to. He's arrogance became the death of him."

Washington opened his mouth to ask Theo to clarify, but he was interrupted by the unmistakable sound of British drums in the distance beating a parley, followed by a tremendous roar of cheers, jeers, and applause. Washington, Lafayette, and Theo immediately left the tent to investigate the source of the raucous, trekking to the top of the hill in the middle of their encampment to look out across the battlefield and the rubble remains of Yorktown just behind it.

Trenches snaked across the battlefield like serpents, occupied by both French and American troops that had been awaiting a shift change later that morning. Those in the trenches were hooting and hollering in excitement, and across the open field, two lone Redcoats could be seen emerging from the main works. One was a drummer, and the other, an officer. In the officer's hand, he waved a crisp white handkerchief in the air for all of the Patriots to see.

"My God," Washington gasped. "They have finally waved the white flag."

Theo felt his knees buckle underneath him, not sure if he was hallucinating, or if he had misheard the Commander's words. Though he had been waiting nearly seven years to hear such a thing, he was reluctant to believe it. From the top of the hill, they watched with bated breath as an American officer from one of the trenches crossed the battlefield to meet the Redcoats outside of their fortifications.

The drummer was sent back into Yorktown while the American took the white handkerchief from the Redcoat officer and tied it around his eyes to form a blindfold before leading him back across the field to the Patriot lines. All batteries and artillery fire ceased immediately, and an ominous silence fell upon the entirety of Yorktown and its surrounding lands.

Within minutes, the blindfolded officer was led to Washington, where he was placed in a chair and the blindfold was removed. Washington stood before him with arms crossed over his chest, while Theo, Lafayette, and several other officers surrounded them. The air was thick with tension as the Redcoat stared up into the Commander's eyes and said with a trembling voice, "Lord Cornwallis requests and armistice. And an appointment of commissioners to discuss the terms of surrender."

Washington deliberated for a moment, glancing all around him to catch the eyes of each of his generals and officers before stating curtly, "I will grant a two-hour cease-fire. But I demand a proposal from Cornwallis in writing."

"Lord Cornwallis asks that he and his troops be paroled and sent back to England."

Washington shook his head stubbornly. "I demand an unconditional surrender."

***

By nightfall, Cornwallis agreed to Washington's conditions, but it would not be until two days later that the surrender was made official. On the morning of the 19th of October, the allied troops assembled in a double line a mile long, with the Americans on the right and the French on the left. Theo, mounted on horseback, stood before the men he was given to command, while Washington placed himself at the head of the American line on horseback and Rochambeau headed the French. After an hour's wait, the British slowly began to march out of the main works with their colors cased in defeat. But even after all of the remaining Redcoats had emerged from the fort, Cornwallis was nowhere to be seen.

That was when Lafayette came trotting by on his own horse to tell Washington in a hushed tone, "Cornwallis has pled illness and remains within Yorktown. He has sent his men to surrender on his behalf."

Washington nearly scoffed and rolled his eyes. "He is just too arrogant to face the ignominy of surrender. Very well, we will commence without him."

King George's men could not bear the thought of having to surrender to the despised Americans, and many were reluctant to display any sort of decorum and respect to Commander Washington and his men as they lined themselves up before their enemies. Most of the Redcoats even went so far as to ignore the American presence all together and fixate their eyes on the French. The Americans were not a real army, after all, the British still believed. They were just a rag-tag congregation of rowdy peasants who did not know their place.

Even still, each and every Redcoat on that field was forced to acknowledge that they had been bested by those rowdy peasants, and in unison, they laid down their arms at their feet, standing in sullen defeat. A General by the name Charles O'Hara stepped forward to present Cornwallis' sword to Commander Washington as a token of surrender, but instead of taking it himself, Washington ordered his own General Benjamin Lincoln to ceremoniously accept the gesture of defeat on his behalf.

By the time the events of Yorktown concluded, the allied French and American forces had taken nearly seven thousand Redcoats prisoner, all of whom were then marched off to prison camps. At the last moment, Washington decided to take pity on his British counterpart and paroled Cornwallis and his principal officers, having them sent back to New York until they could be delivered to England.

The entire siege lasted less than a month, but within that short period of time, the Americans had definitively demonstrated their mettle, their bravery, and their unrelenting desire for freedom. They had everything to lose, and even more to win, and they did not waver until the last shot rang out.

With Cornwallis' sword in the possession of the Patriots, the Revolution was over, and the war was won. The only things that remained to be done were the signing of an official treaty recognizing the colonies as an independent nation from the British empire, and to see the last remains of the Redcoats were evacuated back to whence they came.

***

My dearest Evie,

It is with the most elated heart that I write to tell you the glorious news that the events at Yorktown were a resounding success. After we pounded his fortifications with everything that we had for nearly a month, Cornwallis was forced to surrender unconditionally to us. The war is over, and we have won. Even days after the surrender, it still seems too surreal to me to be true. After so many bloody years, we are finally free. You, me, Liberty, and everyone else that calls these contested lands home is free.

I can recall only two other times in my life in which I was filled with so much joy—the day I became your husband, and the day I became a father.

Though I was honored to be a part of this historical day, it pains me to know that I was not with you on the occasion of the one-year anniversary of our marriage. This past year has been filled with so many triumphs and tribulations, and there is no other woman I could imagine having by my side during those times and the many years going forward. You have told me frequently that I have saved you from a life of pain and torment, but in truth, it is you who has saved me. I haven't the faintest clue where I would be today without you, for it was you who has kept me grounded though every fear, failure, and victory these past seven years. If it were not

Indivisible

for you, I would have felt no desire to change my life for the better, and I surely would not be the man I am today if you were not the woman you have always been.

Cornwallis waved the white flag exactly one year to the day after we became husband and wife, and I cannot think of a better gift for our anniversary than the promise of our freedom. I hope you can forgive me for my absence during the last several weeks, and as promised, I will return to you and our daughter with haste now that the war is won. The concept of liberty and justice for all is no longer just a fantasy—it can now be a reality, if we only remember where we came from and where we wish to go moving forward. This nation was forged in the flames of blood, fire, and fearlessness, and it is my greatest hope that the future holds more peace than we have ever known before.

I long to hold you in my arms again, and to spend the rest of our lives together, no longer living under the iron fist of tyranny as we watch our daughter grow. Tell Liberty and Johanna that I have laid awake every night these past weeks missing you all so much that my heart aches. Tell them I love them, and I love you, with all that I have. And tell them I will be home soon, for good this time.

With all my love,

Your victorious husband, Captain Theo Cunningham

Chapter 24

A Generation Unafraid

November 1781

With the British defeated and much of Yorktown left in a pile of ash and rubble, Washington ordered his men to begin filling in the trenches they had so recently dug so as to prevent an enemy from using them in the future. When that chore was finished, and the bodies of the few casualties that the French and the Americans suffered were removed from the battlefield, the army began to disperse. Rochambeau and his men decided to stay in Virginia for the time being, while Washington's men headed back to the Hudson River to guard against the thousands of defeated and disgruntled Redcoats that remained in New York.

Theo never had any intention of following the other Continentals to New York, and instead began packing what little belongings he carried so that he may return home to Division Point. It was mid-November when he was finally given the chance to leave, and he stood in the middle of the emptying encampment whilst packing and adjusting Artemis' saddle on her back. There was a peaceful quiet in the autumn air, a light-heartedness and excitement that had not been felt since the war began so many years ago. Most of the men that had crowded the encampment just a few weeks ago had already gone, but a few stragglers remained, too intoxicated by the exhilaration of their victory to leave the area. One of those men was Commander Washington himself, who chose to linger near Yorktown while his men began the journey north.

Theo was interrupted in his task of packing Artemis' saddle bags with the provisions he'd need for the long ride home when Washington approached him from behind. Clearing his throat, the Commander quietly said, "Before you take your leave, I would like to speak with you, if I may."

Theo did not look up from the saddle as he mumbled, "Speak quickly."

"I wanted to thank you for your service to the Revolution. We could not have won without men like you. And...I never had the chance to properly make amends for what was done in the past."

Theo paused and turned his head with a raised brow. "With all due respect, Commander, you had plenty of chances. You just could not bring yourself to admit you were wrong."

Washington's lips pressed into a thin hard line before he stated, "My thoughts and prayers are with all of the innocents who were slaughtered during this bloody endeavor."

Theo scoffed under his breath and turned to fully face the Commander. The bandage around his head had been abandoned days ago, and he could now hear loud and clear from his injured ear. His eyes narrowed into aggravated slits as he snapped, "I do not want your thoughts, prayers, or apologies, sir. They will not bring back the innocent people you had slaughtered, and they will not protect the next generation of natives whom your new government will ultimately decide are expendable. I do not want thoughts and prayers. I want change. And you and the other fathers of this new nation are the only men who can bring that change."

Theo and Washington stared each other down in intense silence for several moments before the Commander suddenly looked away, dropping his gaze to the ground and heaving out a sullen sigh. "May I be candid with you, Theo?"

"I wish you would be, for once."

"I know I should be exhilarated by our victory here, and the new future to come. And part of me is. But the other part…feels nothing but regret for the things I have done to get this far." Washington slowly looked up, and when he did, his eyes were glassy with emotion that Theo had never once seen the man display. "There is nothing I regret more in my life than writing that letter to Beavers and ordering the death of those Iroquois. At the time, I truly believed that I was doing what was best for this country. At the time, I was willing to sacrifice a handful of native lives to save hundreds or thousands of colonists, but I have since had time to realize that denying some people freedom in order to give it to others is tyranny just the same. And I would not have realized that if it were not for you opening my eyes to the truth of my hypocrisy.

"And it is the God's honest truth that I did not intentionally bring a plague of smallpox upon your mother's village. My commander merely told me to deliver the supplies to our allies, but he never once informed me of his ulterior motives. And now that I know the truth of what befell the village after I left, I have become overwhelmed with a shame and regret I did not think possible. If I could take everything back, I would. I swear to you, I would. I am sorry, Theo. I do not expect you to forgive me, for I cannot even forgive myself…"

Theo was quiet for a moment as he stared up at the sky and took in the Commander's words. He could hear the sincerity in his voice, and that gave him a sliver of comfort, but it did not change what had already been done.

"I accept your apology," Theo eventually murmured, "but the people who really needed to hear it are the ones you sentenced to die, as well as the generations of their descendants that will now never come to be."

"I understand. But I want you to know that I will spend the rest of my life atoning for my mistakes and forging a better world for *everyone* who calls this place home. A new era has begun, and it will be unlike all of the others that came before."

The corners of Theo's mouth twitched upward into the beginnings of a sideways smirk, and he folded his arms over his chest. "I hope your words are true. For nothing would make me happier."

Washington offered his hand in a gesture of farewell. "I hope you have a safe journey home, and a lifetime of happiness after that, Captain Cunningham. You have earned it."

Theo accepted his hand and gave it a firm shake, feeling some of the anger he had been harboring in his heart begin to dissipate. "The same to you, sir. And I hope you use your power wisely and justly from here on out."

Washington returned his smirk with a gentle nod. "I intend to."

***

December 1781

The familiar and comforting scent of salty sea air greeted Theo like a tight embrace as he rode into Division Point well past midnight. The winds were cold and crisp with both the smell of the nearby Massachusetts Bay and a fresh flurry of snow, and he took them in with a deep breath that brought a sense of peace over his entire being.

The homestead was dark and calmingly quiet as he and Artemis skidded to a stop before the cabin behind the lighthouse, and after penning her in the nearby stable, he took his first step into his home in nearly three months. The journey home from war was thankfully much less eventful than the last, but his mind and body still longed for sleep like his lungs longed for breath.

Closing the front door gingerly behind himself, Theo tiptoed across the front room and poked his head into the doorway of Liberty's nursery to see her sleeping peacefully within her bassinet in the corner. He crept carefully inside until he was standing over her, watching for several minutes as her little chest rose and fell and her eyelids fluttered. Surely, she was dreaming, he decided with a chuckle under his breath.

She had grown so much since he had last seen her and hardly looked like the same child. Now nearly ten months old, it seemed as if she was growing into a woman right before his eyes. He felt a twinge of guilt shoot through his heart as he stood over her bassinet and watched her sleep, and he hated himself for ever leaving her. She looked almost twice as big as she had been when he left, her thick, dark curls now reaching past her ears to frame her chubby tanned cheeks.

How much did he really miss of her life while he was away? Had she learned to crawl? Had she taken her first steps? Could she speak in full sentences, rather than just gibberish babbles? He didn't know, because he wasn't there, and it killed him. And right in that moment, he vowed to himself that so long as his heart continued to beat in his chest, he would never leave her, nor her mother, ever again. Nothing was worth that heartache. *Nothing.*

Theo leaned down to press a soft kiss to her forehead and graze his finger across her cheekbone, murmuring to her, "I know you won't understand it yet, my sweet girl, but our world is about to change for the better. You are about to come of age with a newborn nation—a nation thousands fought and died to give to you."

After watching her sleep for a few more precious moments, Theo turned away and quietly made his way out of the nursery and into the master bedroom next door. As expected, he found his wife fast asleep in their bed, curled up on his side of the mattress in her nightgown with the blankets tangled around her legs and a piece of parchment clutched in her hand. Kicking off his boots and shrugging out of his tattered uniform coat, he silently knelt down at the side of the bed and plucked the paper from her hand to examine it in the light of the moon shining in through the window. Upon closer inspection, he realized she had fallen asleep while reading and re-reading the letter he had last written to her just before he left for home from Yorktown. A warm smile came to his face as he set the crinkled piece of parchment on the bedside table and lowered himself onto the edge of the bed next to her.

She stirred quietly when the mattress shifted with his weight, turning from her side onto her back and slowly allowing her eyes to flutter open. He stared down at her with the slightest of smirks as he took in her beauty—even groggy and disoriented, she was the most beautiful woman he had ever laid eyes upon, and the moonlight streaming into the room from the nearby window gave her an ethereal glow that took his breath away. After being away for almost three months, he could not believe he had gone so long without seeing her face, nor caressing her skin, nor holding her in his arms.

After a minute or two, her eyes opened fully, and she blinked up at him in mild confusion. "Theo?" she asked in a raspy whisper. "Is that really you?"

He nodded with a gentle chuckle, leaning down until their noses were touching. "The one and only."

Suddenly, Evie let out a gasp before shooting up into a sitting position with enough force to nearly knock him off the edge of the bed. Before he could blink, she was on her knees on the mattress, throwing her arms around his neck and pressing her face into his shoulder in the tightest embrace he could ever remember her giving him.

"Oh, God, I was so worried," he heard her sob against his neck as he wrapped his arms snugly around her small frame, pressing her torso against his and rubbing his hand up and down her back. "I received your letter, but I was still afraid that something could happen to you on your way back…"

Theo shook his head and held her tightly, savoring in her scent. She smelled of lavender and freshly washed linens, and he wanted nothing more than to drown in her beauty. "Not this time," he whispered in return. "I told you I would always return to you, didn't I?"

"I prayed for your safe return every day. I was so afraid…"

"It doesn't matter now, love. I am home. And I am never going anywhere without you again."

Evie gently pulled away so that she could look him in the eye, placing a hand upon his cheek as she said, "I saw in the papers what happened in Yorktown after I received your letter. Is it really true? Is the war really over? Are we free?"

Theo's lopsided grin widened as he said, "Cornwallis surrendered like the coward he is. Treaty negotiations will take some time, but the war is over. No more blood shall be shed. We are free."

Another sob escaped Evie's throat as she pulled him close and pressed her lips to his in a feverish kiss. Oh, how she longed to hear those words from him, and how she longed to have him home safe where he belonged. How she longed to kiss him, and feel his arms wrapped protectively around her as they lay in bed together, savoring what it felt like to know that they were no longer prisoners of tyranny.

Breaking their kiss, she murmured coquettishly against his lips, "I suppose I have you to thank for my freedom."

Theo's broad chest rumbled with a hearty chuckle. "Not just me. Thousands of men fought, bled, and died for the moment we could call ourselves sovereign."

Evie tossed her long hair over her shoulder with a smirk before capturing his chin in her hand and pulling him towards the center of the bed. "You are the only man I care to thank," she purred as she placed a hand in the center of his chest and pushed his back against the mattress.

"What...what are you doing?" he asked with a raised brow and flushed cheeks as she began to straddle his waist.

Evie leaned forward to place a soft kiss upon his forehead, the tip of his nose, and then his lips while tangling her hands in the hair at the nape of his neck as she murmured into his ear, "Thanking you for your service, Sergeant Cunningham."

Theo placed his hands upon her hips, grasping fistfuls of the thin fabric of her night gown as he returned, "It's *Captain*, now, actually..."

"*Pardonnez-moi s'il vous plaît,*" she giggled girlishly as she pressed a kiss to the skin of his throat and moved her hands from his hair down to his chest, feeling in the dark for the buttons of his linen shirt so that she could rip it of him in a grand fashion. "Captain it is, then."

After finally finding the buttons she had been searching for, Evie tore open the front of his shirt to reveal his sculpted torso, his tanned flesh marred by several large scars whose histories they both wished they could forget but made him no less perfect in her eyes. She dragged her fingertips down his bare chest while leaning forward to capture his mouth in another kiss, relishing in the sensation of his hands upon her body after so long of sleeping alone. Three months may as well have been a decade without him there to help her warm their bed.

She let out a startled gasp when she felt his grip on her hips tighten before he suddenly sat up and flipped her over onto her back, reversing their position so that he was now the one straddling her waist, and she was at his total mercy underneath him. He quickly shed out of his shirt and tossed it over his shoulder before reaching down to do the same to her nightgown, mumbling the words, "You haven't any idea how long I have waited for this."

"Two months, three weeks, and five days," she returned smartly. "I have been waiting just as long as you have."

Theo let out another rumbling chuckle before slipping her nightgown over her head and pinning her down against the bed with the weight of his own body. He leaned down to kiss her passionately once more, sliding his hands up and down her sides and savoring the glorious way it felt to have her bare flesh pressed against his, with nothing between them to keep them apart. Their bodies fit together beautifully as they reunited after what felt like an eternity, and they never wanted to part.

While she ran her fingertips across his back, grazing each and every shallow scar that painted his flesh from a whipping years past, he pressed hungry kisses across her soft pale skin, beginning with her lips and ending with her hipbones. When he suddenly paused to look up at her from under his eyelashes, she could see in the dim moonlight that his eyes were hazy with a beautiful concoction of lust and adoration.

For several quiet moments, he simply stared at her and marveled at how a man like himself had managed to capture the heart of a woman such as she.

Perhaps there was a God out there, after all.

**

A quiet, contented hum escaped Evie's lips as she rested her head upon Theo's bare chest and snuggled as closely to him as she could manage. He eagerly allowed her to nestle against his side, pulling the blanket up to cover their sweaty, naked bodies as they both sunk into the mattress in peaceful quiet.

"I love you," she whispered after planting a gentle kiss on the scarred skin over his heart and draping her arm over his stomach.

"Prove it," he returned jokingly.

"I believe I just did. Three times."

They both chuckled in unison, but Theo's jovial mood suddenly morphed into one of tense brooding as his laughter faded into silence.

"What troubles you?" Evie asked, her forehead creasing in concern as she gazed up at him.

Theo shook his head and cleared his throat. "It is nothing."

Evie rolled her eyes up to the ceiling before sitting up so that she could look him pointedly in the face. "Please do not lie to me."

After a minute or two of squirming uncomfortably under her intense gaze, Theo let out a heaving sigh and sat up himself, leaning his back against the headboard while nervously fidgeting with the blanket laid across his lap. "I have something I must tell you," he eventually mumbled. "Something happened…at Yorktown."

Evie's concerned expression immediately soured as her eyes narrowed into slits. "Were you…unfaithful?" she asked in a devastated whisper as she brought her hand up to cover her mouth.

"What? No, no. I would never do such a thing," Theo stuttered whilst wildly shaking his head. "You know my heart belongs to you, and you alone."

Evie let out a huff of relief. "Then what did you do?"

"It isn't about me. It's about…Silas."

Evie swallowed thickly and began to nervously curl a lock of her around her finger. Looking away, she mumbled, "What of him? He is long dead."

Theo sullenly shook his head once more. "He wasn't."

Evie gripped onto the nearby headboard to steady herself, her body stiffening as she held her hand over her heart. "You're lying."

"I'm not. I swear to you. He was at Yorktown, leading a charge of Redcoats under Cornwallis' orders. I saw him with my own eyes."

Evie's face grew fearfully pale as she stared at him, eyes widening in terror. The entire earth felt as if it was slipping out from underneath her as she murmured, "That can't be. I saw him bleed out under that tree. I twisted the knife in him myself. I saw his eyes close and his body grow still…"

"He survived his injuries. And he had been plotting our demise ever since."

Evie let out a small gasp behind the hand she placed in front of her mouth. Her heart clenched in her chest, and her body began to tremble in unspeakable terror and disbelief. "Is he…is he still…?"

Theo shook his head morosely, looking away. He had deliberated whether or not it was even necessary to tell her about Silas' true demise at all, but he eventually decided that enough secrets had been kept between the two of them over the years. "He did not survive Yorktown. He is dead for good now."

"How can you be so sure?" she asked with a shaking voice.

"I saw him die myself. He…he took his own life before he could be defeated."

Evie's eyes fluttered closed as she wrapped her arms around herself. Looking up to the sky, she muttered to herself, "A fitting end for a monster like him."

A tense silence fell over the bedroom as they both sat and ruminated, but the silence was suddenly broken when Evie let out yet another gasp and leapt off of the bed to pace anxiously across the floor. She was still completely nude, but that was the last thing on her mind as her thoughts began to spin in a thousand different directions. "Oh, God," she whimpered tearfully, "is our marriage even legal?"

"What?"

"Our marriage, Theo. I was still Silas Porter's wife the day I married you, as he had never really passed! Do you know what this means? This means that our marriage is void in the eyes of the law, and the church! We have been living in sin for the last year, and our daughter—"

Theo abruptly climbed out of the bed, snagging one of the blankets to wrap around both of their naked bodies before silencing her with a kiss.

"In the eyes of the church, and the law, we were living in sin long before our wedding day."

Evie dropped her head onto his chest and began to quietly sob. "What shall we do?"

"There is nothing to do, Evie. We will live our lives as we always have."

"But, the wedding—"

Theo placed both of his hands upon her cheeks to force her to look him in the eye, interrupting her once more. "Nothing about us, or what we have created, is a sin. I do not care what God, the church, or the law have to say about it."

Evie stared up into his fiery golden eyes as a tear slipped down her cheek. "Do you really mean that?"

"I did not risk everything fighting for my freedom, only to be told that it is a crime to love whom I love. That isn't freedom—that is tyranny. And so long as I have you by my side for the rest of my days, I am content."

Evie nodded in agreement and tried to wipe her tears away as Theo gently led her back into their bed, draping the blanket over them once again while holding her tightly to his body. Immediately upon feeling her flesh pressed against his, she relaxed.

"There will always be people out there who despise us," he told her as he held her in his arms and looked up to the ceiling. "To them, our union has committed some kind of unholy crime. But we are free now. We are free to live our lives as we please, because that is what we fought for. We are on the cusp of a new era, an era of change and progress. And do you know who will bring this country into that new era?"

Evie shook her head. "No."

"Us," Theo stated with a smirk as he gazed out the window and into the sky, where he saw a future worth fighting and dying for. "We, and those who come after, are part of a new generation—a generation unafraid to fight for what we know is right and true. A generation unafraid to give our children the world we wish we had. And that starts now, with our family. We are living proof that the world need not be so hopelessly divided."

***

July 1782

"It pains me so to know that she will never remember him," Evie mumbled sullenly as she held Liberty upon her hip and stood between Johanna and Theo in the middle of the graveyard by the church.

Theo raked a hand through his hair before draping his arm across her shoulders, sighing sadly. His eyes were fixated upon his father's headstone at his feet, and though it had been one year to the day since Alistair Cunningham had passed, his heart still ached just the same as it had when they first laid him to rest.

"We will make certain that she knows who he was," he said quietly, clearing his throat. "We will tell her stories. His name will never die in Division Point."

Johanna silently bent down to place a small bunch of flowers before her husband's grave, kissing the tips of her fingers before touching them to the face of the headstone. "I hope you are resting well, my love," she whispered. "After all you have done for us, you deserve an eternity of peace and happiness. I long for the day we can be reunited again at Heaven's gates."

Now a year and a half old, Libby was as talkative as ever, constantly babbling and soaking in new words with every passing day. From her mother's arms, she looked down at the gravestone and tilted her head curiously before pointing and motioning to be put down. Evie bent down to set her on her feet, and she curiously toddled through the grass to the polished stone that stood just as tall as she, tracing her fingers across the engraving that bore her grandfather's name. Theo followed close behind and crouched down by her and Johanna's side.

"Do you see what that says?" he asked her gently, pointing to the inscription. "That is your grandfather, Libby. You won't remember him, but I want you to know that he loved you so very much."

"Papa," Liberty mumbled, following his finger across the words written in stone.

"That's right," Theo said with a sad chuckle. "He was *my* papa. And he taught me what it means to be a father. If it weren't for him, I do not know where any of us would be."

Johanna nodded in agreement while wiping at her eyes with the back of her hand. "I will never love another like I loved him."

Theo placed a gentle hand upon her shoulder as they both remained crouched before the grave. "He would want you to be happy, Jo. He would not want you to spend the rest of your days mourning."

"I know, dear. It is just…even a year later, I cannot imagine my life without him in it."

"None of us can," Theo returned in a whisper, "but we do the best that we know how with what we have been given."

Johanna nodded again, the corners of her mouth twitching upward as she remembered the words her husband had written in his final message to the world. "I suppose we do."

"Isn't that right, Evie?" Theo asked, taking his daughter into his arms and standing before turning to catch his wife's gaze. Except, she was not standing just behind him and Johanna like she had been just a moment ago. "Evie? Where are you?"

He spun in a circle, his eyes scanning the small cemetery for any sign of where she could have gone. That was when he found her on the other side of the graveyard, her back turned as she stood silently over another gravestone.

Johanna and Theo quickly made their way across the cemetery with Liberty in tow, coming to a halt at Evie's side to see that the grave upon which she was gazing belonged to Noah Porter. Her body was rigid as she stared down at the stone that bore her first child's name, and in her glassy blue eyes, Theo could see years of painful memories playing out.

A silent child, an empty cradle, a small pine box being lowered into the ground. Choking back a sob, Evie lowered herself on her knees before the grave while closing her eyes and dropping her head into her hands.

"He would have been seven years in January," she mumbled into her hands, "and he would have had a little sister…"

Theo set Liberty on the ground once more before kneeling by his wife's side, wrapping an arm tightly around her waist. She immediately dropped her head upon his strong chest and clutched at the fabric of his shirt.

"He still does," he whispered to her softly before kissing the top of her head.

"I feel so guilty," Evie admitted between sobs after several moments of silence. "I feel so guilty that I am able to be the mother to Liberty that Noah never had. And that Liberty never had a chance to know him."

"I'm so sorry, my love. But you must know that he still lives on in our hearts, just as my father does."

Evie nodded her head in morose agreement. "I thought with time…it would become easier to come see him. But every time I see his name on that polished rock, my heart shatters into pieces all over again. It still seems like it was only yesterday that I lost him."

Sensing her mother's distress, Liberty teetered toward them and came to stand by her side. "Mama sad," she mumbled, placing her little hand upon Evie's tear-stained cheek.

Evie immediately wrapped her arms around her daughter and held her tightly to her chest. "Oh, sweet girl," she sighed as she wiped away her tears and felt a smile come to her face. "Mama is not sad. She is just…remembering."

Liberty turned in her arms and pointed at Noah's gravestone curiously. "Sad," she repeated.

"Do you know who that is, Libby?" Theo asked softly, tilting his chin toward the headstone. "That is your brother, Noah. He cannot be with us anymore, but he is watching over us every day."

Liberty tilted her head in mild confusion before breaking free from Evie's grasp and waddling toward the headstone.

"Brother," she repeated before staring at the tall polished stone for several silent seconds. She did not know what any of that meant, but it seemed important to Mama, Papa, and Nana Jo. She had seen Nana Jo place a bunch of flowers in front of a different tall rock just a few minutes ago, so she wandered back to the nearest patch of grass and plucked a single wildflower before coming back to drop it before Noah's grave. Just like Nana Jo had done.

Evie let out a small gasp, quickly scooping Liberty up into her arms to give her a kiss on her cheek.

"Your girl already has more empathy as a child than most people will have in their entire lives," Johanna noted with a soft chuckle.

Theo rose to his feet, feeling his chest swell with pride as he looked down upon his daughter beaming up at him. Her dark locks were now past her chin and fell in messy curls into her eyes as she grinned excitedly.

Evie and Theo both glanced back at Alistair's grave and shared a knowing look with one another before Theo pondered, "Perhaps it is just in her blood."

***

November 1783

For many, time seemed to drag on endlessly between the Patriot victory at Yorktown and the official end of the war. That official conclusion would not come until almost exactly two years after the last battle, when a treaty was finally signed by both the young American nation and the British Empire.

The Treaty of Paris was signed on the third day of September 1783, recognizing the former united colonies as the United States and ceasing (in theory) all hostilities between the two signatories of the treaty. All British troops that remained on American soil were made to evacuate the country by the end of the year. The glorious news of the treaty did not reach Division Point until October, yet as soon as the newspapers made their rounds, the homestead could be heard celebrating from miles down the coast.

The war was finally over, for good this time, and it was guaranteed in writing that those in America would never have to bend the knee to a foreign master again. The United States were free to do as they please and order their affairs how they saw fit, without, for once, the fear of foreign reprisal. All that was left to do was build the nation from the ground up, beginning with the final removal of the last remains of the British empire—the few remaining Redcoats that had yet to be shipped back to England and were surely still licking their wounds from the beating they had received over the last nine years.

The two years between the victory at Yorktown and the signing of the peace treaty were quiet and peaceful for Theo and his family, and he cherished every moment he had to watch Liberty grow right before his eyes. While time seemed to drag for the rest of the country, the days flew by for him, and within the blink of an eye, he and Evie were celebrating their third wedding anniversary, and Liberty had grown from a babbling infant to a curious and chatty toddler.

With the peace treaty signed and America's independence formally recognized, celebrations commenced for weeks and even months afterward, and that jovial mood was palpable in the air of New York when Theo, Evie, and Liberty arrived in the city at the end of November. Theo had business in New York in relation to acquiring the materials necessary to finally do the renovations on the homestead's beloved church—a plan that had taken more than nine years to come to fruition—and Evie and Liberty decided to tag along on their first trip away from Division Point as a family of three.

Two years had passed since Alistair's death, and the homestead still had not found someone to take his place as the community's pastor, resulting in the church falling into an even greater state of disrepair. But just because Alistair was gone did not mean that the homestead could not still enjoy the church, so Theo took it upon himself to do the necessary repairs. Alistair would have wanted it that way. He would have wanted to see his friends and family carry on his memory in the place in which he spent most of his time—a house of worship.

After meeting with a lumber supplier at a general store in the city, Theo, Evie, and Liberty took a stroll toward the harbor to watch the ships come and go. Once they reached the docks, however, they noticed that an enormous crowd had gathered in the harbor—a crowd full of civilians hooting and hollering with their firsts in the air. Theo craned his neck to see a large warship opening her sails and raising her anchor, turning slowly in the deep waters of the harbor to head out to sea. She wore England's colors on her mast, and on her large deck, what appeared to be hundreds or thousands of Redcoats soldiers stood, hollering back at the crowd on the docks.

Several other ships were setting sail nearby and flying British colors, and they were filled to the brim with Loyalists who had placed their bets on the wrong side of the war and were run out of town by their outspoken Patriot neighbors. Many of them were fleeing to England or France, and some were trying their luck in Canada or the Caribbean. With the war won and the British gone, there was no place for Loyalists in America.

"Good riddance!" a grouchy old man in the crowd cried at the passing warship.

"No Lobsterbacks on American soil!" another added.

"Go back to England, you yellow-bellied Tories! Let freedom ring!"

"What is happening?" Evie asked in confusion as she held her fidgeting daughter in her arms. Excited by the noise of the crowd, Liberty tried to wiggle out of her grasp and repeatedly asked to be put down.

"Redcoats," Theo answered as he scratched his head. "The last garrison of King George's men is being evacuated back to England."

"It's about time," Evie huffed. "I do not think I can look at the color red ever again."

Theo chuckled lowly under his breath, catching a glimpse of her fiery auburn locks blowing around her face in the wind. He had never minded the color red, especially on her.

The murmur of the crowd was suddenly pierced by a series of gasps, followed by fearful silence, causing Theo to immediately nudge Liberty and Evie behind him. The British warship was now about two hundred yards from the docks, her starboard hull facing the harbor as she released a single cannonball from her guns toward the shore. The crowd on the docks cowered in shock for several moments as the cannonball flew toward them through the air, only to hit the surface of the water one hundred feet out from the docks with an unceremonious and anticlimactic splash. The crowd immediately began to shout, jeer, and laugh again, waving goodbye and snarling curses as the ship finally turned away and eventually disappeared over the horizon.

When the cannonball intentionally hit the water, rather than the docks near which they stood, Theo let out a sigh of relief and relaxed his posture. "They were just trying to frighten us," he told Evie as she and Liberty came out from behind his back. "They cannot harm us without violating the peace treaty."

"One final farewell, I suppose," Evie chortled. "Sore losers, the lot of them."

"They are just cross because they were bested on the battlefield by an army of commoners, rather than an army of soldiers."

Now bored with the events of the crowd and unable to wiggle free from her mother's arms, Liberty busied herself by looking all around at the exciting scenery of the harbor district behind them, her eyes falling upon one area in particular. Tilting her head curiously, she pointed over Evie's shoulder.

"Mama, look," she said. "Look at those people! Why are they sad?"

Evie and Theo both turned in unison to find what it was that had caught her attention, and that was when their eyes fell upon a terrible sight amidst the daily activities of the harbor district. Against the back wall of a nearby warehouse, a platform had been erected, and many smartly dressed men and women had begun to gather around it. Standing upon the platform was a single white man dressed in fine silk garments, and behind him, a line of six downtrodden and malnourished people of African descent. Their skin was dark, their bodies were thin, and their expressions were empty as they stood in rags and chains upon the platform while the white man before them hollered to the crowd below.

An auction was clearly in progress. A *slave* auction.

Theo's posture immediately stiffened, and he swallowed thickly. Evie tried to turn away and draw Liberty's attention elsewhere, but she was fixated upon the scene unfolding just one hundred feet away. Nearly three years old, she had never seen people whose skin was darker than her own tanned complexion, nor had she seen anyone appear so broken and miserable.

"Mama, who are they?" Libby asked curiously. "Papa, they look like us!"

Evie looked fearfully to Theo as she set Liberty on the ground and held her to her skirts. Just a moment ago, Evie had locked eyes with one of the poor souls standing on the auction block, a young girl with large brown eyes who could not have been older than thirteen or fourteen years. Evie stared back at her in horror, feeling her heart clench in her chest at the sight of the girl silently pleading for her freedom. The manacles upon her wrists were heavy and onerous, and they rattled painfully with every move she made.

Immediately, Evie was taken back to a time when she herself had felt just as trapped, when she was a prisoner, when she was someone's *property*. She may have won her freedom after years of struggle, but had everyone else? What of the slaves, and the natives—the people that looked like that little girl on the auction block, or the people that looked like her daughter and husband? Was their freedom worth as much as hers?

Theo tensely cleared his throat again and took Liberty by the hand to lead her away from the vicinity of the auction. "I see, love," he told Libby gently before looking to Evie and saying, "Come, Evie. We shall go back to our room at the inn. You and Liberty should not have to see such things."

Theo turned on his heel with Liberty's hand in his, motioning for Evie to follow. Evie could see the tension in his back as he began to walk away with his head hung low, and she tossed one last look over her shoulder at the auction to see the young girl and another woman, who appeared to be her mother, being led off of the platform by the auctioneer and into the custody of one of the men in the crowd. Their eyes were fixed upon the ground as they hobbled to their new master, their fates sealed with the single exchange of a few coins and a handshake between strangers.

Evie turned away from the tragic sight before her and jogged to catch up to her husband and daughter a few paces down the street. Her heart ached for the poor girl, her mother, and every other soul who had fallen victim to the barbaric practice of human bondage. As a mother, she could not imagine her child being bought and sold like an animal without tears immediately forming in her eyes, and it was not a thought she ever wanted to entertain again.

The moment Liberty was born bearing her father's beautiful tanned skin, Evie knew that her daughter would be subjected to a lifetime of prejudice by those who considered anything different to be dangerous. She had heard the stories of mixed blood children being outcasted and persecuted, of being hunted and prayed upon. They may have now been standing on "free" land, but it was shockingly clear to her now that the same closed-minded people still occupied it. Nothing had really changed yet, and she was not convinced it ever really would.

Once inside the room they had rented for the night at a nearby tavern, Theo closed the door behind them and bolted it shut with a heavy sigh. Evie slowly took a seat on the edge of the nearest bed, and Liberty immediately ran to the window to see if she could catch a glimpse of the harbor district from their room. Unfortunately, much of it was blocked by a row of warehouses. Theo shuffled across the floor to sit next to Evie on the bed, folding his hands in his lap and averting his eyes to the floor. They both sat in tense silence for several moments before he eventually spoke.

"I am sorry you and Libby had to see that," he murmured with a lowered head.

Evie shook her head in disgust and looked nervously over her shoulder to see Liberty still standing at the window with her back turned to them, oblivious to the tension in the room and the tragedy they had just witnessed.

"Do you think she knows?" Evie asked in a saddened whisper. "Do you think Liberty understands what she just saw?"

"No. Thank the stars that she is still far too little to understand the harsh realities of our world."

Evie dropped her head in her hands and squeezed her eyes shut. "That could have been our daughter up there..." she murmured as she felt her blood turn ice cold in her veins. "If she were to fall in the wrong hands, that could be her—"

"Don't," Theo interrupted sternly, wrapping his arm around her shoulders and pulling her into his chest. "Do not even think of such a thing. We would never let that happen."

Evie shook her head again and tried to swallow the tears she could feel brimming in her eyes. "I promised myself I would never let Liberty endure the things that we have," she whispered into her husband's chest, "but I fear that nothing has really changed here. How can we call ourselves free when people are still being bought and sold like chattel at this very moment? That is not freedom. That is just tyranny and hypocrisy cloaked in empty promises of sovereignty."

Theo rested his head upon her shoulder and held her close, feeling his own heart clench painfully in his chest. He should have been elated that the last traces of the British were now gone, and that a new era was about to begin, but all he felt was defeat. He did not fight a long and bloody war to only see the promise of freedom and justice realized for a select few. Was this really to be the new America that Washington and the others had promised? Was anything really different?

"It has been a long, hard ride," Theo said softly in Evie's ear. "But we still have a long way to go."

"How long, Theo? Will another lifetime go by before we have the fair and just country for which we fought?"

"I have no certain answers," Theo admitted sadly. "But I know that our daughter carries in her blood a promise of a better future. I know she will learn from her ancestors' mistakes. If our generation fails to rewrite our tainted history and right the wrongs of the past, then hers will surely stand up to take the lead."

Evie turned in Theo's arms to follow his gaze over to the window, and they silently watched as Liberty gazed innocently across the sea of rooftops stretching out before her. In her pure and un-jaded eyes, everyone was equal, and everyone was human. She and her parents had been named a generation unafraid, a generation hellbent on changing the course of history, but that would only happen when the world realized that different was not, in fact, as dangerous as it seemed.

How long, Theo wondered silently to himself, would it take for the rest of the world to see things as Liberty did? Would that day ever come? Or was history simply doomed to repeat itself forever in an endless cycle of violent injustice?

Only time would tell. But no matter what the future held, Theo knew that they would face it together, Evie, Liberty, and himself. Together, they had endured countless trials, tribulations, and heartbreaks throughout the years, and they would continue to do so for years to come. The world had tried with earnest to tear them apart, but nevertheless, they persisted. They persisted then, and they would persist now, until the end of their days, for they were an unbreakable, indivisible force destined to leave the world a better place than they had found it.

Chapter 25

The Heart of a Hero

December 1783

Snow collected upon the ground in tall drifts throughout Division Point as a bitterly cold wind blew through to jostle anyone who had been unlucky enough to be caught outside when the storm began. Thankfully, everyone in the homestead had sought shelter long before the blizzard commenced, building great fires in their hearths to keep warm through the long winter ahead. Inside the small, quaint home on the edge of the cliff behind the Division Point lighthouse, a cozy fire was roaring in the fireplace, sending a cloud of smoke billowing up though the chimney and into the snowy sky.

"Looks to be a mighty blizzard raging out there," Theo noted as he stood at the window in the parlor that looked out over the frozen Massachusetts Bay. "We will be snowed in for days, it seems."

Johanna sighed from her chair in the corner of the room, setting her needlework aside. "Then we should be thankful you and the girls returned from New York when you did. The roads are treacherous during the winter."

Evie made her way from the kitchen to the parlor, poking her head into the room while lingering in the doorway with Liberty and Gunner following close behind.

"Supper is just about ready," Evie told her husband and mother-in-law, who had been lounging in the parlor by the fire to keep warm. "Stewed vegetables and freshly baked bread."

The smell of the stew for that night's supper had begun to waft through the house long ago, and Theo wasted no time chasing Liberty back into the kitchen so that they could sit down to eat. Evie and Johanna followed them into the kitchen and worked together to set the food on the table, but just before they could sit down, they were startled by a rapacious series of knocks on the front door.

"Who in God's name would be knocking on our door?" Evie huffed as she folded her arms over her chest. "Only a fool would be caught out and about in this weather."

"I'll go see," Theo said as he sauntered back out of the kitchen. "But whomever it is must be truly desperate to be paying visits in the midst of a blizzard."

Liberty let out an excited squeal before hurrying ahead of him and skidding to a stop at the front door. Before she could manage to open the door herself, Theo scooped her up into his arms. He took a moment to peer through the peephole, and when he caught a glimpse of the man standing on his front porch, he nearly choked on his tongue.

Theo opened the door to see none other than Commander George Washington standing on the front veranda, dressed not in his uniform coat, but rather a simple frock coat with dark trousers and boots. He wore a cape around his shoulders to brave the cold, and his attire, as well as his greying, wind-swept hair, were covered in a thin dusting of snow. Much of his face was flushed cherry red, and from his appearance, Theo could only assume he had been traveling through the snowstorm for days.

As soon as Theo opened the door, a gentle smile spread across the older man's face, and he tipped his hat while bowing his head in greeting. "Captain Cunningham. What a pleasure to see you again."

"Commander?" Theo choked out through his shock. "What are you doing at my door? And why in God's name have you come here during a blizzard?"

Washington let out a long sigh, his breath billowing before him in a wispy white cloud. "Conditions were not nearly this terrible when I first set out from Mount Vernon."

"How did you even find my home?"

Washington chuckled lowly and attempted to dust the snow from his shoulders. "Lafayette told me how to find your homestead. And I assure you I have an important reason to be here. May I come in to…warm up?"

Theo was still just as perplexed, and he stood frozen in the front doorway as the cold wind blew through his clothes from outside. After a few moments of deliberation, he nodded his head once and stepped aside to allow the man entry to the front room. Washington graciously stepped into the house after stomping off the snow that had accumulated on his boots. Theo still had very little love for the Commander, but he thought it necessary to entertain him after he had braved the winter winds to travel here all the way from Virginia.

"What are you doing here?" Theo wasted no time in asking as he closed the door behind him.

Washington immediately cupped his frigid hands around his mouth and breathed into them to warm up his fingers before saying, "Well, as you already know, your father and I were once close. I have not spoken to him since the Seven Year's War, and I was hoping to reconnect with an old friend."

Theo's expression immediately soured, and his eyes fell to the floor. "I'm afraid you are too late, sir. Alistair Cunningham is dead."

Washington was quiet for a moment, his jaw going slack and his eyes widening slightly before he cleared his throat and looked away. "I see," he eventually murmured as the air became tense between them. "I am so sorry to hear that. I had no idea. How…how long ago did he pass?"

"Two years. He had been sick for some time."

"My condolences on your loss. Alistair was a wonderful man with a heart of gold. And it is clear the apple does not fall far from the tree."

Theo cleared his throat in mild discomfort and adjusted his hold on Liberty in his arms. Before he could speak, however, Evie and Johanna sauntered into the front room.

"Theo, who was at the—?" Evie started to ask, but she and Johanna both skidded to a stop in the front room when they caught sight of Washington's tall and statuesque figure nearby, his clothes still dusted with snow. "I'm sorry," she quickly corrected herself as her cheeks burned red, "I did not realize we were expecting a guest."

"We weren't," Theo replied, setting Liberty onto her feet on the floor and placing his hands on his hips. "Evie, Johanna, this is Commander George Washington. Commander, this is my wife, Evie; my step-mother, Johanna; and my daughter, Liberty."

Washington bowed his head to the ladies with a warm smile and tipped his hat once more. "Please, call me George. It is a pleasure to make your acquaintance, ladies. I am terribly sorry for stopping by unannounced. I hope you can forgive my tactlessness."

"C-Commander?" Evie and Johanna both repeated, sharing startled looks with one another before quickly lowering themselves into clumsy curtsies. They had never been in the presence of a man with as much power and prestige before, let alone the man that orchestrated the war that had won them their freedom. His reputation clearly preceded him, and he was just as tall, charming, and charismatic as they had heard him to be.

"The pleasure is ours," Johanna stuttered, her cheeks flushing pink as Washington continued to smile at her.

Washington turned his attention to the little girl Theo had been holding in his arms and who was now hiding shyly behind her mother's legs. Kneeling down in front of Evie, he offered his hand out to Liberty with a grin that crinkled his eyes. "Hello, Miss Liberty," he said gently to her. "It is wonderful to meet you."

"Remember your manners, Libby," Evie told her. "Tell Mr. Washington hello."

Liberty poked her head around Evie's hip and clutched onto her skirts, her long dark curls falling into her eyes. Eventually, she murmured the word, "Hello," in a mousy voice before hiding behind her mother once more.

Washington let out a chuckle before rising to his full height and tucking his hat under his arm. "Your daughter is beautiful," he told Theo and Evie.

"Thank you," Theo replied as he folded his hands behind his back. "We are very blessed. Did you come only to inquire about my father?"

Washington shook his head. "No, actually. That was only part of why I came. I wanted to speak with you, in private, if we may."

Theo shared a look with Evie before muttering, "We were actually just about to sit down to dinner…"

"I will be brief, I assure you."

After a few moments of thought, Theo let out a sigh and nodded in agreement, requesting that Evie and Johanna take Liberty into the kitchen to start supper without him while he and the Commander spoke. After he watched them go, he led Washington into the parlor and they both stood before the fireplace.

"I thought I should tell you that I am resigning as Commander in Chief at the end of the month," Washington eventually said after they stood in silence for several minutes.

Theo crossed his arms over his chest and raised his brow curiously. "Oh? What will you do then?"

"Return to Mount Vernon for the time being. Take some time for myself and my family to decide where to go from here."

"And where *do* we go from here?"

Washington shrugged and raised his eyes from the floor. "That is for Congress to decide. I trust they will act in the best interest of our country in paving a path into the future."

"You have more trust than I, I'm afraid."

Washington furrowed his own brow and tilted his head to the side. "Always the cynic, I see. Why are you so cross, Theo? You should be celebrating with everyone else. The war is finally over! We are free."

"Is it really over, sir? You may have won your freedoms, but can you say the same for everyone who calls this place home? My family and I were just witnesses to a slave auction in the middle of New York last month. Human beings, bought and sold like cattle to the highest bidder. How can you call us free when so many still live in bondage?"

Washington tensed, pressing his lips into a thin hard line while averting his eyes back to the floor. "You are not wrong. We have come a long way, but there is still much work to be done."

Theo shook his head in disgust. "It is clear to me whose rights and freedoms have taken precedence throughout this bloody war. It is also clear that there is a great difference in the value of some lives over others. You and your followers promised me life, liberty, and happiness in this new country, but can you honestly promise that my daughter will not be treated unfairly on account of the color of her skin?"

Washington solemnly shook his head. "I cannot promise that. But that is why I came here. I came to tell you that you left an indelible impression upon me during your service under my command. You have left me in awe with your ideals of liberty and justice, not just for some, but for all, regardless of color or creed. I want you to know that I took everything you have said to me over the years to heart, and you have opened my eyes to injustices in our world that I never would have seen otherwise. And for that, I am eternally grateful."

Theo shrugged his shoulders and relaxed his tensed posture, looking into Washington's blue-grey eyes to see that he was just as sincere in his sentiments as he had been the last time they spoke.

"I will tell those things to anyone who will listen. Just because we are no longer under the iron fist of the British empire does not mean that injustice has been eliminated. The rich will continue to grow richer, and the powerful, more powerful. And the people who look like my daughter and myself will continue to be pushed to the side."

"I hope to see all of those things change. Since we last spoke, I have reviewed my position on the matter of slavery, and I realized that you have been right all along. America will not be free until *all* of her people are free. That is why I made the decision to release all of the people held in bondage at my home in Mount Vernon."

Theo stared at him in disbelief, blinking as he asked, "You freed your slaves?"

"I did. They are now free to live and work as they please."

"Even Malgelit?"

"Even Malgelit."

Theo was greatly shocked and slightly taken aback, unable to find his words for several moments. "I hope every slave master comes to see things as you do," he eventually said.

"It will take time. The world has been shaken up enough to last a lifetime already. We cannot expect to right every wrong of our ancestors overnight."

"So many have suffered already. I just long to see the suffering and the sorrow end."

Washington reached forward to place a hand upon Theo's shoulder. "I know, my friend. We have that much in common. But you should take comfort in knowing that history has been made, and I have you and every other Continental soldier to thank for that."

"I did not fight to make history. I fought to protect my family, and to forge a better future for them."

"And that is exactly what you did. You did protect your family, and you protected everyone else in this country. You should be proud. We will forever be indebted to you and the others who risked their lives in the name of freedom."

Theo shifted his weight uncomfortably between his feet, fidgeting under the weight of Washington's compliments. He had never been that comfortable with being showered with praise, especially when he was not so sure he deserved it.

"I only did what any man would do."

Washington shook his head. "Not any man would sacrifice himself the way we both have. You have the heart of a hero, Theo. The war could not have been won without you. I know your father wanted nothing more than to see this divided land united in a stand against tyranny, and he is surely watching over us with his chest swelled with pride."

The traces of a wistful smile tugged at Theo's lips. "I hope so."

Washington suddenly reached into one of the inner pockets of his coat before producing a small indistinct object. "I came all this way to give this to you," he said as he held out his hand for Theo to see in the light of the fireplace.

The object in his hand was a flat piece of thick, dark purple fabric approximately the size of his palm, cut into the shape of a heart. Upon the purple fabric, an intricate filigree design was embroidered in silver thread, along with the word "Merit" in large, striking letters. Looking up from the Commander's hand to his eyes, Theo's brow creased in confusion.

"I do not understand. What is this?"

"A Badge of Military Merit. A medal of honor, for your sacrifices, your triumphs, and your selfless service to the cause of independence."

Theo shook his head with a sigh. "I could not possibly accept this. I have not earned it. I have lied, cheated, stolen, and murdered in the name of war. Nothing I have done is honorable."

"I disagree. I created this medal myself to give to those select few men under my command who have displayed not only instances of unusual gallantry in battle, but also extraordinary fidelity and essential service in any way. And I cannot think of anyone who exemplifies such merit than you. Not only did you fight for me, but you also fought against me when I became hungry for blood and blind to my hypocrisy. I am a better soldier, and a better man, because of you, Captain Cunningham. You taught a stubborn old man something about being human that I had long since forgotten."

Theo hadn't realized how long he had longed to hear Washington say those words until he uttered them in that moment, and he slowly outstretched his hand to accept the medal, a warm feeling of pride spreading through his chest.

"I do not know what to say," Theo mumbled as he held the swatch of fabric in his palm and gazed upon it.

"Nothing else needs to be said. Wear it with pride. Only three other men in the world have been given this honor."

Theo raised his eyes from his hands to meet Washington's gaze, a sideways smirk slowly playing across his face as he said, "Thank you, Commander. I am honored to have this distinction."

Washington chuckled lightly and patted him on the shoulder before turning toward the door to make his exit. "My heart sings to hear you say such things. I think I shall take my leave now."

Washington took a few steps toward the front room before Theo stopped him. "Commander, wait."

"Yes?" Washington asked, glancing over his shoulder.

"I have a question."

"I may have an answer."

"Will you ever...take command of the country that you helped create? You led our army, but would you ever consider leading *us*?"

Washington paused for a moment before chuckling under his breath. "For the time being, I plan to retire to Mount Vernon. But, should the people demand it, I shall be ready to lead this fledgling nation into the future. Only time will tell."

Theo nodded in understanding, his smirk widening. "I would like that very much. If every man in Congress resembles you, perhaps we have a chance at the liberty and justice for which we fought."

"No truer words have been spoken. Well, I have taken enough time away from your family and your dinner. I should set out. It is a long and cold ride back to Virginia."

Washington turned to leave again, but Theo stopped him once more. "Join us."

"Pardon?"

Theo shrugged rather bashfully. "Join my family and I for dinner before you go. We would love to have you."

Washington stared at him in silence over his shoulder for several moments before another wide smile split across his face. Nodding graciously, he said, "Thank you. A hot meal sounds lovely in this bitter cold."

"Come along, then. Evie always makes plenty."

Washington followed him out of the parlor and into the kitchen, letting out a hearty chuckle. "God bless the women in our lives. We could never get along without them, hm?"

Theo nodded in agreement as they entered the kitchen, catching his wife's eye as they all took a seat at the table.

"Yes," he agreed with a lopsided grin as Evie smirked at him across the table. He had never been more grateful for her presence by his side than now, and the mere sight of her crystal blue eyes set his heart on fire all over again. She had captured his heart for the first time nine years ago, and she continued to do so every day since. Without her, he realized in that moment, he would have nothing. Without her, he *was* nothing. "God bless the women."

***

March 1784

The sound of leaves crunching under foot filled the crisp spring air as Theo made his way across the grounds of the cemetery and paused before Alistair Cunningham's headstone. Every other time he had stepped foot in this place, his heart had been heavy, and his head hung low, but this time, there was a peacefulness in his soul and a lightness in his step that he hadn't felt in over a decade.

Theo slowly lowered himself to sit cross legged on the ground in the shadow of his father's grave before reaching into his shirt pocket to produce the medal of honor Washington had gifted him months before. He had carried it in the pocket over his heart along with Alistair's final letter every day, and ever since, he had never felt more content.

Theo tossed the medal between his hands and fidgeted with his fingers, keeping his eyes trained on his lap as he felt the name on the gravestone before him stare back like a pair of old, kind eyes. "Washington came by to see you," Theo eventually said out loud to the headstone. "It is a shame you were never able to reunite, but trust me when I say that you would be proud to call him a friend."

Somewhere deep in his heart, Theo hoped for the headstone to respond in some way, or even yet, for Alistair to come marching through the gates of the cemetery to come sit next to him and deliver one of his many anecdotal lectures. He never realized how much he missed those lectures until there was no one there to give them, and he would have given anything to hear the old man lovingly chastise him once more.

"Washington claims I have the heart of a hero, you know. I am yet to be convinced that is true, but if it is, I think I know whom to thank. If it weren't for you, I shudder to think where I would be now. It pains me to know that I was too stubborn to realize that while you were alive, but I hope I've made you proud, Pa. If I can be half the father to Libby that you were to me, then everything will have been worth it. Tell Mother I said hello, and that I hope you two have found the peace you both sought. As for me, I will see to it that Division Point remains the safe haven you had always wanted it to be. You needn't worry. Your legacy is in good hands."

After sitting in silence in the graveyard for several more minutes, Theo rose to his feet and tucked the medal back into his pocket. He gave the top of the headstone an affectionate pat before exiting through the front gates of the cemetery and wandering back towards the lighthouse. On the way, he passed by Johanna's home, and from the corner of his eye he caught a glance of his axe embedded in one of the posts on the front porch.

He briefly detoured from his original path to approach the front porch, running his fingertips across the surface of the axe's handle as it remained fixed in the post as it had been for the last several years, since he had placed it there in anger and despair in the aftermath of visiting his mother's homeland. For a split second, he considered removing it and tossing it to the side. The war was over, after all. And as Tehwehron had said, the axe was to be removed when the threat of war had been extinguished.

But then he thought better of it. The colonies may now be an independent union of states, but there was still a long way to go before he could call everyone on this land truly *free*. The real war was not yet over, as far as he was concerned, and it would not be truly over until justice and equality became a reality for anyone and everyone who called this place home. After all that had been done, and all that had been sacrificed, it still was not enough. It would never be enough. There was still much work to be done, and until then, the axe would remain where it was, however long that may be.

Theo gave the axe one last glance over and heaved a tired sigh before moving on toward the lighthouse. He took the spiral stairs that lead to the top of the lighthouse tower two at a time, his heart singing with joy when he was met with the sight of Evie and Liberty waiting for him on the catwalk. They were standing hand in hand at the railing, looking out over the Bay and watching as ships sailed by on the distant horizon.

"Look, Papa," Liberty cheered giddily as he came to stand behind them at the railing, "Look at the ships!"

"They sure are beautiful, aren't they?" he agreed while wrapping his arms around Evie's waist from behind and resting his chin upon her shoulder. "Perhaps tomorrow I will take you out for a trip on *The Liberty*, hm? You can finally sprout your sea legs."

"I want to sail the boat! May I sail the boat?" Liberty asked excitedly.

"She's a ship," Evie and Theo corrected in unison.

"Fine. May I steer the *ship*?"

Theo chuckled and reached down to tousle his daughter's hair. "Of course, you may. You shall be an honorary sea captain."

"Will there be pirates?"

Theo shrugged his shoulders with a smirk. "I highly doubt it. But nothing is impossible."

Evie tipped her head back against his chest and stared up at him from under her long eyelashes. "You're in a rather jovial mood today," she noted with a grin.

Theo pressed a soft kiss to the side of her neck and intertwined his fingers with hers, holding up their hands to the sun to admire the matching golden bands they both wore.

"I suppose I am," he agreed.

"Any particular reason?"

He shrugged again, a long, contented sigh escaping his lips as he looked out across the water. "I suppose that I have spent so many years at war with myself that I could not recall what it felt to be at peace. But I can feel that peace returning to me now. And now, it's as if it never left."

Evie pressed a kiss to the back of his hand and closed her eyes in contentment as a light breeze blew through to ruffle her skirts and her hair, the stray locks that had fallen from her braid blowing about and softly caressing her face like Theo longed to do in that moment. They lost track of time as they stood upon the top of the lighthouse and counted the ships that went by on the horizon, but it mattered little. There was no rush. They had the rest of their lives ahead of them.

The world looked so different from so high in the sky, and there was nowhere else he would rather go to see the wave-crashed coast of the Land of the Free stretch out before him. A dark, dangerous, mysterious world existed on the horizon and past the borders of Division Point, but within the confines of their safe little world, nothing else mattered. There was no way to know what the future held, or what monsters lurked in unfamiliar territories, but Theo was reminded of one simple, inalienable truth every time he peered at his wedding band or looked into the eyes of his daughter: come what may, so long as his heart beat in his chest, the *indivisible* would remain exactly that.

* * *

Madison Flores

"They are no longer two, but one. Therefore, what God has joined together, let no one separate."

Matthew 19:6

About the Author

Madison graduated Summa Cum Laude with a full-ride academic scholarship from the University of North Texas in May 2019, earning a Bachelor of Science degree in Integrated Studies with concentrations in anthropology, sociology, and criminal justice, and a minor in history. Madison currently lives in the state of Texas, but she is a native Iowan who hasn't forgotten her Midwest roots. By day, Madison Flores is a preschool teacher. By night, she is a voracious reader and writer. She has loved to write for as long as she can remember, but she chose her senior year of college to officially begin her professional writing career.

In addition to the elements of history and romance, her writing also touches on complex and often hard-to-discuss issues that plague our world to this day. Her favorite part about writing is the fact that she has the power to capture the imagination of complete strangers with her work, with the hope that she could also inspire them to make the world a better place. Those who forget their history are doomed to repeat it, after all. Her goal is not to weave a tale in which two flawless people fall in love within the boundaries of a perfect world, because our world is not perfect, and there is no such thing as a love without obstacles and struggles. To pretend that life and love takes place in a vacuum of perfection is naive, and in her opinion, does a great disservice to the new generations of readers that come long after we are gone. Therefore, Madison's work is targeted to mature, adult readers who are looking for honesty and authenticity in the telling of romance throughout history.

To learn more about Madison and her work, visit her website at www.madisonflores.com, or contact her via her social media:

Facebook: Author Madison Flores
Twitter: @madifloresbooks
Instagram: @author_madison_flores
Goodreads: Madison Flores
Email: author.madisonflores@gmail.com